"I'M WITH YOU UNTIL THE END."

As he said this, he felt the oddest surge of happiness—a feeling with which he hadn't much experience, not since he'd resigned from the army. At that point, Huntley had settled on his makeshift plan to return to England, get an ordinary job, find a sweet wife, and install her in some snug home while they made armfuls of babies, but, strangely, the plan hadn't raised his spirits as he thought it would. But throwing himself headlong into a cause he hadn't known about a week earlier, a cause in which he'd face unknown, supernatural dangers . . . somehow that had done the trick. Huntley felt the blood moving in him, the old excitement of a campaign.

It was made all the better knowing that Thalia Burgess would be by his side.

Hearing his vow, she let out a breath she probably hadn't known she was holding and smiled at him again. Seeing her smile, something hot and animal slid through him. But this wasn't the time, and it wasn't the place; he had his cause and his duty, so he tried to push that roused beast aside. It was a fight, though.

Instead of reaching for her, as he wanted to do, he asked, "And what are these paragons called, who safeguard the world, and save England from herself?"

Before she even spoke, he knew everything was about to change. And change forever.

"The Blades of the Rose."

The Blades of the Rose

Coming Soon

SCOUNDREL

REBEL

STRANGER

Published by Kensington Publishing Corporation

WARRIOR
The Blades of the Rose

Zoë Archer

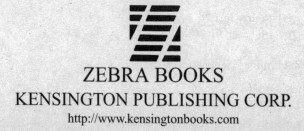

ZEBRA BOOKS
KENSINGTON PUBLISHING CORP.
http://www.kensingtonbooks.com

ZEBRA BOOKS are published by

Kensington Publishing Corp.
119 West 40th Street
New York, NY 10018

All Kensington titles, imprints, and distributed lines are available at special quantity discounts for bulk purchases for sales promotion, premiums, fund-raising, educational, or institutional use.

Special book excerpts or customized printings can also be created to fit specific needs. For details, write or phone the office of the Kensington Special Sales Manager: Attn. Special Sales Department. Kensington Publishing Corp., 119 West 40th Street, New York, NY 10018. Phone: 1-800-221-2647.

Zebra and the Z logo Reg. U.S. Pat. & TM Off.

ISBN-13: 978-1-4201-0679-4
ISBN-10: 1-4201-0679-1

First Printing: September 2010

10 9 8 7 6 5 4 3 2 1

Printed in the United States of America

For Zack:
my warrior,
my hero

ACKNOWLEDGMENTS

Thank you to Kevan Lyon, Megan Records, and the late, great Kate Duffy. The road to the Blades of the Rose has been an amazing adventure because of these daring women.

Thanks to Kent Madin of Boojum Expeditions for his insight on Mongolia, and thank you to Yu-Huei Layton for help with key Chinese words.

And to everyone else who has provided encouragement and support for this eccentric, wonderful series—thank you.

Chapter 1

Trouble at the Docks

Southampton, England. 1874.

Gabriel Huntley hated an unfair fight. He had hated it as a boy in school, he had hated it during his service in Her Majesty's army, and he hated it now.

Huntley ducked as a fist sailed toward his head, then landed his own punches on his attacker in quick succession. As his would-be assailant crumpled, unconscious, to the ground, Huntley swung around to face another assault. Three men coming toward him, and quick, cold murder in their eyes. Their numbers were thinning, but not by much. Huntley couldn't keep a smile from curving in the corners of his mouth. Less than an hour in England, and already brawling. Maybe coming home wouldn't be so bad.

"Who the hell *is* this bloke?" someone yelped.

"Dunno," came the learned reply.

"Captain Gabriel Huntley," he growled, blocking another punch. He rammed his elbow into someone's gut. "Of the Thirty-third Regiment of Foot."

His ship had docked that night in Southampton, bringing him back to British shores after fifteen years away. As he had stood at the bottom of the gangplank, his gear and guns strapped to his back, he'd found himself strangely and uncharacteristically reticent. He couldn't seem to get his feet to move forward. After years of moving from one end of the British Empire to the other, following orders sent down through the chain of command, he was finally able to decide on his fortune for himself. It was a prospect that he had been looking forward to for a long while. After resigning from his captaincy, he had booked passage on the next ship to England.

However, that idea had already begun to pale on the voyage back, with days and weeks of shipbound idleness leaving his mind to pick and gnaw at whatever fancy struck him. Yes, he'd been born in England and lived there for his first seventeen years—in a dismal Yorkshire coal mining village, more specifically. But nearly the other half of his life had been spent on distant shores: the Crimea, Turkey, India, Abyssinia. England had become no more than a far away ideal of a place recreated again and again in company barracks and officers' clubs. He had barely any family and few friends in England besides Sergeant Alan Inwood. The two men had fought side-by-side for years, and when a bullet had taken Inwood's leg, the trusty sergeant returned to England. But he'd written Huntley steadily over the years.

In Huntley's pocket was Inwood's latest missive. He'd memorized it, having read the letter over and over again on the voyage to England. It promised a job working with Inwood as a textile agent in Leeds. An ordinary, steady life. The prospect of marriage. Leeds, Inwood claimed, had an abundance of nice, respectable girls, daughters of mill owners, looking for husbands. Huntley could have a job and a wife in a trice—if he wanted.

Huntley knew how to fight in the worst conditions nature and man could create. Monsoons, blizzards, scorching heat. Bayonets, sabers, revolvers, and rifles. He'd eaten hardtack crawling with maggots. He'd swallowed the most fetid and foul water when there had been nothing else to drink. None of it had broken him. He had nothing left to fear. Yet the idea of truly settling down, finding, good Lord, a *wife,* it turned a soldier's blood to sleet.

After the ship had docked, Huntley had lingered at the foot of the gangplank, jostled on all sides by the shoving and cursing mass of the crowded dock. He had tried to make himself take the first step toward his new life, an ordinary life, and found that he couldn't.

Not yet, at any rate. Instead of rushing toward the inn where mail coaches waited to take passengers to English towns and cities near and far, Huntley had begun to walk in the opposite direction. Though he'd been at sea for months, he needed more time. Time to think. Time to plan. Time to grow accustomed to his strange and foreign homeland. Time for at least one pint.

He walked without real purpose, winding his way through the maze of narrow, lamplit streets that led from the pier. He hadn't gone more than thirty yards from the docks when the crowds thinned, leaving him on a quiet, dark street bathed in seaside mists. A large orange tabby cat slunk by, heading for the docks and promises of fish. At the end of the street was a tiny pub, casting yellow light onto the slick stone pavement outside, and full of raucous laughter and rough talk, not unlike the kind that could be found in any military barracks.

It seemed like heaven.

Huntley had started toward the pub, the desire for a pint of bitters strong in his mouth. At least that part of him was a true Englishman. As he strode toward the welcoming chaos, his soldier's senses alerted him to trouble close at hand. In the gloom of an alleyway leading off the street, he heard it first, then saw it, the sight that turned his blood to fire and overrode all thought: one man, badly outnumbered,

wounded and staggering, as half a dozen men attacked him
and several others stood nearby, ready to throw themselves
into the fray should they be needed. He knew at once that
what was happening was wrong, and that he had to help the
injured man.

Huntley had launched himself into the fight, needing to
even the odds.

Three men now came at him, throwing him against a
damp brick wall. Fortunately, his pack kept him from smash-
ing his head against the bricks. Two men took his arms while
the third pinned his middle. Before any of them could land
a punch, Huntley slammed his knee up into the chest of the
man pinning him, knocking the air out of him with a hard
gasp, then he wedged the heel of his boot against the man's
ribs and shoved. Winded as he was, the man could only
scrabble for a hold before being thrown into a pile of empty
crates, whose sharp edges made for a less than cushioned
fall as the crates broke apart. Huntley swiftly rid himself of
the other two men.

He considered going for his rifle or revolver, but quickly
discarded the idea. Firearms in tight quarters such as alleyways were just as dangerous to whomever wielded them as
they were to the intended targets. Striking distance was too
close, and it would be far too easy for someone to grab the
weapon from him once it was cocked and turn it on him.

Fists it was, then. Huntley had no qualms with that.

Huntley sprinted toward where the victim was being pum-
meled by two men. As Huntley came to the victim's aid, one
of the attackers managed to graze a fist against Huntley's
mouth. But it was nothing compared to the damage the
victim had taken. Blood was splattered all over the man's
shirt and waistcoat, his jacket was ripped at the seams, and
his face was swollen and cut. Huntley had been in enough
brawls to know that if the victim made it through the fight,
his face would never be the same, even under his gingery

beard. He was still swinging, though, bless his soul, as he staggered and struggled.

"I don't like bullies," Huntley rumbled. He grabbed the man who'd just punched him and gripped him by the throat, squeezing tightly.

The man scrabbled to pry Huntley's fingers from around his neck, but the hand that had grown strong gripping a rifle through fifteen years of campaigns couldn't be removed. Still, the man managed to choke out a few words.

"Whoever . . . you are . . . ," he rasped, "walk . . . away. Isn't your . . . fight."

Huntley grinned viciously. "That's for me to decide."

"Fool," the man wheezed.

"Perhaps," Huntley answered, "but since these are *my* fingers around *your* throat"—and here he tightened his hold, squeezing out an agonized gargle from the other man— "it wouldn't be wise to start tossing out names, would it?"

The man's answer never came. From behind Huntley, an abbreviated cry shot out, sharp and dreadful. Turning, Huntley saw a flash of metal gleam in the half light of the alley. One of the attackers stepped back from the victim, a long and wicked blade streaked with bright red in his hand. Blood quickly began to soak through the front of the victim's waistcoat and run through his fingers as he pressed against the wound in his stomach.

"Morris isn't going anywhere," the knife-wielding man said. His accent was clipped and well-born, as neatly groomed as his gleaming blond hair and moustache. He seemed comfortable with the red-smeared blade in his hand, despite his aristocratic air. "Let's go," Groomed Gent commanded to the other men.

Huntley spent half a moment's deliberation on whether to go for the upper cruster with the knife or attend to the fellow who'd been stabbed, Morris. He released his grip on his captive's throat at once and barely caught Morris before the wounded man collapsed to the ground.

The attackers quickly fled from the alley, but not before someone asked, pointing at their unconscious comrade slumped nearby, "What about Shelley? And *him*," gesturing toward Huntley.

"Shelley's on his own," Groomed Gent barked. "And the other one knows nothing. We have to move *now*," he added with a snarl. And before Huntley could stop them, every last one of the assailants disappeared into the night, leaving him cradling a dying man.

And he *was* dying. Of that, Huntley had no doubt. He'd seen similar wounds on the battlefield and knew that they were always fatal. Blood seeped faster and faster through the gash in Morris's abdomen. It would take something akin to a miracle to stop the advance of death, and Huntley had no store of miracles in his pack.

He gently lowered himself and Morris to the ground. "Let me fetch a surgeon," he said. He slipped the straps of his pack from his shoulders so the weight eased off.

"No," gasped Morris. "No use. And time's running out."

"At the least, I can get the constabulary," Huntley said. He recalled the icy cruelty of the knife-wielding gentleman, the sharp angles of his face that likely came directly from generations of similarly ruthless people's intermarrying and breeding. "I had a decent enough look at those men's faces. I could describe most of them, see them brought to justice."

A mirthless smile touched Morris's lips. "That would be the fastest way for *you* to wind up dead in an alleyway, my friend."

Huntley wondered who those men were, that attacked a gentleman in an alley like common footpads but had enough power for retribution. Perhaps a criminal organization. With a well-heeled gentleman as a member of its ranks. Was such a thing possible? He couldn't think on it now. Instead, knowing that his face would be the last that Morris would ever see and wanting to make the remaining time more personal, he said, "Name's Huntley."

"Anthony Morris." The two shared an awkward handshake, and Huntley's hand came away smeared crimson.

"Is there anything I can do for you, Morris?" he asked. Not much longer now, if the dark blood drenching Morris's clothing was any indication.

Frowning, Morris started to speak, but then Huntley's attention was distracted. The remaining attacker, who had been slumped unconscious against a wall, had somehow come to without making a sound. But now he was crouched nearby, whispering into his cupped hands. Looking closer, Huntley was able to see that the man held something that looked remarkably like a small wasps' nest—but it was made of gold. The close air of the alley was suddenly filled with a loud, insistent droning as, incredibly, the golden nest began to glow.

Not once, through the many places around the world he had been posted, had Huntley ever seen or heard anything like this, and he had seen some of the most incomprehensible things anyone could envision. He was transfixed, his mind immobilized by the sight.

The buzzing grew louder still, the nest glowed brighter as the man whispered on. Then something appeared in an opening in the nest, a tiny shine of a metallic wasp. Of its own volition, Huntley's hand came up, trying to reach out toward the mysterious spectacle. A line of wasps suddenly shot from the nest, directly toward Huntley and Morris. And Huntley still could not move.

With a grunt and groan, Morris managed to shift himself around in Huntley's arms and shove him down to the ground. They both splayed out onto the slippery pavement. And just in time. Dozens of wasps slammed into the wall behind them, their noise and impact against the brick like a round of bullets shot from a Gatling gun. Chips of mortar and brick rained down onto Huntley as he raised his arm to shield himself and Morris. He quickly reached out and grabbed a wooden board from a crate that had been broken apart in the fight. Several nails stuck out from one end of the board, and this he hurled at the man with the wasps' nest. The man yelped in surprised pain as the board hit him in the head, then staggered to his feet and scurried away, cradling the nest and pressing a palm to his bleeding scalp. It wouldn't be difficult to catch up with the wounded man, but in those few minutes, Morris would be dead, and Huntley had seen enough death to know it was better with someone, anyone, beside you.

He might have joined Morris in the afterlife, though. Huntley looked up at the wall behind him. Two dozen neat holes had been punched into the solid face of the brick. Exactly where his head had been. If Morris hadn't pushed him, those holes would now be adorning his own skull and his brains would be nicely splattered across half of Southampton, where they wouldn't do him much good.

"What the hell was that?" he demanded from Morris. Huntley heaved himself up into a sitting position, with Morris leaning against him. "Wasps like bullets? From a glowing golden nest?"

Morris coughed, sending another bubble of blood through his fingers. "Never mind that. Something I have to tell you. A message to deliver. Must be delivered . . . personally."

"Of course." Huntley owed Morris his life. That bound him to his service. It didn't matter that, in a matter of minutes, Morris would be dead. It was an unbreakable rule, one that was never questioned, never doubted. Honor was held at a premium when the rest of the world went to hell. "Have you a letter? Something I should write down?" There were a few books in his pack, but of any of these he would gladly sacrifice a few pages to transcribe Morris's message.

Morris shook his head weakly. "Can't write the message down. Even so, there are no mail routes to deliver it."

A message that could not be written. A destination beyond the all-encompassing reach of the British postal service. Things began to get stranger and stranger. Huntley started to wonder if, perhaps, he was lying drunk in a gutter somewhere, already deep in his return to England alcohol binge, and everything that had happened, was happening, was a whiskey-induced delusion. "Where's it going?"

"To my friend, Franklin Burgess." Morris gritted his teeth as a wave of pain moved through him, and Huntley did his best to comfort him, brushing clammy strands of hair back from Morris's forehead. "In Urga. Outer Mongolia."

"That is . . . far," Huntley managed after he found his voice.

Another ghostly smile curved Morris's mouth. "Always is. Was headed to a ship to take me there when," he nodded toward the horrible wound in his stomach as his smile faded. With his free hand, he clutched at Huntley's jacket. The strength left in Morris's grip surprised Huntley, but Morris was growing more and more agitated. Huntley tried to calm him, but to no avail. Morris became nearly frantic, spending the last of his energy as he tugged Huntley closer. "Please. You must deliver the message to Burgess. Thousands of lives at stake. More. Many more."

Huntley hesitated. Inwood's letter was in his pocket. The promise of a quiet future beckoned. What Morris asked was huge, a deviation from plans to settle in Leeds, and yet, to Huntley's mind, an adventure into unknown lands was infinitely preferable to tranquil stability. The fact that he'd thrown himself into a fight minutes after arriving in England told him so. Intelligent, probably not, but Huntley never put much stock in dry logic. And Morris had saved his life, the ultimate obligation. He could not refuse the dying man.

He said, "Give me the message. I'll deliver it to him."

Morris seemed momentarily surprised that Huntley had agreed, but then pulled him down so his ear was level with Morris's mouth. In words barely audible, he whispered into Huntley's ear. Huntley didn't quite know what to expect, but certainly not the two lines of nonsense that Morris faintly gasped. How could the lives of thousands or more rest on something not even Edward Lear would comprehend?

"Repeat them back to me," Morris insisted. He was waxen and pale, his lips growing stiff and awkward. The blood from his wound was slowing now. The source was nearly tapped out.

Feeling not a little ridiculous, Huntley repeated Morris's message—three times at Morris's urging—until the dying man was satisfied.

"Good. You must leave. Tonight. Next ship leaves. Two weeks. Too late."

Huntley, who hadn't been relishing the idea of his return to England, was still surprised by the speed with which he was supposed to leave it. He had some money from his army discharge, but he doubted he had enough to pay for a trip to the other side of the world. Soldiering was not the way any man could make his fortune, though perhaps that was the reason it attracted such a variety of reckless fools, including himself. As if anticipating his objections, Morris added, "In my coat pocket. My papers. Take my place on the ship."

His head still swimming with all that he had seen and heard within the span of an hour, Huntley could only nod. Then a thought occurred to him. "This man, Burgess," he said. "I doubt he'll trust me if I show up at his door with some ridiculous . . . er, coded message, and say that you've . . ." He let his words trail off, even though it was clear that they both knew Morris wasn't going to make it out alive from the alley.

Morris's eyes were dull and sinking into his face. Huntley

could barely hear him when he said, "Waistcoat inside pocket."

As carefully as he could, Huntley reached into the small pocket sewn into the lining of Morris's waistcoat. He pulled from the pocket a small circular metal object that turned out to be a compass. In the dimness of the alley, he was just able to see that the exterior of the compass was covered with minute writing in languages Huntley could not read, though he suspected they were Greek, Hebrew, and, yes, Sanskrit, of which he had a small knowledge. He opened the lid. Each point of the compass was represented by a different blade: the Roman soldier's pugio, the European duelist's rapier, the curved scimitar of the Near East, and the deadly serpentine form of the kris from the East Indies. A classic English rose lay at the center of the compass. Huntley realized that the compass was exceptionally old, with the heaviness of precious metal. Whispers of the past seemed to curl from it like perfumed smoke, and the lure of distant shores beckoned from within it, more powerful than any siren's call. It was extraordinary.

"Give that. To Burgess." Morris's breath grew even more shallow. "Say to him, 'North is eternal.' He'll know."

"I'll do that, Morris," Huntley said, straight and solemn.

"Thank you," he gasped. "Thank you." He seemed to relax at last, no longer fighting the inevitable.

"Is there someone else I should tell about you? Some family?"

"None. Only family I have. Will learn soon enough." And with those words, a final spasm passed through Morris, the body's last struggle to cling to the knowable world. He arched up, almost flinging himself from Huntley's arms as a strangled sound ripped from his throat. Then he fell back, eyes open, and Huntley knew it was done.

He looked down at the dead man's face. Morris couldn't have been more than forty or forty-five, a hale man who, though he wasn't a soldier by trade, had kept himself well-conditioned. He was dressed finely, without ostentation, the quality of his clothing revealing a certain level of status few, including Huntley himself, would enjoy. Shame to have Morris's life end so abruptly, shame to meet death in an ignominious, dirty alley, the victim of an unfair fight.

Huntley reached down and closed Morris's eyes. He sighed. No, he never quite got used to death, no matter how familiar it had become.

Two hours later saw Huntley standing on the deck of the *Frances,* watching the lights of Southampton grow smaller and fainter in the dark of night.

Good-bye, again, he thought.

After Morris had expired, Huntley took the travel papers from the dead man's pocket and saw that the ship on which he was intending to sail would be leaving shortly. There wouldn't be time to call for the police, since a lengthy inquiry would surely follow with the real possibility that Huntley would be forbidden to leave the country until the matter of Morris's death had been resolved. That could take weeks, weeks that Morris had assured him he did not have. So Huntley carefully lay Morris's body upon the ground and used the man's coat to cover his face. His own clothing was utterly soaked in Morris's blood. Getting on a ship in gore-drenched clothes was not an attractive or likely option. He had gone through his pack and found a fresh change, wrapping the ruined garments in a small blanket and stuffing them back into his pack. No point in leaving any clues to his identity when the constabulary did finally discover Morris.

Huntley had felt not a little guilty, leaving Morris alone in that dank alley, but there was nothing to be done for it. When he had presented the papers to the steamship *Frances's* first mate, he was taken at his word to be Anthony Morris, of Devonshire Terrace, London, and was shown to a cabin far more luxurious than the one Huntley had voyaged in on his return. As the ship raised anchor and prepared to sail, the elegance of the cabin, with its brass fixtures and framed prints, could not compete with the restlessness of Huntley's heart, and he found himself standing on the deck with a few of the other passengers, watching the shore of England recede.

"We're going to Constantinople." Huntley looked over and saw a young, genteel woman at his shoulder beaming at him. A sharp-eyed mama stood nearby, watching the flirtation of her charge, but had evidently gleaned enough information about "Mr. Morris" to render him an appropriate target for a girl's shipboard romance. Huntley felt the stirrings of panic.

"This is my first international voyage," the girl continued brightly. "I cannot *wait* to get away from boring old Shropshire." She waited, smiling prettily, for his suitably charming response. A light sweat beaded on his back.

"Knew a fellow from Constantinople," Huntley finally said. "Excellent shot. I once saw him shoot a mosquito off a water buffalo's rump."

The girl gaped at him, flushed, then turned and walked away as quickly as she could toward the protective embrace of her mother. After the mother glared at him, both females disappeared. Presumably they were off to spread the word that Mr. Morris was the most uncouth and ill-mannered man on the ship, including the one-eyed cook who was both a drunkard and an atheist.

Perhaps a little more time away from England would be for the best. Huntley would have to start his bride hunt when he came back, and, if that last exchange was any indicator, he sorely needed some refinement where his conversation with ladies was concerned. Fifteen years out of the company of respectable women tended to leave a mark on one's manners.

He had an even larger enigma on his hands than the workings of the feminine mind. Reaching into his pocket, Huntley pulled out the remarkable compass and stared at its face. He rubbed his thumb over the writings that covered the case as if trying to decipher them by touch, then flipped open the lid to look at the four blades that comprised the four directions. Priceless and old, even he could see that. And full of mystery.

Yes, things were about to get very interesting. No Leeds and job and wife, at least, not yet. A wry smile touched his lips, and he turned his back on the receding English coastline to make his way back down to his cabin.

Chapter 2

A Mysterious Message Delivered

Urga, Outer Mongolia. 1874. Three months later.

An Englishman was in Urga.

The town was no stranger to foreigners. Half of Urga was Chinese; merchants and Manchu officials dealt in commerce and administering the Qing empire. Russians, too, had a small foothold in the town. The Russian consulate was one of the only actual buildings in a town otherwise almost entirely comprised of felt *ger* tents and Buddhist temples. So it was not entirely unexpected to hear of an outlander in town.

But *Englishmen*—those were much more rare, and, to Thalia Burgess, more alarming.

She hurried through what passed for streets, jostling past the crowds. Strange to be amongst crowds in a land that was mostly wide open. Like a typical Mongol, Thalia wore a *del,* the three-quarter-length robe that buttoned at the right shoulder to a high, round-necked collar, a sash of red silk at her waist. Trousers tucked into boots with upturned toes completed her ordinary dress. Though she was English, as was her father, they had both been in Mongolia so long that their presence was hardly remarked upon even by the most isolated nomads. No one paid her any mind as she made her way through the labyrinth of what approximated streets in Urga, toward the two *gers* she and her father shared.

She tried to fight the panic that rose in her chest. Word had reached her in the marketplace that an Englishman had come to this distant part of the world, which, in and of itself troubled her. But the worst news came when she learned that this stranger was asking for her father, Franklin Burgess. Her first thought was to get home at once. If the Heirs had come calling, her father would be unable to defend himself, even with the help of their servants.

As she hurried, Thalia dodged past a crowd of saffron-robed monks, some of them boys training to become lamas. She passed a temple, hearing the monks inside chanting, then stopped abruptly and threw herself back against the wall, hiding behind a painted pillar.

It was *him*. The Englishman. She knew him right away by his clothing—serviceable and rugged coat, khaki trousers, tall boots, a battered broad-brimmed felt hat atop his sandy head. He carried a pack, a rifle encased in a scabbard hanging from the back. A pistol was strapped to his left hip, and a horn-handled hunting knife on his right hip. All of his gear looked as though it had seen a lot of service. This man was a traveler. He was tall as well, half a head taller than nearly everyone in the crowd. Thalia could not see his face as he walked away from her, had no idea if he was young or old, though he had the ease and confidence of movement that came from relative youth. In his current condition, her father couldn't face down a young, healthy, and armed man with an agenda.

Thalia pushed away from the pillar and dodged down a narrow passage between *gers*. Whoever he was, he didn't know Urga as she did, and she could take shortcuts to at least ensure she arrived at her home before him. Thalia had been to Urga many times, and, since her father's accident, they had been here for months. The chaos still did not make sense to her, but it was a familiar chaos she could navigate.

As she raced past the light fences that surrounded the tents, she had to thread past herds of goats and sheep, horses and camels, and dodge snarling, barely tamed dogs that stood guard. She snarled at a dog who nipped at her leg, causing the animal to fall back. Nimbly, she leapt over a cluster of children playing. As Thalia rounded past another *ger,* she caught one more glimpse of the Englishman, this time just a brief flash of his face, and, yes, he was young, but she did not see enough to ascertain more.

Perhaps, she tried to console herself, he wasn't an Heir, merely a merchant or some scientist come to Outer Mongolia to ply his trade, and in search of the language and faces of his homeland. She smiled grimly. It didn't seem likely. No one came to Urga without a specific purpose. And the English-man's purpose was *them*.

At last, she reached the two *gers* that made up the Burgess enclosure. Thalia burst through the door of her father's tent to find him reading. The furnishings here were exactly as they might be in any Mongol's *ger,* with only books in English, Russian, and French to indicate that she and her father were from another country. She allowed herself a momentary relief to see him unharmed and alone. Franklin Burgess was fifty-five, his black hair and beard now dusted with silver, green eyes creased in the corners with lines that came from advancing age and nearly a lifetime spent out of doors. He was her sole parent, had been for almost her entire twenty-five years, and Thalia could not imagine her world without him. She might as well try to picture what life might be like without the sun. Cold. Unbearable.

At her hurried entrance, he set aside his book and peered at her over his spectacles.

"What is it, *tsetseg?*" he asked.

Thalia quickly explained to him what she had learned,

and her father frowned. "I saw him," she added. "He didn't know where he was going, but he wasn't panicking. He seemed used to dealing with unfamiliar situations."

"An Heir, perhaps?" Franklin asked as he removed his glasses.

She shook her head. "I could not tell."

With more calm than she felt, he said, "Be a dear and hand me my rifle." Thalia hastily retrieved her father's gun, one that could open up a nicely sized hole in anyone who sought mischief. Franklin checked to be sure it was loaded, then tucked it behind the chair in which he sat, within easy reach. He was careful not to disturb his right leg, propped in front of him on a low stool. The bones were finally beginning to repair themselves after the accident with the horses, and neither Thalia nor her father wanted any kind of setback to the healing process, not when it had taken so long for the nasty double break to mend at all. It was amazing that, after being trampled by a herd of horses, her father had sustained only a few cuts and bruises in addition to his broken leg. It could have been much worse.

"We don't know if he is an Heir, though," Franklin said. He looked over to the kestrel they kept, perched quietly near the bookcase. The bird didn't seem uneasy, a good sign. "Just in case it isn't an Heir, perhaps it would be wise if you . . ." He gestured toward her *del*. His own clothes were a mixture of European and Mongol, and while it might be more common for European men to adopt some aspect of native dress outside of their home country, it was entirely different for women. Should this strange Englishman turn out to be nothing more than a trader or scholar, it wouldn't do to raise suspicions. To the outside world, Franklin Burgess and his daughter Thalia were simply anthropologists collecting folklore for their own academic pursuits.

Thalia looked down at herself and grimaced. "The things I do for the Blades," she muttered, and her father chuckled. She gave him a quick kiss on his bristly cheek and rushed into her *ger*. Most Mongolian families did not have separate *gers* for parents and children, but as soon as Thalia had turned thirteen, her father thought it best to stray from native custom and give his daughter some privacy.

"Udval," she called to her female servant in Mongolian, "can you please grab my dress? The English one? It's in the green chest. At the bottom."

Thalia began pulling off her *del,* her boots to follow, as the woman set aside her brewing of milk tea to look for the seldom-used gown.

"Here is your dress, Thalia *guai,*" Udval said, holding up the pale blue gown in question. She looked at it, then looked back at Thalia, doubt plainly written on her face. "I think, perhaps, it has grown smaller."

Standing in the middle of her *ger,* wearing a chemise and drawers, Thalia fought back a sigh. "No, it has stayed the same, but I have gotten bigger." Three inches taller, to be more precise. The last time Thalia had worn that gown, she had been fifteen, and though she had been a relatively average-sized girl, she was now a tall woman who stood nose-to-nose with most men. She and her father had purchased the dress ready-made from a Regent Street shop, and it was now the sole remaining relic of their long-ago trip to England. Fashions, no doubt, had changed considerably, but into what, Thalia hadn't the vaguest idea. *The Englishwoman's Domestic Magazine* seldom reached Outer Mongolia.

"We'll have to do the best we can," she said to Udval, who held the dress open as Thalia struggled into it.

"Do Englishwomen have fewer ribs?" Udval asked as she valiantly tried to close up the back of the dress.

"No," Thalia gasped, trying to suck her sides in as far as she could, "they prefer to have all their ribs shoved into their innards with a corset."

"Ah! It is closed now, but do not take deep breaths. What is a corset?"

Thalia tugged at the cuffs of the dress, but unless she wanted to tug the sleeves right out of the shoulder seams, her wrists were going to be pitifully exposed, the cuffs ending in the middle of her forearms. "A torture device that compresses a woman's ribs and stomach."

Udval looked shocked. "Why do the Englishmen punish their women like that?"

"Because the women are much smarter than the men," Thalia answered. She shook out the full skirts that hung limply to the ground. Without a crinoline to support the fabric, the dress looked like a deflated circus tent. Thalia remembered that she hadn't a single pair of the dainty shoes she had worn with the dress, and even if she did, her heels would now hang off the back. She shoved her feet back into her Mongolian boots. There wasn't much time left.

She started for the door, but then remembered her mother's hand mirror, and pulled it from the small box of jewelry and other mementos left to her after her mother had died. Thalia scanned her reflection critically. Englishwomen kept their hair up, so Thalia took her mass of heavy, dark hair and hastily pulled it into a bun that almost immediately began to slide loose. She found a few pins in the box that managed to tame her hair, but just barely. She hadn't any cosmetics, so there would be no way to hide the telltale flush of color in her cheeks, or the gleaming brightness of her jade green eyes, all of which came from years on horseback beneath the expansive Mongolian sky. She recalled that Englishmen liked their women pale and delicate. Thalia failed on both counts.

What did it matter? Her primary concern was making sure that the inquisitive stranger was not an Heir, or anyone else who might cause her and her father harm. Fashion could go hang.

Thalia ran back to her father's *ger,* cursing as the narrow dress bit into her sides. Their other servant, Batu, followed her inside, and he made a choking noise when he observed her dress. She gave him a fierce scowl that would have sent lesser men running for cover, but Batu had known her since she was a child, and only chuckled to himself as he moved to put away the books scattered throughout the *ger*.

When Franklin saw her enter, his eyebrows rose.

"You look . . ."

"Hilarious," Thalia supplied.

"Well, yes," her father agreed. "But I was also going to say 'lovely'."

Thalia went to one of the painted chests and pulled out her father's seldom-used revolver, then checked to ensure it was loaded. "I can't very well be both."

Before her father could answer, there was a knock at the wooden door to the tent. Her father called out, "Enter." The door began to swing open.

Thalia tucked the hand holding the revolver behind her back. She stood behind her father's chair and braced herself, wondering what kind of man would step across the threshold and if she would have to use a gun on another human being for the first time in her life.

The man ducked to make it through the door, then immediately removed his hat, uncovering a head of close-cropped, wheat-colored hair. He was not precisely handsome, but he possessed an air of command and confidence that shifted everything to his favor. His face was lean and rugged, his features bold and cleanly defined; there was nothing of the drawing room about him, nothing refined or elegant. He was clean-shaven, allowing the hard planes of his face to show clearly. He was not an aristocrat and looked as though he had fought for everything he ever had in his life, rather than expecting it to be given to him. Even in the filtered light inside the *ger,* Thalia could see the gleaming gold of his eyes, their sharp intelligence that missed nothing as they scanned the inside of the tent and finally fell on her and her father.

"Franklin Burgess?" he asked.

"Yes, sir," her father answered, guarded. "My daughter, Thalia."

She remembered enough to sketch a curtsy as she felt the heat of the stranger's gaze on her. An uncharacteristic flush rose in her cheeks.

"And you are . . . ?" her father prompted.

"Captain Gabriel Huntley," came the reply, and now it made sense that the man who had such sure bearing would be an officer. "Of the Thirty-third Regiment." Thalia was not certain she could relax just yet, since it was not unheard of for the Heirs to find members in the ranks of the military. She quickly took stock of the width of the captain's shoulders, how even standing still he seemed to radiate energy and the capacity for lethal movement. Captain Huntley would be a fine addition to the Heirs.

There was something magnetic about him, though, something that charged the very air inside the *ger,* and she felt herself acutely aware of him. His sculpted face, the brawn of his body, the way he carried his gear, all of it, felt overwhelmingly masculine. How ironic, how dreadful, it would be, if the only man to have attracted her attention in years turned out to be her enemy. Sergei, her old suitor, had wound up being her enemy, but in a very different way.

"You are out of uniform, Captain Huntley," her father pointed out.

For the first time since his entrance, the captain's steady concentration broke as he glanced down at his dusty civilian traveling clothes. "I'm here in an unofficial capacity." He had a gravelly voice with a hint of an accent Thalia could not place. It was different from the cultured tones of her father's friends, rougher, but with a low music that danced up the curves of her back.

"And what capacity is that?" she asked. Thalia realized too late that a proper Englishwoman would not speak so boldly, nor ask a question out of turn, but, hell, if Captain Huntley *was* an Heir, niceties did not really matter.

His eyes flew back to her, and she met his look levelly, even as a low tremor pulsed inside her. God, there it was again, that strange *something* that he provoked in her, now made a hundred times stronger when their gazes connected. She watched him assess her, refusing to back down from the unconcealed measuring. She wondered if he felt that peculiar awareness too, if their held look made his stomach flutter. Thalia doubted it. She was no beauty—too tall, her features too strong, and there was the added handicap of this dreadful dress. Besides, he didn't quite seem like the kind of man who fluttered anything.

Yet . . . maybe she was wrong. Even though he was on the other side of the *ger,* Thalia could feel him looking at her, taking her in, with an intensity that bordered on unnerving. And intriguing.

Regardless of her scanty knowledge of society, Thalia *did* know that gentlemen did not look at ladies in such a fashion. Strange. Officers usually came from the ranks of the upper classes. He should know better. But then, so should she.

"As a messenger," he answered, still holding Thalia's gaze, "from Anthony Morris."

That name got her attention, as well as her father's.

"What about Morris?" he demanded. "If he has a message for me, he should be here, himself."

The captain broke away from looking intently at Thalia as he regarded her father. He suddenly appeared a bit tired, and also sad.

"Mr. Morris is dead, sir."

Thalia gasped, and her father cried out in shock and horror. Tony Morris was one of her father's closest friends. Thalia put her hand on her father's shoulder and gave him a supportive squeeze as he removed his glasses and covered his eyes. Tony was like a younger brother to her father, and

Thalia considered him family. To know that he was dead—
her hands shook. It couldn't be true, could it? He was so
bright and good and . . . God, her throat burned from unshed
tears for her friend. She swallowed hard and glanced up
from her grief. Such scenes were to be conducted in private,
away from the eyes of strangers.

The captain ducked his head respectfully as he studied his
hands, which were gripped tightly on his hat. Through the
fog of her sorrow, Thalia understood that the captain had
done this before. Given bad news to the friends and families
of those that had died. What a dreadful responsibility, one
she wouldn't wish on anyone.

She tried to speak, but her words caught on shards of loss.
She gulped and tried again. "How did it happen?"

The captain cleared his throat and looked at Franklin. He
seemed to be deliberately avoiding looking at her. "This
might not be suitable for . . . young ladies."

Even in her grief, Thalia had to suppress a snort. Clearly,
this man knew nothing of her. Fortunately, her father, voice
rough with emotion about Tony Morris's death, said, "Please
speak candidly in front of Thalia. She has a remarkably
strong constitution."

Captain Huntley's gaze flicked back at her for a brief
moment, then stayed fixed on her father. She saw with
amazement that this strapping military man was uncomfortable, and, stranger still, it was *her* that was making him uncomfortable. Perhaps it was because of the nature of his
news, unsuitable as it was for young ladies. Or perhaps it was
because he'd felt something between them, as well, something instant and potent. She did not want to consider it, not
when she was reeling from the pain of Tony Morris's death.

After clearing his throat again, the captain said, "He was
killed, sir. In Southampton."

"So close!" Franklin exclaimed. "On our very doorstep."

"I don't know 'bout doorsteps, sir, but he was attacked

in an alley by a group of men." Captain Huntley paused as Thalia's father cursed. "They'd badly outnumbered him, but he fought bravely until the end."

"How do you know all this?" Thalia asked. If Tony's death had been reported in the papers, surely someone other than the captain would be standing in their *ger* right now, Bennett Day or Catullus Graves. How Thalia longed to see one of their numbers, to share her family's grief with them instead of this man who disquieted her with his very presence.

Captain Huntley again let his eyes rest on her briefly. She fought down her immediate physical response, trying to focus on what he was saying. "I was there, miss, when it happened. Passing by when I heard the sounds of Morris's being attacked, and joined in to help him." He grimaced. "But there were too many, and when my back was turned, he was stabbed by one of them—a blond man who talked like a nob, I mean, a gentleman."

"Henry Lamb?" Franklin asked, looking up at Thalia. She shrugged. Her father turned his attention back to the captain and his voice grew sharp, "You say you were merely 'passing by,' and heard the scuffle and just 'joined in to help.' Sounds damned suspicious to me." Thalia had to agree with her father. What sort of man passed by a fight and came to the aid of the victim, throwing himself into the fray for the sake of a stranger? Hardly anyone.

Captain Huntley tightened his jaw, angry. "Suspicious or not, sir, that's what happened. Morris even saved my life just before the end. So when he gave me the message to deliver to you, in person, I couldn't say no."

"You came all the way from Southampton to Urga to fulfill a dying man's request, a man you had never met before," Thalia repeated, disbelief plain in her voice.

The captain did not even bother answering her. "It couldn't be written down, Morris said," he continued, addressing her father and infuriating Thalia in the process. She didn't care for being ignored. "I've had it in my head for nearly three months, and it makes no sense to me, so I'll pass it on to you. Perhaps you can understand it, sir, because, as much as I've tried, I can't."

"Please," her father said, holding his hand out and gesturing for Captain Huntley to proceed.

"The message is this: 'The sons are ascendant. Seek the woman who feeds the tortoise.'"

He glanced at both Thalia and her father to see their reactions, and could not contain his surprise when her father cursed again and Thalia gripped a nearby table for support. She felt dizzy. It was beginning. "You know what that means?" the captain asked.

Franklin nodded as his hands curled and uncurled into fists, while Thalia caught her lower lip between her teeth and gnawed pensively on it.

She knew it was bound to happen, but they had never known when. That time was now at hand. If what Captain Huntley said was true, they would have to move quickly. But that was presuming he *was* speaking the truth.

"We don't know if we can trust you, Captain," Thalia said. She stepped around her father's chair and, despite the tight discomfort of the dress, walked straight up to Captain Huntley, pausing only a few feet away from him. He stiffened slightly at her approach. His gaze flicked down to the revolver in her hand, and he raised an eyebrow.

"A nice welcome for a tired traveler," he drawled.

"Hopefully," she answered, "I won't have to use it."

"Hopefully, I won't have to take it from you," he corrected.

She deliberately eyed him from the tips of his heavy, worn boots to the top of his sandy head—a long journey that, unfortunately, brought her an even greater awareness of his size and strength. He may have been out of uniform, but there was no missing the discipline of his bearing, nor his physicality.

He was no bookish scholar, but a man who made his way through the world with action. Few men who weren't Blades had the same presence. Thalia tried to make herself ignore it, but now that she was within touching distance, the task was impossible. She could smell the dust of the road on him, the scent of wind and leather. A man's scent.

Forcing herself to concentrate, she said, "You could have killed Anthony Morris, yourself, and could be trying to lead us into a trap." Both she and her father glanced at the kestrel on his perch, but the bird seemed untroubled. It wasn't enough of a sign, though.

"I'm tired of your hounding," Captain Huntley answered, his voice a low rumble and his eyes amber fire. He was obviously not a man used to being questioned. Too bad.

"If you know anything of what is at stake," Thalia shot back, "you would understand my need for caution."

"I don't know what's at stake," the captain growled. "But here's further proof." He reached for his pocket, and Thalia's hand tightened on her revolver, moving to cock it. Captain Huntley looked over Thalia's shoulder with a shuttered expression, and she followed his gaze to her father, who now had the rifle trained on the captain's head. As if used to having large guns pointed at him, Captain Huntley calmly reached into his pocket then held out his hand. What she saw there made her gasp.

It was the Compass.

"Morris gave this to me," the captain continued. "I was to give it to you and say, 'North is eternal.'" He handed it to her father.

Thalia stared at the Compass in her father's hand as she felt the gears of a global machine begin to turn.

Everything Captain Huntley had said was true. Their enemy was on the move.

* * *

She and her father managed to remember their manners enough to offer Captain Huntley a seat and some English tea. She handed the captain a cup of the steaming beverage, which he took with large, work-rough hands. Their fingers brushed against each other. The sensation of his touch ran through her like wild horses. He breathed in quickly as her skin went sensitive and alive, feeling everything at once, but mostly *him*.

They stared at each other, manners forgotten. A blaze there, in his golden eyes, and an answering flare within her. Hot and sudden, like wildfire on the steppe after a dry season.

He broke the contact first, pretending to study his cup as he took a sip of tea. Thalia tried, but failed, not to watch the shape of his mouth on the painted rim of the cup. How might those lips feel against her skin? She knew better than this, she chided herself, and as soon as Captain Huntley had finished his tea, she would show him the door and never see the man again.

Though he seemed to have other ideas.

"I can't pretend to know what any of those messages mean," he said to her father. He glanced down at her father's braced and bandaged leg. "But it's clear that you need some help. Let me give it."

"I thank you, Captain," Franklin answered, "but no. We can manage on our own."

Batu had found a small folding camp chair, and now the captain sat in it, but the chair did a poor job of containing him. He kept stretching out his legs and trying to fit himself into the seat that had, in the past, comfortably held Thalia, and nearly every other man who had come into their *ger,* but it was like trying to put a waistcoat on a tiger.

He looked at her father, then at Thalia, sitting nearby. She struggled to ignore the leap her stomach gave when she felt his golden scrutiny.

"I doubt that," the captain said bluntly. "You need me."

Thalia ground her teeth together at his presumption. How like a military man to step in where he knew nothing and didn't belong, and start issuing orders.

"Rest assured," her father replied, "that we do not. You did your duty to Anthony Morris with honor, but now you have discharged that duty and can return home to England."

That prospect did not seem to elate Captain Huntley. He worked the clean square line of his jaw as he contemplated the fragile china in his hand. "Sir—" he began.

"Thank you, Captain," Thalia said, cutting him off, and he didn't care for that one bit. A flare of anger gleamed in his eyes as he looked at her. "We do appreciate your offer of help, but this is personal business."

"Personal enough to get a man killed?"

Thalia stood. She didn't care if she was being rude, violating every principle of Mongol and English hospitality, but she had to get rid of the tenacious, irritating captain immediately. It had nothing to do with her reaction toward this man. It was purely a matter of protection. She walked to the door and held it open.

"Thank you," she said again in a clipped, frosty voice. "Everything you have done has been extraordinary, but you can go no further in your task. My father and I are perfectly capable of managing the situation *on our own*."

Her father kept his expression carefully neutral, providing neither assistance nor resistance.

After a moment, a wry smile curved in the corner of Captain Huntley's mouth, and he set his teacup down on the table with a sharp clack. He unfolded himself from the chair with surprising grace, then picked up his pack and shouldered it. With a slight clicking of his heels, he bowed to her father with a murmured, "Sir." Her father, not much inclined to ceremony, took the captain's hand and shook it.

"You stood up for Tony, which I wish I could have done,"

Franklin said. "And your honor does you credit. Godspeed to you, Captain, and good luck."

The captain offered no similar reply, but shook Franklin's hand gravely. He then strode to the door, stopping in front of Thalia. She kept her gaze trained on the space just over his shoulder, trying to avoid that sharp jolt of sensation that came from looking into his eyes. "I've sailed half way 'round the world," he said quietly, his voice like whiskey, rough and warm, "including chugging through the Bay of Bengal on the leakiest, rustiest, and least seaworthy freighter that ever insulted the ocean, which, after the luxuries of the first steamship, did little for my constitution. I've taken the most damnable journey through China, and most of my coin is now lining the pockets of every single government agent between here and Peking."

"I am sorry about that," Thalia said, and meant it. "We haven't much money, ourselves, but surely we can spare some for your return."

He looked coldly at her. "I don't want sympathy, and I don't want your coin."

"What *do* you want, then?"

"Tell me what Morris's message means."

She shook her head. "That is one thing I cannot give you, Captain. It would imperil not only you, but many others as well."

Though her answer clearly didn't satisfy him, he pressed for no more. He gave Thalia a small bow, but there was an intangible something that was deeply ironic about the gesture. He stared at the ground for a moment, and Thalia followed his gaze to the tops of her muddy, heavy boots, which stuck out from the hem of the dress. Yes, she was a genuine elegant English rose. Thalia drew herself up to her full height and resisted the urge to twitch the gown's fabric over the boots. Their gazes met and held. *Dangerous,* she thought. He might not be a Blade, but he was a man, and not any man, but one who could inflict serious damage on her, if she let him. She could see that plainly. Oh, God, she was glad he was leaving. She would have had to be on her guard constantly, had he stayed.

"Miss Burgess," he rumbled.

"Captain," she said coolly.

With a nod, he placed his hat upon his head and walked out into the dusk. He never hesitated, instead moving straight and steadily through the still-crowded lanes. Without any urging on his part, the throngs parted to let him pass. Rather than watch him disappear into the mass, which she felt possessed to do, Thalia shut the door, then turned and looked at her father. The confines of the tent, or, more accurately, the confines of her own body, still vibrated with Captain Huntley's presence. He lingered there, the sun's afterimage burned into her.

"You may be a Blade," she said to her father, "but you also have a broken leg. Both of mine are whole and hale. The responsibility now falls to me."

"Only *you,* my dear?" Her father found the crutches next to his chair and pulled himself up, waving away the solicitous Batu. He limped toward her, his expression concerned and dark. "This will be a dangerous task. I cannot send my only child, my only daughter, into such peril."

"There's no choice, Father," she answered levelly. "I must go."

"But you aren't a Blade, Thalia," he countered. "I am."

Thalia knew he was trying to protect her, but his words still stung. "You cannot ride, not as fast as you need to go. I can ride fast, I can shoot straight, and I will make sure that whatever needs protection will be kept safe."

After a few moments, her father sighed and shook his head. She knew then that, though he did not like it, he understood that she spoke the truth and was giving her leave to carry out the work of the Blades. As she had longed to do ever since she was ten years old and had first learned of their existence.

He pulled out a chain that hung around his neck. Hanging at the end of the chain was an old locket. "You recognize this, don't you?"

Thalia nodded, stepping forward. Her father had never been without that locket, not once. Carefully, he unclasped the chain, put the locket in his palm, and then opened it.

Her and her father's faces were bathed with a soft glowing light. On both sides of the locket appeared a pair of tiny people, barely two inches high. They smiled and waved, though neither of them seemed really to see either Thalia or her father.

"Your mother," her father murmured. "And you."

Thalia bent closer, even though she had seen the locket many times. It still sent a shiver through her. One of the little figures was Thalia herself, and it was strange to see herself in miniature form. But the most amazing thing was Thalia's mother, healthy and happy. It had been years since Thalia had seen her mother as anything other than this small magical image. Looking at Diana Burgess's tiny figure, Thalia felt her throat ache.

The locket enabled the wearer to see whomever they loved most dearly. It wasn't always such a gift.

"I shall look at this every day while you are gone," her father said quietly.

He shut the locket and then refastened the chain around his neck.

She tried to make herself smile, but her heart was pounding with mingled fear and anticipation. Nearly everything she knew about the world of the Blades had been related to her by her father or other members of the group. Their activities were shrouded in danger and mystery. Some Blades never returned from their missions. She might soon be added to that number. But there was no room for failure. There was much more than her own life at stake.

"I set out at first light," she announced.

Chapter 3

Followed

Though it was only September, the predawn air was bitterly cold. Huntley stood in the darkness, hidden from view by a fence surrounding one of the large felt tents, his breath curling in warm puffs before dissipating in the chill. He kept his icy hands in his pockets and didn't stamp his feet to warm his almost-numb toes, since he was too well trained to make any noise while lying in wait.

The same couldn't be said for his horse. The animal chuffed softly behind him, moving restlessly and tugging on the reins. You've gone through the trouble to get me awake, she seemed to say, so why not make use of me? Huntley stroked the horse's softly bristled muzzle and murmured soothing words into her ear to quiet her. The mare seemed appeased, but only slightly. She wanted to move. He couldn't blame her.

Huntley had spent the better part of yesterday evening tracking down a horse large enough for him to ride comfortably. Mongol horses were sturdy beasts, adapted well for the steppes and hard weather, but they were also remarkably small, almost the size of ponies, and unless Huntley wanted his knees knocking against his jaw as he rode, he needed to find a horse that could fit his tall frame. He'd also bought himself a Russian saddle of soft leather. The wooden Mongol saddles were beautifully ornamented, but deuced uncomfortable.

He hadn't any idea how many miles he would cover on the journey ahead, but he wanted to be prepared for any eventuality. He tried to think of anything that could happen, be ready for whatever came his way, for good or ill. That was something else that had enabled him to rise to the rank of officer when others who'd enlisted at the same time languished as sergeants.

Huntley was no longer an officer, no longer a soldier, but his senses in the frigid morning were still sharply alive as he kept watch over Franklin Burgess's compound. After sleeping a few hours in a hospitable Mongol's tent in exchange for splitting firewood, Huntley had taken up position opposite Burgess's own group of tents to wait. The man had insisted that he didn't need Huntley's assistance, but it was clear that the blasted message Huntley had delivered yesterday meant that trouble was coming, and a middle-aged man with a badly broken leg wouldn't be able to face it properly on his own.

Though Burgess wasn't entirely on his own. There had been his daughter, too. Julia. No, that wasn't her name. Thalia. A young woman with bold eyes and a bolder mouth, neither of which he had been able to forget, even while he had slept. His mind also kept circling back to those muddy boots peeking out from under the hem of her dress, what they meant, and why he'd even care about some girl's boots.

He hadn't expected to find a young Englishwoman in such a wild place as Urga, and her presence inside Burgess's tent immediately threw him when he entered. He had been so focused on delivering the message, finally learning what it meant, that Huntley had never considered that Burgess might not be a single man like himself, but a father, and worse, the father of a daughter. Huntley didn't like having genteel ladies around. He didn't know what to say, where to look. Genteel ladies seldom had much to do with enlisted men, but when he had become an officer, he'd had to associate with the other officers' wives. Their fripperies and fragility made him nervous. Somehow, he almost always wound up offending them, though God only knew how.

Strangely, he hadn't offended Thalia Burgess, but they riled each other. He wasn't used to being questioned. Fifteen years of steady and good service for Her Majesty meant something.

Damned aggravating, how difficult it had been to tear his eyes from her, how, from the moment he had set foot inside Franklin Burgess's tent, Huntley had been aware of her, every movement, every word, even, for the love of the devil, her breathing.

His only explanation was that it had been six months since he'd taken a woman to bed. He had to think for a moment, and then only barely remembered Felicia, Lieutenant Colonel Calvin's wife. Huntley generally avoided sleeping with married women, but everyone in the camp knew that Calvin kept at least two native mistresses and had given each of them a handful of babies. When Huntley had sold out, he finally gave in to Felicia's advances. They'd spent a single pleasant, but not particularly remarkable, night together. And that was really six months ago? Great Gideon! Being near *any* woman was bound to attract his attention, and Thalia Burgess was definitely a woman. That had to be the reason.

He'd found her manner to be a peculiar mix: on one hand, she was trussed up in a dress that looked ill-fitting. Wrinkled and seldom worn. The fabric had been tight across her bosom, but he'd tried like hell not to look. He'd tried, and failed. She could fit quite nicely in his large hands, filling them but not spilling over.

He clenched his hands into fists, as if the feeling of his fingers curling into his palm might erase the desire to peel that damned dress off Thalia and see if his intuition was right.

That didn't stop his mind from wandering back to her, though. It didn't help that he had nothing to do but wait, no task to keep his thoughts busy but think of her.

Thick, dark hair, meant for tangling in a man's fingers. Her cheeks were so full of lively color, her green eyes so vivid and brilliant, she must wear some of the womanly paint that ladies always claimed they never used but often did. And then there were those boots, spattered with mud and soft from use, though the dress's hem was clean. A strange tangle of contradictions.

Besides the way she looked, he had also been struck by her manner. He remembered the officers' wives, even Felicia, complaining about the heat or their servants, and trying so hard to be genteel and pleasant and proper in the middle of "heathen backwaters," as they called them. Thalia Burgess had said nothing derogatory about Mongolia, never apologized, and didn't yell at her native servants.

He and Thalia Burgess had stood close to each other, within touching distance. His body had reacted immediately to her nearness as he saw that she was tall for a woman and prodigiously pretty. She wasn't a smooth and oval-faced porcelain doll, but had high, clear cheekbones, a strong chin, and an equally strong, straight nose. A full, rosy mouth. Even her annoying mistrust of him couldn't shake his interest.

Damn it, he needed to get a hold of himself, and he needed to do it *now.* Which meant he couldn't think about Thalia Burgess any longer.

Think about the message, he told himself. It was important, whatever it meant, and Franklin Burgess was going to do something about it. And when he did, Huntley would be right there, giving the stubborn man and his even more stubborn daughter the help they needed. He couldn't just turn around and head back to England, to Leeds, which probably had more than its fair share of textile merchants. He was needed *here,* halfway around the bloody world, picking apart dangerous enigmas that had already cost one man his life. Despite Burgess's insisting that Huntley had performed his duty to Anthony Morris, there was too much unresolved in Urga.

To keep his fingers from freezing off, Huntley counted the number of bullets in his kit, and reviewed his preparations from the night before, including taking his guns apart and cleaning them thoroughly. All routines he'd done more times than he could remember.

It didn't seem likely that the task at hand, whatever it was, would be done in the chaotic maze of the city. Broken leg or no, Burgess would be traveling, and when he did, Huntley would be shadowing him. He'd be remiss in his duty if he let Burgess venture out into danger without reliable protection.

With that in mind, Huntley now waited near Burgess's compound, eyes adjusted to the dark, trying to calm an impatient horse, freezing his goddamned rump off, and looking for signs of activity from the tents.

Finally, there was movement. The door to Burgess's tent opened and a man in native dress came out. Huntley recognized him as Burgess's Mongol servant. The servant walked quickly to where several horses were tethered and began saddling two of them. As he did this, another man came out of the tent. Huntley didn't recognize him; he was taller than the servant, but he wore native dress, also, and carried saddlebags. It couldn't be Burgess, since this man walked easily and confidently, not a crutch in sight. His long, dark hair was pulled back, and he wore a small wool hat. In the quiet of the morning, Huntley heard the man speak softly to the other in Mongolian, and realized with a start that it wasn't a man, but a woman, and no ordinary woman, but Thalia Burgess.

She moved much more comfortably now than she had the day before, striding around the yard that surrounded the tent, confident and intent. She made several trips to and from the tent, easily carrying bags and equipment, as the servant finished saddling the horses. The final time she emerged from the tent, she carried a rifle, the same heavy old Beattie that Burgess had pointed at Huntley yesterday. She put the rifle in a scabbard hung on her saddle. The servant took an ancient muzzleloader and also hung it from his saddle. Thalia Burgess and the servant loaded the horses together, hardly speaking, working quickly. They put most of the bags onto a third, unsaddled horse, keeping the smaller items for the horses they planned on riding. It was clear they had packed for a journey before.

As they were finishing, Burgess himself came out of the tent, a crutch propped under one arm and using the other to lean on a Mongol woman beside him. His daughter gave her reins to the male servant before stepping forward, just in front of her father. Burgess handed her something, and she stared at the object in her hands for a moment. Burgess then wrapped one arm around his daughter's straight shoulders and held her tightly as her arms came up to clasp him. She pressed her face against his shoulder, and he struggled with his crutch as he caressed the back of her head with a loving and protective hand. It was the embrace any parent, regardless of nationality or race, gives his child before he or she sets off on a dangerous journey. The servants watched, emotion plain in their faces. The female servant dabbed at her eyes with her sleeve. Feeling like an interloper, Huntley almost looked away from the intimate family scene.

He reminded himself that whatever that message meant, it surely was something important if Burgess was willing to let his *daughter* embark on the mission, since he could not. That meant that Huntley was going to be stuck with her for some time now. May the Archangel Michael descend from the skies and kick Huntley straight in the rocks.

After finally breaking away from her father's embrace, Thalia put the object her father had given her into her pocket. She then moved without hesitation toward one of the saddled horses, taking back the reins. She put her booted foot into the stirrup and swung herself up into the saddle with a fluid ease that would make any cavalryman proud. The male servant also mounted up. Burgess raised his hand in a farewell as his daughter and servant wheeled their horses about and kicked them into a canter. They disappeared into the remaining night.

Huntley waited until Burgess and the female servant went back inside before mounting up on his own horse. The mare responded eagerly to the press of his heels into her flanks, leaping into her gallop and ready to run. Mongol horses needed movement, needed freedom. For Huntley, the feeling was mutual. He wasn't familiar with this city, and knew nothing of this country; however, despite all this and the darkness, he could find Thalia Burgess's trail.

She may have been one of the more confounding women he'd ever known, but, whether she wanted his help or not, he was sticking with her. No matter where the journey took them.

"We're being followed."

Batu turned in his saddle and looked around, but aside from the rolling hills full of gently browning grass and the huge expanse of blue sky, they seemed to be alone as they rode west from Urga. The sun had risen several hours ago, and they had slowed their horses to a brisk trot to conserve the animals' energy.

"I see no one, Thalia *guai*," Batu said.

"He's too skilled to let us see him," Thalia answered. She kept her eyes moving across the landscape, touching the undulating hills, the scattered rocky outcroppings, the shadows of clouds slipping over the steppe, blown on dry winds from the northwest. She breathed in deeply, felt the crisp autumn air fill her and cleanse away the dirt of Urga. God, it was good to be out of the city!

"Who?"

"Captain Huntley."

"The man with the golden hair and golden eyes? He seemed fierce."

Thalia gave a clipped nod, remembering darkly not only the captain's extraordinary appearance and manner, but his immediate effect on her, as well. "He's been following us since we left Urga," she explained. She tried to tell herself that what she was feeling was irritation. She had not the time nor energy to worry about an annoyingly persistent soldier. And she had even less room for her own unwanted reaction to him. "It seems he did not take my father's refusal of help to heart. The captain is determined to sneak after us and force his assistance on us."

She briefly entertained the idea that perhaps her father had sent Captain Huntley after them to ensure that she and Batu were protected on their mission, but just as quickly rejected the idea. As much as Franklin Burgess didn't like it, the safety and secrecy of the Blades came first.

"Are you sure?" Batu looked around again. "We seem quite alone."

"I am sure." Thalia patted the neck of her horse in encouragement. They had only just begun their voyage, and the animals would need their spirits bolstered to make it the whole distance. She pointed to a rise, and she knew that a small, clear stream flowed at the base on the other side, sheltered in a small valley. "We'll stop and water the horses once we reach there, maybe have a little something to eat, ourselves.

Once we do, we'll wait for the captain to catch up and politely but firmly tell him to leave us alone."

Batu still looked dubious that anyone was on the steppe besides themselves and the occasional herd of gazelle, but Thalia's instincts for such things were seldom wrong, so he did not pursue the matter any further.

She had become aware of someone's presence behind them shortly after they had ridden past the outskirts of Urga, when the *gers* had begun to thin into more and more remote *ails,* or encampments. It could only be Captain Huntley, and though he had been very good at remaining quiet, keeping his horse from kicking up too much telltale dust, she had known he was there.

She had been all too aware of him since he stepped into her father's *ger.* He was big and commanding and unapologetic about both of those qualities, and though Thalia had always been at ease in the presence of men, there was something about Captain Huntley, something so specifically *masculine,* that she could not feel comfortable around him. His golden eyes, his whiskey voice, his very physical nature that the tent could barely contain—these things combined like a drug in her body, a drug on which she could not become dependent. She could never trust such an opiate as Captain Huntley. Her swift and strong reaction to him was unnerving. The very fact that he *did* bother her bothered her even more, until she felt as though she was chasing her own ghost, grabbing at something that would always slip from her grasp.

In a few more minutes, it would no longer matter. She would confront Captain Huntley and insist that he return to England. Truthfully, it didn't matter where he went, Brazil or the Maldives or anywhere else, so long as he wasn't following her in Mongolia. And then her interest in him would disappear, as it must.

She and Batu crested the rise, then rode down into the

small valley where she planned on watering and resting the horses. Water was always scarce, even far north of the vast Gobi desert. It would not benefit her and Batu to push the horses, despite the time concerns, since thirsty horses tired quickly. Better to lose a few minutes here and there than to face a larger obstacle later on.

The valley that contained the stream was shaped like a cup, surrounded on all sides by low, rocky hills. A few larch trees dotted the valley, most of them clustered near the water's edge. As they approached the stream, she and Batu dismounted and led the horses to the water. The animals gratefully dipped their muzzles into the cold, fresh stream, and Thalia crouched near the bank, cupping her hands to take her own drink. She closed her eyes, tasting the sweet and bracing water. Its purity was never in doubt. To pollute a lake or stream was a great sin for a Mongol, and all nomads took great care to preserve the cleanliness of the water, since it was so precious. Drinking deeply from the stream, Thalia remembered the sludge and rubbish floating in the Thames, the children and women walking up and down its muddy banks, looking for anything of value that had been discarded and then churned up. She had heard tales, too, of a noxious fog that rose up from the Thames, blanketing London with a thick yellow haze that made it impossible to see or breathe. She had no idea how anyone could live like that, why Londoners never saw the direct relationship between clean water and the health of themselves and their city.

As if her thoughts had conjured up another Englishman, Thalia heard the rattle of rocks kicked up from the ground behind her. It had to be the captain. She rose, preparing to be very polite but exceedingly firm in her assertions that she and her servant would proceed alone. As she turned, the polite refusal vanished as her blood chilled.

Henry Lamb stood twenty feet away. Impeccably groomed and blond, he smiled without warmth. He was accompanied by an unsmiling Jonas Edgeworth, his black hair gleaming with tonic, his moustache clipped and severe. They were both attired in the most expensive expedition clothing that Bond Street could provide, as well as armed with revolvers on their hips. Nearby stood three Mongols of dubious appearance holding the reins of a half dozen saddled and packed horses. One of the Mongols was exceedingly big—a barrel-chested man with powerful arms and a rapacious look. His *del* was threadbare, and he wore a battered European hat, with a wicked hunting knife hanging from his belt. He could probably tear a camel apart with his bare hands. However, the large Mongol did not frighten her nearly as much as the well-groomed Englishmen. She instinctively stepped back, trying to reach the rifle strapped to her saddle.

"Please, Miss Burgess," Lamb said, holding up his hands and giving her another bland smile, "it isn't necessary to resort to base violence."

"I believe Tony Morris might disagree with you," Thalia answered. She tried to hold her voice level, keep the fear out of her words, but she couldn't keep her thoughts from Tony, lying dead in an alley in Southampton, with only Captain Huntley to bear witness to his passage from this world to the next. Would Batu play the same role for her?

Lamb's smile faltered only slightly. "An unfortunate, but necessary, casualty." He took a step toward her, and she lunged toward her rifle. Before she could pull the gun from its scabbard, Jonas Edgeworth and two of the Mongols had their own guns pointed at her and Batu. Lamb did not bother to draw his own weapon, and actually looked a little bored as he drawled, "I think it will be much more civilized if we conduct our conversation without your being armed, don't you agree? Take your hand off of your gun."

Thalia obeyed but did not bother to answer. Her mind whirled, trying to figure out how she and Batu could get away, if she could pull her rifle in time. She understood that it had been Lamb and Edgeworth, along with their hired muscle, that she had observed following her, and not Captain Huntley. If only it *had* been him. She would much rather tell the attractive, persistent captain to go away than face down two Heirs and their brutes.

"What do you want?" she asked, stalling.

"You know what we want, girl," Edgeworth barked. Unlike Lamb, he hadn't mastered the art of polished menace, and his pale skin was already reddening with anger.

Again, Lamb held up one finely manicured hand. "Enough, Edgeworth. We don't have to resort to anything unpleasant. Yet." Edgeworth reddened further, but clamped his lips together to keep his silence. Lamb continued, tipping his head toward the giant Mongol, "Our friend came to us a few months ago with a riddle about where to find the Source."

"Then you know where to find it," Thalia answered.

"Not quite. But you know this miserable country very well." He picked at a minuscule piece of dirt on his lapel. Thalia nearly smiled at the Sisyphean labor. "Come now, Miss Burgess," Lamb added, attempting to sound appealing, "don't be difficult. You can prove yourself a credit to your sex, and do your country a great service as well, by telling us where the Source is. I am prepared to make it worth your while."

"So you can enslave the people of Outer Mongolia?"

"With the power of the Source at our disposal, Mongolia would be conquered," Lamb snapped. "We'd force these shiftless nomads into *real* work. Mining."

"And those that resisted?"

"Disposed of."

"Killed, you mean."

Lamb shrugged, unconcerned about the possibility of slaughter. "Yellow barbarians don't matter."

Instead of answering Lamb, or running up and shoving her knee into his groin as she longed to do, Thalia turned toward the three Mongols standing nearby. "Do you know what these Englishmen mean to do?" she asked them in Mongolian. "They will steal the heart of your homeland and use it against you, to subjugate you, murder you if you resist them."

Two of the Mongols shifted uneasily. But the large Mongol grunted in an approximation of a laugh. "Who do you think sold them the information about the prize in the first place?" he said.

"But your country," Thalia protested, shocked, "your way of life as a nomad—"

"Doesn't buy me a herd of camels," the Mongol said. "Or put mutton in my belly or women in my *ger.*"

Batu looked disgusted, and Thalia could not blame him. She was horrified that someone could trade his life and culture for a handful of pound sterling.

"That's enough of that," Lamb cut in, speaking in English. He was irritated and impatient, his polish beginning to rub away, revealing greed, ambition, and something uglier, something cruel and brutal, beneath. "I'm tired of niceties. I'll let my men get the answer out of you." He gestured toward the Mongols, waving them forward. His men leered at her, concerns about their way of life forgotten in exchange for a chance to assault her, and began to advance. Thalia knew she couldn't get to her rifle in time, so she went for the knife at her waist just as one of the Mongols reached out to grab her.

He never touched her. There was a loud *crack,* and the man fell to the ground, blood seeping from a hole in the middle of his chest. He was dead within seconds. Everyone, including Thalia, whirled around, looking for the source of the gunfire. She and Batu immediately drew their weapons from the scabbards on their saddles and crouched low, having no time to register shock.

Lamb ran for the shelter of his horses. A bullet whined, and a small patch of ground exploded near his feet as he sprinted. Edgeworth began firing wildly at the top of the valley as he, too, headed toward the cluster of agitated horses. The large Mongol unshouldered his Russian rifle as he squatted behind some brush. When another gunshot pierced the air, grazing the Mongol's cheek, the man merely dabbed at the line of blood on his face and shouted at the remaining Mongol thug. The big Mongol pointed at the rise of the hills to the east, and ordered his compatriot to ride up there and take out the marksman while he provided cover fire.

The man looked dubious at first, but the large Mongol shouted that he would tear his insides out and feed them to the hawks, and looked as though he meant every blood-thirsty word. So the man leapt into the saddle to obey. The giant Mongol began firing at the crest of the hill as the other rode closer to whomever was shooting from the valley's rim. It wasn't a deep valley, and the rider would reach the crest within a moment. The marksman, whoever he was, could not defend himself against the rider and the huge Mongol's fire at the same time, and then Thalia and Batu would be on their own.

Another shot rang out, and the rider was pitched from his horse. He groaned, clutching his chest, and went still. The animal reared in fright and sped away, leaving behind the body of its rider. The large Mongol turned toward Thalia with a snarl as she swung the barrel of her rifle away from the dead rider and toward the Mongol's head.

"My accuracy is even better at this distance," she said to him as more shots rang out from the top of the valley.

With a vicious sneer, he began to unfold from his crouch, heading toward her.

"Tsend!" Lamb shouted at the big Mongol. He and

Edgeworth were struggling to keep the horses under control, the animals snorting and shoving each other as they tried to break free and run away. "We'll get her later!"

The Mongol, Tsend, looked torn. He clearly wanted to smash the butt of his rifle into her face, and maybe do worse, but another shot from the sniper just missed Tsend's head. The lure of coin and threat of bullets from the hidden marksman both won out, and the Mongol ran for his own mount. The two Englishmen and their Mongol brawn rode furiously away, bent low over the saddles and casting fearful, angry glances over their shoulders. Batu tried to fire at them, but his muzzleloader was too old and slow to be very accurate when he was hurried. It did not seem to matter as the Heirs disappeared over the ridge, the sounds of their horses' hooves echoing in retreat.

As soon as they vanished, Thalia leapt to her feet but kept her rifle close. She shielded her eyes from the sun as a figure of a man appeared at the top of the valley, the light behind him turning him into a golden-ringed titan.

"Nice shot," he said with a familiar gruff voice as he made his way quickly down the side of the hill. "But I could've taken him with my revolver had he made it over the ridge."

Thalia lowered her rifle and tried not to sigh with relief.

"You are an extremely stubborn man, Captain," she said.

He came down into the valley with long-legged strides, forming from a shape of light into a very real man. A man who was almost smiling as he approached her and she almost smiled back.

"In your case," he answered, "that's a very good thing."

She wanted to say something clever and stoic, something a battle-hardened veteran might pronounce while calmly lighting a celebratory cheroot, but that was precisely the moment her mind and body both realized that she had just shot a man. Killed him. Not an animal, but a human. Her legs gave out from under her as her vision dimmed. She was a murderer. Nausea clutched her stomach.

But then she felt something warm and solid beside her, around her, as she was lowered gently to the ground. "All right. Everything's right, lovely," the captain murmured, his arms cradling her as he eased her onto the grass. She let him hold her as she tried to find some air but couldn't find enough anywhere in the world to fill her lungs, let alone take a simple breath. The world retreated. She felt the rifle slip from her fingers, and it was only the quick reflexes of Batu that kept it from clattering to the ground.

"Now, just be calm, lass," the captain said, quiet and steady. "Have a look at me and be calm." With one large, callused hand cupped around her head, he turned her to face him. His hat was off, and, through the mists that gathered inside her head, she could see him, as close as he had been the other day, no, closer. She could see the hard planes of his face that seemed, at that moment, just a little softer, the bump on the bridge of his nose that revealed at least one break, the contrast with his beautifully formed mouth, and the small lines that fanned out from the corners of his amber eyes. His eyes, she realized, were not nearly as cold as she had first thought them, but full of living energy, almost animalistic in its intensity. It was that immediate connection to life that started to bring her back from wherever she had been drifting.

"Tell me something," the captain said.

Thalia tried to make her mind focus. "What?"

"Tell me about your first pet," he said. "You had one, I'd wager. A cat, perhaps."

"No . . . ," Thalia murmured. "It was . . . a dog."

Her brain kept trying to bring her back to the dead man on the hill, but Captain Huntley wouldn't allow it as his voice interrupted her thoughts.

"A dog then. Was he small? A little lap dog?"

Thalia heard herself laugh. "No, God, no. Thief was huge. Paws the size of wagon wheels." Her thoughts shifted away from death and toward the animal that had been her constant companion for years. "He was . . . some kind of mastiff. No one knew *what* he was, maybe part bear. The least subtle dog you ever met. Bashed into everything. Could knock you over with just a wag of his tail." She laughed again, remembering.

"That's why he was called Thief," the captain deduced.

She smiled at him. "Yes. Exactly." She finally drew in a breath. Her vision cleared. And she became aware that the captain was practically cradling her against the hard breadth of his chest while her hands had managed to grip his jacket, holding him as tightly as one might hold a vow. She pried her fingers loose and tried to move away from him, but, given the strength of his arms, it was no simple task.

"I'm perfectly well," she said, and hated the slight tremor in her voice.

"You are, at that," the captain answered easily, "but you've also killed someone, which you don't have much experience with. Give yourself some time."

"Do you?" She was breathing better now. And she was loathe to believe it was because of him, his reassuring presence, but she had a bad feeling that that was the very reason.

"Do I what?"

"Have much experience killing people?"

"I didn't become a captain by knitting socks," he said, and Thalia had no answer to that. He loosened his hold on her, taking her by her shoulders. "Come on, let's try and get you on your feet."

"I can stand on my own," she said immediately.

His mouth quirked. "Indulge me."

So she allowed herself to be raised up, trying to bear as much of her own weight as she could. The ground wobbled slightly, but not for long. The captain stepped away, which made her sorry. At last, everything had righted itself. Even so, she could not look at the form of the fallen man's body as it slumped on the hillside.

Captain Huntley stared at her for a few moments, as if waiting for her to crumple to the ground again, but then he seemed satisfied. He turned to Batu.

"Speak English?" he demanded.

"Russian, too," Batu answered.

The captain gave a clipped nod. "Good." He pointed at Thalia. "Keep an eye on her. I'll return in five minutes."

"Where are you going?" Batu asked.

"I hobbled my horse on the other side of this valley," was the reply. "I'll get her and then I'm coming back."

Thalia stopped as she was reaching down to retrieve her rifle. "Back?"

"Yes, back." He took up his hat and set it on his head, the broad brim shading his face. She felt, rather than saw, his eyes on her, the interplay of determination and, oddly, humor. "You aren't taking another step on this journey of yours without me. *Someone's* got to knit the socks."

Chapter 4

Captain Huntley's
Mysterious Disappearance

He didn't expect her to wait for him, but when Huntley came back into the valley, riding his horse, there she was, her servant nearby. Huntley had expected a long chase across the rolling steppes of Mongolia—it seemed like her contrary nature to do something along those lines—and maybe had been perversely looking forward to it, but she had stayed. Another surprise from the continually surprising Thalia Burgess. The bigger surprise, and one he hadn't welcomed at all, was how much he'd enjoyed holding her, how good she had felt in his arms. The woman had been in *shock,* for God's sake, and there he had been, stealing her touch like a randy schoolboy. Sometimes, he thought disgustedly, he just wanted to punch his own face in.

When Huntley returned, she did not look up from repacking the horses. Some of the baggage had fallen from the horses during the skirmish. They had been frightened by the gunfire, unused to the sound, but they hadn't been the only ones.

He watched Thalia as she worked, how she stayed with her task and forcibly kept her gaze from straying toward the dead man on the hill and the other body nearby. She wasn't a killer. Drawing blood had marked her, stunned her. Though she'd handled herself with admirable calm and nerve during the fight—he was still shaking his head with respect at her marksmanship, to take down a man galloping up a hill with one shot—it was in the aftermath that the facts had been laid bare. Her innocence was gone. She was left on the barren plain of guilt and horror.

So he'd done for her what he had done for his men, what he'd had to do for himself, so many years ago: showed the way back from that bleak place. One time, he'd made a trembling private, covered with the enemy's blood, tell him all the bawdy limericks he knew, until the boy had tears in his eyes from laughter. There was another, a lance corporal, who'd had to hold down his best friend while the surgeon cut off an infected leg. The lance corporal hadn't been able to sleep for days, hearing the screams of his friend whenever he closed his eyes in the quiet of night. Huntley had sat with him one night and told him to describe each variety of apple grown on his father's farm in Essex, each tree and leaf, until the lad had slipped off to sleep.

None of them had he commanded to look at him, none of them had he held, but that was something both for Thalia and himself. Seeing guns pointed at her made him need reassurance that she was whole and well. The world for her might one day return to normal, but, he hoped, she would never grow thick-skinned when it came to killing, the way he'd had to in order to survive. He didn't want her to become like him.

That didn't seem to be the case, not yet. She was still riding close to the border of shock. The best way to get her fully back to herself was not to coddle her too much. He knew that much about her.

"Don't fiddle with those packs for much longer," he said

from atop his horse. "Your friends might come back to finish what they started."

She turned her remarkable green eyes to him as she finished tying down the bags, and that strange, unwelcome flash of heat shot through him. He pushed it down, tried to make himself ignore it, but he recalled the lush late summer color of her eyes when he'd held her after the skirmish. He'd learned then that he had been wrong: she didn't wear cosmetics. The gem-like brilliance of her eyes and the rosy color in her cheeks were hers through nature and not art. On top of everything else he was discovering about her, about his response to her, it wasn't a comforting thought.

"How did you know?" she asked. She walked toward her horse and stared at him over the saddle.

Huntley found himself momentarily thrown, and wondered if one of her other unusual qualities included mind reading. That was an even *less* comforting thought, and he struggled to think only of sunshine-filled meadows and kittens playing with dandelion puffs. "Know what?" he stalled.

"About . . . about . . ." She gestured toward the bodies of the men but still could not look at them.

"The ambush?" He shrugged, dismissive. "I knew they were following you just after Urga."

She recovered enough to glare at him. "You knew all the way back then?" she demanded. "And you didn't do anything until now? Why the hell not?"

Huntley had never before met a respectable woman who cursed. Despite her unconventional attire and her ability with a rifle, Thalia Burgess *was* a respectable woman, and to hear such language come from her edible-looking mouth was something of a thrill for Huntley, not unlike going to a prayer meeting and finding it full of unrepentant strumpets.

"I needed to see what they wanted before I made any moves," he said. "And there were five armed men against myself. The best chance was to take them by surprise."

"But it wasn't five against one," she protested. "It was five against three."

"I never count on an untested ally."

She shook her head, muttering something about soldiers, then swung up into the saddle with a fluidity that caused another unwanted flare of interest to spark inside him. Gone was the awkward, confined miss he'd met the day before. This other Thalia Burgess had grace and confidence in her movement, even in her long robe and heavy boots. She walked her horse beside his until they were side by side. Her leg brushed against his, and his grip on the reins tightened, causing his horse to move and bump their legs again. His night with Felicia seemed very long ago, now. In his mind, he called himself many colorful names that would shock even a sailor.

"I thought they were you," she said grudgingly. "That is why I was unprepared when they appeared."

"You wouldn't know I was coming." It wasn't a boast, merely a statement of fact. Huntley had learned years ago how to track and follow without being detected, something else that had come in useful more times than he could recall. Somehow, despite his abilities, Huntley couldn't manage to avoid touching this one woman. He guided his horse so that there was a decent distance between himself and Thalia Burgess—for now.

"I'm not certain whether that is supposed to comfort or terrify me," she replied. "But I do thank you for coming to our aid. If you hadn't been there . . ." She could not hide the shudder that moved through her slender body, the body he remembered pressed against his own.

"I recognized them," Huntley said. "The dark-haired bloke and the other one, the blond toff."

That sharpened her attention. "From Southampton?"

"It was the toff that stabbed Morris."

A look of fury hardened her features, an impressive sight.

She was a woman who gave herself fully to her passions. "Henry Lamb. I should have killed *him,* too," she growled.

"That's the trouble with bloodlust," Huntley remarked. "It's a thirst that's never quenched."

She finally looked at the man on the hill and the other cooling corpse, still lying on the ground where he had fallen from Huntley's shot.

"Should I bury them?" Huntley asked.

Thalia shook her head and turned away. "Bodies of the deceased aren't interred in Mongolia. They're taken to a hillside and left to nature, returned to the earth and heavens that created them. It's called 'sky burial.'"

That explained why Huntley had seen human remains out in the open in Urga. "All the same, I'd rather have my bones covered," he said. "I'd be right sore if I knew some jackal was running around with one of my ribs in his mouth."

"If I'm around for that unfortunate event," she answered, "I'll be sure to keep the dogs away."

Before he could reply, she set her heels to her horse. Batu followed right behind her, and, after checking to make sure that none of the attackers were returning, Huntley also kicked his horse into a canter. He came over the rise and saw Thalia and her servant continuing to ride west. She rode well, straight and tall, standing in the stirrups as the Mongols did.

Huntley trailed after them, keeping his gaze alert and attuned should the Englishmen and their giant slab of a Mongol decide to finish their business within the day. Even as he watched for trouble, and as his eyes kept traveling to the slim back and shoulders of Thalia Burgess, the trim span of her waist bound with a silken sash, he could not help but marvel at the landscape. He had had no idea what to expect when he learned he would be traveling to Mongolia; all his mind had come up with was a gray, featureless plain. But what he now saw changed that. He rode a spread of grass and sky so wide and open that he could believe that he was

sailing across a stretch of green ocean, an endless banner of
azure sky above. And the dark blue robe of Thalia Burgess
riding ahead of him was the star by which he set his course.

He was no sailor. He was a soldier. Escort and guardian
for a reluctant Thalia Burgess, a woman he hadn't known existed until yesterday, and who now occupied a goodly portion of his thoughts. His life was a strange one, all right. It
didn't bother him nearly as much as it should. Bloody wonderful to have a mission again, a purpose beyond Inwood's
promises of work and wife in a country that hadn't been his
home for fifteen years. He forced away thoughts of the
letter, still residing in his pocket.

He nudged his horse, and the mare responded instantly,
ready to gallop across the steppes with almost no encouragement. Within seconds, he had ridden abreast of Thalia. She
glanced at him over her shoulder, her dark hair catching the
wind and light, but said nothing.

"You're going to have to tell me what this is about," he
said after they had ridden together for a few minutes. "Who
your attackers are, why Morris was killed, where we're
headed, what's at stake. All of it. I can't do my job properly
unless I know everything."

"You don't *have* a job," she reminded him and tried to
push her horse farther ahead.

"Everything that happened back in that valley says I do."
He didn't have to see her face to know that she was scowling. The curse words she muttered in Mongolian were also
something of a giveaway. Huntley's mare sped up without
urging, as if goaded by the lead Thalia's horse had, until the
two were again side by side. "Like me or don't, Miss Burgess,
it doesn't matter to me. But either way, I'm protecting you
until we see this through."

Her jaw tightened. Then released. He already knew what
she was thinking. Damned strange. He'd never been particularly attuned to any woman's mind before.

"Losing me won't work," he added, and by the way she clenched her teeth he knew that he had been correct. With a jolt, he felt himself slipping inside of her, her mind, her body, and it bound him to her, suddenly, powerfully, in a way he'd never experienced with another woman. A tight knitting of self to self. He'd killed for her, and he'd do it again, kill anyone who tried to harm her. Even Morris's mission meant less than keeping her safe. The revelation stunned him.

"I've lived in Mongolia since I was a small child," she said. "I know this country better than you, Captain. It wouldn't be difficult to elude you."

He tried to collect himself. "Doesn't matter where we are," he answered. "A trail is a trail. And you'll leave one."

"You sound awfully sure of yourself."

Huntley almost laughed, but wisely checked the impulse since it would only rile her further. "I once tracked down the notorious brigand Ali Jai Khan to his gang's secret hiding place in the Aravali Mountains of Rajasthan, and *that* bloke knew how to disguise his trail." He realized too late that discussing brigands with ladies was probably unwise, but he kept forgetting that Thalia Burgess was a lady. On further reflection, after the hem of her robe flipped back in the breeze, revealing a long, shapely leg in trousers, he was very much aware that she was a woman. The term "lady," however, which brought to mind images of painted china and cramped rooms full of overstuffed furniture, didn't seem to apply.

And, far from being horrified at his anecdote, Thalia Burgess seemed reluctantly impressed. "I wouldn't mind learning how to track," she said so quietly he almost didn't hear her above the sounds of the horses' hooves and rushing wind.

"I may show you, someday," he answered. He didn't know if he ever would, but the prospect seemed almost pleasant. He tried to steer his thoughts back toward the matter at hand,

and not to the idea of spending long hours crawling on forest floors with her, just them alone, in the cool damp seclusion of the woods. "So you may as well face facts: I'm sticking with you. Tell me everything. Better for all of us if you do."

"I wish I could," she said after a pause, and there was real regret in her voice. He found that he liked to hear her speak. She had an unusual accent, not fully English, tinged with a husky, almost Russian flavor. It sounded of long nights under fur blankets.

But despite her remarkable voice, Huntley felt his patience begin to fray. "Look, Miss Burgess," he growled, "whoever or whatever you're protecting—"

"Is far more important than your sense of obligation," she finished. She turned and looked at him directly. "I take my own responsibilities very seriously, Captain. And one of them is maintaining my silence."

Huntley didn't respond, nor did she expect him to. They rode on without speaking, but he was a patient man. When he'd tracked Ali Jai Khan, he and his men had had to lie in wait for days, barely moving, making no noise, even when it rained for an entire day and they'd been lying in mud and mosquitoes, until the time for the bandit's capture was exactly right. It had been hell, but worth it. The situation he was in now would be a paradise by comparison. Though that might not be true, either. He was a soldier, she was a gentleman's daughter, they were on a dangerous journey together, and no matter what his body wanted, he was going to force himself to keep his hands, and other parts, off of her. There were things he needed to know, things that didn't involve the taste of her mouth or the feel of her skin.

He'd have to content himself with finding out her secrets. Where they were headed. What they sought. And why. But those mysteries were much easier to solve than the ones presented by Thalia Burgess. And while he knew he shouldn't learn her secrets, they were becoming much more intriguing to Huntley than anything else he'd ever come across in his jumbled life.

Sunrise was not for some time, but Thalia was already awake. Despite the long hours in the saddle and her physical exhaustion from the trying day, her sleep had been shallow, her dreams troubling. She kept seeing the face of the man she had killed, kept watching him ride up the hill over and over, and each time she raised her rifle and the shot fired sounded louder than disaster. But in her dreams, the man would fall off his horse and roll down, down the hill, until he lay sprawled at her feet, and his face would no longer be his face, but her father's. Blood, bright and accusing, covered her hands.

Many times, over the course of the night, she would wake, gasping and sick. Then she would turn her head toward where she knew Captain Huntley was sleeping, and, somehow, he was always awake when she was, because she would hear his voice say to her softly, "Easy, lass. The dreams will stop, in time."

It didn't seem that way. It didn't seem that she could ever fall asleep again, but she would, after hearing the captain. She didn't know why she found his presence nearby comforting, and it disturbed her that she did. Even so, she did drift off again, back to the nightmare. Would it always be this way? He didn't think so. She wanted, at least, to believe that much.

Thalia now lay still as she fully wakened, looking up at the dark sky, marshalling her strength and her cunning. She and Batu would have to be extremely quiet, more quiet than silence itself, if they were to evade the captain. She supposed they could knock him unconscious with the butt of Batu's heavy muzzleloader, but after everything that Captain

Huntley had done for them, it would be unforgivable for her to physically hurt him. He'd helped save her from the Heirs' violence, and she could not repay him with more of the same. But she did need to be free of him, for the sake of the Blades and everything they protected. She had no choice in the matter.

She would have to move soon. Thalia watched as one star, and then another, began to wink out with the approach of morning. They had camped for the night, wrapped in blankets that had been packed on the horses. Had she been traveling for any other reason, she would have stopped at a nomad's *ail* for the evening and saved herself and Batu the discomfort of sleeping on the hard, bare earth. She understood that she could receive hospitality at any *ger,* whether she knew the family or not. It was the Mongol way never to refuse food or lodging to anyone. But she hadn't the time to stop, pay the usual respects, socialize over a meal, and perhaps perform a few chores to repay her hosts. So she had gone out of her way to avoid any *gers,* making sure that she and her party could not be seen by anyone at the encampments. To pass a *ger* without stopping was highly peculiar and almost rude. Better to stay out of the line of sight and avoid any speculation or unpleasantness.

It would be unpleasant to abandon Captain Huntley, but she saw no alternative. As befitting a soldier, he had traveled well and kept his council, only asking her now and again to identify certain animals or plants. She rather liked his curiosity, how he seemed interested in even the ridiculous marmots who would stare at them from their holes. He was focused on their journey, but had an expansiveness of mind that allowed for taking in new things. It was dreadfully appealing.

For their evening meal, she had handed out typical Mongol foods for travel: *borts,* dried mutton, and *aaruul,* dried cheese from goats' milk, nothing that required a fire for cooking. Out on the steppe at night, a campfire shone like a beacon, and if the Heirs were out there, Thalia could take no chances in giving away her location.

"You're not eating," the captain had noted after she had distributed some food to him and Batu.

She had shaken her head. The idea of putting food into her mouth, chewing and swallowing it, after what she had done earlier in the day, seemed impossible. She didn't think she could hold down anything.

Captain Huntley had gotten up and walked to the bag holding their provisions. He took a measure of *borts* and *aaruul,* and pressed them into her unwilling hand. "Eat," he had commanded. "You can't bring that man back by starving yourself, and you wouldn't want to, anyway."

"I can't," Thalia had answered, but he would not take the food back.

He had insisted. "You can and you will. If we have to sit here all night, I'll make sure you finish those rations."

"Don't talk to me as though I'm a child," she snapped.

"You're not a child, and I don't think of you as one," he replied. "But after a soldier's first kill, he can hurt himself. Not eating, not sleeping. I make sure that doesn't happen. Not with them, and not with you." He sat down opposite her and watched, waiting, until she began to nibble at the dried meat. At first, it had been difficult, and she nearly gagged, until he had said, "Breathe through your nose. Go slowly. And keep drinking." She'd taken sips of *airag,* fermented horses' milk, and gradually, bit by bit, finished her small meal. Despite her resentment toward Captain Huntley for his high-handed way of commanding her, she had ultimately been glad to have eaten something, recovered some of her strength because of it, which annoyed her. She didn't want him to be right, not where knowing her own body's needs was concerned, but he had been. She had a strange, unwanted thought—how well did the captain know women? Probably very well, indeed, with a face and form like his. Not that it mattered to her at all.

At the least, as they readied their beds for the night, he hadn't pressed her for further answers. She appreciated his discretion, yet she also had an idea that he would take another tactic to learn the truth. He might not believe it, but for his sake, she could never tell him everything. And she had to lose him. Immediately.

With that in mind, Thalia now slowly, slowly pulled off her blankets and rolled into a crouch. It was too dark to see much, but she knew that Batu slept not but a yard away to her right. She crept toward him and woke him with a hand on his shoulder, another hand over his mouth to keep him from speaking. Thalia pointed toward where Captain Huntley slept, and Batu nodded with understanding, then got to his feet. They both tiptoed toward where the horses were hobbled and began packing them as noiselessly as possible, using touch, rather than sight, as their guide. The animals snorted and stamped to warm themselves for impending travel. Thalia glanced over her shoulder, alarmed. Nothing from the captain.

The horizon turned pink and the rocky hills around them began to burn with dawn light. It wouldn't be long before the sun's rays reached their position, which would undoubtedly wake Captain Huntley. Even though he'd been awake whenever she had roused from a nightmare, he seemed to sleep soundly now. Maybe she had worn him out, with her frightening dreams. At least she could be grateful to the nightmares for that. She couldn't rely on the captain's exhaustion, though. They had to move quickly.

Thalia debated with herself whether or not she would take the captain's horse. No Mongol liked to walk. Even small children learned to ride soon after taking their first steps. But the steppes were not uninhabited, nor uninhabitable. Taking Captain Huntley's horse was not a death sentence. If he set out on foot, he could reach a *ger* within a day, if not less. She could surely lose him if she deprived him of a horse, and do him very little harm in the process.

As quietly as she could, she moved through the horses to find the tall mare he rode. Yet something was very strange. The mare was somehow eluding her, because she kept finding only her own horses. She fumbled toward Batu and whispered into his ear, "Where is the captain's horse?"

Batu had been raised as a nomad and knew horses better than most people knew their parents. After a cursory examination, he whispered back, "The horse is gone."

Thalia was alarmed. The captain had hobbled his horse when they had made camp, and she had discreetly watched him to ensure that he'd done it properly, which he had. So where in blazes was his animal? It couldn't have wandered off on its own. Had it been stolen?

A strange intuition had Thalia cautiously approach where Captain Huntley slept. As she did, the first rays of light began to illuminate the basin. And that was when she saw it.

The captain was gone.

There was a slight depression in the ground where he had lain, but that was all that remained of him. His horse, his gear, everything had vanished. She found herself crouching down, touching the earth where he had slept, as if trying to catch the lingering warmth of his body, perhaps judge how long it had been since he left. Of course, the ground was cold.

She felt a stab of panic. What if something had happened to him? Had the Heirs kidnapped him from the camp, as she and Batu slept on, unaware? No. He was a soldier, and a good one. Nothing ill had befallen him. There was another explanation for his absence.

She straightened. "He left us," she said to Batu as he came to stand beside her.

"Without saying anything?"

"It appears so." Irritation flared as she contemplated this

development. "All his protestations about accompanying us, that we needed his help—I suppose they had no weight." Annoyed with the captain for leaving, more annoyed with herself that she should care, Thalia stalked back to her horse and adjusted the saddle.

"Or perhaps," Batu suggested, following, "he finally took your words to heart and headed for home. A man will only wait around so long while a woman holds him at bay."

Thalia scowled at her old friend, who merely looked back at her with a calm, unperturbed expression. She took out her frustrations on her poor horse by giving the saddle cinch a hard tug, and the animal snorted and pawed at the ground in protest. Thalia patted it, contrite.

"We should get going," she finally said. "Morning is here and we have at least three more days of traveling."

Batu agreed, and together, they finished packing, then mounted their horses and began to ride west. They had camped in a wide gulley, and had to crest a small line of hills to continue on their way. Thalia felt strange and out-of-sorts, and tried to dismiss it as the result of a poor night's sleep, but, deep inside herself, she knew it was because she had not said a proper farewell to Captain Huntley. He was gruff and commanding, yes, but he had also shown her an unexpected compassion. Between that and the insistent pull she felt toward him whenever he was around, she could have compromised herself badly had he stayed. He could have been more dangerous than Sergei. A letter shouldn't hurt, though. If she only knew more about him, where he was headed, she might be able to write him a letter, thanking him for his service. But she knew almost nothing of him besides his name and rank, and finding him could be nearly impossible.

Thalia shook her head, clearing her thoughts. She needed to focus her attention on the task at hand. The Heirs would be hard on her heels, and she had to protect the Blades, do their work. This was the opportunity she had longed for, and she would be damned if she let anything, including herself, get in her way.

Yet all of her carefully constructed resolve fell away just as she and Batu came over the top of the hills.

Captain Huntley was waiting for them.

He was atop his horse, and, judging by the sheen on the animal's hide, they had been riding for some time. As he wiped some dust from his face with a kerchief, he did not look at all surprised to see them, unlike Thalia, who felt a confusing mixture of happiness, relief, and anger.

"Good, you're up," he said as she and Batu trotted to meet him. "I've scouted the area and it looks clear, so we can move ahead."

Thalia vowed to herself that she could be just as sanguine as the captain, while her heart, clearly not receiving the telegram from her head, capered inside her chest. "There's a narrow gorge about three miles from here," she said. "It could be a good place for an ambush."

"Already secured it," he answered.

"And a stand of larches a mile beyond could hide a group of riders."

"That's been taken care of, as well. Your friends don't appear to be anywhere in the vicinity. I spotted a grouping of tracks, but they were headed north, not west."

Thalia took a breath, scanning the horizon. She finally allowed herself to look at him directly, and found that the morning light turned his eyes to burnished coins. He must have slept less than she did, yet seemed to suffer no lingering trace of tiredness, no ill effects. In fact, with the golden sunlight playing across his cheekbones, the hard line of his jaw, and the slight fullness of his bottom lip, he looked quite enticing. It didn't seem quite fair, not when Thalia was certain that she looked like the underside of a saddle.

"You're quite thorough," she said after a moment.

"Always am." An almost teasing glint appeared in his eyes, warming them, warming her. "In everything."

"Ah," she cleverly answered. Thalia actually felt herself blush, something she hadn't done since . . . since Sergei. And look how well that had turned out.

She resisted the urge to rub at her face, to try to hide the signs of her awareness of him, which would only draw further attention. *His* attention. Which she did not want. For so many reasons. Including the fact that she could easily respond to his attention, easily and eagerly. She would have to be careful, watchful, as much toward herself as toward him. Which meant that there would be no more blushing. There was a sizable difference between telling herself something and actually having it happen, however. She would have to take action, beginning immediately.

So: no flirtatious remarks from her. "We cannot stay here all day," she said instead, and put her heels to her horse. The animal leapt into a gallop. Behind her, she heard Captain Huntley and Batu kick their horses into motion. As she listened to the horses' hooves, felt the cool morning air against her face, something strange and surprising began blossoming within her, something she only later recognized as a secret happiness.

Chapter 5

The True Hammer of Thor

The servant, Batu, shouted something in Mongolian to Thalia. He sounded anxious. Her somewhat calmer answer was also in Mongolian, so he had no way to know what they were talking about. Huntley wasn't sure if he should ask. Ever since that morning, when she had practically frosted over in response to his attempts at flirtation, Huntley had wisely decided to give her some room, and speak seldom.

Perhaps her father kept her isolated from the company of men. It might explain why she was skittish and abrupt with Huntley. Or, he thought wryly, perhaps his own ham-handed efforts at seduction could attract only the most jaded trollop that ever followed a regiment. Maybe he should have taken care of his sexual needs back in Peking. There had been a lot of opportunities, but Huntley had never been especially fond of paying for female company, which was the most available option, and he was also pressed for time. So he had ridden on, and now it seemed he was paying the real price. Clumsily flirting with a woman who would rather he had the good manners to be thrown from his horse and kicked in the head.

Their company of three had ridden in silence for the

better part of the day. They hadn't even stopped to eat, but instead, still in the saddle, they gnawed on more of the dried meat that Thalia had handed out. Thalia held the lead, while Huntley continued to ride at the back of the group, keeping his eyes and ears attuned to any sights and sounds. Occasionally, they passed a nomad herding sheep, and a few clusters of those large tents that Thalia called *gers* appeared in the distance, but she seemed intent on giving them a wide berth. Huntley admitted to himself his interest in the woman kept growing, and not only because she had a strong-featured beauty he'd seldom seen before. She campaigned well, almost as well as a seasoned veteran, and while no one would ever call her masculine, she wasn't fragile. Perhaps the fact that he found this appealing was even more reason for him to get back to England as soon as this mission was over and find himself a tranquil wife whose favorite pursuits included embroidering slippers and pillow covers. His value system, as it stood now, was badly in need of repair.

The talking between her and the servant was growing more animated, and Huntley followed Batu's finger as he pointed toward the east. The sky, which was clear overhead save for a few high, wispy clouds, appeared gloomy and threatening on the eastern horizon, behind them. Batu was clearly disturbed by this.

"A storm is coming," Huntley said.

Thalia and Batu both looked at him as they reined in their horses. "Yes, a storm," Batu agreed. "A bad one." He spoke again to her in rapid Mongolian, and she shook her head.

"I thought there was hardly any rain in Mongolia," Huntley said.

"There isn't," confirmed Thalia. She frowned at the northern sky, a worried line appearing between her straight black eyebrows.

"But the wind is blowing southward," Huntley pointed out. "It should give us no trouble."

The servant shook his head. "No. It heads toward us."

"I don't see how that could be possible."

"But it *is* possible," Thalia said, her voice tight. "It's drawing closer. And I suggest we try to outride it."

She was right. Even in the few minutes since their group had stopped, the small belt of darkness that had only occupied a narrow fraction of the sky had grown three times as big. On the open space of the Mongolian steppe, the torrents of rain that the storm was unleashing could be plainly seen, a gray column that stretched between the clouds and the soaked earth. The storm seemed to be traveling as quickly as a steam engine hurtling straight toward them. At that rate, they would be soaked in thirty minutes.

"The devil," Huntley cursed.

"No, Captain," Thalia corrected, grim, "something worse." She kicked her horse into a gallop, with Huntley and Batu close at her heels.

The wind began to pick up almost at once, turning from a gentle breeze into a punishing gale that tore tears from the eyes. The bright day quickly faded into gloom as the storm raced nearer. Despite how hard they rode the horses, the giant wall of dark clouds advanced on them, taking over the sky and shadowing the ground. Across open pastures they rode, over rocky fields, trying to put as much distance as they could between themselves and the oncoming squall.

Huntley managed a brief look over his shoulder, and pulled automatically on the reins. He nearly caused his horse to rear up before he recollected himself and spurred the animal forward. In all the years he had served, with all the strange weather he had ever lived through, Huntley had never seen anything like the thunderhead that, he could almost swear, *chased* them now. The clouds were as tall as mountains, black as the grave, roiling and tumbling with unchecked rage.

Just as the edge of the clouds reached over their heads, rain slammed into them. Their clothing was soaked in an instant. Racing through the downpour, it was almost impossible to breathe—water kept pouring off the brim of Huntley's hat and into his nose and mouth. Squinting, Huntley could barely make out the forms of Thalia and Batu ahead as they, too, struggled against the shredding wind and punishing rain. A thunderclap tore open the air with a report so loud, Huntley would have sworn a cannon had gone off right beside him. His horse did rear up then, and it took all of his strength to control the animal and continue their flight.

They climbed up a hill, trying to seek shelter in a small overhang of rocks. Thalia had already reached it, and Huntley and Batu soon followed. The rocks provided a tiny measure of relief, but not much, as the horses jostled each other in fear while their riders panted and watched the storm.

"We can't stay here long," Huntley shouted above the rain. As if to emphasize his words, a tumble of rocks, loosened by the downpour, clattered off the overhang and landed at the already nervous horses' feet.

"There's a cave not very far from here, on the other side of a river," Thalia shouted back. Her dark hair was plastered against her face, which she shoved back with an impatient hand. She snatched off her soggy hat and shoved it into a saddlebag. "We can set out as soon as the horses have gotten their wind."

Huntley started to answer, but was cut off by a bolt of lightning striking the ground a few hundred yards away. The flash was enormous, and Huntley had to shield his eyes from the glare. Another titanic thunderclap slammed through the air. Huntley felt it through the ground, in the marrow of his bones and recesses of his mind. It was as though he was under bombardment. The edge of the storm was passing overhead, but the dark center drew nearer. He couldn't believe that any storm could have so much power. Then he saw something which made him doubt his sanity altogether.

There, in the clouds the size of a canyon wall, a man's face formed. Huntley rubbed at his eyes, trying to clear the water from his vision, but no matter how much he pressed at his eyes, the image did not fade, but rather took greater shape and clarity. It was, in fact, the fierce and angry face of a man that appeared within the clouds, and not an ordinary man, but one with a long moustache and braided beard, a Norse helmet atop his head. A Viking. As Huntley watched, incredulous, the clouds also massed into the shape of a huge arm, and held in its fist was a hammer. The Viking opened his mouth with a bellow of thunder and brought the hammer down onto the ground, unleashing another bolt of lightning that struck a small stand of trees. The trees exploded, leaving only charred stumps in the rain. Huntley swore violently.

"What the hell was that?" Huntley demanded, turning to Thalia. Her face was white, her eyes wide, but she did not appear as though she was witnessing something extraordinary. Instead, she looked as though this was something she had anticipated. But that couldn't be. No one could anticipate the impossible.

"We cannot wait," she shouted over the roar. "We must ride for the cave now!"

There was no time to press for answers. The storm would be directly overhead in minutes, and surely the rocks would crumble around them when it hit. They broke from the minuscule shelter of the overhang, riding hard over the hills. Huntley spared only a moment to glance behind him, daring his eyes to show him what could not be there. But his sight was either lying, or the impossible was now very real, because the Storm Viking had not vanished. He was still in the clouds, his mouth twisted in rage, his eyes burning, and his arm upraised to strike again. Huntley urged his horse to gallop harder, though the mare needed no encouragement.

Huntley almost said a prayer of thanks when he spotted the river that Thalia had mentioned, with a hill just beyond it, and halfway up the hillside, the welcome dark of a cave. The river's waters were swollen from the rain, its banks flooded, but it did not look too deep to ford—yet. A few more minutes was all they had.

Huntley led the group as the horses struggled down the bank and into the river. The water surged around them, trying to pull them from their saddles and tearing at the horses' legs. As they managed to reach the middle of the river, the air was filled with an almighty roar that even obscured the wind and rain. Huntley had been pulling the reins of the pack horse to get the terrified animal to move forward, and he looked up with a vicious oath as the roaring grew even louder.

Hurtling down the river was a wall of water. It moved forward with an unquenchable hunger, tearing up the few trees that grew on the river's banks and pulling huge rocks from the earth and adding them to its arsenal of water, mud, and debris. But there weren't only rocks and trees swirling within the flood. Huntley saw beasts, demonic combinations of animals with gaping maws and pointed talons, made of water. As they hurtled down the river, the beasts tore at the land with their claws and teeth, destroying and consuming everything in their path. Already frozen from the rain, Huntley was chilled further when he saw that these water creatures were headed straight toward them.

Thalia managed to get her horse across the river, maneuvering the animal skillfully through the surging water. Huntley's mare was fighting to reach the riverbank, but the pack horse was too frightened to do anything besides pull on the reins and roll its eyes. The water was rising higher and higher, and now surged up to Huntley and Batu's thighs as they both pushed and shoved at the fearful animal. The force was so great that some of their bags came loose from their moorings and were quickly pulled into the turbulent water and submerged. Huntley hoped they didn't contain anything irreplaceable.

"Get to the cave," Huntley shouted at Batu. "I'll take care of the horse!"

The manservant shook his head. "I will help," he yelled back.

Huntley cursed stubborn Mongols, but kept working. They both bullied the pack horse toward the shore, until it finally reached the riverbank, where Thalia grabbed its reins and pulled it behind her as she rode up the hill to the cave, moments ahead of the oncoming wall of water. Huntley was not satisfied until he saw Thalia ride into the mouth of the cave, then turn and wave back to signal her safe arrival.

He had no time to breathe easier as Batu's horse struggled to reach the muddy bank, its head tossing wildly with fear and exertion. Huntley took hold of its reins and dragged on them hard, his arm burning. The horse was almost to the bank when the wall of water, and the beasts within it, struck.

He felt as though he was being slammed, over and over again, by columns of marble. Water surged all around, and he felt hundreds of claws tearing at him, trying to force him from the saddle. One hand on the saddle horn, and the other desperately gripping the reins of Batu's horse, Huntley fought to stay mounted. He couldn't breathe, he couldn't see, he knew nothing beyond the rage of the river demons battling to drown him. His thighs ached in agony as he kept them clamped hard around the flanks of his horse. The only hope he had to survive was to move forward, out of the hellish river.

He dug his heels into his horse. It pushed against the current, sidestepping, and, after what seemed like ten lifetimes, the mare breached the water and made it onto the bank. Though Huntley felt as though his arm was going to fly out of its socket, he continued to pull on the reins of Batu's horse. The animal burst through the water as the creatures within it continued to claw at its flanks, leaving marks on its hide. Batu bent low over the horse's neck, urging it forward. They had nearly broken free of the galloping river when a talon reached out and plucked Batu right from his saddle. The man disappeared into the water.

Huntley immediately let go of the horse's reins, barely noticing when it galloped away. He didn't care what happened to the beast, but he had to find the man. Through the pounding of the rain and the rising water, he searched for any sign of Batu, barely daring to believe that the Mongol might still be alive. He shouted the servant's name, trying in vain to be heard above the almighty din.

Thalia's voice joined his. He turned in his saddle and was furious when he saw her beside him, on her own horse, calling for Batu.

"Get back to the cave, damn it!"

"I can't lose him," she shouted, and called Batu's name again.

Under any other circumstances, Huntley would have forcibly returned Thalia to the cave, but a man's life hung in the balance. He, too, shouted for the Mongol as they searched, their horses moving gingerly down the bank. Thank God that the wall of water had moved on a bit, the beasts inside as well, leaving churning floodwaters in its place. They called and called for Batu until their voices gave out, and Huntley was almost resigned to the fact that the loyal servant had drowned, when he felt Thalia reach over and grip his sleeve.

"There," she shouted, pointing a little further downstream. "He's there!" He followed her direction. It was true. Batu clung to the branches of a partly submerged tree that was moments away from being torn from the ground by the water. He looked exhausted, barely able to hold on for much longer. As one, Huntley and Thalia kicked at their horses and rode toward Batu's precarious salvation.

They reached Batu, and Thalia managed to get him to

release his grip on the tree, but not without prying his fingers loose from the branches. Huntley grabbed Batu's waist and swung the battered man in front of him, knowing that the nearly drowned Mongol had hardly any strength left and would not be able to hold on without support. Huntley gripped Batu, holding tightly to keep the servant from sliding off the saddle and into the river. The horses were also worn out, and Huntley and Thalia weren't faring much better. Huntley nodded at Thalia. It was time to seek their shelter.

With a final burst of effort, Thalia and Huntley pushed their horses enough to get them up the hill and into the cave. It was a blessed relief to be out of the punishing rain at last. Everyone slipped from the horses' backs to the ground. Freed from the burden of their riders, the animals retreated to the rear of the cave, their hooves clattering on the rocky ground. Batu's horse no longer made up the caravan, having disappeared in the storm.

From their vantage, they could see down into the gorge, where the river continued to rage. The banks had completely overflowed, and the river itself looked to have been changed from a quiet stream of a foot's depth to a torrent over seven feet high. The storm kept at it, howling winds swirling around the mouth of the cave. What had been a relatively peaceful day had been torn to pieces by a vengeful, sentient storm.

Huntley held on to Batu, who could not stand on his own. Both Huntley and Thalia helped lower Batu to the floor, leaning him against the wall of the cave. The servant's breathing was shallow and labored, his eyes closed. Thalia cast Huntley a worried look, and Huntley held up his hand to ask for patience. As Thalia carefully held the manservant's lolling head, Huntley produced his flask of whiskey and dribbled a little of the alcohol into Batu's mouth. Batu coughed twice, but managed to revive a bit.

Thalia, kneeling on the ground, sagged with relief. She said something to Batu in Mongolian, and he answered, smiling at her weakly. He then looked at Huntley, crouched to his left, and spoke again in Mongolian, before closing his eyes, completely sapped.

"He says that his English washed away in the river," Thalia translated. "But he wanted to thank you for saving his life. And," she added, "I want to thank you, too. You saved us both, again." She fought to keep her eyes level with his. "You humble us with your courage when we've asked nothing of you."

Huntley, battered, soaked, tired beyond comprehension, sank beside Batu. His legs stretched out in front of him while his arms hung limply to the ground. He wrung out his last remaining ounce of strength to tip the flask to his own mouth, gratefully sipping at the warming whiskey. He offered the flask to Thalia. She took it and put it to her lips. Huntley closed his eyes. He didn't want to watch her drink from exactly where his mouth had been.

"Now's the time you repay me," he rasped. When he heard the cap replaced on the flask, he opened his eyes. A slight flush stained Thalia's white cheeks, but he didn't know if it was a result of the whiskey or his demand.

"Very well," she said. "Name your price."

Huntley forced his arm up and took hold of her wrist as she was returning the flask. Her skin was cold and smooth under his grasp. Her eyes flew to his.

"The truth," Huntley growled. "We don't take another step further until you've told me everything."

Fortunately, some nomads had used the cave to camp recently, leaving behind a decent-sized pile of dry wood that Huntley used to build a fire. The blankets were relatively dry, but their clothing was soaked, and they knew that if they wanted to prevent sickness, they would have to let the clothing dry near the fire. Huntley first saw to the horses, removing their saddles and packs. Afterward, Thalia shyly retreated to the back of the cave and removed her wet clothes, while Huntley and Batu promised not to watch. Huntley made himself stare at the fire, trying not to listen to the sounds of Thalia disrobing, but he could mark each garment as it was taken off: first the robe, which would uncover her shoulders and arms; then the boots and socks, revealing her feet; trousers next, peeling off of her legs, one, then the other. There was a moment's hesitation, followed by the sound of smaller cotton items being removed. Great God, she'd taken off her underwear, too.

Her bare feet slapped gently on the rocky floor of the cave as she approached the fire. Huntley saw that she had wrapped a blanket just above her breasts, holding it up with her free hand while the other spread her clothing in front of the fire. He knew he shouldn't stare, and there were other, larger issues to deal with, but he was moonstruck by the sight of Thalia Burgess's bare shoulders, her slim arms and creamy neck. Her black hair hung down, as she tried to shield her blushing face with its dark curtain. She didn't have the arms of a lady of leisure, and he couldn't help but admire the small bunching of muscles that moved there as she arranged her clothes.

She eased down next to the fire, drawing the blanket tight around her. As she did so, he caught a flash of slender, strong leg and hoped that he was too tired and cold to let that affect him. He felt his body stir, his cock lifting. Apparently, he was going to have to be suspended in the middle of an ice floe to be unmoved by her. If only one were handy.

Huntley helped Batu to his feet, and the servant had enough energy to take himself to the back of the cave and disrobe. After Batu had returned, also swaddled in a blanket, it was Huntley's turn to strip. It didn't take long, and soon there were three groups of clothes drying in front of the fire. Huntley noticed that Thalia's eyes kept straying to him and the parts of his body that his blanket showed. It was the same pattern, over and over again: her gaze would wander to him, fasten on him—his shoulder, the length of his arm—then, as if chastised, skitter away. Yet never for long. This repeated itself many times. He wondered how many partially clad men she had ever seen. Doubtful if any of them were built like a common laborer . . . or soldier.

"It's hard to know where to begin," she said, after they were all settled.

"Let's start with that Norseman in the storm and the beasts in the water." Huntley could hardly believe he was saying such words, but it had been a day that defied imagination, and seeing Thalia Burgess partially dressed was only one part of it. "Tell me what the hell that was."

She stared at the fire, as if readying herself for his response, his disbelief. "The storm and flood were summoned by Mjolnir, the True Hammer of Thor," she said after a moment. "Whomever wields it can call forth a storm that would tear Asgard from its very foundations. The rains it causes create a flood more savage than a hundred wolves. It was stolen from its sacred burial mound in Norway two years ago, but this is only the third time it has been used."

"Someone found an old hammer in a pile of dirt," Huntley said, "and just used it to try to drown us." Patent disbelief dripped from his voice.

Thalia looked up sharply at him. "You asked for an explanation, and I'm giving it to you. Whether or not you believe me isn't my concern."

"Fair enough," Huntley conceded. "Let's assume that what you've told me is true. For now. Who stole this hammer?"

She tightened her jaw. "I'm not supposed to tell you this."

"Think you can't trust me?" Huntley scraped out a laugh that had no humor in it. "Sweetheart, I've been shot at, not only by bullets, but with metal wasps that punched through solid brick. I've been abandoned on the steppe, nearly struck by lightning, and come *this close* to drowning, and all in service to you and your mission, whatever the hell it is. I'm more trustworthy than the damned Archbishop of Canterbury."

"I could tell you some colorful stories about him," Thalia said with a tiny smile.

He wouldn't be distracted by that enigmatic smile of hers, though he wouldn't mind seeing it more often. "Some other time. Now, you were telling me about who took this hammer."

Seeing that he would not give up, she nodded. "I think it would be best if I started at the beginning. Or as near to the beginning as I can."

"You're stalling."

"It may be hard for you to believe, Captain," she said after casting him an annoyed look, "but the world is filled with magic. Actual, genuine magic. What you saw today was just a hint of the power that is out there. That which we call myths or legends is, in fact, the lore that has developed around this magic. Including the stories about the Norse thunder god, Thor."

"They write children's books about him," Huntley said, recalling some of the stories he'd learned in the dame school he had attended long ago.

"And to most people, the realm of magic is just that, the stuff for nursery tales and academic research," she continued. "But it is quite real and quite dangerous. All over the world, there are repositories of this mystical power, objects imbued with magic, like Mjolnir, the hammer that belonged to Thor. These repositories are known as Sources. They can be found in every country, amongst every people. England, Scotland, Spain, India, the Americas. Even here, in Outer Mongolia."

"If that were true," Huntley cut in as his mind fought to understand, "then how is it that the world hasn't been destroyed by power-mad dolts? And why don't more people know about them?"

"Not for lack of trying," she said. "But the Sources are kept well hidden to ensure that doesn't happen. They are protected and sheltered from the world at large."

Huntley thought for a moment. "By men like your father. And Morris."

She nodded. "There is a group of men and women who seek out and protect the Sources, wherever they are. This group has been around for over a thousand years, but when the nations of Europe began to turn their eyes to distant shores, racing one another to create giant empires, the group became more organized. They had to ensure that the Sources were not taken from their native homes and exploited, not only for the sake of the local people, but for *everyone's* sake." She looked utterly serious, and grim, staring into the fire. "Mutual destruction would be assured if the great nations of Europe were able to harness the Sources for their own blind advancement."

"That never stopped fools from trying," Huntley added.

"And they do try," she confirmed. "Napoleon's escape from Elba would never have succeeded without the use of Nephthys's Cloak, which shielded him from the British patrols of the island."

"But he failed at Waterloo."

"The Cloak was recovered before the battle."

Huntley leaned back and considered. He had never thought himself to be very clever, had been an average student, and relied on his gut instinct when it came to soldiering. His instinct didn't know what to make of the yarn Thalia was spinning, though he was becoming more and more aware that it wasn't a yarn, but the truth. He felt the surface of reality growing soft and porous like an orange, peeling away to reveal a world underneath the one he thought he knew.

"Those men who killed Morris and attacked you," he said as things shifted and moved into their new positions. "They're in on it, too."

"They are part of an organization called the Heirs of Albion."

"Heirs, hm?" Huntley mused, thinking of the murderous, gently born piece of shit who murdered Morris and who led the attack against Thalia. "*They* are England's chosen sons? Upper crust men who kill unarmed men in alleyways and assault women? I hate them already."

She smiled ruefully. "Trust me, you will come to hate them more. The Heirs are one of the largest and most powerful groups who seek out the Sources for their countries' benefit, and they don't care who they step on, or kill, along the way. The Heirs will stop at nothing to ensure the supremacy of England, even if it means murdering their own countrymen." Thalia looked at him guardedly. "But you're a soldier. You have served Queen and country for many years. Perhaps you think the Heirs are in the right, that England should reign supreme over all other nations."

"I served my country," Huntley shot back, "but I never stood for bullying. I didn't in the army, and I don't now. That goes for men, women, *and* nations. It was them, the Heirs, who stole the hammer and used it against us today."

She seemed relieved to hear his answer, though it galled him a little that she would've believed he sided with those blue-blooded bungholes. "Yes."

"How close would someone have to be to use it?"

"No one knows for certain, since it hasn't been studied thoroughly, but it's been figured that the hammer can be employed from as far away as a hundred miles."

"So, the Heirs are close to us now."

"Within a hundred miles. But I fear that using the True Hammer is just the beginning. The Heirs know that there is a Source here in Mongolia, but they don't know exactly where. That's why they killed Tony, to keep him from find-ing out and getting to it first. And that's why they attacked Batu and me yesterday."

"What will they do when they have the Source?"

Bitterness hardened her voice. "With the Source's unlim-ited power, Mongolia will belong to them. Its steppes will be plowed and plundered. The people yoked to pull the great machine of Britain forward, crushing everyone in its path, with the Heirs at the whip."

"That's what Morris's message meant, 'The sons are as-cendant,'" Huntley figured.

Thalia smiled at him again, warming him faster than the whiskey ever could. "You're a remarkably quick study, Cap-tain," she said with real admiration in her voice. "I should think you would have keeled over with shock after learning all this."

"I'm hard to shock." He was, in truth, reeling inside from all this information. Magic. Sources. Heirs. Things that would have given him a good laugh only a few days ago. But now seemed real and serious. He thought of the metallic wasps in the alley in Southampton, piercing a brick wall and then vanishing. Another Source, perhaps. One that had almost taken his life. Years of going into battle had trained him well enough to keep from showing fear or shock, or at least, not too much. Wouldn't do for his men to see his jaw hit the floor when confronted with a surprise counterattack. This wasn't much different, only instead of an assault by the warriors of Tewodros II, he had a young woman revealing to him the existence of actual magic.

"So Morris and your father are part of the group that keep the Sources out of the Heirs' greedy paws," he said. "You, as well?"

She looked somewhat abashed. "There are women mem-bers, but . . . me, no. Not yet. You have to . . . prove yourself before you are made a member. My father is, but he is injured. So it fell to me. I *wanted* to go," she added with a sudden ferocity, no longer embarrassed.

Interesting. Thalia Burgess, a young woman who burned with need to prove herself to this group. If Franklin Burgess hadn't been hurt, would Burgess have let his daughter accompany him on this dangerous journey? Perhaps the old man had been trying to protect his child more than she would have liked for longer than she wanted. But the needs of the many outweighed his own fatherly instinct, and he'd had to let her go. What was Burgess feeling right now? Probably an agony of worry. Huntley wished he could write Burgess and let him know. Huntley wasn't going anywhere. He would stay and ensure the mission was completed, but, more importantly, protect Thalia. That had become Huntley's purpose. She was a brave woman, he wouldn't deny that, seeing courage and determination shining in her glittering emerald eyes. She'd fought that supernatural storm without once backing down or showing fear, and she'd pushed through her own guilt and doubt that had threatened to swamp her after she'd killed. Huntley could count on one hand the number of men he knew who could withstand as much.

But, with the exception of Batu, who was no fighter, she had started her journey alone against a very powerful, ruthless enemy. Her solitude made her vulnerable. She wasn't alone in her fight anymore.

"So, Captain Huntley," Thalia said, breaking the silence, "what I've told you has been kept a secret for generations, but you've proven yourself more than trustworthy. Now that you know everything, what do you intend to do?" She stared at him, intent and slightly afraid of what he might say.

He held her gaze. "I'll say this one last time. I'm with you until the end. Whoever and whatever comes our way."

As he said this, he felt the oddest surge of happiness—a feeling with which he hadn't much experience, not since he'd resigned from the army. At that point, Huntley had settled on his makeshift plan to return to England, get an ordinary job, find a sweet wife, and install her in some snug home while they made armfuls of babies, but, strangely, the plan hadn't raised his spirits as he thought it would. But throwing himself headlong into a cause he hadn't known about a week earlier, a cause in which he'd face unknown, supernatural dangers . . . somehow that had done the trick. Huntley felt the blood moving in him, the old excitement of a campaign.

It was made all the better knowing that Thalia Burgess would be by his side.

Hearing his vow, she let out a breath she probably hadn't known she was holding and smiled at him again. Seeing her smile, something hot and animal slid through him. But this wasn't the time, and it wasn't the place; he had his cause and his duty, so he tried to push that roused beast aside. It was a fight, though.

Instead of reaching for her, as he wanted to do, he asked, "And what are these paragons called, who safeguard the world, and save England from herself?"

Before she even spoke, he knew everything was about to change. And change forever.

"The Blades of the Rose."

Chapter 6

Karakorum

Captain Huntley by firelight, partially covered by a woolen blanket, was one of the finest sights Thalia had ever seen, and that included sunrise over the red cliffs of Bayanzag, a Kazakh hunting eagle soaring in flight, and the gilt sculptures of the divinely inspired Bogdo Gegen Zanabazar.

She knew she wasn't supposed to stare—there were *some* English concepts that had been impressed upon her from an early age, including modesty and a decent amount of decorum, as well as a love of a decently made cup of tea—but it was very, very difficult to keep her eyes where they were supposed to be. The captain had wrapped the heavy blanket around himself like a toga, so she had a perfectly lovely view of his broad, sculpted shoulders, and his lean, muscled arms. Oh, princesses had abdicated kingdoms for lesser arms. The light from the fire played across the burnished gold of his skin and caught in the dusting of fair hair on his forearms. Unfortunately, he'd wrapped the blanket so that his chest was hidden from her sight, but even the glimpses of his collarbones, the shadow in the hollow of his throat, and the strong column of his neck could keep her well satisfied. For now.

And there were his hands, his feet, capturing her attention. Large, capable, unmistakably masculine, and so powerfully suggestive that Thalia felt herself spellbound. She wanted those hands on her, touching her, wondered what they would feel like. Rough? Gentle? She wouldn't mind, either way.

He knew what effect he was having on her. She saw the gleam of amusement and interest in his eyes whenever her gaze lingered on him too long. She saw, too, the way he looked at her from across the fire. They had survived a harrowing ordeal together; they were both young and healthy, and far from the structures of social custom. It was only natural that desire was there, in the cave with them, making the air thick like smoke.

Men were creatures she understood. Their motivations were more direct, purer than women's. Sex was a matter of simple bodily needs for them. They wanted. They took. She might not be a classic beauty, but the captain would not refuse her if she asked to lie with him. It wouldn't take much. Batu was asleep. All she had to do was beckon to Captain Huntley, or stand and let her blanket drop. The rest would take care of itself.

Thalia, however, wasn't a man. She had desires, just as they did, but satisfying them was not so uncomplicated. She had almost taken a man to her bed, and had paid dearly for even that brush with sex. If she actually gave her body to a man, she could not protect her heart, could not treat the matter lightly, as if she was simply eating an apple when she craved something sweet. Men, especially beautiful, physical creatures like Captain Huntley, had the luxury of walking away and remaining intact. She did not.

So she might look, but she would not touch, would not taste, and would try as best she could to be content. Though it was deuced hard.

She attempted to distract herself by focusing on her mission, and telling the captain everything he might need to know as they pursued their goal of protecting the unknown Source. Night had fallen, the rain had slowed. The cave offered a momentary illusion of safety and peace.

"In my *del*," she said, "you will find the Compass Tony asked you to give to my father."

Captain Huntley leaned toward the pile of her drying clothes—ah, Earth Mother Etugen! the muscles in his back, shoulders, and arms seemed made of rough satin as they flexed with movement—and rifled through the pocket of her coat until he produced the object in question. It sat in the palm of his hand, appearing small and ancient in contrast to the living energy of his skin. Thalia moved closer and took the Compass from him, her fingers brushing against his palm. She fought the impulse to shiver.

Flipping open the lid, she showed him the inside of the Compass. She remembered her father giving it to her in Urga, the pride in his eyes. She was not a Blade yet, but the Compass would be both her protection and duty.

As the captain leaned in to look, she could smell him, his flesh warmed by the fire, the water that still dampened his hair, even his breath mingling with her own.

She made herself speak in a level voice. "The blades that mark each direction on the Compass symbolize the span of our mission: to traverse the world and protect the Sources. In the center of the Compass is a rose, which bids us to be merciful and compassionate in our mission." Thalia closed the Compass and ran her thumb along the writings etched into the case. "These messages are from our ancestors, urging us to do right, even when faced with . . . temptation." She struggled a little over that last word, knowing what temptations she wrestled with that very moment. She and the captain were sitting very close to one another now. She could lean forward slightly and brush her lips against his throat where, she saw, his pulse moved steady and strong beneath his skin.

"Each member of the Blades of the Rose carries this Compass," she continued. She made herself concentrate on the Compass. "They are the Blades' most prized possession, and no one, including the Heirs of Albion, knows of their existence. Even the threat of death cannot induce a Blade to part with it."

"Morris gave it to me." She felt the dry brush of his breath on her cheek.

"So you would give the Compass to my father. There are many Blades all over the world, but they don't always know each other. The Compass lets them see that they are amongst friends. But that isn't enough. An object can be stolen, no matter how well it is guarded. So there is another way."

Captain Huntley nodded with understanding. "That was why Morris had me say, 'North is eternal.'"

"Yes. It is the first part of the Blades' catchphrase. When a Blade meets another Blade, the first must say, 'North is eternal.' The response is: 'South is forever. West is endless. East is infinite.' It helps them to know one another, and reminds them of the scope of their responsibilities."

"Someone might not answer correctly, though. Someone who's trying to infiltrate the group. How can Blades protect themselves against enemies?"

"They are not called the Blades without having more than a little fighting skill." She glanced at him, now leaning even closer, and felt herself drawn into a warm cocoon that surrounded them both.

"Even the women?" Humor danced in his amber eyes.

Thalia felt her mouth curve in a smile. "Even the women."

As their gazes held, the moment stretched out between them, growing heavy and almost languid. Thalia could hear, faintly, the popping of the fire, Batu's quiet snores, the horses as they slept standing up at the back of the cave, and the trailing off of the rain outside. But everything sounded so far away, so distant, and Captain Huntley was so near, he became all she saw, all she heard. His pupils widened, darkening his eyes. A muscle flexed along the square line of his jaw.

He reached out, and she started to close her eyes, thinking he would touch her, but instead he took hold of a lock of her hair. It was still damp, just beginning to dry at the ends, and he wound it slowly around one long, blunt-tipped finger. Thalia lost the ability to breathe. Her dark hair wrapped around his finger was the most intimate thing she had ever seen.

When he bent his head down and lowered his mouth to hers, she did not move back. Nothing felt more natural, and yet, the feel of his lips gently brushing against her mouth was something she could never have anticipated. Some semblance of self-preservation kept her from opening to him, but his gentleness was deceptive. Gradually, inexorably, he took small tastes, sampling her and in so doing, growing more hungry, more demanding. As was she. Thalia could not resist, and let her lips part. It was enough of an invitation for him to take the kiss further, deeper. And he did. They opened to each other. A tender, warm invasion, barely civilized but never brutal.

She didn't know. Hadn't known. That a simple kiss could wreak such delicious havoc. It never had, before. But this. This was opening the atlas to find a whole, unexplored world within its familiar pages. She was an explorer, and needed more.

She set the Compass down. Her hands came up and caressed his wide shoulders, danced up his neck. His skin was marvelous, almost fever warm, and his body was knit together with hardened muscle. She threaded her fingers into his damp hair and pulled him closer. In her mouth, he growled, and the vibrations jolted straight through her, right down to the place between her legs, which grew moist instantly. Desire had never hit her so hard or so quickly. She pressed her thighs tight against each other.

He must have released the ribbon of her hair, because his own hands came up, stroking along her shoulders. The rough fabric of the blanket frustrated him, and he pushed it down, partially uncovering her skin. When he touched her again, it was the meeting of flesh to flesh, his palms along her collarbones, across her sensitive upper back. The skin of his palms and fingers was work rough, rasping against her, and she felt in them such strength, such capability and ferocity, but also the hint of an unexpected gentleness. She wanted him everywhere, and let the blanket drop so it gathered in heavy folds at her waist, so she was bare to him.

He didn't pull back to stare at her. Instead, he let his hands look for him. One pressed tightly against the small of her back, and the other, oh, the other, curved around her breast. Thalia heard a mewl as it arabesqued from her throat. She'd never made that sound before. A deep rumbling from low in his chest was his response, like a feral creature calling from another nighttime mountain. The large pad of his thumb brushed against her tight nipple, and though she tried to keep her knees locked together, hot, vivid sensation caused them to drift open. She began to lean back, pulling him with her.

Batu's snore, heavy and unaware, was the dart that pierced the bubble of her fever spell. Her trusted friend slept only a few yards away.

Thalia pulled away. She did not want to, but she had to, and she tugged the blanket back up over her shoulders with clumsy fingers. She wanted what she knew she should not have. As she gulped for air, she looked at the captain with dazed eyes. His jaw was tight, his eyes had a hard gleam, and he, too, seemed to lack for air. He did not look dazed. He looked sharp, painfully focused, and not a little riled. It had been a long time since Thalia had been close to an aroused man, but she'd forgotten how potent they could be, just by revealing their desire. Especially *this* man.

"I shouldn't . . . have let it go so far," she said. Thalia had never heard her voice this way before, so breathless, so close to seduction. "I'm sorry."

"We took the path together," he growled.

"Yes, but—" But what? She had been foolish. Men could turn desire on and off like a lantern, blinking in the dark, but she should have known it would be different, more consuming, for her. She'd wanted him inside of her, wanted him there now. It was a shock to her. Even the pleasure she'd had from Sergei's touch faded into a dying ember compared to the uncontrolled blaze that now moved beneath her skin. She hadn't counted on that, not at all. "We should get some sleep, Captain," Thalia finally said. "Much of today has been lost. We'll need an early start tomorrow if we're to make up time."

He gave a single, clipped nod. He looked so fierce, she wondered if he would simply reach out, grab her, and finish what they had started. She almost, almost, wished he did. But he must have seen something in her, fear, perhaps, that kept him at bay. Yet, his exercise of honor was taxing him. She saw it in the straining muscles of his arms that seemed to hold him back, felt it in the waves of barely leashed hunger that rolled off of him. It would be so easy, so easy to lean toward him . . .

"I feel odd calling you 'Captain,'" she said instead. "So formal."

In a low rumble, he said, "I've been just 'Huntley' or 'Captain,' or 'sir,' for a long time."

"Can I not call you by your Christian name? And you can call me by mine. You are not here as a soldier." She was amazed she could string that number of words together.

"If that's something you want."

"I . . . do."

She felt strange, awkward, vaguely embarrassed. He wasn't making things any easier, simply staring at her with that undisguised need in his eyes. "Do you want something to eat?" she asked. "I think most of the provisions were washed away in the river, but we've a little left."

"No."

"Ah." The silence stretched tightly. "I'm not hungry either." Still nothing. She put the Compass back into the pocket of her *del*. Finally, she said, "Good night, Gabriel." His name felt wonderful in her mouth.

"Good night, Thalia."

She shut her eyes to the picture he made, speaking her name, but the sound of it lingered just behind her heart. She had done the right thing by ending their kisses and caresses. Captain Huntley—Gabriel—was far too dangerous.

Thalia did not open her eyes until she heard the rustle and shift of the blanket. When she did look again, he had moved so that the fire was between them. In his hand was a piece of sodden paper. He tossed it into the fire, and the flames hissed and sputtered briefly before consuming the paper entirely.

"What was that?" she asked.

He shrugged. "Something unimportant."

Thalia saw he would speak no more on it, but watched as he lay on his back, and stared up at the roof of the cave that had been cold and damp but was now impossibly close, impossibly warm. Thalia also lay down and pulled her own blanket around herself as tightly as she could, as though swaddling herself. Restricting her movement. Keeping her from getting up and lying down beside him.

This had been one of the most draining days Thalia had ever experienced. Chased by a deadly storm, fighting a flood before helping to save Batu from drowning, revealing the secret world of the Blades. And Gabriel's kisses, his touches, whose power eclipsed everything else that had come before.

As she fell into an exhausted sleep, Thalia wondered if, on this journey, the greatest threat would come from the Heirs, or from herself.

"Tell me where we are going."

Thalia glanced over at Gabriel riding behind her. They had set out before dawn and ridden in silence. She took the lead, Batu held the middle, and Gabriel kept watch from the back. Her few attempts at conversation had died, so she had resigned herself to listening to the birds call to one another as they wheeled in the clear sky. She had been wondering if he was angry with her, but she would not apologize for protecting herself from certain injury. Now, at least, he was breaking the silence that had accompanied them for most of the day.

"The message from Tony said that we were supposed to 'seek the woman who feeds the tortoise,'" Thalia said.

"I've a feeling there's more than one tortoise in the whole of Outer Mongolia," he answered dryly.

"Yes," she agreed, "but I doubt any of them would harbor one of the Sources, whatever it is. But there is one place where I think we can find a special tortoise." She looked around, as if the Heirs might be hiding behind some scrub, eavesdropping. But, of course, Gabriel had already done a thorough reconnaissance of the area, and she knew with confidence that it was secure. Even so, she lowered her voice. "The city of Karakorum. It's another day's ride from here."

"And do the Heirs know of this place?"

"Doubtful, otherwise they wouldn't have tried to beat it out of me. It seems that their Mongol is more concerned about his own interests than the geography of his home country."

"Not much of a home to him, if he's willing to sell its treasure to the highest bidder."

"He should be horsewhipped," Batu said angrily. "That *yamaa* is no son of Mongolia."

"If we ever find him, Batu," Thalia answered, "we will give you that privilege."

Batu held up his *tashuur,* the whip all Mongol horsemen carried. "With this, I will take the skin off his miserable face."

Gabriel looked at Thalia, one eyebrow quirked. "He's just bloodthirsty enough to be a naval officer."

"Not so surprising, since Batu claims to be a direct descendant from Genghis Khan, himself," Thalia said with a laugh. "But, given that the Great Khan sired probably whole cities of children, almost everyone in Mongolia is his descendant."

Refusing to be baited, Batu merely sniffed and held up his *tashuur* again with a threatening air while Gabriel chuckled. Thalia wondered if this meant that the tension between them had gone. She surely hoped it had. It would be a long journey to Karakorum otherwise.

Everyone fell quiet until a few minutes later, when Gabriel sped up so that his horse was beside Thalia's, and said, "I don't *usually* kiss or fondle the men I campaign with."

Thalia looked at him and was relieved to see him genuinely smiling. She had thought him attractive before, but the smile transformed him into something mythically handsome, which was less of a relief. "And do *they* kiss or fondle *you?*"

"They try," he said with a negligent shrug. "I'm devilishly good-looking."

Honest laughter bubbled up from inside her; she felt release from the tension she had been carrying.

"Thalia." She still had not gotten accustomed to his speaking her name, and it curled warmly in her belly. "I'm not sorry for what happened last night."

"I'm not, either," she said, though that wasn't entirely

true. She was only sorry because she had been given a glimpse of a country she could not explore. "However, you have to understand, Captain—"

"Gabriel," he reminded her.

"You have to understand, Gabriel," she continued, "that it cannot happen again."

He looked chagrined, but not, it turned out, with her. "Damn," he muttered. "Been out of decent company too long. I forget that a bloke isn't supposed to paw a woman he fancies."

She felt absurdly happy that he should admit to fancying her. Still, it could not lead anywhere outside of her own secret, feminine gratification. Perhaps there was a way that ladies usually let men know that they did not welcome their amorous attentions, but Thalia had never learned it. Her father, it turned out, had not covered that when supervising her education.

"Let's just stay focused on the task at hand," she said. It was the best she could do without inventing a complete fabrication or, worse, telling him that he could easily leave her heart battered and bleeding without much effort on his part. She understood men enough to know that such a confession would strike a man dumb with terror. "We have enough to concern ourselves with. Agreed?"

He cursed some more. If he ever *did* plan on mixing with "decent company," as he called it, something would have to be done about his language. That was a topic for another time, however.

"Agreed," he finally grumbled.

That should have made her feel better. But knowing that she would never again experience the marvel that was Captain Gabriel Huntley's kisses, Thalia didn't feel at all better. She felt . . . lonely.

* * *

At the very least, after she and Gabriel had settled matters between them, the travel became less fraught with internal tension. Thalia did not lose her awareness of him, not at all, but it was an awareness with which she could come to terms. The whole of the day was spent riding in watchful readiness should the Heirs attempt another strike against them. They skirted around several *ails* to ensure speed and secrecy, even though Thalia wanted nothing more than to rest and enjoy some hot food and tea. Once they had reached Karakorum, it would be easy enough to replenish their supplies at the nearby monastery of Erdene Zuu. For now, they had to settle for rationing out their remaining *borts* and *aaruul* and try to ignore both the monotony and scarcity of their diet.

The past months in Urga had robbed Thalia of some of her usual stamina. When she and her father had lived out on the steppes, days of riding hard would not bother her. But city life had softened her. So when it came time to bed down for night, Thalia tumbled into an immediate and dreamless sleep. Somewhere, out on the steppe, the Heirs were watching, waiting, and that alone should have kept her awake. Yet having Gabriel nearby, knowing that she and Batu were both safe while he was around, allowed her to give in to her fatigue completely. One moment, she had closed her eyes, the next, she was being gently awakened by Gabriel's hand on her arm, dawn light gilding his shoulders. She couldn't think of a better way to greet the morning.

"We should reach Karakorum today," Thalia said after she had rinsed her mouth with water.

"Thank God," Gabriel muttered. "I've nearly pulled out half my teeth chewing on that dried mutton."

As Thalia swung up into the saddle, she grinned. "The Mongol horsemen used to soften *borts* by putting it underneath their saddles as they rode. We could try that to make it more palatable."

Gabriel made a face. "Dried mutton and horse sweat? Even enlisted men were fed better. It's grounds for mutiny."

"I hope not," Thalia answered. "Flogging is so time consuming."

By late afternoon, they had entered a broad valley, through which flowed the Orkhon River. Thalia had been to the Orkhon Valley before, but its beauty always filled her heart with lightness. Small stands of trees clustered on riverbanks bright with sun. Scattered throughout the valley were groups of *gers,* smoke rising from their chimneys into the sky. A shepherd on horseback tended his cattle, and the echoes of their lowing could be heard across the basin. A few monks from the monastery had left its walls and were taking their leisure by sitting in the sun on the grassy knolls, their robes spots of flaming color against the green.

"A lovely spot," Gabriel said. "But where's the city?"

"This is it," Thalia answered. She gestured to the wide plain. "Karakorum."

"But it's . . ."

"A ruin. Yes."

She kicked her horse into a gallop, and, with Batu and a mystified Gabriel following her, they descended into the valley that had once held the great city of Karakorum. Now it was a barren field, empty of everything except a few weed-covered rocks. The only sounds of civilization came from the temples inside the monastery, where the many monks went about their lives and prayers.

They walked their horses around the desolate plain. "There's nothing here," Gabriel said.

"Karakorum was once the capital of the Mongol Empire, built by Genghis Khan's successor, Ogodei Khan. It contained the royal warehouses, where all their plunder was housed." Thalia looked around as if trying to conjure up the long-destroyed walls from her imagination. "Treasure came from everywhere: China, Persia. Anyone wanting an audience with the Great Khan had to come to Karakorum, even envoys from the kingdoms of Europe."

"That must've been a long time ago," Gabriel murmured. "Just rocks and weeds now. Not even a battlement left."

"Six hundred years can rob anything of its greatness," Thalia said.

"So what happened to this place? Doesn't seem to be a spot you could easily defend, out in the middle of a valley."

"Most of the soldiers who had defended it left when the capital was moved by Kubilai Khan to Peking. A little over a century later, Karakorum was razed by Manchu soldiers. The treasure disappeared. Nothing remains of the great capital."

He gazed around at the empty space where once a marvelous city and palace stood, the center of one of the greatest empires the world had ever known, and shook his head. "A man spends his life chasing power and glory, something for the world to remember him by. He thinks it'll last forever, but . . ." Gabriel shrugged. "It's just dust and weeds. And sheep," he added, hearing one nearby bleat.

"So what *should* a man, or woman, chase?" Thalia asked.

Gabriel stared at her with a strange intensity that was almost too much for her to withstand, before turning away. "Damned if I know." He gave his horse free rein, letting the mare amble over the grassy field, while Thalia and Batu slowly trailed after him. Strange, but she could swear that the ruins had provoked a small fit of melancholy in the tough-skinned captain. "There's nothing here," he said at last, "that's for certain. So why come?"

"Not *everything* was destroyed by the Manchus." Thalia urged her horse into a brisk, brief canter, nearing a large stone shape that stood close by. As their group drew closer, it became more clear what the shape represented, and it made Gabriel chuckle.

"A damned tortoise," he said, rueful.

Thalia dismounted and walked up to the stone animal.
The wind and centuries had worn away much of its elaborate carving, but the tortoise was still easily identifiable as
it stared with unseeing eyes up at the sky. The sky looked
down, ageless, far removed from the concerns of empires,
khans, and stonemasons. Around the tortoise's neck were
bright scarves of blue silk, tributes left by travelers and
nomads. As Thalia ran her hand over the sun-warmed stone,
she heard Gabriel dismount and walk up beside her. She
watched his hand also run along the back of the tortoise,
touching the stone with surprising reverence.

"There were four of these tortoises once," she said quietly. It was difficult to find her voice when she was somewhat hypnotized by the strength of his large hand, its
movement across the stone. A vivid sense memory of his
hand on her skin, on her breast, pulsed through Thalia.
"They marked the boundaries of the city and guarded it."

"Odd to pick tortoises for the job, and not something
fierce, like lions or dragons."

"Tortoises represent eternity, longevity."

"Not so eternal now, eh, friend?" Gabriel asked the tortoise. When there was no response, he gave the stone animal
a friendly, consoling pat. "Not much to say. That's all right,
lad. We're here to talk to the lady that feeds you."

Thalia frowned. She still could not puzzle out what that
part of the message meant. "I knew that Morris's clue directed us here, but I thought something about the old capital might be revealed to us once we arrived. There once was
so much treasure here, I thought for certain that one of those
objects must be a Source."

"If it *was* here," Gabriel said, turning around and leaning
against the tortoise, "it's long gone, now." He patted the
stone again. "This chap isn't talking, though."

"What should we do, Thalia *guai?*" Batu asked.

Thalia contemplated the tortoise. She honestly did not

know if there was something, or someone, they should look
for. "Let's ask at the monastery," she said after some time.
"Perhaps they know of someone who 'feeds' the tortoise."
They all agreed that this was the best plan and set off to see
it through.

Several hours later, however, Thalia was ready to tear out
her eyelashes in frustration. Discreet inquiries at the monastery led nowhere. None of the monks they had quietly
spoken with knew anything about a woman who had anything to do with the stone tortoise, let alone fed it. Most of
them stared at Gabriel with undisguised fascination, having
seen few white men in this isolated part of the country.
Thalia, Gabriel, and Batu were given some *buuz,* steamed
dumplings, which were wolfed down by their party in a
matter of minutes, and washed down with cups and cups of
milk tea.

When they finally emerged from the gates of Erdene Zuu,
all they had to show for their efforts were full bellies and
Batu's pockets laden with juniper incense, purchased from
the monastery, which he intended to give his parents the next
time he visited them. The afternoon was gone, and night had
turned the sky indigo. The only sources of light in the
Orkhon Valley came from the *gers* dotting the fields and the
torches burning inside the monastery.

"I suppose we could ask at some of the *gers,*" Thalia said
tiredly, trying to keep irritation from hardening her words.
"But I'm concerned that if we do, it means more trails for
the Heirs to follow."

"There was this bloke in Jhansi, ran a lamp shop,"
Gabriel said. He reached into his inside pocket and produced
a cheroot, which he proceeded to light. The brief flame from
the match gilded the plane of his jaw before being shaken
out. "Knew everybody and everything. Including, it was
whispered, the location of a secret stash of weapons that
were going to be used against the Maharajah in a bloody

uprising. So I went to the bloke and asked him. But the cussed man gave us nothing. It was damned nasty. Still, I didn't want to beat it out of him, the way my superiors wanted. I got what I was after, though." He took a draw on the cheroot and exhaled a cloud of fragrant smoke.

Thalia was blindsided by a vivid memory of him tasting of tobacco and whiskey. "How did you manage that?"

"By waiting." He grinned around the cheroot between his teeth. "Stood outside his shop for days. Didn't say anything to him. Or anybody else. I leaned against the wall opposite the shop, arms crossed like this and face like this." He demonstrated, folding his arms across his chest, and suddenly looked quite intimidating with only a tightening of his jaw and lowering of his brow. No one could disobey Gabriel if he summoned menace so easily. Even Thalia felt momentarily cowed by this brief demonstration. And just as quickly, the menace was gone, and it was Gabriel again, talking easily about the past. "Just stayed there, watching him. And after three days of this, the blighter drags me inside and tells me everything I needed to know. Pressure got to him. We found the guns, ended the rebellion before it began."

"So," Thalia said slowly, "you're suggesting that we wait and see before charging off to do something foolhardy."

Gabriel tapped the ash off the end of his cheroot before answering. "I'm not *suggesting* it."

"I might point out," Thalia said, bristling, "that you are not in the army here in Mongolia, nor are you in command of our party."

He shrugged. "You might. But you strike me as a clever lass, one who wouldn't let her stubbornness and pride muck up an important mission."

Thalia muttered something in Mongolian that made Batu choke. It wasn't particularly flattering toward tall, fairhaired, and high-handed former army captains, of which Thalia knew only one. "All right," she said in English. "If nothing happens by morning, we head out and track down this woman."

"Sensible decision," Gabriel said with a nod. "And watch your language." At Thalia's questioning glance, he answered, "Don't have to speak the language to know when somebody's calling me a rotten bastard."

Unfortunately, that made Thalia smile, so her annoyance with Gabriel was nearly gone by the time they hobbled their horses and hunkered down next to the stone tortoise. For a few hours, the three of them sat together, backs against the tortoise, and spoke quietly, trying to pass the time. Gabriel smoked half of his cheroot before putting it out and saving it for later. As each hour passed, and the lights in the surrounding *gers* winked out as their inhabitants went to sleep, Thalia became more and more convinced that coming to Karakorum had been a mistake. Perhaps the clue referred to something else besides the stone tortoise? If so, what? Maybe the Heirs had learned the clue and deciphered it, and were even now in possession of the Source. Had she failed the Blades so soon?

"Steady," Gabriel murmured into her ear. He nudged her with his shoulder. "You're keeping the horses awake with your fretting."

Thalia did not reply. There was nothing to do but wait in the dark, watching the moon rise, and she did not realize that she had fallen asleep until she became aware of the fabric of Gabriel's coat against her cheek. Not only that, but she was clasping his arm, holding it between her breasts as she leaned against him. His very hard, very strong arm. She came fully awake with a start, throwing herself backward in an attempt to put some distance between them.

In the silver gleam of the moonlight, she could make out Gabriel's lopsided smile as he watched her flop around on the grass. She wondered if he was going to say something horribly cutting about her throwing herself at him, but was spared that ignominy when his expression sharpened, and he began to stare fixedly out into the darkness.

"What is it?" she asked, but he held a finger to his lips without so much as a glance her way.

Thalia pushed herself up and tried to focus on whatever it was he saw. At first, she thought he was funning her, or, at the least, had simply spotted a wolf out prowling for prey. But just as she was about to dismiss his intense concentration as the byproduct of too much military training, Thalia saw movement at the edge of the field. Movement that was definitely *not* an animal. Thalia heard the soft clink of metal against metal. She didn't even know Gabriel had gone for his revolver until she saw it in his hand.

"It's just one person," Gabriel muttered. "Are those bastards really that cocky?"

"Can you tell who it is?"

He shook his head, still peering out into the dark. "Get your rifle," he growled to Thalia as he rose into a crouch. He nudged Batu's foot. "You, too. Take my Snider carbine, not that antique you've got. And both of you, don't leave the tortoise," Gabriel added, looking pointedly at Thalia. When she nodded, he started to move away soundlessly.

"Where are you going?" Thalia hissed.

"To surprise our friend."

Chapter 7

The Tortoise Speaks

It was a damned hard choice to make. Either stay with Thalia and possibly suffer what the approaching Heir had planned for them, or trust that she could take care of herself and venture into the night to catch the Heir off guard. Gabriel had made tough decisions before, but he'd never had a woman to protect. Gabriel always hated waiting while the enemy advanced. It put a man in a tight spot. He'd much rather take the initiative. It was a better tactic, and gave him the advantage. If Thalia had been a man, he would have gone after the Heir with no hesitation. But not only was she a woman, she was *her*. He could still taste her, feel the satisfying, perfect weight of her breast.

Gabriel had a much better chance of safeguarding Thalia, though, if he went after the Heir, rather than letting the bloke come to them. So he'd swallowed his fear and stalked his prey. At least Thalia was a good shot, and he had given Batu his own rifle rather than leaving him with that obsolete, inaccurate muzzleloader the Mongol carried, since it was unlikely that their advancing enemy was a drunk whale.

The moon was a slice of silver in the dark night sky, giving him just enough light to see where he was going as he edged around the field. His plan was to circle back and steal up behind the approaching Heir as the enemy's attention was focused on Thalia and Batu. Ares's bollocks—he didn't like using Thalia as a distraction, but if everything went the way it was supposed to, she wouldn't be in danger.

Gabriel crept through the tall grasses, keeping one eye trained on the Heir. He didn't recognize him from the attack outside Urga, but it was hard to know for certain in the darkness. Whoever the hell this gent was, he wasn't too keen on keeping quiet. Some kind of metal pieces were hanging from the Heir's clothes, jingling with each step. And the Heir was muttering, too. Words Gabriel couldn't understand.

No time to think about anything but ambushing the prey. Gabriel doubled back behind the Heir and stole forward, behind the enemy. As he got closer, he ducked down to hide in the grass, peering up every now and then to make certain of the Heir's position. The Heir never stopped, keeping up his steady progress toward Thalia, and unaware of Gabriel's presence. They were a hundred paces from the tortoise. Nearing the Heir, Gabriel saw that the man was smaller than the two English toffs, and less than half the size of the giant Mongol they'd hired. Someone else, then, some other paid muscle. But no less a threat, regardless of size.

Gabriel pushed forward, feeling not a little like some giant cat stalking its dinner. Both he and the Heir were only fifty feet from Thalia. Gabriel would have to make his move now, before the Heir got too close. He'd take the Heir down then wring some answers from the bastard's neck. He took a steadying breath, then launched himself at the Heir.

And hit the ground, having thrown himself at nothing but air.

Gabriel leapt to his feet at once. It was impossible. The sodding bloke had been right in front of him one moment. And the next . . . gone.

No, not gone. Gabriel broke into a run when he saw that

the Heir had appeared right in front of Thalia. He'd never run so fast in his life, not even when he was being chased by khukri-wielding bandits in Central India. Gabriel wasn't exceptionally skilled at running and shooting with a revolver—his rifle suited him better—but there wasn't any choice. Thalia, damn it, hadn't even drawn her weapon. Instead, it looked like she was actually *talking* to the Heir. Gabriel swore. He was going to have to teach her that as soon as she could take a shot, she bloody better well do it and not waste time or opportunities by *talking*.

It would be impossible to take his own shot now, not with any accuracy. There was too great a chance he might hit Thalia or Batu. He didn't hear Thalia as she cried out, "Gabriel, wait!" Instead, Gabriel threw himself at the Heir and tackled him to the ground.

Only to have Thalia and Batu grab Gabriel's shoulders and pull him away. The three of them went tumbling backward in a heap of struggling limbs. The Heir lay flat on his back, trying to right himself.

"What the bloody hell do you think you're doing?" Gabriel growled, struggling to peel Batu off of him.

"A mistake, Huntley *guai*," Batu panted. "Don't hurt her."

"I'm not going to hurt her," Gabriel snarled, shoving Batu away. "I'm trying to *protect* her." He started to take aim with his revolver as the Heir got to his feet.

"Not me," Thalia gasped as she grabbed Gabriel's arm and shoved, pushing his gun away. *"Her."* She pointed to the Heir as she and Gabriel struggled. "Look."

Gabriel did look, then went still. The Heir wasn't an Heir at all, but a Mongol woman. Her gender was confirmed by her voice, as she chuckled and dusted herself off. Gabriel saw that her sex had been hidden by the large robe she wore, which appeared even bigger because of the heaps of ribbons covering the fabric. Silver charms and mirrors dangled from the sleeves and the hem of the robe, as well as from the leather apron wrapped around her waist. The woman's face was mostly hidden by the ribbons trailing down the front of her headdress, and it was hard to tell how old she was, though her hair hung loosely around her shoulders. She carried a small drum, also draped in ribbons that glinted palely in the moonlight, and a drumstick with a horse's head carved into the end. In the weeks Gabriel had been in Mongolia, he'd never seen anyone dressed so peculiarly.

"A shamaness," Thalia whispered to Gabriel. They both rolled to their feet. "There aren't many left in Mongolia, not since Buddhism came three hundred years ago."

"Some kind of witch?" Gabriel asked.

The shamaness spoke, a long stream of Mongolian that Thalia quickly translated. "Not a witch," the shamaness said, and Gabriel could only wonder how she had understood his English words. "One who speaks with the spirit world. Everything in nature has its own spirit, not only men and animals, but every plant, every stream, every mountain. And they are all part of a living whole. Even you," continued the woman, pointing at Gabriel with the drumstick, "are connected by the World Tree. Shamans and shamanesses cross into the mirror world of the spirits, speak with them, listen to them."

Thalia spoke to the shamaness, and the woman answered. "I asked her why she is here in Karakorum," Thalia translated. "She told me that she brings offerings to the past."

The shamaness reached into the folds of her robe and pulled out sticks of incense as well as a small metal bowl. The woman filled the bowl with *airag* and set it before the tortoise, then struck a flint to light the incense. Pungent smoke curled into the air.

Gabriel finally understood. "She's feeding the tortoise."

"You're right," Thalia nodded, amazed.

He'd seen people make offerings before, at shrines to deities in temples and by the sides of roads, always wondering what they saw in cold stone or statuary that inspired faith. A hard life in Yorkshire and what he'd seen as a soldier had convinced Gabriel that he'd little to believe in besides himself. Ever since brushing up against the world of the Blades, though, his understandings of truth and reality tottered. As they did now. Why make an offering to a statue of something that wasn't even a god?

Whatever the shamaness's purpose was or was not, it didn't matter, not where the mission was concerned. "Then she's the woman we want," Gabriel said.

Thalia started to step forward. "I will ask her about the Source."

"She looks a bit busy at the moment."

The shamaness had begun pounding on her drum, first softly, then with growing strength and loudness. As she did this, she chanted to herself and began turning in circles. Gabriel watched, fascinated, as this went on for several minutes, the drumming, chanting, and turning never ceasing.

"She's entering a trance," Thalia explained quietly. "It is how she crosses over into the spirit world. I have never seen this before, only heard of it."

"My grandfather spoke of shamans," Batu added. The usually fearless servant was standing behind Gabriel as if looking for protection from the chanting woman. "They are powerful and strange."

Gabriel had to agree. Just listening to the shamaness's chanting made every nerve in his body shiver. Even though he had been stationed in remote parts of the world, as an Englishman and soldier, he'd never had much chance to witness native spiritual rituals, but had been inclined to dismiss them as just another variation of the religious nonsense he'd been force-fed as a child. Hindu ceremony or Anglican rite—it all seemed the same. Empty gestures.

There was nothing empty here in the dark plain of Karakorum. As the shamaness continued to chant and spin, beating on her drum, Gabriel could actually feel a change in the air. Something seemed to stir to life. An unseen energy pulsed beneath the surface of the world, working into his skin and mind. The night crystallized, sharpening and expanding at the same time. He almost jumped when he felt Thalia's hand on his arm. His senses were alive to her touch, almost painfully so.

"Do you feel it?" she whispered. Her eyes were wide and glittering, beautiful.

Somehow, he managed to nod.

The chanting grew faster, the shamaness's voice swirling around them. She twirled so fast, she became a blur of glimmering mirrors and ribbons. Her drumming and chanting pierced Gabriel's brain, making it impossible to think or move. He could only stand, amazed, as something began to glow and pulse *inside* the tortoise.

A warm red light gathered in strength within the stone. While the shamaness continued in her unearthly chant, the light began to move. It traveled from the center of the tortoise, moving up through its body, its neck, then into its head and finally its mouth. Gabriel felt Thalia's hand clutch at his sleeve as the light danced out of the mouth of the tortoise and into the mouth of the shamaness. The woman suddenly stopped her chanting and drumming. The drum dropped from her fingers, as did the horse-headed drumstick. She stopped spinning, swaying on her feet as the red light glided to the center of her chest.

Afraid that the shamaness had been possessed by some dark spirit, Gabriel moved toward her. He wasn't entirely sure what he could do to help her against a magical energy, but it seemed better than standing by and just watching. Thalia stopped him, however.

"I think this is what she wants," Thalia breathed.

"Is it what *we* want?"

"Please be quiet," Batu whispered. "She speaks."

Yet when the shamaness opened her mouth, she did not talk, didn't even chant. Eyes closed, she sang. It was an uncanny song that dipped and swayed, curving itself down into valleys and up again into mountains. Gabriel couldn't understand the words, but he felt the song stretch out all around him like a banner unfurling itself under his feet, showing him an entire landscape. He was taken across the whole of Mongolia, could see and touch its rolling steppes, the secluded vales, the unforgiving beauty of the rocky hills, the dark, pearl-blue lakes. It was all contained in the breadth and shape of the song. He had never experienced anything like it, not in all his travels. There weren't many words, but each one extended on for miles.

Thalia, gazing at the shamaness with undisguised amazement, quietly translated the song, but it was almost unnecessary, since Gabriel *felt* its meaning.

I have seen the world change
Many times over.
A life, a breath, drawn in and exhaled.
They are the same.
I am stone. I never yield.
And though I carry the universe upon me
I do not move.
The sky sees everything, He tells me
Everything. What He sees amazes
Even Him!
A crimson field. No matter the season, the soft springtime,
The brief heat
Of summer, the brittle autumn, the long
Cold snows of winter—
The field burns crimson always.
Though it is constant, it does what I cannot.
It moves.

When the last syllable of the last word died away, the shamaness gently began to fall to the ground like a blown leaf. Gabriel, his reactions slowed by the power of the song, leapt forward to catch her. But when he reached her side, his arms came up empty.

The shamaness had vanished completely.

Gabriel wished he had more whiskey. After the shamaness had disappeared, he'd completely drained his flask to steady himself, but it still wasn't enough to get him used to the idea of magical songs moving from stone to person. And then the total disappearance of that person, vanishing into nothingness, right in front of him. But there was *airag,* and its slight fermentation would have to do in place of whiskey's direct assault on his nerves.

They had returned to the monastery and found a room for the night. Thalia had gone out to tend to her private needs. Batu saw to the baggage by the light of a single lantern, while Gabriel paced next to his sleeping mat and made steady, but unsatisfactory progress through his flask. He could take his liquor, and the few sips of whiskey he'd had did nothing to help brace him after witnessing a woman blink into air. Batu, bless him, had found some *airag,* and Gabriel was making decent progress through it now. Still, it wasn't quite enough. He wondered if he could ever get used to this new world that had been uncovered, where words were magical and solid flesh could disappear.

The door to their room opened, and Thalia entered quietly. She didn't have a lantern or candle. After checking the corridor, she closed the door behind her. Gabriel strode immediately to her and took her into his arms. It wasn't only because he had been scared out of his wits earlier, thinking that she was about to be attacked by an Heir. He also needed to feel her real, living self, the truth of her body and scent.

Her hands came up to cup his shoulders, and she leaned into him. She breathed deeply, pressing her face against his neck, drawing him in just as he was doing with her. Ah, God, she felt so damned good. Too good. His body's reaction to her was fast and earth-bound, and though he knew he couldn't have Thalia, some comfort was taken in his need for her.

Not quite enough comfort, though. She wouldn't appreciate being jabbed in the belly by his now stiff cock. Gabriel not-too-gently pushed himself away and turned to fake an interest in a carved chest, muttering something about being glad she was safe. He listened as Batu and Thalia spoke quietly in Mongolian, hearing in their tone that they were discussing him and how well he was faring after the night's events. No shots had been fired, but she was worried about him. The idea was awful, silly . . . and touching. Damn it.

He grabbed up his cup of *airag* and took another drink. When he was satisfied that his tool was no longer at attention, he sat down, leaning against the wall with his legs stretched out in front of him.

The tone of Batu and Thalia's conversation shifted, grew tense and curt. Almost as if they were quietly arguing. Gabriel wasn't sure what they were arguing about, but, judging by the quick looks they were both casting toward him, he was the topic. Why?

Thalia said something to Batu that meant she wouldn't hear another word. Batu tried to speak, but she refused to hear him. Instead, pointedly ignoring the servant, Thalia sat cross-legged beside Gabriel with a swift and smooth grace that made his breath catch in his throat. Without speaking, she reached out and took his cup of *airag,* then took a sip before returning it to him. Gabriel held the cup tightly in his hand. He was sodding done for if just watching her drink from his cup sent blood straight back into his groin. He hadn't stumbled around with so many unwanted cockstands since he was a spotty-faced lad.

"How are you?" she asked softly.

"Not too poorly, what with a person literally disappearing from my very hands," he answered. He didn't want to be touched by her concern, but, bloody hell, he was. "You?"

She gave him a slightly wobbly smile that hit him in the dead center of his chest. She was a little frightened, but prepared to face her fear, and that struck him harder than sheer bravado. "Strange night."

"You're an old hand with this kind of thing," he pointed out.

"Theory only," she said wryly. "Seeing the magic, watching it, *feeling* it, is . . . very different from hearing tales. I'd wanted to see it for myself for a long time now."

"Did it pass muster?"

Her smile was stronger now, and that much more potent. "Can something *surpass* muster?"

Thank the blighted star Gabriel was born under, Batu was still in the room and fully conscious, otherwise Gabriel would have taken hold of Thalia Burgess and given her a thorough kissing, and probably more. Gabriel was suddenly attacked by a powerful, fierce desire for her, wanting to pull her onto the nearby sleeping mat and peel the robe from her, to cover her body with his own. He wanted to finish what they'd begun the other night in the cave, sink into her welcoming warmth. Both his cock and his mind were in agreement. He couldn't remember wanting a woman so badly.

Unaware that he was wrestling with the angels of his better nature, Thalia said, "Now you understand. The magic you felt tonight is nothing compared to what the Sources can do. And if the Heirs get hold of these Sources—"

Right. Gabriel brought his mind back to the reason he was even with Thalia in the first place. Finding and protecting a Source from those mealy bastards, the Heirs. "They won't get the one in Mongolia," he said at once. He'd protect Thalia, too, from the Heirs and anyone or anything else. He wondered if that would include himself. "Whatever it is."

"The song mentioned a moving field of crimson," she mused.

"Seasons don't affect it," Gabriel added.

Thalia frowned in concentration as she thought. He wasn't used to seeing a woman thinking deeply. Most of the officers' wives usually looked bored and vacant. It surprised him how much he liked seeing a woman— Thalia—think. He knew many men were on edge around clever or thoughtful women. Probably because it made them feel small or stupid. Gabriel didn't feel either of those things as he watched Thalia thinking. He felt . . . warm. Hungry.

"Because of the song, we know it's extraordinary that this field can exist in all seasons," she mused. "Something natural, then. Something usually only seen during a certain time of year."

"An animal," Gabriel said, "or a plant."

She considered this. "A herd of animals moves, not plants."

"I'd wager moving plants are right extraordinary," he said dryly.

"Wager?" She smiled. "I could never resist a gamble."

He grinned right back at her. "Never could resist a betting woman."

"The odds are too steep," Batu interjected from the other side of the room. Gabriel caught the man's barbed stare, which was aimed directly at him. What the devil?

Thalia said something hard in Mongolian to Batu, and whatever it was, it had enough bite to make the servant scowl and fuss with the baggage. She turned back to Gabriel and made herself appear calm and untroubled. Before Gabriel could puzzle out why he was suddenly a bone of contention between Thalia and Batu, she continued with her musing. "A herd of red animals, or a field of plants. We could be looking for either. Though I haven't heard of a Source being any of those things."

"You're our sharpshooter," said Gabriel. "It's your know-how that's going to find what we're looking for."

She grimaced. "I may fire wide. Outer Mongolia is a big country. With the clue about the tortoise, I knew where we needed to go. But this . . ." She held her hands open, as if they could encompass the whole of the country.

Gabriel took a drink of *airag* and considered. He didn't have much experience figuring out mystical clues that led to magical power sources—he had exactly none—but he did know a thing or two about strategies and buried information. Bandits plagued the hills of India, and more than once Gabriel had uncovered their secret networks of communication to prevent raids. One of the clever buggers had even used baskets of fruit to send messages—each fruit had been given a specific meaning, and together, they made up a whole message. Finally, Gabriel had been able to crack the code, and none too soon. The local villages were at the brink of destitution because of those thieving sods.

He picked over in his mind all the aspects of the song. Something was hidden within it. That was certain.

He started to speak, then stopped.

"Come, now, Captain," Thalia chided. "Don't be shy with *me*. You can't forget that we were all naked in blankets together. You were about to say something. Tell me."

He didn't want to be reminded of that. Just hearing her say the word "naked" was a test of his resolve.

When he didn't speak, Thalia sighed and looked up at the ceiling, addressing the heavens. "He issues orders left and right, but can't seem to take them himself. If this was the army, he'd be drummed out for insubordination." She turned back to Gabriel. "What if I was your commanding officer and ordered you to speak?"

"If I told my commanding officer what I was thinking now, I'd be sent to a lunatic asylum," Gabriel said, sardonic.

"Especially if you mentioned mystical singing stone tortoises and vanishing shamanesses," she countered.

She had a point there. Magical objects, demon Viking storms—nothing was too strange. Taking a breath, he finally admitted, "I was going to say that when the shamaness was singing, I . . ." Never a man comfortable with words, he struggled, trying to find the right ones. "It was like I could *see* the song."

Instead of laughing right in his face, Thalia nodded thoughtfully. He liked her acceptance. Liked it more than was good for him. "See?" she repeated. "In what way?"

"I saw . . ." He fought to give words to what had been a strange, almost indefinable experience. "The land unrolled all around me."

Admiration and understanding lit Thalia's lovely face. "Mongolian tradition has many songs sounding like the land itself. The notes and tones reflect the landscape. Rivers, steppes, mountains. One could actually *sing* a place."

"This is true," Batu said, coming to stand beside them. He still seemed angry, but not so put off that he couldn't lend a hand. "I will demonstrate." He sang out a few wordless notes, surprising Gabriel with his skill, and in those notes, Gabriel heard the flowing of water over rocks, tumbling down into a large pool.

Almost at once, a monk opened the door and glared at them. He spoke a few hard words at Batu and Thalia before shutting the door. Batu looked sheepish.

"Let me guess," Gabriel said dryly, "we're being too loud. A common barracks complaint." Batu merely shrugged, continuing to be sore with Gabriel. If Thalia hadn't been there, Gabriel would have hauled the other man by his collar and rattled him until he confessed what had gotten him so riled. And then they'd settle it with their fists. That's how it was done in the army, and it worked fine. No grudges.

"But what you just sang," Gabriel continued. "It sounded like . . . like a waterfall."

"Yes," Batu said stiffly. "Near where I was born, there is a beautiful cataract, and I sang it to you."

"Can you remember what the shamaness's song sounded like?" Thalia asked Gabriel. When Gabriel nodded, she moved from sitting cross-legged onto her hands and knees and crawled to the baggage. Gabriel tried to make himself stare at his hands instead of watching her well-formed, edible behind sway temptingly across the room, but he didn't do a very good job of it. A man couldn't resist looking, unless he was quite dead and buried beneath several feet of hard-packed dirt. However, Batu was glaring at Gabriel again, and understanding finally hit. It was a wonder it had taken him so long to puzzle it out.

Gabriel had almost half a foot on the other man, and outweighed him by three stone, an uneven match if it ever came down to it. But Gabriel, despite his growing lust for Thalia, didn't want to hurt her, and in that, he and Batu shared the same goal.

Thalia came back with some paper and a piece of drawing charcoal that she gave to Gabriel. She seemed unaware of Gabriel's ogling as well as her servant's silent efforts to shelter her. "Try to draw what you felt when you heard the song," she urged.

"An armless baboon can draw better than me," Gabriel objected.

She tried to look stern but couldn't hide the smile that curved the corners of her mouth. "Just try. It might help if you close your eyes."

Grumbling, Gabriel did as she suggested. He closed his eyes. "I don't see anything," he said at once.

"Were you the man who counseled patience to me at Karakorum? Give yourself a little while." He heard the laughter in her voice and couldn't keep from laughing a little himself. Her voice turned soft and coaxing. "The world you're in now, it isn't the same as where you were before. Let the soldier part of yourself go. There's no training here, no right and wrong way to do something. All right?" When he nodded, she continued. "Now, bring the song back into your mind. Don't rush. It will come when it's ready. And when it does, fall into it."

None of his commanding officers had ever made such a bizarre request of him before. But he kept his eyes shut and let his mind wander back to the song. He didn't think he could recall it very well, and at first struggled with frustration and a need to know *right now*. But once he let go of that impatience, the song seemed to release itself into him, as though it had been buried somewhere and needed a moment's stillness to come forward. He heard the notes filling him up, let them take him wherever they needed to go. There was a wild, harsh beauty in the melody, as there was in the land. He'd never been particularly moved by scenery— always too busy with a job to do or trying to uncover the geography's secrets when planning a mission—but something stirred inside him when he handed himself over to the steppes and rocky hills of Mongolia, and how right, how fitting it was that Thalia Burgess was part of that land. The more he saw of it, the more he understood that she would live in such a place, and how forbidding both the land and the woman could be, if one didn't know how to survive in their harsh climates.

"You've done it!" Thalia said, wonder and pleasure in her voice.

Gabriel opened his eyes.

Here was another impossibility. He had drawn something. Not just a paper full of meaningless scrawl, but an actual tree that stood where two streams forked. He hadn't even been aware that his hand holding the charcoal had moved, let alone created an actual picture.

With this small success, they decided to call it a night, and soon everyone was settled on their sleeping mats, the lantern doused, the room dark and quiet.

It was a hard night. He'd grown somewhat used to sleeping near Thalia, but never in a room. Having four walls and a roof enclosing them, instead of the limitless steppes and sky, changed things. He tried to remember when the last time was that he'd slept beside a woman, and couldn't. With Felicia, he'd slipped from her bed, dressing quickly and quietly in the dark, and the dawn had found him sprawled in his own bunk.

In the monastery room, Gabriel could hear Thalia breathing as she slept. Those soft sounds from her were more intimate than the cries of pleasure Felicia had made as she and Gabriel had impersonally fucked. The result of having Thalia near him, even with Batu close by, was a damned long, uncomfortable night and too little sleep.

He was grateful for the morning, grateful to get back into the open spaces. They rode in a southerly direction, which Gabriel had said *felt* right. He hated trusting the lives of Thalia and Batu to something beyond his understanding, but they had little to go on besides impressions of the shamaness's song. For hours, they rode, no one speaking much as Gabriel tried to concentrate on how the song had felt. It was bloody frustrating.

Just before noon, with no sign of the tree or the rivers, he became positive that he'd led them all down the wrong path. He was a man of tangibles, not a believer in impressions and feelings. Here was proof of that. They were wandering around Mongolia with no set destination. And somewhere out there were the Heirs, ready and eager to spill blood. Gabriel fumed.

Pulling up the reins on his horse, he grumbled, "Hell's arse, this has been a waste of time."

"Don't be so sure," Thalia counseled. "Let's ride a little further, just over the next hill. After that, we can think about what we should do." She nudged her horse on with Batu close behind.

Grudgingly, feeling like a fool, Gabriel put his heels to his horse. He let Thalia keep the lead as he scanned the land, looking for enemies or something that resembled his drawing. When Thalia and Batu reached the crest of the hill and then stopped abruptly, alarm prickled the back of his neck. Had his ridiculous ideas about how a song *felt* taken them straight into an ambush? He kicked his mare into a gallop and reached for his rifle.

Thalia looked over her shoulder at his approach, a smile touching the corners of her mouth. "You aren't going to need that," she said, eyeing the weapon. "Unless you plan on hunting cottonwoods."

Puzzled, Gabriel brought his horse alongside hers, then followed her gaze into the valley ahead.

Nestled peacefully between the hills, a cottonwood tree stood on a grassy bank that lay where two small streams forked into their separate directions. Everything was quiet and undisturbed. Gabriel fumbled in his pocket, then produced the scrap of paper on which he'd drawn the night before. He held the picture up, stared at it, then looked back into the valley. The scenes were the same.

"The song has not misled us," Batu said.

"*Gabriel* has not misled us," Thalia corrected. "You shouldn't doubt yourself," she added, looking at him meaningfully.

Gabriel couldn't speak. For the first time since beginning this strange mission, since being all the way back in

Southampton, Gabriel felt part of something much larger than himself or another person. This other world that Thalia had shown him, he had seen it, but never felt it, never been inside of it, nor it inside of him. But through that song, the magical force that pulsed beneath the skin of the everyday joined with him, used him as a channel. The results were right there, drawn onto a scrap of paper. And in the valley with the forked rivers. Not until that very moment did Gabriel understand how very large and very powerful magic could be. He felt humbled, awed. Yet also, being a part of it, he felt expansive, strong.

"Bugger me," he said quietly.

What followed was the strangest tracking mission Gabriel had ever undertaken. Since both Thalia and Batu insisted that the song spoke most clearly through Gabriel, at their behest he would continue to lead them toward their destination. And by "lead," they meant: have him sit quietly and think about the shamaness's song, each note following the next. Whatever bit of geography sprang into his mind he would describe or draw, and they would set off in search of it.

"This is a damned silly way to run a campaign," he grumbled after they had left the cottonwood tree behind in search of a hill with three tall, rocky spires.

"That's not what Lord Raglan said at the battle of the Alma," Thalia answered, riding beside him.

Gabriel stared at her. "I knew men who saw action at the battle of the Alma, and not a one said any magic had been involved."

"None that *they* were aware of," she replied. She must have seen his look turn black, because she answered quickly, "Yes, the troops fought bravely, and the Alma wouldn't have been won without them, but Lord Raglan had a little bit of assistance from Fatimah's Guiding Hand, recovered in Constantinople the year before."

"This Guiding Hand—the Heirs gave it to Raglan?"

"They did."

"And the defeats that followed—what happened to the Light Brigade, the losses in the winter of '55, the Malakoff, and the Redan—because the Blades took the Guiding Hand back?" He heard the cutting steel of his voice, but didn't try to temper it.

She looked horrified. "God, no! The Blades would never take back a Source, knowing it could cost soldiers' lives. They tried to get the Guiding Hand back long before it had been brought to the battlefield. It was, unfortunately, pure military mismanagement of the Source and of men that caused those defeats. Fatimah's Guiding Hand was lost somewhere in the Crimea, and hasn't been recovered."

Gabriel shook his head and muttered, somewhat calmed. It was bloody well difficult to get his bearings, now that he knew about the Blades and the Heirs and the rest of their lot. He didn't know whether to be pleased or troubled when, after riding the rest of the afternoon, the three rocky spires were sighted, glowing with the setting sun's last rays.

Thalia, however, wasn't troubled at all. When they came upon the pinnacles of rock, a smile lit her face and lit something inside of Gabriel, too. In his experience, women grew less beautiful the more time he spent with them. But somehow, being with Thalia disproved that. It wasn't a theory he was happy to refute, not in this case.

They all dismounted and walked toward the spires. The rocks looked like three old men, watching the world pass by and finding it all rather lacking. It was eerie, having seen them so clearly in his mind, and then, there they were, no longer thought or sound but real stone.

"Well done, Gabriel," Thalia cried, exultant, and took hold of his hand. Without any thought, his fingers wove with hers. They were palm to palm. He could feel her everywhere. Touching her like this felt impossibly *right*. It was wonderful—and unsettling.

And over quickly. She suddenly pulled away, frowning, her color high, or maybe the light from the setting sun was burnishing her skin. No. She was upset. Wonderful. Not only was the servant angry with him, so was the woman Batu served.

Damn it, he cursed to himself, what the hell did she want? Everything had been going right lovely between them, and now she was angry because they held hands. He couldn't figure out the maze of the female mind. Just because he got along better with Thalia than he had with any other woman didn't change the fact that she *was* a woman, with all the mental tangles and inconsistencies of her gender. It could drive a man out of his gourd.

"Night's falling," Gabriel said roughly. "We'll make camp soon."

She nodded and peered along the rolling hills. "I think there's a sheltered spot about a mile south."

"Can you and Batu find it on your own?"

Alarm flared in her eyes. "Yes, but where—?"

Gabriel quickly headed toward his horse and mounted up. "Good. I'll find you. Need to do some reconnaissance, make sure those sodding Heirs aren't on our trail."

He didn't wait for any response from her, just pulled hard on the reins to bring his horse about before kicking the mare into a canter. Gabriel focused hard on the landscape, looking for telltale signs that their enemies were close or following. He saw without seeing the oceanic beauty of the dry grassy plains, the isolated stands of scrub and trees, the smoke of a distant *ger's* chimney rising in a white plume into the indigo sky. They had no meaning to him, beyond indicating whether or not the Heirs were nearby. All he cared about was ensuring the safety of their small riding party, the success of their mission. He couldn't understand the changeability of women, and, at that moment, he told himself he didn't bloody well care.

Chapter 8

A Curious Means of Seeing

"I can't see anything," Gabriel muttered, stalking back to the campsite.

Thalia watched him as he threw himself down to the ground, moodily stretching out and staring up at the sky, his arms folded behind his head. She honestly didn't *want* to stare at him—how he moved with an athletic energy, or the long, sinewy form of his body that she knew felt hard and solid with muscle. But what she wanted and what she actually did were sadly two different things, and she drank in the sight of him with a greediness that made her light-headed.

He had arrived at the campsite she and Batu had made in the sheltered glade, having found no sign of the Heirs. This didn't console her much. She never doubted Gabriel's abilities as a tracker, but the Heirs had no qualms about using Sources or other forms of magic to hide themselves. It was entirely possible that Lamb or Edgeworth would still be able to stalk them without a seasoned soldier such as Gabriel being aware of it. Even so, the Heirs presumably could only observe them remotely, and weren't bodily nearby. That gave Thalia some reassurance.

Not a minute after Gabriel had arrived at the campsite, the

news good but his mood black, he had grabbed something to eat then headed off into the darkness to commune with the shamaness's song. Apparently, he hadn't been successful. Thalia and Batu exchanged speaking glances, and Batu bent his head to his task of repairing a hole in a saddle blanket and said nothing. For that, she was grateful. Thalia had had enough of her old friend's opinion on Gabriel. She didn't need Batu's thoughts crowding her own, which were already packed to capacity.

"Give yourself a chance," she urged Gabriel.

He snorted. "This whole damned thing is a big, bloody waste of time."

"That isn't true," she countered. "You've led us this far."

"And where the hell are we?" he grumbled. "Haven't seen a single blasted Source. Maybe that old witch from Karakorum wants the Source for herself, sent us on a fool's errand."

"She wouldn't do that."

Gabriel sat upright and, even in the deepening twilight, she could feel the heat of his golden eyes. "And you know this because you and she are bosom chums," he snapped.

Thalia wouldn't be baited. "You sound as though you've swallowed a bowl full of nettles."

In response, he ran his hands through his hair, causing it to stand in rather charming tufts that lent him an uncharacteristically boyish appearance, contrasting with the golden beard that had come in during the last few days. Hard travel left little time for such personal niceties as shaving, though she found herself wistfully wishing she could watch him attend to this mundane task. Applying lather to the planes of his cheeks, the deliberate, methodical progress of the razor moving across his face, slowly revealing his skin with each stroke. Thalia grabbed another saddle blanket and pretended to inspect it for more tears to keep from reaching out and putting her palm to his face, feeling the hard bristle of his whiskers and the juxtaposition with his soft mouth.

"I'm not used to going on like this," he said after a pause. She understood that the admission cost him, his acknowledgment that he was outside the realm of his expertise. "Knowing that the enemy is out there, but being unable to do anything about it. Picking out clues from the air to lead me toward something I don't even understand. It's not how things are done."

"This isn't the army," she reminded him. "Once we find the Source, then you'll be able to go back to that life." A bright knife of pain gleamed through her, as she thought of the time when she and Captain Gabriel Huntley would part company to resume their usual lives. In just a few days, he had come to occupy a large part of her thoughts, of herself; her body even now demanded his touch, and it distressed her to think how quickly she'd carved out a space for him. Batu had noticed it, too. He'd said as much at the monastery of Erdene Zuu. Reminded her what she had suffered because of Sergei, the danger she was facing now of having it happen again. Thalia had insisted that she wouldn't repeat her mistakes, confident that she could be much smarter where her heart was concerned. Yet each minute she spent with Gabriel threatened that confidence. She had taken his hand when they had discovered the three rocky spires, touched him because she needed to. Without thinking. And she had been furious with herself when she had discovered what she had done, pulling away from Gabriel, trying to imprison the wild creature of her heart in its cage.

Perhaps Batu was right, after all, damn him.

When Gabriel returned to the army, they would likely never see each other again, and she would be left with a self-inflicted emptiness. Time had helped her recover from Sergei, yet somehow Thalia sensed that it would take much longer, hurt that much more, when Gabriel took his leave. Her anger with Batu was anger with herself.

"Not going back," Gabriel said.

Her heart leapt up, and she tried to wrestle it back down again. He would desert? "Not going back to what?" she asked, trying to sound unmoved.

Gabriel picked up some twigs at his feet and began snapping them into small pieces, his broad hands fast and efficient even at this task meant to waste time. "To the army. I'm done. Resigned my captaincy." He snapped twigs as punctuation.

Thalia gaped, felt herself flounder. "When? Why?"

"Four months ago." Snap. "Passed over too many times for promotion." Snap. "Too much of a collier's son," he said, deepening the rough music of his accent. Snap, snap.

"So, your ambitions were thwarted." Each broken twig danced along her nerves.

"Yes." Snap. "No."

She reached over and stilled his hands, causing him to look up sharply. She made herself ignore the answering warmth in her belly, and pulled her hands back. She should know by now that skin to skin contact with him felt much too good. "Which is it?"

"I did want to be a major," he admitted. "But even if I'd become a general, I couldn't see myself sitting in the officers' club twenty, thirty years down the road, blowing steam and boasting about how many men's lives I'd lost in a battle. So, I chucked it in." He forced out a laugh. "Became another civilian."

"When I met you in Urga, you said you were in . . ."—she cast her mind back, trying to recall—"the Thirty-third. But you weren't."

"Been serving Queen and country for fifteen years," he answered. "Takes more than a few months to unlearn half a lifetime's lessons. It wasn't my aim to mislead anyone."

"I don't feel misled," Thalia said quickly. "Just . . . surprised." She tried to readjust her perception of Gabriel, knowing now that he was no longer a soldier. It didn't seem right, somehow. Even in the short amount of time she had known him, she could see how much he thrived on challenge, how his every movement and word was as sharp as a bayonet. He wasn't bloodthirsty, but he had the air of a warrior about him, something as inseparable from his identity as his hair or eye color.

Those golden eyes were watching her carefully now, waiting to see how she'd react. "In the army or no, I'm sticking with this mission."

"I never thought otherwise," she answered truthfully. It didn't matter in what capacity he served, civilian or soldier, Gabriel Huntley was a man of honor. She'd met very few, outside of the Blades. "But, once the mission is over, what will you do?"

He began methodically arranging the pieces of twigs he'd broken, as if lining up troops. "The objective is to go back to England. Supposed to find work in Leeds. Settle down."

Thalia's mouth dried, even as she wondered at his strange use of the term *objective,* which sounded awfully military. "You mean, get married."

He nodded without looking at her, not hearing the change in her tone. Batu did, though, and her loyal servant glanced at her with raised eyebrows. It was the look he always gave her when he was right and she contradicted him. Faintly smug and self-congratulatory, and also pitying. Thalia wanted to scream. Instead, she said to Gabriel as levelly as possible, "Your future bride must have been somewhat angry when you postponed domestic bliss and headed off to Outer Mongolia." Then, she could not keep her words from turning hard and brittle. "Did you write to her during your voyage here? Does she know about the fight in Southampton?"

"I haven't written to anybody," Gabriel said.

That was something of a relief. "She might be worried about you."

"She who?"

Thalia wondered how someone as perceptive as Gabriel could be so obtuse. "Your fiancée," she said with enforced patience, when all she wanted to do was howl.

The thunderstruck look on Gabriel's face nearly made Thalia laugh, but she was in no mood for laughter. She'd never seen him so thrown. "I've never proposed marriage to any woman."

Relief hit Thalia so hard, she thought she might lose consciousness. But this was followed by dismay at the strength of her reaction. There were many ways that Gabriel was different from Sergei, though she hadn't been able to stop the anger and fear that had risen inside of her at even the slightest hint of duplicity. She refused to look at Batu.

"Not yet," she echoed. "But you will." She had to make herself face the unpleasant truth as soon as possible, and, in so doing, protect herself from certain pain.

"At some point, when the mission dictates." He threw a handful of twigs into the fire.

Again, he used oddly detached, military terminology for what should have been deeply personal. "You have someone in mind."

Gabriel gave another hollow-sounding laugh. "Not at all. Been soldiering almost half my life. No time to meet ladies. At least," he added, rueful, "not the kind one marries."

"I don't think I want to explore that last comment," she said dryly.

A frustrated growl rumbled out of his throat. "I'm always saying things I oughtn't in front of women. It's going to be bloody disastrous if I go back to England and start scouting for a bride."

That was exactly what Thalia needed to hear. Once their work together was finished, he would return home and find himself someone suitable. Not a tall, Mongolian-raised woman with ties to dangerous secret societies, but a sweet, biddable girl who would keep a neat home, presiding over the teapot and serenely watching their children play on the rug. Dear Lord, the prospect of Gabriel's making children with some faceless simp of a female churned in Thalia's stomach like rancid mutton. Yet it was a truth she had to face.

"I can't instruct you on proper behavior when courting," she said, "since I'm not precisely the model of genteel manners."

"I'm glad you aren't," he answered with a candor that surprised her. "This mission wouldn't go too smoothly if I had to watch what I was saying, or if you needed to be coddled."

It was a compliment, of sorts. He didn't strike her as the kind of man who doled them out with a liberal hand. Thalia started to rise, needing to stretch her legs and gain some distance from him. "For the sake of the mission, then, it's a good thing I'm not a real lady."

This time, he was the one who reached out, putting a hand on her thigh, which caused her to stop in the action of getting to her feet. "I didn't say you weren't a lady, just that you didn't require cosseting or a bunch of other silly tripe. One doesn't have to entail the other."

Thalia could only stare at his hand on her leg, aware of the heat of his touch even through her *del* and trousers, a heat which rose up her thigh and settled immediately between her legs, and in her breasts, which suddenly felt heavy and sensitive. She hated her body's traitorous response, which seemed to have no consideration for her head or heart.

He followed her eyes to his hand, then pulled back, but not without a slight lingering touch, an almost imperceptible increase of pressure from his fingertips, as if he was trying to imprint the feel of her into his skin before forcing himself away. Thalia sunk back to the ground, avoiding Batu's too-knowing gaze. She didn't think she could walk just then.

"I've no wish to talk about brides or manners or any other rot," Gabriel said gruffly, curling his hands into fists and then pressing his knuckles into the dirt. "Not when I can't figure out where to take us next."

She wondered if her skin glowed where he had touched it. It certainly felt as if it should. Had any man ever affected her so strongly? No, none had, not even Sergei.

"We've had a long day and should get some rest," she suggested. "Perhaps things will be clearer in the morning."

"Perhaps," he agreed, but she doubted if either of them believed her.

It was no better at dawn. Gabriel tried repeatedly to conjure up images of the landscape, but either too much time had passed since he had heard the song, or there were no more embedded clues within its fabric of sound. Both Thalia and Batu also tried to envision the geography of the song, but with no success.

"We *must* be close, though," Thalia insisted with more conviction than she felt.

"But 'close' in Mongolia could mean a hundred miles or more," said Gabriel, more than a little frustration in his voice. He was cleaning his short-barreled rifle unnecessarily, since Thalia had watched him painstakingly clean it the night before. He needed something to do, some way to be useful. She tried to imagine him behind a desk at a bank, or carrying sheaves of important documents in a leather case down a city street, but none of those images seemed at all appropriate. Not to her, anyway. Maybe he thought differently of himself.

He finished wiping down the barrel of the rifle and got to his feet. "You and Batu stay here," Gabriel announced. He sheathed the rifle in its scabbard, then shouldered his pack and started toward where his horse was hobbled. "I'll scout the area further, see if I can't locate the crimson field, whatever that is."

"Two things, *Captain*," Thalia said, planting her hands on her hips and herself in front of Gabriel. He stopped and gazed at her with an impatient frown. "Firstly, you aren't in command here, so you cannot order me and Batu around."

His jaw tightened. He might have resigned from the army, Thalia understood, but he hadn't lost any of his commanding ways. Irritation with the current lack of progress only shortened his temper.

"And the second?" he growled.

"*None* of us need to ride halfway across creation looking for something when we have a means of bridging distance at our disposal." She stepped around him and headed toward one of the saddlebags. "Fortunately, the item I need wasn't washed away by the True Hammer of Thor." Thalia rummaged through the bag, searching.

"I have a spyglass," Gabriel said behind her.

"That cannot see nearly as far as this," she proclaimed, and, locating what she was searching for, removed it from the saddlebag with a triumphant smile. She quickly unfolded it with Batu's assistance.

It was a contraption of painted canvas stretched over a shaped wooden frame. But the paint on the canvas revealed an extraordinary artistry and attention to detail. Gabriel stared at the object in her hands. "A cloth eagle," he said at last. "Life-sized, too." He gently touched the fabric as if to convince himself it was real. Thalia had to admit that the canvas bird was indeed beautiful in an almost dreamlike way, each feather ready to feel the wind, the glint in the eagle's eye as bright as anything living.

"This will help us see much farther away than we ever could, even with the best spyglass," she declared.

"If it can help us see, we could've used it earlier."

"The conditions weren't right. Perhaps you can't think of

the next part of the song because it had reached the end. Now we have to do the work."

He studied the beast made of canvas and wood. "Do you have some magic that will make the eagle real?"

She shook her head. "I do not, and Blades avoid using magic that is not their own. But we do have something almost as powerful." At her nod, Batu retrieved a leather case from the saddlebag and brought it to her. She opened it to reveal a large prism, which was connected via brass chains to a series of round lenses several inches in diameter. Thalia suspended the prism from a hook on the eagle's body while Batu supported the weight of the lenses.

"Graves *guai* would be very unhappy if we had lost this," Batu said.

She glanced up from her work to find Gabriel watching her intently, his eyes as keen as cut topaz. Instead of battering her with a litany of questions, he let her continue to assemble the device, observing with a focus that was almost unnerving.

"It's ready," she finally announced. Thalia took several steps away from Gabriel and felt the breeze on her face. It should be strong enough. She held the fabric bird up and started to run. The prism and lenses were somewhat ungainly to carry, but she continued to sprint across the autumn grasses. When she felt confident, she let go. The canvas eagle soared up into the air, while Thalia held on to a long, stout, waxed twine line wrapped around a wooden reel. The prism hung beneath the fabric body, while the lenses dangled beneath the prism. She stopped running and let the line play out. It tugged in her hands, but she kept her grip strong, knowing that there would be no replacements if she should let go.

Behind her, Gabriel laughed. "Good God, a kite!" He came to stand beside her, watching the eagle kite reach up into the morning sky. The line was exceptionally long, and the kite hovered several hundred feet in the air. "It's beautiful. Only . . ."

She couldn't help smiling along with him, caught up in the joy of the kite in flight. There was something giddy and jubilant about watching it dance upon the sky, removed from terrestrial concerns. She finished his question. "How will it help us see? Look there." She pointed to the ground thirty yards ahead of them and enjoyed Gabriel's exclamation.

"Let me hold it," Batu said, taking the wooden reel from Thalia. "You go look."

Thalia sprinted ahead, with Gabriel close at her heels, then stopped at the edge of a bright circle, twenty feet across. The edges of the circle were blurred, but it was the center that captured both Thalia and Gabriel's attention. It was a projected image of the countryside, taken from the kite's vantage point high in the sky. They could see the steppes and hills they had ridden through the previous day— all visible at their feet, like an enormous picture window.

"Behold the work of one of the Blades' most valuable members, Catullus Graves," Thalia said, unable to disguise the pride in her voice. "Catullus and his family have been creating devices and contraptions for the Blades for generations. This viewing kite was invented by Catullus himself."

"Unbelievable," Gabriel breathed, staring at the image of the countryside displayed on the ground. He gingerly stepped inside the projected circle, as if worried he might disrupt the image, but it did not move, and he strode into the center. He was bathed in the strange light of the image, fields and mountains covering him like a tattoo, and looked up at the kite. "The prism," he said, understanding causing the corners of his eyes to crease.

Thalia joined him inside the circle, and they were both illuminated, two living maps. She felt as though they were somehow suspended between the earth and the sky together. "Exactly. The prism suspended just below the body of the kite captures the image of the landscape, which passes through those lenses hanging beneath. The image is projected onto the ground, allowing us to see for miles in any direction. I can demonstrate." She signaled to Batu, who shifted the line, bringing the kite around, and casting an image of another part of the landscape onto the earth.

"This Graves bloke must be brilliant," said Gabriel.

Thalia nodded. "His whole family, too. His great-great-grandmother Portia designed the Compass which all Blades carry, and you should see some of the inventions his great uncle Lucian created. Rather terrifying, actually, to be around someone so hopelessly clever."

"I know the feeling," Gabriel said, flicking a glance toward her.

She rolled her eyes. "You're just as intelligent as I am. Even so, I'm a whimpering pudding compared to Catullus."

"Always had a taste for pudding," he murmured to himself.

Thalia decided it would be best not to address that last statement. She directed her attention back to the projected image of the distant landscape. It was incredible to see a picture of the hills and plains many miles distant, as though a dream had been made real. "I don't see anything even remotely red toward the east."

"Try another direction."

At her signal, Batu shifted the line, and they followed the image as it changed with the kite's placement. Slowly, laboriously, they combed the surrounding geography until—

"There!" Gabriel said, pointing.

A large *ail* of *gers* was situated at the base of some rocky hills. The rhythms of everyday life pulsed around the tents. Children performed chores or played on the ground. Women were drying curds of cheese on top of the *gers*. Herdsmen chatted over their pipes as they tended their flocks of sheep and herds of horses. And surrounding this whole encampment, spreading out in a corona of vibrant color, were acres of crimson flowers. Against the faded greens of autumn grasses they glowed like constant fire.

"Those hills," Gabriel said. "You can just see them on the horizon, there."

Thalia looked up from the projection toward where Gabriel pointed. Sure enough, what appeared to be large rocky crests in the projection were barely perceivable bumps against the sky.

The red flowers lay nearly a day's ride from Thalia, Gabriel, and Batu, but there was at last proof of their existence, just as the song had described. It was truly wonderful to see. She felt a heady pleasure, sharing the enchanted moment with Gabriel.

"If I should ever meet this Catullus Graves," Gabriel said in wonderment, "I'd like to buy him a pint."

Thalia's mood abruptly pitched down. The likelihood that Gabriel would meet Catullus was practically nil. Thalia knew that Gabriel's first mission for the Blades would be his last. Once they had located and secured the Source, Gabriel would have no more contact with her or the Blades. He would return to England to begin a life free of Heirs, Sources, Blades—and her.

She had refused to cry. That's what Batu remembered from his first meeting with Thalia. He had not known her as a baby, but his acquaintance with Thalia had begun early in her childhood. When he first met the Englishman, Franklin Burgess, and his then-little daughter, the girl had been nearly eight summers old, shy as a deer as she clung to her father's side. Her mother had died the year before, and her father had tried to outrun his grief by taking the child to a distant place, far away from familiar sights that only served to remind him of what he had lost. The girl, according to her father, had not yet shed a tear for her dead mother, convinced that holding back her sorrow would somehow bring Diana Burgess back from the place of shadows.

Back then, Thalia spoke no Mongolian. Batu's English was even worse. The only thing they could understand was their mutual love of horses, and, after he observed the girl watching him cut horses from the wild herd every day, they gradually bridged the gap between them. He taught her to ride the Mongol way, helped bandage her bruises when she was thrown, and wiped her tears when she finally cried for her mother.

Batu had served her and her father ever since.

He and Thalia had taken many voyages together across the whole of the country, but neither of them had ever undertaken a mission for the Blades of the Rose. When Franklin Burgess had eventually revealed the existence of this society, and the role he played in protecting the magic of the world, Batu accepted his own responsibility immediately. Having been a youth on the steppes that fairly hummed with mystical power, knowing that shamans crossed from this world into the world of the spirit, Batu never doubted the existence of Sources. He knew that Burgess would shield them from men who would use the Sources for their own gain, and Batu gladly took up the task to do the same. If necessary, he would die to protect them, and he almost had. If Thalia and Captain Huntley had not saved him.

The work of the Blades was his work. Batu had no daughters, but he had sisters and nieces. Thalia was both to him. He bore a double burden: to protect the Sources, and to protect Thalia. It was a sacred charge, one he would never abandon.

He signaled to her now. It was midday and time to rest the horses as well as themselves. Thalia nodded and searched for a river where they could find good water and grass. She understood. The horses were already showing signs of strain, even though they had not ridden particularly far this day. Mongol horses spent part of the year roaming wild on the steppes. If taken too far from familiar land, they grew restive and melancholy. It was the price one paid for such a sturdy, spirited animal. Already the three horses had traveled hundreds of miles from their home. As soon as he was able, Batu would find replacement horses, and let theirs go free. They would return home on their own. Having faced the powerful magic used by the Heirs of Albion, Batu wasn't sure that he would also be making the return journey to Urga. Thalia, however, would. Batu had promised her father to get her back to him safely. And he always kept his promises.

With that in mind, Batu waited until they had stopped to rest, and Thalia had gone off to seek some female privacy, before approaching Captain Huntley. The tall, fair Englishman was crouched down near where the horses were hobbled, carefully reviewing his weapons and equipment with a practiced eye. Batu had known many soldiers in his life, mostly Russians and Chinese, and many were braggarts and bullies; some of them had been capable men, but only a handful had ever truly impressed him with their skill and intelligence—as the captain had. Having spent nearly a week with Captain Huntley, Batu knew that not only were soldiers such as Huntley rare, civilian men were, as well. That did not make him any less of a threat, however.

"In the army, you were a cavalry officer?" Batu asked.

The Englishman cast him a quick, wary glance before returning to his task. "No, foot soldier," he answered.

"Then you must be unused to riding for so long."

"I'm fine," the captain said, terse.

"You must be careful, Huntley *guai*," Batu said.

"I'm always careful, Batu," the captain said without looking up.

"With the business of being a soldier, yes," Batu agreed. "But Thalia *guai* is not a war campaign."

That got the Englishman's attention. He looked up with those curious gold eyes, frowning. It was an intimidating sight, even though he remained crouched and Batu stood. "Never said that she was."

Batu would not let himself be cowed, as he fought the urge to put some distance between himself and the captain. He had already seen that the Englishman was as ferocious as a lion. "Perhaps, though, you think to conquer her, or that she is a warrior's prize to serve as your reward for service. She is a lovely girl."

Captain Huntley surged to his feet, angry, and Batu could not help taking a step back. "You're a decent enough bloke," the captain growled, "so I won't smash your head in. *Nobody's* going to touch Thalia without her consent. Not you. Not me."

"I do not think of her that way," Batu shot back. "She is *ger bül* to me."

"And what the hell is that?"

Batu struggled to recall the English word. "Family. She is family. And I must protect my family."

"I'll keep her safe," the captain said at once.

"From the enemy, from the Heirs, yes, but what about you?"

The captain scowled. "All those looks you've been shooting my way since that night at the monastery. And this." He snorted, a sound both angry and bitterly amused. "You're warning me off her."

"What does that mean, 'warning off'?"

"Chasing the mongrel away from the prized bitch."

"Ah, I understand. Yes, that is what I am doing."

"I haven't laid a finger on her since—"

"Since when?" Was Batu too late? But that was impossible. They had not been apart since they left Urga. Perhaps sleeping had been a mistake.

The captain shook his head. "Doesn't matter. I've been a bloody gentleman, and I'll stay that way until this mission is finished."

"I do not know that word 'gentleman.' If it means 'a man who looks with longing at a woman,' then you are a gentleman."

Batu could have sworn that the captain's face turned a little pink. "You're out of your sodding mind," Captain Huntley grumbled, but he did not look away.

Feeling slightly more emboldened, Batu persisted. "When she returns to her father, she will be untouched by any man, just as when she left."

The words that came out of the captain's mouth were words Batu had never heard before in all the years he had served Franklin Burgess and his daughter. They involved something that had to do with the offspring of unchaste female dogs, and some actions that Batu was quite sure were physically impossible, even for a circus contortionist.

"I will do none of those things," Batu answered. "Yet I was there when you made mention of marrying when you return to *Angil* . . . England."

"Not *yet,* and I *don't* have a damned fiancée. Good Christ, Batu," snarled the captain, "I'm not going to bed Thalia."

"You would not be the first man to try."

The Englishman suddenly towered over Batu, more terrifying in his fury than Batu recalled. "Some man assaulted her? Give me his name. I'll find him and kill him."

"Not assaulted, Huntley *guai,*" Batu gulped. He did not doubt that the captain would make good on his threat, and prayed that he would not be around to see it. "What is the word? Seduced?"

Captain Huntley still looked ready to commit the foulest of murders. "Tell me what happened," he commanded.

Batu glanced around to be sure that the woman in question had not returned. When he felt certain that he and the

Englishman were alone, he cleared his throat and explained, "Three years past, her father met a young Russian who was studying Mongol plants. The young Russian was handsome and well-spoken, and soon became a good friend to Franklin *guai* and Thalia *guai*. When it became clear that this Russian wanted to pay court to Thalia *guai,* both she and her father were quite pleased. The Russian looked at her the way you do, and she looked back. They seemed very much in love." Batu stopped when the look on the captain's face turned even more fierce. He thought Captain Huntley might break his neck.

Instead, the Englishman rumbled, "Go on."

"The Russian never mentioned taking Thalia *guai* as his wife, and Franklin *guai* became suspicious. We finally learned the truth."

"How?"

"One of the Russian's friends from home spotted him in the market," Batu explained. "I was with him and Thalia *guai* at the time. The Russian tried to avoid his friend, but he could not."

"Bringing news from home," the captain guessed.

"Yes, including news of the Russian's wife."

More of the strange, angry words came from the captain as the muscles in his neck faintly pulsed with rage. "Already married."

"A wife and two small children in Moscow, a boy and a girl." Batu nearly trembled with remembered fury, thinking of how miserable Thalia had been in those bleak weeks after the truth had been uncovered. But she had not cried, the same as when she was a little girl mourning her mother. Instead, she wore a strange, empty look, as though she was nothing but dust blown across the expanse of the southern deserts. It had chilled both father and servant.

"Franklin *guai* beat the Russian until the man was almost dead, and the miserable coward slunk away back to his family. We never heard of him again. Hopefully, he died from his injuries." Batu shivered slightly. Mongols were highly superstitious about speaking of blood and death, but he could not contain his desire for revenge against the weak Russian.

The captain was silent for some time, his jaw clenched tight and his hands curled into fists. He tilted his head, as if listening to something, but Batu could see nothing nearby, only the trees and water.

"I won't do that to her, Batu," the captain said lowly.

"You are a good man, Captain Huntley," Batu answered, "and I owe you my life. But you will be returning to England when we have finished our task. And if you tempt Thalia *guai* into lust and then leave, then there is no place you can hide. Not England. Not anywhere. Franklin *guai* and I will find you and make you wish your mother had remained chaste."

"And what *Thalia* wants, that means nothing?"

"She wants you." The simplicity and directness of the statement had the captain blinking in surprise. "Yet she has been wounded before. I do not let my cattle graze too long simply because they want to. If they eat too much, they get sick."

"Now she's a damned cow," grumbled the captain.

"You understand my meaning," Batu said. The Englishman gave a short nod, but did not argue. He was a powerful warrior, yet that would not save him from the wrath of Franklin Burgess or Batu. Even the other Blades of the Rose would seek vengeance if it came to that. And the captain understood.

They both turned when they heard Thalia approaching. She smiled brightly at them, and Batu was relieved. She had not heard what they had been discussing. Everyone then shared a quiet midday meal. When they were confident that the horses had rested enough, they mounted up and began to ride in the direction of the distant field of flowers. With the horses refreshed, they should reach the encampment by nightfall.

Batu glanced over at Thalia as she rode alongside him. "Why did you tell him that?" she asked in Mongolian. Her voice had gone hard as frost, the way it did when she was especially angry.

He scowled. So much for being discreet. "You heard us."

"You didn't need to tell the captain, Batu," she answered. She cut her eyes toward Captain Huntley, but he was riding behind them and seemingly unaware of the nature of their conversation. "You already warned me back at Erdene Zuu."

"But you did not heed my warning," Batu countered. "I have seen how you continue to look at him, how you enjoy his touch."

"I don't want to talk about that with you," she muttered, reddening.

"We must," he insisted. "These are steps that lead to disaster, Thalia *guai*. If you will not protect yourself, then I must take up the task."

"By disrespecting the captain? He's been nothing but honorable."

"He *is* honorable, but he is also a man."

"Men aren't beasts, Batu."

"They can be ruled by the animal part of themselves."

"And women?"

"Women, too."

"That's right. We're *cows*," she said bitingly.

Ah, that was not good. She had heard too much. "The words were clumsy, but the meaning held true."

For some time, she was silent, but her mind was not still. At last, she said, "He didn't need to know." She shook her head. "Trusting Sergei was *my* mistake, Batu. My mistake and my *private* shame."

She was as headstrong as she had ever been. It was one

of many reasons why Batu loved her like blood. "Do you remember when you first learned to ride the Mongol way?"

She gave a cautious nod.

"Do you remember when you were thrown, and you lay in the dirt, looking up at the sky, and you refused to cry, even though the fall was bad and you cut yourself?" She did not answer, but Batu could tell by the tightening of her mouth that she did remember. "I picked you up and used the sash from my *del* to wrap your cut."

"I still have that sash," she said after a pause, and now her voice wasn't hard with frost, but rather rough with river gravel. She would never be a woman who gave in to tears easily. "And the scar on my leg."

"That was the first time I cared for your injuries, but it wasn't the last," Batu said solemnly. "Yet I will do everything in my power to make sure I never have to tend your wounds again."

Without looking at him, she said, "Cows or no, you're a good friend, Batu." She reached across the space between their horses and gave his arm a squeeze, then let go and put her heels to her horse as if trying to outride her own heart.

Chapter 9

The Lion and Lamb

The small whirlwind of dust finally began to gather in strength. It grew from as tall as a man's knee to almost reaching mid-thigh. A faint, damp smell curled from within it, the slightest breath of life. But the triumph was short-lived. Within less than a minute, the whirlwind collapsed back down to the ground, nothing more than a pile of dirt. The medallion also fell to the earth, sending up a puff of dust.

"Hell and harlots," Jonas Edgeworth barked, surveying the failed test, "I almost had it that time." He picked up the medallion and glared over at Henry Lamb, who was sitting on a folding camp stool, next to the fire but far enough away so the wood smoke wouldn't scent Lamb's clothing. Edgeworth continued, spitting in the dust. "I don't know what the bloody hell I'm doing wrong."

Lamb scarcely spared Edgeworth a glance as he packed the bowl of his pipe with his favorite, custom-blended tobacco that came straight from a tiny shop on Jermyn Street. Inhaling the scent of the tobacco, Lamb wished that he was back at his club, relaxing over a pipe and paper, and far away from the primitive backwaters of Outer Mongolia. Partnered with the loutish Jonas Edgeworth, Lamb would have to endure for the sake of the Heirs and England. Lamb, Edgeworth, and the Mongol Tsend had voyaged from England to China on a steamship hired by the Heirs, a long trip made longer by the boorish company.

"Try again," Lamb suggested, barely containing his annoyance. "And this time, don't rush the chant. You spit it out as if you were speeding through school lessons. But, before you do," he added, waving a piece of paper, "I've received a letter through the Transportive Fire. Very good news from headquarters."

"What is it?"

"Our team in Africa was successful. The Heirs are now in possession of the Primal Source." Lamb waited for Edgeworth's jubilation at the news.

Edgeworth stared blankly.

Holy God, *how* could this dolt be part of the Edgeworth family?

"The Primal Source is the first Source," Lamb explained. "When mankind was born and formed civilization, it created magic, it created Sources. From the Primal Source, all magic arises. The power it contains cannot be grasped by the mortal mind. And now the Heirs have it. Trouble is," he added with a grumble, "we don't know how to use it."

"So get some of our frightful sorcerers to have a go at it."

"They are working on unlocking the Primal Source as we speak." Lamb cast a critical eye at Edgeworth. "Which means that you need to return to your own work."

Edgeworth scowled, and went back to his task, cursing under his breath, and not a few of those curses were meant for Lamb himself. Ah, well. It didn't matter if he and Edgeworth wouldn't be punting down the Thames together when they returned to England. Lamb actually would not be overly distressed if, for some reason, Edgeworth met with a tragic but heroic death while pursuing the Mongolian Source.

Edgeworth's father would be furious, however, and Lamb was determined to avoid the wrath of Joseph Edgeworth. So, he would have to keep young Jonas safe as they worked to obtain the Mongolian Source.

Lamb had used the True Hammer of Thor to stop Thalia Burgess and her escorts. When that had failed, Lamb realized there was a better use of the girl and her friends. She and that annoyingly steadfast Yorkshire soldier were actually doing the most difficult part: locating the Source. And, judging by the speed and directness of their southerly route, they were very close. Which meant that the Heirs were also close. The Sumatran Obfuscation Charm was short-lived, but it allowed Lamb, Edgeworth, and Tsend to ride just three miles behind the Burgess girl and her group without detection. Any closer, and the magic wouldn't function. Lamb wasn't worried. On horseback, he could breach those three miles within minutes. Knowing that Thalia Burgess had no idea how close he was, how easily he could reach out and take her, hurt her, and her soldier powerless to stop it, gave Lamb a delicious, dark shiver of pleasure.

"How does this work?" asked the giant Mongol. He pointed at the small round mirror, resting on its stand. Within the mirror, tiny images of the Burgess girl and her retinue of two flickered in and out. Lamb was annoyed. He had made a mistake in not killing the soldier back in Southampton, little knowing that the base-born ruffian would take it upon himself to complete Morris's work. Now, Lamb had to pay for his own lack of judgment, which was nearly intolerable and shortened his temper considerably.

The Mongol, Tsend, reached out with a huge, meaty paw and snatched the mirror up to look more closely.

"Careful with that, idiot," Lamb snapped as he jumped to his feet. He strode over and plucked the mirror from Tsend's hand, then carefully returned it to its brass stand while the Mongol growled. "I cannot very well rush down to Algiers and get another thousand-year-old enchanted mirror." He wiped the reflective surface with an embroidered handkerchief, removing traces of the Mongol's grimy fingerprints.

Tsend looked unimpressed. He did not value age or rarity, only costliness and size. Which was good, since it was the lure of heaps of money that secured not only the Mongol's information, but his loyalty. Though, Lamb corrected himself as he eyed Tsend's brutish hands and the knife at his belt, his "loyalty" only went as far as the strings of his coin purse.

"How does it work?" Tsend repeated.

"Birds are very susceptible as well as sensitive to magic," Lamb explained. "So I can easily control one using a binding and viewing spell. I just find a bird and tell it to follow the Burgess girl, then I see what it sees through the mirror. A simple enough process."

A curse from where Edgeworth stood let Lamb know that his partner still had not succeeded. Edgeworth was still young and, despite his impressive lineage within the Heirs, largely untested. If the situation with Edgeworth's inexperience grew dire, Lamb would step in. Until then, he would let Jonas Edgeworth fume and cuss like some Billingsgate fishmonger, though Lamb's refined sensibilities shuddered with distaste to hear such language. How had Joseph Edgeworth, one of the most influential and revered members of the Heirs, sired this boor?

Speaking of boors, Lamb cast a suspicious eye toward Tsend. The Mongol had worked on a steamship that took him to Southampton. From other sailors he learned that the Heirs paid good money for reliable information about magic. Tsend approached the Heirs, claiming that he could lead them to a powerful Source in his home country. For a price. Lamb wondered how long he would have the Mongol's loyalty, or if the faintest whiff of money could draw Tsend away to another camp. Not the Blades. Those imbeciles considered themselves too superior to use financial inducements. But there were other organizations, other countries and nations who sought the Sources, and it would not be difficult for Tsend to locate them and sell the Source, and possibly members of the Heirs, to the highest bidder.

Those other organizations—France's *Les privilégiés,* or that German cabal, to name just two—would all kill to have the Mongolian Source. But Lamb would kill to make sure they didn't, and that it belonged to Britain alone.

"The thing we are looking for," Tsend said, lumbering over to where Lamb sat, "it will also help us control birds?"

Lamb mentally rolled his eyes. The Mongol had come to the Heirs with the knowledge of a riddle, but no idea its exact meaning or value. Tsend had assumed it possessed some worth, because he'd had to beat it out of a shaman. The shaman had finally yielded the riddle, and only then because Tsend promised to kill him quickly. Unfortunately for the shaman, Tsend hadn't kept that promise. Or so the Mongol had boasted at the Heirs' London headquarters.

It didn't take long for the Heirs to figure out what the Mongolian Source could achieve, however. Once they did, Lamb and Edgeworth were dispatched immediately. Failure wasn't permitted, not with such a powerful Source at stake.

"What we are after has a far greater power." Lamb drew on the stem of his pipe, taking the fragrant, wonderfully English smoke into his mouth. God, he loved his country! It had the best of everything—land, food, language, monarchy—and the finest, most intelligent minds all working toward a single goal: ensuring that Britain's empire would expand until there wasn't a single nation that wasn't under her flag. He honestly could not fathom why anyone, particularly anyone who happened to be English, would ever knowingly and deliberately hinder the work of the Heirs of Albion. Every Briton stood to benefit from their nation's global advancement, though the ruling class—Lamb's class—benefited more than most. But, infuriatingly, not everyone seemed to share the goals of the Heirs.

The Blades of the Rose were dangerous subversives, anarchists, probably reformers. They sought to destroy the foundation of British culture and its civilizing influence all over the world. A strange and motley collection of men from all walks of life. Worse, they even allowed *women* in their ranks, taking them from the sacred protection of home and husband, and imperiling their lives on fools' pursuits. And Lamb would not allow himself to think of Catullus Graves and his whole blighted family. A shame, really, since they had the finest minds in the world, and, but for the singular problem of their skin's pigment, the Heirs would have tried to lure them away from the Blades long ago. It was grotesque, maddening.

Lamb made himself take a calming puff from his pipe. As it always did, the smoke helped soothe the temper within him that, he knew, at most foul could grow blacker and more vicious than anything Edgeworth could produce.

"This thing we chase," Tsend persisted, "what sort of power will it have? Can it bring us wealth?"

"Better."

"What is better than money?"

"Power. The same power that let Genghis Khan rule almost the entire known world. From China to Arabia, all the way to Hungary, the Mongol army destroyed any who opposed them and brought every nation to heel, and he used a Source to do it."

Tsend frowned, trying to understand things beyond his limited comprehension. "What does the Source of the Great Khan do?"

"It might make a small army great in size and devastation," Lamb speculated. "A hundred men may have the strength of a thousand. A single regiment could conquer and destroy nations." Lamb could not contain his excitement just theorizing about the prospect. "The British Army is the best in the world, but we only have so many soldiers. Once I seize the Source, Britain will be able to conquer and control the globe, starting here, in Outer Mongolia, where Genghis Khan's rise to power began. We continue to Russia, finally crushing that gadfly, and move out from there."

"Will this Source be so powerful?"

"It must," Lamb said fiercely. "Back in England, the Heirs have the Primal Source. It takes the power of all Sources and heightens it, so that every Source is imbued with a thousand times more strength. Including the one we search for here, in Mongolia." He did not add that unlocking the Primal Source was still a mystery, but it did not matter. The power would be Britain's, would belong to the Heirs and to Lamb himself.

Almost giddy, Lamb began to pace. "Every country, every nation will become a British colony. And not merely in Asia and Africa, but in Europe and the Americas, too. No more France. No more United States." The British lion would reign supreme, as it was always meant to do. With Lamb and the Heirs of Albion commanding it all. In such a world, the Blades of the Rose would be annihilated, completely and utterly.

"Will I get to kill that Englishman with the girl?" Tsend asked, unconcerned with global domination. "He shot at me, and I want him dead."

"My good man," Lamb said, happily puffing on his pipe, "when we find that soldier, you may grind him into an unrecognizable paste with my blessing." He wouldn't make the same mistake again where the soldier was concerned. Lamb had a few plans for Thalia Burgess before she was also disposed of, though he kept those ideas to himself.

A shout of glee broke into Lamb's thoughts. He and Tsend both looked over to a triumphant Edgeworth, who yelled over his shoulder, "I've done it! Come and see, Lamb!"

Both Lamb and the Mongol walked toward Edgeworth, who waved his hands at his creation. "Very good, Edgeworth," Lamb said. The lad wasn't entirely a simpleton.

For once, even Tsend looked awed as they all stared at what Edgeworth had summoned. The smell of earth was strong. And beneath that, the living fire of magic.

Gabriel couldn't shake the feeling that they were being watched. Even though he had scouted and thoroughly investigated a wide swath of land all around them, something prickled along the back of his neck and down his arms, as if unseen eyes followed their progress across the rolling steppes. He trusted his instincts too well to simply ignore the feeling, but hadn't evidence to back it up. There was no way to prove it, no way to dismiss it. Something *was* wrong, though, and it angered him, not knowing what or why, or how he could protect Thalia from this invisible threat.

Perhaps a gun couldn't do the job against magic, but it never hurt to have a little insurance. Gabriel now rode with his rifle across his lap, ready to be used. The closer he, Thalia, and Batu got to the Source, the greater the chance that the Heirs would try something. And when they did, Gabriel would be ready for them. He almost wished that the Heirs would launch an attack, just so it would end the waiting and uncertainty. He could finally act, instead of biding his time. But ever since the storm caused by the True Hammer of Thor, the Heirs of Albion had remained quiet. Gabriel didn't trust that silence.

But there was one silence he could end. Glancing over at Thalia, her dark hair like a silk standard fluttering behind her, he urged his horse beside hers, until they were riding side-by-side.

"If I could," he said to her, "I'd go back in time and butcher that Russian. Or hunt him down now."

She looked over with a flash of surprise. Thalia shook her head at herself. "I should have known you knew I was within earshot." Her shoulders drew down as she sighed, no longer holding up a burden of tension. "That's good. I was tired of pretending. And," she added, with a small smile, "thank you, for your bloodthirstiness on my behalf."

"I'm not speaking tripe, Thalia," he said. "I'd slowly kill that vodka-steeped bastard if it was possible. Stomach wounds are good. Takes a long time to die from them."

She stared at him for a moment. "I believe you," she said at last. "And, maybe it's wrong to revel in your thirst for vengeance, but it's a better gift than a bouquet of posies."

"You want his guts tied up with pretty ribbons, I'll do it for you."

"Such a lovely gift." But she didn't look too bothered by his imagined grisly offering. "Although, you might want to save such ribboned presents for your future bride."

"Something's wrong with your eyesight. You keep seeing a bride where there isn't one."

"I'm no shamaness, but I can see into your future based on the plan *you* made. And it included returning to England and finding a wife."

He swore roundly—his natural compulsion whenever he was frustrated. "I hadn't a bloody idea what I wanted to do with myself after I left the army."

"So you went to England without any plan?"

"Not exactly. Do you remember the night we spent in the cave? After the storm from Thor's Hammer?" When she nodded, he continued. "I burned something that night, and you asked what it was."

"You said it wasn't important."

"It was a letter."

"A love letter?"

Gabriel snorted. "Hardly. From an old friend, promising me a job and the possibility of a bride. If I wanted it."

"And did you? *Do* you?"

"Now . . ." Gabriel felt the sun on his face, the wind tugging at his clothing and breathing life into his whole self. He was alive. Here and now. "I burned it that night because the rain had turned it to useless pulp. Now I think it was for another reason. I don't know what tomorrow brings. Soldiering taught me that. But I know that a job behind a desk, an ivory doll for a wife who knows only embroidery and babies—such things aren't for me."

"Ah," she said, and couldn't quite hide the hope and happiness in her voice. "That makes things . . . very different." Thalia quieted, turning her thoughts inward, as if trying to reach an important conclusion. If only he could climb inside that clever brain of hers and know what she was thinking. Then she seemed to come back to herself, away from larger schemes. "But we cannot make any kind of plan with certainty, not while we search for the Source, and the Heirs are out there, somewhere, trying to claim it for themselves."

"Certainty is for milksops."

She smiled, and he felt it plain throughout his whole body. "We are definitely not milksops, are we, Captain?"

"No, ma'am, we aren't." She didn't object or pull away when he brought his horse up beside hers, then took her hand. A slim woman's hand, but definitely strong and able. With just the touch of her skin to his, heat roared through his body. He had the urge to take her sweet fingers in his mouth, lick them, or guide them to where he needed touching most. Instead, he made himself what he never thought he could be: a gallant. He kissed her hand. But he wasn't completely transformed into some cavalier. Her eyes widened as he pressed his mouth to her palm, then she flushed as his tongue came out quickly to lap at the sensitive skin.

Gabriel made himself release her hand and put a little distance between their horses, otherwise, he'd drag her right off her saddle and give in to what his body and heart demanded—claiming her for his own.

Fate was a contrary bitch, bringing him to Thalia when every day meant facing mortal peril. Gabriel had never known another woman like her. It wasn't his own possible death that bothered him—though he wasn't particularly keen on the idea of his final muster, not when being alive was pretty damned pleasant—so much as knowing that *she* was in danger. Well, he'd just have to stay twice as vigilant.

Yet she had sharp eyes, too. "There it is," Thalia said, pointing ahead into the broad plain. Her voice came out a bit breathless, which gratified him even if he wasn't satisfied. "It's beautiful."

As Catullus Graves's distance-viewing device had shown, there were almost a hundred acres covered with small red flowers, with a large encampment of *gers* in the midst of them. The flowers weren't of themselves extraordinary, but in the entire time Gabriel had been in Mongolia, he had seen only small sprinklings of these flowers, and never in this abundance. A soldier wouldn't note them outside of what they might indicate about the season, the quality of the land, or whether there was water for horses nearby, and that's what his mind went to first. But then, at Thalia's comment, he *did* see the flowers for their bright beauty, a carpet of flame that dazzled between the lush green grasses and the blue sky.

There wasn't much time for poetic fancy, though. "Do these nomads follow the flowers, or the other way around?" he asked.

"We're going to find out," Thalia said. "However, we cannot simply stop and examine the flowers without first paying our respects to the tribe. That would be suspicious and rude."

"I don't know the first thing about Mongol customs," Gabriel admitted.

"Don't worry," she said. "Just follow my lead."

Since his promotion to captain, he hadn't much experience being directed by anybody else, and certainly never by a woman. Even so, he was out of his element here in Mongolia, and had enough brains rattling around inside his skull to understand it was best to let Thalia take charge. For now.

As they rode into the encampment, they were met with naked stares of curiosity from the people who lived there. Men tending herds of livestock and horses watched them from the backs of their saddles, while women stopped in the middle of their chores to gape. And a flock of children chased after them like ducklings, jostling and peeping amongst themselves. Almost everyone was looking at Gabriel, not at Thalia or Batu. Their interest didn't unsettle Gabriel too much. He was familiar with being the first white man locals had ever seen. Some soldiers never got used to it, or felt that the color of their skin somehow made them better than a country's natives, but Gabriel wasn't one of them. So he returned everyone's stares with a polite nod.

"This is the chieftain's *ger,*" Thalia said as they neared the largest tent. "We shall speak with him first."

Riding up, they were met by a barking dog, who danced his guard in front of the *ger,* and Thalia called out, *"Nokhoi khor!"* A little girl darted out and grabbed the dog by its neck, but that didn't stop the animal from continuing to bark. As Thalia, Gabriel, and Batu dismounted, a boy came from behind the tent and took hold of the horses' reins. He and Thalia spoke for a moment before she gestured for their party to go inside.

It took some moments for Gabriel's eyes to adjust to the darkness. The only light came from an opening at the top of the tent. At first he was reduced to using his ears, listening to Thalia exchange pleasantries with a man, the sounds of someone preparing a meal, two children playing on the floor. But then the haze that filmed Gabriel's sight disappeared, and he looked around. He hadn't been inside a *ger* since he'd left Urga, and was curious what he'd find. And he was surprised, but for a different reason than he'd originally believed.

"Yes," Thalia said softly at his side, sensing his question. "It looks the same. All *gers* are arranged exactly the same way as one another. The stove is at the center, while the door must always face south." She made a small movement toward the left side of the tent, where a woman was stirring a fragrant kettle of milk. "That is the women's side, where food is prepared and the children sleep. The right is where men sit." Sure enough, a man stood on the right-hand side near some saddles, ready to greet the visitors. Everything else, from beds to red-painted cupboards, to the shrine that decorated the north part of the *ger,* was just as Gabriel had seen in Urga. "It is an ancient custom that is never broken," Thalia explained. "And this way," she added, "you always feel as if you are home."

Having spent the last fifteen years in tents and barracks, none of them remarkable, comfortable, or at all homey, the idea that a man could find his home anywhere and with anyone strangely pleased Gabriel.

The man Thalia had been speaking with started to talk to Gabriel, but he could only shake his head in response. Thalia immediately stepped in and began to talk, while Batu quietly provided an ongoing translation.

"He is my cousin from England, and speaks no Mongol."

"You are welcome to my home, cousins," the man said, with Batu translating. Gabriel noticed that his *del* was slightly finer than everyone else's, with silk trim along the cuffs and hem. The chieftain.

Not content with playing mute, Gabriel repeated what he had heard Thalia call out earlier. *"Nokhoi khor,"* he said, with a small bow.

The chieftain looked puzzled, while Thalia suppressed a

smile, and the children giggled. "You just told him to hold his dog," she whispered.

"I'll shut my gob, then," Gabriel muttered as he felt his face grow hot. So much for international diplomacy. He'd stick to shooting and scouting from here on.

More pleasantries were exchanged, including questions about livestock fattening, horses, and family members, in that order. After this, Gabriel was waved toward the northern part of the tent, which, Thalia murmured, was the seat of honor. He sat on the ground, with Thalia to his right and Batu on his left. While small talk was made, the chieftain approached Gabriel and pulled a silken pouch from his *del* while also going down on one knee. The chieftain touched his right elbow with his left hand as he pulled a small bottle from the pouch and held it out to Gabriel expectantly.

"A customary snuff exchange," Thalia said when Gabriel looked at her. "All men do this when they greet one another."

"I don't have any snuff. Just cheroots."

"It doesn't matter. It's custom, a sign of friendship." She offered quiet guidance as Gabriel did what she instructed. "Take a pinch of the snuff using your thumb and forefinger, that's right, now sniff it. Bless you," she added when he sneezed. The chieftain laughed good naturedly. "Return the bottle to him, and mime handing him your own bottle. Yes, just like that." Gabriel tried not to feel like a dolt as he pretended to give the Mongol chieftain a snuff bottle, but no one seemed to think it odd, and the entire ritual was enacted one more time in pantomime.

"What about you?" Gabriel asked Thalia.

"Only men."

The ritual was repeated with Batu and the chieftain.

After this, the chieftain turned to Thalia, and, as he spoke, Batu continued to provide an ongoing translation. "We have heard of you. My brother has gone to Urga and made mention of the English Mongol and his daughter." It *did* seem an

apt way to describe Franklin and Thalia Burgess, since they
weren't one nationality or the other, but some kind of mix.
It wasn't rare for people living away from home to go native
in one way or the other—sometimes the efforts were absurd,
and sometimes the expatriates turned more native than the
actual natives, as if trying to lose themselves in someone
else's culture. Somehow, Franklin Burgess had struck just
the right balance, and his daughter was proof. Gabriel was
beginning to wonder if he could ever get used to seeing an
Englishwoman cinched into a corset or dragging a bustle
behind her after seeing Thalia's freedom of movement. And
freedom of self. She was so different from the girls his comrades in arms used to moon over, those gentle creatures who
were trained to serve, docile and obliging. What the hell had
he been thinking, even to consider having a girl like that as
his bride?

Batu interpreted Thalia's answer into English, so Gabriel
might follow the conversation. "You honor us," she replied,
but the chieftain waved away the compliment. A woman,
whom Gabriel assumed was the chieftain's wife, stepped
forward with her eyes downcast. She held out a bowl of
steaming tea to Gabriel, which he took and sipped from,
before returning the bowl to her. She offered the same hospitality to Thalia and then Batu, before returning quietly to
the women's side of the *ger.*

Gabriel burned with questions about the flowers, but he
knew that the polite rituals would have to be observed. Even
so, he longed to leap up and run outside. It felt strange to be
in a shelter again after living and sleeping in the outdoors.
The monastery of Erdene Zuu had been but a small break in
the routine. Inside again, Gabriel was becoming much too
aware of Thalia's nearness, the sweet soft femaleness of her;
the sound of her voice, contained as it was by the felt walls
of the *ger,* played low and hot in his belly.

"*We* are honored by your presence at our humble *ail,*" the chieftain said through Batu. "Whatever I have is yours, my sister." A small child toddled up to him and began playing with the frogs that fastened the side of his *del,* and the chieftain accepted his baby's mischief with good grace. "Have you joined us for our *nadaam?*"

"Forgive me, but are not the *nadaam* festivals held in July?" Thalia asked. She repeated the question in English for Gabriel's benefit.

"Yes, but our tribe has a special custom. Each year, the strongest and bravest men from nearby *ails* come in the autumn to compete for a special honor."

"What is this special honor?" she asked in Mongol and then English.

The chieftain, whom Batu told him was named Bold, called to his wife. The woman, named Oyuun, immediately left the tent. "I shall show you. It will take just a moment."

"While we wait," Thalia said, again in two languages, "I must remark on the flowers that surround your *ail*. I've never seen anything like them."

Bold grinned. "I am so used to them that I never see them. I did not realize until I was nearly a man that not every *ail* had its own field of scarlet flowers throughout the year. They go where we go, even if we change settlements."

"Does anyone know what makes them grow?"

The chieftain shrugged. "No one knows. They feed our livestock, no matter if the frost is very deep, so we do not delve too deeply into their mystery. The Buddhist priests cannot say, and the shamans will not. It may have something to do with the ruby."

As Batu translated the word "ruby," Gabriel's senses sparked into awareness. Both he and Thalia exchanged glances.

"Here," Bold said as Oyuun returned to the *ger,* a strapping young man following her. In an instant, Gabriel had sized the man up and knew he could be an impressive fighter. And better guard. In his hands, the man held a small red wooden chest covered with elaborate carvings, which someone had clearly labored over for a long time. Bold signaled to the man, and the chest was opened. It took all of Gabriel's will to keep from cursing with astonishment when he saw what it held.

"This is our tribe's glory and our prize," Bold explained, pride weighting his voice, and Batu echoed the sentiment in his translation. The chieftain looked up at the man holding the chest as if asking permission, which was odd, since Bold was clearly the man in charge of the tribe. When he received a nod, Bold reached into the chest and pulled out its contents and held it up to the light.

Gabriel felt Thalia's hand on his arm, as if she, too, were trying to restrain herself. Taking a quick glance at her, he saw a flush stain her cheeks, her eyes widened with amazement. Even though he was trying to remain calm, he probably looked the same way. Sometimes, a soldier's training only went so far.

It was a ruby. Not an ordinary ruby, but one as large as a child's hand, and a deep blood red that caught the light, shimmering and hypnotic. The stone was uncut, but even without polished surfaces, it was one of the most incredible objects Gabriel had ever seen. Surely it had to be worth hundreds of thousands of pounds, if such a thing could have a price.

"This is what the champion of the *nadaam* wins," Bold continued through Batu. "For a year, he lives with our tribe and has the honor of guarding our ruby. Each year, he must defend his honor or yield it to a stronger, better champion. Unlike other *nadaam* festivals, ours is held as a tournament, so we may find the best man for the task."

The man holding the chest said something to Bold, which Batu did not translate. And again, the chieftain seemed to obey the man, returning the ruby to the chest, where it lay on a blue silk pillow. At once, the man closed the chest and left the *ger,* looking about him with alert eyes. He would have made an excellent soldier.

Thalia spoke in Mongol, then said in English to Gabriel, "I told him I am awed by his ruby," Thalia said.

"It is not mine," answered Bold, Batu interpreting, "but belongs to our tribe. We have had it in our possession for many generations, and each is taught to revere and protect it."

"Where does it come from?" Again, she spoke in two languages so Gabriel could follow.

Batu translated the chieftain's response. "We do not know. There are stories, of course, but none that have been confirmed. Where it comes from does not matter. All that matters is keeping it safe."

The toddler that had been sitting in Bold's lap suddenly fell over and began to cry. As Oyuun and Bold picked up the boy and soothed him, Thalia turned to Gabriel.

"It must be the Source," she said in English, quiet and urgent.

"You sure?"

"How could it not be?"

"It surely is the ruby of Genghis Khan," Batu added.

"There is a legend," Thalia said quickly, "that when Genghis Khan was born, he clutched in his hand a blood clot, and this was the secret to his power. Some have speculated that it wasn't a blood clot at all, but a ruby." She looked over to the door of the *ger,* where the ruby's guardian had been minutes earlier. "*This* ruby. It must be what causes the flowers to follow the tribe and bloom all year."

Before Gabriel could answer, the squalling child had been attended to, given a dumpling to keep him quiet, and Bold returned his attention to his guests.

Thalia spoke to the chieftain, but didn't translate her words for Gabriel.

"She wants to compete in the *nadaam,* Gabriel *guai,*" Batu said, eyes wide.

"What?" asked Gabriel.

Bold said something in Mongol at the same time that sounded very much like, *"You?"*

Thalia turned to Gabriel. "How are you with a bow and arrow?" she asked in English.

"Never shot one," he answered, thrown. "Guns only. A cannon, once."

She pointed to herself as she spoke to Bold.

"Sister," the chieftain said, Batu translating, "you cannot enter. You would have to live with our tribe for a year if you won. But, more importantly, our *nadaam* is for men only."

Gabriel had gathered his scattered wits enough to growl, "The *hell* you're competing. I don't know what the damned tournament is, but you aren't entering. I'll do it."

Thalia shot him an angry look, but he wouldn't back down. He had already committed himself to protecting her, no matter what it cost him. And if there was *physical* danger, he damned well wouldn't let her get involved. He might not have Catullus Graves's brains, but Gabriel did have brawn in his favor.

Thalia began to speak to Bold, without repeating herself in English, so Gabriel had to rely on Batu to provide him with her words. "In England, it is quite common for women to be warriors." She ignored Gabriel's curse of dissent. "There is even the famous warrior queen, Boudica, who waged glorious war against the Romans." To Gabriel, she hissed in English, "No orders from you, Captain. If we want to win the ruby, then I *must* compete."

Knowing that it would be impossible to get answers from her, Gabriel looked at Batu. The servant looked just as appalled as Gabriel. After their talk, they had reached an armistice, and were united in their need to keep Thalia safe. "Tell me what else happens at these *nadaams.*"

"It is a celebration of the three manly arts," Batu explained. "Horse racing, archery, and wrestling. Usually, children compete in the horse race, and women may enter the archery competition, but it must be different here. I should mention that there are no weight classes in the wrestling competition, as there are elsewhere."

Wrestling? "You are *not* entering the tournament," Gabriel repeated to Thalia. He looked to Batu for reinforcement.

"Your father would not allow it," Batu added. "And he would be furious should I let anything happen to his only child."

"I'm a grown woman, not a child," Thalia said through gritted teeth. "He would also know that the Source must be protected at *all* costs."

"Not if the price is your life," Gabriel growled. "*I'll* enter."

"*You* can't shoot a bow and arrow, and *I* can," she fired back.

"*You* can't wrestle a fully grown man and win," he countered. "And sure as the devil, I won't let you get hurt, which you would."

They both glared at each other, with Bold looking on quizzically, until Batu cleared his throat. "If I may suggest, should Bold allow it, perhaps you could enter as a team," he offered in English. When Gabriel and Thalia began to sputter their protests, Batu continued, "Alas, I am only a fair archer and even my younger brothers can beat me at wrestling, thus I should not enter. Either one of you might win the horse race, but only Thalia *guai* can win the archery, and only the captain can win the wrestling. So you must enter together. The captain will ride in the race and wrestle, while Thalia *guai* will shoot in the archery competition."

Everyone was quiet as they mulled over this proposition. "Will *that* satisfy you?" Thalia finally asked Gabriel hotly.

"I'd rather you were ten bloody miles away from the damn tournament," Gabriel grumbled. Anything to avoid the possibility that she might get hurt. Someone could fire wildly, or, hell, a nearby horse could get spooked by the hubbub and trample her. Who knew what might happen in the midst of a Mongol athletic contest?

"That isn't an option."

"Then yes, it'll do."

In rapid Mongolian, which Batu did not translate, Thalia made her case to the chieftain. Bold continued to look skeptical about the whole idea, perhaps even more so than when he thought Thalia would enter the competition alone. Gabriel could try to take the ruby from the man guarding the jewel, but it would be far better to get it without resorting to violence. He knew that the best way to get the ruby was to win it, and it steamed his pudding knowing that not only couldn't he do it on his own, but that Thalia would have to be put in danger. He wished Batu could guarantee a win in archery, but the absolute certainty in Thalia's eyes that she not only *could* win but *would* win convinced Gabriel that she was their best hope.

"Wait," Gabriel said, breaking into Thalia's appeal, "tell him this: it might seem strange to you. Go on, translate," he urged, and Thalia reluctantly translated as he spoke. "A man and a woman competing together? Why shouldn't I enter on my own? It's because . . . ," he struggled to find the words, not used to or comfortable with talking eloquently. Finally, he said, looking at the chieftain, "She and I are like flint and gunpowder. Each are strong, but together, they're explosive."

Bold only frowned. So Gabriel kept talking. "We're the bow and the string. Useless alone, but strong together. Or . . . uh . . . we're the knife and the blade." He stopped as the chieftain began to laugh as he nodded his head. Bold spoke first to Gabriel, then to Thalia, wiping tears of mirth from his eyes.

"It appears that you and I are competing in the *nadaam* as a team," Thalia said, turning to Gabriel.

"What did I say that convinced him?"

At this, Thalia's own mouth quirked in a little, rueful smile. "None of it. But he found the idea of a man and woman working together so amusing, that he's letting us enter. He thinks that the tribe could use a good laugh."

Gabriel couldn't help but chuckle, too. "My brief career as a diplomat—over before it started."

"That's all right, Captain," she said warmly while giving his hand a squeeze. "I prefer you as a man of deeds."

He grinned, thinking of the tournament. His blood hummed with excitement, relishing the prospect of real stand-up fighting. No hidden ambushes from underhanded enemies. No magic. Just straight man-against-man competition.

But not only man-against-man. There was a woman involved, too. Thalia. She'd never been in battle, but she was a warrior, just the same. The perfect woman to have at his side in the competition. Soon, they would fight together. And nothing felt more right.

Chapter 10

Another Form of Magic

The timing could not have been more auspicious. Bold informed them that the *nadaam* tournament would be held the following day, and in the meantime, there would be a celebration that night, with Thalia, Gabriel, and Batu as guests of the tribe.

Batu was given a bed in a kinsman's *ger,* since it was discovered that, in one of those coincidences that happened with a strange frequency in such a vast country as Mongolia, he was related by marriage to the chieftain's second cousin. Even beyond a Mongol's usual endless hospitality, this further endeared Batu to the hearts of the tribe. He was plied with food and drink immediately, pounded with a hundred questions about his family as well as about the English man and woman who accompanied him. Thalia and Gabriel received the honor of sleeping in the chieftain's *ger.* But sleep was a long time away. In the meanwhile, there was the feast.

Thalia and Gabriel walked out of Bold's *ger,* and the *ail* was bustling with activity as tents went up all around them.

"Seems like every man within miles wants to try for the ruby," Gabriel remarked.

Thalia watched as several people walked by, leading

camels laden with all the necessary equipment to erect *gers*.
"It's an honor that many seek. Bold said that people from
ails nearby would be arriving all evening."

Gabriel rubbed his hands together. "Should be a good
show."

She couldn't help smiling at him. "It appears you're looking forward to it, Captain."

He grinned back. "Ma'am, I am, indeed. Nothing like a
little old-fashioned competition to get the blood hopping.
But," he added, turning serious, "I don't like that you have
to get involved. Not looking forward to that."

His protectiveness both annoyed and secretly delighted
her. Before she had time to fashion a reply, Oyuun appeared.
"We could use another woman's hands in the preparation of
the feast," the chieftain's wife said.

Thalia glanced at Gabriel and translated. Batu was off
somewhere, sharing gossip, and, with her off to attend to the
feast arrangements, Gabriel would be alone amongst people
with whom he shared no common language.

"Go on," he urged her, gently nudging her with his shoulder. "They need you, and it looks like these fellows"—he
nodded toward a group of men assembling a very large
ger—"could use some help, too."

"Will you be all right?"

A delicious, rather cocky smile tilted the corner of his
mouth. "Warms my heart when you worry about me."

She longed to throw something heavy at his head, but he
was gone before she could grab the nearest cauldron.

"Come, sister," Oyuun said. "I know that the others want
to meet you. Every woman is delighted to meet the English
Mongol lady who will compete against men."

Thalia let Oyuun lead her away toward a sizable group of
chattering women, all eager to press her with questions, but
not before casting a look over her shoulder to see how
Gabriel fared with the men.

He was already in their midst, as comfortable as if he'd been born on the steppes. The men had already laid down the floor and furniture, and, communicating through gestures, were showing Gabriel how to put up the trellis walls. The whole process could usually be done in less than an hour, but this *ger* was exceptionally big.

"For the feast later," Oyuun explained.

Nodding with understanding, Thalia followed the chieftain's wife to the gathering of women, who were busy preparing the mountains of food and drink that would be consumed that night. Cooking wasn't one of Thalia's favorite pursuits, and her father had never expected her to fill the traditional female role, but she knew enough about cookery to keep from embarrassing herself. Exchanging greetings with the tribeswomen, Thalia began filling sheep carcasses with hot rocks which would cook the mutton— a favorite festival dish.

"Do you really believe you can beat a man in the *nadaam,* sister?" asked one of the women.

"I should think that any one of us could shoot a bow as well as, if not better than, our husbands," Thalia answered.

"Is *he* your husband?" a younger girl asked, looking over Thalia's shoulder.

Even though Thalia knew who the girl was talking about, she felt compelled to look behind her. Gabriel and several other men hefted the roof posts for the festival *ger.* A grin spread across her face as she watched him. Though he spoke no Mongol, he responded readily to the others' signals, and was absorbed in both the work and the camaraderie. It did not hurt that he was able-bodied, strong, and clever, quickly understanding what needed to be done and accomplishing his tasks with almost no trouble. Once or twice, the nuance of fitting one of the roof poles provided a momentary obstacle, but those difficulties were overcome nearly before they had begun. Despite the language barrier, he laughed with the

Mongols and made them laugh in turn. A few of the men slapped his shoulders, the universal sign of male approval.

"He is a kinsman," Thalia said, turning back to the group. As tolerant as Mongols were, even they would look askance at an unmarried man and woman traveling together.

"So, he is available?" an older woman asked. "I have daughters."

"And my husband is old," another tribeswoman added with a wicked grin. Her comment set off a chorus of feminine giggles, like doves rising into the air.

She didn't know how to answer that. Thalia scanned the faces of the women, and only few of them were paying attention to their cooking tasks. Instead, most of them were staring past her. Unable to help herself, Thalia looked back again, and lost her ability to think rationally.

Along with some other hale young men, Gabriel unrolled the large swaths of wool felt that made up the *ger's* walls. Somewhere along the way, he had shed his coat and vest, unbuttoned the top buttons of his shirt, and rolled up his sleeves. The sight of his tanned forearms and neck, combined with the athletic grace of his body underneath the cotton shirt, transfixed Thalia. He moved with pure masculine beauty, an economy and purpose of action. It was impossible to keep her eyes from him as he threw the felt covering over the top of the *ger's* wooden skeleton, his muscles hard and sure beneath the woven lawn of his shirt. Her gaze trailed lower. Without his coat to cover him, she could see the tight firmness of his buttocks, the toned thickness of his thighs, everything moving, working perfectly together. She recalled vividly the feel of his skin, how hard and alive he'd been beneath her hands.

But more than the aesthetic glory of Gabriel, his energy and enthusiasm entranced Thalia. He threw himself into the task, observing with a keen and intelligent eye, carefully following the instructions he was given while also taking chances. If he made a mistake, he corrected it and moved on. There was a real pleasure living in him. Pleasure in trying something new. Pleasure in letting his body and mind align. Here was someone who would never hold himself back, and his joy in life became the joy of those around him, including Thalia.

Catching her watching him, Gabriel gave her a cheerful wave before getting back to work.

"'Kinsman,' hm?" Oyuun asked pointedly.

Thalia made herself return to her own tasks, but her hands felt clumsy. "A distant kinsman," she said.

The chieftain's wife smiled, knowing, but did not go further. Instead, as everyone cooked, she readily absorbed Thalia into the world of her tribe, filling her in on the latest scandals, who pined for love for whom, which man wasn't speaking to his brother-in-law because of the loss of several goats. By the time most of the food had been prepared, Thalia felt as though she had known this tribe all her life. Thalia became so engrossed in conversation with the women, she hardly noticed when Oyuun disappeared.

It was only when Oyuun returned and stood next to Thalia that she'd become aware of her absence. "Come with me," the Mongol woman said.

Thalia followed Oyuun back to the chieftain's tent, where she found a steaming tub of water waiting. Knowing that water was scarce, Thalia looked at Oyuun with wide eyes. "I couldn't . . ." she started to protest, but the woman would not have any part of it.

"You may be an English Mongol," she said, "but you are still English. And from what my husband tells me, the English love their baths. Come," she insisted, putting her hands on Thalia's shoulders and gently pushing her toward the tub, "you have been traveling hard for many days, and we shall have you clean for the feast and your 'kinsman.'"

A few half-hearted protests later, and Thalia had stripped

out of her dusty clothes and sunk into the bath with a pagan moan. Oyuun left the *ger*, giving Thalia some much-needed privacy. It felt sinfully wonderful to wash the grime from her skin, using a bar of sandalwood soap that probably came from Russian traders. Thalia dunked her head under the water and washed her hair as well, which had made considerable progress toward resembling a diseased marmot. She dunked her head again, rinsing the soap from her hair. When she came up, water streamed into her eyes, and she felt around for the towel that Oyuun had left nearby.

The towel was placed in Thalia's searching hand. "Thank you, Oyuun," Thalia said as she wiped at her face.

"You're . . . welcome."

The sound of English in a familiar deep voice had Thalia's eyes flying open. Gabriel stood beside the tub, staring at her with amber fire. For a moment, all Thalia could do was stare back at him, seeing a slight glaze of perspiration gleaming on his skin, his discarded jacket and vest hanging from his hand. Even though he was at rest, his breathing was shallow, strained, as his gaze moved down to the bath water.

Belatedly, Thalia realized that the cloudy water did almost nothing to hide her naked body from him. She could even ask him to take off his clothes and join her in the small tub. His skin . . . wet . . . But this was Oyuun and Bold's *ger*, and she couldn't, not when anyone could wander in at any moment. Understanding it would be best not to start something she would not be able to finish, she crossed her legs and held one arm tight over her breasts, shielding herself.

This seemed to break him out of a spell, and he turned his back to her. He seemed to understand as much as she that this was not the time or place to play with their attraction. "Bold said I might . . . ah . . . clean up before the celebration," he said, hoarse. "I didn't know . . . he didn't tell me you . . ." He headed toward the door.

"No, please," Thalia said quickly. He stopped in his tracks

but did not turn around. Tension emanated from the wide breadth of his shoulders, his hands curled into fists at his sides. "The water is still warm. We can share. I mean," she added hastily as he gave a start, "I'm just finished. If you don't mind somewhat used bath water."

"No, I don't mind." His voice was strained, a rough rasp. "I'm very . . . dirty."

"I won't be a moment." Thalia stood, sloshing water, and hastily wrapped herself in the towel with shaking hands. It wasn't the first time she'd been almost completely naked near Gabriel, but she was by no means accustomed to the experience. If anything, her attraction to him had grown even more potent in the ensuing days, and she was bodily fighting with herself to keep from walking over to him and pressing her nude body against the broad muscles of his back. Frantically, she looked for her discarded clothing, but could not find it. Oyuun must have taken the clothes to be cleaned. For the first time, Thalia cursed Mongol hospitality.

Knowing that she could not very well walk outside in nothing but a towel, Thalia pulled a *del* and trousers from the clothes chest, then threw them on. It wasn't a particularly good fit, since Thalia was considerably taller than Oyuun, but for now it would do.

"All done," Thalia said, trying to make herself sound bright and unaffected. "You can turn around now."

Gabriel did so, slowly. He looked everywhere but at her. With his shirt unbuttoned at the collar, she could see the tight column of his neck, the movement there as he swallowed. Then he did glance over at her, and inhaled sharply as his eyes narrowed. He looked positively dangerous. His jaw hardened, and he thrust the bundle of his jacket and vest in front of him. Thalia wondered what the matter could be, since she was dressed, but looked down and saw that, in her haste, she had not dried herself completely, and the clothing clung to her body in a way that revealed every curve, more suggestive than complete nakedness. Oh, hell.

"Thalia," Gabriel growled.

"Yes?" she squeaked.

"Get out."

Grabbing her boots, Thalia ran from the *ger,* even though every part of her demanded she stay.

Life on the steppes was never easy—dry, short summers; long, harrowing winters with their threat of *zud,* the killing frost—so every celebration was enjoyed to its fullest. For this tribe, the feast before the ruby's *nadaam* was also the farewell to warmth. Autumn would turn quickly to winter, the green pastures disappear under cold white blankets for months while the blue sky froze overhead and the sun shone with icy crystalline light.

There was enough heat inside the celebratory *ger* to fuel the nomads for another winter. The special large tent Gabriel had helped set up just for the feast, despite its size, was crammed full of celebrating herdsmen and women. The air was thick with laughter and music, the smoke of pipes, scents of roasted mutton, and the wafting aromas of the continual supply of potent *arkhi* to drink, which turned cheeks red and shy men into heroes. Several hundred people had stuffed themselves inside the huge tent. It was raucous, noisy, and crowded, the furthest thing from a genteel cotillion or sedate afternoon tea.

Home, Thalia thought to herself as she stepped inside the tent. This was her home. She could not imagine herself anywhere else. As she moved through the throng, weaving deftly between warm bodies, exchanging cheerful greetings, she felt an overwhelming sense of love and tenderness toward the nomads, people who accepted her far more readily than her own supposed countrymen. She had to help protect the Mongols, protect this world, this place, especially from the Heirs. They would turn Mongolia into another corner of England—pie shops on every corner, English-language newspapers reporting on the latest British triumph, frock coats and bustles instead of *dels*—and destroy everything unique and wonderful about it in the process.

"Are you nervous about tomorrow?" Oyuun asked as she came to stand beside Thalia.

"Not at all," Thalia answered. With a rueful laugh, Thalia realized that she had been so absorbed in thoughts of defeating the Heirs, she had not even considered the possibility of losing in the *nadaam*.

"I will tell you a secret," Oyuun said, cupping her hand over her mouth. When Thalia leaned closer to hear better, Oyuun whispered, "I hope you win."

"Why?"

"Because no one thinks that a woman can best a man. I know that Gabriel *guai* will compete with you," she said to Thalia's objections, "but the fact that you dare to enter when no other woman has ever done so before—that, to me, is wonderful."

"Perhaps next year, you should try," Thalia suggested, but Oyuun laughed.

"You think I haven't enough to worry about, between my children, my husband, and the well-being of this tribe? I should add the ruby to my burden, too? No"—she chuckled—"I leave such tasks to the young and free. Although," she added with glittering eyes, "perhaps you are *not* free."

Thalia knew immediately that Oyuun was speaking of Gabriel, and her face flushed. There was no point denying it. The wild creature of her soul had finally yielded to the calloused hand of one man.

The chieftain's wife smiled wickedly, looking toward the entrance to the tent. "And here is your handsome Englishman, and I am glad to know that you are not related, especially given the way he looks at you." Before Thalia could offer up a rejoinder, Oyuun had disappeared into the crowd, acting as hostess for the enormous party.

Thalia watched from the other side of the tent as Gabriel entered. Her heart leapt like an unbroken horse to see him, even after merely an hour apart. He'd shaved, and his face was starkly handsome in the glow of the lanterns, sculptural and piercing. His hair, now a dark gold with damp from his bath, was brushed back from his forehead, so that nothing hid him from view. And he'd managed to find some clean clothing, only slightly rumpled from being stowed in his pack. She didn't doubt that, in his uniform, he would have been a sight to tempt any woman to profligacy. As it was, even with him in his travel-creased jacket, vest, and shirt, Thalia was willing to give him whatever he wanted. He looked around, as if trying to find someone. She almost waved to him, but then held back. She wanted to see him on his own in the realm of the herdsmen.

As soon as Gabriel came into the tent, he was greeted boisterously by several men. Some of them, already deep into their third or fourth bowl of *arkhi* and in good spirits with the universe, threw their arms around Gabriel in a hearty, manly embrace. Gabriel didn't stiffen or pull away. He seemed startled at first, but then returned the gesture at once, smiling and laughing. Thalia let go the breath she hadn't known she held.

Gabriel was quickly commandeered by some of the tribe's younger men, and escorted through the tent. The men with him beamed with borrowed glory. Whatever trepidation both Englishman and Mongols had toward one another was long gone, lost beneath the joined experience of setting up a *ger*. A liberal quantity of *arkhi* didn't hurt the cause of fellowship, nor the fact that, on the morrow, Gabriel would be competing in the *nadaam* not only as a foreigner, but as the partner of a woman. Thalia saw that, with great good humor, the tribe had decided to informally adopt him. A bowl of *arkhi* was put into his hand. Someone put a velvet-trimmed, pointed Mongol hat on him, and he didn't take it off.

But he continued to look around. For her. Had any woman wanted to be found more than Thalia did at that moment? Yet she wanted to prolong the game a little longer, and ducked behind some women when his gaze moved in her direction. When she felt that he'd moved on, she peered around the women to watch him some more.

Gabriel was talking animatedly to some herdsmen, and they laughed rowdily together, the kind of uninhibited laughter men reserved for each other. Batu stood next to Gabriel, translating, though by the looks of things—everyone's arms slung around each other's shoulders—a translator wasn't really necessary.

She felt the strange twin sensations of joy and jealousy. Joy to see Gabriel so light of heart, after days of focus and skirting danger. Jealousy to share him even with these good people, after all this time when he had been hers alone. Seeing him across the smoky interior of the *ger*, his tall, lean body loose with relaxation, his face truly glorious as he smiled and laughed, she was dizzy with longing. There wasn't a man she wanted more. Not even what she had felt for Sergei could match this hard hunger, this need. She barely recognized herself beneath its bright radiance. Always before her mind had held dominance, but now her body and heart had taken control.

As if sensing the hot pulse of her desire, Gabriel suddenly looked right at her. Sharp, golden, unavoidable. His smile faded and was replaced by something much more intent. A soldier again. No, not a soldier—a man. He murmured something to Batu without breaking eye contact with Thalia, then moved swift and straight toward her on the other side of the tent. He was an amber arrow headed for her, and she the target that could not, did not want to, move. The crowds swirled in a tide around him. She waited.

He stopped a foot away from Thalia, then raked her up and down with his gaze, saying nothing. It became difficult to catch her breath as she stared back.

"You've changed," he finally rumbled.

"Not particularly," she answered, "I'm the same Thalia you've always known."

A small smile appeared in the corner of his mouth. "Same biting tongue. But the feathers are different." He gently touched the strands of pearls and coral that draped from her silver headdress and curved in a low, graceful swath from temple to temple. The headdress itself was a band that encircled her head like a diadem, studded with more pearls and coral. She had taken the unruly mass of her dark hair and braided it into a single, heavy plait that reached the middle of her back, bound at the end with a silver clasp. Gabriel's eyes moved lower, taking in the fine emerald silk *del* she now wore, covered with intricate embroidery, and the golden sash around her waist. Unlike the *del* she wore every day, this one was longer, lightweight, cut to show a woman's figure. The flare in Gabriel's eyes showed her that he liked what he saw of hers.

"Oyuun," Thalia explained. Realizing that something had changed between them, she suddenly felt awkward and shy, a young girl only recently admitted to the company of men. "Actually, her sister-in-law, who's closer to my size."

"I'll have to thank them both later." He lightly traced the embroidery running along her collar, his fingers brushing against her neck. Liquid heat gathered between Thalia's legs.

To keep herself from dragging him against her and demanding his kisses right in the middle of the crowded feast, she tried some distracting pleasantries. She looked up at the Mongol hat he wore. "Seems the tribe has taken you as one of their own."

He pulled his hand away to touch the hat, as if he'd forgotten it was there. "More like a mascot," he said wryly.

"No, it's respect. It's a rare foreigner who falls in so easily. You work hard. And tomorrow, you compete in the *nadaam*."

"With a woman as my partner."

She grew tense, guarded. "We agreed—"

"If there was another way, I'd do it," he said at once and without apology. "But there isn't, and if anybody can trounce these blokes, it's me. And you. Besides," he added with a disarming grin, "I'd wager they'd all want to be on a team, if their partners could be as pretty as you."

His compliment turned her cheeks crimson. "Flatterer," she chided playfully.

Gabriel scowled. "I don't know flattery from a tiger's arse."

"Well . . . thank you." Her attention snagged on the activity of the feast. "The singing is about to begin," she said.

A small space had cleared from the middle of the tent, and several men with *morin khuur,* the horse-head fiddle found everywhere in Mongolia, seated themselves on the floor while the crowd quieted. Smiling, laughing, a few men and women were pushed in front of the musicians as their friends and relatives playfully demanded songs.

"This won't make me fall into some kind of magic trance, will it?" Gabriel whispered in Thalia's ear as he stood behind her.

"No magic," she whispered back. "Music only."

Bows were drawn across the fiddles resting between the musicians' knees, and at once the tent was filled with the keening, plaintive sound of the open steppes. Then a woman began to sing an *urtïn duu,* a long song. An old favorite, one that Thalia had heard many times before, but it never ceased to touch her deeply.

"She sounds so sad," Gabriel whispered. "Is it a love song?"

"She's joyfully calling praise upon the lush green fields that sustain her people," Thalia translated.

"Doesn't sound so joyful to me."

"There's always a hint of melancholy in Mongolian music, no matter what happy event or thing it describes."

"Like life," he murmured.

Thalia turned her face to one side, so that she was breaths away from Gabriel's mouth. As she contemplated his lips, she understood that every day brought more uncertainty. "Just like life."

In groups and alone, the people of the tribe sang, and Thalia realized that she had lied to Gabriel. There *was* a kind of magic in this music, binding the multitudes within the tent together through sound and collective experience. Even if one couldn't understand the words, the power of human voice and instruments worked their enchantment, drawing deeply upon the place within oneself that had no language, no shape, but simply was. She'd heard both European music and Mongolian music, and each meant something important to her, but in different ways. One spoke to her mind, the other, her soul.

"Do you like it?" she asked Gabriel quietly.

He frowned, considering. "I can't say just yet. But I'd rather listen to this than the damned bagpipe corps."

"Faint praise." But at least it wasn't outright condemnation.

After two brothers finished singing about the heavenly blessing of horses, Oyuun, who had been standing close to the musicians, called out to Thalia. "Sister, please honor us with a song," she cried, a mischievous glimmer in her eyes. Everyone in the tent turned to look at Thalia, who felt fairly certain she would immolate herself from embarrassment.

Thalia felt Gabriel tense, and he moved quickly to stand in front of her, shielding her. "It's fine," she said, placing a hand on his arm. "She just wants me to sing."

"Do you want to?" He seemed ready to defend her against anyone and anything, which broke her heart just a little.

"I'd rather listen to bagpipes. But it would be unspeakably rude if I said no." She stepped around him, but not before giving him a small smile of reassurance.

She edged through the crowd until she was standing in front of the musicians, careful to keep from looking up and seeing the hundreds of faces staring back at her—including Gabriel's. Everyone in Mongolia sang. Herdsmen on horseback tending their flocks would sing to keep themselves company on the lonely steppes. Babies and children were coaxed to sleep with lullabies, camels and horses serenaded to persuade them to nurse their young. People sang with their families, friends, to their animals—a way to fill the vast skies with sound. Even Thalia would sing, and thought it as natural as the earth, but always in small groups or by herself. Feeling the presence of many eyes upon her now, she was beset by a new and painful modesty.

"What shall I sing for your pleasure?" she asked Oyuun as she stared at the tops of her boots.

"Something for every blushing young maiden and brave young man, I think," Oyuun answered, and Thalia could hear laughter in her voice. "A love song."

Without meaning to, Thalia's glance shot up to catch Gabriel's across the tent, then quickly returned to a thorough contemplation of the floor. At least Gabriel spoke no Mongolian, so he would have no idea what was being said just then. But he had to see the meaning in her eyes.

She felt dizzy—not with fear about singing in front of strangers, not from the heat of the tent—but with understanding. It had happened to her. When she had least anticipated it. She'd thought that the process would be slow and gradual, taking months, years, but it had happened in a span of weeks, and it had grown from a sapling to a forest, thick and lush. And now she stood in the midst of it, the unknown land. Love, at last.

Her pulse raced. Despite the revelation of her feelings for

Gabriel, she wasn't quite prepared to announce them to several hundred people. "How about a song to welcome autumn?" she suggested as an alternative.

"A love song," shouted a man.

"Yes, a love song," a woman cried. "Tell our men how it should be done!"

Soon, the whole tent was filled with demands for a song of love. Thalia wished that she could, perhaps, ride naked through a field of brambles while simultaneously chewing on carrion, but since that pleasant option was not available, she had no choice but to yield.

"I cannot deny the request of my generous hosts," Thalia finally said, and the crowd fell silent in anticipation.

Knowing she couldn't sing to her boots, Thalia raised her head and closed her eyes. All the better to block out the undivided attention she was receiving. Taking a deep breath, she started to sing, then her voice caught, and she stopped. After clearing her throat, she began again. It was an old, old song that everyone in the tribe had heard a hundred times already, about a courageous horseman who rode through the heavy snows of winter to reach a beautiful maiden on the other side of the mountains. Thalia's voice was at first thin and reedy, but after a verse, she gained courage and strength, and let the words come out without hindrance. She opened her eyes and looked directly at Gabriel as she sang.

It was a well-known song, but often sung because no one could grow tired of hearing about the power and perseverance of love over obstacles. Thalia thought of her own heart, that battered, proud animal, darting over the steppes, and the fierce creature of Gabriel's heart, and how strange and yet right that they should meet. But there was doubt, too. Brought about by dangerous enemies. The ambiguity of an unknown future. Since he could not understand the lyrics she sung now, she let them speak for her. Her longing. Her fear. Her need for him that she could not deny.

As she sang, she watched him. His jaw was tight, his nostrils flared slightly, and his chest rose and fell with quickening breaths. And his eyes. Burned her. He was carnal, predatory, impossibly desirable and yet desiring *her*. His eyes made promises, dark promises, that she longed to fulfill. Even standing in front of all these people, she felt a slick dampness gathering between her legs, and her breasts felt full, sensitive beneath the silk of her *del*. It would have been embarrassing, if she hadn't been so thoroughly aroused and focused on Gabriel alone.

When the tent filled with loud applause, Thalia realized that she had finished the song. Glancing around, Thalia saw Oyuun beaming at her and Bold nodding his approval. Batu frowned, knowing not only the meaning of the song's lyrics, but how she had sung them and to whom. He wanted to protect her, but there was no shielding her now. Thalia had made her choice. She looked for Gabriel. But he was gone.

She moved out of the circle and into the crowd. Behind her, three girls were challenging each other to a contest balancing full bowls of *arkhi* on their hands, heads, and feet, while the other guests rowdily urged them on. After searching for him in the tent and finding no sign of Gabriel, Thalia quietly slipped outside. The crisp, cool air pleasantly stung after the oppressive heat inside. Because of the brightness of the *ger,* it took some moments for her eyes to adjust to the black night.

Peering into the darkness, she searched for Gabriel nearby. No sign of him. A thread of panic unwound inside her. Had something happened to him? The Heirs? Or maybe she was just being unreasonably afraid. He could have gone off to take care of his bodily functions. Even now, a few men ambled past her and into the *ger,* adjusting their trousers, ready to launch into another round of drinking.

Yet after she waited a few minutes, allowing plenty of time for tending to any and all bodily needs, there was still no Gabriel. Her internal debate lasted only a moment before she went to find him. She quickly checked to make sure her hunting knife was still tucked inside her sash.

At the chieftain's *ger,* Thalia found only Bold's elderly grandmother watching the small children as they played. The woman hadn't seen Gabriel but urged Thalia to rejoin the feast.

"You won't find a husband out here with the old people and babies," she chuckled.

Thalia thanked her for the advice and left. Instead of heeding the grandmother's recommendation, Thalia ducked her head into other *gers,* but they were either empty or contained only the elderly or very young. No one had seen Gabriel. From one of the *gers,* she borrowed an oil lantern.

She stalked through the *ail,* searching, the lantern held aloft. She told herself not to be alarmed—he was a soldier and more than capable of taking care of himself—but a man didn't simply vanish from a crowded tent without explanation. The Heirs could have used any number of Sources or spells to spirit him away. For the first time, Thalia wished that the Blades had more flexibility in their moral code. She would like nothing better than to summon some vicious demon to track the Heirs down and rip their miserable carcasses apart. On second thought, if anything were to happen to Gabriel, Thalia would greedily break the Heirs' bones with her own hands.

Her breath came in frantic puffs that misted the cold air as she started to sprint. The pearls and coral beads hanging from her headdress swayed and clicked with a frenzied rhythm that matched her heartbeat. Yellow light swung back and forth as the lantern danced in her hand, turning the still night into a dreamlike tableau. She didn't know where she was running, only that she had to find Gabriel.

In the corner of her eye, she caught the faint gleam of blond hair. Thalia skidded to a halt as she saw Gabriel sitting on a large rock, watching a herd of horses nosing at the ground and huddling together in the evening chill. Relief hit her so hard she nearly cast up the roast mutton eaten earlier. She waited for her breathing to calm, feeling the sweat cold upon her back, even though she wanted to run to Gabriel and throw her arms around him, confirming that he was real and safe.

The light from the lantern suddenly felt too bright, too intrusive, so she adjusted the wick to dim it to a faint glow before walking toward him. She knew he heard her coming by the slight stiffening of his shoulders as she approached. Perhaps he'd come out to find some solitude. She didn't want to disturb him, but, after the absolute terror she'd felt just moments earlier, it would be impossible for her simply to turn around and leave him alone. Not without saying something, or at least being near him. Selfish of her, maybe, but she needed reassurance just then, even if it cost Gabriel a few seconds of privacy.

Coming to stand next to him, Thalia glanced over at Gabriel. A trace of panic unwound inside her. Had she gone too far with her song? Was it possible she had misconstrued his feelings for her, and he'd needed to put welcome distance between them? He did not look at her, but continued to watch the horses leading their peaceful lives under the starry blanket of night. Something, some wave of energy, barely contained, radiated out from him. The dim illumination from the lantern turned him into a creature of dusky gold and shadow, slightly menacing. Now her heart beat strongly again, but not quite from fear. She set the lantern on the ground.

"Is my singing so dreadful?" she asked with a lightness she didn't feel.

She didn't even see him move. One moment, he was sitting silently, and the next, he stood before her and—oh, God.

He was kissing her. But not so much a gentle caress of mouth to mouth as it was a devouring. He pulled her tightly against him, his hands large and firm, one on the back of her neck, the other on her hip as she was pinned against the taut span of his body. There would be no retreat for her. She felt captured, pinned, but in the most exquisite way. The intensity of his kiss would have frightened her, if she had not matched it with her own unfettered desire. She needed him with a desperation that could destroy fields, level cities.

He tasted warm, wonderful, his mouth both velvety and relentless. She wanted to crawl inside him. Against the curve of her belly she could feel the hard length of him pressing into her. Instinct had her rocking her hips against his, and their combined groans were swallowed each by the other. The sensation seemed to shred whatever scrap of restraint he'd held. His hands were now everywhere: palming the swell of her behind, stroking the sides of her ribs, cupping her breasts through the silk of her *del*. His fingers played across her already tight and sensitive nipples. She leaned into the lightning-hot pleasure, lost to everything but him. Before tonight, before the stolen time in the shelter of the cave, it had been so long. So long since any man had touched her like this. But not like this. Something that approximated it, but all other touch was a candle and this was the sun. She would burn to oblivion.

Touching him was as necessary as life. Thalia quickly relearned, as her hands roamed over his body, that there wasn't a part of Gabriel that was not solid with muscle. His shoulders, back, thighs, buttocks. Stomach. Ridged, sculpted, but sensitive to her fingers as they splayed across his abdomen. He twitched beneath her hand. And when her hand moved lower, caressing his rigid thickness through the fabric of his trousers, the breath was drawn from her mouth as he sucked his own breath in. Thalia reveled in this evidence of his desire, growing powerful, more feminine than she had ever felt before.

They were on the ground before she was aware of moving.

He pulled her on top of him as he stretched out in the dust. She pulled off the headdress in one impatient move, heedless of pins ripping from her hair, and let the ornament fall to the ground. Thalia's legs opened. She straddled him. Moved against him, their hips meeting and pulling back, and, even with fabric separating them, he fit perfectly, rubbed her exactly as she craved. Something bright and strong began to build inside her. She reached toward it the only way she knew how. He growled as she pressed even closer. At her waist, his fingers shook as they tried to untie the fastening of her trousers.

Then his hand stopped. He panted with the effort.

"Why . . . ?" she murmured, deeply swathed in the spell of desire.

"Not in the dust," he growled. "Not you."

She would have been touched by his concern if she hadn't been so damned close to tearing his clothes off. "Maybe we could find an empty *ger*."

"And have someone come in to get an eyeful." He shook his head.

He was still hard and alive beneath her. She blazed with desire, needing him with a desperation that was painful. Words of love formed on her lips, but she couldn't let herself speak them. Not yet. For now, there were needs that had to be satisfied. "Gabriel, please. I don't want to wait for you anymore."

With sinuous speed, he rolled to his feet, pulling her up with him. He reached down and turned the lantern off completely, and for a moment, Thalia was in utter darkness. But her eyes adjusted quickly, enough to see him backing toward the large rock on which he'd been sitting earlier. It was tall enough so that he could sit with his legs comfortably stretched out in front of him, and he sat down now. He tugged on her hands, drawing her forward, so that her legs straddled his as she stood in front of him. She understood.

Thalia wrapped her arms around his shoulders, bringing her and Gabriel together for another deep, greedy kiss. Her hips cradled his so that when the length of his erection slid up and down, he pressed perfectly against her sex. His fingers resumed untying the drawstring of her trousers. Thalia managed to collect herself enough to move away. Frantically, she pulled off her boots, then her trousers, and in seconds, she was naked beneath her *del*. Cool night air was a sweet sting as it touched her most hidden places; the earth was rough under her bare feet.

She stepped close again, and both she and Gabriel fumbled to unbutton his pants. A hiss escaped his lips as he sprang free from his constricting clothing, and then he groaned as she took him, bare, in her hand. He was thick and large. Could she take him? She had to.

"I wish," she whispered as her hand glided up and down his shaft, "that it wasn't so dark. I want to see you." A tiny bead of moisture escaped from the very tip of his penis, and she used it to ease her progress.

"Sweetheart," he gritted, "I wouldn't last . . . ah, that's it . . . two seconds if I could see your pretty hand on my cock."

"No more waiting," she gasped. "I want you inside me."

Smiling against her mouth, he said, "Thank God I know when to obey orders." He placed his broad hands on her hips. Then, with a strength that left her breathless, he lifted her up easily and held her above him. She braced her feet on the cool surface of the rock, one on each side of his hips, as she held tight to his shoulders.

"Tell me your full name," he rumbled.

"What?"

"Do it."

"Fine. Thalia Katherine—ah!"

He brought her down so that he plunged up into her with one deep thrust. After almost a lifetime spent on horseback, there was no tearing, yet she felt an intense internal stretching that made her eyes sting. "You said to tell you my *full* name," she gasped as she learned the new experience of having a man, Gabriel, deep within her. It hurt more than she expected.

"I'm . . . impatient," he growled against her neck. Then he kissed her. "Sorry, sweetheart, but I had to distract you. Does it hurt too much?" He started to pull away, but she held him fast.

"Stay, stay inside me," she said in labored puffs. For a few moments, neither of them moved, Gabriel gripping her securely as he kept his legs anchored to the ground. They were both breathing heavily, even though they remained still. She could feel him shaking with effort, holding himself back. Thalia experimented by moving her hips up and down. He slid almost completely out, then all the way back in again. Discomfort faded and pleasure began to take its place, faster than she would have anticipated. "Oh!"

Something like a laugh thundered deep in his chest. His hips rose up as he surged into her, and he guided her, with his hands, as she found a rhythm. "Better?"

"Yes . . . much . . . oh, God . . ." Thalia tried to keep her voice down, knowing that, even though the *nadaam* feast was a noisy affair, someone in a nearby *ger* might hear her moans and investigate the sound. But it was almost impossible to stay silent as she rode him. Again and again. She wrapped her legs around his waist, needing to be as close to him as possible. Clenching him, feeling his girth, an extraordinary, blinding pleasure began to build.

"That's it, Thalia," he gritted, bucking. "Come for me."

He thrust again, and it began to roll over her, starting deep inside her and spreading out in growing surges, bigger and bigger, until it hit her fully, a crashing torrent of rapture that she threw herself into with a recklessness she never knew she possessed. Her jaw ached from holding in her scream.

Just moments after she was lost to the flood, he stiffened beneath her with an agony of bliss.

He held her close as she collapsed against him. And though a heavy quilt of drowsiness threatened to drag her into sleep, Thalia kept her eyes open. She wanted to see the stars.

Chapter 11

Nadaam

Nearly four dozen men on horseback were lined up at the edge of the encampment. A large crowd stood close by, already cheering. The horses sensed the excitement, and were eager to run, Gabriel's mount included. His stallion tugged at the reins, wanting to let loose the power of his legs. Familiar faces from the night before greeted Gabriel as he took his place between some riders. He called out his own greetings in painfully awkward Mongolian, but no one seemed to mind his butchering of the language. Everyone was too caught up in the thrill of the moment. Gabriel even felt himself smile. He loved action, loved *doing,* and after waiting and agonizing over the Heirs' next move, finally taking charge of the situation was bloody marvelous.

Bloody marvelous didn't come close to describing the night before. Thalia. Finally. After an eternity of days, a misery of wanting but not having. Good Christ, even waiting for the race to begin, when he should be thinking about how best to take the course, his body demanded more, his pulse sped with desire. He wanted nothing more than to gallop up to Thalia, throw her over the saddle, and ride away with her to some secluded spot where he could take her sweet body again and again, making her come relentlessly, until she was hoarse from screaming, until they were both tapped dry. Last night hadn't even approached dulling his hunger for her.

When he'd cleaned himself later, he'd been surprised not to find any blood. But there had been no tearing, either. She had been a virgin. He knew that completely. But she was also a horsewoman and no English sidesaddle for Thalia, and he was grateful that had tempered her pain. He couldn't stand causing her any pain.

Gabriel's attention snapped back to the moment when Bold came forward. He addressed the riders, saying something in Mongolian that Gabriel could only assume meant, "Ride well, and watch your arse."

He saw Thalia and Batu join the crowd, and his heart knocked into his ribs to see her and the encouraging smile she gave him, but he made himself focus on scanning the territory ahead, learning the landscape so he could be prepared. But nothing prepared him for what he saw next.

Muscling between two riders, mounted on his own wild-spirited horse, was Tsend, the Heirs' henchman. Jesus, how close were the Heirs, to send their thug? They'd kept themselves hidden, somehow, and belated recognition of danger turned to fire up Gabriel's back. So near. The Heirs had been so near, and Gabriel unknowing the whole time. Christ and devils.

The large Mongol mockingly saluted Gabriel with his riding crop, then flicked his greedy eyes to where Thalia stood. Gabriel followed his gaze, and saw that a surprised and angry Thalia recognized him, too. She took a step toward them, as if she could somehow fight the vicious Mongol herself. But Tsend just smiled coldly. Black rage poured through Gabriel. Not only was Tsend leering at Thalia, but the bastard was going to vie for the ruby. Probably easier than trying to steal it outright from several hundred tribesmen. He'd win the Source and give it to the Heirs.

"Like hell," Gabriel muttered. He started to wheel his horse toward Tsend, maybe try to knock him down, but there was a shout from Bold, and suddenly the race had begun.

Every day in the army hadn't been a battle. In fact, there could be months on end when almost nothing happened, and the soldiers had had to find a way to amuse themselves or else go barmy from boredom. Horse races had been just one of the entertainments they'd devised. Gabriel had competed in, and won, his fair share.

But none of those races had the urgency, the necessity, of this one. Only the first eight men to finish this race would advance to the next stage in the tournament, and Gabriel had to be one of them.

Sounds of hooves beating hard into the earth rumbled on every side as riders galloped hard across the fields. Gabriel bent low over his horse's neck, while dust rose up in huge, choking clouds. The first part of the course was nearly flat, half a mile of steppe without interruption. Gabriel pressed his heels into the stallion's sides, kept the quirt resting lightly on its flank as a reminder for speed. He didn't want to tire his horse too soon, but had to establish an early enough lead to separate out from the throng of riders.

He chanced a quick glance around and saw that already half of the competitors had fallen behind. That still left nearly two dozen men, all of them whipping hard at their horses. Tsend was among them.

They forded a stream. For half a moment, Gabriel wondered if the Heirs might summon more water demons to sweep the riders from their saddles, but, in an instant, everyone had crossed the stream. Flat steppe swelled up to rolling hills dotted with birch trees. Gabriel wove his horse through the trees, nimbly dodging them. By the sounds of horses neighing and men shouting, followed by a few crashes, other riders hadn't been so careful.

He ducked under a low-lying branch and felt a few twigs

brush his hat, which almost came loose. From the corner of
his eye, he saw a few other riders keeping pace deftly, including Tsend. Somehow, the Heirs' Mongol had found a horse
large enough to support his bulk. Folded awkwardly over his
own knees, Gabriel wished he'd been able to do the same.

Abruptly, the hills and trees gave way to a steep and rocky
slope. Some of the horses were unprepared, and they and
their riders stumbled as rocks blocked their descent. One
pair even toppled over completely, rider and horse somer-
saulting together. Gabriel almost swung his own mount
around to help, but saw the fallen horse immediately get up
and trot away while the dazed rider tottered to his feet.

Gabriel leaned back in the saddle as his horse careened
down the hill. Without a firm hand on the reins, the horse
would have galloped madly, directionless, heedless, but
Gabriel held tight, guiding the beast around rocky outcroppings when possible, or urging it to leap over smaller obstacles in his path. The bright blue sky seemed to reach
down to meet him as wind pushed against his body. A
strange, wild joy thundered in his chest in those brief, air-
borne moments. His mind and body both pulsed with life.
He laughed aloud.

He took that thrill and directed it toward staying on his
horse and toward the head of the pack of riders. The stone-
covered slope ended, stretching back into grassy steppe,
which meant it was time to bring the horse about and complete the course. Quickly, Gabriel counted eleven other riders,
with Tsend part of that number. At least three riders couldn't
cross the finish line ahead of Gabriel, or the battle would be
lost. This wasn't just for the ruby, not merely for the Blades of
the Rose, but for Thalia. The thought spurred him on.

Like a booming flock of birds, the competitors wheeled
around en masse. The rest of the course was flat steppe, so it
was an all-out sprint to the clusters of *gers* off in the distance.
Gabriel lifted up, crouching in the stirrups, and his horse

caught his urgency. The sight of the other horses around it spurred it onward, ears folded back, neck stretched out, sandy hide flecked with foam. Tsend managed to pull up alongside Gabriel. The Mongol's horse's flanks were striped with red welts from his indiscriminate use of the whip.

Then Tsend moved closer, snarling. Gabriel anticipated the blow, and caught the strike of the whip on his forearm as he shielded his face. Tsend struck again and again, the force of the blows almost knocking Gabriel from the saddle. He grimaced in pain as the leather bit through the fabric of his jacket, catching flesh. He cursed, as the attacks were causing his horse to fall back, losing ground. More riders passed, either unable or unwilling to help, and Gabriel had to act.

The next time Tsend slashed with the whip, Gabriel managed to wrap his hand around it. A struggle ensued as the Mongol mercenary and British soldier fought for dominance, their bodies suspended over the racing grasses beneath them, each tugging furiously on the whip. Gabriel felt as though his arm, burning with exertion, was about to be torn off. With a growl, he pulled hard. Tsend shouted. The whip went flying, cutting the air, and was lost somewhere on the steppe behind them.

Gabriel spared neither the lost whip nor the swearing Mongol any further thought. He was a few hundred yards from the finish line, could already hear the crowds shouting encouragement, but there were ten riders ahead of him. The race could be lost or won in the next moments. He nudged his heels into his horse, and the animal, wanting to taste victory, hurtled forward.

Shapes of the other riders slid past Gabriel as he bridged the gap between himself and his competition. He didn't look to his left or right, didn't look behind. His sole focus was the blue silk banner that marked the finish. As he pushed onward, sweat formed and cooled on his back. Closer. Closer. He felt himself, his horse, begin to flag. Now he could give the horse's flank a swat with the quirt, and did so. The animal broke out of its complacency, drawing upon reserves of energy Gabriel had carefully tended throughout the race. The crowd's indistinct roaring became individual voices as he neared. And in the midst of that sound was Thalia, yelling in English, "That's it, Gabriel!"

Her voice was all he needed. With a final push, he dug in. A flash of blue silk moved and was behind him. The crowd shouted. It was over. He'd crossed the finish line, but not knowing in what position he'd placed. Had other riders passed him at the last minute, edging him out?

Pulling up on the reins, Gabriel eased his horse into a canter, then a trot, and finally a walk. He brought the horse around, and in the haze of dust kicked up from so many other riders, it was impossible to know. He squinted through the swirling yellow dust.

Then, appearing like a summoned spirit, Thalia ran toward him. She dodged the horses milling in excited confusion, never breaking stride, until she was beside him, beaming up at him with a beauty and radiance that stung his eyes. He'd made her happy.

"You've done it," she cried. "Tied for second. Wonderful, wonderful Gabriel."

He bent down, wrapped an arm around her waist, and hauled her up so that her hip touched his. And then he kissed her. Hard.

She seemed startled at first, hands suspended in the air like birds, but then she gripped him, kissing him back with the same ferocity. The race had his heart already thundering in his chest like heavy artillery. And now, he was sure every cannon in the British army fired simultaneously underneath his ribs. The excitement of the race was nothing to holding Thalia, kissing her.

When her hands gripped his upper arms, pressing into the fresh cuts from Tsend's riding crop, he couldn't help the hiss of pain that escaped between his teeth. Hearing this sound, Thalia broke the kiss and leaned back. When she saw the injuries he'd sustained, she scowled and wriggled free until her feet touched the ground. He hated letting go of her, but she was determined, and he was more than a little sapped from the race and from defending himself against the Heirs' Mongol. He swung his leg over the saddle and dismounted.

"I'll rip his guts out, starting at his toes," she growled, gently examining Gabriel's wounds.

He couldn't help but smile at the fierce panther that was Thalia. "Against the Blades' rules, isn't it?"

"Not if it's justified." She shook her head at his bleeding skin. "I can bind these, put some herbs on them to help the healing. Do you think you'll be up for wrestling later?"

Gabriel decided he wouldn't tell her about the time he'd almost had his arm shot off, though he had the scars on his shoulder to prove it. Bragging never did anybody any good, except make him or her look like a bleating fool. "That shouldn't be a problem."

Just then, Tsend rode slowly past them, chuckling. Gabriel started after the Mongol, but a restraining hand from Thalia stopped him. "He finished just after you. So save that fight for later. If he places in the top four of the archery competition, you'll get your chance. Besides," she added when Gabriel let out a stream of rather unpleasant oaths, "we don't know what the Heirs are planning. If we simply take out their heavy muscle, they'll surely have someone or something else ready. At least Tsend is a known commodity, and one that can be bested."

It wasn't as satisfying as beating the Mongol's skeleton into a paste, but it would have to do for now. Other things also left Gabriel unsatisfied, such as the kiss he and Thalia had just shared, the kiss that flooded him with thick heat.

She seemed to recall it at the same moment he did, because her already pink cheeks turned nearly ruddy as she blushed. Kissing in public wasn't something she was familiar with. "Come on," she said. "Let's get you bandaged. The archery is about to start, and I don't want to be distracted by thinking about you." Thalia turned and began to walk toward the chieftain's *ger*.

After handing the reins of his horse to a waiting boy, Gabriel followed, watching the sway of Thalia's hips. He knew it would take more than a few bandages to keep *him* from thinking about *her*.

Thalia rubbed her palms against her thighs, trying to dry them. She'd shot a bow many times in her life—it had been one of the first things Batu had taught her, soon after she'd arrived in Mongolia, and not long after that, she'd surpassed him in ability—so she didn't doubt that she *could* shoot well. But Thalia had only hunted, as well as shot at targets for amusement. Now, if she failed in this task, she and Gabriel would be out of the running for the ruby. If they didn't win the Source they might have to steal it, or make a stand out on the exposed steppes against the relentless Heirs; the mission might be a failure with all its attendant disaster, and her first opportunity to join the Blades would be her last.

To keep her mind from dragging her under, Thalia checked and rechecked her bow. It wasn't the one she usually shot with, but it would suffice. She'd borrowed it from Bold's youngest brother, who smiled at the thought of a woman competing against the area's most skilled men. Thalia shook her head to clear more doubts. It was a typical Mongolian recurve bow, once the weapon of the unstoppable Mongol horde. She, like those warriors and any self-respecting herdsman, could shoot both on the ground and from horseback. But all she needed today was distance and accuracy on her own two feet.

After checking the fit of the leather bracer she wore on her right forearm and the ring of horn protecting her thumb, she glanced around the *ger* that had been set aside for the archers to prepare themselves. Every now and then, one of the competitors would look over at her and shake his head, yet, so far, no one had outright complained about or disparaged her presence in the tournament.

No, she'd been premature in that assessment. Tsend stalked into the *ger,* carrying a bow, and glared around the tent. Thalia wanted to run up and shove her elbow into his throat. The wounds that Gabriel had suffered at his hands hadn't been severe, but any injury that Gabriel sustained was one too many, and to have the Heirs' bully be the cause of those injuries was beyond endurable. She managed to restrain herself, though. Brawling wasn't allowed in the *nadaam.* All her hate would have to be channeled into winning the archery competition.

When Tsend's eyes fell on Thalia, he burst out into harsh laughter and pointed derisively. Most of the other competitors looked away in embarrassment.

"You?" he snorted. "Are Englishmen so feeble that they must have their women fight for them?"

"And you must doubt your own skill," Thalia countered coolly, "to belittle someone so clearly beneath your attention."

"I doubt nothing," he snarled back. Clearly, he was a man unused to being called out.

"Today is a good day to start."

The giant Mongol took a threatening step toward Thalia. He was easily a foot taller than she, with a sizable weight difference. She did not back away, but stared straight at him, looking just a little bored. When he saw that she wouldn't be easily cowed, he turned away and muttered something under his breath, and made a big show of adjusting his bow.

Thalia slowly let her breath out and forcibly kept her hands from shaking. She would not let him rattle her.

A tribesman poked his head into the *ger.* "The competition begins now. Please come out to the field."

She and the seven other archers filed out of the tent, each carrying his or her bow and a quiver of marked arrows. Thalia made sure to put several men between her and Tsend. She refused to let him bully her, but she also wasn't stupid. The crowd erupted into cheers at the emergence of the archers. Immediately, Thalia sought out Gabriel in the multitude. He was difficult to miss. Tall, broad-shouldered, radiating a soldier's focused energy, and looking directly at her with crystalline, alert eyes. An immediate hunger curled through her like incense, and her trepidation about the archery contest disappeared under the thick blanket of desire. Just after the horse race, that kiss . . . and the night before, the things they'd done . . . how he'd made her feel . . .

That way led to madness. If she misplaced her concentration before this, possibly the most important moment of her life, everything would be lost, including her own self. And then it wouldn't matter if she could have Gabriel touch or kiss her like that again. Nothing would matter.

She spared him a slight nod, which he returned, but his was just as terse. Even from a distance, it was impossible to miss how tightly he held his jaw, the fists he clenched at his sides. Did he doubt her?

Thalia turned her gaze upward, and she watched the clouds as they slipped across the sky. To make sure she had the wind's direction exactly right, she scooped up some dust and let it scatter in the breeze. Her mind went through its quick series of calculations. The wind wasn't strong, but it was enough to make a difference, and she would need to make adjustments with her arrow.

Steeling her shoulders, she turned her attention to Bold, who addressed the competitors.

"Your targets are there," he said, gesturing almost a hundred yards away. Thalia noted the small leather targets, placed at a greater distance than at most *nadaam* festivals. She'd never shot a target at that distance. "You may shoot three times. Only four of you will move on to the next stage of the tournament. Fire only on my signal, and may the gods guide your arrows."

Thalia swallowed hard as she and the other archers took their positions. The sun was hot on her shoulders and back. She positioned her arrow, lifted her bow, and drew back the string with her thumb, but it was more difficult than usual. Her arm shook a little. It felt as though every member of the Blades of the Rose, plus the Heirs of Albion, as well as Gabriel and her mother were all holding tight to the string, weighting it with their own expectations and agendas. Worse still were her own hopes, now building to a pressure that was almost insupportable.

Two hundred people watched her. So did Gabriel. And, from hundreds of miles away, so did her father. Her breathing grew shallow. The point of the arrow dipped and danced as her grip faltered. Could she do this?

Thalia lowered her bow and again rubbed her hands on her *del*. She refused to look at Gabriel, but felt his eyes on her all the same.

"What's the matter, girl?" sneered Tsend from the end of the line. "Something wrong with your equipment?" He grabbed his crotch and laughed. Thalia remembered his bearing down on her beside the river outside Urga, the menace in his eyes, his very real threat. She felt cold.

From the corner of her eye, she saw Batu restrain Gabriel. She struggled with the impulse to run to him, hide behind him. No. Thalia would do her own fighting. She closed her eyes, focusing on the sounds of the wind ruffling the grass. She imagined herself an eagle, wings open, riding the currents of heat and air, lifting up and high over the plains.

I am a Blade of the Rose, she thought. *I help protect the world's magic.*

Opening her eyes, Thalia raised her bow high. She drew back the string as she aimed. It pulled easier now. The world was quiet, her mind was quiet. The target waited, silently calling to her.

"Now!" Bold shouted, and at almost the same time, the crowd yelled, "Hit the target!"

Thalia fired, as did the men standing on either side of her. Arrows whistled as they split the air, hurtling up in an arc before sweeping back down to earth. Then came the distant, meaty sound of the arrows hitting the targets. The crowd cheered. She wanted to look at Gabriel, but knew that the sight of his face would only distract her.

There was no time to know how she'd done. Bold signaled for the archers to raise their bows and aim. Thalia let herself think only of the target and her arrow, the movement of the wind, the feel of the bow in her hands, the strength of her arms as she drew back the string. And then Bold cried out to fire, the crowd yelled, and her arrow sang in its voyage across the field.

Two of the archers groaned as their arrows fell short. Unfortunately, Tsend was not one of them. Thalia could tell that she, Tsend, and the other four competitors had struck the targets, but only the judges would be able to tell who was the closest to the center. At this distance, she could not see. She'd hit the target, yes, but she could still be edged out. She grappled with an uprising of fear and doubt. What if she failed the Blades? Failed Gabriel? What if she failed herself?

She heard Gabriel shouting his support from behind her, yet, while his words warmed her, she didn't take her encouragement from him. It had to come from within. If she relied on something, someone, outside of herself, then she would be no good to the Blades. She must be strong on her own.

The signal came to raise bows. Thalia did so, keeping her eyes trained solely on the target. She would be her arrow, and when she released the string, she would fly strong and true. The archers were commanded to shoot. The string leapt forward, propelling her arrow. How beautiful it sounded, whistling like a child.

Every arrow struck home, and the judges came hurrying out to examine the results. The judges consisted of Bold and several tribal elders. Four of the judges carried blue silk banners, which they would wave next to the winners' targets. She and the other archers, with the exception of Tsend, exchanged concerned looks as the judges gestured and shook their heads. That could mean anything. Thalia risked a glance back at Gabriel, and the smile he offered her, small but proud, broke her heart a bit. No matter the result of the competition, he knew she'd done her best, and that was enough to satisfy him.

But *she* would not be satisfied if she cost them the ruby.

Thalia clutched at her bow as the first blue banner unfurled next to one archer's target, a small sapphire flag waving across the grasses. The man grinned triumphantly as his family applauded. Then the next banner was waved beside another target, and the winner couldn't stop himself from dancing in place with glee. As this was happening, Tsend muttered and swore under his breath. Only two more competitors could progress to the next round of the tournament. But when a judge ran next to Tsend's target and waved the blue silk, he stopped muttering and laughed at Thalia with a vicious spite.

"Looks like your English fool should have left the shooting to the real Mongols," he jeered.

A hard knot lodged in Thalia's throat. She and four other archers remained, vying for a single slot. She wanted to close her eyes and pray to whatever deities listened, but she dared not look away from the judges. Bold, carrying a banner, walked slowly past her target, and she felt her eyes burn. She had failed.

Then Bold stopped, and turned back. As her breath abandoned her, Thalia watched as Bold ceremoniously unfurled his silk banner next to her target. He grinned, enjoying his theatrics.

The cheer that rose from the crowd was louder than any that had come before. Turning, Thalia saw that all the women watching the *nadaam* were yelling with an almost manic delight, while the men appeared more than a little puzzled. All except Gabriel, who was making so much euphoric noise—clapping, whistling, and even, good Lord, cussing—that she felt her face heat with happy embarrassment. Joy careened inside of her. She'd done it. Really done it. They were another step closer to the ruby.

Thalia turned to Tsend, who looked ready to commit murder then and there, if not for the presence of the tribesmen. She gestured to her *del*. "This is not a costume," she said to him. "I *am* a real Mongol. More than you, traitor."

With a foul oath, Tsend stormed off, shoving people out of his way.

Thalia barely noticed, because Gabriel was suddenly beside her, wrapping her in an embrace so tight, she saw stars. She tried to think of a time when she'd been happier, but couldn't.

Thalia was already exhausted, wrung dry from the horse race and archery, but there was still one more competition to go before the ruby's guardian could be determined. Even the short pause while everyone had some food and drink wasn't enough to revive her. But her hardest work was over. The final challenge belonged to Gabriel alone.

"Does your Englishman know how to wrestle the Mongol way?" Oyuun asked Thalia. The chieftain's wife and she waited with the rest of the crowd for the competitors to change their clothing and emerge once more.

"Batu and I explained the rules to him," she answered.

"Explaining and doing are quite different things," Oyuun

pointed out. Thalia shot her a warning look, already close to her breaking point. She didn't need anyone adding to her anxiety.

"He was a soldier for most of his life." It still felt odd to speak of Gabriel's military service in the past tense. In her mind, in her heart, he was a warrior, and always would be. "He knows how to fight." She hoped his skills, and determination, would be enough.

The spectators cheered as the wrestlers began to come out of their private *ger.* When Tsend emerged, as massive and terrifying as fear itself, Thalia gulped. In the skimpy traditional wrestling costume, he appeared a barely civilized brute who used higher reasoning only when all other options had failed, and even then with resentment.

"I do not know who this Mongol is," Oyuun whispered, "but his eyes are terrible and dead."

For a moment, Thalia almost confessed that she, Gabriel, and Batu knew Tsend all too well, but then Gabriel came out from the *ger,* also wearing the prescribed wrestling costume. Her own ability to use higher reasoning disappeared instantly.

"Ah," Oyuun said on a breath, "*that* man is not dead. And neither am I."

Having been to numerous *nadaam* festivals, Thalia was well-used to the clothing that the wrestlers wore, even if other Europeans found the outfit somewhat shocking. Classical Greek and Roman statues were only slightly more bare. Mongol wrestlers were shirtless, except for a very short jacket that was completely open in the front, and instead of trousers or even breeches, the wrestlers wore trunks much smaller than even the scantiest pair of men's underdrawers. Typical boots and the pointed hat completed the rest of the costume, such as it was.

When she'd started to come of age, Thalia had been intrigued by male bodies, so unlike her own. There was a degree of openness and frankness with the Mongol people that allowed Thalia to see and learn as much as she wanted—

within reason. She *did* have a father, after all. Then she and her father had traveled to Britain. What English girls knew, or rather, how much they *didn't* know, about men and sex had shocked her, and she had happily returned to Mongolia. Certain gaps in her education had been mostly filled in, not literally, of course, by Sergei. They had never seen each other naked, but through their heated pettings and pawings, Thalia came to know the feel, shape, and size of a man. All of him.

And then there was Gabriel. She'd seen him partly covered the night they had taken shelter in the cave. The night before, he'd been almost completely clothed, but she'd felt him, their bodies pressed as close as possible, and him, inside of her. Thalia had a fairly good idea what he looked like undressed. It was a very pleasant idea, and one she couldn't stop herself from returning to again and again in quieter moments.

Sometimes imagination did not do justice to reality. Gabriel in the extremely revealing wrestling costume was one of those times.

He was the mythic Warrior, the protector of magic, defender of causes, even those not his own. His body was a weapon, and a beautiful one.

Every year he had spent as a soldier showed. Each of his muscles were developed to their apotheosis, the ideal of form and use—the defined shape of his chest, made even more seductive by the light dusting of golden hair, the ridges of his stomach, undimmed by extraneous fat or flesh, some delicious muscles that curved from his hips under the waist of the trunks. Thalia had touched them through fabric, and they had felt marvelous, but she hadn't known that they could rob her of the ability to remember her own name.

And what the wrestling trunks covered . . . Heaven and Earth . . . the man wasn't even aroused, and Thalia couldn't keep herself from staring. She'd touched him, he'd filled her, but she hadn't seen, and was almost glad she hadn't. She would have been terrified. At least she had the comfort of knowing she could accommodate him. Dimly acknowledging that she shouldn't leer at Gabriel's crotch, she forced her eyes lower, taking in his legs, tight and powerful. No wonder he rode horses so well, with thighs like those. They had been beneath her, between her legs. She had been the one riding him last night. A hot shudder of blazing desire coursed through her.

"You say he was a soldier?" Oyuun asked beside her. Thalia managed to pry her gaze away to look at the chieftain's wife and nod. "I can see that now. He carries stories on his body."

Thalia turned her attention back to Gabriel and saw, in the golden light of afternoon, that scars marred the perfection of his form. There, on his left shoulder, a round, puckered mark showed he'd been shot. And stretching from just under his ribs, on the right, a long, raised ridge made by—a jagged knife? The flesh there had closed without finesse, and Thalia winced to think of the lengthy, unpleasant recovery from such a wound. But these were only the two most obvious. There were more scars, more tales of battles and meetings with death, on his legs, his back. Horrible. Her fingernails bit into her palms as she realized, at last, what Gabriel had been doing every day for the past fifteen years. It was miraculous that he was alive.

Not miraculous, but a testament to his capability, his will to survive.

Gabriel caught Thalia staring at him. Her face turned completely and obviously red, but she did not look away. For the barest moment, he seemed a little discomfited, despite their intimacy of last night. He would probably never consider wearing such an outfit in front of a European woman. But that awkwardness lasted less than a blink, and he slowly smiled at her. A carnal, deliberate smile. He knew she liked what she saw, and seemed more than ready to let her look her fill. And later, more than look.

He started walking toward her. In motion, barely clad, he would make any woman renounce all vows. Thalia couldn't suppress a measure of pride as women, from the blushing maiden to the wizened grandmother, watched him pass, but he saw no one but her.

"Perhaps there is a camel that needs milking." Oyuun laughed, and mercifully slipped away.

"You think the British army might take this up as their new uniform?" Gabriel asked, coming to stand in front of her.

"Only if they want to inspire lust in their enemies," she answered.

He grinned. "Is that what I do?"

"I won't answer that. I don't want you to get a swollen head."

"Keep looking at me that way, and my head won't be the only thing swollen."

Thalia laughed, and said, lowly, "Hang on to that costume. It might be useful later." Her smile, she knew, was pure feminine provocation.

Something like a growl rolled from the back of his throat as he stepped nearer.

"Huntley *guai*," Batu said, jogging up. "I am to serve as your *zasuul*, your second. You will face that man"— he gestured toward a competitor—"and if you win, you will wrestle whomever wins that match." He pointed toward where Tsend glowered at a rather intimidated-looking wrestler. "Let us hope that the Mongol defeats the Heirs' ruffian."

Gabriel looked toward Tsend. "I've got something that he doesn't." He turned back to Thalia, his eyes golden vows. "Someone to fight for."

Chapter 12

Surprising Outcomes

It was, Gabriel thought as he flapped like a bird around the field, the stupidest he'd ever acted without the influence of alcohol. He was painfully sober. Gabriel didn't really consider himself a drinking man, and hated the times in his life he'd been truly fuddled. Still, a measure of good whiskey right then would have done him a world of help. Here he was, definitely not drunk, in clothing even smaller than what he'd worn as a snotty child, prancing before a crowd of two hundred Mongols. For the love of hell, if anyone wanted to know if he was cold, they didn't have far to look. The humiliation didn't end there, however. Thalia had explained that all wrestling matches started with the competitors performing a dance that imitated the glorious phoenix. He performed the dance, but Gabriel felt that he didn't resemble a phoenix so much as an ass.

Focus on the prize, Huntley, he told himself, as he waved his arms and circled like a wheeling bird. His bloody pride could take more than a few kicks to the stones. His stones might even *be* kicked, given how unprotected his goods were.

Finally, Bold came forward and announced that the

contest would begin. The wrestlers stopped their dance and offered gestures of respect to Bold, who would serve as judge, the other competitors, and the crowd. Gabriel already knew that, of the four men entering the wrestling competition, only one would emerge victorious. That man had to be him. He couldn't fail, not the Blades, and not Thalia.

She watched from the sidelines, Batu at her side. She didn't seem to find his bleeding costume ridiculous. In fact, she'd liked it. Quite a bit. It took every drop of self-control he had to keep from showing her just how much he enjoyed seeing that naked lust in her face. If he wasn't careful, he'd pop right out of the damned trunks and give every one of the tribesmen an eyeful of genuine English sausage.

Thoughts of lust scattered quickly when it was time to face off against his opponent. Gabriel had watched the man throughout the *nadaam* festival and knew that, even though he was shorter than himself, he contained a lot of power in a small package. The Mongol also had the advantage of a lifetime spent wrestling, whereas Gabriel had spent his years shooting rifles. Gabriel had done his share of hand-to-hand combat, though, including the time he'd had to defeat a giant of a mercenary near Kanpur with nothing but a broken bayonet. Almost lost his damn hand to that bastard.

Gabriel and his opponent faced each other and placed their hands on each other's shoulders. At Bold's command, the competition began. They strained against each other, testing resistance, learning each other's strength. Gabriel gritted his teeth. The chap was a sturdy one, all right. He tried to grab the back of Gabriel's jacket, twisting so he could flip him, but Gabriel muscled himself free and narrowly avoided touching the ground with his knee as he regained his balance. If any part of his body except the soles of his feet contacted the ground, he would lose.

For a few minutes, they shoved and danced back and forth. Their movements might have been small, but they cost quite a lot. Sweat stung Gabriel's eyes as he repelled another attack. He and his opponent locked in another hold, pushing against each other. The crowd, clearly expecting the foreigner to lose immediately, roared its approval. Thalia shouted something, but seemed to recall in her excitement that Gabriel spoke no Mongol, and switched to English.

"Thrash him, Gabriel! Send him crying to mama!"

His arms were already tired from the horse race, but, hearing Thalia cheer for him, they came back to life as his mind planned his strategy. He lessened his hold just enough so that his opponent's center of gravity shifted. Gabriel could see it in his legs. In that tiny moment of instability, Gabriel quickly moved his arms, grabbed the man by the waist, and tossed him over his shoulder. The man went down on his back with a grunt.

This time, when Gabriel performed the phoenix dance, he didn't mind so much. Victory was victory, even if he did have to flap around like an ailing chicken. As the onlookers cheered, Thalia and Batu jogged up. She handed him a bowl of tea to refresh himself. It wasn't whiskey, but he'd take what he was given, especially from a beaming and proud Thalia.

"Your challenger was his tribe's best wrestler," Thalia grinned.

"He was a tough little bugger," Gabriel answered. When the man himself walked by, Gabriel grabbed hold of his hand and shook it respectfully. "Nice job, gov'nor," Gabriel said. "Maybe next year."

The Mongol looked a bit confused, not used to shaking hands, but he took it in stride, smiling and bowing. He said a few things to Gabriel, which Thalia translated. "Those muscles of yours aren't for show," he said. "And you use your brain, too. You would make an excellent Mongol."

"Much thanks," Gabriel answered, oddly touched by his

opponent's praise. Thalia, too, seemed affected, her own smile getting a bit wobbly around the edges.

They all moved aside as Tsend and his opponent took the field. No doubt about it, the Heirs had done well finding themselves a bruiser. Even the good-sized man who was wrestling Tsend found the double-crossing bloke intimidating. The crowd itself sensed something sinister about Tsend, quieting a little and shuffling back just a bit as if trying to gain distance.

"Look," Thalia whispered, nudging Gabriel. She frowned, and pointed out a host of birds taking flight from their perches in the grass and crimson flowers. They dotted the sky with their dark retreating forms. A strange and ominous shiver ran down his neck as he watched them disappear.

"What does that mean?" Gabriel asked.

"Birds are sensitive to magic," she explained quietly, though almost no one nearby spoke English. "They must sense the Heirs' presence around Tsend."

Gabriel almost dismissed this idea as daft, but remembered that the world he once knew, the world without magic, was gone. He understood differently now. It was magic he was fighting for.

Taking the field again, Bold eyed Tsend with barely concealed mistrust. But a legitimate place had been won in the tournament, so the wrestling competition had to proceed. The two wrestlers placed their hands on each other's shoulders and waited. Then Bold called out for the contest to begin.

Gabriel settled back to watch a wrestling match as involved and lengthy as the one he had just fought. Yet in less time than it would take to sneeze, the match was over. Gabriel barely saw it happen. Tsend sneered as his opponent was suddenly sprawled on the ground, wide-eyed with shock. Even the crowd and Bold were stunned into silence. Thalia went white.

"Good Christ," Gabriel muttered in the quiet. "That was faster than a private with his first whore."

At his words, Tsend turned to Gabriel and bawled out a laugh. "You are next, English fool."

Gabriel nearly snarled back his own retort, but figured that only cowards and bullies felt the need to belittle their opponents. The more a man bragged and taunted, the more afraid he must be. So, without saying anything, he started toward the field.

"Gabriel, wait," Thalia cried behind him. She grabbed at his arm.

He tried to quell a flare of temper as he turned back. "You've got to believe I can win," he said lowly. "I need you to have faith in me."

"I *do* have faith in you," she answered readily, which gave him sizable comfort. "But I don't know if you can win against someone who's cheating." She looked meaningfully at Tsend, who was making a big show of being bored, staring at the distant mountains.

"Cheating?" Gabriel repeated. "I don't see how. We all watched him throw the other wrestler. He didn't cast any spells. He's not wearing an amulet or some such object."

"You don't have to cast a spell or have an object to use magic. Look." She gestured slightly and Gabriel followed her direction. "He isn't wearing any boots."

"That gives him a *dis*advantage. Less traction."

"Except the magic he's using requires him to have bare feet. I just saw it, painted on his soles. The Mark of Antaeus."

That didn't sound promising.

"Is your woman too frightened for you to wrestle?" Tsend shouted.

Gabriel scowled at the Mongol, but ignored him. The crowd, however, started to get a bit fidgety. "Tell me what it is and how to defeat it," he said to Thalia.

"Antaeus was the giant in Greek mythology who derived his strength from touching the earth," she explained quickly. "He was impossible to defeat, because every time he was thrown down, he rose up even stronger than before. Only Heracles was able to vanquish him by holding him aloft until his strength drained away. If the Mark of Antaeus is painted upon flesh which contacts the ground, the wearer gains the giant's strength. That's how Tsend defeated the other wrestler."

"You must take your positions now," Bold announced.

Gabriel moved away from Thalia, and he heard the panic in her voice as she called after him, "It's impossible to beat him."

"I've learned that nothing is impossible," Gabriel said over his shoulder, "since I met you."

Late afternoon sun blazed low in the sky. No wind stirred the grasses and flowers at the edge of the field. Even the sounds of the animals, the soft chuffing and bleats of horses and sheep, faded away as Captain Huntley and Tsend faced each other. The world seemed to be holding its breath, knowing what was at stake as operatives from the Blades of the Rose and the Heirs of Albion prepared to fight for magic on the open steppes of Mongolia.

The Heir Lamb had commanded a hawk to serve as spy in the *ail* of red flowers. The bird, following Lamb's orders, discovered this tribe's prize—a massive ruby. Surely the gem was what the Heirs sought, so Tsend was dispatched to win it.

After Huntley and Tsend briefly performed the phoenix dance, they crouched opposite each other. Tsend smirked, confident in his superiority. Even if the Englishman had known about the Mark of Antaeus on the soles of his feet, it wouldn't have mattered. The mark gave him power.

Undefeatable power. Unless the Englishman used some magic of his own, there would be no way to conquer Tsend. But the blond man simply stared back, showing no fear. That made him a fool. There was always something to fear.

He and the Englishman placed their hands on each other's shoulders, and Tsend was unpleasantly surprised by the strength he felt in the other man. It didn't matter, he told himself. Even if his foe was the strongest man in all of Mongolia, he would be unable to best Tsend. He happily anticipated thrashing the man in front of the dark-haired Englishwoman, who watched with anxious eyes from nearby. Unfortunately, she was promised to Henry Lamb, so Tsend could only enjoy watching defeat in her face. Later, perhaps, when Lamb was tired of her, Tsend would have his chance to take his pleasure. Then, a new fear and horror would fill her face, making Tsend's pleasure all the sweeter.

"Begin!"

Enjoying his advantage, Tsend let the Englishman push hard against him. He could still feel his opponent's strength, but it was as if Tsend was at the bottom of a well, and the other man simply dropping pebbles rather than boulders. Huntley gritted his teeth and strained, shoving against him with enough force to knock any number of large men over. Any man except Tsend. He didn't bother hiding his laughter. So pitiful, the futile efforts of the Englishman. But the experience quickly grew boring for Tsend. The sooner this wrestling foolishness was over, the sooner Tsend could claim the ruby, give it to Lamb, and receive his rewards. Although, with the strength of the Mark on his feet, there was no need to surrender the ruby to Lamb or his snarling friend. Why not keep it for himself? Then the power of Genghis Khan would belong to Tsend alone. Tsend had always felt, ever since he was a child without parents in the muddy lanes of Urga, that he was owed something, that the world conspired against him, cheating him. The ruby would change everything, finally give him what he deserved. Yes, that was an even better plan. Tsend smiled.

The Englishman must have sensed Tsend's decision to end the match. Huntley let go of Tsend's shoulders. With a quick shuffle, the Englishman moved back, out of reach. Tsend chuckled. So, Huntley had finally learned fear. It didn't make any difference, not now.

Tsend took a step toward the Englishman, but as he did so, Huntley moved with a hidden speed, so quickly Tsend barely saw him move. Lumbering closer, Tsend took a swipe at Huntley, but the blond man ducked. Then the Englishman was right in front of him, wedging his boot underneath Tsend's lifted foot. Huntley grunted under the weight, but he didn't move away. Idiot. Tsend picked up his other foot, determined to put his full weight onto the Englishman's boot and hopefully break some bones.

Just as he did so, Huntley shoved his other boot underneath Tsend's foot. With a start, Tsend realized what the Englishman was doing. He knew about the Mark on Tsend's feet, and was trying to separate him from the power of the earth. Already, with the contact broken, the magical strength started to ebb. Tsend tried to move back. He couldn't. Huntley had grabbed him around the waist and, with an almighty groan, picked Tsend up and held him suspended a few inches above the ground.

Tsend struggled and thrashed. He easily outweighed the Englishman by at least fifty pounds, but Huntley would not let him go. It felt as if thick ropes were tight around Tsend's middle, crushing the breath from him. Not only stealing his breath, but his strength, too. Tsend felt it draining from his body as if he was slowly freezing. He bucked and twisted, trying to break free. Somehow, with his own natural strength, Huntley continued to grip him tightly and hold him away from the earth.

Panic flared. Huntley's fingers were laced together, so Tsend awkwardly reached back and clawed at them. Nothing. Even as the Englishman sweated and grunted with the effort of holding Tsend aloft, he wouldn't let go.

From somewhere, the Englishwoman shouted encouragements, and that only fueled Huntley further. No matter how hard Tsend fought to free himself, swinging his fists and kicking, Huntley held fast. Tsend even bloodied the Englishman's face with a strike from his elbow. It made no difference. The blond man continued to hold him, dangling Tsend above the one thing that would replenish his power. Nearly gone. Tsend writhed. He was so close to the ground. All it would take was one touch. But, no. The magical strength from the Mark shivered once, then disappeared completely.

Sensing this, Huntley hefted Tsend up, then tossed him onto his back on the ground. The crowd screamed its approval. Tsend blinked, stunned.

He'd lost.

A surge of strength from the earth filled him, but before Tsend could jump back up to his feet, Thalia Burgess rushed forward with a large bowl and splashed its contents onto the soles of his feet, destroying the Mark. As quickly as it had come, the power of the earth was gone.

Struggling to sit up, Tsend choked as Huntley's arm wrapped around his neck. Tsend flopped around, his vision dimming, while his lungs screamed for air.

Dimly, he heard the Englishwoman cry out, "Gabriel! No! Not here, not now!"

"When, then?" Huntley growled.

Tsend did not hear her answer, but whatever she said made the Englishman release him with a shove. Tsend sprawled face first into the dirt, coughing and gagging.

"Go back to your masters, dog," Huntley snarled. "And I promise you, the next time we meet, I'll kill you."

As Tsend crawled away, filled with rage and shame, he

heard the chieftain proclaim the English man and woman as the winners of the tournament, and the new guardians of the ruby. Tsend wanted to rush back, steal the ruby for himself, beat Huntley lifeless and take the girl. But he barely had enough strength to slither on the ground, let alone rip the Englishman apart. He hated feeling weak. He destroyed weakness.

Yet, as he concentrated on placing one trembling hand in front of the other, Tsend couldn't help the cold smile that tugged on his mouth. He *would* meet Huntley again. And when that happened, nothing anyone said or did would be able to stop Tsend from gleefully, slowly killing the Englishman. While his woman could only watch, and suffer.

Some things, a man got used to. Like, say, being awakened by rifles firing at close range. Or learning to go without food for days at a time. Or, worst of all, sharing a tent with Lieutenant Thatcher, who snored like a steam engine. Gabriel became inured to all of that, even the snoring. But he didn't think he would ever get used to seeing Thalia laugh and smile. She turned from merely beautiful into something celestial, goddess-like. No, that wasn't right. She was too tied to the earth, too full of real life and body and self to be heavenly.

As Thalia finished tending to Gabriel's latest wounds— this set a few nasty cuts and bruises on his face courtesy of that cheating bastard, Tsend—she tried but could not contain her delirious joy, her exhilaration that she and Gabriel had won the tribe's ruby. And he couldn't stop his own pleasure at seeing her so happy.

"We should take it straight away to my father," she beamed as she dabbed some healing salve on his cheek. "He'll know the best thing to do with it, how to protect it from the Heirs. And, at last, I'll be a Blade." This last fact made her glow with euphoria.

"Haven't been given the ruby, yet," Gabriel pointed out. At least Gabriel had changed back into his normal clothing from the skimpy wrestling costume. Despite the fact that Thalia enjoyed it, the tiny scraps of silk offered less protection from the elements than a handkerchief.

"But we will have it in a few minutes," she countered with a smile.

"The ruby belongs to Bold's tribe." He didn't want to be contrary, but it was an important fact. "They're not going to let us waltz off with their prized possession without having something to say about it."

A small frown furrowed her brow. "Maybe if we explain . . ."

She didn't get to finish this idea before Oyuun, Bold, and the ruby's current, but soon to be replaced, guardian came into the *ger.*

"It is now time for you to accept your honorable duty," Bold said as Thalia translated. Both Gabriel and Thalia started to rise from sitting on the ground, but Bold waved them back. "You must kneel to show your respect."

Both Gabriel and Thalia did so. "Aren't we supposed to do this in front of the tribe?" Gabriel asked, and, when Thalia translated this question for Bold, the chieftain shook his head.

"The glory comes from winning the responsibility," he answered gravely. "What happens here is a private matter between yourself and your own sense of honor. Once the ruby is under your protection, we must trust you in all of your decisions involving it."

Gabriel made sure not to glance at Thalia, kneeling beside him. That would surely give away that they had something planned. Conscience stabbed at him. Could they take the tribe's most sacred and valuable treasure? Even if it meant protecting the greater good?

The ruby's guardian stepped forward, opening its case. Once again, Gabriel marveled at the size and lustrous deep red color of the uncut gem. Many men would cheerfully murder babies and nuns in order to possess such an incredible object, regardless of whether or not it held any magic.

"You are to repeat after me," the protector commanded. "I swear beneath the eternal sky and upon my own immortal soul that I shall not suffer to part from this, the pride of generations, for the next cycle of the sun. For a year and a day shall I do this. May I endure the torments of a thousand flaming arrows if my greed or foolishness causes the jewel any harm in the course of my guardianship."

After a pause, Thalia repeated the oath in Mongolian, while Gabriel answered in English. He tried to rationalize that, technically, he wasn't going to let anything bad happen to the ruby, but it wasn't much comfort at all. Maybe Thalia was right, and if they just told the tribesmen what kind of untapped power they held . . . but then there was the possibility that the Mongols would want to use that power for themselves, and not let the Blades safely house it. Yet, it rightfully belonged to this tribe, not to the Blades of the Rose.

Gabriel inwardly grimaced. Though there were always areas of gray when serving in the army, he wasn't used to such complicated issues of right and wrong.

Then Bold said something, stepping forward, and Thalia held out her hand. The hiss of a knife leaving its sheath caused Gabriel to spring to his feet. He didn't have a gun or a knife of his own just then, but fists worked, too.

Thalia's hand on his leg stopped him before he knocked the blade from Bold's hand. "It's a blood oath," she said quietly. The ruby's guardian also held out his hand, and Gabriel saw the faint scar that traced across his palm.

"There's no need to cut you too," Gabriel growled.

"I will also guard the ruby," she answered. "So I must. I'm not afraid."

Gabriel muttered, but knelt back down again. He did not look forward to seeing Thalia cut. Bold took the knife and scored the flesh of his own hand so that a line of bright blood flashed there; he hissed slightly in pain. Without a flinch or tremor, Thalia presented the chieftain with her palm. Gabriel gritted his teeth as the blade cut her skin, but she made no noise. Only a slight tightening of her mouth betrayed that she felt any pain. She pressed her palm to Bold's, saying a few words in Mongolian as she did so.

Then it was Gabriel's turn, and he made sure to bear the incision stoically. He took Bold's hand, commingling their blood. "I swear that I will protect this treasure and the woman who guards it with my life," Gabriel vowed.

Thalia, the only one who understood what his words meant, turned startled eyes to him. But the gravity with which he said the words seemed to satisfy Bold, Oyuun, and, most importantly, the ruby's protector. With a bow, the box holding the ruby was presented to Thalia and Gabriel. As soon as it had been taken from the guardian's hands, he visibly relaxed and smiled for the first time. He said something to Thalia and Gabriel, then spoke with Bold and Oyuun before quickly leaving the *ger* with a noticeable spring in his step. Gabriel couldn't help but wonder what the hell he'd gotten himself into.

Oyuun came forward, beaming, and spoke with Thalia and Gabriel excitedly. "Now you receive another honor," the chieftain's wife said. She began to lead them outside. "All of the ruby's guardians have their own *ger* for the duration of the year. Our children will move your belongings."

"What about Batu?" Gabriel asked as they followed Oyuun.

Blushing, Thalia answered, "He continues to stay with his cousin. So you and I will be . . . alone."

Alone, with Thalia. Sweet Christ in Heaven. He'd been given a gift.

Oyuun stopped outside a *ger*. The door was open, and it was, indeed, empty of people, though typical furnishings were inside including, Lord Almighty, beds. Two of them. Oyuun waved Thalia and Gabriel inside.

He swallowed hard as he followed Thalia into the tent. Blood oaths and moral ambiguities seeped out of his brain as other, more animal, needs prowled forward.

"Come to our *ger* for dinner tonight," Oyuun chirped before disappearing, closing the door behind her. Gabriel could have sworn he saw a wicked twinkle in the woman's eyes, but she was gone before he could prove it.

So, there they were. Thalia and Gabriel truly alone together for the first time. It was time that he didn't want to waste. He closed the distance between himself and Thalia, already reaching for her.

The door banged open, and Oyuun and Bold's two older children came in, staggering under the weight of their baggage. Gabriel and Thalia jumped apart, then quickly came forward, relieving the boy and girl of their burden. Shyly, the children left without speaking, casting curious glances over their shoulders.

Reminding himself that he had a duty, Gabriel made himself concentrate on the box in his hands. He sat upon the ground and opened the lid, revealing the dazzling splendor of the ruby. Noiselessly, Thalia sat opposite him and stared at the gem. He waited to feel a thrum of magical power coming from the ruby, but all he felt was a hot need for Thalia building inside of him.

"The tribesmen have had this thing for generations, but none of them seem to know it's magic," Gabriel said, his voice little more than a growl.

Thalia reached over and picked up the ruby, testing its weight. Dark red glimmers glided across her face as light penetrated the jewel's surface. "Perhaps there is some chant, or a phrase, that must be used." She turned the ruby over and over in her hand with long, tapered fingers. They weren't the fingers of a woman whose sole labor consisted of lifting teacups and writing up guest lists. He wanted them on him, wrapped around him.

He forced his concentration to the stone and not the woman holding it. "Could be anything."

Thalia frowned as she thought. "To begin, we ought to test its strength."

"Another device by the talented Mr. Graves?"

She shook her head as she rose to her feet. Carefully cradling the ruby, she waited by the door for Gabriel to join her, then slipped the gem back into its case. Gabriel opened the door first, then, after checking to make sure that no one lurked outside and no Heirs were approaching from the horizon, nodded for Thalia. She stepped outside and walked toward the perches of a few hunting eagles tethered nearby, Gabriel following. The noble creatures took little notice of them, beyond shaking out and settling into their feathers.

"You know now that birds are sensitive to magic," she said, standing next to one of the eagles. "So we can use these eagles to test the ruby. The more strongly they react, the more powerful it is. That way, we can know if its magic is dangerous, and what it might be capable of."

With a nod, Gabriel opened the case and held it near the bird. He and Thalia waited.

"Nothing's happening," he muttered.

"Give it a moment," Thalia answered.

They waited more. The eagle turned one gleaming eye toward the gem, then began preening, deucedly uninterested in either the ruby, Thalia, or Gabriel.

"Maybe this buzzard can't feel magic," Gabriel suggested.

"But *all* birds respond to magic," she said grimly. "That has been true ever since magic was discovered. However, just in case . . ." She held the ruby near another hunting eagle, and then another, then another, but the reaction was always the same. Nothing.

Thalia looked baffled. "I don't understand."

"The last bloke who guarded the ruby might've switched it out."

"I don't see a stockpile of giant rubies around here, do you?" Thalia snapped, then rubbed her face contritely. "Sorry. It's just that . . . this, this . . . *nothing* . . . isn't supposed to happen."

"Might not be a Source."

"It *has* to be," Thalia almost cried. "We followed the directions given to us by the stone tortoise. We found the moving field of crimson. And then this tribe happens to have an enormous ruby, just like the one Genghis Khan may have held when he was born. If this isn't the Source, I don't know what is." She turned bleak eyes to Gabriel. "I can't have failed the Blades. I can't have failed Mongolia. Not when I'm so close."

He wanted to pull her into his arms and shield her from disappointment, but knew that she would not want, nor accept, being sheltered. Words of comfort would only ring hollow and false.

They needed time to think, and, just then, neither of them seemed capable of deep contemplation. "We'll take our supper with Bold and his family," he said. "Afterward, we can go back to our tent"—he relished those words, *our tent*—"and figure this out, you and me." He tipped up her chin and was glad to see not tears shining in her eyes, but fierce determination. God, she was extraordinary.

"I'm famished," she said.

If Bold and his family noticed something preoccupying their honored guests, they didn't mention it. Thalia and

Gabriel ate mutton and drank tea without speaking much. The *ger* was filled with the chatter of the family, especially the grandparents talking with the excited children about the unusually thrilling *nadaam*. No one could quite believe that both a white man and a woman had won, and as a team. Then, there had been that big man who had competed, the one who didn't wear boots during the wrestling matches. Something hadn't been right about him, and they all agreed that everyone breathed easier when he'd gone.

Several times throughout the meal, Gabriel saw Oyuun look between Thalia and himself, speculative. The chieftain's wife kept her counsel, however. Gabriel wondered what kind of confidence she and Thalia had shared. More of the female mystery that was both terrifying and intriguing.

When the meal was finished, Bold said to Gabriel, "Join me for a pipe, and we shall have some singing and storytelling."

Gabriel exchanged looks with Thalia, torn. They needed to get back to their *ger* and figure out what, if any, kind of power the ruby had. Then there was the pressing matter of the fact that they hadn't touched in over an hour.

Oyuun seemed to sense their dilemma, though she didn't quite guess all of the reasons for it. Gently, she said to her husband, "Perhaps our guests are tired after such a trying day." When she looked back at Gabriel, she winked. Bless her.

"Of course!" Bold said, getting to his feet. "There will be chances enough for pipes and stories."

He and Thalia wished their hosts a good night before leaving as quickly as possible. Hand in hand, they strode through the encampment, but were delayed often by different people's coming up and congratulating them on winning the *nadaam*. Gabriel was starting to get some basic words, and was able to clumsily thank everyone who was so damned gracious and admiring. If only the Mongol people were a little less sociable, Gabriel could be peeling Thalia's *del* off by now and stroking her bare skin.

By the time he and Thalia were within twenty yards of their *ger,* and still *another* herdsman tried to stop them and wax rhapsodic about the wrestling tournament, Gabriel couldn't make himself stop or even slow down. He grunted his thanks to the gawking man, tugging Thalia behind him.

"That was rather rude." She laughed as they entered their tent. She went to light a lantern.

Gabriel slammed the door shut and dragged a chest in front of it. He set down the case with the ruby. "Don't care." Then he stalked over to Thalia—feeling clearly the blood pulsing through his body, aware of everything about hers— and pulled her to him, one hand on her waist, the other cupping the back of her neck. She breathed in once, deeply, green eyes wide and shining as she looked up at him, her hands on his forearms. And then he took her mouth with his.

Open, wet. Neither of them held back. Last night had done nothing to sate his hunger for her. If anything, last night had made it sharper; he was desperate for more. He tasted the tea they had drunk on her breath, and the milky sweetness of her. But he wasn't satisfied just to kiss her mouth, delicious as it was. Trailing down, running his lips along her neck, until he met with the heavy fabric of her *del.* He made deft work of undoing the fastenings, then pushed the *del* open. Underneath, she wore a light cotton camisole. No corset.

His hands slid over her breasts, small but full. The nipples tightened and beaded under the nearly sheer fabric. When he bent down and flicked his tongue over them, one and then the other, she moaned and clasped his head to her.

"Not enough," he muttered. He shoved the *del* off of her, onto the floor, and tugged at her camisole until, impatient, he tore it right down the middle. Her aroused gasp was alive on his skin. Soft scraps of fabric drifted down to the ground, but he didn't notice, he was licking her, swirling his tongue over her breasts. Her hips surged against his. Gabriel swore. He didn't want to swear, not at that moment, but he'd no other way of expressing this, this tidal wave of sensation and emotion that her unrestrained response awoke in him.

As he nipped gently at the tip of her breast, Thalia moaned again and began to pull at his clothes.

He broke away from her and was next to one of the mattresses in an instant. Another instant, and he'd tossed the mattress across the *ger* so that it lay beside the other sleeping mat, doubling the size.

"Now," he said, turning back to her with a feral grin, "we've got a proper bed."

Chapter 13

An Expanding Knowledge

She'd known that when Gabriel turned his mind to something, he gave himself up to it completely and with a thoroughness that would shame most men. When he was a soldier, he was the consummate soldier. When he took the field in battle—or horse racing, or wrestling—he was unstoppable, ferocious. And when he was preparing to make love to her . . .

Thalia was stunned, a little giddy, as Gabriel stood by the large bed he'd just made and systematically removed his clothing, all the while holding her gaze with his own. First his jacket. Then his waistcoat. Braces, next, pushed off his shoulders. And when he unbuttoned his shirt, he revealed that he wore no undershirt beneath it. His chest, an expanse of tight golden muscle, marked here and there with puckered scars like a treasure map. Earlier that day, she had marveled at his masculine beauty, not marred but made more perfect by the numerous scars that crossed his flesh. New marks had been added since then, put there because he helped fight for her cause. And as each bit of his skin was revealed to her, sharp, greedy desire flowed in her own body, until she felt gathered dampness soaking between her legs.

When he started to pull off his boots, Thalia realized she

was wasting valuable time, and shucked the remainder of her clothes with no thought to where the garments would land once she'd taken them off. What did she care of tidiness when Gabriel was now standing completely naked but two yards away?

Fully nude, fully aroused, Gabriel could not have been more beautiful. Thalia did not stop herself from staring at his erect penis. The head gleamed as it reached toward his navel, and there, at the very tip, a slight glisten of fluid. He was thick, but not frighteningly so. It was a marvel of perfect shape, perfect for being inside of her, claiming her. Thalia tore her gaze from his erection and looked her fill, all over. He was the essence of Man, a warrior who would possess his woman. And his woman, at that moment, was Thalia.

She was naked now, too. His jaw tightened, while his eyes glittered like dangerous magic. She watched as those eyes moved up and down her body, and everywhere they looked, she blossomed and blazed.

"You're too far away," he rumbled. He pointed to the bed. "Lie down."

That was an order she wouldn't disobey. Thalia hurried to the bed and lay down upon it. He stretched out beside her. Their bodies touched.

Perhaps they might, at some future date, be tender with one another, slow and deliberate, taking their time to learn and explore with the patience of scholars. Not today. They wrapped arms around each other, tight enough to bruise, as their mouths, demanding and urgent, met. His fingers tangled in her hair. Their tongues touched, stroked, and Thalia opened for him, as much as she could, trying to take him in all at once and be drowned in him.

Leaving the chaotic mass of her hair, his hands skimmed down her neck, down her shoulders and arms, then returned to the delicate place beneath the hollow of her throat. This was so far beyond what normal touch ever felt like, to Thalia it seemed as if she'd been given a fresh, new body that just now learned the world. And when his large, rough hands curved over her breasts, possessing them, she could not stop the febrile moan that rose up in her throat. He knew precisely how to touch her.

Then one of his hands moved over her breast, down across her belly, and slid lower. Already damp and ready, when his calloused fingers brushed between her thighs, her lips, Thalia arched up from the ground with a choked scream. One fingertip rubbed against her opening whilst another stroked her most sensitive place. Thalia could not set two thoughts beside each other. All she knew was that Gabriel, this man who was an expert shot and had waged brutal war, touched her and gave her pleasure as though he was born to do only that.

"I have to—" she said on a moan, then reached out and took him in her hand. The words that poured from his mouth were a combination of the foulest curses and the highest of blessings. He filled her hand. Her thumb and forefinger could not meet as she circled him. He felt satiny and rigid and exactly right. As Gabriel touched her, his fingers delving just inside her opening, she slid her own hand up and down the length of his shaft, using the drop of moisture from the tip to glide her progress.

"Ah, Jesus," Gabriel breathed. "Too good. Too goddamned good."

He took her mouth again. Just as he did so, one long, blunt finger entered her as the heel of his palm pressed against her pulsing nub. Thalia bucked and cried out, gripping him tighter. Before she could draw another breath, one finger became two, widening her. She gasped and flung her legs apart.

Gabriel pumped his fingers into her, all the while rubbing against her clit. Thalia had heard that word before, knew there was something wicked and crude about it, but just then, in her mind, that's what that sensitive bit of flesh had become, as base and sinful as anything in creation. Names for parts of her body fled as Gabriel continued to work her, and she couldn't keep hold of him any longer. She threw herself into the blinding pleasure and it hit her, all at once, breaking over her like a tidal wave of fire. She bowed up from the mattress as she cried his name.

The world shimmered around them, growing vaporous and gleaming. She felt her skin tighten and become, if possible, even more receptive.

Panting, barely coherent, Thalia watched as Gabriel took the fingers that had been inside of her, and slid them into his own mouth. "I want to taste you, sweetheart," he said, licking them clean, "but later. Now, now, I have to get my cock inside of you."

"Yes, now," she urged, opening her arms to him. A gilded haze enveloped them, sparkling like a shower of coins, but to Thalia, it seemed natural, right.

He was between her legs in an instant. His weight settled over her as the head nudged at her opening. Thalia looked up into his face, dark and tight with desire. Love saturated her. She wanted to brand him into her mind, into her body, for now and tomorrow and all the days that followed, whatever they might bring.

The thrust of him into her sent her up from the bed, bending into an arch. At the same moment, the world dissolved. The *ger* disappeared and became, instead, the canopy of the night sky. But the stars took on a shine beyond their normal glitter. Instead, they had the crystalline perfection and sharpness of diamonds.

He drew back, sliding, then drove into her again. A wordless syllable jumped out of her as he groaned. God, to be this full, to envelop him like this—almost too pleasurable. And with each stroke, with each fevered kiss they shared, more and more of the world shifted and changed. She didn't know if the change happened in her mind only or if there was something more.

"Gabriel," she moaned. "Gabriel . . . look . . ."

Lifting his head, his forehead slick and his hair damp, Gabriel took in the protean landscape, which had changed again. Night was gone, day was gone. Instead, it was as if the skin of the world had been peeled back to show the magic beneath. Everything pulsed with it, in different colors and tones. The earth itself hummed with rich green energy, and each tree, every drop of water that coursed across the surface of the land, gleamed and sang.

He didn't stop thrusting, rubbing himself along her. "What . . . ?" he panted.

"I don't know." Yet she wasn't afraid.

The earth was covered in a webwork, a net of power, from each animal, each human and flora, pinpointed with bright, heated loci that revealed the hundreds of Sources scattered across the globe. Thalia could see them all, wanted to reach out to them and hold them in her hands. But she would not release Gabriel. She gripped his shoulders tightly.

"Beautiful," he breathed. His hips drew back, then forward, another plunge, and the Sources gleamed brighter. "I want to see. Everything. You. Beautiful Thalia."

She mewled a protest when he slid out of her. Rising up onto his knees, he rolled her over, onto her stomach, then gently pulled her up so that she was on her hands and knees. As he maneuvered her, the landscape dimmed, the Sources began to fade. But when he took hold of her hips and pumped into her, everything blazed brightly again. Thalia could watch the swirling, living planet while Gabriel claimed her, took her without restraint, embedding himself in her dark secret places. Mating, like animals. She began to expand with ecstasy.

He was a clever animal. One hand left its grasp on her hip to reach forward, finding the flushed, full nub that nestled in her sex. His fingers stroked, rubbed. All the while, he kept his strong, sure pace. Thalia was consumed with limitless pleasure. She heard the insistent sounds of their flesh meeting, his hips to her buttocks. And as she neared closer and closer to the pinnacle, the energy of the world and the Sources grew brighter and brighter.

It hit her, the culmination. Her scream couldn't be stopped. She felt herself completely torn apart, but in the best possible way. The frame that contained Thalia Burgess disappeared and was replaced by pure sensation. Moments later, Gabriel followed, stiffening, groaning her name. And she came all over again, hearing her name on his lips, feeling him pulse within her.

And as they both careened into fulfillment, everything expanded to dazzling, blinding brightness, until they were swallowed by it. All Thalia could think was, *Yes, this is right, and even more so because my love is inside me.*

Then, in the darkness that followed, she and Gabriel slept, two slick bodies twined together as if nothing could ever separate them.

It was the best morning of her life, and also the strangest. Thalia awoke in the warm shelter of Gabriel's arms, both of them quite naked under the covers. Feeling the firm heat of him, nestled close behind her, she recalled the events of the night before. Every moment of their sex came back to her with such vibrant clarity, she shivered.

For a long time, Thalia had wondered what it would be like to go to bed with a man. She'd known since adolescence the mechanics involved, but even the frantic groping she'd had with Sergei hadn't prepared her for what it would truly be like to have a man fill her with his body, and not any man, but Gabriel. Whatever old ideas Thalia had about sex were gone, destroyed in the wake of the pure wonder they had shared. Though she'd enjoyed their sex outside the *nadaam* feast, within the sanctuary of their own *ger,* they'd been able to let themselves fully go, and go they did. Into a place she could not describe.

Had she imagined it, the dissolving of the tent, the revelation of the Sources? Could it have been an enchantment?

His voice behind her came as a husky surprise. She'd thought him asleep. She should have known by now that his soldier's senses were too sharp to let him sleep deeply.

"It wasn't a dream," he rumbled, and she felt the low vibrations of his voice everywhere. His hand pressed low and warm on the curve of her stomach. She responded immediately to his touch as heavy desire tumbled through her. His words alone dampened her.

Thalia rolled to face him, and in the faint haze of dawn light that filtered in through the top of the *ger,* the planes of his face were slightly smoother, less hard. To lie with him like this, skin to skin, was an intoxication she had never imagined. And his smile, sweet Heaven, was an intimate promise.

"You felt it, too?" she asked.

She moved so that one of her legs draped across his, and she could feel the heat and soft skin of his genitals brushing against her thigh. He wasn't fully erect, but she vividly recalled the feel of him in her hands, in her body.

His arms tightened around her. "I felt everything," he said, gravelly with morning. Within moments, he was almost completely hard, pressing into her skin, hot and ready. "Your mouth," he said, nipping at her lips, "your neck," he continued, trailing his tongue down and then over her collarbone, "your delicious, delicious breasts"—large, warm palms covered them, her nipples stiffening into sensitive points, then his hand moved lower, between her legs, which she began to spread without thinking—"and your silky, tight—"

"No," Thalia panted, trying to keep her mind clear, which was nigh impossible when he touched her. "The . . . other part . . . the stars and the . . . Sources."

His hand stilled, and he rested his head in the curve of her neck. "That, too," he said.

"What was it?"

"I can't figure."

"Maybe the ruby."

He rubbed the slight bristle of his beard against her, and the abrasion was exquisite. "The birds didn't react to it," he murmured. His fingers caressed the back of her leg in slow, liquid strokes that gathered heat in her sex.

Thalia's eyes began to drift shut, but she forced them open. "Gabriel, please, you have to stop. I can't concentrate when you . . . oh, God . . . do that."

Unfortunately, he listened to her, and rolled onto his back with his hands behind his head. "Can't seem to help myself," he admitted ruefully, "where you're concerned. But you're right," he continued. "We need to figure out two things. If the ruby isn't a Source, what is, and what happened to us last night."

He sat up, a tight focused expression on his face. "I need to question Bold and his family. They must have fed us something. Maybe our food was drugged."

"Drugged?" Thalia repeated. "They ate exactly the same food we did. Drank the same tea."

Gabriel threw back the covers and rose to his feet before starting for his clothing, which, Thalia noted, was strewn around the *ger* as if wild animals had attacked their luggage. But no, *they* had been the animals. She recalled his taking her from behind, like a stallion. Ah, she'd have to keep her mind away from last night, or else she'd forget everything and demand he return to bed immediately. Gabriel seemed to transition well enough, she noted dryly. He'd returned to the role of soldier, and while Thalia again drank in the sight of his superb nude body, he paid no attention to his state of undress. Instead, he quickly gathered his garments and put them on, muttering just loud enough for her to hear. "They could have taken some kind of antidote beforehand," he said, dragging on his trousers. "So they wouldn't be affected."

"Why would they do that?" Thalia asked, also rising up from the bed. The covers fell away, and the cool morning air inside the *ger* touched her nakedness. Her nipples tightened.

In the middle of buttoning his shirt, Gabriel glanced at her, and his fingers stilled while his eyes narrowed. He growled—there was no other word for it. A primitive thrill coursed through her.

Focus, Thalia, she commanded herself. She hunted down her clothes. Trousers, drawers, *del,* socks and . . . scraps of cotton? She held up the pieces and realized that the fabric was all that remained of her chemise, which Gabriel had torn off her body. He recognized the chemise, too, judging by the flush creeping up his neck.

Gabriel returned to the buttons of his shirt, which for some reason seemed a difficult task for his agile fingers.

"Maybe," he began, but his voice was too full of gravel, so he cleared his throat and tried again. He busied himself with the last of his shirt buttons, then pulled on his waistcoat. "They didn't want foreigners guarding the ruby, getting close to its magic, using it." Gabriel checked the ruby's case and was satisfied when he found it safe.

"They could have just prohibited us from entering the *nadaam,*" Thalia pointed out.

"Probably, they didn't think we could win," he said, rumbling. He pulled on his boots, strapped on his revolver and knife, and donned his jacket. "The Heirs might have had a hand in it, too."

Thalia plucked a fresh chemise from her pack and finished dressing, shaking her head. "We should *talk* to Bold and Oyuun," she said. "Not question or interrogate them. They have been our generous hosts until now, and I cannot insult them." Fully clothed, Thalia faced Gabriel, placing her hands on his chest as he started for the door. "*I* will do the talking."

He grumbled at this, but saw that she would not be dissuaded. "If there's anything suspect," he vowed, "then *I'll* be the one breaking bones. *You* stay out of danger." Thalia started to protest, yet his will matched her own. "Is that clear?"

Seeing that there was no way around him, she answered dryly, "Yes, sir."

He looked down at her hands on him. Gone immediately was the toughened soldier, and his expression turned to something much more warm, and so incredibly wonderful it felt like pain. He picked up her hands in his own and kissed the backs of each, but it wasn't exactly gallant, not the way his golden eyes glinted with undisguised sexual hunger. For her.

"I like this very much," he said, nibbling on the tips of her fingers. "An army of two."

"Who's in command?" she answered as she fought for breath.

What a wicked smile he had. "Let's take turns."

There was no way to make her questions sound anything but accusatory, so Thalia figured the best approach was to be as straightforward as possible. Naturally, Bold and Oyuun both denied having put anything into Thalia or Gabriel's food or drink. Oyuun, particularly, looked hurt by the questions, and Thalia could not blame her. Mongols took their hospitality quite seriously, and their guests had cast doubts on one of the most important tenets of their culture. It wouldn't take much for word to spread from herdsman to herdsman that the white Mongol woman was one of those strange and foul creatures known as an ungrateful guest. Thalia and her father would not be welcome anywhere.

"That big man from yesterday at the *nadaam*," Thalia quickly explained, "whom Gabriel *guai* wrestled at the very end—he is part of a group of men who want to hurt us, who want to hurt the whole of Mongolia. We are trying to stop them."

"What do they want?" Bold asked stiffly.

"I cannot tell you, for your safety." She turned pleading eyes to Oyuun, who had treated Thalia as a younger sister rather than guest and now looked betrayed. "Please understand, these men are dangerous and ruthless. They might have persuaded or even forced you to drug Gabriel *guai* and me."

Oyuun said nothing, her mouth taut.

"These men might have treated our food without you knowing it," Gabriel added, which Thalia translated.

"I cooked it myself and never once left anything alone," Oyuun said. "I even brewed the tea myself in this kettle." She marched over to the hearth and snatched up the object in question, an old, battered piece of metal that looked as though it had been in use for literally generations. "I boiled the meat in this pot," she continued, striding to her well-used cooking vessel, which, even then, boiled milk for cheese.

Thalia's attention snagged on something. "Might I see the tea kettle?"

Without a word, Oyuun thrust the kettle into Thalia's hands, then she crossed her arms over her chest.

Gabriel was immediately at Thalia's side, making her color. "Tell me what you see," he murmured.

She made herself focus on the iron vessel in her hands, even though she couldn't stop her reaction to Gabriel's nearness. "This kettle," she answered quietly as she turned it over in her hands. "It isn't Mongolian. It's Chinese. The shape is different, so is the metal. Strange." It was also, she realized, incredibly old. Having studied many objects and artifacts from Mongolia and nearby regions with her father, Thalia knew how to date a piece based on clues from its appearance. The heft, the way it was made, even the small dents and rubbings on its surface all told her one thing: the kettle was hundreds of years old, maybe even more. And it felt . . . alive . . . in her hands.

"Maybe they got it from a Chinese trader," he suggested.

"What can you tell me about this?" Thalia asked Oyuun. "When did you get it?"

The chieftain's wife looked at her husband, who answered, "We've always had that kettle. I remember my grandmother brewing tea in it, and she said it belonged to *her* grandmother. But we have made tea for everyone in our tribe using it, and no one has ever become ill afterward."

"And any visitors?"

"None of them, either."

"Do you know if any of them . . ." Thalia could not bring herself to look at Bold. Concentrating on a painted cabinet that stood behind him, she cleared her throat and felt her cheeks heat. "Did any visitors . . . sleep with anyone . . . after?"

"We all sleep in the *ger* together."

Everyone stared at Thalia; she wondered if it was possible to will oneself out of existence by sheer embarrassment alone. Mongols were open about their sexual lives, but there was a part of Thalia, a very English part, that couldn't quite be comfortable with such complete candor. Even Gabriel, who was as unpolished as a wolf, looked a trifle red.

"Not sleep," she said through her teeth. "Share a bed. Two people. In a bed. Together."

The smile the chieftain and his wife shared made Thalia long for a herd of stampeding horses to come through. "Ah," said Oyuun, momentarily forgetting her tension. "If they did, no one said so, and we did not see it." Her husband nodded to confirm this.

Despite her embarrassment, a strange current began to run up and down Thalia's neck as she stared down at the humble object in her hands. "I would like to borrow this for a moment."

Before Bold or Oyuun could reply, Thalia was already outside, with Gabriel easily matching her long strides with his own. "What are you thinking?" he asked.

"Not sure, yet," she said. "It's only a feeling. But I believe we triggered something last night." When she turned and headed toward where the hunting eagles were perched, he nodded with comprehension. Thalia smiled to herself. She did not need further words with Gabriel. He understood her.

As she and Gabriel neared the eagles, the birds began shifting on their perches and ruffling their feathers. The closer they came to the birds, the more unsettled the animals became.

Standing in front of the birds, Thalia and Gabriel exchanged glances. He nodded at her, and she held up the kettle so it was no more than a few inches away from the eagles. Their screeches flared out over the steppes, causing horses, camels, and sheep to look up from their grazing. Even the men and women who were performing their daily chores paused to see what was causing such a commotion.

Thalia quickly took the kettle away, and the eagles quieted. As a test, Gabriel held up the ruby again. The birds remained silent. Once more, Thalia presented the eagles with the kettle, and people, including Batu, came out of their *gers* to investigate the birds' renewed shrieks. Bold and Oyuun were also watching from the doorway of their tent, mystified.

"Oh, my God," Thalia breathed. "The Source isn't the ruby."

Gabriel put the ruby into the inside pocket of his jacket. He held her eyes with his as the weight of their discovery

settled over them. It was both ridiculous and also pro-
found. "The bloody Source everyone's chasing," he said
with a shake of his head and rueful smile. "It's a damned
shabby kettle."

"Magic?" Bold repeated. "That cannot be."

"It seems strange," said Thalia, "but the test with the birds
is always accurate. Your tea kettle holds a powerful magic."

"We would have known," Oyuun put in. She examined the
kettle as if it were a familiar dog that had suddenly begun to
speak. She turned questioning eyes to Thalia and Gabriel.
"Wouldn't we?"

Since Gabriel was almost entirely unfamiliar with the
realms of magic, he stood with his arms crossed over his
chest and let Thalia do the explaining to Bold, Oyuun, and
almost the entire tribe, most of whom were now gathered
inside the large *ger* that had been used for the feast before
the *nadaam*. Instead of engaging in raucous merrymaking,
however, the large assembly of people were almost completely silent, save for a few babies and children fussing.
Everyone wore similar stunned expressions. Except Thalia,
Gabriel, and Batu.

"Not necessarily," Thalia explained. Batu provided
Gabriel with a running translation. "Sometimes magic is
contained in an object and it takes a special set of words or
actions to release it. But we already know that this kettle
contains some kind of power. Gabriel *guai* and I felt it last
night"—though she did not explain under what circumstances—"but more than that, the crimson flowers that
follow the tribe come from that power."

A murmur of startled understanding rippled through the
crowd.

"How can we release the magic?" a man asked.

Now it was Thalia's turn to look mystified. She honestly

had no idea. Whenever she had discussed the use of Sources with her father and other Blades, they had never mentioned exactly what one might need to do to access a Source's power. There were many combinations of words and rituals, too many to know where to begin. Then a horrible thought occurred to her. Would she and Gabriel have to make love in front of the entire tribe to bring forth the magic? That was a spectacle in which she had no desire to participate.

"Water," Gabriel said behind her.

Surprised, Thalia turned to face him. "What's that?"

He strode forward, taking the kettle from Oyuun. "It has to do with water, I'd reckon. Why else place magic inside something that heats water?"

"But they boil water inside the kettle every day," Thalia pointed out. "And nothing has happened."

Gabriel considered this for a moment while staring intently at the kettle. "Water's scarce in Mongolia," he finally said. "So they might not have used enough or," he added, brows drawn down in concentration, "perhaps they used too much." He turned to Oyuun. "We'll need water and a fire."

Oyuun nodded at the translated command and gestured for some women to assist her, which made Thalia smile a little to herself. Ever the soldier, Gabriel could order around even a chieftain's wife with no resistance. His air of authority would not allow questioning or disobedience. Thalia recalled how he'd demanded that she repeat her full name to him a few nights before, and ordered her to the bed, how she'd been unable to deny him. In the middle of the large *ger,* with hundreds of eyes surrounding her and the mystery of the Source unfolding, she couldn't stop the rush of pleasure, remembering him buried deep inside of her.

Pressing a hand to her fluttering stomach, Thalia watched as a fire was set up and the kettle filled. Gabriel placed the kettle onto the fire.

"And now?" Thalia asked him.

He did not take his eyes from the kettle. "Now, we wait."

In the strained silence of the tent, the noise of water gradually coming to boil could be heard like a soft song. Steam rose up from the spout as the water heated. After several minutes, the water evaporated, and the steam disappeared. Still, Gabriel would not take the kettle from the fire. Thalia shifted her gaze back and forth from the tea kettle to Gabriel, wondering what each would do next. It seemed somewhat useless to continue to heat the kettle without more water.

"I should refill it," Thalia said, stepping forward.

Gabriel held out his hand, a wordless imperative to stay where she was.

Both she and the assembled tribe grew restive as they continued to wait. Yet no one would disobey Gabriel or even dare to move more than necessary.

After what seemed like lifetimes, the kettle heating over the fire, Thalia gasped. She reached out and gripped Gabriel's arm. "Do you—?"

"I see it," he answered, clipped.

It started as a small puff, but within a moment, thick, sweet-smelling steam began to pour out of the kettle. Nothing could be left inside the kettle to create that steam, and certainly not so much of it. But it continued to flow from the kettle unchecked, warm and fragrant. It formed a heavy cloud just above their heads. Figures began to appear within the cloud, gathering shape and substance.

Thalia's pulse raced, and she felt Gabriel's steady fingers intertwine with hers as the Source finally revealed its secrets.

Chapter 14

Within the Clouds

Gabriel hadn't thought, but had instinctively taken Thalia's hand in his own. When the world fell apart and reshaped into something new, the only thing that felt right and balanced was her. He needed the touch of her skin, having her close and under his protection, as a warm vapor shaped itself into a thick cloud within the tent. Gabriel didn't know what the hell the cloud was, what it might be capable of doing—good or ill—and had to be sure he could safeguard Thalia.

He waited, tensed, as shapes congealed within the mist. Gabriel's other hand hovered over his revolver, just in case. Maybe a bullet couldn't stop a magical steam creature, but it might, and he'd be ready.

Instead of a beast or something sinister, the figures revealed themselves to be people. They sharpened into focus, as did the world around them, until it was like watching a stage play hovering over the ground. The crowd watching the display shouted out as one, and even Gabriel had to swallow an oath. The figures in the clouds were the tribe themselves. Gabriel recognized several of the faces, including those of the chieftain and his wife. And, Great Gideon, Gabriel himself and Thalia, as they had competed in the *nadaam* and taken a meal with Bold's family. Bizarre, to see himself manifested within the steam.

Everyone in the tribe appeared to be going about his or her normal life, performing chores, tending to the animals. And cooking. Oyuun gasped nearby as she watched herself in the mists, filling the tea kettle. Yet, these ordinary tasks were odd because—

"Everything is going backward," Thalia murmured beside him.

"Like a zoetrope spinning in reverse," Gabriel answered.

And in that strange pattern, the ordinary life of the tribe played out topsy-turvy, the sun setting and rising, west to east, and odder still, foals disappearing back inside their dams, tall grasses retreating as seeds into the earth, thaws turning to snow. Yet, through it all, the shadow play kept returning to the kettle as Oyuun and then many other women, old dames growing young, boiled water inside it as their families moved across the steppes. Always, the bright carpet of red flowers surrounded them, wherever they camped.

"My grandmother," Bold exclaimed as one of the cloud women brewed tea. Then she disappeared and more women took her place. Whole generations, hundreds of years, passed in a moment. Even the kettle itself grew slightly less battered. The unceasing rhythms of life, even in reverse, made Gabriel feel humbled and small, knowing how brief his own time on this earth was in comparison to the bigger world. He gripped Thalia's hand more tightly.

Then there was a shift within the clouds. The kettle left the tribe and was now carried backward in a horseman's pack. A soldier, judging by his armaments. But he carried no firearms, only a blade and bow. It seemed to be far back in the past, possibly more than five hundred years. He sped through the steppes, through territory which seemed recognizable to Gabriel, and quickly he realized why. A thriving city appeared in a familiar valley.

"It's Karakorum," Thalia breathed.

"Except alive."

The ruin was now the center of a flourishing Mongol Empire, and the whole stone tortoises supported pillars to mark the limits of the city. Carts, merchants, scholars, ambassadors, traders, and holy people from all over the known world streamed into Karakorum, and the riches on display made Gabriel's eyes sting. Even the wealth of the gilded palaces in India could not compare to the piles of gold, jewels, and silks that flowed like a swollen river. And included in that opulence was the humble kettle, carried in by the soldier, where it found its home within one of the vast storehouses of treasure and plunder.

But it didn't stay within the warehouse for long. Along with tapestries, polished blocks of jade, and scroll paintings, the kettle was placed into a cart and taken backward with a great army heading southeast. Even an old soldier like Gabriel could not stop the whistle of appreciation to see the size of this army, a huge column of riders and horses, stretching to the horizon and beyond. The ease and comfort of the men in their saddles marked them as the finest horsemen Gabriel had ever seen—and he'd been witness to incredible feats of horsemanship over the years. The vision within the mist moved along the enormous army, until it reached a single armored man, trailed by generals and guards, at the head of the troops. A man with ruthless intelligence glinting in his dark eyes as he surveyed the lands around him, missing nothing, assessing everything for his empire. Gabriel's heart seized. The man's power was a palpable thing, certain.

A name rose up from within the tent, passing like a torch amidst the tribe watching the steam clouds. "Khan," the herdsmen murmured. "Genghis Khan."

"Oh, my God," Thalia gulped. "It really *is* him."

Gabriel said nothing, stunned. He, Thalia, Batu, and the

tribe were the first people to see the conqueror's face in over six hundred years or more. There was no denying the man had the air of command about him, worn with complete assurance. And yet, the Khan was a man only. Not a myth, or a creature of magic, but flesh, as faulty and fragile as any other living thing.

Still, Genghis Khan knew warfare. And Gabriel witnessed its cruel machine as the kettle's clouds showed smoking ruins turn into thriving towns, villages, and cities, the result in reverse of having the Khan's army pitilessly subjugate and pillage with no concern for human life, only acquisition. Whatever settlement foolish enough to try to hold out against the Khan met with a gruesome, bloody end. Those who conceded defeat were spared, but those that defied him were destroyed utterly. The tribe, watching such scenes of slaughter, screamed and wept. Even Gabriel, who had witnessed things that would drive most men mad, felt his gorge rise to see men torn to pieces, women and children skewered, kings and ministers tortured to death. Thalia pressed her face into Gabriel's shoulder as she shuddered. He stroked the back of her head, offering what comfort he could. It was made worse because it was going backward, and a mutilated corpse became, in a moment, a man fighting for his life.

"You must think me a coward, not to watch," she gulped.

"I think you're a good woman who hates death and suffering. No shame in that." He was glad that he could still be troubled by such brutality. If it left him unmoved, *that* would disturb him.

Everywhere the Khan vanquished, he took. Not only treasure and goods, but people, too. Learned men and craftsmen were taken prisoner, added to the spoils. Yet the kettle continued on with the army, taken past the grassy steppes until the terrain grew barren and rocky, thirsty plains swept by the wind. A vast and pitiless desert.

"The Gobi," said Thalia, who'd lifted her head from the shelter of Gabriel's shoulder. Shining wet tracks marked her face, and he brushed away the moisture with gentle fingertips. "I've only visited the very edge with my father a few times."

"A harsh place," Gabriel replied.

"But beautiful, from what I saw."

He had to agree that it was, in its desolate way. People lived there, too, tending short-legged camels and sheep. The isolated herdsmen were left undisturbed by the Khan, who passed them by. Through the hard desert rode the huge army, covering miles and miles, the porous border between Mongolia and China, until, appearing on the horizon, rose a craggy peak. At the top of the peak stood a thickly walled building with the distinctive sloped ceramic roofs of Chinese temples. The army was making its way, backward, toward the temple. A cold ember settled in Gabriel's stomach. Monks and holy men would be no match for the Khan's soldiers.

"Look away, Thalia," he commanded her quietly.

She complied without a word of protest, pressing her closed eyes into the curve of his neck, so he had the strange double feeling of watching the army of Genghis Khan slaughter a temple full of Buddhist monks while Thalia's warm breath fluttered over his skin. She smelled of grasses and sandalwood.

"They've gone now," Gabriel said, after a time, "and the kettle stayed behind."

Thalia raised her head to watch. "I wonder if the monks knew what the kettle was?"

"If they didn't, they're taking damned good care of a simple teapot." It wasn't used in daily routine, but was kept in a locked cabinet in the head monk's chambers; the head monk held the key. Seconds earlier, a Mongol soldier had smashed that same cabinet as a monk tried to defend it.

Moments later, just before the killing blade stopped him, the monk stood before the cabinet, hands in the air. Bright energy glowed briefly. He'd been trying to cast a protective spell.

"Oh, God," Thalia said, under her breath. "They *did* know it was magical."

What, exactly, the powers of the kettle wasn't revealed, for it stayed safely hidden for still more generations. Until, one day, the cabinet was opened, and a monk took the kettle far into the depths of the temple, through courtyards and passageways. Then sparks and flame. A man, stripped to the waist, pounding metal into shape. The kettle was made and then unmade over the blacksmith's anvil. A swirling ball of light was released as the kettle became raw material. Close at hand, a senior monk chanted, drawing magic from the fires of the forge. The kettle and its power was then unborn.

The thick clouds of steam shrank quickly, retreating into the kettle, until nothing was left of the history everyone had just seen but a lingering damp warmth.

For long moments, no one spoke. Not even a baby fussed.

Gabriel turned to Thalia. "Looks like we're going to China," he said.

"I will send my best horsemen and hunters with you," Bold insisted. "We may no longer be soldiers in the khan's army, but, if we have to protect the magic from wicked men, we can fight."

A small council had gathered in Bold's *ger* to discuss what should happen next. It was certain that after Tsend's defeat at the *nadaam,* the Heirs would come soon. They still believed the Source was the ruby, would kill for it, but when they did learn that the ruby had no power, they would destroy everything and everyone in the search for the true Source. There was little time to spare. The kettle had belonged to the tribe for generations, but everyone had agreed that it needed to be returned to its place of origin, the Chinese temple on the other side of the Gobi, and safeguarded by those who had created it. The temple survived, or, at least, it had at the time the khan's army left it. They had to take the chance that it still stood, hundreds of years later. There was no alternative.

Through Thalia, Gabriel said to Bold, "The men we had spoken of before, they're dangerous, and they'll be hunting the magic, to take it by any means necessary. Including killing. I can't ask you to risk your men's lives."

Bold drew himself up proudly. "It is our decision to make. All of us would gladly sacrifice ourselves to defend our country, our families, those that we love."

Gabriel understood. He glanced over at Thalia, her face serious and focused as the literal fate of nations was being decided. She showed no fear, no hesitation, only a burning desire to see the just thing done. If all Englishwomen were raised in Mongolia, they'd be formidable creatures. That wasn't right. There was only one Thalia, and no nation could claim her as its exclusive handiwork. It was her uniqueness that made him all the more determined to see no harm come to her, no matter the cost to himself.

"Fine," Gabriel said, his voice clipped. "Get your men together. We leave in an hour. Some must stay behind to protect the *ail* if the Heirs return."

With a nod, Bold left the *ger*, taking the men who had gathered for the council with him. Gabriel could hear the chieftain, issuing orders as his tribesmen hastened to do their duty.

"Batu," Thalia said, turning to him as he stood nearby, "you must ride for Urga immediately and let my father know everything that has come to pass."

"Everything?" Batu repeated, looking from Thalia to Gabriel and back again. So, the man knew what had happened between them. Gabriel supposed it wasn't that hard to figure out, given that every time he looked at Thalia he felt as though he'd drunk pots of wine. He probably had damned stars in his eyes, like some fool in a Walter Scott epic. But he didn't feel like a fool. He felt . . . her.

"Everything about the *Source*," Thalia said firmly. Still, a deeper blush stole into her cheeks as she spoke. "Tell him where we are going."

Batu narrowed his eyes, but agreed. "I will pack my belongings now and be off at once." He took a few steps, then stopped and held out his hand to Gabriel. "This is how it's done?"

Gabriel swallowed his momentary surprise. He would have figured Batu would have tried to castrate him instead of shake his hand. "Yes," he said, taking Batu's hand and giving it a shake. "You're a fine man, Batu. A fine soldier."

"You, as well, Huntley *guai*," was the solemn answer. "We would have been quite lost without you. *I* would have been dead many times over." With a meaningful glance at Thalia, he added, "And I trust you to do what is right."

"Batu!" Thalia yelped.

"I will try to do right," Gabriel replied. "In everything."

That seemed to satisfy the loyal servant. Releasing Gabriel's hand, he turned to Thalia and quickly enfolded her in a tight embrace, which she returned. Batu said something in Mongolian, before saying in English, "Be safe, child." His voice sounded thick.

"I will. And you, too," Thalia said, and murmured something else in Mongolian. She held him close, this man she had known almost her whole life and who was to her as close, if not closer, than blood. He'd taught her to ride and helped her move past the silencing grief of her mother's death, felt her injuries, and struggled to keep her from harm. Gabriel, jaded as he was, felt his own eyes grow wet to see the unconditional, fierce love between these two old friends.

Then Thalia forcibly stepped away, pain and resolve

warring in her expression. "Tell my father I love him. And I will do him and the Blades proud. I swear it."

"You have already, Thalia *guai*," Batu said, blinking. After dragging his sleeve across his eyes, he strode hastily from the *ger,* as if afraid another moment would see him disgraced.

Now Gabriel and Thalia were alone in the *ger.* They stared at each other for a moment before he crossed over to her and put his arms around her. She felt strong and alive. They knew what the Source was now, and what they had to do with it. The Heirs would be coming, and they would be desperate. Which meant they would do anything to claim the Source for themselves. Including killing anyone, even a woman, who stood in their way.

He was glad women weren't soldiers. If he'd fallen in love with a female soldier, each day in the army, each day facing death, would've been hell, knowing that a precious life could be lost.

"Don't try to send me with him," she said, willful.

"I want to, yes," Gabriel answered, and when she started to protest, he continued, over her objections, "but I won't try. It's your right to protect the Source. Just as it's my right to protect you, whether you want that protection or not."

Her expression softened as she linked her fingers behind his neck. "I wish I knew what tomorrow might bring. I wish I knew we had a future together."

For the first time in a long while, Gabriel understood what a torture it was to *want* a future. Especially knowing there was a high degree of likelihood that it wouldn't come to pass. In war, there were always casualties. All he could try to do was make sure that she wasn't one of them.

Wars required soldiers, and Henry Lamb knew that he, Edgeworth, and Tsend, even driven as they were, made up a piss-poor, meager army. To that end, Lamb had dispatched Tsend to find them a decently sized batch of mercenaries. The Mongol had grumbled about being sent on such a menial task, but Lamb needed to punish the bastard for failing to win the ruby.

Turned out that the ruby wasn't the Source after all. Ironic, that. The enchanted hawk that Lamb had circling the herdsmen's settlement had kept Lamb and Edgeworth partially informed. He'd seen it himself, albeit from a distance, when the hunting eagles had nearly torn themselves from their perches when presented with the genuine Source. Definitely strong power there, perhaps the strongest Lamb had ever seen. As Lamb sat at his folding camp desk, penning a letter to the Heirs back in England, he wondered how to best phrase, "The Source is a grubby old tea kettle," in a way that didn't sound completely ludicrous, or, worse, make him look like a buffoon.

Hell, he hadn't gone to Cambridge for nothing. Lamb managed to cram several polysyllabic words into a few sentences, obfuscating the truth just enough so that the higher members of the Heirs' inner circle would consider Lamb, and themselves, very clever. It was a trick Lamb had mastered years ago at King's College, and even earlier, when he'd written letters to home while at Harrow.

"Where the hell is that filthy bugger?" snapped Edgeworth, pacing.

Lamb blotted his letter with a grimace. He felt honor-bound to correct Edgeworth's abominable swearing habit, but knew he couldn't cross the younger man. His father was too important to make an enemy of the son. Besides, Lamb needed to stay in Jonas Edgeworth's good graces. As soon as they returned in triumph to England, Lamb planned on calling on Edgeworth's sister, the cumbersomely named Victoria Regina Gloriana London Harcourt, née Edgeworth, and more familiarly known as London. She was a pretty woman, perhaps a little too clever, but kept ignorant of the existence of the Heirs through scrupulous manipulation. London's husband, Lawrence Harcourt, had been an Heir, and it had been on an assignment three years ago that Harcourt had died at the hands of a Blade, Bennett Day. London never learned the details of her husband's death. If Lamb could secure the widow London's hand in marriage, he'd be that much closer to Joseph Edgeworth and the inner circle.

With that in mind, Lamb was careful to keep his tone unruffled. "He'll be here soon with the men we need." Lamb rose and walked with the letter to their campfire. He reached into his pocket and produced a sprinkling of dried flowers.

"But the Burgess bitch and that tyke soldier are already on the road," Edgeworth complained. He pointed to the seeing mirror, which indeed revealed Thalia Burgess, the Yorkshireman, and a dozen Mongols riding south, toward the desert. "We don't know where they're headed, and we're out of spells and Sources to slow them down."

Lamb tossed the letter and flowers into the fire at the same time. The letter curled up quickly, then disappeared in a small cascade of glowing ash. It would reach its destination within hours: a continual fire, burning in the study of the Heirs' headquarters in London. Such communication was kept to a minimum, since the dried flowers that enabled the spell were exceedingly rare, but Lamb knew that the inner circle would need to know about the latest development in the pursuit of the Mongolian Source.

"The imbeciles only use magic which belongs to themselves, pretty puny stuff, so it stands to reason that they're going to try to take the Source someplace safe, someplace they believe we won't be able to breach," Lamb explained to his short-tempered protégé. "It's true, I don't know where that might be, but it doesn't signify. We'll catch them before they secret it away. They are merely a bunch of sheepherders led by a woman, with some brute of a common soldier providing muscle. Nothing to fuss about."

Any further complaint from Edgeworth was drowned out in the sound of approaching hoofbeats. Both Lamb and Edgeworth watched as Tsend rode up. Mongols were largely, and disgustingly, loyal to their homeland, and Lamb had entertained not a little fear that Tsend would be unable to find men desperate and greedy enough to betray their motherland. But gold always seemed to unearth the rapacious, like pigs rooting in shit.

"Where are the men?" Lamb snapped, looking past Tsend.

Wordlessly, Tsend pointed down the road. What Lamb saw there made him truly smile for the first time in weeks, and even Edgeworth shuddered.

Gabriel had been lulled into a false sense of calm. For those few, brief days with Bold's tribe, he hadn't been a campaigning soldier. There were those incredible, but brief, hours with Thalia that reminded him he was a man. True, competing in the *nadaam* hadn't exactly been a seaside holiday, but Gabriel had been focused on one goal at a time, instead of keeping constant vigilance. The way he was doing now, back on the road, racing toward uncertainty with enemies in pursuit.

Or so he believed. "One of the bloody frustrating things about the Heirs," he growled to Thalia riding beside him, "is that you can never *see* them until it's too late."

"I'd say that maybe they aren't following us," she said, "but that would be hopelessly naïve. But I have to ask: are you sure?"

Gabriel glanced around. They were moving too quickly for him to do proper reconnaissance, which scorched his sausage. How was he supposed to protect Thalia *and* the

Source if he couldn't get a feel for the land, or sniff out those inbred Heirs? It was enough to make a man chew on his own bullets.

"They're out there," he said. "Thanks to their damned magic, I don't know *where,* exactly, but they're on our tail."

"It's been nearly a week since we left," Thalia pointed out. It had been endless hard riding until the horses were half-dead. The end of each day saw Thalia, Gabriel, and their escort collapsing into brief, exhausted sleep; then they rose before dawn to ride even more. It had been tough going, but no one, including Thalia, had complained. Gabriel's body, on the other hand, was grumbling something fierce, being so near to her but denied the pleasures of her skin.

"Doesn't matter. Maybe they're gathering strength. Maybe they're playing with us. Any of that could be possible." He tightened his jaw. "I hate running away instead of standing and fighting."

"We're not running away," she answered. "This is a . . . strategic retreat."

His smile was wry. "You sound like a commissioned officer covering his arse."

"Commissioned?" She snorted. "Hardly."

"That's right. You're too smart." He said, thoughtful, "You'd have made a first-rate soldier." But he was glad she hadn't been.

Thalia laughed quietly. "I can't take orders, or haven't you noticed?"

"I've noticed." And he liked it.

Had Batu reached Urga by now? Gabriel tried to imagine what the servant was telling Franklin Burgess, not only about the quest for the Source and its uncovering in the most unlikely place, but about him and Burgess's daughter. He didn't know how someone told a man that his daughter had taken a lover. Seemed deuced uncomfortable. But what about the return? Gabriel wouldn't let himself think of what would happen after the Source had been brought back to the Chinese monastery. If he did, he would start having hope, making plans—both surefire ways to meet disaster and pain.

The best way to avoid that was to stay on guard. That proved difficult with long days in the saddle and not a single opportunity to be alone with Thalia. Their riding company was all men, and while Gabriel didn't think any of them would blame him for sharing her pallet for the night, he sure as hell didn't want to treat any of them to listening to a rendition of that particular sound Thalia made, high, in the back of her throat, moments before she came.

Gabriel then treated himself to the longest and most elaborate streak of mental cursing he'd ever embarked upon. He couldn't let himself remember the sounds she made, or he'd lose his godforsaken mind.

In his saddlebag was not just the kettle, but the ruby, as well. Both objects weighed on him constantly. Just before he'd left Bold and his tribe, the chieftain had reminded him that the ruby was still his and Thalia's charge for the year. Which meant that it would have to be guarded and returned. Gabriel was no stranger to duty and responsibility, but he felt himself stretched thin. He wouldn't allow himself to break.

After a few more days, the grassy steppes began to disappear, replaced by long stretches of rocky, scrub-dusted plains. Whatever moisture was in the air vanished just as the greenery did. It wasn't hot, but light bounced off the arid earth, and biting winds raced unimpeded to choke them with dust. Still, it was beautiful, the way a knife was beautiful, spare and brutal in its precision. Gazelles, white-tailed and spry, leapt in herds like laughter, or grazed on the scarce grasses. Their curious black stares followed the group as they kept up their tough pace. Overhead, falcons wheeled in the sky. They had been keeping constant company with the riding group, only sometimes diving down to snatch tiny, unlucky prey from the plain.

"Amazing anything can live out here," Gabriel said to Thalia.

"People do, too," she answered. "If life on the steppe is hard, the Gobi is harder. And this is just the outlying lands. I've never traveled so deep into it before."

"Suppose that puts us on equal footing, then." He smiled.

"You have no equal, Captain."

They had just crossed a rock-strewn rise, when Gabriel wheeled his horse around. The other riders cantered on, but Thalia stopped and brought her horse back. Both mounts stamped impatiently, edging back and forth.

"What is it?" Thalia asked as Gabriel stared at the sky.

"Birds."

She followed his gaze. "There are always hawks and falcons."

He shook his head. "Something's not right. Feels like they've been following us." He took a spyglass from his saddlebag and trained it on the birds of prey. "I could swear they look familiar." He handed her the glass, and she looked as well, but could only shrug her shoulders.

"I can't recognize them."

Gabriel couldn't shake the feeling, a cold awareness prickling his scalp underneath his hat. Even as his horse tugged on the reins, impatient to join the rest of the group riding southeast, he kept scanning the sky, the horizon. Both the sky and the earth felt immense, stretching into eternity. Nothing could hide here. Except—

"There!" The shimmering surface of the ground danced in waves, then broke for a moment, revealing the truth beneath.

"Oh, my God," Thalia breathed, standing up in the stirrups.

No need for a spyglass. Even a nearsighted clerk could see them. Only a few miles away and headed straight for

Thalia and Gabriel. With nothing between them except rock and scrub.

"They bought themselves a whole damned army," Gabriel spat.

He'd anticipated that, in their push to claim the Source, the Heirs would find a handful of men to add to their strength. Instead, hammering across the stark earth like vengeance itself was a thick, dark swarm of riders.

"How many?" Thalia asked.

A quick calculation. "Seventy-five, maybe more." Gabriel glanced over to where their own Mongol complement had stopped, waiting for Thalia and him to catch up. Two dozen men of their own, and, despite their willingness to fight for and defend their home, likely no match for nearly a legion of mercenaries. Mercenaries fueled by greed and magic.

Without another word, he and Thalia kicked their horses into gallops, heading as quickly away as the already tired animals would allow. Gabriel's mind raced faster than the horses as he cursed himself. He'd no idea how long the Heirs had been following them, and, had he known, wouldn't have let them get this close. There was no way to outride them. No way to lose them. The land was too flat, leaving no place to hide. Maybe, if he . . .

"No," Thalia shouted at him over the pounding of their horses' hooves.

Bent over the neck of his mount, Gabriel looked at her.

"I won't let you sacrifice yourself to help us gain time!" she yelled.

He scowled. Holy hellhound, she'd read his bloody mind. "I don't see any other damned alternatives," he snarled back. He wanted to give her the ruby and kettle, and send her ahead whilst he provided a distraction. Clearly, she didn't care for this plan.

They had reached their own group of riders, who, catching sight of Thalia and Gabriel racing toward them, inferred that they were being pursued. Thalia let their men know what they were up against. Eyes widened in surprise, but not fear. They began talking amongst themselves. Twenty of the men jumped down from their horses and began gathering fallen branches and sticks from the low saxaul trees. And while they did this, the Heirs' army thundered closer.

"Come on, damn it," Gabriel bellowed at them. "We're riding, now!"

But the men paid him no mind, even as Thalia urged them on in Mongolian and Gabriel swore at them with every foul word he knew in English. They tied the branches to their horses' tails, then remounted. One of the men, whom Gabriel remembered from the *nadaam,* spoke tersely with Thalia before setting his heels to his horse. The twenty men then rode off with him, veering toward the west. The branches tied to the horses' tails dragged on the ground, kicking up enormous clouds of dust. The air became thick and yellow.

"What the *hell* do they think they're doing?" Gabriel demanded. "They're leaving a trail."

"But not *our* trail," Thalia answered with a shake of her head.

A gruff laugh sprung from Gabriel. She was right. Their Mongol allies were creating a huge screen of dust, not only creating the illusion that Thalia and Gabriel were headed west, but hiding them in the process and drawing the Heirs away. "An old trick from the days of Genghis Khan," one of the remaining riders explained. Gabriel couldn't help but admire their ironclad bollocks. No time to waste on admiration, though. He, Thalia, and the other riders wheeled their horses about and sped on their way, deeper into the unforgiving desert.

Henry Lamb was a ponce, or so Jonas Edgeworth thought. He'd complained to his father about being sent to

Mongolia with a man who had more starch in his underwear than most blokes had in their entire wardrobe, including shirts for church. For Christ's sake, Lamb didn't even follow *cricket*. But Joseph Edgeworth had insisted that his son accompany Lamb.

"Ponce or not," his father said, "Lamb is a valuable Heir. He can show you a few things out in the field that you can't learn at home."

Jonas was just now learning that you never, ever made Henry Lamb angry. The man might've been a ponce, but when he was enraged—devils protect Jonas. Satan himself would piss in his brimstone drawers from fear.

When Lamb discovered, after a whole day of chasing Thalia Burgess and her band of supporters, that he had been tricked, only God or Queen Victoria could have inspired so much terror. The eighty battle-hardened, heartless fiends Tsend had found cowered meekly as Lamb ranted and raged, actually tearing small trees up from the ground and using their trunks to bash in the head of an unlucky decoy they'd managed to catch. The others fled, but they had to hear the stomach-churning gurgles coming from their dying comrade.

Jonas, no stranger to brutality, couldn't even watch as Lamb's immaculate clothing became spattered with brains and blood. When the chap was quite dead, Lamb wasn't done with him. Lamb's prized Sheffield knife, polished and gleaming, was used to cut him into bits, which were left for the animals. Jonas would've been sick, but was afraid that, in Lamb's frenzy, any sign of such activity would send him off on another berserker rage. So, instead, he swallowed his gorge and looked away as the true face of Henry Lamb was revealed.

After a half an hour of this, Lamb seemed to have sufficiently calmed for Jonas to speak to him. "Jesus, Lamb," he said as they both mounted up, "all that wasn't necessary, was it?"

Lamb barely spared the desecrated remains a glance. Of greater concern to him were the stains on his Bond Street clothing. He tsked and frowned over them like a disapproving valet surveying the night's damage to a dinner jacket.

"Oh, that," Lamb drawled. "That's nothing compared to what I plan to do to that Yorkshireman."

"And the girl?"

The gleam in Lamb's eyes caused Jonas's stomach to clench. "She won't go quite as quickly."

With that, Lamb ordered the men out, and no one complained about how tired and hungry they were, not a single man. Jonas rode alongside Lamb and wondered what, if anything, he could tell his father.

Chapter 15

Allies or Enemies?

The reprieve would be temporary. As much as Thalia admired the courage and ingenuity of their tribesmen compatriots, nothing could keep the Heirs away forever, except outright defeat. She didn't know how that might be possible. Only six remained in her company. The Heirs had many, many more, and she didn't doubt that whatever men Henry Lamb had found were likely the sort who killed readily and happily for money. She, herself, had killed only once in her life, and never wanted to repeat that experience again. But being able to keep her hands unspotted with blood now seemed doubtful.

As the Heirs drew closer—and she knew they couldn't be more than a day behind—she felt her first true taste of fear, finally understanding the extraordinary danger one faced when joining the Blades of the Rose. It was entirely possible that either she or Gabriel, or both of them, wouldn't survive the mission. She shook her head, trying to clear it of the terror of losing him.

"You can still ride for Urga," Gabriel said to her. They had stopped in the shadow of one of the large cliffs that had been rising from the earth for the past few miles to rest their horses, which were half-dead with thirst and fatigue. She pitied the poor animals, but they could not afford to let them go and attempt the remaining trek on foot.

Thalia, sitting on the rocky, barren ground with her arms braced on her knees, looked up at him wearily. She took the canteen he offered and allowed herself only a few sips of water, though she wanted to finish the whole thing. Everyone's rations, not only those of the horses, were low.

"No," she croaked back. "Stop asking me to." She returned the canteen.

Caked in red dust, lips dry, tiredness turning his face into hard planes of bronze, Gabriel had never looked more beautiful. Campaigning sat well with him. Lean, sharp as a cutlass, capable of anything. He easily folded down to sit beside her and capped the canteen, despite the fact that he'd barely touched any of the water himself. Saving it for her.

"Have to ask," he said without apology.

"Make this the last time."

He shook his head with a rueful smile. "You're stubborn as hell."

Despite her own bone-deep weariness, Thalia couldn't help but return the smile. She reached over and ran her hand along the sculpted lines of his cheek, his jaw. She felt it, even exhausted and thirsty, the insistent pull whenever she touched him. The pull that demanded she touch him more, until they were bare of everything except desire. She struggled, still, with the knowledge of her love. Impossible to tell him here, in the midst of danger. She did not believe he would run from her love, yet she also understood that knowledge of it whilst fighting for life and magic would be a distraction neither of them could afford. She hoped that, one day, and one day soon, she could tell him how he filled her heart. Instead, she said, "And you, my dear Captain, are one of the most biddable men I've ever met."

Clasping her hand with his own, holding her to him, he asked, "Biddable, or beddable?"

"Both," she chuckled, then sighed. "What I wouldn't give for a few gallons of water, a bath, and a nice, green place for us to lie down together."

His eyes glinted with hunger as his fingers tightened around hers. "I'd kill for that."

"We might have to." She refused to consider that now, though her desiccated blood turned to sleet to think of what lay in store for them, what chased them. "So odd," she murmured.

"What's that?"

"After all this time, after I'd given up hope. To meet you now. Here." She waved her hand at the austere beauty of the Gobi, silent except for the wind stirring the coppery dust. It was very far, in distance and feel, from the lush steppes on which she'd grown and lived. Whether or not they had actually crossed into China was a matter of debate. Borders, like so much of life, never remained fixed, but shifted without warning or reason.

"Not so odd." He pressed the palm of her hand to his mouth. "Just right. For people like us." Then his eyes sharpened, his body tensed. He stood, pulling her up with him. Their four remaining escorts looked at him, questioning, as he pulled his rifle. "Someone's coming."

"The Heirs?" Thalia asked. She was already heading toward her saddle for her own firearm.

He tilted his head, listening. "Too few. Not on horseback. Something else."

Finally, Thalia was able to hear it, too. Coming closer. But the cliffs made it almost impossible to tell where the sound was originating from, or how near. Gabriel tucked the wrapped bundle of the kettle under one arm and the ruby into a pocket. He motioned for everyone to gather in a circle, facing outward with their weapons drawn. Thalia's heart knocked into her ribs. Perhaps the Heirs had found a way to bribe more men into tracking them down.

The wind picked up, raising clouds of dust. Thalia squinted into the swirling grit. Voices. Footfalls, but heavy. She tightened her grip on her rifle, her finger hovering over the trigger. And then large, dark shapes emerged. They made a hideous sound, an awful, hoarse bellowing.

"Stop!" Thalia shouted out in Mongol. "We are armed and have nothing of value."

"*You* are valuable, English Mongol woman," a voice atop one of the large shapes responded. The brief eddy of dust settled, revealing ten men mounted on shaggy, short-legged camels. One of the camels let out another terrible bray. Heart sinking, Thalia saw that the men were armed, too, with Russian rifles all pointed at her group.

"I think you must be valuable, indeed," continued the man who'd spoken. He kicked his camel forward, so that only a few feet separated the unknown man and her. Gabriel immediately stepped in front of her, deliberate fury tightening his jaw as he kept his rifle trained on the man. "See how you are guarded?" the man said. "And you are chased by almost an entire army."

"Did they send you?" Thalia shot back.

The man shook his head, but she would not yet feel relief. They were outnumbered, and, she realized as several of the men drew pistols from their belts, outgunned. "Tell your English friend that we will shoot him and then you if he does not lower his weapon." Thalia had no choice but to convey the message.

Gabriel swore, but he could see, just as clearly as she could, that there was no way out of the situation. Everyone in their party was too tired and thirsty to put up much more than token resistance before being killed. With another oath, he lowered his rifle. Several of the men on camels dismounted and came forward, relieving everyone of their guns, then looked to the man who was plainly their leader.

"We are sent by no one but ourselves, and we would like to know," the man said, bending over his saddle with an assessing stare, "just *what* it is that makes you so worth pursuing."

The camp crouched in the maze of ravines, rising gold and red all around them. Winds had carved grooves into the cliffs, and sang through these ridges with an eerie, sad lament. As she, Gabriel, and the tribesmen slowly rode, the bandits behind them, pushing them forward, Thalia saw more men perched in these cliffs like nimble-footed goats. Goats who were also armed. She turned her gaze back toward the camp they approached.

"They don't know what the kettle is," Gabriel said lowly, glancing at his saddlebag where it lay. "Maybe we can give them something else."

"But what?" Thalia asked, also careful to keep her voice down. "All we have of value is the ruby." Glancing over at him, she realized that was exactly what he was thinking. She hissed, "We cannot! We swore to protect it."

"The Source, and our lives, come first," he pointed out, expression impassive. Thalia scowled, but he wouldn't be dissuaded. "I had to make these damned decisions almost every day when I was in the army. The greater good. The lesser of two evils, and all that tripe. But," he added, "as you've pointed out before, I'm muscle, and *you're* in charge of this mission. The final choice is yours."

"And you'd honor that choice?" She looked at him in disbelief.

"Your judgment is sound. However," he added, a corner of his mouth tilting up, "that doesn't mean I won't try to convince you otherwise, if you've made the wrong choice."

Thalia rolled her eyes. She should have known that, just because she and Gabriel had become lovers, he wouldn't surrender his military arrogance. "None of this matters," she said, "if we don't leave here soon. We could lose what lead we have on the Heirs."

"Might have an idea or two about that," Gabriel murmured.

They had reached the camp. Far from a civilized *ail,* with families and animals, this was a place of basic necessity only. Thalia saw no women, no children. Only men slung with bullets, gathered around fires and watching the newcomers, appraising. Their clothing was a mixture of Mongol, Chinese, and Russian, taken, obviously, from the few remaining traders and merchants that traversed the old silk trade routes. Camels, not horses, were the mounts of choice in such an arid place. Shelter was comprised of makeshift tents, rather than *gers.* Hard living for a harsh clime, and the men were just as remorseless.

She couldn't help but longingly stare at the bowls of tea the bandits drank, and the smell of roasting meat made her dizzy. Everyone dismounted, tensely watching one another. The leader of the bandits came forward. He was the same height as Thalia, but brawny, dark from the desert sky, and sharply intelligent. That mental agility glinted like obsidian in his eyes. He said something to another man nearby, who scuttled off quickly to do his bidding. "Have something to eat and drink," the bandit leader said. At Thalia's look of surprise, he said, laughing, "We are thieves, but we are Mongols, too. It's more wrong to deny a guest than to take their belongings."

They were herded toward a fire, where bowls of tea and meat were given to them. Gabriel eyed his suspiciously, and would not let her eat or drink until he saw some of the brigands eating and drinking the same food. "Strange code of honor," he said over the rim of his bowl. They both watched as their horses were given water.

Thalia, busy gulping tea down her parched throat, could only grunt in agreement. Nothing had ever tasted quite so wonderful. But as her thirst was quenched, trepidation took its place. The bandits were not friendly, open tribesmen of the steppe. They weren't even reserved but benign desert-dwelling nomads. For all her experience in Mongolia, as much as it was her home, she'd never had any interaction with men whose sole means of living was through thievery and other unsavory means. They could be capable of anything.

She glanced over at Gabriel, whose expression revealed nothing. Thalia tried to take some comfort in knowing that Gabriel probably had faced men such as these bandits many times over when he was in the army. She hoped he had some plan, because, short of bribing their way out of the bandits' lair with the ruby, Thalia could think of nothing to extract them. Catullus Graves, no doubt, would have created some terrifying new contraption within seconds from nothing more than a few rocks and a piece of mutton. Bennett Day would have charmed everyone, and soon had them telling bawdy stories of conquest over shared drinks of *arkhi*. But Catullus wasn't there—he was probably safe in Southampton, tinkering on his latest diabolical design—and neither was Bennett—sneaking out of some married woman's bedroom window, no doubt—so it was left to Thalia and Gabriel to escape unharmed on their own.

The leader of the bandits stood across the fire, lighting his pipe. After a few puffs, he said, "Now you must repay my generosity by telling me what those Englishmen and their army want with you."

Telling the truth was impossible. Fortunately, none of the tribesmen were willing to betray their precious cargo, and they kept silent, as did Thalia.

"A race," Gabriel said in Mongolian.

Quite possibly, Thalia was more surprised than anyone. Next, he would start tatting lace. "I didn't know you could speak Mongol," she said in English, turning to him.

He shrugged dismissively. "Been picking up a few words here and there. Always had a head for languages."

"What kind of race?" the bandit leader asked.

"Sponsored by a rich lord. For treasure," Gabriel answered. "Much treasure."

"Like this?" prompted the leader. He strode forward and, striking as quickly as a snake, plucked the ruby from Gabriel's jacket pocket. Thalia and the tribesmen all yelped in horror, but a quelling look from Gabriel held them all back.

"That is nothing," Gabriel said, indifferent. "Compared to what awaits."

The leader considered the glow of the fire through the ruby, casting deep red light across his face and beard. "Then you will tell me where the finish for this race is."

"At a temple."

"Which temple?"

Gabriel, as if he had all the time in creation and didn't care that the Heirs could ride up within moments, or that the bandits might slit their throats without hesitation, reached into his jacket. The bandits clustered around their leader tensed, but were held off by a restraining hand. Thalia thought she might shatter with tension. Gabriel wouldn't possibly try to shoot their way out with a hidden pistol, would he?

But all he produced from his pocket was a cheroot. He bent forward and lit it, as casually as if he was in the officers' club and not some brigands' encampment in the middle of the Gobi cliffs. Nothing could disrupt his sangfroid. After taking a few draws from the cheroot and exhaling the smoke, he reached out and offered it to the leader.

Intrigued, the man took it, still holding his pipe. He puffed on the cheroot, then, magnanimously, offered his pipe to Gabriel. With the same casual air, Gabriel took the pipe and placed the stem in his mouth. Such strange masculine courtesies that communicated worlds more than simple words.

"We need fresh mounts," Gabriel said around the stem. "Food and water. And we need to leave soon. Or we might lose the race." He breathed out a small cloud of smoke.

The bandit leader smiled, wry. "Ah, I see. We give you those things, and you tell us where to find the treasure." He took a few more puffs from the cheroot, then took it from his mouth and contemplated the smoldering tobacco. "This is very good. But I think I have a better idea."

"What's that?" Thalia couldn't stop herself from asking.

"My men and I will come with you."

The horses were freed to find their way home. How ridiculous was it that Thalia envied them? Fed and watered, the animals cantered away without sparing their former riders a single glance. She watched them go, coveting their liberty.

"We've exchanged one problem for another," she said to Gabriel as their baggage was transferred to camels. "Or rather, we now have a whole *new* problem, in addition to the Heirs."

"Always something," he commented. "Made a deal once with some Manipur warlords. Safe passage to Imphal in exchange for a case of Enfield rifles. A damned hard choice, but without them watching our backs, we'd never have made it."

"But we've no rifles or anything else to give this lot." Thalia indicated the milling group of brigands, who saddled their camels and prepared for a long journey. "Assuming they don't just slit our throats during the trip, once we get to the temple, they'll know they've been duped. Between the Heirs and these bandits, we're going to have a hell of a fight on our hands. What?" she asked, as Gabriel grinned at her.

Stepping in close, so that no more than an inch separated them, he said warmly, "I love it when you talk flinty."

"Skirmish," Thalia whispered, husky. "Trounce the bastards."

Under his lowered lids, his pupils dilated, and he slowly licked his lips. Despite the fact that they were standing in a bandits' encampment, the Heirs close behind them, and every part of her ached with weariness, Thalia wanted him so badly her knees shook. And not only because he was strong and alive and handsome, but because she was fully herself with him, and he didn't turn away. He embraced it, the whole of her. And wanted her, too.

Now, though, was not the time. Visibly collecting himself, he moved away. "The leader isn't trusting anyone with the ruby. He keeps it in his coat. I'm no pickpocket, so he's going to have to keep it for now."

"What if we made tea in the kettle and gave it to the bandits?" Thalia suggested. "The magic could distract them long enough for us to make an escape."

A corner of his mouth turned up. "Sounds good. After we give them the tea, you can suggest to them that they just start buggering each other so that the magic can take effect."

"Perhaps I'll formulate another plan," Thalia mumbled, reddening. She had no desire to see a brigand orgy.

His smile faded as he kept a watchful eye on their captors. "We might not be serving them tea, but I'm going to make sure nobody's filched the kettle," Gabriel said, then strode off.

Thalia, too, set to work. She ignored the stares of the bandits as she helped pack the camels, and, within the hour, everyone was on the road. Thalia hadn't much experience riding camels, but she soon grew used to the cantankerous beasts. Weaving their way through the labyrinth of canyons, they emerged into late afternoon, when the setting sun set the cliffs to flames and everything glowed like burning dreams. The sky, too, had caught fire as trails of golden fleece danced around the sun. In this light, Gabriel, riding beside her, his eyes shaded by the brim of his hat, was living myth.

The camels took the terrain better than horses. Rocky, dusty land flew beneath her as she rode. Having something decent to eat and drink had revived her considerably, and she took in the spare landscape with an appreciative eye. Gabriel looked over at her, and they exchanged smiles. It was absurd, but she was actually enjoying herself. It seemed that he was, too. Something must be wrong with them. Or perhaps, Thalia amended, other people were too tame in their needs for happiness.

This was no holiday, however. She, Gabriel, and the steppe tribesmen kept to themselves when it came time to stop for the night. More than once, the tribesmen muttered about the bandit chief possessing the ruby, but Gabriel assured them that he'd find some way to get it back. There was no way to know how long the brigands would be content simply to accompany them to the temple, rather than kill them and try to seize what valuables they could.

They watched as Altan, the bandits' leader, ordered his men around with the same directness and surety as any military officer.

"If he wasn't a bloodthirsty thief," Thalia whispered to Gabriel, "I'd say you two would have a jolly time together."

"I'll save my jolly for you, thanks all the same," he answered.

Over the evening meal, Thalia and Gabriel stayed close together while the bandits laughed and shared *arkhi*. "We could try to sneak away," she suggested, "after everyone goes to sleep."

"Men like these don't sleep all at once," Gabriel answered. "They'll keep watch."

Thalia noticed that some of the bandits were already asleep, camped a little ways from the communal fire. In a few hours, one of their comrades would wake them to take a later shift. Hell. "What if we got them drunk enough?"

He shook his head. "Even if we could get away, this desert is their home. They'd find us before we had time to wipe our noses."

"They can't come with us all the way to the temple," she protested, but she wasn't saying anything he had not already considered. Even though they were simply eating a meal at the end of a very long day, his mind was never at rest, always assessing, considering.

"I'll think of something."

"No," Thalia corrected. "*We* will."

His smile was private, meant for her alone. "We will, indeed."

She slept right beside Gabriel that night. He kept his arms wrapped around her, and even though he wasn't armed, Thalia knew he'd fight hard if anything happened to her during the night. She dreamt of kettles, rubies, and a golden lion, pacing back and forth without tiring.

When they woke the next morning, it was to news that the Heirs had been spotted by a scout a day's ride behind them. Somehow, their cloaking magic had stopped working, rendering them visible. But this was a small comfort, knowing how close they were. Which was worse? The known threat of the Heirs, or the unknown potential of Altan's men? If only she, Gabriel, and the tribesmen could elude the bandits, at least one threat could be eliminated. Yet escape seemed impossible, and they were too untrustworthy to try to forge a true alliance.

Opportunity came in a strange guise the following day. One moment, the entire group was riding their camels, the day placid and still. Within minutes, a fierce wind began to scour the dry, rocky plains. Thalia had no idea where it came from. It pulled like claws at their clothing and threatened to topple them from their saddles. She clung to the reins of her camel, ducking her head from the onslaught. Clouds of grit and dust scraped at any exposed skin. Gabriel gave Thalia a kerchief to wrap around her mouth and nose, while he took a spare shirt from his pack and used that to protect the lower half of his face. The brigands were well prepared, having lengths of fabric stuffed into their coats for just such an event.

Through the punishing winds, they continued on, until one of Altan's men turned and pointed. Everyone turned to look behind them.

"Oh, hell," Thalia said, but her words were lost in the wind.

A wall of flying sand hurtled toward them, billowing, as tall as a cliff and just as terrifying. Red and impenetrable, it bore toward them with an awful, quiet inevitability. A protean killer that had no body but was all sharp claws and teeth.

"The Heirs?" Gabriel called to her.

"No, just your average deadly sandstorm," she yelled back. "I don't think we can outrun it."

"Do what they're doing," he shouted back, pointing to Altan and his men, who were dismounting and making their camels sit. The large beasts folded their legs underneath themselves and tilted down until they were sitting upon the ground. Each camel's reins were staked to the ground. As if used to such storms, the bandits immediately hunkered in the lea of the camels, pulling their coats close to keep out the racing sand. The animals themselves didn't seem to mind the sand, viewing it with boredom through their long eyelashes.

The four tribesmen quickly imitated the bandits, sliding off of their camels and finding shelter in the creatures' bodies. Gabriel did the same, but Thalia could not get her blasted camel to cooperate. She wrestled with the stubborn animal, pulling on the lead ring in its nose to get it to sit, but she did not want to pull too hard and tear the ring right from the tender flesh. So she pushed. The camel bellowed at her, and if the wind had not been gusting so hard, she would have been covered with foamy camel spit. She desperately missed horses.

Glancing between the camel's humps, Thalia saw that the sandstorm was almost upon them. Cursing, tears torn from her eyes, she shoved and coaxed her mount. No doubt the bandits were having themselves a good laugh at her expense. Meanwhile, she could barely breathe or keep her eyes open.

Then Gabriel was beside her, taking the reins from her. "Sit your bloody arse down or I'll put a damned bullet in it," he roared at the camel.

The animal stared at him for a moment, and then placidly sat.

In the next moment, the sandstorm slammed into them. It hit like a million stinging wasps, biting without mercy at any unprotected flesh. Sight was nearly impossible. Even if she had been able to open her eyes fully, only a few feet would have been plainly visible. Everything else was swallowed in the crimson air.

Gabriel started to pull her down next to the camel, but they both stopped moving when an animal bawl rent the air, followed by a human scream. A bandit's camel, spooked by the storm, had torn itself free from its stake and galloped away into the punishing clouds of sand. But the camel's rider had tangled in the reins, and now dragged behind the animal as it ran in a panic. Thalia clutched at her throat. If the storm itself didn't kill the man, then tumbling and pounding across the rocky earth would. Altan and his men half-rose from behind their camels, clearly torn. Saving their comrade meant risking their own lives, or getting hopelessly lost in the disorienting blizzard of dust.

A hard hand shoved on Thalia's shoulder, pushing her behind the camel. "Don't move," Gabriel snarled at her, before he ran off, disappearing into the storm. She did not even have time to say no nor clutch at his sleeve. The sand had taken him.

He was a jelly-brained fool. What the hell compelled him to run into a sandstorm just to save the life of a thieving scoundrel who'd likely stab him in the throat, given the opportunity? He'd done it, just the same. Gabriel had made sure that Thalia was secure—at least *some* part of his mind was functioning properly—before rushing into what felt like the devil's breath, hot and brutal and capable of tearing flesh from bone.

Only the flood of water demons from the True Hammer of Thor came close to the torture of pushing through the swirling, howling sand. Gabriel ran, squinting into the red darkness, trying to pick out the terrified man's screams above the wind. Thank God his hearing was good. There. Faint and growing fainter. Instinct shoved Gabriel along, through the biting void, fighting to stay on his feet, until, yes, the form of the terrified camel came into view. His rider still skidded behind, but what condition the man was in, Gabriel had no way of knowing. Face and back probably cut to shreds by now. And he'd stopped hollering. Not a good sign.

Gabriel threw himself forward, grabbing hold of the camel's saddle. He dug his heels into the ground and pulled to the side with every ounce of strength he had left. The camel was young, saints be praised, and relatively small, so it stumbled when Gabriel pulled back. He shouted at it, though he hadn't a single idea what stream of abuse poured out of his mouth, all the while pulling to the side so that the camel moved in a circle. As soon as the animal began to slow, Gabriel pulled his knife from his belt and hacked at the reins tangled around the rider.

The man came free, going limp, at the same time that the camel decided it'd had enough running around. Gabriel wrapped one arm around the man, and was relieved to discover he was unconscious but alive. He looped his other arm around the camel's neck and tugged the beast down. It staggered, then sat.

Immediately, Gabriel crouched next to the camel, also pulling the insensible man into the shelter of the animal's body. He tugged the man's coat up, covering the brigand's face, before doing the same for himself. And that was how he spent the next who knows how long, tucked into himself like a giant tortoise, as the sandstorm continued to scream and tear.

Gabriel lost track of time, could hear only his own breathing and the roiling sand, as he waited and waited, and continued to wait some more. He hoped like hell that Thalia had been intelligent enough to sit out the storm, unlike his own moronic self. Jesus, if anything happened to her . . . No, he wouldn't let himself think about that; otherwise he'd do something even more stupid like dash off into the storm again, trying to find her, and get either lost or buried in the process.

After minutes, hours, or maybe even days, the winds calmed. Carefully, Gabriel unwound himself from his shroud and lifted his head. Sand poured from his shoulders. The swirling cloud of dust retreated toward the horizon as the sun reemerged. Gabriel checked the man next to him, relieved to see that not only was he relatively unharmed, save for a goodly sized black eye and cuts on his face, the bastard was snoring.

"Reveille," Gabriel growled, shaking the man awake.

The bloke blinked and slowly roused. When he realized that he was alive, he began babbling a stream of indecipherable words, throwing his arms around Gabriel.

"Don't need another sweetheart," Gabriel snapped, shoving the man away. He rose to his feet, and the man did the same. The camel stared at them both, chewing its cud, then continued to stare at the barren landscape. There had not been many landmarks even before the storm; the sand had further erased anything that might look familiar.

Gabriel looked up at the sun, then down at the earth, checking shadows. An hour. The whole damned thing had lasted only an hour. Before the sandstorm had hit, he'd made sure to check the position of the group, and now he drew upon his directional and tracking skills to get him and his new best chum back to their companions. There wasn't enough room for two on the camel's back, so both he and the other man had to walk as they set out to find everyone else.

Some half a mile later, he found them. Bless his beer, Thalia was with them, whole and well. The bandits had gotten back onto their camels, as had the tribesmen, but Thalia was not mounted. Altan was yelling something at her, and she was shaking her head, her feet planted, refusing to get into the saddle. She was shouting something back at him. Then a few of the brigands caught sight of Gabriel and their compatriot and began shouting all at once. Everyone turned, including Thalia. She ran toward him.

"Lost my damned hat," he started to say, before she launched herself at him. Already weary from fighting the storm, not to mention wrestling with a camel, Gabriel almost lost his footing as her arms wrapped around him. She gripped him tightly, her body shuddering. A soft stream of Mongolian bubbled from her lips, and though he didn't catch all the words, he knew words of thanks just the same.

"It's all right, sweetheart," he murmured as his own arms came up. "I'm—ow!"

She'd punched him. In the shoulder. Hard.

"Did the wind blow away your damn *mind?*" she shouted. "Don't ever do anything that stupid again!"

"No promises about my stupidity," he said. "You giving me orders?"

Her lovely face was tear-streaked and furious. "I'll bloody well tie you to the sodding ground, you mad, brave idiot!" She started to stomp away. "Lord protect me from heroes!"

He didn't let her get very far. One hand shot out, grabbed her arm, and pulled her back, hauling her against him. She began to launch into another string of abuse. His mouth on hers prevented it.

The hooting of the bandits brought them back to their surroundings, and then only after a goodly while. Breaking the kiss, Gabriel saw that the whole company was watching him and Thalia with enormous grins plastered on their faces, like fond uncles at a wedding. Christ, what he wouldn't give for a quiet, dark room with a bed and plenty of privacy.

Altan walked his camel to where Thalia and Gabriel stood, with the man Gabriel had rescued trotting beside. The bandit chief looked at Gabriel for a few moments. Gabriel stared back, keeping one arm tight around Thalia's waist.

"You did not need to do that," Altan said at last. "We would not have endangered our lives to save you."

"I know."

"Foolish. We are your captors."

"He would have died unless someone did something."

"And that someone was you."

Gabriel shrugged. "You all seemed pretty busy protecting your own arses."

Altan barked out a laugh. "That is our first rule. But, it seems, not yours." He glanced at his men behind him. "None of them have your courage."

"You need to find better men."

"Or make better allies." Shaking his head, Altan reached

into his *del* and produced the ruby. He tossed it to Gabriel, who caught the large gem with one hand. "There is no race."

"No." Gabriel slipped the ruby into the inside pocket of his jacket. He did not miss the looks of relief exchanged by the tribesmen.

"Nor treasure."

"Not exactly."

"Yet you are chased, just the same."

"We are trying to protect something more valuable than the ruby, to take it someplace where it will be safe," Thalia said. She wiped her wet cheeks on the sleeve of her *del,* erasing the traces of her relief and terror. She displayed more resilience than most men Gabriel knew. He didn't quite understand how fate had been so kind to him. "But," she continued, "if it falls into the hands of those men who pursue us, you will lose it all. The freedom you love. Your control over your own destiny. They will take everything that gives you pride."

Altan tugged on his moustache while he contemplated this. His eyes scanned the northern horizon, seeing things even an experienced tracker like Gabriel never could. As much as Gabriel admired the unsparing landscape of the desert, the rolling steppes called to him more. Maybe because the steppe was Thalia's home and always would be.

"Go on, then," Altan said, tugging the reins of his camel so that he walked back toward his gathered men. He shouted something at a handful of his men, and they dismounted, carrying several packs. The men handed the packs to Gabriel. He opened them and found the kettle and all of their pistols and knives. Two more men came forward and handed Gabriel and Thalia their confiscated rifles. Gabriel carefully checked each and every gun to ensure they were still loaded. With an inward sigh of relief, he strapped on his revolver, sheathed his knife, and shouldered his rifle. Thalia and the tribesmen did the same.

"Go save the world," Altan said.

"Are you setting us free?" Thalia asked.

"Free?" Altan repeated, shifting in his saddle so he looked at them. "Yes, you can go free." He turned back to his men and said something so quickly, Gabriel couldn't translate it. Whatever it was, the men agreed to it, and with great enthusiasm.

No point in questioning the gift. Gabriel and Thalia hurried to their camels, mounted, and, after Gabriel rechecked their position, started in the direction of the temple. Hopefully, it wasn't more than another day or two away. The kettle hadn't been forthcoming in mundane details like distance. Whatever the distance, Gabriel wanted it traversed speedily. The storm might have bought them more time—with any luck, the bleeding Heirs were buried under mountains of sand, though that happy outcome was unlikely—yet if they did make it to the temple before the Heirs caught them, it still wouldn't be time enough to prepare for a siege. If the temple still stood, Gabriel wondered how many monks were there, and if any of them were fit for battle. He prayed that was the case. Otherwise it would be him, Thalia, and four herdsmen against an entire army.

Thalia, Gabriel, and their companions began to ride south. But they were making a hell of a lot more noise than a handful of camels might. Gabriel looked over his shoulder. Altan and his men rode with them. The whole pack of brigands rode along, peaceful as lambs.

"This does not feel very free," Gabriel said to Altan.

"Oh, you have your liberty," the bandit chief answered. "But my men and I have decided that we are fond of our own freedom, as well. So we will help you in your task. Besides," he added with a wry smile, "when I asked if there was treasure, you said, 'Not exactly,' which is better than 'No.'"

"The men that chase us are killers," Gabriel said.

"So are we. In fact, we are very good at it. And, in truth," he admitted, "we have been a bit bored with our prey. They put up so little fight."

"If you join us," Gabriel warned, "you will have plenty to fight."

Altan grinned. "Good." He kicked his camel so that the beast broke into a canter. "I hope it will be soon," he called over his shoulder.

It was Thalia's soft chuckle that next commanded Gabriel's attention. She wasn't fearful, or angry or even annoyed. No, she was actually *amused*. He looked at her, and she saw the question in his eyes.

"Men," she said, rueful, "are the most absurd creatures on this green earth."

"But there are camels," Gabriel pointed out.

"Believe me," she answered, "I've taken camels into consideration."

Chapter 16

Oasis

He'd had enough. Since Gabriel had saved the life of their comrade, the brigands had treated him like a lost brother, urging food and *arkhi* on him with abandon. Thalia and the steppe tribesmen weren't neglected, and given more than their share, but it was Gabriel who held pride of place around the campfire. His Mongol wasn't strong enough to keep up with the endless male bluster that comprised most fireside talk. Still, it satisfied the bandits' needs, so they could laugh and cuff each other like friendly bears.

But this had been going on for hours. Meanwhile, the night was growing darker and a quiet Thalia sat close, her legs touching his. In the glow of the firelight, the dusky desert behind her, she shined with beauty like an elemental fairy. Time in the Gobi sun had gilded her skin, and strands of copper and chestnut glimmered in her dark hair. He swayed precariously close to losing his wits if he didn't have some time alone with her.

Yet, no matter how jovial the bandits were, Gabriel hadn't any certainty that their allegiance would not change as quickly as the wind changed directions. Getting up from the fire with Thalia in tow might rile Altan and his men, something that they needed to avoid. So, like a boy stuck in a classroom, agonizing after a girl in the front row, Gabriel sat and ached. He tried to turn his thoughts to the mission.

"Tell me what you know about the monastery where we are heading," he said to Altan. "You have heard of it?"

The bandit chief mulled, tugging on his beard. "Yes, but it has always been too far away for our interests."

"So, it still stands?" asked Thalia.

Altan nodded. That was a relief. "It is called the Monastery of the Mountain. An isolated place. Only a few pilgrims go there."

"It must be rather empty," Thalia remarked.

"I do not think so," Altan said. "Some of my brother bandits tell me that several dozen monks live at the monastery, those that want to be far from the world."

Gabriel mulled over this, considering what it meant for their future battle site. It was hard, though, to concentrate on anything besides the hunger for Thalia that pulsed through him.

"Are the *arkhi* and mutton not to your liking?" Altan demanded during a lull.

Gabriel immediately drained the skin he'd been given. The potent alcohol left a trail of heat in his throat. "Both are good. Damned better than the weak stuff served to me by the Maharajah of Kalam."

Altan nodded with approval, glad to have bested a maharajah in something so important.

"Our Englishman has another hunger," chortled another bandit, flicking his eyes toward Thalia.

Gabriel fought the urge to leap up and grab the leering bastard by his throat. Thalia seemed more sanguine, saying nothing but smiling a little. Her smile, Gabriel noticed, showed a hint of strain in the corners.

"Do you know, I was born in the Gobi and have never left it, not once," Altan said suddenly.

"It is a beautiful place." Gabriel thought it best to be as complimentary as possible, even though he had no idea why the bandit chief thought to mention this not particularly interesting fact about his upbringing.

"A beautiful bitch," Altan agreed. "One moment, she will flay you with her claws, and the next, she welcomes you into her soft cunt."

The crude language didn't bother Thalia in the slightest. She didn't stiffen or act insulted. Gabriel could have told the brigands that she wasn't a woman who shocked easily, something he liked beyond measure.

"For example," Altan continued, "just today, that sandstorm wanted to rip us apart and would have killed stupid Dorj here if you had not come to his aid. And yet," the chief went on, "not but a few hundred yards south of here is a small oasis, a little sheltered spot hidden amongst the rocks."

This sounded rather promising. "Why are we not camped there?"

"It is not large enough to hold more than two people."

"Sheltered," Gabriel mused aloud.

"Private." Altan did not smile, but it was clear in his voice. "And safe."

He'd suffer the consequences, if there were any. But that was doubtful. Altan was giving Gabriel a gift. He wasn't so thick-skulled to refuse a present. Gabriel took Thalia's hand and rose to his feet. The revolver still hung from his belt, and he had a knife, as well. If anything happened, he would be prepared.

Looking up, Thalia saw the intent in Gabriel's eyes, and stood. Her own eyes glittered, fire-warmed emeralds, as her grip tightened in his.

"Good night," Gabriel said to Altan.

The chief nodded and drew on his pipe, keeping silent.

As Thalia and Gabriel left the group, knowing laughs and some coarse words trailed behind them, but neither he nor she paid attention. Gabriel collected the kettle, the ruby, and a blanket from the packs while Thalia waited, then, claiming her hand again, he strode off with her into the dusk.

They didn't speak as they walked. Already, breath came fierce and fast in his chest. In the darkness, he could not see Thalia's face, but heard her shallow breathing, felt heat suffuse her hand. Jesus, he wasn't even sure they could make it as far as the oasis.

Nimble as mountain sheep, they leapt over the rocks, sometimes stopping to help one another traverse a particularly uneven bit, seldom letting go of one another unless absolutely necessary. The going was slower than Gabriel would've wanted, his anticipation already priming him like a pistol. Better to tread carefully than risk a twisted ankle. If only he had the power of flight, just to speed them on their way. At least his eyesight was well adjusted to the darkness, so that everything became shades of gray and purple, including Thalia, a shapely form keeping pace alongside him.

"Oh, thank Tenger," she breathed. "I thought we'd never get here."

The rocks encircled a pool, no bigger than a *ger,* with grasses and a few saxaul trees rustling softly in the breeze as they gathered close to the water. The banks surrounding the pool were narrow and pebbled. Overhead, the dark blue bowl of the sky reached infinity, evening stars coming out like coy birds. Altan was right. There was only enough room for two people. The rocks that surrounded the oasis couldn't be traversed by a camel or horse. Anyone approaching would be heard. Utter privacy, for once. Merciful bloody heavens.

Gabriel leapt down from the rocks into the enclosure. He set down the blanket, kettle, and ruby, then turned, placing his hands on Thalia's waist. He swung her down to join him. Once her boots touched the ground, he didn't release her. She twined her arms over his shoulders, pulling herself against him, and the moment their bodies touched, desire exploded.

They took each other's mouths, open, withholding nothing. It really was a taking, no use trying to make it sound pretty or delicate. Two people prodigiously hungry for each other. He stroked her mouth, its warm, willing sweetness, and she touched her tongue to his without restraint. He felt the slim strength of her waist and lower back. Just there, that small dip of her spine. He wanted to lick it. Gabriel pressed her close, and she made a sound that had only one meaning: more.

Stepping back, Gabriel pulled at his clothing. Everything came off. Thalia, clever and avid, did the same. All the while, they stared at each other, at their bodies being revealed, garment by garment. Soon, a pile of their combined clothes formed on the bank of the pond. She was a tall woman, but her clothing looked so delicate and feminine beside his own, and something as ordinary as her sock became ethereal and tender when draped over his rough leather boot.

When they were both completely naked, Thalia started toward him, but he shook his head and began backing toward the pond with his hands outstretched.

"Am I so bedraggled that you won't touch me unless I bathe?" she asked, wry.

"I want to clean you." His voice was barely more than a growl. "Everywhere."

With deliberate steps, Thalia followed him into the pond, her hair dark and loose over her bare shoulders, brushing over the pink tips of her breasts. The water touched his ankles, and it was cool, almost bracing, but she kept coming toward him, so that when the water reached his calves, then higher up his thighs, he barely felt it. It was only her he knew.

They were both in the pond now, the water reaching their bellies. It was a measure of how much he wanted her that his cock did not flag or shrink in the chilly water, but stood upright, reaching for her. Thalia tried to take hold of him, but he edged away.

"I'll see to you first," he said.

Cupping his hands, he filled them with water, then poured it onto her shoulder. She gave a small shriek and laughed. "Ah, that's cold!" She hit the water with a palm, splashing him.

So much for tender, worshipful ministrations. He should have known Thalia wouldn't submit like some untouchable temple priestess. She was a witch taking a lover to invoke lusty magic, far too earthy for distant worship.

Gabriel splashed her back, dragging his fist through the water. Thalia stared at him, then pushed both hands across the surface of the pond, soaking his chest. In moments, they chased each other around the pond, dashing water back and forth. They laughed and taunted like children. Soon, neither noticed the temperature of the water. Gabriel hadn't played like this since he was a lad swimming in the quarry pool. It was bloody marvelous.

Both of them sopping, Gabriel lunged. Thalia yelped as he snared her legs. They both toppled completely into the water, submerging briefly. When they came back to the surface, they twined and sported like otters, swimming in the shallow pond in a tangle of wet limbs. When Thalia tried to grab him to duck his head underwater, he seized her wrists and hauled her against him. Then he kissed her.

Hot, so hot, her mouth. For long minutes, they kissed as water swirled around them. Thalia kissed as though there was nothing else on earth that gave her more pleasure, and only he could give it to her. He stroked her sleek body, she caressed him, pressing the wet flesh of her breasts into his chest, her nipples taut points brushing against him, erasing thought. When she wrapped her legs around his waist, the heat of her sex cupping his rigid, pounding erection, he groaned.

Gabriel scooped her up and strode from the pond, water

churning around him. He set her down just long enough to unfold the blanket. She didn't wait to be invited. Thalia lay herself down and held her arms out to him. But he had plans.

He knelt between her legs, his hands spreading her thighs. She raised herself up on her elbows to look at him with wide, aroused eyes. "Been wanting to do this since I saw you wearing only a blanket and a blush," he rumbled. And before she could say anything, he lowered his head.

"Gabriel," she cried as his tongue touched her. "God!"

The pond hadn't washed away her desire. She was slick and full and tasted of sweet midnight. Gabriel traced the shape of her lips, delved deeper, pushing his tongue inside her, then out, swirling over the firm bud of her clit. He held her down as she thrashed against him, barely able to keep screams from uncoiling deep in her throat. Her legs draped over his shoulders, her heels pressing into his back as she arched up from the blanket. He reached up and rubbed the tips of her breast, and she gasped, thrusting her chest high. He could come from this alone.

"Stop, stop," she mewled.

He immediately stilled, looking up with her juices glistening on his mouth and chin. "What is it, love?"

"I want to try," she panted. "I want you in my mouth." His cock jumped. Thalia lifted herself up and began crawling to him. She pushed him down onto the blanket. He went willingly.

Thalia knelt between his legs as he had hers. She stared at his impatient cock, licking her lips. "Tell me what to do," she breathed.

"Take it," he rasped, "take it in your hand. That's right . . . oh, Jesus. Now, run your hand up and down. You can go harder than that. Yes." He tried, without much success, to keep his head up so he could watch her. She looked so incredible, his cock in her hand, her eyes glazed but sharp with lust. It didn't take her long at all to find the right pressure, the right rhythm.

"When can I take you in my mouth?"

"Now . . . now would be good. Start with your tongue. The head. That's the most sensitive." He groaned as her tongue flicked out to twirl around his penis, lapping at the fluid that leaked from the tip. Up and down she licked him, as if he was barley candy, while her hand stroked him. "Bloody Christ. Holy God."

"I want you *in* my mouth," she said between tonguings around him.

"Yes, in."

She went slowly, adjusting to the feel of his cock in her mouth, first the head and then, when she grew more bold, further. When he felt himself engulfed in the heat of her, her tongue wrapped against his shaft, Gabriel's hips bucked. "Fucking hell!"

He felt her smile around him. "Such language."

"I can't—ah, sweet Jesus—stop." He gritted his teeth as she sucked, pulling at him, giving him an incredible pleasure he'd never experienced. Gabriel propped himself on his elbows, needing to see her, desperate for the sight of her lips wrapped around him. He swore again as he saw her thighs rubbing against each other while she sucked his cock. She wanted touching there.

"I'll do that," he growled.

Thalia lifted her head, dazed, but understood readily when Gabriel pulled her up and turned her around. He lay on his back and she straddled him, her thighs on either side of his head. She faced his legs. With shaking hands, he gripped her thighs and lowered her closer to his mouth. At the feel of his tongue against her folds, Thalia gasped, then sank down, taking his penis back into her mouth.

God, he was so close. So close. He tried to concentrate, licking, suckling, drawing on her clit, her pussy so unfathomably wet, so beyond delicious. He'd never heard a sound so wonderful as Thalia screaming her climax around his cock. But he wasn't satisfied. Not until she screamed again, and again, panting around him. When the last tremor subsided, Gabriel flipped her onto her back, placed himself between her legs, and plunged into her with one, fierce thrust. She bowed up from the blanket, moaning.

He showed no mercy, not to her nor to himself, as he fucked her with hard, deep strokes. Thalia writhed and clawed, wrapping her legs around his waist, unable to form words except long trills of sound. Gabriel pounded into her, giving her everything. "So good," he rumbled. "Goddamn it."

Wrapping one arm around her waist, the other hand braced against the ground, raised up on his knees, Gabriel held Thalia tight and let his body speak what he never could articulate with enough satisfaction. Inside her. Forever. That's all he wanted. That's where he belonged.

Thalia screamed once more, clenching around him. Then his climax hit him, so hard he almost lost consciousness. Anyone within miles could hear him, but he didn't bloody care. He cared for only one thing, one person, and she was beneath him, singing out her own pleasure.

"Thalia," he gasped. "I love you. I love you so goddamn much."

He kept himself from collapsing on top of her, but only barely. She sighed when they rolled onto their sides, facing each other, with him still inside of her.

The sun had long since set, but she glowed, as brilliant as her soul. She trailed her fingers through his damp hair. "Gabriel, my warrior," she murmured. "I never knew I could love anyone the way I love you."

"And how is that?" he asked, languorous but exhilarated by their declarations.

She pressed kisses against his jaw and snuggled close. "Without fear."

But as they drifted in a dream bliss, Gabriel could not say

the same. He loved her. She loved him. And that scared the hell out of him.

Neither Thalia nor Gabriel were quite ready to return to the encampment, so they wrapped themselves in the blanket, body pressed to body, warm and alive in the shelter of the rocks. Full night had fallen. She wasn't sure how long they had been at the oasis—time seemed to lose its weight. Minutes, or years. It didn't matter to her.

"Why did you join the army?" she asked. He was snug against her back, cupped, with his arms around her waist, his wonderful rough hands stroking the curve of her belly. Thalia felt such peace, such rightness, being with him this way.

She felt his breath in her hair as he spoke. "Not much choice in Brumby. Work in the mines, or don't work at all. I was lucky to go to school most days instead of working in the pit, like other children."

"I don't know much about coal mining," Thalia admitted. "Sounds . . . dark."

"And dangerous, and filthy. There were floods, collapses, explosions. The chokedamp and afterdamp that could kill if you breathed it." His voice sounded flat, as if he was used to such horror. "So I enlisted after my da died. He was my last family."

Thalia shuddered to think of Gabriel, who radiated light and life, shut down into sunless mines where every moment was peril. She knew that in the army he faced danger nearly every day, but there was something so relentless and futile about clawing fuel from the depths of the earth, where the enemy wasn't another country's soldiers, but the work itself.

Whatever darkness took him, she wanted to chase it back. "You must have liked the army, to stay for so long."

"Well enough. Fine days and bad, like anything. Sometimes, I do miss it. I didn't like killing, but I liked being on missions, having a purpose. And the day-to-day life could be good. I remember," he said, growing a bit more relaxed, "think it was in Nagpur, and the rains had come. Months and months of it. Hard to imagine in a place like this."

"I like being wet with you."

Gabriel's eyes glittered with hunger. "This won't be the last time, sweetheart."

Her body, much as she wanted him again, was spent. She tried to turn the conversation back. "So, the rains in India?"

He understood her tiredness. "Months of this, constant rain, and we were ready to lose our taffy. One day, me and Lieutenant Carlyle start thinking of everything we're going to do once the rain stops. Things outside. Paint a picture. Write a letter. Tune a piano."

"Do you know how to tune a piano?"

"I'd learn, just so I could do it outside."

He puzzled her, after all this time, but in a way that delighted her. "So, did you learn?"

"No. But this went on a while, Carlyle and me trying to top each other with our after-the-monsoon plans, until somebody, Reynolds, I think, told us to either get off our arses and *do* something, or shut our gobs. So we went out and played football. After a bit, some more men came out and joined us. Sepoys, too."

"In the rain?"

"In the rain. The pitch was muddy."

"Who won?"

"My team. Made Carlyle polish my boots every evening for a month."

"That doesn't sound so bad."

"With his pillowcase."

Thalia heard herself actually giggle, for the first time in years. "I hope you got them good and grimy."

"Always walked through the stables before coming back to my quarters."

Now she shook with laughter, and Gabriel joined her. It felt so good, to share this with him. When he'd first come into her father's *ger* in Urga, Thalia never would have suspected he could be this light, this playful, yet the more she learned about him, the more she felt right in giving him her love. She felt light, too, having at last spoken of her feelings to him. And he loved her. *Loved* her. Such a blessing.

"I can't believe I can get a laugh out of you, talking about muddy football and horseshit," Gabriel chuckled.

"Doesn't speak very highly of me," Thalia said wryly. She felt herself turned so that she faced Gabriel, and, even in the dark of night, his eyes burned golden and serious.

"I'm a bloody lucky bugger," he said with a guttural rasp. "A rough soldier who's known little of softness or niceness. Never thought I'd find a woman I could talk to without making a complete ass of myself. But you don't expect me to have dainty manners, and you even like being with me, just as I am." He sounded genuinely surprised, and he was not a man to devalue himself.

"Just as you are," she repeated solemnly, then kissed him, her hands on the archangel sculpture of his cheekbones. "I never thought I would find the same, either."

"Any man would be daft not to want you."

Her laugh was low and rueful. "Wanting and loving are very different. I know that men can *want* quite easily."

Gabriel muttered something about Russian bastards that needed castrating.

"Yes, him," Thalia said, rather appallingly pleased with his desire for vengeance on her behalf, "but most others, too."

"Your father is so honest with you?"

"Oh, no. He never wanted to remarry after my mother died, and he had plenty of opportunity. And when it came time to discuss . . . family matters . . ." She grimaced. "I think he was more embarrassed than I. But most of my friends are male, and they've been good enough to be candid about themselves. And their appetites. Which almost never include things beyond the most basic and physical. Whenever I see Bennett—"

"Who?" Gabriel demanded.

Thalia kissed him again. "Bless you for your jealousy. But I've known Bennett Day since I was fourteen. He's a Blade. He could have very easily been recruited to the Heirs. Extraordinary with maps and codes, and from a good family, too. And, to my father's unending disappointment, but vicarious thrill, the worst libertine. By 'worst,' I mean successful and unrepentant. God, the stories Bennett tells over pipes late into the night. My father always sends me to bed so my delicate ears aren't harmed, but I listen outside."

"Burgess should keep you locked up whenever that Day is around," Gabriel grumbled.

"To Bennett, I'm more of a younger sister than potential seduction," she said. "And, though I admit to a small childish infatuation with him when I was around sixteen, I've not once been tempted, nor has he tried. He's perfectly happy moving from one conquest to another. I wish I could say that, underneath it all, he's desperately lonely, but that isn't the case."

Gabriel rolled onto his back, pulling Thalia with him so she lay partially atop him. He ran his hands up and down her back, and she shivered with pleasure at his touch. "Not every man is like this Day bloke."

"Thank God for that. Or we would be faced with a population explosion." She let her hands drift over the healthy brawn of his chest, feeling the dusting of hair, the puckered flesh of scars. The body of a man who'd lived with energy and purpose, and would continue to do so. At least, as long as circumstances kept him alive. It was horrible that, possibly within a day, the Heirs would do everything in their power to crush out Gabriel's life, and hers. Horrible for so many reasons.

"Thalia," Gabriel said, "I'm not the sort of man who's ever had to think of anybody but himself."

"You're not selfish, if that's what you're saying."

"Maybe not. But what I mean is"—he turned his head to look at her—"what I mean is, I don't mind the battle that's ahead, but the thought of your being hurt or worse—"

"That's not going to happen," she said immediately.

He shook his head. "Years of combat taught me. I can fight and fight, but that might not be enough." His voice rusted and caught, but he cleared his throat. "Now that I've found you, it scares me witless to think of anything happening. To you. I'm not used to being . . . afraid."

A sudden realization came to her. "So this is love," she said quietly. "The daily prospect of joy or disaster."

For a long time, neither of them spoke as they considered this, touching each other with gentle caresses. Then touch warmed, grew heated. Her tired body revived itself. Gabriel's hands moved from her back to cup the curves of her bottom while her hands also moved down, from his chest to lower, where she wrapped her fingers around his stiffening erection. He stroked her breast and between her legs, and soon they were both gasping. Wordlessly, Thalia mounted him, thrusting him deep inside of her, wanting to take him as far into her as she could, as if there was a place, protected by the intimate bond of their joining, where they could take shelter and know with conviction that they would share tomorrow, and the day after that, and the day after that, and all the days that followed.

There was no certainty to be found, but as their bodies and hearts moved together, pleasure overtaking them both, Thalia hoped that even this small moment of rapture caught the dispassionate gaze of the world's magic, and that, somehow, there might be just enough enchantment to keep her and Gabriel safe.

Chapter 17

A Good Place to Stand and Fight

The rider approached, and his face looked grim. As he neared the waiting group, he shook his head.

"They are no more than a day behind us," he said. "And their numbers are growing."

"Is your friend sure?" Gabriel asked.

The rider looked over his shoulder, to where another man on camelback rode away. "He saw them himself, and his cousin did, as well. There are over a hundred men now. Impossible to miss on these gravel-covered plains."

Yes, the huge stretches of barren expanse would do little to hide an advancing army. And there was no way for Gabriel to hide the tracks of his party. Everything stirred up dust, making their trail blaze like lightning. If they could outrun the Heirs, it would only lead them straight to a battle. He glanced at the assembled group. Two dozen brigands, four tribesmen, himself and Thalia. Against over a hundred. Possibly the monks at the monastery might fight, but Gabriel couldn't count on that. He'd faced tough odds before. But he'd never gone up against an enemy that not only outnumbered his own forces, but had magic as a weapon.

"And the monastery?"

"It is known as Sha Chuan Si, and it is fifteen miles from here, so says my kinsman."

"Can we do it?" Thalia asked. She tried to keep the worry from her voice, but wasn't completely successful.

He turned to her, and there it was. The sweet, sharp pain of loving her in the midst of madness. "We will," he answered, and had to believe it or else lose his mind. "But we ride hard."

"I thought we had been," she said, her smile weary.

"A Sunday promenade, compared to what we have to do." When she nodded, he put his heels to his camel. Altan and his men immediately followed.

As they rode, Gabriel's mind filled with a hundred different scenarios. If the Heirs overtook them en route. If they reached the temple but could not get inside. If they could get inside but the monks conspired against them. If the monks would not fight. If the monks would fight. The permutations were endless. And through it all, Gabriel twisted his insides, trying to figure how he could keep Thalia safe throughout all this. She wouldn't agree to shutting herself up in some locked room while a battle raged around her. He loved her for her fighting spirit, but that same spirit put her in harm's way.

No. He had to turn his thoughts to something else. So he reviewed past sieges, trying to find the best possible strategy.

Midday came and went, and they stopped briefly to rest the already tired camels. The sturdy beasts were being pushed to their limits. One of them had already died earlier that morning from the hard pace, and a pack camel had taken its place. After everyone shared a quick meal, it was back into the saddle. Gabriel estimated they'd traveled over ten miles.

"Not too much farther," he said to Thalia.

"You're an optimist at heart," she answered.

"If I was an optimist, then I'd say that not only was the temple close, but that they likely had fifty cannons, two hundred rifles, and a huge canopied bed."

"A bed won't do much in a battle."

"I'm thinking about after."

She smiled wickedly as her cheeks flushed. "I'm beginning to embrace positive thinking myself."

As she rode ahead, Altan drew up alongside Gabriel. "Are most white women like her?" the bandit chief asked. "If so, perhaps I should consider moving west. Or go to Russia."

"You won't find *any* other woman like her," Gabriel said tightly. He didn't care for the way Altan looked at Thalia, not so much a leer as speculation. If Gabriel had his way, he'd make the whole damn party wear blinders.

"That is too bad," Altan said. "Is she for sale?"

"You *do* want to keep your testicles," Gabriel replied. "Or maybe you want to wear them as jewelry."

Altan chuckled. "Fair enough. But if you change your mind—" He broke off when Gabriel stared at him. "Ah. You mean it."

"And tell your men."

"Judging by the way you look at her, they already know."

"Oh, thank Tenger," Thalia sighed hours later. "We made it."

Gabriel kept his relief in check as he surveyed their destination. He wasn't certain that the monks would even let them inside the front gate, let alone let them use their monastery as the location of the upcoming stand against the Heirs. Assuming that the monks did welcome them and were somehow willing to take on the Heirs, the monastery of Sha Chuan Si was formidable and well-situated. All the gilded temples in Urga, even the busy sprawl of Erdene Zuu, couldn't equal the impressive sight of the desert monastery perched at the summit of a broad, flat-topped rock. Though other large rocky outcroppings rose nearby, the temple on its hill stood alone, the square fist of man in the middle of stark wilderness. Wide, dun-colored walls surrounded the temple, topped by curved red Chinese roofs. A tall, round tower stood just inside the front wall. A single steep escarpment led up the side of the rock to a giant, heavy door. Gabriel saw no windows, either. It seemed impenetrable.

"A good place to stand and fight," he said to Thalia and Altan.

"Hopefully, our welcome will be a little less fearsome than the building itself," Thalia answered.

"Do you speak Chinese?" Gabriel asked.

"A little."

Gabriel turned to Altan. "And you and your men?"

"We can say, 'Throw down your weapons,'" Altan replied.

"I'll need you to translate," Gabriel said to Thalia.

There would be no hiding their approach. As the camels struggled up the slope, getting closer to the front gate, Gabriel saw several shaved heads peering at them quizzically over the top of the wall. Judging by the number of guns his party carried, they couldn't be mistaken for pilgrims, unless pilgrims judged devotion by number of bullets.

Once they were a few dozen yards away, Gabriel dismounted. "I need you and your men to stay back," he said to Altan.

Grumbling, the bandit chief and his men obeyed.

Thalia and the tribesmen stayed close and dismounted. Gabriel tucked the wrapped kettle under his arm, put the ruby in his pocket, and kept one hand resting on the butt of his revolver. It might not be the most friendly stance, but he was willing to make a bad impression to save lives.

Thalia walked beside him as they neared the massive gate. He resisted the urge to take her hand, since he needed to keep himself ready for any possibility, but he wanted her close.

"It's very quiet," she murmured. Their boots on the gravel crunched loudly. "Should we be concerned?"

"Always."

"Not particularly reassuring."

"Realistic."

Nearing the thick wooden gate, he saw there was a small door set into the surface. No doubt to make entering and exiting easier. He didn't like simply approaching head on, it was too vulnerable a position, but there was no other choice. Just as he wondered whether he was supposed to knock, the small door opened. But instead of a monk waiting for them, they were met by a white man. In English clothing.

Gabriel immediately pulled his revolver. Too bloody late. Somehow the Heirs had gotten to the temple ahead of them.

Then Thalia yelled, bolted from his side and ran toward the man. Jesus, did she think to tackle the bloke herself? "Wait, damn it!" Gabriel shouted, but she flung herself at the Englishman, throwing her arms around him. "Get out of the way!"

Thalia glanced over her shoulder at Gabriel, the smile on her face freezing. "Put the gun away, Gabriel," she said with enforced calm. She let her arms fall from the Englishman's shoulders. Gabriel was aware of other people coming through the temple door, but he remained focused on the Englishman, who was smiling with remarkable good humor, considering he had a revolver pointed at his handsome face.

"A new friend, Thalia?" the unknown man asked with a quirked brow.

"Who the hell are you?" Gabriel demanded.

Thalia took the stranger's hand and drew him forward, reaching toward Gabriel with the other. As politely as if they in a drawing room, she said, "Bennett, may I introduce Captain Gabriel Huntley, late of Her Majesty's Thirty-third of Foot. Gabriel, this is Bennett Day. Of the Blades of the Rose."

"A pleasure, I'm sure," murmured Day as he held out his free hand, though he didn't release Thalia.

"The libertine?" Gabriel asked, turning to Thalia. She reddened, but Day laughed.

"Is that what they call me? What a charming name. Most people just call me bastard."

Gabriel grudgingly gave Day his hand to shake, eyeing the man without attempting to hide his mistrust. He didn't quite have Gabriel's height, but he was a pretty collection of bones, dark haired, light eyes, and built like a boxer. Day might smile and twinkle like a beau, but Gabriel didn't doubt he could lay out a decent right hook. His grip was strong enough.

Day turned to Thalia with an easy smile that probably charmed scores of women. "Desert living must agree with you, Thalia. You look positively radiant."

She made a face while Gabriel considered how far down the man's throat his foot might go. "You mean, I look sunburned and haggard," she corrected.

"A bit more golden, perhaps—" Day conceded, "but lovely, just the same. Or perhaps"—he turned a considering eye to Gabriel—"it isn't the desert, so much as the company."

Thalia must have sensed how close Gabriel was to pummeling Day, because she quickly changed the subject. "What are you doing here?" Even though it was a perfectly ordinary question, it rankled a bit to see how much pleasure Day's presence gave her. This was the man she had admitted to fancying once. The man who bedded women as often as most men put on their boots. Who still held her hand.

"Your father sent us," Day answered.

"Us?" Gabriel repeated.

"Yes, us," said a deep voice behind them.

Everyone turned, and Thalia let out another girlish yell to see the newcomer, breaking free from Day. "Catullus!"

One of the most elegant men Gabriel had ever seen

smiled down at her as he embraced her. He looked as though he'd just stepped off the pages of a fashion journal, complete with dark green embroidered waistcoat, perfectly fitted gray coat and trousers, and sparkling boots. He wore neat, wire-trimmed spectacles that barely hid the powerful intelligence in his dark eyes.

"Gabriel, this is Catullus Graves," Thalia said, stepping back. "The Blades' scientific wizard."

Gabriel couldn't stop himself from blurting, "But, you're Negro."

"I know," Graves answered, his gaze hooded.

"Sorry," Gabriel said, shaking his head, "just a little thrown." He stuck out his hand. "Damned glad to meet you, Mr. Graves. That viewing eagle you created is brilliant. Really saved our arses. You'll have to tell me how you came up with the idea."

Relaxing, Graves shook Gabriel's hand. "Glad it came in handy, Captain. It's a design I've been refining for the past few years."

"Hsiung Ming," Thalia said brightly as she turned to a lean Chinese man who had come forward, "you here, as well? This is quite a reunion."

"Graves and Day collected me in Peking," he answered with a smile. His English was perfect, better than Gabriel's; it spoke of private tutors and exceptional intellect. "Graves, brilliant as he is, has no ear for the Chinese language, so I have accompanied them from there."

Thalia introduced Gabriel to this man, adding that he represented the Blades in Northeastern China. It was certainly one of the most strange experiences of Gabriel's life, standing outside the walls of a Buddhist temple in the Gobi Desert, cordially shaking hands with men who were all part of a secret society with as much pleasantry as if they were meeting by a punch bowl.

Before any of them spoke any further, Thalia, Graves,

Day, and Hsiung Ming gathered in a circle, with Gabriel looking on curiously. The four linked hands.

"North is eternal," Thalia said.

"South is forever," said Graves.

"West is endless," said Day.

"East is infinite." Hsiung Ming was the last to complete the watchwords. At their conclusion, everyone seemed to breathe just a bit easier. Then Day turned a shrewd gaze toward Gabriel.

"Can he be trusted?" he asked Thalia as he kept his eyes fixed on Gabriel.

A reasonable question, given the circumstances, but Gabriel still wanted to plow his fist into Day's well-formed face, perhaps see how well he'd fare with a broken nose. Although, a small bump already marred the bridge of Day's nose, so maybe someone, a jealous husband, had already enjoyed the privilege.

"I trust him completely," Thalia said with absolute sincerity. She laced her fingers with Gabriel's, and he felt at once the effect of her touch and words, like warm satin sliding over his skin.

An older man in monk's yellow robes approached and spoke with Hsiung Ming, who quickly translated. "Have you the Source?" he asked Gabriel.

Unwrapping the fabric that swaddled the kettle, Gabriel revealed it to the monk, whose eyes widened. "Please, inside, everyone," said the monk. "And quickly."

"But who are these men?" Day asked, looking at the tribesmen.

"Friends," Thalia answered.

"Pretty rough bunch," Day murmured, looking at Altan and his men further away.

"The Heirs have over a hundred men," Gabriel said. He drew Thalia close, until her hip touched his. It wasn't the most subtle signal, but Gabriel didn't give a damn. "Being snobbish isn't an option."

The head monk began to look frantic, waving his arms. With a groan, the giant gate was opened so everyone in the party, including their camels, was able to enter the monastery. Monks of every age watched the strange parade of brigands, steppe tribesmen, Englishmen, including one of black skin, a Chinese man, and a white woman in Mongol clothing filing into the large outer courtyard of the temple. Once everyone was inside, the door was shut as quickly as possible, which wasn't very fast at all, and bolted.

"Impressive defenses for a place of worship," Gabriel remarked. He noticed that the stone pagoda he had seen earlier was seven stories high. It stood just inside the walls, close to the gate, and would make for an effective lookout station.

"It is not uncommon for the monastery to be attacked by bandits," the head monk said, casting a wary eye at the brigands. The men in question looked around at the gilded pillars that supported the interior buildings, as if trying to figure out how to pry the gold from the columns. Gabriel wondered if the bandits would simply cut the pillars down and strap them onto their camels' backs.

"Then you're prepared for a siege."

The monk shook his head. "We are not equipped for warfare, only for protecting ourselves."

Gabriel cursed as he surveyed the monastery, trying to determine the best ways to fend off an attack. Their numbers had increased slightly, but that only barely increased the probability they could not only keep the Heirs back, but defeat them as well. As he scanned the courtyard, Thalia spoke with the Blades.

"Tell me how you got here," she insisted.

"Found out about poor Tony the morning after he was murdered," Graves explained, somber. "We knew he was heading to Mongolia, so Day and I took the first ship we could, but it was weeks later. Like Hsiung Ming said, we met up with him in Peking and went to your father in Urga. He told us that you and Captain Huntley were already on the trail."

"While we were there," Day continued, "Franklin's servant Batu showed up and told us all what had happened, and that you and the captain were trying to get the Source to a place of safekeeping. Quite a tale. You've done an incredible job, Thalia. You and Captain Huntley both have, and neither of you are even Blades."

Thalia didn't seem to focus on his praise, though Gabriel knew it meant quite a bit to her. "How on earth did you get here so quickly?" she asked. "We nearly killed ourselves covering the same amount of distance."

"Graves," Hsiung Ming said, admiration plain in his voice. "He built . . . I suppose you might call it a ship that sails upon the land. It took us here much faster than any horse or wagon, and never tired."

Gabriel turned and couldn't help gaping at the inventor. "*That* is something I need to see."

"Perhaps later," Graves said with a smile. "First, you and your party need to get something to eat, and then we can discuss strategies. I believe Lan Shun, the head monk, wants to be involved. This is *his* monastery, after all, and he knows more about the Source than any of us."

"The Heirs aren't more than a day behind us," Gabriel said, grim. "And I don't know if this place is going to have what we need to defeat them."

"Captain, there is something you should know." Graves took off his spectacles and carefully cleaned them with a fine lawn handkerchief, embroidered on the corner with *CAG*. "If there's one word to describe me, it's resourceful."

* * *

Thalia hadn't any actual experience with war councils, but she found it difficult to believe that a finer collection of minds had ever been assembled, though the location was a bit unusual. Buddhist monasteries were places of peaceful contemplation and prayer, yet there was nothing peaceful or contemplative about the discussion going on at that moment inside Sha Chuan Si's temple.

Statues and images of the Buddha and his disciples stared out from altars, unruffled and unconcerned with earthly matters, as the council sat on the floor to debate their strategy. Hsiung Ming provided an ongoing translation for Lan Shun, the head monk. Since Gabriel was deeply mired in the conversation, Thalia translated the English for Altan. Catullus sketched out a plan of the monastery's layout, which consisted of the temple, several halls, courtyards, and smaller living quarters and spaces for meditation. The tall, round pagoda soared seven stories high close to the front wall. Even though it was plain that Gabriel didn't much care for Bennett, he'd set aside his ill feelings so they might confer on the placement of what Gabriel kept referring to as "troops," although Altan took umbrage at the idea that his men were so weak-minded they needed to be in the army.

A mechanically minded intellect, a seasoned soldier, a code breaker and expert strategist, a Chinese scholar, a Buddhist monk, a bandit chief, and an Englishwoman more at home on horseback than in a salon. All talking battle strategy. It sounded like the beginning to a bizarre joke. Yet there wasn't much amusing about the situation they faced. The Heirs would most likely be at the monastery by the following morning, just over twelve hours hence.

Thalia kept glancing at Gabriel as he was deep in discussion with Altan and Bennett, translating back and forth from Mongol to English and back again. Focused, intense, Gabriel reviewed options and proposed ideas, sharply alert so that his eyes glittered like golden coins. She watched the play of muscle in his arm as he pointed out an area on the monastery map that would need particular attention, and wondered at the strange design of the world, to give her the man she needed but at a moment when everything was uncertain. Such a short amount of time they had left together. She knew they needed to plan for the battle that lay ahead, but she wished desperately that the hours they had remaining could be spent more privately.

Every now and then, Gabriel would look over at her, and their gazes would lock and hold. The paired intoxicants of desire and tenderness overwhelmed her each time. It amazed Thalia that he could be at all jealous of Bennett, when everything she felt for Gabriel was plainly written in her face, her eyes. The polished charm of Bennett Day meant nothing to her compared to the real emotion one gruff soldier had shown her.

The Blades were her brothers, but Gabriel was her heart.

"They'll try to breach the outer wall," Gabriel said, interrupting her thoughts, "through the door, but we should also consider their coming over the walls themselves."

"Grappling hooks?" Bennett asked.

"Most likely, since they won't have time or resources to build siege towers or ladders."

"Perhaps we could cut the lines attached to the grappling hooks," Thalia suggested. "Though I don't know with what."

"I believe I have an answer to that, though it doesn't involve *cutting* the ropes, exactly," Catullus said. On another piece of paper, he drew up a diagram and quickly explained how the idea he had in mind worked. Everyone agreed that this invention would make itself very useful, so a few monks were given direction by Hsiung Ming on how to assemble the devices.

"My men can take up sniper positions on the outer wall," Altan offered.

"That will be helpful," Gabriel said. "But we need to consider what will happen if the Heirs get inside the monastery. How are they with hand-to-hand combat?"

The bandit chief grinned. "It is one of their favorites."

"And Blades receive training in close combat," Bennett added. "Although Thalia—"

"Will be fine," she said firmly. The idea that she might, and probably would, kill someone soon set her stomach to flipping over and over, but if it was a choice between the life of an Heir or their mercenaries versus someone she cared about or an ally, she knew she could make the right decision.

"You should have seen her at the *nadaam* festival," Gabriel said, pride warming his voice. "She could out-shoot Genghis Khan."

They shared an intimate smile. Only Gabriel could make a compliment on her archery sound like the wickedest kind of flirtation. She felt herself already growing damp.

Catullus cleared his throat, reclaiming their attention. "I will construct some incendiary devices for outside the monastery walls. I've also been working on a weapon that I think will be effective for closer combat, should the walls be breached." He showed them another drawing that made Thalia gape like a baby at the circus. "The construction of it will be somewhat involved," Catullus continued, "so I believe I will have to take care of it myself as soon as we have finished here. Operating the weapon is a two-man job so Hsiung Ming and I will commandeer it during the battle."

"Holy hell," Gabriel said with a shake of his head. "You must be running a fever, to keep the machinery in your brain going so fast."

The smile Catullus gave Gabriel was rueful. "A family blessing and curse. I never get a full night's sleep, since I'm always jumping out of bed to write something down."

"Perhaps you need a better reason to stay in bed," Bennett suggested.

Catullus rolled his eyes. "I'm surprised *you* get anything done, since you're always in the prone position."

"Not just prone, but standing, and sitting, and—"

"Gentlemen," Thalia said, interrupting. "We're discussing warfare, not Bennett's acrobatics."

"We'll need to find someplace safe for the monks," Gabriel said. "One of these dormitories could work."

"Excuse me," Lan Shun interjected through Hsiung Ming. "The kettle is ours to protect. We will not meekly hide while you risk your lives to defend us and the kettle." The object in question was cradled in his arms.

"You said that you weren't equipped for warfare," Gabriel said. "Only for protecting yourselves."

The head monk nodded. "That is true. But we have a special way of protecting ourselves that, I think, will be more than useful." He rose and bade everyone follow him into the courtyard outside the temple. When they had assembled, Lan Shun called two monks, who gathered in their bright robes and bowed, first to Thalia and her party, and then to each other. Only Hsiung Ming seemed to understand what was about to happen, but he kept silent.

"I don't see how that is much of a defense," Bennett said dryly. "Unless the monks plan on 'courtesying' the Heirs to death."

Lan Shun paid Bennett no heed. "Watch." At his signal, the monks tucked their robes close to their bodies and bowed to each other again. Then one monk, slightly taller than the other, advanced on his brother with a series of flying kicks that happened so quickly, Thalia could barely see them. The shorter monk nimbly dodged the blows, then launched his own attack. With powerful fists, he struck out, and the taller monk barely avoided catching one in his chest. The tall monk tried to sweep his leg under the short monk and knock him to the ground, but again, the short monk danced out of reach. When the tall monk advanced, throwing sharp punches with the sides of his fists, the short monk leapt forward, grabbed his opponent's arm, twisted it around, then flipped the tall monk onto his back. While the tall monk lay on the ground, the shorter one brought the side of his hand down onto his throat, just pulling up so that he did not actually make contact, but the intent was clear. If the shorter monk had wanted to, he could have hit his opponent with a choking strike.

Then the short monk backed away, the taller one stood, and they faced each other again before bowing. They left silently when Lan Shun dismissed them.

Everyone, with the exception of Hsiung Ming, gawked. "What the bloody hell was that?" Gabriel demanded after a pause.

"Shaolin kung fu," Hsiung Ming said, and Lan Shun nodded. "An ancient art of defending oneself and harnessing the body's magical energy that the monks practice. I have seen and studied it, myself."

"I want to learn," Gabriel said.

"Me, too," seconded Thalia, simultaneously with Bennett.

"As would I," added Catullus.

"It takes many years," Lan Shun said. "Which we do not have. But you will not shoulder the burden of protecting the kettle alone."

"How many monks reside here?" Gabriel asked.

"With myself, fifty-three."

"And do you have any weapons, or are you trained only in hand-to-hand combat?"

"Spears and short swords. I retain the key to the armory."

Gabriel nodded. "We'll need someplace to keep the kettle so that it remains secure."

"It will do its part," Lan Shun answered.

Thalia asked, "You'll use its magic?" When Lan Shun nodded, she turned to Catullus. "Can Blades do that?"

"The code of the Blades prohibits them from using magic

that is not their own, but it allows for the Source's original owners to do so," he answered.

Intrigued, Thalia asked Lan Shun, "What does it do?"

"As I said, it will do its part," was all the head monk would say.

"Can you not tell us anything about it?" Catullus asked. "Its purpose, its age?"

Lan Shun walked from the courtyard, everyone following, into a smaller building, stocked to the rafters with scrolls of paper. A library. The room whispered of ancient knowledge and smelled of ink. Though Thalia read no Chinese, she would have loved to spend at least a few hours pouring over the scrolls, feeling the power of the words they contained. Lan Shun spoke with the monk who tended the library, and the librarian took a ladder to scale the walls. At the very top was a locked cabinet, which the librarian opened using a key tied with yellow silk around his wrist. He took from the cabinet a fragile scroll, brittle around the edges, and carefully brought it down to Lan Shun.

With reverence, the head monk spread the scroll out on a table. Painted upon its surface were Chinese characters, accompanied by small detailed paintings. In the first, a man was shown with his arms spread wide as he stood beneath the nighttime sky. "The kung fu that you just witnessed is part of our belief in harnessing chi, the energy of the body. Chi does not merely exist within the human body, but within every living thing." He looked up to see if any of the strangers or Westerners would debate this notion, but if he wanted an argument against the concept of living energy, he wouldn't find it amongst the Blades of the Rose. Even Gabriel seemed to accept the idea readily. Thalia smiled to herself, thinking how much he had changed since she first met him weeks ago, and yet the essential core of him had not altered.

"Over a thousand years ago," Lan Shun continued, "one

man known as Po Tai thought to harness as much chi as he could and contain it within himself."

"Why would he do that?" asked Thalia.

"Po Tai was not the first nor the last man to covet power," Lan Shun answered. "So he performed many forbidden rituals to gather chi." He pointed to the next illustration, of a man glowing with energy, but the man, instead of looking triumphant, was bent over and clawing at his own flesh, agony clearly evident in his face. "There is a reason why no man should claim that much chi for himself. It can drive a human mad. The chi destroyed him, but when Po Tai was obliterated, the chi did not simply disappear back into the universe."

The next illustration showed what looked like a beast, made of many animals, rampaging through the distinctive tall peaks of Chinese mountains as tiny people fled in its path. "The chi could not be stopped. Finally, the emperor called forward the monks from this temple to find a way to contain it." Another illustration depicted a small army of brightly robed monks chanting, their eyes closed, as they arrayed themselves in front of the beast. "It cost nearly all of them their lives, but they managed to bind the chi to a physical object. In order to ensure that no one would ever be tempted to use the gathered chi for his own selfish purposes, it was contained in the most modest of things, using the humblest materials."

"A tea kettle," Altan said.

Thalia looked at him with surprise. "How did you know?"

The bandit chief smiled. "I can always tell if something is valuable, and the way you carried that thing like a treasure told me just that."

Lan Shun nodded, gesturing to the final illustration of a monk at a forge, and with a start Thalia recognized the scene as the same she had witnessed in the kettle's steam. She met Gabriel's eyes and saw his recognition, as well. "The kettle was kept by the monks here," Lan Shun said, rolling up the scroll, "and carefully studied, until Genghis Khan and his horde took it, never knowing what they stole. A good thing, too, for if the khan had possessed an idea as to what the kettle could do, how much power it contained, he would have destroyed the world in his quest for dominance. Though the kettle has not been at our monastery for over six hundred years, tales of its power were passed to each head monk. We were all taught, should the kettle ever be returned, how to control it so that no harm befell anyone. And it is capable of a very great harm."

Thalia shivered and found herself pressing close to Gabriel for the reassurance of his solid body. God, if the Heirs managed to obtain the kettle, the resulting disaster would be unfathomable.

"Why not simply destroy the kettle?" Catullus asked.

"Once chi has been gathered, it cannot be diffused. We would only destroy the physical cage of the chi. If the kettle ceased to exist, then the concentrated chi would be unleashed, and we would have to find another object to which we could bind it. Then the cycle would begin again."

Everyone was silent as they absorbed this information. They all stared at the kettle which Lan Shun held. So odd. It still looked like an ordinary kettle, useful only for brewing tea, and for generations, that was exactly what it had done. Yet it contained such power that even those most familiar with magic—Bennett, Catullus, and Hsiung Ming—looked a bit awed. Thalia was sorry that her father could not be there just to see it, but then she was glad he was far away, and safe. Should the Heirs know what the kettle might be capable of doing, they would stop at nothing to make it theirs. She might have to witness the death of her good friends, of the man she loved. Icy with fear, Thalia wrapped her arms around Gabriel's waist.

He seemed to understand her, his own arms coming up to

hold her close. He felt strong and real, and she had to believe that they would make it out alive, together. She had to believe, because the alternative was too awful to comprehend.

"Enough standing around and gabbing like fishwives," Gabriel said in the silence. "We've a battle to prepare for."

Chapter 18

The Siege Begins

Thalia wiped the perspiration from her face as she finished burying the last of Catullus's incendiary devices outside the monastery wall. After the war council had broken, Catullus immediately went to where herbs and chemicals were stored for making medicine and tinkered with them until he was satisfied. Though he had explained to her how the combinations of substances worked, she did not quite fathom all the complex reactions or how they could produce explosions. It did not matter. All that mattered was that they reduce the number of the Heirs and their mercenaries.

Sentries were posted on the ramparts, keeping watch and guarding those working outside the safety of the walls.

"I believe we are finished with this stage," Thalia said to Catullus, who stood nearby and directed the placement of his device for cutting grappling hook lines. Monks strung thick lengths of rope, soaked in chemicals, all the way around the monastery's exterior wall. Each rope was suspended midway up the wall, held in place by metal spikes.

Since night had fallen, everything was done by torchlight, and Catullus thoroughly surveyed his handiwork. "Careful," he shouted to a monk and waved his arms. "Don't get the torches close to the rope!"

Though the monk did not speak English, nor Catullus Chinese, the words and gestures had their intended effect. The monk moved the torch away from the rope.

Catullus dabbed at his forehead with his handkerchief. "We don't want to blow ourselves up," he said to Thalia. "So mind where you walk, as well." He eyed the mounds of dirt that subtly marked where each incendiary device was buried.

"I must admit," Thalia said, "I'm surprised to see you away from Southampton."

Catullus smiled faintly. "I can fight as well as any Blade."

"I don't doubt that," she said quickly, afraid she had insulted him. "But, you are so valuable to us—to the Blades, I mean." She wasn't a Blade herself, at least, not yet, but if she survived the siege and kept the Source safe, then surely she would be inducted into their ranks. But all of that was too distant even to consider. "If anything were to happen to you . . ."

"My sister Octavia is just as adept as I am when it comes to devising new contraptions. She can easily take my place if I am killed."

"The prospect of your death does not seem to bother you," Thalia said.

His smile was larger, but no less rueful. "Believe me, I'd rather not die. There are so many inventions I've considered but haven't had the opportunity to create. Yet when we take the Blades' Oath, we must keep the possibility in mind that serving the cause could result in injury or worse. Not just for ourselves, but our friends as well. Those that serve with us."

"Have you heard from Astrid?" Thalia asked quietly.

Catullus's smile faded, and he looked tired and despondent. "No. Not a letter from her in nearly a year. She never recovered from Michael's death."

Thalia's mind immediately went to Gabriel. He, Bennett, Hsiung Ming, and Altan were busy within the monastery walls, planning more strategy and troop placement. She and Gabriel had not had a moment alone together since they'd arrived at the monastery, many hours ago. It felt like years.

"Would you excuse me?" Thalia asked Catullus.

He seemed to understand exactly what she meant, and did not mind when she left him to go back into the monastery. Thalia strode through the outer courtyard, passing monks, bandits, and a few tribesmen in furious preparation for the siege. Yet she could find no sign of Gabriel. Thalia went into the central courtyard, and even ducked into the temple, but still, she could not locate him. In the walled monastery garden, where food for the monks was grown, Thalia found Bennett and Hsiung Ming with a map of the monastery. They both looked up from their discussion when Thalia appeared at the entrance to the garden.

"He isn't here," Bennett said before Thalia could speak. "Try the walkway around the outer wall. There are stairs that lead to it in the northwest corner."

She barely breathed out her thanks before heading for the stairs. They were steep, but she took them two at a time to reach the walkway. Sha Chuan Si's outer walls were constructed with parapets, much like a castle, so that a monk could observe the surrounding landscape in relative safety. Sentries stood atop the ramparts, but Thalia's gaze was drawn to one man.

Gabriel leaned against the parapet, staring out at the moonlit desert. It wasn't quite bright enough for her to be able to make out the details of his face and dress, but she knew his wide, strong shoulders, his soldier's bearing, the hard beauty of his long-limbed body that contained the potential for both action and pleasure. Though he did not move when she approached him, she knew he heard her boots on the wide, rough stones. Thalia stood beside him, also leaning against the parapet, to take in the dark plain. With the silver glow of the moon bathing everything in pearly luminescence, the Gobi appeared to be as other-worldly as the moon itself. A cold, dry breeze danced over the surface of the desert, up the mountain and the walls of the monastery, until it stroked Thalia's face and ruffled Gabriel's hair. Atop the wall, darkness gave them only a temporary sort of privacy from the sentries, but she would take it, just the same.

She did and did not want to touch Gabriel. She wanted to feel him, his skin, his self, but feared that if she did, she would never want to let him go. Would plead with him to run away with her, leave the defense of the Source to the Blades, and find some secluded corner of the Mongolian plains where they could be safe and untroubled. A *ger* only for them, where they could spend their nights making love, their days on horseback, with the sky above and the steppe below.

"I wish the morning would never arrive," she said softly, without looking at him.

"Can't come soon enough for me," he answered. His voice was so low, such a gravelly rasp, she could barely hear him.

Thalia turned to him, resting her hip against the parapet, and crossing her arms. Temper, strained by anticipating the siege, flared. "Are you so eager for battle? Perhaps you were too hasty in leaving the army."

His profile was a gold and silver coin, his jaw tight, as he continued to study the desert. "The sooner it's morning, the sooner the Heirs get here. Once they get here, I can fight them. Once I can fight them, I can crush them. And then," he continued, turning to her, his eyes gleaming in the night, "as soon as the Heirs have been defeated to the very last man, I'm going to ask you to marry me."

Her heart slammed inside her chest, and her mouth dried.

For one of the first times in her life, Thalia felt as if she might faint. "Only then will you ask?"

"Only then. I'm not fool enough to court disaster by asking now."

"Would it . . . be tempting fate, if I said that when you do ask me, I would say 'yes'?"

"It might," he answered with a growl. "But I don't give a damn." He pulled Thalia against him and kissed her, open-mouthed, as if trying to draw her completely inside of himself, and she pressed herself to him, kissing him back with a frantic hunger. "I need to be alone with you," he rumbled against her mouth. "I've an idea."

Taking her hand, Gabriel led her down the stairs, through the bustling courtyards, until they reached the pagoda. Silently, they climbed all seven stories, until they reached the very top. Moonlight poured in through the open windows, and the sounds of battle preparations were far away. A sanctuary, for now.

He took her in his arms. He was warm and alive and all she would ever want to know of love. "Haven't got any gift for words," he murmured in the shadows. "But my body can tell you what my words can't."

In that place of light and darkness, they made love, and even though Thalia never demanded pretty avowals of devotion, she understood everything in the way Gabriel touched her, his mouth against hers, on her skin, hands and flesh communing. She let her own body speak for her, as well. Each caress was a promise, and each moan and sigh was a vow. Their climaxes, when they came, sealed their bond.

While Gabriel was still inside of her, her mind could not help but drift to Astrid Bramfield, burying herself alive somewhere in the depths of the Canadian wild. When Thalia had first learned, several years ago, that Astrid's husband Michael had been killed on a mission for the Blades, Thalia had been sorry for her friend, comprehended her loss, but could not fully understand how grief completely shattered Astrid. Surely, Astrid would mourn for a time and then move on, for her own sake. But she hadn't. And now Thalia understood why.

When Gabriel and Thalia regained some measure of calm, they reluctantly disentangled themselves. After rearranging his clothing, Gabriel helped clean and dress her, his ministrations economical but tender. They both stood.

She felt her legs weaken, and she tottered. Gabriel immediately supported her. He swung her up into his arms easily. Thalia murmured a protest but hadn't the strength to fight him.

He walked down the pagoda's stairs, then headed toward the dormitories. "Sleep," he said.

"I can't," she objected, though her words were slurred. "Too much to do. Doubt I could sleep, anyway." She could barely lift her head up to see the quizzical expressions of the monks in the dormitory as Gabriel strode into the room.

He laid her down upon an unoccupied mat. Though the monks did not usually share their quarters with women, these were doubtless special circumstances, and no one in the room complained as Gabriel pulled a blanket over Thalia.

"Rest then," he commanded her softly. He brushed the hair back from her face, and she struggled to keep her eyes open, just to look at him a few moments longer. He appeared tired, preoccupied, but there was no mistaking the love that softened his expression. Gabriel bent forward and brushed a kiss against her mouth. "Think of where you'd like to go for our bridal tour."

A foolish idea, she thought, when they might not survive the morrow. Even so, Thalia fell asleep smiling.

He was no stranger to the morning of a battle, though it had been many months since he'd experienced one. Sometime, in the hours before dawn, he'd managed to catch a little sleep. Soon after enlisting, he had faced his first night before combat. All night, he'd shook with a combination of fear and excitement, so that when the actual conflict began, he was already exhausted. Only several cups of coffee and his own nerves kept him upright. After barely surviving that battle, Gabriel learned it was better to sleep than stew.

So, after finalizing preparations with the Blades and Altan, Gabriel returned to the dormitory and stretched out next to a completely slumbering Thalia, setting his rifle down beside him within reaching distance. He wrapped an arm around her waist, and, in her sleep, she sighed and burrowed close to him. Even though he knew better, he tried to keep his eyes open, stay awake so he could memorize the feel of her, but his body demanded rest, and he slept hard for a few, brief hours.

Next thing he knew, Bennett Day was shaking him into wakefulness. Day had a rifle in one hand and a spyglass in the other. "They've been spotted," Day said, quiet and urgent. "About an hour's ride from here."

Gabriel forced himself upright and nodded his thanks when a cup of steaming tea was put into his hand. Another was provided for Thalia, who was rubbing her face. "Five minutes," Gabriel said.

Day nodded and quickly left the dormitory. As Gabriel sipped his tea, he studied Thalia over the rim of his cup. She looked pale and worn, and the sun had barely begun to lighten the sky. Knowing that the enemy was nearly at the gates, Gabriel waited for the sense of calm to come over him that usually did in the hours before combat. But it didn't come. His hands were shaking. And he knew why. In order to survive the day, in order to protect her, he would have to think of her as another soldier and nothing more. Otherwise, he very well would lose his godforsaken mind.

"You should eat something," he rumbled, his voice still hoarse from sleep.

She shook her head. "I couldn't possibly keep anything down." She glanced at him as if expecting him to argue, but he didn't.

"Finish your tea, at least," he said, and she complied. Once they had both drunk the last of their tea, he set their cups aside and rose to his feet. He didn't help her up, even though he wanted to. Instead, he shouldered his rifle.

Thalia stood, looking at him quizzically. Before she could speak, he turned and left the dormitory. He heard her follow. Dawn turned the sky violet and pink, and the air was cold. Gabriel's breath turned to white puffs in front of his face. Gathered in the central courtyard were the monks, the bandits, the tribesmen, and the Blades, wearing expressions that varied from eager to terrified, to, in the case of the Blades, alertly ready. Everyone turned to Gabriel when he entered the courtyard, looking at him expectantly.

"Given that you've years of military experience," Graves said, "it would be best if you went over the final preparations. Hope you don't mind."

"Not a bit," Gabriel answered. "I like telling people what to do."

Graves smiled a little at this. With Hsiung Ming translating for the monks and Thalia translating for the brigands and tribesmen, Gabriel addressed the crowd. He didn't bother standing on a box or anything else to elevate him and demand attention. His voice could do the job.

"We have a slight advantage in our location," Gabriel said. "High up, with only one true entrance. First line of defense will be Graves's devices, and half of Altan's men on the parapet. But the Heirs will find a way to breach the wall, and when they do, you monks and tribesmen will do your best to disarm the mercenaries. Graves and Hsiung Ming have their weapon, which is mounted on top of the blacksmith's building. Altan and I will guard Lan Shun, who will be in the temple with the kettle. Some of Altan's men will serve as skirmishers and the rest with Altan and me in the temple. Everyone clear?"

"What about me?" Thalia asked. "Where shall I be posted?"

He addressed her as if she was an infantryman. "You and Day are our best shots, so you'll both be in the pagoda, sniping." He pointed to the tall, round structure. "It has windows on all sides, so the position is excellent both for defending the front gate and for getting shots at anyone who should breach the walls." Gabriel didn't add that it wasn't only her excellent aim that earned her the post. Out of everywhere in the monastery, it was the most protected location, the one furthest from the actual battle, and he would only have to look up to know exactly where she was at all times. Having Day serve as her guard was a bonus. Gabriel might not like the charming bastard, but he knew that Day would do his utmost to keep Thalia safe.

Thalia seemed to guess the other part of Gabriel's rationale for situating her in the pagoda, but at least she didn't argue. Gabriel quickly went over a few of the final directions for the siege. "I believe that's everything," he said when he finished. He wanted to take up his position as soon as possible and get on with this damned fight.

"Not everything," Lan Shun said, coming forward. He carried the kettle under one arm, and in his other, he held a gold silk pouch. A younger monk took the pouch from Lan Shun and began distributing its contents to everyone. Gabriel could not tell what they were being given, but when the monk approached Gabriel and motioned for him to hold out his hand, he did so. The monk set something tiny and round into Gabriel's palm before moving on. Looking closely, Gabriel saw that he had been given a plant seed.

Even the Blades appeared puzzled as they studied the seeds in their hands. Lan Shun and his assistant both took seeds, as well.

"Place the seed here," Lan Shun instructed, pointing at

the hollow of his throat. Everyone obeyed, and Lan Shun started to chant.

No sooner did the words start to leave the head monk's mouth, but the seed between Gabriel's fingers became incredibly warm. He moved to drop it, but the seed didn't move from where it nestled at the base of his neck. Instead, it began sprouting at an accelerated rate. He couldn't see it happen on himself, but watched Thalia as she underwent the same experience, her eyes wide with surprise. Green tendrils curled out of both sides of the seed, curving up and around their necks like serpents. Gabriel tried to pull at it, but Lan Shun called out, "No! Let the seed do its work."

Not particularly fond of snakes, even if they were actually plants, Gabriel struggled to keep from wrenching the seed away. But he endured the sensation of slithering, coiling plant shoots wrapping around his throat, until they met at the back of his neck. A living necklace.

"Do not, under any circumstances, remove the seed," Lan Shun commanded. "It will protect you."

"From the Heirs?" Altan asked.

"From this." Lan Shun held up the kettle.

Thalia, Gabriel, and the Blades exchanged looks. What the hell were they getting themselves into, unleashing the power of the Source? But Lan Shun appeared confident, and, since Gabriel had almost no experience with Sources of any variety, he didn't challenge the head monk.

"The Heirs will be here soon," Graves said, checking his pocket watch.

Gabriel cocked his head to one side, listening. "I can hear them coming." The hooves of their horses made a dim thunder, nearing the monastery. He knew the sound well. "Everyone, to their positions."

As the assembled crowd dispersed, Thalia threaded through the men to Gabriel's side. She reached for him, but he edged away from her touch.

"I can't," he growled. At her unspoken question, he continued. "I have to tell myself that you're just another soldier. If, for even a minute, I thought of you as Thalia, the woman I love, the woman I want to be my wife, then I'd—" His voice hitched, cracked, and he squeezed his eyes shut. When he opened them again, she'd taken a step back.

Her lips pressed tightly together, her eyes glistened, while twin spots of red stained her cheeks. "No kiss, then," she said on a rasp.

Gabriel shook his head, not trusting himself to speak. Thalia nodded, looking not angry but determined, and then walked off in the direction of the pagoda. He curled his hands into fists to keep from reaching for her, and would only find much later the cuts his fingernails had made in the flesh of his palms.

Armed with a rifle and plenty of ammunition, Thalia climbed the stairs of the pagoda, Bennett following. Her feet took the steps as she ascended seven stories, but her mind was down in the courtyard with Gabriel. As much as she wanted one final embrace, one last kiss before the battle, she could not find fault with his decision to distance himself. If pushing her away was what it took to ensure his survival, then she'd let him. Anything to keep him alive.

Upon reaching the top floor of the pagoda, Thalia tried to suppress her potent memories of making love with Gabriel in that same room the night before. She looked out of the arched windows. As Gabriel had pointed out, the pagoda provided a view of every part of the monastery. She glanced down into the monastery to see people taking up their positions, and from her high vantage point, everything looked small and removed. Except for Gabriel. Her eyes went to him immediately—he commanded her attention, moving confidently and decisively through the monastery.

"You aren't going to start sighing and languishing, I hope," Bennett said dryly.

Thalia shot him a look as she moved toward the windows that faced the front monastery wall. "I should think you're quite familiar with that."

He grinned at her. "I'm long gone by the time the sighing and languishing begins."

Her retort died on her lips as she and Bennett looked out the front windows. The Heirs and their mercenaries massed at the foot of the escarpment. They were a thick, bristling mob, a dark wound against the desert's red plain. A handful of riders broke off to circle the mountain, but within minutes they returned. Scouting for a way up besides the front slope, and unsuccessful. Thalia spotted Lamb's fair head at the front of the mob as he consulted with the riders. Seeing no other way up, he waved for the mercenaries to take the escarpment. The men surged forward.

"I see Henry Lamb is taking up his usual location at the rear," Bennett muttered. "Protecting himself. What an ass."

"Jonas Edgeworth is with him, as well."

"That belligerent puppy? I suppose that's Lamb's punishment. And who's that enormous heap of a man riding with them?"

"Tsend," Thalia answered darkly. "The one Gabriel wrestled. A betrayer of his homeland. He sold his knowledge of the Source to the Heirs."

"And Huntley defeated *him?* Good Lord, remind me not to get your captain angry."

The sounds of the advancing horses grew louder as the Heirs and their army neared. Individual faces began to form from the crowd, all of them cold and ruthless, ready to kill for the promise of gold. As she fingered the strange necklace of plant shoots around her neck, Thalia wanted to crawl away to the other side of the pagoda and hide. She also wanted to throw boulders at their foes. Instead of doing either, she settled into position, shouldering her rifle and training the barrel on the approaching men. Bennett did the same in the window beside her.

Closer, closer. Thalia kept her finger on the trigger, though she knew she would have to wait until exactly the right moment to begin firing. Bullets were not in endless supply, and the moment she shot, her position would be revealed. She was no happier about having to kill, but she had no choice. One more mercenary alive meant one more person able to hurt Gabriel.

The mercenaries halted their advance fifty feet away from the monastery's front gate. Horses pawed the ground, restive, and the men shifted in their saddles, ready for war.

"Last chance," Lamb's voice boomed out. It was so loud, Thalia's teeth rattled. "Give us the Source, or you will all be slaughtered."

"How can he do that with his voice?" she asked Bennett, her ears ringing.

"Caesar's Clarion," Bennett answered grimly. "A charm used by conquerors to intimidate their enemies."

But those protecting the Source would not be cowed so easily. Stony silence met Lamb's demand.

"Death, then," Lamb thundered, sounding almost pleased at the opportunity to kill. He shouted to his men, and, with a collective roar, they surged toward the monastery gate.

"Now?" Thalia asked Bennett.

"Wait."

The mercenaries drew nearer.

"Now?"

"A moment longer."

The pagoda shook with the force of an explosion. Horses reared, and mercenaries were thrown as Catullus's incendiary devices, buried in the ground, were trod upon. They were clay pots filled with an exact proportion of chemicals that combined and detonated when pressure was put on them. One after the other, the advancing mercenaries triggered the devices, which heaved dirt and chaos as they blasted. Confusion struck, and some tried to retreat while their brethren pushed forward.

At the same time, the brigands stationed along the front wall began firing into the group. Smoke and noise. Men pitched backward off of their mounts.

"Now!" Bennett commanded.

She and Bennett fired. Thalia tried to pick her targets wisely, only taking shots she knew she could make. Some men went down. Between each shot, she ducked down as the mercenaries returned fire. Chips of stone flew from the window as bullets flew overhead.

But there were only so many bandits stationed at the wall, and she and Bennett were only two, versus well over a hundred men intent on getting inside the monastery. Before too long, the mercenaries were at the front wall and swarming around the sides. As Gabriel had predicted, they had ropes attached to grappling hooks, and Thalia soon heard the clank of the metal hooks thrown up the walls and finding purchase.

Thalia continued to shoot, watching as the mercenaries began to scale the walls. When the attackers were midway up, a few monks tossed burning embers down. The mercenaries laughed as the embers grazed passed them, but their laughter cut off abruptly. Flaming embers caught on the ropes that Catullus had wrapped around the monastery walls. Soaked in a chemical solution, the ropes burned quickly, then exploded. Men toppled from their severed grappling lines like ants.

"Remind me to kiss Catullus later," Bennett shouted over the din.

"You'll have to queue up," Thalia yelled back. "I'm first."

"Don't think your captain would appreciate that."

"He'll be second in line." Thalia reminded herself that

Gabriel was ensconced in the temple, protecting Lan Shun and the Source, and, for now, he was safe. Turning her attention to the action outside the monastery wall, she continued to shoot, reload, and shoot. Even though their grappling lines had been cut, the mercenaries continued to swarm up the walls with makeshift lines.

Knowing that bullets were precious, Thalia scanned the advancing mob, trying to find the Heirs in the midst of the pandemonium. If she could wound or kill Lamb and Edgeworth, the mercenaries might turn. Go for the officers, she remembered Gabriel telling her once. An army without leaders couldn't fight.

But Lamb, damn him, was elusive. Never staying anywhere for long, ducking in and out of the attacking mercenaries, he kept himself well hidden behind a human shield. And Edgeworth . . .

"I can't find Edgeworth!" she shouted at Bennett.

Bennett scanned the horde, using his spyglass. "Where did that squirrelly bugger get to?" he muttered. "Wait—I see him! But what the hell is he doing?" He handed Thalia the glass, and she followed his direction.

Kneeling in the dirt, far at the back of the invaders, Edgeworth focused on the soil at his feet. Something metal glinted on the ground. It looked as though he chanted, and, as he did so, a small whirlwind of dust began to gather and twist in front of him. Edgeworth continued to chant as the eddy grew and gathered momentum. Soon, the whirlwind was taller than a man. And it glinted and glittered with the presence of magic.

"He's casting some kind of spell," Thalia said darkly as she returned the spyglass.

"Not if I can stop him." Bennett took up his rifle, aimed, and fired. "Damn! He's too far to get a decent shot."

"Maybe I can get closer," Thalia said. "If I went down to the wall, perhaps I could—"

"No." Bennett, his gaze still fixed on Edgeworth, rose from his crouch. "I'll go."

"He told you to keep me up here, didn't he?"

Bennett didn't bother asking who she meant or denying the charge. He headed for the stairs, with Thalia at his heels. "I'm a better shot than you," she protested, following. They reached the sixth floor. Sounds of battle drew closer as the bandits continued to fire on the mercenaries, while the enemies fired back. A man screamed.

"Don't flatter yourself," Bennett threw over his shoulder.

"I'm not. But be reasonable."

Bennett barked out a laugh. "There's nothing reasonable about the way your captain feels about you. Get back to the top of the tower, Thalia." Fifth, then fourth floors.

"But—"

Shouts and yells interrupted her, louder than the terrible and typical noise of warfare. Thalia and Bennett raced to the window on the fourth floor of the pagoda to see what caused the uproar. Shocked at what she saw, Thalia gripped Bennett's arm without knowing that she did so.

"Sweet sinners," Bennett muttered. "The bastard did it."

As tall as two men and entirely the same reddish hue as the Gobi soil. A giant. At Edgeworth's command, the creature moved slowly, lumbering steadily toward the monastery's outer wall. Mercenaries, hardened men frightened of nothing, scattered in the giant's oncoming path. The creature moved like an automaton, without thought, but direct and awful in its progress. Bullets pierced its clay flesh, yet had no effect on the giant, and it took no notice of them. It continued forward, nearing the front gate. Thalia shuddered at the sight.

"A golem," Bennett snarled. He turned and began racing back up the stairs, with Thalia shortly behind. "From Jewish folklore. A man, made of earth, enchanted and unstoppable."

"What if we killed Edgeworth?" Thalia panted. "That might halt it."

Bennett shook his head. They took up their original positions on the top floor of the pagoda. From there, they watched as the golem shambled toward the front gate. With enormous fists the size of cannonballs, the golem pounded on the gate, shaking the huge wooden structure as if it were pasteboard. Monks and bandits gathered on the other side of the gate, bracing themselves against it, trying to keep the gate standing. Each pound of the golem's fists nearly threw the defenders backward.

"Only way to stop a golem is to remove the Star of David amulet on its chest," Bennett said. "Which means someone has to get close enough to that thing to grab the amulet."

Slam, slam, slam. Thalia watched with an awful sense of inevitability as the golem continued its relentless assault on the front gate. There was nothing she nor Bennett could do to stop it. An enormous, awful splintering rent the air. The gate flew apart into kindling, monks and bandits flying through the air, as insubstantial as dandelions. As soon as the gate was breached, the invaders flooded inside, shouting for blood. And that's when the battle truly began.

Chapter 19

The Walls Are Breached

The entire monastery shook. Gabriel knew the gate had been breached. But by what? No trees to use for battering rams. Maybe the Heirs had their own explosive devices. Didn't matter how the gate had fallen. He had to check and make sure Thalia was unharmed.

He ran through the central courtyard, shoving his way through the thickly clotting mercenaries as they fought with the monks and the few steppe tribesmen. Everywhere was a jumble of yellow robes and the dark clothing of the Heirs' hired muscle. Bodies already littered the ground. Gabriel ducked as a mercenary's fist flew in his direction. He slammed the butt of his rifle into the man's face and sped on, not noticing or caring when the attacker crumpled to the ground.

Men screamed, and several monks and a few brigands flew up and over Gabriel's head. He didn't wonder long what had caused them to be thrown into the air. A clay giant steadily and ruthlessly plowed through the monastery's defenders, knocking men aside as if they were ninepins. There wasn't any time to goggle at the sight. Gabriel fired at the thing, but, even though he shot it straight between the eyes, the giant didn't stop or even slow. Bloody Christ, he had known the Heirs wouldn't play fair, but he had had no idea to what lengths they would go.

Gabriel looked and saw that the pagoda was not only still standing, but that Thalia and Bennett had now trained their rifles away from the outer wall and into the center of the monastery, where they were effectively picking away at the invading mercenaries. He allowed himself only a moment's relief at her safety before turning and heading back toward the temple. Lan Shun and the kettle needed safeguarding, and the clay giant was clearing a path for the mercenaries.

Gabriel burst through the temple entrance and slammed it shut behind him, ignoring the brigands who had jumped to attention, guns ready. "We're moving you someplace safer," he said, whirling around. Lan Shun wouldn't understand the words themselves, but he could figure out their meaning.

Instead of heeding Gabriel's command, the head monk was bent over a small lit stove, on top of which was the kettle. He sprinkled several handfuls of dried roots into the kettle, continuously chanting. But the clay giant lumbered closer.

"No time for that now!" Gabriel shouted, but Lan Shun paid him no mind.

Gabriel started forward, then stopped. A heavy smoke poured from the kettle, even more impenetrable than the smoke that had revealed the kettle's history. Dense white clouds swirled and snaked up to the tall roof of the temple, forming a heavy serpentine shape. The brigands shouted, and retreated against the temple walls. Lan Shun continued to chant.

Smoke congealed, took shape, and danced through the air. A roar came from its huge jaws while its claws scratched at the temple floor. White eyes burned and scales gleamed. Gabriel could scarcely believe it. A dragon. A real, live dragon, made of smoke and cloud, but real, nonetheless. The beast swam through the air and pressed its nose against the cowering brigands before turning its attention to Gabriel.

As the dragon advanced, Gabriel forced himself to stand and face it. Its head was enormous, the size of a wagon, with a mouth that could swallow three men whole. Hot breath puffed from its nose and mouth, smelling of water and herbs, enveloping Gabriel. The dragon shoved its face against Gabriel, nearly toppling him over, but the moment its nose touched the plant necklace at his throat, it moved on. Gabriel let out the breath he hadn't known he'd been holding. If he had not been so battle-trained, he would have pissed himself for certain.

One of the monks attending Lan Shun hurried to the temple door and flung it open. The Smoke Dragon roared again before swimming through the door. Outside, the same pattern repeated itself. The dragon would check each man for the protection of the seed necklace, but if it didn't find that protection, God help the unfortunate soul. Claws tore, the jaw snapped, and gurgling screams ripped from the throats of the mercenaries.

Over a dozen men met their deaths swiftly from the clean savagery of the dragon. Other men scattered, trying to avoid similar fates. Within moments, the clay giant and the Smoke Dragon faced each other in the cleared space. The dragon didn't bother checking for the seed at the giant's throat, recognizing threatening magic immediately. The dragon circled the giant once before descending. They tore into one another, crashing into walls and buildings, sending timber and stone flying. It was something out of a myth, to see such enormous monsters battle, with chaos and death all around.

Myth or no, Gabriel could not stand and marvel at it.

He turned to Altan, who had run into the temple. "I'll lead some skirmishers. Can you guard Lan Shun and the kettle?"

"Rather watch the teapot than face that beast," the bandit chief said.

Wasting no more time, Gabriel gathered a group of brigands and took them out into the seething courtyard in front of the temple. Scores of attackers faced off against monks, and while the holy men's use of fist and foot was powerful, both throwing foes and spitting them with spears, the mercenaries had firepower. Chi couldn't stop a bullet. Gabriel rammed his way through the mercenaries. His rifle did him no good in close combat, so he shouldered it and pulled his revolver and knife. Then he plunged into battle.

His movements were practiced, familiar. He knew how to fight, and even months away from his last such combat, his skills did not fail him. When a mercenary's blade cut across his face, he didn't feel it. He punched the sword from the man's hand, sunk his own knife into the mercenary's chest, then pulled out the blade and moved on. Beside him, three monks went down in a heap of gold cloth and crimson blood as a mercenary shot them at close range. Gabriel ducked a flying fist then brought his attacker down quickly. He fired and reloaded without breaking stride. More mercenaries crumpled.

A loud whooshing, followed by more men's shouts of pain, made him look up, then shake his head in amused disbelief. Standing on the roof of the blacksmith's shop were Graves and Hsiung Ming, putting to use another of Graves's diabolical devices. The mechanical genius held a crimped shotgun barrel, pointing it toward the invaders below, while Hsiung Ming poured a basin of spirits into the rifle's breach. A lit fuse attached at the opening of the barrel and ignited the liquid as it shot through the rifle, sending out jets of flame. Burning mercenaries howled as they ran in circles, trying in vain to douse the fires on their clothing. The air, rent by the roars of the Smoke Dragon, smelled of smoke, gunpowder, and charred flesh.

Gabriel slammed into the ground as a large mercenary plowed into him. They wrestled, vying for control of Gabriel's revolver. Pinned to the ground on his back, he tried to lodge a foot in the man's stomach and shove him off, but the bugger was too heavy and strong. Gabriel gritted his teeth as he attempted to pry the mercenary's fingers from the gun's handle. The man reared up, pulling on Gabriel's arms and his muscles screamed in protest.

Suddenly, the mercenary stiffened as a bullet neatly pierced his chest, and he pitched forward. Gabriel managed to roll out of the way before fifteen stone of dead mercenary collapsed onto him. Getting to his feet, Gabriel followed the trajectory of the bullet and traced it to the pagoda. Thalia nodded at him briefly from a window before returning to her sniping. Pride and gratitude swelled in his chest. Jesus, he loved that woman.

But his admiration turned to horror as the pagoda began to shake and list. Thalia disappeared from the window, knocked to the floor by the quaking. The Smoke Dragon, sensing that the kettle was threatened, had abandoned its attack on the giant and now circled the temple, snatching up in its jaws any mercenaries that neared the temple. With the dragon's focus diverted, the clay giant, directed by an unseen hand, had turned its attention to the snipers and was trying to topple the pagoda, shoving against its base. Stones from the tower's circular walls began to fall. The giant would destroy the tower in moments.

"The hell it will," Gabriel snarled to himself. Even if he couldn't shoot and kill the creature, he'd draw it away from Thalia.

Gabriel started toward the tottering pagoda. And barreled right into the massive chest of Tsend. Around his neck, the Mongol wore a seed necklace, clearly taken from a monk. The Smoke Dragon tore through the unfortunate monk just behind Tsend before moving on to more mercenaries. No divine intervention would come to Gabriel's aid. It was might against might.

Thalia crawled to the window. She could just make out Gabriel, Tsend looming over him. She tried to aim for the enormous Mongol, but the shaking of the tower made it impossible. Walls buckled around her, and beams collapsed from the ceiling. The golem did not cease its attack below. And the dragon's interest lay in guarding the Source.

"You have to get out!" Bennett shouted at her.

"The only exit is down," she yelled back.

He looked pointedly at the window.

"We can't jump seven stories, Bennett!"

"It's not jumping, it's climbing. And *we* aren't. *You* are."

"I bloody well won't without you!"

Bennett sent her a grin. "Captain Huntley has had a disastrous effect on your vocabulary, my dear. Better get out and lend him a hand." With a wink, he disappeared down the stairs, heading straight for the golem.

Thalia made to follow him and provide what assistance she could, but a beam tumbled from the ceiling, blocking the stairs. She had no choice. Shouldering her rifle, Thalia took a breath and straddled the window. The ground looked impossibly far down. She couldn't tell if her head spun or the pagoda was collapsing. Casting a quick look toward the courtyard, Thalia saw Gabriel grappling with Tsend, the two of them locked in desperate combat. She had to help him however possible.

She gripped the windowsill, then began to lower herself down the side of the pagoda. She found footing, then slipped as the tower shook. Her palms grew damp. Concentrate, she told herself. Slowly, painfully, Thalia worked her way down, a story at a time. She prayed no one on the ground paid her any mind. She made a perfect target, clambering down the tottering pagoda like an awkward spider.

More than halfway there. Thalia risked a glance over her shoulder, but Gabriel and Tsend had disappeared. Damn. She returned her focus to her climb, but then the pagoda leaned sharply, and she lost her grip. The thick air swirled around her as she fell.

Clawing at Tsend's bruising fingers around his throat, Gabriel watched Thalia tumble from the sky like a fallen angel. Hot ice flooded him. Nearly two stories up. Could she survive that fall? His body shook with rage and fear. It was no use. He couldn't pretend that she was just another soldier, and he prayed he hadn't squandered their last moments together with his protective impulses. He had to get to her.

Tsend followed Gabriel's gaze and laughed. "I hope there's enough of her left for Lamb. He is not too particular, though." He released Gabriel's throat long enough to punch him hard in the ribs. Something cracked. "I will enjoy killing you."

Burning with fury, Gabriel ignored the pain and wrested himself free of the enormous Mongol. He unslung his rifle and smashed it into Tsend's grinning face. Blood shot from the Mongol's nose and gathered in the corners of his mouth. "Now you're as ugly as your mother," Gabriel snarled.

Tsend wiped at his face with his sleeve, scowling. Seeing his own blood infuriated him, and he lurched forward. Gabriel leapt out of the way and kicked the small of Tsend's back. The Mongol shouted in pain and stumbled around. Rage made Tsend clumsy as he swung at Gabriel. But Gabriel's own wrath and fear for Thalia sharpened him, made him as precise as a blade. He had to beat the Mongol to reach Thalia.

His fists plowed into Tsend, his aim direct. A jab to the

throat cut off the Mongol's breathing. Another blow to his gut bent Tsend over, retching. Gabriel went for his revolver, but Tsend recovered just enough to kick at Gabriel's leg, causing him to stagger. From his belt, Tsend pulled a long, wicked knife and swung at Gabriel. Gabriel blocked with his own blade. Metal against metal hissed and screeched. Gabriel shoved hard, then lost his balance as a running mercenary knocked into him. Tsend seized the momentary advantage and threw Gabriel to the earth, then ground the heel of his boot into Gabriel's hand, forcing the hilt of his knife from his fingers. Tsend laughed again and lunged with his own blade, aiming for Gabriel's eye.

A shot from Gabriel's trusty revolver stopped the Mongol in his attack. For a moment, Tsend seemed puzzled, as if he couldn't quite understand how a bullet came to be lodged in his chest. A second shot struck him in the center of his forehead. Then his eyes glazed, his expression slackened, and he fell to earth.

Gabriel did not waste a minute gloating over his kill. He leapt to his feet and headed toward Thalia, praying he wasn't too late.

For several moments, Thalia could only lie on the ground, staring at the sky, and struggle to regain her breath. She'd tried to take the fall well, rolling as she did when thrown from a horse. But horses weren't two stories high. Still, she needed to get up quickly and find Gabriel.

A dark shape hovered over her, blocking her view of the sky. "Already on your back for me," Lamb drawled. "Thank you for saving me time."

"You're not welcome," Thalia growled, pushing to her feet and facing her enemy.

Henry Lamb, slightly dirty and bruised, his fair hair mussed and far from a barber's attentions, grinned at her. "I don't mind if you put up a little fight. Makes my job so much more enjoyable." In his elegant, refined hand, he brandished a knife that glinted in the morning light.

Bitter disgust flooded Thalia's mouth. "I won't let you touch me, bastard."

"Charming. But that decision isn't up to you." He surged toward her.

Thalia danced away, but Lamb grabbed her hair and roughly tugged her back. Pain exploded in her eyes as her hand automatically came up, trying to loosen his hold. Lamb gripped her waist, pulling her against him. She almost gagged when she felt his erection pressing into her from behind. He held the knife to her throat while his other hand gripped her breast. As she struggled, the edge of the knife cut into the tender skin. Wetness trickled down her neck.

"This really is marvelous, Thalia," Lamb panted in her ear. "Exactly what I'd hoped for. I can take my pleasure with you while that dragon exhausts its magic protecting the Source."

Thalia kicked out behind her, trying to land a blow to his groin. He anticipated this, however, and turned just enough so that her heel only caught on his hip. Then she yelped as the knife cut deeper. She stilled, not wanting to slit her own throat.

"Yes," Lamb hissed. "A fight is good, but I don't want to kill you, Thalia. Not for a while. I have such plans for you."

She made herself go slack against Lamb. He ground into her. The hand on her breast moved, and she felt him reaching for the buttons on his trousers. With his attention diverted, the blade of the knife moved slightly away from her neck.

Thalia reached up and grabbed the blade with her bare hand. She bit down her scream as the knife cut deeply into her palm, and pushed the weapon away. Lamb cursed in his genteel accent, calling her a bitch and a whore, as Thalia twisted in his grasp. As they both grappled for the knife, she thought of Tony Morris, murdered and abandoned, of the Heirs' greed for empire and dominance, of the threats she and Gabriel had faced many times over. Gabriel, whom she loved ferociously, powerfully. He fought for her. He might die for her. But not if Thalia could do anything about it.

Fueled by anger and love, Thalia pushed harder as she fought with Lamb. The knife slipped in his fingers, and she muscled it around so the blade pointed toward him. Her mind flashed to the wrestlers at the *nadaam,* their technique. Hooking her feet around one of Lamb's ankles, Thalia threw him to the ground. He fell, and the knife he held caught him between the ribs. Thalia stumbled backward, staring at the hilt as it pointed up from Lamb's chest, scarlet staining his expensive waistcoat.

He lay there, pinned and choking, while his hands clawed at the hilt. Blood seeped from his aristocratic mouth. He tried to speak, gasping out unintelligible curses, but then a paroxysm hit him. He gurgled, then fell still, eyes open and staring at the blue Gobi sky. Thalia watched this, her gaze dispassionate, as her own wounds bled into the dust.

A mercenary saw Lamb's body and shouted. "He's dead! The English chief is dead!" Other nearby mercenaries turned at this. They met each other's eyes. No leader meant no payment. There wasn't a reason to risk their lives any further. Like bleating, terrified sheep, the men pivoted and ran. It wasn't long before the monastery was emptying out as mercenaries fled in panic.

"Thalia!" She turned at Gabriel's voice, and there he was, living and whole, racing toward her. Stunned, Thalia let his strong arms enfold her, and she realized with dim shock that Lamb was dead, and she had killed him. Even more surprising, she was glad.

Then she clasped Gabriel tightly. Lamb was dead, but Gabriel was alive. Wetness coursed down her cheeks. "I tried to get to you," she whispered. "I saw Tsend attack you, but I couldn't get to you."

"He's as dead as Lamb," Gabriel said, holding her close, cradling her head.

"What about Edgeworth?"

"Gone," Catullus said. He and Hsiung Ming, both bloodied but largely unhurt, strode toward them. "I saw him sprinkling some dried flowers into a fire, then he dove in and disappeared. Some means of transportation, I believe. But I don't know exactly where he went."

"Let him go to the devil," Gabriel said. She felt him shaking, and held him tighter. She wanted to crawl inside of him just to assure herself that he was real and unharmed. They were all here, all safe, except—

"Oh, God," Thalia cried. She looked toward the pagoda, which, miraculously, still stood. "Bennett!"

The man in question appeared at the doorway of the now barely standing pagoda, covered in red dust. Slapping at his sleeves and wiping at his face, he walked out, limping a little.

"If any of you ever want to wrestle a golem," he coughed, "I highly discourage you from doing so. More trouble than a pack of nuns." Bennett held up the Star of David in his battered hand. "This needs to be returned to whomever it was stolen from, I believe."

Thalia glanced up at Gabriel and saw him regarding Bennett with a new respect. Yes, Bennett was an incorrigible flirt, but he was a fighter, too. All of them—Gabriel, the Blades, the monks, the bandits, even the tribesmen—were fighters. Including herself. And soon, she would have the scars to prove it.

It was a bloody mess. The monastery courtyard filled with the wounded and monks attending to them, the destroyed buildings, camels and horses wandering around. Altan oversaw the tending of his men as his own wounds were bound. Not much different from the aftermaths of countless battles, but different for so many reasons. Gabriel had never witnessed a Smoke Dragon being corralled back into a tea kettle until this very day. It was a bit trickier than one would have first supposed. He'd seen things he would never have believed just a month ago. A giant of clay. A rifle that could shoot flame.

The woman he wanted to marry having her wounds dressed after she'd fought to the death with a black-hearted son of a bitch.

Thalia submitted patiently and without complaint as Lan Shun applied poultices to the cut on her throat and the deep gash across her palm. Gabriel could barely bring himself to look at her injuries. Every time he saw them, the crusts of her blood on her skin, he wanted to bring Lamb back to life so he could eviscerate that highborn maggot. But Thalia, bless her fierce heart, had already done the job of killing Lamb. Gabriel contented himself with holding Thalia's uninjured hand as they sat on the floor of the temple. He had no plans to release her any time soon. Like, say, for the next century.

"Will Edgeworth come back with more Heirs?" Thalia asked Graves, who stood nearby, critically examining the crooked earpiece of his spectacles.

"Doubtful. He already knows that the Source won't be taken without a messy fight; it already cost the life of one Heir. And if he does," Graves continued, straightening the earpiece, "we know we can best them."

"The Blades will come back, if they are needed," Day said to Lan Shun.

The head monk nodded.

"What will happen to the kettle now?" asked Altan.

Lan Shun, finishing dressing Thalia's wounds, gathered up

the kettle and wrapped it in yellow silk. "We shall keep it, as it had been kept for generations, before the khan came."

"But will it be safe?" Gabriel demanded. He hadn't risked Thalia's neck and his own just to have a Source left unguarded for some other greedy fool to stumble across and covet.

"Our lesson was learned the first time it was stolen," Lan Shun said with a half smile. "Trust me, there will be no breaking the charm we set over our treasure." He bustled from the temple, with several monks serving as guards for the kettle.

Gabriel muttered to himself, but he had to believe the head monk. It had to be maddening, being a Blade of the Rose, knowing that all over the world were unprotected Sources and being unable to safeguard them all. But how much worse was it, loving a Blade, understanding that he or she would constantly have his or her life in jeopardy.

He glanced over at Thalia, who was contemplating a statue of an equally thoughtful Buddha. She'd grown quiet since the battle, drawn into herself. He tried not to worry overmuch about this. She was exhausted, and had just undergone the nasty experience of warfare, had killed several men that day. It was bound to leave her not quite her usual self. He wasn't entirely certain, though, why she wouldn't meet his eyes. Left him more than a little edgy.

The close council of the Blades didn't sit any easier with him. Graves, Day, and Hsiung Ming were gathered in a corner of the temple, talking lowly amongst themselves and looking at Thalia. When the three men nodded and then began walking toward her, Gabriel got to his feet, placing himself in front of her.

"What the hell are you planning?" he growled at the Blades. He didn't like the serious looks on their faces one bit. It meant trouble.

None of the men seemed offended by Gabriel's brazen

question. Day actually looked at him with a touch of fondness. "It's time," he said simply.

"For what?"

"For what I've been waiting for," Thalia said, standing up and placing herself at Gabriel's side. "To finally become a Blade of the Rose." Her bright green eyes glistened, and her pale cheeks flushed. She removed the Compass from her pocket. "To make this mine in truth."

"You've wanted this your whole life," Gabriel said softly.

She nodded. "Ever since I learned about the Blades. But, Gabriel," she said, turning to him, "you understand what that means."

The burning in his throat told him everything he needed to know. "It means that you can be called at any time. Every day brings you close to danger."

"Not unlike being a soldier, I imagine." She smiled, bittersweet.

"I'm not a soldier anymore." His gaze burned down at her. "Something you want to ask me, Thalia?"

She glanced over at Graves, Day, and Hsiung Ming, all of whom promptly began examining the walls of the temple as if they'd never seen something as miraculous as walls before. In Thalia and Gabriel's small, illusory bubble of privacy, she turned back to him. "Are you going to make me choose? Between the Blades and you?"

It took him a minute before he could speak. "Jesus, Thalia," Gabriel swore, stunned and a trace angry. "I'm not so small a man that I'd do that. You can't think I would."

Relief shone in her eyes. "I did not think so, but I wanted to be sure. There are so many risks."

"Sweetheart," he said firmly, taking her chin in his hand, "don't doubt me. I've run all over hell and back, seen things and faced things I never would've believed, including the kind of fear I'd never felt before. And I did all of that because I love you. That's not going to change no matter what you do, whether you're a Blade or not."

She blinked, droplets shining in her eyelashes. "Thank you."

"Don't thank me yet." Releasing her, Gabriel stalked over to the Blades. Despite the fact that they were supposedly spellbound by the temple's walls, each man smiled, the eavesdropping buggers. "Me, too," Gabriel said.

"You, what?" Graves asked.

"I want to become a Blade too. Think I've earned it."

Surprised, Thalia flinched behind him, while Graves, Day, and Hsiung Ming exchanged glances. "Be sure," Day said, serious. "This isn't a momentary fancy, Huntley. It's a lifetime's responsibility."

"Don't lecture me about responsibility, lad," Gabriel growled. "I know where my priorities lie. With Thalia. Her cause is mine. And I'll fight for her until there's not a damned breath left in my body."

"If you're certain, then," Graves said after a moment.

Gritting his teeth, Gabriel said, "I can't get any more certain. You want me to bleed, I'll do it." He pulled the knife from his belt, put it to his forearm, and moved to cut himself as Thalia yelped in alarm.

Day's hand on the hilt of the knife stopped Gabriel. "Not necessary. Blades don't require blood oaths."

"Thank God," Thalia said, coming forward and wrapping her arm around Gabriel's waist. She smiled up at him, and in her face he saw everything he ever wanted in life, and more. So much more. "I think we've seen enough blood for one day."

"If you will give us a few minutes," Hsiung Ming said, "we will prepare for the initiation." He and the two other Blades quietly excused themselves and slipped away.

Once they had gone, Thalia and Gabriel left the temple. Neither of them asked where they were going. They knew, without speaking, their destination. Together, hands interlaced, they climbed the stairs that led to the parapet. From their vantage, Gabriel and Thalia could see the whole of the monastery, damaged from the siege. The gate had been shattered, the pagoda would need to be demolished and rebuilt, and several other buildings sported cracks in the walls and chips in the masonry. The monastery would be restored and serve to guard the Source for centuries more. But the battle site didn't hold their attention for long.

They looked out over the Gobi. Afternoon sunlight blazed across the desert, and the sky was a cold blue fire above. With Thalia warm at his side, Gabriel closed his eyes and felt the dry wind sweep over his face, smelled the hard-baked earth. Beneath it all, he could feel, like a pulse, the magic of the Source, not only here, at the monastery, but everywhere in the world. He'd never noticed such things before. It had taken Thalia to open him.

"Yes," she said quietly. "I will marry you."

He chuckled as he felt a happiness he'd never believed he could experience. Opening his eyes, he brought the back of her hand to his lips. "It was a good wind that blew me to your door," he said.

"Do you think it was magic that brought us together?" she asked him, leaning her head against his shoulder. He smelled smoke in her hair and, underneath, the sweetness of her skin.

"Warriors such as us don't need magic," he said. He turned and clasped her in his arms, looked down into her dusty, tired face, so lovely he ached. "We make our own."

Epilogue

Winter's Benefit

The bullet whizzed past Thalia's ear and plunged into the snow behind her, sending up a spray of ice. She crouched behind the fence of the sheep enclosure, then, when the Russians' shots momentarily stopped, she rose up slightly, took aim and fired. Someone cursed in Russian, and she smiled to herself.

"Get him in the hand?" Gabriel asked, hunkered beside her. At her nod, he grinned. "There's a lass."

"Last I checked, I was your wife, not a lass."

He leaned forward and kissed her. "You're both." Another round of shots rang out, splintering the wood at the top of the fence. Fortunately, the sheep inside the pen crowded together, bleating in annoyance, far away from the threat. While Thalia reloaded, Gabriel fired on the band of five Russians who'd come for the ruby. A yelp sounded.

"Shoulder?" Thalia asked when Gabriel bent back down to load more ammunition. When he nodded, they shared a smile. Fighting with her husband by her side under the icy azure sky, in the diamond snow—she loved her life. She loved him. More each day.

She made herself ignore the sharp winds that tried their

best to find some bit of unprotected skin. Her fur-lined *del* and thick woolen hat ensured that she stayed relatively insulated, but gave her enough freedom of movement so that when fools like these Russians came around, seeking the tribe's ruby, she had no trouble defending the gem. Treasure hunters were infrequent, but showed up often enough so that she and Gabriel stayed busy.

"I forgot to ask," Gabriel said, between salvos. "Everything all right with Oyuun?"

"She's convinced that her niece is going to enter the *nadaam* next year. Thank you," she added, when he fired on an advancing Russian, who then had the good sense to run back to his companions as they huddled behind an empty *ger*.

Gabriel's mouth quirked in amusement. "Will she?"

"If she does, she won't be the only female in the tournament. I've heard from three others that girls from surrounding tribes are already training."

"The *nadaam* is in October," he pointed out.

More shots. She rolled her eyes. "This is growing tiresome, and I'm getting cold."

"Ready, then." Gabriel counted to three, and they charged the Russians. Not expecting a frontal attack, the would-be thieves were unprepared. Thalia, using some of the Shaolin kung fu taught to her by Lan Shun, kicked one man in the chest and struck another with a blow to the stomach. They both collapsed into the snow, groaning.

Gabriel took a more traditional approach with his fists, sending them crashing into jaws and ribcages. "You sure none of these sods is Sergei?" he panted as he easily avoided one of the Russian's punches.

She glanced around quickly. "Sorry. He's not here."

Gathering up a fistful of one man's coat, Gabriel slammed a punch into the Russian's face and the man groaned before lapsing into unconsciousness. "Damn."

"Enough! Enough!" the Russians shouted in terror. "We yield!" They covered themselves with their arms for protection.

"Leave, then," Gabriel said, using the small amount of Russian he'd learned from Thalia.

"And tell no one about the ruby," Thalia added, "or they'll suffer a similar fate."

With whimpers and moans, the Russians agreed, then stumbled toward their horses, dragging their insensate comrade, before clumsily getting back into the saddles. Thalia and Gabriel held hands as they watched the Russians ride away. Once the thwarted thieves disappeared over the horizon, Gabriel turned to her. She caught her breath at the sight of him. How he permeated the space of the steppe with his bold presence, and how she marveled every time she saw him in all his golden masculinity. With his broad shoulders filling his *del,* his fair hair now a bit longer, and carnal smile meant for Thalia alone, her husband was a vision of rugged virility that never ceased to stir her.

"Let's get you inside and warm," he rumbled.

They walked back to their *ger.* She smiled to herself when she saw sturdy horses grazing on the crimson flowers that poked through their frozen blanket. The kettle had long since been returned to China, but its magic still flowed strong in the people who had kept it for centuries.

A cheerful column of smoke rose up from their *ger.* They entered the tent and shut the door fast behind them. It took Thalia's eyes a moment to adjust to the soft light inside the tent after the dazzling brightness of outside. While she waited for her eyes to acclimate, she felt her heavy *del* removed by unseen hands, her hat plucked from her head. And a warm kiss on the tip of her chilled nose.

"Go warm up," Gabriel instructed her. Thalia nodded and moved to the stove that blazed at the center of the *ger.* She sighed when the fire's heat began to thaw her numb fingers.

"They do hold the *nadaam* in October," she said,

continuing their earlier conversation, as if the fight with the Russians had been a minor interruption. "Which means we'll be with the tribe, guarding the ruby, for months more."

"Your father said we might be called back to England before then."

She nodded with a concerned frown. "Something is brewing. The Heirs now have the Primal Source, but no one knows how or when they will use it, so we must be ready. But, until then, we must stay with the tribe. Are you content with that?"

"Hm, let's see," Gabriel mused. He began leading her toward their sleeping pallet. "Months of endless, freezing cold. Nothing but mutton and dried cheese to eat. Cantankerous horses and grumpy sheep. Oh, and fighting off any idiot who wants the ruby for himself. Does that content me?"

They reached the sleeping pallet, and Gabriel sank down, drawing Thalia with him. He pulled off her boots and then his own, then started to work at the fastenings of her tunic. Just the brushing of his fingers over her covered skin sent Thalia's pulse speeding, more so than the skirmish minutes earlier.

Although she was desperate for his touch, she covered his hand with her own, stilling him. "Does it?" she asked, looking into his topaz eyes, seeing her world and her heart reflected there. "I don't want you to have regrets."

He did not hesitate in his reply. "None. I'm never so happy as I am when we're out on the steppe together, battling side by side. Although," he added, that wicked smile curving his delicious mouth just before he brought it down onto her own lips, "this cold weather makes me damned fond of keeping warm with you."

His hand stroked down her neck, grazing the chain and locket she wore at her throat. It had been a gift from her father on her wedding day. Thalia knew, without even looking, that if she were to open the locket she would see the magical representations of those she loved most. Her father. Batu. And especially Gabriel. Forever close to her heart.

Don't miss the rest of
The Blades of the Rose series,
coming this fall!

In October, let SCOUNDREL whisk you away to the shores of Greece . . .

The Blades of the Rose are sworn to protect the Sources of magic in the world. But the work is dangerous—and they can't always protect their own . . .

READY FOR ACTION

London Harcourt's father is bent on subjugating the world's magic to British rule. But since London is a mere female, he hasn't bothered to tell her so. He's said only that he's leading a voyage to the Greek Isles. No matter, after a smothering marriage and three years of straitlaced widowhood, London jumps at the opportunity—unfortunately, right into the arms of Bennett Day . . .

RISKING IT ALL

Bennett is a ladies' man, when he's not dodging lethal attacks to protect the powers of the ancients from men like London's father. Sometimes, he's a ladies' man even when he *is* dodging them. But the minute he sees London he knows she will require his full attention. The woman is lovely, brilliant, and the only known speaker of a dialect of ancient Greek that holds the key to calling down the wrath of the gods. Bennett will be risking his life again— but around London, what really worries him is the danger to his heart . . .

"Save those slurs for your grandmother," said a deep, masculine voice to the vendor. He spoke Greek with an English accent.

London turned to the voice. And nearly lost her own.

She knew she was still, in many ways, a sheltered woman. Her society in England was limited to a select few families and assorted hangers-on, her father's business associates, their retainers and servants. At events and parties, she often saw the same people again and again. And yet, she knew with absolute clarity, that men who looked like the one standing beside her were a rare and altogether miraculous phenomenon.

There were taller men, to be sure, but it was difficult to consider this a flaw when presented with this man's lean muscularity. He wonderfully filled out the shoulders of his English coat, not bulky, but definitively capable. She understood at once that his arms, his long legs, held a leashed strength that even his negligent pose could not disguise. He called to mind the boxers that her brother, Jonas, had admired in his youth. The stranger was bareheaded, which was

odd in this heat, but it allowed her to see that his hair was
dark with just the faintest curl, ever so slightly mussed, as if
he'd recently come from bed. She suddenly imagined herself
tangling her fingers in his hair, pulling him closer.

And if that thought didn't make her blush all the harder, then
his face was the coup de grace. What wicked promises must
he have made, and made good on, with such a face. A sharp,
clean jaw, a mouth of impossible sensuality. A naughty, thoroughly masculine smile tugged at the corners of that mouth.
Crystalline eyes full of intelligent humor, the color intensely
blue. Even the small bump on the bridge of his nose—had it
been broken?—merely added to the overall impression of pro-
found male beauty. He was clean-shaven, too, so that there
could be no mistaking how outrageously handsome this
stranger was.

She may as well get on the boat back to England immediately. Surely nothing she could ever see in Greece could
eclipse the marvel of this man.

"Who are you?" the vendor shouted in Greek to the newcomer. "You defend this woman and her lies?"

"I don't care what she said," the Englishman answered
calmly, also in Greek. "Keep insulting her and I'll jam my
fist into your throat." The vendor goggled at him, but wisely
kept silent. Whoever this man was, he certainly looked capable of throwing a good punch.

Yet gently, he put a hand on London's waist and began to
guide her away. Stunned by the strange turn of events, she
let him steer her from the booth.

"All right?" he asked her in English. A concerned, warm
smile gilded his features. "That apoplectic huckster didn't
hurt you, did he?"

London shook her head, still somewhat dazed by what
had just happened, but more so by the attractiveness of the
man walking at her side. She felt the warmth of his hand at
her back and knew it was improper, but she couldn't move

away or even regret the impertinence. "His insults weren't very creative."

He chuckled at this and the sound curled like fragrant smoke low in her belly. "I'll go back and show him how it's done."

"Oh, no," she answered at once. "I think you educated him enough for one day."

Even as he smiled at her, he sent hard warning glances at whomever stared at her. "So what had his fez in a pinch?"

She held up and unfolded her hand, which still held the shard of pottery. "We were disputing this, but, gracious, I forgot I still had it. Maybe I should give it back."

He plucked the piece of pottery from her hand. As he did this, the tips of his fingers brushed her bare palm. A hot current sparked to life where he touched. She could not prevent the shiver of awareness that ran through her body. She met his gaze, and sank into their cool aquatic depths as he stared back. This felt stronger than attraction. Something that resounded through the innermost recesses of herself, in deep, liquid notes, like a melody or song one might sing to bring the world into being. And it seemed he felt it, too, in the slight breath he drew in, the straightening of his posture. Breaking away from his gaze, London snatched her glove from Sally, who trailed behind them with a look of severe disapproval. London tugged on the glove.

He cleared his throat, then gave her back the pottery. "Keep it. Consider it his tribute."

She put it into her reticule, though it felt strange to take something she did not pay for.

"Thank you for coming to my aid," she said as they continued to walk. "I admit that getting into arguments with vendors in Monastiraki wasn't at the top of my list of Greek adventures."

"The best part about adventures is that you can't plan them."

She laughed. "Spoken like a true adventurer."

"Done my share." He grinned. "Ambushing bandits by the Khaznah temple in the cliffs of Petra. Climbing volcanoes in the steam-shrouded interior of Iceland."

"Sounds wonderful," admitted London with a candor that surprised herself. She felt, oddly, that she could trust this English stranger with her most prized secrets. "Even what happened back there at that booth was marvelous, in its way. I don't *want* to get into a fight, but it's such a delight to finally be out here, in the world, truly experiencing things."

"Including hot, dusty, crowded Athens."

"*Especially* hot, dusty, crowded Athens."

"My, my," he murmured, looking down at her with approval. "A swashbuckling lady. Such a rare treasure."

Wryly, she asked, "Treasure, or aberration?"

He stopped walking and gazed at her with an intensity that caught in her chest. "Treasure. Most definitely."

Again, he left her stunned. She was nearly certain that any man would find a woman's desire for experience and adventure to be at best ridiculous, at worst, offensive. Yet here was this stranger who not only didn't dismiss her feelings, but actually approved and, yes, admired them. What a city of wonders was this Athens! Although, London suspected, it was not the city so much as the man standing in front of her that proved wondrous.

"So tell me, fellow adventurer," she said, finding her voice, "from whence do you come? What exotic port of call?" She smiled. "Dover? Plymouth? Southampton?"

A glint of wariness cooled his eyes. "I don't see why it matters."

Strange, the abrupt change in him. "I thought that's what one did when meeting a fellow countryman abroad," she said. "Find out where they come from. If you know the same people." When he continued to look at her guardedly, she demonstrated, "'Oh, you're from Manchester? Do you know Jane?'"

The chill in his blue eyes thawed, and he smiled. "Of course, Jane! Makes the worst meat pies. Dresses like a Anglican bishop."

"So you *do* know her!"

They shared a laugh, two English strangers in the chaos of an Athenian market, and London felt within her a swell of happiness rising like a spring tide. As if in silent agreement, they continued to stroll together in a companionable silence. With a long-limbed, loose stride, he walked beside her. He hooked his thumbs into the pockets of his simple, well-cut waistcoat, the picture of a healthy young man completely comfortable with himself. And why shouldn't he be? No man had been so favored by Nature's hand. She realized that he hadn't told her where he was from, but she wouldn't press the issue, enjoying the glamour of the unknown.

His presence beside her was tangible, a continuous pulse of uncivilized living energy, as though being escorted by a large and untamed mountain cat that vacillated between eating her and dragging her off to its lair.

In November, get lost
in the Canadian wilderness with REBEL . . .

*On the Canadian frontier in 1875, nature is a harsh
mistress. But the supernatural can really do you in . . .*

A LONE WOLF

Nathan Lesperance is used to being different.
He's the first Native attorney in Vancouver,
and welcome neither with white society nor his sometime tribe.
Not to mention the powerful wildness he's always
felt inside him, too dangerous to set free.
Then he met Astrid Bramfield and saw his like
within her piercing eyes. Now, unless she helps him through
the harsh terrain and the harsher unknowns of his
true abilities, it could very well get him killed . . .

AND THE WOMAN WHO
LEFT THE PACK

Astrid has traveled this path before. Once she was a
Blade of the Rose,
protecting the world's magic from
unscrupulous men, with her husband
by her side. But she's loved and lost, and as a world-class
frontierswoman, she knows all about survival. Nathan's
searing gaze and long, lean muscles mean nothing but
trouble. Yet something has ignited a forgotten flame inside
her: a burning need for adventure, for life—and perhaps
even for love . . .

He had looked into her. Not merely seen her hunger for living, but felt it, too. She saw that at once. He recognized it in her. Two creatures, meeting by chance, staring at one another warily. And with reluctant longing.

Yet it wasn't only that immediate connection she had felt when meeting Lesperance. There was magic surrounding him.

Astrid wondered if Lesperance even knew how magic hovered over him, how it surrounded him like a lover, leaving patterns of nearly visible energy in his wake. She didn't think he was conscious of it. Nothing in his manner suggested anything of the sort. Nathan Lesperance, incredibly, was utterly unaware that he was a magical being. Not metaphorical magic, but *true* magic.

She knew, however. Astrid had spent more than ten years surrounded by magic of almost every form. Some of it benevolent, like the Healing Mists of Ho Hsien-Ku, some of it dark, such as the Javanese serpent king Naga Pahoda, though most magic was neither good nor evil. It simply *was*. And Astrid recognized it, particularly when sharing a very small space, as the Mounties' office had been.

If Nathan Lesperance's fierce attractiveness and unwanted understanding did not drive Astrid from the trading post, back to the shelter of her solitary homestead, then the magic enveloping him certainly would. She wanted nothing more to do with magic. It had cost her love once before, and she would not allow it to hurt her again.

But something had changed. She'd felt it, not so long ago. Magic existed like a shining web over the world, binding it together with filaments of energy. Being near magic for many years made her especially sensitive to it. When she returned from Africa, that sensitivity had grown even more acute. She tried to block it out, especially when she left England, but it never truly went away.

Only a few weeks earlier, Astrid had been out tending to her horse when a deep, rending sensation tore through her, sending her to her knees. She'd knelt in the dirt, choking, shaking, until she'd gained her strength again and tottered inside. Eventually, the pain subsided, but not the sense of looming catastrophe. Something had shaken and split the magical web. A force greater than anyone had ever known. And to release it meant doom.

What was it? The Blades had to know how to avert the disaster. They would fight against it, as they always did. But without her.

A memory flitted through her mind. Months earlier, she'd had a dream and it had stayed with her vividly. She dreamt of her Compass, of the Blades, and heard someone calling her, calling her home. Astrid had dismissed the dream as a vestige of homesickness, which reared up now and again, especially after she'd been alone for so long.

The jingle of her horse's bridle snapped her attention back to the present. She cursed herself for drifting. A moment's distraction could easily lead to death out here. Stumbling between a bear sow and her cub. Crossing paths with vicious whiskey runners. A thousand ways to die. So when her awareness suddenly prickled once again, Astrid did not dismiss it.

A rustle, and movement behind her. Astrid swung her horse around, taking up her rifle, to confront who or whatever was there.

She blinked, hardly believing what she saw. A man walked through tall grasses lining the pass trail. He walked with steady but dazed steps, hardly aware of his surroundings. He was completely naked.

"Lesperance?"

Astrid turned her horse on the trail and urged it closer. Dear God, it *was* Lesperance. She decocked her rifle and slung it back over her shoulder.

He didn't seem to hear her, so she said again, coming nearer, "Mr. Lesperance?" She could see now, only ten feet away, that cuts, scrapes, and bruises covered his body. His very nude, extremely well-formed body. She snapped her eyes to his face before they could trail lower than his navel. "What happened to you?"

His gaze, dark and blank, regarded her with a removed curiosity, as if she was a little bird perched on a windowsill. He stopped walking and stared at her.

Astrid dismounted at once, pulling a blanket from her pack. Within moments, she wrapped it around his waist, took his large hand in hers, and coaxed his fingers to hold the blanket closed. Then she pulled off her coat and draped it over his shoulders. Despite the fact that the coat was quite large on Astrid, it barely covered his shoulders, and the sleeves stuck out like wings. In other circumstances, he would have looked comical. But there was nothing faintly amusing about this situation.

Magic still buzzed around him, though somewhat dimmer than before.

"Where are your clothes? How did you get here? Are you badly hurt?"

None of her questions penetrated the fog enveloping him. She bent closer to examine his wounds. Some of the cuts were deep, as though made by knives, and rope abrasions circled his wrists. Bruises shadowed his knees and knuckles. Blood had dried in the corners of his mouth. Nothing looked serious, but out in the wilderness, even the most minor injury held the potential for disaster. And, without clothing, not even a Native inured to the changeable weather could survive. He was in shock, just beginning to shake.

"Lesperance," she said, taking hold of his wide shoulders and staring into his eyes intently, "listen to me. I need to see to your wounds. We're going to have to ride back to my cabin."

"Astrid . . ." he murmured with a slow blink, then his nostrils flared like a beast scenting its mate. A hungry look crossed his face. "Astrid."

It was unexpected, given the circumstances, yet seeing that look of need, hearing him say her name, filled her with a responding desire. "Mrs. Bramfield," she reminded him. And herself. They were polite strangers.

"Astrid," he said, more insistent. He reached up to touch her face.

She grabbed his hand, pulling it away from her face. At least she wore gloves, so she didn't have to touch his bare skin. "Come on." Astrid gently tugged him towards her horse. Once beside the animal, she swung up into the saddle, put her rifle across her lap, and held a hand out to him. He stared at it with a frown, as though unfamiliar with the phenomenon of hands.

"We have to go *now,* Lesperance," Astrid said firmly. "Those wounds of yours need attention, and whatever or whoever did this to you is probably still out there."

He cast a look around, seeming to find a shred of clarity in the hazy morass of his addled brain. Something dark and angry crossed his face. He took a step away, as if he meant to go after whoever had hurt him. His hands curled into fists. Insanity. He was unarmed, naked, wounded.

"Now," Astrid repeated.

Somehow, she got through to him. He took her hand and, with a dexterity that surprised her, given his condition, mounted up behind her.

God, she didn't want to do this. But there was no other choice. "Put your arms around my waist," she said through gritted teeth. When he did so, she added, "Hold tightly to me. Not that tight," she gasped as his grip turned to bands of steel. He loosened his hold slightly. "Good. Do not let go. Do you understand?"

He nodded, then winced as if the movement gave him pain. "Can't stay up."

"Lean against me if you have to." She mentally groaned when he did just that, and she felt him, even through her bulky knitted vest, shirt, and sturdy trousers. Heavy and hard and solid with muscle. Everywhere. His arms, his chest, his thighs, pressed against hers. Astrid closed her eyes for a moment as she felt his warm breath along the nape of her neck.

"All set?" she asked, barely able to form the words around her clenched jaw.

He tried to nod again but the effort made him moan. The plaintive sound, coming from such a strong, potent man, pulled tight on feelings Astrid didn't want to have.

"Thank . . . you," he said faintly.

She didn't answer him. Instead, she kicked her horse into a gallop, knowing deep in her heart that she was making a terrible mistake.

And in December, STRANGER
brings the adventure back to London . . .

*He protects the world's magic—with his science.
But even the best scientists can
fall prey to the right chemistry . . .*

LOOKING FOR TROUBLE

Gemma Murphy has a nose for a story—
even if the boys in Chicago's newsrooms would rather
focus on her chest. So when she runs into
a handsome man of mystery discussing how
to save the world from fancy-pants Brit conspirators,
she's sensing a scoop. Especially when he mentions
there's magic involved. Of course, getting him
on the record would be easier if he hadn't
caught her eavesdropping . . .

LIGHTING HIS FUSE

Catullus Graves knows what it's like to be shut out: his
ancestors were slaves. And he's a genius inventor with
appropriately eccentric habits, so even people who love
him find him a little odd. But after meeting a certain red-
headed scribbler, he's thinking of other types of science.
Inconvenient, given that he needs to focus on preventing
the end of the world as we know it. But with Gemma's
insatiable curiosity sparking Catullus's inventive impulses,
they might set off something explosive anyway . . .

Now was her chance to do some investigating. Surely she'd find something of note in his cabin. A fast glance up and down the passageway ensured she was entirely alone.

Gemma opened the cabin door.

And found herself staring at a drawn gun.

Damn. He *was* in. Working silently at a table by the light of one small lamp. At her entrance, he was out of his chair and drawing a revolver in one smooth motion.

She drew her Derringer.

They stared at each other.

In the small cabin, Catullus Graves's head nearly brushed the ceiling as he faced her. Her reporter's eye quickly took in the details of his appearance. Even though he was the only black passenger on the ship, more than just his skin color made him stand out. His scholar's face, carved by an artist's hand, drew one's gaze. Arresting in both its elegant beauty and keen perception. A neatly trimmed goatee framed his sensuous mouth. The long, lean lines of his body—the breadth of his shoulders, the length of his legs—revealed a man comfortable with action as well as thought. Though, until now, Gemma had not been aware *how* comfortable. Until she saw the revolver held easily, familiarly in his large hand. A revolver trained on her. She'd have to do something about that.

"Mr. Graves," she murmured, shutting the door behind her.

Behind his spectacles, Catullus Graves's dark eyes widened. "Miss Murphy?"

Despite the fact that she was in danger of being shot, it wasn't until Graves spoke to Gemma that her heart began to pound. And she was absurdly glad he did remember her, for she certainly hadn't forgotten him. They'd met but briefly. Spoke together only once. Yet the impression of him remained, and not merely because she had an excellent memory.

"I thought you were out," she said. As if that excused her behavior.

"Wanted to get a barometric reading." Catullus Graves frowned. "How did you get in?"

"I opened the door," she answered. Which was only a part of the truth. She wasn't certain he would believe her if she told him everything.

"That's not possible. I put an unbreakable lock on it. Nothing can open it without a special key that *I* made." He sounded genuinely baffled, convinced of the security of his invention. Gemma glanced around the cabin. Covering all available surfaces, including the table where he had been working moments earlier, were small brass tools of every sort and several mechanical objects in different states of assembly. Graves was an inventor, she realized. She knew her way around a workshop, but the complex devices Graves worked on left her mystified.

She also realized—the same time he did—that they were alone in his cabin. His small, *intimate* cabin. She tried, without much success, not to look at the bed, just as she tried and failed not to picture him stripping out of his clothes before getting into that bed for the night. She barely knew this man! Why in the name of the saints did her mind lead her exactly where she did not want it to go?

The awareness of intimacy came over them both like an exotic perfume. He glanced down and saw that he was in his shirtsleeves, and made a cough of startled chagrin. He reached for his coat draped over the back of a chair. One hand still training his gun on her, he used the other to don his coat.

"Strange to see such modesty on the other end of a Webley," Gemma said.

"I don't believe this situation is covered in many etiquette manuals," he answered. "What are you doing here?"

One hand gripping her Derringer, Gemma reached into her pocket with the other. "Easy," she said, when he tensed. "I'm just getting this." She produced a small notebook, which she flipped open with a practiced one-handed gesture.

"Pardon—I'll have a look at that," Graves said. Polite, but wary. He stepped forward, one broad-palmed hand out.

A warring impulse flared within Gemma. She wanted to press herself back against the door, as if some part of herself needed protecting from him. Not from the gun in his other hand, but *him,* his tall, lean presence that fairly radiated with intelligence and energy. Keep impartial, she reminded herself. That was her job. Report the facts. Don't let emotion, especially *female* emotion, cloud her judgment.

And yet that damned traitorous female part of her responded at once to Catullus Graves's nearness. Wanted to be closer, drawn in by the warmth of his eyes and body. An immaculately dressed body. As he crossed the cabin with only a few strides, Gemma undertook a quick perusal. Despite being pulled on hastily, his dark green coat perfectly fit the breadth of his shoulders. She knew that beneath the coat was a pristine white shirt. His tweed trousers outlined the length of his legs, tucked into gleaming brown boots. His burgundy silk cravat showed off the clean lines of his jaw. And his waistcoat. Good gravy. It was a minor work of art, superbly fitted, the color of claret, and worked all over with golden embroidery that, upon closer inspection, revealed itself to be an intricate lattice of vines and flowers. Golden silk-covered buttons ran down its front, and a gold watch chain hung between a pocket and one of the buttons. Hanging from the chain, a tiny fob in the shape of a knife glinted in the lamplight.

On any other man, such a waistcoat would be dandyish. Ridiculous, even. But not on Catullus Graves. On him, the garment was a masterpiece, and perfectly masculine, highlighting his natural grace and the shape of his well-formed torso. She knew about fashion, having been forced to write more articles than she wanted on the subject. And this man not only defined style, he surpassed it.

But she was through with writing about fashion. That was precisely why she was on this steamship in the middle of the Atlantic Ocean.

With this in mind, Gemma tore her gaze from this vision to find him watching her. A look of faint perplexity crossed his face. Almost bashfulness at her interest.

She let him take the notebook from her, and their fingertips accidentally brushed.

He almost dropped the notebook, and she felt heat shoot into her cheeks. She had the bright ginger hair and pale, freckled skin of her Irish father, which meant that, even in low lamplight, when Gemma blushed, only a blind imbecile could miss it.

Catullus Graves was not a blind imbecile. His reaction to her blush was to flush, himself, a deeper mahogany staining his coffee-colored face.

A knock on the door behind her had Gemma edging quickly away, breaking the spell. She backed up until she pressed against a bulkhead.

"Catullus?" asked a female voice on the other side of the door. The woman from earlier.

Graves and Gemma held each other's gaze, weapons still drawn and trained on each other.

"Yes," he answered.

"Is everything all right?" the woman outside pressed. "Can we come in?"

Continuing to hold Gemma's stare, Graves reached over and opened the door.

Immediately, the fair-haired woman and her male companion entered.

"Thought it was nothing," the man said, grim. "But I *know* I've caught that scent before, and—" He stopped, tensing. He swung around to face Gemma, who was plastered against the bulkhead with her little pistol drawn.

Both he and the woman had their own revolvers out before one could blink.

And now Gemma had not one but *three* guns aimed at her.

LECTURES
ON CONTEMPORARY
SYNTACTIC THEORIES

CSLI
Lecture Notes
Number 3

LECTURES
ON CONTEMPORARY
SYNTACTIC THEORIES

AN INTRODUCTION TO GOVERNMENT-BINDING THEORY,
GENERALIZED PHRASE STRUCTURE GRAMMAR,
AND LEXICAL-FUNCTIONAL GRAMMAR

Peter Sells

Postscript by Thomas Wasow

 CENTER FOR THE STUDY
OF LANGUAGE
AND INFORMATION

CSLI was founded early in 1983 by researchers from Stanford University, SRI International, and Xerox PARC to further research and development of integrated theories of language, information, and computation. CSLI headquarters and the publication offices are located at the Stanford site.

CSLI/SRI International
333 Ravenswood Avenue
Menlo Park, CA 94025

CSLI/Stanford
Ventura Hall
Stanford, CA 94305

CSLI/Xerox PARC
3333 Coyote Hill Road
Palo Alto, CA 94304

Library of Congress Cataloging-in-Publication Data

Sells, Peter.
  Lectures on contemporary syntactic theories.

  (CSLI lecture notes ; no. 3)
Bibliography: p.
Includes indexes.

  1. Grammar, Comparative and general–Syntax.
2. Government-binding theory (Linguistics) 3. Generalized phrase structure grammar. 4. Lexical-functional grammar. 5. Generative grammar. I. Title. II. Series.
P291.S36   1987   415   87–10243
ISBN 0–937073–13–X
ISBN 0–937073–14–8 (pbk.)

Author's Preface

This second printing incorporates several minor changes of text and references, but does not differ in any substantial way from its predecessor. There has been some minor reformatting, and indexes of names and subjects have been added. The changes that have been made are due in large part to the comments I have received from many people over the past year; my thanks to them all.

In the Spring of 1985, I gave a series of lectures on contemporary syntactic theories at the University of California, Santa Cruz, covering Government-Binding Theory, Generalized Phrase Structure Grammar, and Lexical-Functional Grammar. The material presented here is based on my notes from those lectures. I have tried to provide enough background so that the non-linguist might understand the concepts and motivations in each of the theories. To that end, I include a short introductory chapter. In addition, Tom Wasow has generously provided a Postscript to my own presentation which gives a more general historical and methodological overview.

I should emphasize that the three theories discussed here by no means exhaust the inventory of syntactic theories deserving the label 'contemporary'; rather, these are the ones of which I have enough knowledge to be able to discuss them in a serious way. I have not made any effort to compare analyses of particular constructions; such an enterprise would require another separate book in itself. Rather, I have tried to present the most important aspects of each of the theories. I have also limited myself (except where forced by expository obligations) to discussion of purely syntactic aspects of these theories.

Syntactic theories change rather rapidly, and nothing presented here represents the current state of the art within any theory; moreover, I have not attempted to provide definitive analyses, but rather representative ones. The version of Government-Binding Theory presented here is roughly that in Chomsky (1981) and Chomsky (1982), and does not incorporate recent developments documented in Chomsky (1986a, 1986b). The version of Generalized Phrase Structure Grammar is that given in Gazdar, Klein, Pullum, and Sag (1985), and does not include recent developments stemming out of the work of Pollard (1984). Finally, the version of Lexical-Functional Grammar is based on that presented in Kaplan and Bresnan (1982), with some more recent modifications added. In each case, I have chosen the particular formulation of the theory that seems to me to be most internally consistent and accessible to the non-specialist. I have not provided extensive references, though it has been my intention that from the references I do provide, the reader will be able to work back to a wider literature.

I would like to thank everyone connected with the Syntax Research Center at Santa Cruz for their hospitality and kindness, especially Victoria Liptak, who organized the lecture series. The presentation of the material here has benefited greatly from comments on an earlier draft by Joan Bresnan, Carol Cleland, Edit Doron, Ron Kaplan, David Perlmutter, Geoffrey Pullum, Ivan Sag, Tim Stowell, Tom Wasow, and Annie Zaenen, though I remain solely responsible for all errors, inconsistencies and misstatements that persist. The writing and preparation of this work would have been much more arduous without the support of Geoffrey Pullum, Ivan Sag, and Tom Wasow, and without the aid of Masayo Iida and Dikran Karagueuzian, who, in their own ways, suffered uncomplainingly in their dealings with an impatient author. I would also like to thank Emma Pease for her work on my final draft, to bring it into its present form.

The published version of these notes was prepared at The Center for the Study of Language and Information, and was made possible by a gift from the System Development Foundation.

–Stanford
February, 1987

Contents

Chapter 1

Basic Concepts of Syntax

The different syntactic theories that I will describe here have a shared ancestry and a common core domain of concepts and terminology. This chapter will provide a backdrop against which the remaining chapters will be set, and will cover the basic vocabulary and the shared assumptions that are basic to contemporary syntactic theory.

In fact, for many readers of this book, the very idea of syntax as it is conceived of here may be somewhat unusual; the various rules of syntax—or of grammar—that we remember from high school are usually of a pre-scriptive nature. Probably the most salient and common is the supposed prohibition against splitting the infinitive: against saying, for example, *to boldly go* rather than *to go boldly*. The factors that govern the distribution of these two alternatives are partly historical and, in our current society, partly sociological. From the point of view of syntax—and from this point on I use both the terms 'syntax' and 'grammar' in a technical sense—forces of history and sociology are largely irrelevant. For syntax concerns itself not with the distinction between a possible phrase in English such as *to go boldly* and a passable (if somehow dispreferred) variant; syntax concerns itself with the possible and the *im*possible phrases of English, or of any other human language for that matter. The key datum in syntax is a difference that a native speaker will assent to, that some sentence A is possible while sentence B is under no stretch of the imagination acceptable as a sentence of the language in question. If one is developing a theory of gravity, the key datum is that things fall and very rarely rise. The difference between possible and impossible sentences is in principle no different from the point of view of constructing a theory to explain some observed behavior as the difference between attraction to a large body and repulsion from it, and in practice that linguistic difference is at least as hard to discern as is 'pure fall,' with all external effects and disturbances removed. In the following section, I would like to elucidate the nature of syntactic data as conceived by practitioners of the theories to be described below.

However, before moving on, I would not like to leave the reader with the impression that the study of syntax is of necessity divorced from perhaps more tangible considerations of history, sociology, and whatever else contributes to human experience. Ultimately, when we know much more about all these things, syntax will have its place in larger theories of human action and human interaction; until then, it is probably wise, and from my current exegetical point of view essential, to leave such larger considerations out of mind. One of the compelling things about syntax is that while the study of it is a highly abstract theoretical enterprise, syntacticians are discovering and refining their understanding of phenomena that are arguably quite real.

1. Syntactic Competence

The beginning point of the syntactic enterprise as conceived of currently is the question "What do we know when we know a language (say English)?" The answer given by Noam Chomsky in his book *Syntactic Structures,* published in 1957, brought about a whole new discipline within the larger field of linguistics; his answer was that what we know is a collection of words and rules with which we *generate* strings of those words which we call sentences of our language. Any string of words that cannot be produced in this way is not a sentence of the language. Moreover, while there are only a finite number of elements in this collection, say several thousand words and no more than a few hundred rules, they will generate an infinite number of sentences, some of them very long. This will happen as some of the rules will be recursive, i.e., they apply to their own output to produce the same structure over again. For example, any linguist will tell you that *George thinks that it never rains in Tulsa* is a sentence of English, and that we can continue to produce new sentences of English by embedding that under the sequence *George thinks that* .... We will end up with sentences of the form *George thinks that George thinks that ... George thinks that it never rains in Tulsa*; if we collect all of these sentences we will have a boring, somewhat useless, but nevertheless syntactically impeccable subset of English.[1] These will all be, then, *grammatical* sentences. The subfield

---

[1] It is important to note that it is the *structure* that is generated over and over here; with a few more words we could add to our set structurally identical

of linguistics that takes this point of view, that what is important is this conception of generating sentences, is known as *Generative Grammar*.

1.1. Grammaticality

Language ultimately expresses a relation between sound at one end of the linguistic spectrum and meaning at the other. I produce sounds—or, in the present context, graphic symbols—which you perceive and derive some meaning from. Somewhere in the middle of this process lies syntax. It is a fact of English, for instance, that the sequence *The women sold the paintings* can convey a certain meaning that *The women the paintings sold* can not. Two points are relevant here: one, it is not the case that we couldn't guess what this last example would mean—what it should mean is relatively clear; the point is, one is not speaking English if one chooses to convey that meaning in that way. Secondly, there are many languages of the world in which the word-for-word translation of the second example is indeed a grammatical (and in some cases the only grammatical) way of arranging the words in question to convey the meaning in question. Thus, there is nothing inherent in the message conveyed that could explain the impossibility of that sequence as being a sentence of English.

In *Syntactic Structures,* Chomsky gave the now-famous example (1) to illustrate the importance of investigating syntax independently (in part) of other considerations:

(1)   Colorless green ideas sleep furiously.

This is meaningless in any usual sense yet, again, syntactically impeccable. In contrast, (2) is as senseless, yet also syntactically deviant:

(2)   *Furiously sleep ideas green colorless.

The asterisk (*) preceding the example indicates that it is syntactically ill-formed; thus our rules for English should be set up so as to produce (1) but not (2). We see the syntactic distinction again if we replace the words in these examples with others so that the whole thing makes sense, as in (3).

(3)   a.   Revolutionary new ideas appear infrequently.

      b.   *Infrequently appear ideas new revolutionary.

---

but rather more useful sentences like *George thinks that Max said that Betty believes that it never rains in Tulsa.*

In these examples, I have replaced some words with other words belonging to the same part of speech—or, as I shall say here, in more usual linguistic usage—belonging to the same *syntactic category*. In fact, this switch indicates another aspect of syntax that Chomsky emphasized—the structure of sentences. For the real syntactic truth underlying the contrasts in grammaticality seen above is that while some sequences of the form

Adjective-Adjective-Noun-Verb-Adverb

are syntactically well-formed in English, sequences of the form

Adverb-Verb-Noun-Adjective-Adjective

are not. Plugging in certain combinations of words will also lead to sentences that are meaningful in the former case, but this is not a relevant consideration if we are just concerned with syntactic well-formedness. A more subtle grammatical (i.e., syntactic) contrast is seen in the examples in (4):

(4) a.   The book seems interesting.

  b.   *The child seems sleeping.

Again, it is obvious what (4)b means; but again it is not English (the closest acceptable example is *The child seems to be sleeping*).

Although I have spoken here of strings of words, the most important aspect of the syntax is its structure, and not simply the strings. I will discuss the concept of structure in more detail in the following section.

1.2. Universal Properties of Language

I have so far talked mainly about data from English; yet what I have said would hold, other things being equal, for any other human language too. Thus it is a fact of English sentence structure that it has the basic order subject-verb-object (*The man read the book*), while Welsh, for instance, has verb-subject-object (*Gwelodd – y dyn – y llyfr*), and Japanese has subject-object-verb (*Sono otoko ga – hon o – yonda*).

When someone knows a language, any language, that person is considered to possess a certain competence such that they can distinguish between grammatical and ungrammatical sequences of words in that language. Actually, we must be a bit more precise here, and note that we are talking about the grammaticality of sequences of words *qua* sentences.

For example, the sequence *the man the woman was accidentally* is not a grammatical sentence, but it can be part of a grammatical sentence: *Ferdinand rescued the man the woman was accidentally chained to.* (Anyone still having difficulty should imagine a *that* between *man* and *the woman*.)

Digressing briefly, I should point out that I will use the words 'word' and 'sentence' without providing a definition of either. These particular terms appear to resist all scrutiny, and while I know of countless definitions and counter-definitions in the literature, I know of none that accord with intuition in all cases. Yet in the case of sentences, which is what we are primarily interested in here, we can be sure that we are restricting ourselves in our syntactic work to a subset of English sentences. While we might not be able to claim (as no one can at present) to have an understanding of all of English, we can claim to have an understanding of some of it.

So, while studying and making hypotheses about the syntax of, say, English or Irish, we must be careful to keep in mind a range of potential variation. It is a goal of syntactic theory to provide a descriptive space within which the range of variation that we find among languages is precisely captured. That is, we would like to have a theory which is flexible enough to allow us to characterize all the fine variation we find, while still not allowing us to even consider certain possibilities; to choose a common example illustrating the last desideratum here, there are no languages in which questions are formed from normal sentences by reversing all the words in the sentence, as if (3)b were an interrogative form of (3)a.

Ultimately, knowledge of this sort would lead us to various new reseach areas concerned with the mind—we might ask questions like "What can we find out about the computational procedures and capacities of the brain given that we know that it never has to deal with operations reversing all linguistic symbols in a given sequence?" or "How is it possible that language is learned?" This latter question is considered very important and has been very influential in shaping research programs in syntax. Chomsky certainly conceives of linguistics (i.e., syntax) as a part of cognitive psychology in that ultimately we are probing properties of the mind. There is a large and healthy sub-discipline of Psycholinguistics which relates our knowledge of the mind and of language.

Again, it is not necessary to go into detail on these matters here, for the matters of syntax that I will discuss below are (or can be considered) largely independent of psycholinguistic concerns; the only point is that 'universal' in the sense that it will be used in this work refers to properties ultimately attributed to mental phenomena, rather than, say, social ones. There is a wide range of variation among linguists as to how psychologically real they conceive their syntactic theories to be, and in a presentation like this I think it is better to err on the side of caution. So when I speak of syntactic explanation I will initially be speaking of a system of description that covers the most facts with the minimum number of independent assumptions and postulations. I leave it up to personal preference whether a theory of syntax is to be viewed as a direct account of our linguistic knowledge, or as a description of a system whose behavior models our linguistic behavior.

1.3. Data

In this subsection I would like to address two matters, one of substance in the theoretical sense and one of substance in the material sense. Each distinction of syntactic structure that we find is the result of a little experiment—we find our native speaker of Irish or Hopi or whatever we want, and we try to tap that person's sense of grammaticality of certain strings of words. Linguists refer to these judgements as *intuitions*. Intuitions are, unfortunately, not presented to us in any obvious way, and often they are not simple matters of 'ungrammatical' (*) versus 'OK.' Consider the examples in (5): how do we describe a book belonging to Martha and me?

(5) a.   Martha and my book

    b.   Martha's and my book

    c.   Martha and me's book

    d.   Martha and I's book

There are many more possibilities here. We may also have some prescriptive idea of how to say this. My sense, for what it is worth, is that (d) is not acceptable and that all of the others are clumsy but I could imagine producing them. From these facts alone, then, we don't know exactly how to describe the rules for putting together English noun phrases (for that is what these examples are; a noun phrase usually contains a noun and maybe some modifying adjectives and determiners). Yet some things seem clearly no good—for example, *Martha's and me book* is surely impossible, and should be excluded. So even this apparently failing little experiment can give us some useful data.

Fuzziness of intuitions is noise in the data to the syntactician, and one must simply find ways to deal with it. Linguists live with this fuzziness and try to stick with clear cases as much as possible; and as intuitions are not something the normal speaker of English has any conception of, linguists have to learn to tap into their intuitions. Linguists are in a sense language-experts, for they, if anyone, have some idea of what is English and what isn't. Consequently, it is quite possible that some of the judgements of grammaticality that I will indicate in the following chapters, while accepted by a body of professional linguists, will seem opaque and perhaps perverse to the reader. I shall therefore take a little more space below in elucidating the notion of intuitions.

First, let me try a little experiment on your intuitions. Imagine that I'm asking questions about a movie that you saw and the man who directed it.

(6)   a.   Which movie did you meet the man that directed?

      b.   Which man did you see the movie that directed?

Both of the sentences in (6) are ungrammatical,[2] yet one can still sense a contrast—(b) is somehow *worse* than (a). You will probably experience a structural effect in (b)—it seems to want to have the interpretation where the movie directed the man, which is silly given our real-world knowledge. I would note that although this is a feature of the interpretation of the example, it is nonetheless a syntactic feature, for it derives from a decision about what should be the subject and what should be the object of the verb *direct*.

There are two further points about intuitions that I would like to make; the first concerns the relationship between intuitions of grammaticality and our actual linguistic usage. It is not a claim of theoretical syntax that people actually speak all the time in fully grammatical sentences—clearly this is not so; there are innumerable mental and physical obstacles to be overcome in any given speech-situation. Does this undermine the foundation upon which the study of syntax is based?—not in the least, for what is important is that once the rigors of actually producing speech are abstracted away from, one can get fairly reliable data about what is and what is

---

[2] It is a strange quirk of linguistic terminology that leads me to be able to speak of 'ungrammatical sentence,' for these should be mutually incompatible terms. It is, of course, a potentially significant fact that English (or any other language to the best of my knowledge) does not provide a word meaning 'thing that would be a sentence if only it weren't ungrammatical.' As this is even more unwieldy than 'ungrammatical sentence,' I shall be sloppy and stick to the shorter phrase.

not English. Using a close analogy, philosophers and semanticists concern themselves a lot with truth-conditions when talking about meaning. Thus one would normally use the sentence *It is raining in Tulsa* if indeed it were true that it was raining in Tulsa, and any native speaker would assent to this. Yet it is not a semantic fact of any human language that its speakers (always) speak the truth; again, quite clearly they do not. (This is not to deny that there is in general some communicative utility to speaking the truth, and usually people do; big liars are people who tell big lies, not who lie with every utterance. Similarly, most utterances are grammatical, especially in careful styles.)

The last point about intuitions is more of a caveat. The intuitions we have are intuitions relative to a structure assigned to the example under consideration. Given enough imagination and time, it is probable that most of the sequences of words deemed ungrammatical in this work could be found to be acceptable. For example, any linguist will tell you that (7) is ungrammatical:

(7)   *Reagan thinks bananas.

Why? For the verb *think* takes as its complement (i.e., the sequence that follows it) something that is of a sentential, or clausal, nature, as in *Reagan thinks that it never rains in Tulsa*. Yet we have apparently given *thinks* a direct object noun phrase, as if it were *Reagan sells bananas*. Assigned this syntactic structure, the example is ungrammatical because it has failed to conform to the rules of English.

Now the string *Reagan thinks bananas* is in fact acceptable, as will be apparent in (8):

(8)   What is Kissinger's favorite fruit?
         —Reagan thinks bananas.

We understand this with the clausal complement, as our rules say we must; the interpretation of the example is something like *Reagan thinks (that) bananas (are Kissinger's favourite fruit),* with the parenthesized words omitted. In confirming that the complement of *think* really must be a sentence, this again demonstrates the importance of investigating the structure assigned rather than the string.

At the beginning of this subsection I said I would talk about the theoretical and material substance of judgements and example sentences and phrases. All of the above has been the theoretical part; now I will say a few words about material substance.

Example sentences in syntax are used to make specific points of theoretical relevance, though the same sentence may of course be used to demonstrate different points. In general, examples are constructed by the linguist, often on the spur of the moment (an ability to produce relevant examples quickly is a definite asset), and become data objects through publication in the literature and subsequent discussion and analysis. For example, it is part of many people's syntactic training to learn about the 'sonata-sentences' and to understand why they are important. (Their importance is too much buried in complex theoretical issues for me to display it here.) Consequently, most of the examples here will probably strike the reader as unimaginative at best; this is precisely what they are, for again we are not concerned with usage, but with underlying knowledge. In fact, the different theories described below use slightly different styles of example, and I have done my best to make each chapter representative in that regard too—though I defer to my reader a theory of what those differences indicate.

2. Constituency

I have been speaking of the structure assigned to a string of words; one thing that is clear is that the job of syntax is not simply to characterize strings of English, but also to assign them an appropriate structure. Exactly how one goes about deciding what structure is correct in any particular case is a very complex matter that I could not describe here. And in the context of the present discussion of syntactic theories, this matter is again not crucially relevant, for there is a fair amount of agreement on what structures to assign, in general. Differences of opinion arise, though, over what information those structures carry and how the theory relates occurring structures in the language to non-occurring ones.

Pieces of syntax that are constructed out of smaller pieces of syntax are called *constituents*. For example, the noun phrase *several smelly fish* is a constituent, consisting of a determiner, an adjective, and a noun. Another constituent is the verb phrase (a phrase usually containing a verb and some other stuff) *bothered Nigel*. Combining these two constituents, we can get a sentence, whose minimal constituent structure is shown in (9):

(9)

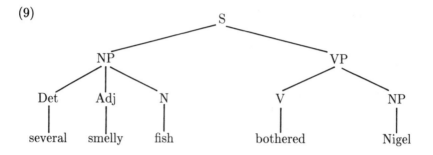

The sentence (S) consists of a noun phrase (NP) and a verb phrase (VP).[3] Rules which affect noun phrases will, under ideal circumstances, affect the NP *several smelly fish* or the NP *Nigel* equally. On the other hand, we expect to find no rules that affect the sequence *fish bothered,* for that is not a constituent. In fact, if we did encounter such a rule, that would count as evidence for the hypothesis that these things really did form a constituent, perhaps contradicting other observations.

Often it is convenient to suppress the internal structure of a constituent, where it is not relevant to the point at hand, and this is represented in the following way:

2.1. Tree Diagrams

The structure shown in (9) is known as a tree diagram, or more usually simply a *tree* that represents the syntactic structure of the sentence or phrase in question. Various important technical terms are stated in terms of tree-geometry (continuing with (9) as an example), such as:

---

[3] Many terms used in syntax have standard abbreviations; linguists, for example, nearly always speak of "an NP" rather than "a noun phrase." It is also a common practice to introduce abbreviations for names of theories and principles which are used over and over again. The non-linguist might find this a little disturbing, and so I have provided at the end of this work an appendix of the abbreviations used throughout.

- A sentence of the language is a string assigned a syntactic structure that is *rooted* in the category S (i.e., S is the topmost category label). There may be additional occurrences of S within the entire S.

- The *node* of the tree labelled S *dominates* everything else in the tree. S *immediately dominates* NP and VP. The relation of domination is very important in that lots of syntactic rules and operations refer to it.

- The node S is the *mother* of NP and VP, and NP and VP are *sisters* (i.e., NP and VP have the same mother). Note that N and V are not sisters.

- A *constituent* is any section of tree that has a single mother.

These are some of the basic features of syntactic trees.

2.2. Labelled Bracketing

Sometimes it is convenient, and sometimes it is more revealing, to use a different representation of constituency. This involves the *labelled bracketing* representation, which encodes the same information as a tree but presents it linearly. The labelled bracketing of the example (9) is shown in (10):

(10)   [$_S$ [$_{NP}$ [$_{Det}$ several][$_{Adj}$ smelly][$_N$ fish]] [$_{VP}$ [$_V$ bothered][$_{NP}$ Nigel]]]

These representations will undoubtedly be quite hard to follow at first for those readers unfamiliar with them, but are very commonly used in syntactic description, and I mention them for that reason. Where possible, I will use trees in the rest of this work, but sometimes the labelled bracketing has much more utility, and in those cases I will use it.

3. Phrase Structure Rules

Trees represent the structure of phrases and sentences of the language. The next question is then, Where do the trees come from? That is, how does our syntactic theory tell us which structures are well-formed and which are not? The basic answer to this question is that we specify a set of rules which *generate* trees; our knowledge of syntax consists in a knowledge of such rules. For what we have seen so far, the *phrase structure rules* (PS-rules) shown in (11) will generate the tree under consideration.

(11) a.   S   →   NP VP

   b.   NP →   Det Adj N

   c.   VP →   V NP

Technically, the arrow means 'rewrites as' (i.e., if you have an S, you can 'rewrite it as' NP and VP). For purposes here, we can interpret the arrow as 'expands as' (i.e., 'dominates in the tree').

There are two variations on the little system in (11) that I wish to consider here; the first introduces recursion and the second introduces optionality. Some verbs, like *think* as discussed above, do not take NPs as their object (as specified by rule (11)c), but rather sentences (Ss). If we add to our little grammar the rule in (12), the size of the set of trees generated becomes potentially infinite.

(12)   VP →   V S

For now this rule can 'feed' (11)a, and we will generate Ss within Ss, and we now have a system that generates as many objects as we could possibly want. (Of course, the hard work still remains—we have to get the rules to generate exactly the right structures, not simply any old structures.) This is an important step towards capturing the nature of the flexiblity and creativity of language.

The notion of optionality is perhaps less impressive. Consider the first set of rules in (11). While an English NP is grammatical if it contains a determiner, an adjective, and a noun, this is not the only option. In fact, just having a noun would suffice (as in *Fish bother Nigel*), and so we will want to make the determiner and adjective optional. Similarly, within the VP, some verbs can get by without an object (e.g., *sneeze*), and so we should make the NP optional. In English, neither category on the right-hand side of the S-rule is optional, but in other languages the NP is arguably optional (e.g., Italian *verrò* 'I will come'). So we can revise the rules in (11) to those in (13), according to the variation we find in English, and we use parentheses to indicate an optional constituent:

(13) a.   S   →   NP VP

   b.   NP →   (Det) (Adj) N

   c.   VP →   V (NP)

This gives an overview of the way we produce trees; but sentences are trees with words on the bottom, and so the next step is to get the words in.

4. The Lexicon

Part of our linguistic knowledge involves knowledge of a large number of words, which constitute our vocabulary, or the *lexicon* as linguists have it. In general, the elements of the lexicon are what we might think of as words, although different syntactic theories have slightly different conceptions of what a 'lexical item' is, and so it is not always safe to think of the lexicon as just a stock of words. In particular, the lexicon of a generative grammar may contain a listing of various affixes, such as the -*s* verbal affix in English (the affix that distinguishes *the sheep walks* from *the sheep walk*). The study of word-formation, e.g., 'verb+*s*,' is known as *morphology*, for it relates to the form of words. The study of *phonology* is the study of the way things sound; thus it is a fact of English morphology that the 3rd-person singular present tense affix is -*s*, and a fact of English phonology that it is pronounced 's' in some environments and 'z' in others (compare the last sound in *stinks* with that in *stings*).

4.1. Lexical Insertion

When lexical entries of the appropriate category are inserted onto the bottom of a tree, we then have a sentence. Lexical entries, like *fish* and *tall* and *suddenly*, are known as *terminal symbols*; the tree stops there, in a sense. Categories like V and N and Adj are known as *preterminals*. We can express lexical insertion in our PS-rule format as below in (14); I also introduce a bit more notation: curly brackets indicate a choice point. So (14)a says that V can immediately dominate *sneeze* or *sleep* or *cook*, etc.; and I use A for 'adjective,' which is the more usual notation.

(14) a.   V   →   { *sneeze, sleep, cook, tell, ...* }

    b.   N   →   { *fish, man, despair, bathtub, ...* }

    c.   A   →   { *smelly, tall, confident, fake, ...* }

Nothing prevents what looks like the same word from appearing in different categories—so *sneeze, sleep,* and *cook* are all nouns as well as verbs. In such cases, it is safest simply to consider that we have two different, though related, lexical items that happen to sound the same.

4.2. Subcategorization

Lexical entries carry lots of different information about lexical items—think of the average entry in a good dictionary. For example, the entry of the lexical item *give* will contain the information that it belongs to the syntactic category of verb, that it is pronounced in a certain way, that its past tense form is irregular (*gave* not **gived*), what it means, and so on. I will cover some of these kinds of information in the following chapters. One very important piece of information that some lexical items carry is the information linguists call *subcategorization*. The simplest illustration of this is the difference between a transitive and an intransitive verb; a transitive verb must have an object in order to be grammatical, and an intransitive verb cannot have such an object. This is illustrated in the examples in (15).

(15) a.   Caesar died.

   b.   *Caesar produced.

   c.   *Caesar died four children.

   d.   Caesar produced four children.

The rules we have given so far, if augmented with the appropriate lexical items, would generate all four of these examples. What we need to do is to divide the class of verbs into *subcategories,* such as the intransitives, the transitives, etc.; we must add into the lexical entry for *die* the restriction that it can *only* be inserted into a syntactic structure with no object following the V, and the opposite for *produce*. (Again, verbs may belong to more than one subcategory, and commonly do—*eat* is a popular example of a verb that may be either transitive or intransitive.)

Some sample lexical entries of verbs are shown in (16), followed by some example verb-phrases.

(16)   die, V, _

            sneeze, V, _

            eat, V, _

            eat, V, _ NP   *eat fried shrimp*

            produce, V, _ NP   *produce four children*

            devour, V, _ NP   *devour the meatball*

            give, V, _ NP PP   *give a cookie to Sam*

            think, V, _ S   *think that Max likes fish*

            tell, V, _ NP S   *tell Susie that elephants fly*

The sixth line here, for instance, says that *devour* is a verb, and that it must appear in the environment (the ' _ ') immediately preceding an NP. We say that it *subcategorizes for* the NP, and the last part of the entry (following the second comma) is called the *subcategorization frame*. As another example, the seventh line says that *give* subcategorizes for a noun phrase (NP) and a prepositional phrase (PP), in that order.

5. Transformations

In *Syntactic Structures*, Chomsky gave various arguments to show that PS-rules alone were not adequate to give a reasonable description of English, and by extension, any human language. I will not go into these arguments here, for they will arise naturally in the chapter on Generalized Phrase Structure Grammar, which *is* a theory of syntax that tries to use only (mechanisms equivalent to) phrase structure rules. The fact of history is that, from the early 1960s until the 1980s, the dominant theory of grammar was Transformational Grammar, developed originally by Chomsky. A transformational grammar takes a lexicon and PS-rules and augments the system with *transformations,* which take structures created by PS-rules and transform them into new structures.

For example, questions[4] in English are different from normal sentences in that (a) a *wh*-word or -phrase (such as *who, how many fish,* etc.) appears initially, (b) some position within the clause (the 'body' of the structure) is missing a phrase where you would expect one in a normal sentence, and (c) an auxiliary verb (*do*) appears in the structure. Thus, in a certain sense, (17)b is a 'question-version' of (17)a:

(17) a.   The police want to arrest that man.

b.   Which man do the police want to arrest?

What happens with the auxiliary is not uniform in all cases, and I will switch examples slightly to control for it; in embedded questions in English, nothing corresponding to part (c) above happens. The hypothesis of transformational grammar is that (18)b is derived by letting PS-rules and the lexicon generate (18)a, with a transformation ('Question Formation') altering the structure so that the *wh*-phrase is initial within its S, which I indicate by square brackets.

---

[4] Excluding 'yes-no' questions like *Did Max fall?*.

(18) a.   Maxine wonders [the police want to arrest which man]

     b.   Maxine wonders [which man the police want to arrest]

I will not go into detail about the formulation of transformations here, as there is nothing resembling them in the contemporary theories. A first approximation to 'Question Formation' would be (19).

(19)   Any structure that can be analyzed

$$[_S \text{ X}-wh\text{-NP}-\text{Y}]$$

is transformed into

$$[_S \text{ } wh\text{-NP}-\text{X}-\text{Y}]$$

In (19), X and Y are variables over any sequence of structure, possibly null; so the transformation simply finds a *wh*-phrase somewhere in the structure and puts it at the front.

The classical transformational grammar developed in the 1950s and 1960s was built around this basic scheme; PS-rules and the lexicon create *deep structures,* which are then (possibly) transformed into *surface structures,* which are the output of the grammar. For example, (18)a is the deep structure of (18)b. With an active sentence like *The police arrested that man,* the deep and surface structures will be identical, while its passive counterpart will have the deep structure of the active version, and the Passive transformation will derive from this the surface structure *That man was arrested by the police.* Classical transformational grammar embraced a whole set of transformations, applying in a cyclical order, such as those just discussed, and others such as 'Raising,' '*There*-Insertion,' and 'Relativization' (to produce such pairs as *It seems that Harold is asleep / Harold seems to be asleep, A pig was rooting in the bushes / There was a pig rooting in the bushes,* and relative clauses like *the continent that Columbus discovered*).

Everyone is agreed that simple PS-rules as I gave them above are not adequate to the task of natural language syntax, and that the work done by transformations must be done somehow. The framework of Transformational Grammar is the common ancestry which the three theories to be described here share, and each preserves different aspects (possibly very few) of that framework in attempting to go beyond it. Moreover, Transformational Grammar produced a massive body of data and set certain standards of adequacy with respect to that data that any contemporary theory must match. For the interested reader, Newmeyer (1980) gives an excellent historical account of the developments that took place in generative grammar from 1955 up to 1980, and Newmeyer (1983) presents an overview of the assumptions and concepts of generative grammar.

Chapter 2

Government-Binding Theory

Government-Binding Theory (GB) was developed initially by Chomsky and is in a sense the immediate descendant of Transformational Grammar. In fact, one feature of Government-Binding Theory that distinguishes it from the other theories presented here is that it makes use of transformational operations. However, the 'transformational' nature of these operations is not their most important aspect, and little rests on it. So while there is a direct historical chain from Transformational Grammar to Government-Binding Theory (GB), many of the ideas of GB either alter or in some cases turn around completely their apparent counterparts in earlier theories.

Similarly, much of the terminology that remains from Transformational Grammar (TG) has been revised in Government-Binding Theory. In Chapter 1 I discussed how TG posited two levels of analysis, deep- and surface-structure. As the range of the theory increased during the 1970s, two other levels of representation were brought in; these are now (usually) called *phonetic form* and *logical form*. The levels which persisted from Transformational Grammar (TG) have been renamed *d-structure* and *s-structure*, for they play roles similar but not identical to the TG notions of deep- and surface-structures. The overall organization of the GB grammar is shown in (1). I give below an example that demonstrates each level.

(1)

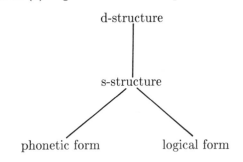

d-structure

s-structure

phonetic form   logical form

Again, to save confusion with other uses, phonetic form and logical form are usually referred to as PF and LF respectively. PF ('phonetic form') is the level representing the actual string that is the output of the grammar at the 'sound' end; LF ('logical form') is the corresponding level at the 'meaning' end. The properties of PF have not been the focus of much attention in GB, and so I shall say little about them, and concentrate on the other three levels and the relationships among them.

We can now begin to look at those relationships. The TG rule for expanding S (sentence) that came to be widely accepted was slightly more complicated than I have so far suggested, namely:

(2)   S   →   NP Aux VP

In this rule, the new category Aux dominates material carrying information about such things as tense, aspect, verb agreement, and modality in the clause (often carried in English by a 'modal' verb like *might* or *could*). (There has in fact been a long debate over whether there is evidence of syntactic constituency of Aux and VP, though I will not go into the issues here.) Even if there is no modal, information about tense appears under Aux, and these elements are inserted into the tree from the lexicon; for example, the 'underlying' structure of (3)a is shown in (3)b:

(3)   a.   They fired Mary.

      b.   They PAST fire Mary.

In GB, the node Aux is called INFL (for 'inflection'). (3)b would be the structure manipulated by transformations (note too that the lexicon must include elements like PAST, which (arguably) never occur in English as separate words). In GB, (3)b would be both the d- and s-structure of the sentence, for no transformations apply to it. Between s-structure and PF the PAST element is joined with the verb, and is 'spelled-out' as the -*ed* ending on the verb.[1] Here is a case, then, where the s-structure of an example and its PF representation are different. Other typical operations in this part of the grammar are the rule of Auxiliary Reduction (*He is* ⇒ *He's*, etc.) and subject-verb agreement (**Lucy sing* vs. *Lucy sings*). Both

---

[1] In LGB, this operation is called 'Rule R.' Throughout this chapter, 'LGB' refers to Chomsky (1981).

of these are syntactically conditioned in the sense that their s-structure representation will contain the information necessary to their operation, but that operation itself (e.g., the 'spelling-out') takes place in the PF part of the grammar.

The levels of d- and s-structure are related by the transformational operation of Move-α. Here α is understood to be a variable over syntactic categories, and the fundamental idea is that a structure may be altered in any way by 'moving anything anywhere'; independent principles will dictate just what can move and where it can move to, allowing the transformation itself to be stated in a maximally general way. Another way of thinking of it (one that is historically accurate) is that many of the transformations proposed within TG have been factored into elementary operations, one of which is Move-α, which expresses the 'movement' part of a relation between two structures.

For example, passive sentences are derived via Move-α as illustrated in (4) and (5), *Mary was fired* (ignore for now the *e* and the subscript *i* symbols that appear in the trees—they will be explained later):

(4)   d-structure

(5)   s-structure

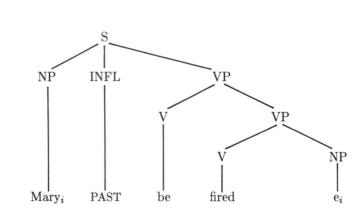

One motivation for this analysis is that we need to ensure that Mary in this example is interpreted as the object upon which the action was performed, that she was the one who got fired, not who did the firing. By having *Mary* in the position of the object of the verb at d-structure, this NP is assigned the status of the semantic object in exactly the same way as in (3)b; however this is actually done for (3)b will carry over directly to the present passive example.

A very important aspect of GB is that it assumes that there are no construction-specific rules, and this is an important departure from TG; while TG has rules (transformations) of Passive, and Question Formation, GB eschews this point of view. So, for example, Passive essentially moves objects to make them subjects; it does not move objects and make them prepositional objects. Exactly the wrong thing to do, as far as GB is concerned, is to set up a rule, which you call Passive, which says to make an object a subject. The GB point of view is not that movement to the subject must be specified, but rather that movement to any other position must be prevented. Thus the GB analysis of passive is that Move-α moves anything anywhere, and that other independent (universal) principles and constraints rule the example out unless the movement happens to be from object to subject position. So passive is the epiphenomenal result of the interaction of various aspects of the grammar, these aspects being direct functions of properties of Universal Grammar (see below). What we find in Universal Grammar, then, is not a rule of Passive, but rather more abstract things like constraints on movement applying across the language as a whole.

Completing the picture, LF encodes information relevant to the semantic interpretation of the example in question—in particular, such matters as quantifier scope and the scope of question-words are dealt with at this level. As illustration, the sentence *Two languages are spoken by most people* has two LFs, as seen in (6):

(6)   a. $[_S$ Two languages are spoken by $[_{NP}$ most people]]

      b. $[_{NP}$ most people$_i]$ $[_S$ two languages are spoken by e$_i]$

The representations are intended to bear a similarity to the representations used in first-order logic, in which left-right order indicates the relative scope of quantifiers. The first LF represents the interpretation where everyone who knows two languages knows the same two languages; the second interpretation is where maybe each knows different languages. The first LF comes from leaving the s-structure alone, the second from applying Move-α to it, moving the NP *most people* to a position outside the original S (known as the 'wide-scope' interpretation for that NP). So the same transformational rule, Move-α, relates the levels d- and s-structure and the levels s-structure and LF. LF itself feeds into the semantic part of the language faculty, though there is no uniform consensus among practitioners of GB as to what the nature of that part is.

While GB conceives of the relations between d- and s-structure and s-structure and LF as matters of syntax, I will alter the current usage slightly, as a certain unclarity often arises in that usage. When speaking of something that happens in the mapping from d- to s-structure, I shall say that it happens *in the syntax*; for between s-structure and LF, I shall say *in LF*. When speaking of operations that are defined on the levels themselves, rather than the mapping between them, I shall say *at s-structure*, and *at LF*.

It is an important and potentially distinguishing feature of GB that it maintains that such interpretive mechanisms as quantifier scope are governed by the same principles of grammar (e.g., Move-α) that govern the form of such constructions as Passive (whose form differs visibly from the corresponding active) or interrogatives. GB proposes that the grammar itself consists of a series of 'modules' that contain constraints[2] and princi-

---

[2] I come to the notion of a 'constraint' shortly.

ples which govern the well-formedness of the output. Such constraints as we might find supporting evidence for on the basis of overt movement of constituents, as in the case of Passive, will also be expected to apply (in the unmarked case) to these more abstract cases of movement (movement in LF, as in (6)b), such as the assignment of quantifier scope. (By 'abstract' here I refer to the fact that the two different interpretations of the sentence *Two languages are spoken by most people* are not distinguished by any overt marking in the output string itself.)

The organization of the GB grammar, with all its different components, is shown in Figure 1. During the course of this chapter, I will illustrate each of these parts of the overall theory.

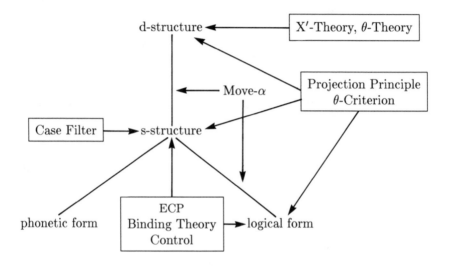

Figure 1.   Government-Binding Theory

Before getting into more detail, I would like to touch on some rather broader points, which again might be viewed as potentially distinguishing features of GB.

Syntax and Universal Grammar

What is it that we are trying to describe when we are doing syntax? All theories are very much concerned with 'the big picture,' that is, with a characterization of what it is to be the syntax of a human language. The point of view of practitioners of GB is that the human mind comes with quite a lot of linguistic knowledge 'wired in,' and that experience with one particular language or another is a kind of fine-tuning within that predetermined range. The endowment of a language faculty is known as UG (for 'Universal Grammar'). Now let me not mislead here: it is certainly *not* a particular feature of GB that it concerns itself ultimately with the study of UG, for I think that all contemporary syntacticians believe that we have some kind of endowment of this nature; but what differ across the theories (and of course across syntacticians) are (a), what the nature of the information UG supplies is and (b), how much we can infer about the properties of UG from studying properties of individual languages.

The fundamental grammatical notion in GB is that of a constraint. The working assumption is that everything is possible and that gaps in the data reflect the operation of some constraint;[3] this assumption is not peculiar to GB, and many theories adopt it in some form. In fact, the constraints will be so strong as to limit very severely the actually realized possibilities. A constraint is something which is part of the grammar which disallows certain logical possibilities in the data. As an example, in studying the syntax of a certain construction in a certain language, we typically find ourselves wanting to say something like 'Move-α moves NPs unless they are in a certain structural position.' This would be stated in the grammar by letting Move-α apply with full generality and then ruling out (i.e., deeming ungrammatical) those examples where the moved NP had started out in the offending position. Again, this conception is not particular to GB. What is perhaps more particular to GB is the inference from this to UG. At this level, the logic goes as follows: our syntactician here has just proposed a constraint on the application of Move-α that is crucial to the proper description of the phenomena under consideration. How might speakers of the language become sensitive to this constraint?—Well, hardly through exposure to the relevant data, for all the relevant data is *un*-grammatical and therefore unavailable. (Even if it occurs, it will hardly come with a 'flag' indicating that it is in fact ungrammatical.) Yet if speakers know the constraint (though not consciously, of course), and they cannot learn it,

---

[3] In addition, the idea that each rule or principle should be as simple as possible motivates this view; complexity in the data is taken to reflect complex interactions of simple (i.e., overgeneral) principles, rather than complex principles.

then the only other option is that it is part of the very nature of language itself, i.e., given to us in UG.

Next, suppose we look at another language and find a similar constraint—the NP cannot be moved from some specific, but different, structural position.[4] For this, GB invokes the notion of a *parameter*. What UG specifies is something like 'A constituent cannot be moved from position X,' where X is a variable over a range of specified values (typically, some small number of values $X_1, \ldots, X_n$). So once one example with movement from position X_1 is encountered, the language-learner knows that the language is a language with X_2 as the value for this parameter (i.e., that movement is possible from position X_1, and not possible from X_2). Cross-linguistic variation is thus conceived of in terms of parameterized variation, the idea being that setting all the switches in UG one way gets you French and another way gets you Chinese.

Given this conception, there is every reason to expect that the effects of parameter-setting will show up in different constructions in the grammar; for example, the effects of setting the parameter hypothesized in the previous paragraph to X_2 would mean that every construction that is analysed by movement would lack movement from the X_2 position.

Related to this overall outlook is the matter of the range of data assumed to be the domain of syntax. Language-particular details of description typically go uncharted in GB, for there is no obvious way in which their study would yield interesting hypotheses about the nature of UG; for example, the Rule R which puts together elements of INFL and the verb is at best tricky to state (and some would argue impossible). There is no statement or definition of the operation of Rule R in LGB (Chomsky (1981)), for it is presumably considered that nothing would be gained by such a statement—for instance, the rule obeys none of the constraints that apply to Move-α, and so Rule R is taken to be a rule of a rather different character than the members of the family characterized by Move-α. As another example, it is a fact of English that the word *aren't* can only appear with the subject *I* if the sentence is inverted (i.e., the auxiliary verb precedes the subject). So we have *Aren't I the one?* but not **I aren't the one*. It again seems unlikely that GB will ever want to say anything about this fact (Generalized Phrase Structure Grammar, in contrast, describes

---

[4] This is a slightly artificial example, in that the usual case is that, say, movement in language A takes place from a subset of the positions allowed in language B; cf., the discussion of English and Italian in Section 5.4.

this fact and uses it to motivate a particular feature (see Chap. 3, Sec. 3.2)).

These are, of course, matters of philosophy in a certain sense. Chomsky once said in a class lecture (I'm sure he's said it many times) that it would be a mistake to come up with a grammar of English full of lots of rules and little riders that got all the facts right, down to every detail. The reason it would be wrong is not that it would not be an honorable scientific endeavor, but rather that you'd be so bogged down in little details that you'd find nothing of sufficient generality that would lead you to make hypotheses about UG. I will say no more about this except to note that not everyone shares this point of view.

1. X′-Theory

X′-Theory (pronounced 'X-bar Theory'[5]) was developed in the 1970s and plays an important role in GB. The idea is that when one looks at the structures internal to different phrases in a language, one typically finds a similar pattern within each. For example, in English the verb precedes its object and a preposition precedes its object; in Japanese exactly the opposite situation is the case (hence, Japanese has *post*positions). By abstracting away from particulars of one syntactic category or another, we can talk about a language-wide template for characterizing phrasal and sentential structure. This is X′-theory.

1.1. The X′-Scheme

A fundamental and central concept in all contemporary syntax is the concept of a *head*. The head of a linguistic unit is that part of the unit that gives its essential character. In the present context, the head of an NP is the noun; it is in virtue of the fact that it is headed by a noun that the phrase is a noun phrase. Similarly, a verb heads a VP, and so on for adjectives (I will use the category symbol A for adjective) and prepositions (category P). The phrase is said to be a *projection* of the head. Standardly, two levels of

---

[5] The name here derives from the original formulation of the theory, in which the notation was $\overline{X}$. However, overbars are also used in a different way (meaning set-complement) in other parts of the GB grammar, and so I will use prime-notation for X′-Theory in an attempt to avoid confusion.

projection are countenanced; the phrasal level (e.g., NP) is assumed to be related to its head by an intermediate, semi-phrasal, level.

The X′-scheme for English proposed by GB is shown in its bare outlines in (7). The phrasal level is characterized by being a second-order projection of the head, i.e., X″; this is equivalent to the notation XP (second-order (phrasal) projection of any head), and I will use the latter in general throughout. The highest level of projection is called the *maximal projection*; hence AP is the maximal projection of A, etc.

(7)

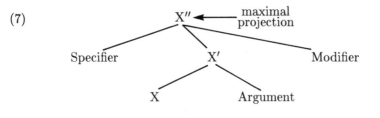

(I should note that there are many different versions of this scheme to be found in the literature; I am choosing what is the simplest for expository purposes, without claiming that it is the absolute best for English.) The categories that are sisters to the head (often called the 'lexical head') in the syntactic structure are its *arguments*; *arguments* are those constituents that a head subcategorizes for, the prototypical argument being the object of a verb. At the higher levels of structure come *modifiers*, and *specifiers*. Specifiers are things like determiners in NPs and degree modifiers (like *very*) in APs. Things are not entirely cut-and-dried; the distinction between modifiers and arguments is notoriously difficult in certain cases, for instance. And the position of modifiers is somewhat variable in English—so many adjectives, for example, precede the noun (e.g., *happy man*), while *asleep* follows the noun (*asleep man). This is not problematic for GB, as what is important from (7) is the hierarchical structure; this is factored out from, and hence theoretically separate from, the relative order of constituents. Order is fixed by other principles of the grammar, such as Case assignment. So, ultimately, one might hope to abstract slightly further than in (7), and just have the information that arguments are sisters of the head and that modifiers and specifiers are sisters of X′. Then any further ordering restrictions would be stated independently.

Some sample instantiations of the X'-scheme are shown below:

(8)

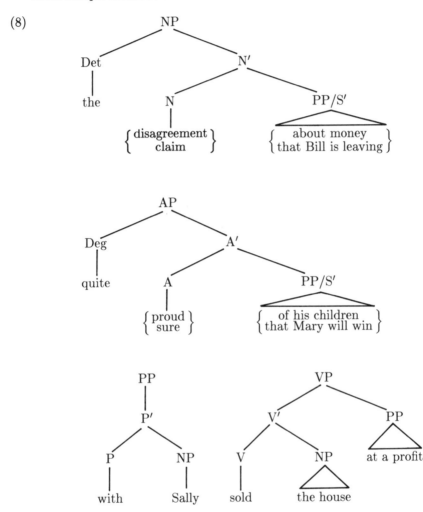

I should note that in practice (as a typographical convention) it is usual to leave out the intermediate levels of structure if they do not branch; so for example the usual way of representing a PP would just have PP immediately dominating P and NP.

Next we come to the structure of sentences. INFL is taken to be the head of S, and in many versions of GB S is taken to be the intermediate projection, the maximal projection being called (for historical reasons) S′. This is an unfortunate clash of terminology, for we should really be talking about INFL′ and INFL″. However, S and S′ are what one finds in the literature, and I shall use these. A sample S′-structure is shown in (9):

(9)

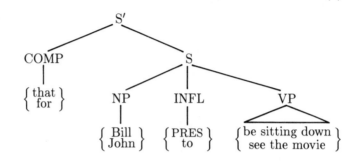

The specifier of S′ is COMP (for 'complementizer'), which dominates the presentential material like *that* and *for*. If the complementizer is *that* the clause must be tensed; if the complementizer is *for*, the clause is untensed. Untensed clauses are called *infinitives*. For purposes of exposition, I will take the particle *to* to be of category INFL. (There has been and still is a lot of debate about the relationships between S′ and COMP and S and INFL; in Chomsky's more recent work (e.g., Chomsky (1986a)), he takes COMP to be the head of S′ and INFL to be the head of S. Stowell (1981) presents evidence for this view.)

The X′-equivalences are summarized in Table 1:

Table 1
X′-Equivalences

X	X′	X″
N	N′	NP
V	V′	VP
A	A′	AP
P	P′	PP
INFL	S	S′

In addition, the categories N, V, A, and P are assumed to be defined in terms of two two-valued features, N (nominal category) and V (verbal category). This is shown in Table 2:

Table 2

Categorial Features

	[+N]	[−N]
[+V]	A	V
[−V]	N	P

This classification allows the statement of generalizations across categories; for example, [+N] categories appear as the complement of *consider*, so we have *consider Bill sick/ a fool* but not **consider Bill under the table/ singing*.

These X′-structures (partly) characterize well-formedness at d-structure. GB, in another departure from classical TG, has few or no phrase-structure rules, just the X′ template. The idea is that any structure can be built out of any categories, but only those conforming to (7) will be well-formed; so if for instance, an A heads an NP, that will simply be ruled out at d-structure (or ruled out 'in the base'). Phrase structures, like entire constructions, are viewed as arising out of complex interactions of different principles, and are not assumed to be generated in any traditional way (i.e., by a set of rewriting rules as illustrated in Chap. 1). (In fact, it is not even clear if GB is a 'generative grammar' any more, but I will not dwell on this issue.)

1.2. Subcategorization

In the late 1970s it was realized that there was a large redundancy in the system of phrase structure rules and subcategorization frames; for example, the information that a transitive verb is followed by an NP object was encoded both into the rule expanding VP *and* in the subcategorization frame of the verb. The GB view on this is that it is another reason for thinking that PS-rules are simply not appropriate theoretical devices, and the burden of the work has been shifted to the subcategorization frames of heads.

As an illustration, it is fairly uncontroversial that any maximal projection (that is, AP, NP, PP, S′, or VP) can be the argument to a head, in principle. Typically, different heads select different elements from the set of maximal projections as their arguments. The verb *kick* selects NP, *think* S' (as in *think that tea is ready*), *wax* AP (as in *to wax lyrical*), and so on. Often there are idiosyncracies—so the verb *discuss* looks like a verb that should take an S' argument, but it only takes NP (as in *We discussed the problem* but not *We discussed that there was a problem*). Using terminology adopted in Chomsky (1986a) (proposed in Pesetsky (1982)), we can say that each verb *c-selects* ('c' for 'category') a certain subset of the range of maximal projections.

The subcategorization is then used as a filter on randomly generated phrase structures in the following sense: if we try, for example, to do lexical insertion of *discuss* in a structure where it is sister to an AP, that structure with that head will be ruled out, for its subcategorization requires NP.

Another important feature of GB is the relation between subcategorization and the appearance of subjects. The subject NP (in English) does not appear sister to the head of the VP and therefore cannot be subcategorized by that head. The domain of subcategorization is limited to the domain of the maximal projection containing the head, and it is really this notion of the domain within the maximal projection, rather than the notion of being a sister, which is important here. Given the X'-theory assumed, the subject is not within the domain of the verb as the maximal projection of the verb is VP. This leads to many important predictions about differences in syntactic behavior of subject and non-subjects (the latter being the class of things subcategorized for). The relevant phenomena here are usually, and slightly misleadingly, called 'subject/object' asymmetries. Ultimately all of these reduce in GB to the fact that the subject is *external* to the VP (see (9)).[6]

It is not a necessary feature of X'-theory that it be set up this way; for instance, in Generalized Phrase Structure Grammar, V is the head of S and so the subject is, in a certain sense, in the domain of the verb. But in GB much rests on setting up the theory this way, and the indirect relation between the verb and its subject is a crucial aspect of the overall theory; this will be present in any analysis.[7] Finally, I should make a point about

---

[6] An alternative view is that the subject is out of the domain of the verb due to it being to the left rather than the right (in English). Work by Kayne (especially "Connectedness," Chap. 8 of Kayne (1984)), among others, explores this as a means of deriving subject/object asymmetries.

[7] For example, in the Celtic languages, the order of constituents is verb-subject-object; the GB account of this is to propose a d-structure like English,

my usage of the terms 'subject' and 'object'; in GB, these are not primitive notions, but are assumed to be structurally defined. The subject is the NP immediately dominated by S, and the object is the NP immediately dominated by VP (technically, this should be V'). This is usually represented by the notations [NP,S] and [NP,VP] respectively. I will continue to use the terms 'subject' and 'object' in this chapter, understanding them as abbreviations for the structural definitions. So in the case of a passive construction, for example, we say that the d-structure object moves to become the s-structure subject.

2. Projection Principle

What I discussed under the heading of 'subcategorization' in the previous section about the way the syntax respected lexical selection was really part of a more general principle about the relation between the requirements of lexical items and the syntax which fills those requirements. An overarching constraint on syntactic representation in GB is the *Projection Principle*, which is given in its initial form in (10).[8]

(10)   Projection Principle
          Representations at each syntactic level are projected from the lexicon, in that they observe the subcategorization properties of lexical items.

The Projection Principle is a fundamental tenet of GB; it is responsible for many deductions that lead to hypotheses that are distinctive features of the theory. For example, it states a constraint on the mapping between d- and s-structure and LF to the effect that if there is an NP-position in a certain structural configuration at one level, that NP-position must be present at all levels. (Though, as we will see, that position may be *empty* in the sense that it dominates no lexical item.) Certain transformations in TG had exactly the property that the Projection Principle rules out, and so these transformations have no analogs in GB. For instance, a transformation

---

with the verb moving out of the VP to an initial position at s-structure. For discussion of such an analysis, see Sproat (1985).

[8] This is Chomsky's formulation (LGB, 29). Later, he revises it to include thematic structure as well (LGB, 38ff), and this revised version is now the accepted formulation; see Section 3.2.

which takes a deep-structure subject and makes it into a surface-structure object has enjoyed much support over the years—but this is ruled out in GB, for the idea of the Projection Principle is that if the object is there at one level, it must be there at all levels.

While this expresses the basic intuition, there is more to say here. In a passive construction the d-structure object can move to the subject position; the subject position is there by an extension to the Projection Principle, discussed shortly below. The object position is there as the verb subcategorizes for it. In the case of a subject moving to object position, we will see below in Section 3.2 that nothing can sanction a comparable empty object position, and hence the movement cannot take place. Returning to the case of legal movement as in passive, the d-structure subject position is empty, and after movement the s-structure object position is occupied by an empty category (see Section 5.1); the Binding Theory will determine what type of empty category this is. The empty category will need to be there to satisfy thematic requirements (see Section 3). However, for our current concerns, what is most relevant is that the Projection Principle forces the existence within the theory of empty categories, for otherwise, any kind of movement structure would violate the Principle.

The conception of syntactic structure that comes out of the Projection Principle is that some position will exist in syntactic structure just in case some lexical item requires it to exist. In such cases, the lexical item is said to *license* the category in the structure. Not everything can be licensed via the Projection Principle, and recently there has been much emphasis on, and study of, this concept of licensing,[9] such that one really can end up with a theory in which each bit of structure is there because some other bit of structure requires it to be there, or else the second is dependent on the first for its own well-formedness.

Note that this leaves a problem with subjects—subjects are not subcategorized, so why do they appear at all? The solution given in Chomsky (1982) is to add in a second clause to the Projection Principle (giving the *Extended Projection Principle*) which simply adds that all clauses have subjects. The more recent work on licensing has looked for ways to derive this as a consequence of other requirements rather than leaving it as a bald stipulation.

There will be more to say about the effects of the Projection Principle after the discussion of θ-theory.

---

[9] See, for discussion and references, Chomsky (1986a).

3. θ-Theory

The theory of θ-roles (or 'thematic relations' as they are more generally known) was developed in the 1960s and 1970s (though it has antecedents in the work of ancient grammarians) but has only been brought into syntactic description in a general way in recent years. While subcategorization in its core conception provides information about the syntactic form of arguments, θ-roles provide essentially semantic information. For example, while the verb *find* subcategorizes for an NP, it has two θ-roles: Agent and Theme (or Agent and Patient in some terminology); these are notionally the one responsible for the action and the thing upon which the action is performed, respectively. These properties are written into the lexical entries of heads, and are known as the *argument structure* of the head; each syntactic argument of the head will receive one θ-role.

3.1. θ-roles

Many different theories make reference to θ-roles (under one name or another) yet there is unfortunately no presently available theory of what the range of possible roles is and how you might tell in a given context which one you're dealing with; one must, for the present, rely on intuition in large part. There are some aspects of semantic interpretation that are apparently sensitive to thematic relations and these too can be used as heuristics.[10]

There is presumably some relatively small finite number of θ-roles from which heads will pick a few for their argument structure; here I will just look at the argument structure of verbs. It is unusual to find a verb with more than three basic arguments, though others may be added by various word-formation processes. Some sample lexical entries are shown in (11); note that while verbs do not subcategorize for subjects, they may assign θ-roles to them (I use 'may' here as there are in fact verbs with 'non-thematic' subjects, which do not receive a θ-role). Often the subject is the Agent argument, but not always. For example, in *Bill received the package*, *Bill* is arguably the Goal argument. The θ-role assigned to the subject needs to be distinguished in some way, and I have followed the convention of Williams (1981) in underlining (though I am not presenting Williams' particular views on the whole topic of θ-roles). I represent

---

[10] See Jackendoff (1972) for a classic discussion of such phenomena, following work by Gruber (1965).

subcategorization (categorial-selection) in angle-brackets and the argument structure (semantic-selection) in parentheses.[11]

(11) a.   sneeze, V, (<u>Agent</u>)

      b.   devour, V, <NP>, (<u>Agent</u>, Theme)

      c.   donate, V, <NP, PP>, (<u>Agent</u>, Theme, Goal)

Each θ-role is assigned by a head within its domain (e.g., within VP for a verb) with the exception of the underlined argument, if there is one. This is known as the *external* argument; the others are *internal* arguments. The external θ-role is taken by many to be 'compositional,' in the sense that its nature is determined not just by the verb but by the whole verb-phrase. I will not dwell on details here, for they are not important to the matter at hand; what is important is that some sort of thematic argument position for the subject must be encoded into the lexical entry of the verb.

The assignment of θ-roles to internal arguments is known as *direct* assignment; the external θ-role is *indirectly* assigned, the process mediated by VP. θ-roles are assigned at d-structure. (12) indicates the assignment with a simple transitive verb.

(12) θ-role Assignment

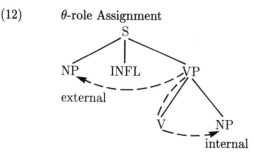

Nothing that I have mentioned so far ensures that there is a match between the number of places in the argument structure of a head and the number of phrases around to host the θ-roles assigned by that head. This is taken care of by the θ-Criterion, which is our next topic.

---

[11] The parenthesized terms are those used in Chomsky (1986a). The angle-bracket notation for subcategorization is something that I have invented for expository convenience.

3.2. θ-Criterion

The idea behind the θ-Criterion is that if the syntax is to be a 'projection' of lexical properties, as is the GB conception, then there should be a requirement to the effect that each head gets exactly the number of arguments that are lexically specified for it. Moreover, each such argument should be assigned exactly one θ-role, and hence, in a sense, have a unique function in any given syntactic structure.

While θ-roles are assigned at d-structure, the θ-Criterion applies at all levels (LGB, 112ff), ensuring that heads and their arguments are in suitable configurations. In its simplest form, the θ-Criterion says:

(13)   θ-Criterion
        Each argument bears one and only one θ-role, and each θ-role is assigned to one and only one argument.

Finally, there must be a principle that relates subcategorization and the assignment of θ-roles (usually called 'θ-marking'). This principle makes the two subsystems interact in very important ways.

(14)   If α subcategorizes the position occupied by β, then α θ-marks β.

Note that subcategorization is for a position, e.g., an NP, while θ-marking is to the lexical content dominated by that position (i.e., its 'semantic' content).[12] The requirement in (14) is built into the revised Projection Principle (LGB, 38); that principle is also revised to say that it is thematic requirements that are projected at each level. This interacts with (14) to ensure that both thematic and subcategorization requirements are projected at each level.[13]

The requirement that subcategorization entails θ-marking provides a very strong restriction on the mapping between levels (i.e., the mapping mediated by Move-α), for movement can never take place from one subcategorized position to another. This is impossible as the argument that

---

[12] Actually, in LGB Chomsky defines θ-marking as to both positions and to the material that they dominate, but we need not worry what any implications this might have.

[13] The revised Projection Principle requires the existence of thematic subjects, for these are lexically required by predicates. However, the 'extended' part of the principle is still necessary to ensure the presence of subjects that are non-thematic (such as the empty d-structure subject position in a passive sentence).

moved would have two θ-roles, in violation of the θ-Criterion; for it would get one θ-role in its pre-movement subcategorized position, and another in its post-movement subcategorized position. I will discuss the positions that are *open* for movement (positions to which movement may take place) in the subsection below on 'Landing Sites.'

It is important to note that different tokens of the same θ-role are distinct from the point of view of the θ-Criterion. If there were a case where, say, some NP moved from a position assigned a Theme role to another position assigned a Theme role, this would violate the θ-Criterion, for these would be Themes assigned by different heads. In fact, some people like to think of θ-roles as relative to a head, and so will talk about "Theme of this occurrence of the verb *slice*," etc.

To complete the survey of well-formedness at d-structure, one last point is that d-structure is conceived of as a 'pure' representation of argument structures, and that θ-roles are assigned to arguments at this level. All the thematically relevant configurations will then be present at d-structure. Along with this, a d-structure satisfying the subcategorization and X' requirements will be well-formed.

4. C-Command and Government

Many processes in syntax are known to be local, in that they only make reference to relatively small sections of tree-structures at any one time. For example, I have used above the notion of 'domain' of a head, namely its containing maximal projection, in the description of subcategorization and θ-marking. *Government* is a fundamental concept in GB that is used to get at this notion of a local domain; following quite traditional usage, the idea is that some category β is in the domain of some other category (typically a head) α just in case α *governs* β. Thus we require that subcategorization and internal θ-marking are satisfied *under government*; a verb cannot subcategorize for an NP in another clause, for instance.

The relation of government is defined in terms of a more primitive notion, that of *c-command*, which states a relation defined on tree-structures ('c' for 'constituent'). Originally motivated by studies on anaphora[14] and other types of structural dependency, the notion of c-command now enjoys wide acceptance and will be found, in one guise or another, in many

---

[14] A survey of the data supporting the notion of c-command can be found in Reinhart (1983).

different syntactic (and in some cases semantic) theories. The notion of c-command expresses something like the notion of that subpart of a tree which a given category α is hierarchically superior to.[15]

There are several different definitions of c-command that have been proposed in the GB literature, motivated by different empirical concerns, to the point at which a valid and interesting topic for a research paper might be (in fact, has been) a survey and critical evaluation of the different versions. Here I will present two different definitions, both of which have been proposed to deal with topics that I will discuss; it is sometimes suggested that some components of the theory will use one definition and others the other (or variations thereon).

(15)   **C-Command** (preliminary definition)
         α c-commands β iff
         every branching node dominating α dominates β.

This is the definition originally proposed by Reinhart, but currently the revised definition in (16) is more widely used.

(16)   **C-Command** (revised definition)
         α c-commands β iff
         every maximal projection dominating α dominates β.

Note that these are alternative definitions, not two clauses of the same definition. The first definition is often known as the 'strong' definition of c-command, and the second as the 'weaker,' as it allows more cases. Most of the appeals to c-command that I will make below will be to the latter, revised definition, and I present the former just to give the idea upon which the current formulation is based.

These different definitions can be illustrated in the simple tree in (17):

(17)

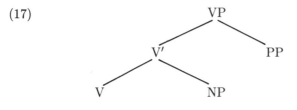

---

[15] As c-command can be mutual, it would be more accurate to say 'not inferior' rather than 'superior.'

Under definition (15), V c-commands NP but not PP; under (16), V c-commands both NP and PP. Note that in the latter case, c-command cannot go upwards through a maximal projection, for then a maximal projection would dominate α (e.g., the verb) without it also dominating β. So, for example, a verb cannot c-command its subject, which is outside the VP, under the latter definition; however, with the former definition, this is possible if the VP does not branch, as in the structure in (18):

(18)

This should be enough to illustrate what c-command is about. *Government* is a localized version of c-command; while c-command may hold between α and some β that is arbitrarily far down in a tree, government is defined over a much 'flatter' domain.

(19)   Government
    α governs β iff:
    (a) α c-commands β, and
    (b) α is an X^0, i.e., $\alpha \in \{N, V, P, A, INFL\}$, and
    (c) every maximal projection dominating β dominates α.

So government is in a sense a special version of c-command;[16] the governor must be one of the five X' head categories, and no maximal projections may intervene between it and the governee: this last requirement comes from clause (c). If a maximal projection did intervene, there would be a maximal projection (namely, the intervening one) dominating β but not α, in violation of (c). In the literature, this is summarized as 'maximal projections are barriers to government.' Government is essentially restricted to the sisterhood relation, with one important exception. This is in the case of verbs which take clausal complements (clausal arguments); in GB theory,

---

[16] With the revised definition of c-command, government is roughly a case of mutual c-command.

some take S′ complements while others take S (e.g., examples (50)a and (50)c below). As S is not a maximal projection, a verb taking an S complement will govern the subject NP of that S (though not relevant for our concerns here, it also governs the INFL and VP of the S). In the case of an S′ complement, the verb will govern nothing in that complement, for the S′ is a barrier to government. The possibilities are illustrated in (20). (More recently, Chomsky, and others, have suggested that COMP might be governed by the higher verb in such structures; see, e.g., Chomsky (1986a, 1986b).) However, no version of the definition of government would allow the subject NP in (20)b to be so governed.) It is in exactly the case of an S-complement that the relation of government departs from the sisterhood relation.

(20) a.

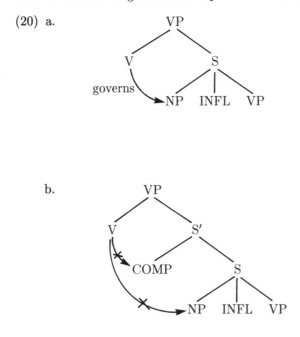

b.

Government and c-command are used in the definitions of other principles and constraints; for example, by the end of this chapter, the reader will have seen that it is in the configuration of government that the following happen (some of these concepts have not been presented yet):

- subcategorization is satisfied

- internal θ-role assignment takes place
- Case assignment takes place
- the Empty Category Principle (in part) is satisfied

In addition, government is important for dictating the distribution of the empty category PRO, and both government and c-command play a crucial role in the statement of the Binding Theory.

5. Move-α

The relation between levels of representation is mediated by the transformational operation, Move-α ("Move anything anywhere"). As we have seen, θ-theory and Projection Principle restrict many logically possible cases of movement. In this present section, I would like to cover three main points: what happens when Move-α occurs, where Move-α may move a category to, and what structural constraints apply to restrict the application of Move-α. In among these, I will discuss the notation of coindexing and its place in the grammar.

5.1. Trace Theory and Empty Categories

Given the Projection Principle, once some syntactic position exists, it must always have existed and must always continue to exist, within the context of a deriviation (a 'derivation' in this usage is one d-structure—s-structure—LF sequence). This entails the existence of *empty categories*; an *empty category* is typically an empty NP position that has been vacated by Move-α. Such empty categories are called *traces*, and traces come in two varieties, as I will outline shortly. In addition, GB recognizes two more empty categories that are essentially pronouns. These four types of empty category will be discussed in detail in the section on the Binding Theory.

In the late 1970s, Chomsky proposed that there were two basic types of transformational movement, which at that time were called 'NP-movement' and '*wh*-movement.' As the names indicate,[17] the former affects only NPs, and the latter only phrases with *wh*-morphology (a class not restricted to

---

[17] The presentation here is not strictly correct, for cases of 'NP-movement' of non-NPs have been suggested (e.g., in Stowell (1981)), and GB posits the existence of abstract *wh*-elements which have no morphology at all. However, these are beyond the range of the presentation here.

NPs). I will continue to use these names as sub-instances of Move-α, for the sake of clarity.

A typical case of NP-movement is what we find in a passive construction. The GB analysis of passive is that a d-structure object moves to become an s-structure subject. I indicate this in the strings in (21); *-en* indicates the passive morphology on the verb (i.e., the fact that the verb is a passive participle).

(21)

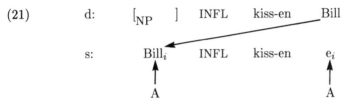

(I will discuss the meaning of the A notations below.) The verb *kiss* is a transitive verb that assigns two θ-roles. The analysis of the passive morphology is that it attaches to the verb and causes the external θ-role to be suppressed.[18] This allows subject position to be empty at d-structure, for no θ-role is assigned to it. However, the syntactic position will exist, due to the Extended Projection Principle ("all clauses have subjects"). Move-α may apply, moving the object into this subject position, without violating the θ-Criterion; this is why the external θ-role must be suppressed. The movement will leave behind an empty category, which I will refer to as *NP-trace.*

Let me comment some more on the notation and introduce some new terms. The trace of movement is coindexed with the NP that moved, to indicate that movement has occurred. When Move-α applies, it always creates indices in this way. The pair (more generally, the n-tuple) of NP_i and e_i are known as a *chain*, and the θ-Criterion is revised to apply to chains: All θ-roles are assigned to chains, and each *chain* has exactly one θ-role. The chain is represented thus: (Bill, e).

Continuing, it is useful to have terminology to distinguish positions that are assigned θ-roles from those that are not. Those that are, are called 'θ-positions'; those that are not are called '$\bar{\theta}$-positions' (known as

---

[18] As we will see below in Section 7, the passive morpheme takes away the ability of the verb to assign Case, forcing movement. The suppression of the external θ-role is a precondition for this movement, as explained here.

'theta-bar' positions). (Here the overbar is the set-complement overbar, and is not the same concept as the 'bar' in 'X-bar theory.' For that reason, I used primes in the X′ discussion, and will continue to reserve the overbar for contexts where it approximates to set-complement.) One of the characteristics of NP-movement is that it is movement from a θ- to a $\bar{\theta}$-position.

In addition, a similar distinction is used for structural positions; the theory distinguishes the 'core' grammatical positions where subject, object, indirect object etc. are located, from more 'peripheral' positions such as the clause-external position COMP. These are known as A- and $\bar{\text{A}}$-positions, respectively ('A' for 'argument'). The distinction here is left rather up to intuition, but a fruitful way to conceive of it is that A-positions are those positions to which a θ-role *may* be assigned, given some suitable head; the rest are $\bar{\text{A}}$. Both positions involved in the passive example are then A-positions, as indicated in (21).

The case of *wh*-movement is again movement from a θ-position to a $\bar{\theta}$-position, as in fact all movement must be—for some item to be in a position in d-structure, that must be a position assigned a θ-role, so the only way to satisfy the θ-Criterion is if movement is restricted to movement to a $\bar{\theta}$-position. Moreover, movement will always start out from an A-position, for only A-positions are filled at d-structure (though in some cases they are 'filled' with an empty category). With *wh*-movement, we have movement to COMP, and so the movement is distinguished from NP-movement in that this time we have movement to an $\bar{\text{A}}$-position. A sample *wh*-movement case (the embedded question *who Bill saw*) is shown in (22).

(22)   d: [$_{\text{COMP}}$]   Bill   INFL   see   who

        s: [$_{\text{COMP}}$ who$_i$]   Bill   INFL   see   e$_i$

              $\uparrow$ $\uparrow$
              $\bar{\text{A}}$ A

This kind of movement, *wh*-movement, will leave behind an empty category that I will refer to as *wh-trace* (many GB practitioners refer to this as 'variable').

5.2. Coindexing

Coindexing is used to represent many important relations in GB. There are three coindexing mechanisms that will be important in the present discussion, which I will introduce here without too much comment; the only relatively novel coindexing is that given in (23)a below, which is responsible for subject-verb agreement. AGR is the 'agreement' component in INFL.

(23)   Coindexing
  (a) Coindex [NP,S] and AGR at d-structure.
  (b) Move-α creates and preserves indices.
  (c) Freely index all A-positions at s-structure.

Clause (c) ensures that all A-positions have an index at s-structure;[19] this will be relevant for the Binding Theory. We have seen clause (b) above; so at s-structure, all A-positions will have received an index, and those $\overline{\text{A}}$-positions to which movement has taken place will have an index. I assume here that the free indexing in (c) does not reindex NPs indexed by Move-α, though it would be quite possible to alter the theory slightly to allow for this, if any motivation were found.

Clause (a) is of a rather different nature, in that it indicates not a purely formal relation but in fact one that has overt realization, as agreement on the verb.

The category INFL is assumed to be a complex bundle of information, and in particular it contains tense and agreement information. Every d-structure has the following schematic form:

(24)

The rule coindexes the subject NP and AGR, and by convention INFL shares that index. Two points to note: one, it is the NP *position* that is indexed—the position (as in the case of passive) may be empty at d-structure; and two, while only tensed clauses show agreement in English,

---

[19] The exclusion of $\overline{\text{A}}$-positions is motivated by some very interesting and important facts, but it would not be appropriate to go into them here. For discussion, see Chomsky (1982, 59ff).

there are languages—such as Portuguese—in which infinitive (non-tensed) clauses show agreement with their subjects, motivating the distinction between TNS and AGR.

5.3. Landing Sites

As we have seen, only certain positions are available for movement to take place to—these are known as 'Landing Sites'; the main discussion of these can be found in Baltin (1982). One potential Landing Site is the subject position, just in case it is a $\overline{\theta}$-position; this is straightforward. On the other hand, movement to COMP is often taken to involve a slightly different operation, known as *adjunction* (I will say more about movement to COMP presently). Adjunction of β to α creates a new instance of α which immediately dominates α and β. For example, another instance of adjunction occurs in the movement of a quantified NP in LF; this involves adjunction of the phrase to S:

(25)   s: $[_S$ an oak$_i$ INFL grow from every acorn$_j]$

         LF: $[_S$ every acorn$_j$ $[_S$ an oak$_i$ INFL grow from e$_j]]$

In this example, *every acorn* has undergone this operation, which is known as QR (for 'Quantifier Raising'). (According to one's theory of quantification, one may want some NPs to undergo QR obligatorily, some optionally, and some not at all; that is not important here.) It is a general property of adjunction that it appears to violate the Projection Principle, in that it creates positions out of nowhere; however, the Projection Principle does not say anything about non-subcategorized positions, and so adjoined positions are outside of its purview.

Other instances of Move-α in LF involve '*wh*-construal,' which moves to COMP all *wh*-phrases that have not been moved in the syntax; this is again motivated by interpretive considerations—*wh*-phrases have 'scope' just like quantified NPs. In English, one *wh*-phrase must be in COMP at s-structure (movement in the syntax); GB assumes, following earlier work in TG, that the rest in a multiple interrogation (e.g., *Who gave what to whom?*) move in LF.[20] This time, Move-α adjoins the *wh*-phrase to COMP; we can assume

---

[20] This may be analyzed as a parameter of variation. Some languages, such as Chinese and Japanese, have no movement of *wh*-phrases in the syntax,

that all movement to COMP is adjunction, with the first movement being a trivial kind of adjunction, in that COMP may not be branching. Consider the following derivation (of *Who ate what?*); I have assumed adjunction to the left in this case, following LGB (p. 232):

(26)   d: $[_{S'}[_{COMP}\ ][$who INFL eat what$]]$

         s: $[_{S'}[_{COMP}\ who_i][e_i\ $INFL eat what$]]$

         LF: $[_{S'}[_{COMP}\ what_j\ [_{COMP}\ who_i]][e_i\ $INFL eat $e_j]]$

We have now seen the cases of movement listed below, to which I add one final case (adjunction to VP); note that all are $\overline{A}$-movement except the first.

The set of possible movements is:

- movement to [NP, S] position (NP-movement)
- adjunction to COMP (*wh*-movement/*wh*-construal)
- adjunction to S (QR)
- adjunction to VP

The typical example of adjunction to VP involves the 'post-verbal' subject that we find in Italian and Spanish, among many other languages. Thus we find alternate word-orders as illustrated in (27) (Italian):

(27) a.   Molti studenti telefonano.   'Many students telephone.'

     b.   Telefonano molti studenti.

     c. $[_S\ e_i\ [_{VP}\ [_{VP}\ $telefonano$][_{NP}\ $molti studenti$]_i]]$

The structure of (b) is shown in (c) (ignoring INFL); the [NP, S] subject moves and adjoins to VP.

This concludes what I will say about Landing Sites; many of the examples discussed here will come up again.

---

and all move in LF (see Huang (1982)). English moves one. Some East European languages, such as Polish, Rumanian, and Serbo-Croatian, appear to move all *wh*-phrases to COMP in the syntax, but this is a matter of some controversy.

5.4. Subjacency

The notion of *subjacency* is relatively old, having been around for 15 years or so, and deriving in part from earlier work. This topic is often currently referred to as 'bounding theory.' Most languages display what syntacticians call *island constraints*, a name which derives from restrictions on the operation of transformations: certain constructions are syntactic 'islands' in the sense that it is impossible for a transformation to apply between a position outside them and one inside them. In the present circumstance, what we are dealing with are restrictions on the application of Move-α. Subjacency provides such restrictions, by requiring that each application of Move-α not operate over too large a distance; though applications of Move-α may iterate, so the movement is a series of smaller hops. The idea of subjacency is that domains of rule application must be relatively close to each other—not as close as *ad*jacent, but rather one step removed, hence *sub*jacent. Subjacency may be stated in the following way, though much of the work is embedded in the notion of *bounding node*.

(28)   Subjacency
        Any application of Move-α may not cross
        more than one *bounding node*.

An interesting analysis of movement constraints, which also illustrates the idea of parametric variation again, is due to Rizzi (1982).[21] If we take the bounding nodes for English to be NP and S, we can explain the following typical facts. First, 'long-distance' movement out of a complement clause is possible:

(29)   the man who$_i$ [$_S$ I think [$_{S'}$ that [$_S$ you said

        [$_{S'}$ that [$_S$ you had seen e$_i$]]]]]

The analysis of this relative clause is that the *wh*-phrase *who* moves from its d-structure position indicated by *e* to the COMP at the top. This cannot be in one swoop, due to subjacency, but must proceed 'COMP-to-COMP' as indicated, in order that each step respect subjacency; in GB, the

---

[21] See Rizzi's paper "Violations of the *Wh*-Island Constraint and the Subjacency Condition," Rizzi (1982, Chap. 2).

moving phrase literally hops through each COMP. (Some linguists refer to this as the 'pit-stop' property.) COMP is the only position which allows itself to be hopped through, and hopping is not prevented by the presence of the complementizer *that*.

(A historical note: in the 1970s, there was a big theoretical debate over whether movement hopped like this or took place in one swoop. More recently, morphological evidence (see, e.g., Goldberg (1985) and Zaenen (1983), and references therein) has been found that suggests that this basic view of hopping is correct. However, other theoretical outlooks and considerations have now led to a quite common conception that not just every intervening COMP might be affected by—and therefore show signs of—movement (or the counterpart of movement in other theories), but that in fact every intervening *node* is so affected, in that it bears information of the movement that has taken place over it. Thus many linguists (GB[22] and non-GB alike) favor a view in which there is some kind of abstract 'path' between the two positions related by movement (e.g., between *who* and *e* in (29)).)

In contrast to (29), movement (to form, in these examples, a relative clause) cannot take place out of a relative clause, or an embedded question; this is shown below, and is predicted if NP and S are bounding nodes.

(30)   *the man who$_i$ [$_S$ I identified [$_{NP}$ the dog

          [$_{S'}$ which$_j$ [$_S$ e$_j$ bit e$_i$]]]]

(31)   *the man who$_i$ [$_S$ I wonder

          [$_{S'}$ which woman$_j$ [$_S$ e$_i$ married e$_j$]]]

In each case, the lowest COMP is filled by a *wh*-phrase, and is not available as a temporary stopping-point for *who* (though I will not go into details, the difference in allowing hopping between *wh*-phrases in COMP

---

[22] See Kayne (1984, Chap. 8 ("Connectedness")) and Pesetsky (1982).

and *that* is that the latter is not indexed). Other cases confirm that NP is a bounding node:

(32)   *the man who$_i$ [$_S$ I started [$_{NP}$ the rumor

[$_{S'}$ that [$_S$ John would sue e$_i$]]]]

We can again explain the ungrammaticality by blocking movement in one swoop across NP and S or two Ss.

Now in the work cited, Rizzi was trying to explain a difference between English and Italian. For while movement out of an NP is generally bad in Italian just like English, movement out of an embedded question (cf., the English (31)) is good in Italian (34):

(33)   *questo incarico, che$_i$ non sapevi   la novità
         this   task   which$_i$ [$_S$ I didn't know [$_{NP}$ the news

                che   avrebbero   affidato   e$_i$ a te, ...
         [$_{S'}$ that   [$_S$ they would   entrust   e$_i$ to you, ...]]]]

(34)   il   incarico   che$_i$ non sapevi
         the   task   which$_i$ [$_S$ I didn't know

                a chi   avrebbero   affidato   e$_i$
         [$_{S'}$ to whom   [$_S$ they would   entrust   e$_i$]]]

To account for the difference between the two languages, Rizzi proposed that the bounding nodes are parameterized, and that Italian chooses NP and S′ while English chooses NP and S. This will predict that movement out of NPs containing S′s is impossible, while movement out of embedded questions, which are S's, will be acceptable in Italian; in this latter case, the movement (in (34)) crosses two S-nodes, but only one S'.

As I have noted above, GB treats naturally any parallels that might be found between movement in the syntax, of the kind I have just discussed, and movement in LF. In this regard, some Japanese data brought to light in recent years provide intriguing evidence. In Japanese, all *wh*-phrases stay in their d-structure position in the syntax, though the clause is marked by a final particle indicating that it is interrogative (*ka* in the examples below). A simple Japanese embedded question has the form indicated in the bracketed part of (35).

(35)   Boku-wa [$_{S'}$ dare-ga   kuru   ka] sirimasen.
        I-topic   who-subj come   Q   know-not
        'I don't know who will come.'

'Q' indicates the interrogative marker, and *ga* is (for our purposes) the subject marker. Now *wh*-phrases may appear inside of relative clauses, which, given the hypothesis that there is movement in LF, would lead to the conclusion that subjacency is not operative in Japanese.

(36)   [$_{NP}$ [$_{S'}$ dono   kyoozyu-ga   suisen siteiru $_{S'}$] hito $_{NP}$]-ga
                which professor-subj recommend   person-subj

                saiyoosare   soo desu ka.
                employed   likely be Q

There is no translation of this into English that is not awkward. The best we can do is something like "Which professor's recommended person is most likely to get the job?" The sentence is literally "The person that which professor recommends is likely to get the job?" Now what makes this example interesting in the context of subjacency is the pattern of answers that are possible for it. For while it is normally possible to truncate answers in Japanese, as in English, it is only partly possible in response to (36). Some logically possible answers are given in (37):

(37) a.   Suzuki kyoozyu-ga   suisen siteiru hito   desu.
           Suzuki professor-subj recommend   person be
           'It's the person that Professor Suzuki recommends.'

     b.   *Suzuki kyoozyu   desu.
           Suzuki professor be
           'It's Professor Suzuki.'

However, in these cases one must repeat (at least) the entire containing NP to give a good answer. Although a certain amount of inference is necessary to argue from the answers to questions to claims about syntactic structure, these facts strongly suggest a subjacency account. If subjacency is operative in Japanese, and applies in LF in this purely abstract way, as is the unmarked GB assumption, then the only way to respect subjacency (assuming bounding nodes of NP and S′ or S[23]) would be to move the entire containing NP (the top line of (36)). The structure at LF is apparently reflected in the answer. The assumption is that the whole containing NP inherits the *wh*-feature from the contained *wh*-word, and is moved in LF.

To the extent that there exist strong parallels in between syntax and LF, this would support a GB-view that there is more than one structural level of syntax (specifically, that syntactic properties of LF and the mapping to it have 'overt' counterparts). Neither Generalized Phrase Structure Grammar nor Lexical-Functional Grammar acknowledge a level of interpretation like LF whose syntactic or configurational properties have analogs in the surface syntax, and, as this lack of such a level is axiomatic in both cases (though for different reasons), it might not be a trivial task to extend them accordingly.

6. Case Theory

We have so far seen what conditions apply at d-structure and what the mapping relation between d- and s-structure is, amongst other things. The remaining parts of the theory all characterize well-formedness at s-structure, or LF, or both. *Case Theory* is responsible for determining in large part the distribution of NPs, and possibly other maximal projections too. Here I will concentrate on NPs.

The notion of Case in GB is based on the traditional notion of case, which is manifested in many languages. English is rather impoverished in this regard, with only personal pronouns retaining case distinctions: for example, *they* is nominative, *them* accusative or objective, and *their* genitive. In GB, each NP must be assigned Case (the capitalization indicates that we are dealing with a technical notion of Case here), with the possible exception of some empty categories. If some NP fails to be assigned Case,

---

[23] It would require a much more thorough study than the few facts I have presented here to determine whether S or S′ is the correct choice for Japanese.

or more strictly, fails to be in a position to which Case is assigned, then the structure is ruled ungrammatical. This is expressed in the *Case Filter*, given in (38):

(38)   Case Filter
         *NP, if NP has phonetic content and no Case.

This applies at s-structure;[24] having 'phonetic content' means having some physical realization, as opposed to being an empty category. Actually, in the general case, the Filter must apply to chains; each chain must have exactly one Case-marked position if it has NP as its first member. The Case Filter is like the θ-Criterion in that having two Cases is as bad as having none at all; there is quite a large similarity in the operation of the θ-Criterion and the Case Filter, and more recent work (Chomsky (1986a), following ideas in LGB) revises the θ-Criterion to subsume the Case Filter. However, it is important to understand what the Case Filter does, even if current formulations of the theory do that grammatical work in a slightly different way. The notion of Case assignment remains a central part of GB.

The basic instances of Case assignment (in English) are the following:

- if INFL contains TNS, Nominative Case is assigned to the [NP,S] position
- a verb assigns Accusative Case to [NP,VP]
- a preposition assigns Accusative or Oblique Case to [NP,PP]
- nouns and adjectives ([+N] categories) do not assign Case
- Case is assigned under government with the exception of Genitive
- Genitive Case is assigned in the structure $[_{NP} - X]$.

The category INFL assigns Case to the subject under government if it is tensed; the infinitival INFL *to* does not assign Case. Verbs and prepositions assign Case to their objects; in English, it is the same Case, but typically, prepositions assign some kind of oblique Case, such as Dative.[25] With Genitive, there is no assigner; rather it is a property of the structure, as in *John's book*, *Lucy's betraying Maud*, etc. Exactly which Case is assigned

---

[24] There is some debate in the GB literature as to whether the Case Filter applies at s-structure, PF, or LF; I will assume that it is s-structure.

[25] As discussed in the following section, verbs and prepositions also assign Case across an S boundary to an NP, so long as government holds.

is not a matter of much importance in GB; it is the fact of having *a* Case that is significant.

In English, Case is further restricted to be assigned under *adjacency*, for in general, nothing may intervene between a Case assigner and its assignee. (I will discuss some counterexamples below.) The basic picture of Case assignment is shown in (39):

(39)

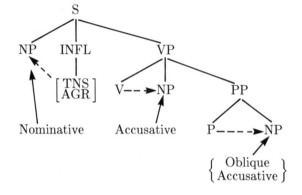

The idea of an adjacency condition is to account for facts like the following:

(40) a.   I like flowers very much.

    b.   *I like very much flowers.

    c.   I smell gas very strongly.

    d.   *I smell very strongly gas.

    e.   I believe very strongly that you will win.

    f.   I gave the book to Bill.

    g.   *I gave to Bill the book.

Examples (b) and (d) and (g) indicate that nothing may intervene between a verb and its NP argument; (e) and (f) show that this does not hold of other arguments, such as S′ and PP. The requirements of Case as outlined above will account for this; S′ and PP do not need Case.

The adjacency condition on Case assignment is also assumed to be a parameter; for example, the French translation of (40)b, *J'aime beaucoup les fleurs*, is grammatical (see Stowell (1981) for more discussion).

Two obvious kinds of counterexample appear against the adjacency idea for English. One is the class of 'ditransitive' verbs, as exemplified by something like *We sent Mary the letter*; I will return to this shortly. The other kind involves the fact that if the NP is 'heavy,' linguistically speaking, it may (and may be preferred to) follow other things in the VP:

(41)   I gave to Bill [my last copy of the third-quarter report].

Although I will not go into details, there is an analysis of these examples in which Move-α has applied to adjoin the NP to the VP, leaving a trace adjacent to the verb which is assigned Case. Chomsky (1982, 47ff) presents evidence that movement has occurred here. It is worth noting too that this rule does not apply out of PP (*I talked about to Sue my latest ideas on physical fitness*); given some further constraint to the effect that the shift rule applies within the domain of the Case assigner, this would be predicted: in moving out of the PP into the VP, the NP has passed out of the (government) domain of its Case assigner, which is the preposition in this case.

With the ditransitives, there is more of a problem.[26] It may just be prudent to add to the grammar some additional way of assigning Case in just these configurations (e.g., Case may be a property of the structure, as with Genitive); for the sake of discussion, let me assume that this is so. What the GB analysis now predicts is that, however the second NP does get Case, it does not get it from the verb, and again there seems to be evidence for this. We will come to this below.

Another important function of Case Theory is to force movement. For example, in passive, the NP moves from object- to subject-position; but nothing that I discussed above forces this movement to happen. Yet the movement is obligatory—otherwise English would allow sentences of the form *There was arrested John*. The analysis of the passive morpheme *-en* is that it has two effects: it takes away the verb's ability to assign Case, and also the ability to assign an external θ-role. The Case Filter now renders movement apparently obligatory—for if the NP remains in object position, it will violate the Case Filter at s-structure. Movement must be to subject position, for this is the only free position for movement, and in that position Case is assigned, so all is well. In general, cases of NP-movement (of overt NPs) are instances of movement in order to get Case. On a more

---

[26] For discussion of these constructions, see Kayne (1984, Chaps. 7 and 9 ("Unambiguous Paths" and "Datives in French and English")) and Stowell (1981).

general level, it is very much part of GB to handle obligatoriness in this way—obligatory application of some operation is explained by positing a principle that is violated by the pre-application structure but satisfied by the post-application structure.

Returning to the ditransitives, if only the first NP gets Case from the verb, then only it should be forced to move in passive. That is, the GB analysis predicts that only the immediately post-verbal NP should be allowed in the passive construction, and this is so:

(42) a.   We gave Mary the envelope.

b.   *We gave the envelope Mary.

c.   Mary was given the envelope.

d.   *The envelope was given Mary.

The first two examples show that it is the Goal argument that must follow the verb in this construction; and the latter two show that only this NP passivizes.

I will conclude this section with an illustrative example from (Mandarin) Chinese, which will show the potential interaction between θ-role assignment and Case assignment; I will also introduce the idea of a *directionality* of assignment. The basic generalization about the order of arguments of the verb in Chinese (i.e., only those constituents assigned a θ-role by the verb) is shown in (43), ignoring INFL:

(43) $[_S$ NP $[_{VP}$ PP V NP$]]$

We are only concerned with order within the VP here. Arguments except the direct object NP precede the verb, with one additional wrinkle; sometimes the direct object may appear as the object of a preposition, *ba*, in which case it precedes the verb. The GB analysis of this is as follows:

- at d-structure, θ-role assignment is from right-to-left (i.e., the VP is head-final)

- at s-structure, Case is assigned from left-to-right.

Directionality is a parameter along with adjacency (I do not know enough about Chinese to state whether adjacency is relevant in that language or not for Case assignment). All subcategorized arguments must be to the left of the verb at d-structure. To get Case, an NP argument must move to the right of the verb, adjoining to VP; only NPs need Case so only NPs move. (To be fully correct, we should also require that PPs and the like *resist* Case, to prevent them from moving arbitrarily. Such proposals have been made in the GB literature; see e.g., Stowell (1981).) However, the NP need not move if it can get Case in some other way; the analysis of the *ba* would be that it is semantically inert and just functions as a Case assigner, and so *ba*-NP sequences would appear preverbally.

7. Summary of Types of Movement and Complement Structures

This would be a good point to summarize the kinds of movement that are allowed in GB. The simplest is perhaps the *wh*-movement kind, that is, movement to an $\overline{\text{A}}$-position. This type of movement has the following abstract properties:

(44) $\overline{\text{A}}$-movement:
        Movement from a position that is assigned both a θ-role and Case; the movement creates an adjoined position, which is an $\overline{\text{A}}$-position, and lacks a θ-role and Case. The resulting chain (α, e) receives exactly one θ-role and one Case, both assigned to the empty category created by movement.

Examples of this kind of movement are, in English, overt *wh*-movement in the syntax, as in questions and relative clauses; and in LF, QR and *wh*-construal. In each case movement is forced by some external principle—say the necessities of interpretation in the case of a quantified NP, or by an additional requirement that a question in English is only well-formed if it has one *wh*-phrase in COMP.

The other kind of movement, A-movement, is movement forced by the Case Filter, and so affects only NPs. It has the following abstract properties:

(45)   A-movement:
        Movement from a position assigned a θ-role but no Case; the NP must move to get Case, and so must move to a position that has Case but no θ-role. The only possible candidate here is subject position, which is an A-position. The resulting chain (α, e) receives exactly one θ-role and one Case, the former assigned to the empty category created by movement, and the latter to α.

The effect of the passive morpheme -*en* can now be fully demonstrated. Attachment of the morpheme affects a verb's properties in the way seen in (46).

(46) a.   kiss, V, <NP>, (Agent, Theme), assigns Accusative Case

b.   kiss-en, V, <NP>, (Theme), assigns no Case

(The form *kiss-en* turns into *kissed* in PF.) The fundamental property of passive is that the verb loses its ability to assign Case (not having this ability is the theoretical reconstruction within GB of the notion of 'intransitive verb'). It still subcategorizes for an NP and assigns an internal θ-role. Concomitant with the loss of Case, the external θ-role must be suppressed, for otherwise movement will take place to a θ-position. For independent reasons, namely the Binding Theory (see Sec. 9 below), movement cannot pass out of the clause in these cases, so movement must be to the local subject position if it is to be possible at all.

The other construction where we have NP-movement, in English, is the so-called 'Subject-to-Subject Raising' construction. This terminology derives from the original transformational analysis which related examples like (a) and (b) below by moving the embedded subject up to the subject position of the main clause (and performed a few operations on tense, etc., at the same time).

(47) a.   It seems that Max is sick.

b.   Max$_i$ seems e$_i$ to be sick.

This is A-movement and so the GB account forces the following conclusions: the position of e in (47)b must be a Caseless position, and the subject position of *seems* must be a $\bar{\theta}$-position. This latter conclusion is confirmed by (47)a; the 'non-referential' *it* is one of two NPs that are stipulated not to require a θ-role. (The other NP is *there* as in *There is a woman in the room.*) So what we want to say for *seem* is that it takes one argument, some kind of proposition. The difference between (47)a and (47)b is reduced to the category of the complement; in (a) it is S', in (b) it is S. I will explain below how this works. The actual implementation of this in LGB is to say that *seem* takes an S' complement but allows the S' node to be deleted, leaving an S complement. So the following might be the lexical entry for *seem*:

(48)   seem, V, <S' $\Rightarrow$ S>, (Proposition)

I have again invented notation to indicate the S'-deletion property; the material within the angle-brackets says that the verb subcategorizes for an S' that may be 'pruned' to an S.

Now, as I mentioned above, the Binding Theory only permits NP-movement to take place within the clause. As 'clause' is identified with the maximal projection S', movement will be allowed just in case S'-deletion takes place. The account of raising, then, is as shown in (49):

(49)

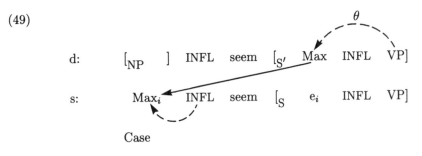

$$d: \quad [_{NP} \quad] \quad INFL \quad seem \quad [_{S'} \quad Max \quad INFL \quad VP]$$

$$s: \quad Max_i \quad INFL \quad seem \quad [_{S} \quad e_i \quad INFL \quad VP]$$

Case

Here movement is forced again; the NP *Max* must move in order to get Case, for *seem* does not assign Case. The θ-role of the subject is determined entirely by the lower VP, and may even be non-thematic with respect to that, as in *It seems to be raining* or *There seems to be a fly in the soup*.

In contrast to this raising operation, GB posits no movement in the corresponding 'Subject-to-Object Raising' construction; in the classical TG analysis, a raising transformation of the general type just discussed would relate the first two examples in (50), the movement this time being to object position.

(50) a.   I believe [$_{S'}$ that Mary is a genius].

b.   I believe Mary$_i$ [$_{S}$ e$_i$ to be a genius].

c.   I believe [$_{S}$ Mary to be a genius].

Note that (b) is not acceptable in GB, for movement cannot take place to object position, due to the θ-Criterion. Yet there is a clear sense in these structures in which *Mary* acts simultaneously like the subject of the lower clause and object of the higher clause. GB again employs the mechanism of S'-deletion in these cases, assigning the s-structure (50)c. The lexical entry for *believe* is as follows:

(51)   believe, V, <S′ ⇒ S>, (<u>Agent</u>, Proposition),
         assigns Accusative Case

The verb does not subcategorize for an NP argument, but does have the ability to assign Case. Given the definition of government, a verb governs across an S boundary but not S′. Hence *believe* can assign Case to the lower subject; this is known as *Exceptional Case Marking*:

(52)   s: I   INFL   believe   [$_S$ Mary   INFL   VP]

Thematically, *Mary* is the subject of the lower S, for it gets its θ-role from the embedded VP; yet it is Case-marked by the higher verb, and so in that sense is its object.

In these cases of S′-deletion, the only option if deletion does not apply is to have a tensed clause as complement, and no raising structures will be possible. I will not go through the details of this. The advantage of this analysis is that two subcategorization frames are not necessary; both Generalized Phrase Structure Grammar and Lexical-Functional Grammar would posit two different subcategorization frames for these verbs, say S′ or the sequence NP VP for the examples in (50). GB proponents would regard such 'surfacy' analyses of the syntax as being too superficial to uncover the underlying unity of the two cases.

Continuing with the *believe* example, there are other examples which look superficially similar, as in (53).

(53) a.   The men prefer the women to cook.

     b.   John wants Bill to win.

These verbs have demonstrably different properties; for example, the NP following *believe* passivizes, while that following *want* (or *prefer*) does not:

(54) a.   Mary is believed to be a genius.

     b.   *Bill is wanted to win.

In GB, the difference between the two verbs in (54) is that *want* does not allow S'-deletion; passive is NP-movement, which we know can cross S but not S'. If this is so, then a question arises as to how the postverbal NPs in (53) get Case, for government cannot cross the S' boundary. With verbs like *want*, a *for* complementizer appears if the complement clause is separated from the verb, and it is this that is responsible for the Case to the subject (*for* is a prepositional complementizer and hence can assign Case like other prepositions):

(55) a.   *John wants very much Bill to win.

   b.   John wants very much for Bill to win.

Case is assigned, under government and adjacency, as shown in (56):

(56)

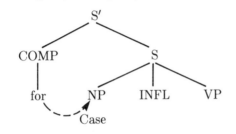

In case the *for* is adjacent to the verb, there is a deletion rule which removes it (some dialects allow things like *I'd prefer for you to go now*); if there is no adjacency, the *for* stays. As an additional piece of evidence, Chomsky notes that the rule shifting heavy NPs applies with *believe* but not *want*,[27] which would follow (with a few other assumptions) from the fact that the NP was shifting out of a non-maximal S in the one case but a maximal S' in the other:

(57) a.   They'd believe to be foolish any candidate who would take the trouble to run in every primary.

   b.   *They'd want to win any candidate who would take the trouble to run in every primary.

Again, these facts would be potentially problematic for any theory that assigned a simple NP VP sequence in both cases.

---

[27] This observation is originally due to Paul Postal.

8. Empty Category Principle (ECP)

The ECP is a well-formedness condition applying to empty categories created by movement (i.e., the two kinds of trace), and it is this principle that is responsible for many of the subject/object asymmetries that GB predicts.[28] The main idea behind the ECP is that subject position is not in the domain of any lexical head (i.e., one of the categories defined by the features [N] and [V]) and that this is an important difference; while other A-positions are governed by a lexical head, the subject position, if governed at all, is governed by INFL. The ECP is formulated so that government by INFL alone is not enough to license the existence of an empty category; INFL is not a *proper governor*.

(58)   Empty Category Principle
           A trace must be properly governed.

           Proper Government:
           α properly governs β iff
           (a) α governs β and α is lexical (N, V, A, or P), or
           (b) α locally $\overline{\text{A}}$-binds β.

The first clause here is the 'core' case, with the empty category properly governed by a lexical head. The second clause is primarily for the case of subjects, and is best illustrated with an example. I will discuss what 'locally $\overline{\text{A}}$-binds' means below.

One of the main empirical motivations for the ECP was the following set of facts:

(59) a.   Who$_i$ do you think that Bill saw e$_i$?

     b.   Who$_i$ do you think Bill saw e$_i$?

     c.   *Who$_i$ do you think that e$_i$ left?

     d.   Who$_i$ do you think e$_i$ left?

The generalization here is that the complementizer may be optionally absent with movement from any non-subject position, but must be obligatorily absent with movement from a subject position. In the former

---

[28] I have assumed for the purposes of presentation that the ECP applies both at s-structure and LF, to emphasize the parallel constraints applying at both levels; many GB practitioners believe that it only applies at LF, for reasons that are too complicated to go into here.

examples, we have proper government by the verb, and the facts in the latter examples suggest that the complementizer is implicated in the proper government of the subject. Let us look at the structure of (59)d first.

(60)

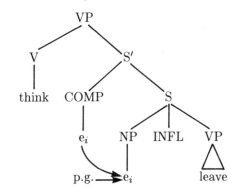

While INFL governs the subject position, it does not properly govern it, for it is not a lexical category; rather, it is the empty category left behind in COMP as the movement hopped through that is the proper governor. The configuration shown is the configuration of binding[29] as required by clause (b) of (58), and hence the subject empty category is properly governed. The crucial difference between (59)d and (59)c is that in the bad example COMP branches, as the *that* is in there already; this prevents a binding relation. The internal structure of COMP in the bad case is:

(61)

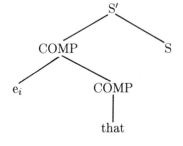

---

[29] The definition of binding is given in (71) below.

Now part of the definition of binding, which I will give in the next section, involves the notion of c-command; in the case where COMP branches, c-command will not hold between the empty category in COMP and the one in subject position, and so binding and hence proper government will not hold either. (59)c is therefore an ECP violation.

The requirement that the proper governor in these cases is a 'local $\overline{\text{A}}$-binder' prevents the *who* in (59)c from properly governing the subject empty category. For our purposes here we can understand 'local' to mean 'within the same S'.' An $\overline{\text{A}}$-binder of some category α is some category that is in an $\overline{\text{A}}$-position, is coindexed with α, and c-commands it. An extensive discussion of this kind of proper government can be found in Lasnik and Saito (1984).

There are many different ways within the GB framework that have been proposed to handle these data, and so what I have given is just an illustration of one possibility. Yet there is an interesting point to be made about the way the theory develops in response to these data. It is taken to be the case that (59)c is an ECP violation. Ultimately this reduces to a failure of c-command in (61). The strategy is then to *define* c-command in such a way as to make it fail in (61). Given the strong definition of c-command that I gave above, this is straightforward; COMP branches, and so the empty category cannot "see" out of it. With the weaker definition, things are not so clear, for the next maximal projection up is presumably the S'; in that case, we have to modify our understanding of the definition such that only heads c-command in their domain. This would mean that only the *that* would c-command the empty category in subject position, for it is the head (the head of COMP is the first thing that was there); but *that* is not a proper governor.

Similarly, although the prepositional complementizer *for* governs and assigns Case to subject position, it is not a proper governor as indicated by the contrast in (62):

(62) a.   *Who$_i$ do you want for e$_i$ to leave?

   b.   Who$_i$ do you want e$_i$ to leave?

Some typical ECP effects in LF are the ones relating to the phenomenon known as 'Superiority'; the generalization is that, given an s-structure with multiple *wh*-phrases, it is the leftmost ('superior') one that must move in the syntax:

(63) a.   Who saw what?

   b.   *What did who see?

The account of these provides support for the idea that it is the head of COMP that governs subject position, irrespective of the branching of COMP. If we look at the LF in each case, we see that (63)b is an ECP violation.

(64) a. $[_{S'}$ [what$_j$ [who$_i$]]$[_S$ e$_i$ INFL see e$_j$]]

b.   *$[_{S'}$ [who$_i$ [what$_j$]]$[_S$ e$_i$ INFL see e$_j$]]

In (64)a, *who* has moved in the syntax and therefore is the head of COMP, and remains so even when *what* adjoins in LF. Hence the subject empty category is properly governed from COMP and the object empty category by the verb. In (64)b the order of movement is the reverse; the subject empty category must be properly governed from COMP, but its potential governor is not the head of COMP, and so proper government fails. Again the object empty category is properly governed by the verb.

Evidence of this correlation between syntax and LF can be found in other languages. The following data and analysis are again from Rizzi,[30] extending some observations and proposals made by Kayne. In Italian, it appears that the so-called 'COMP-trace' effects such as we have just seen (in (59)) are not present.

(65)   Chi$_i$ credi   che   e$_i$ verrà?
          Who you-think that   will-come
          'Who do you think will come?'

However, if Italian did not obey the ECP, then the following facts of LF would be mysterious. The interpretation of an Italian sentence like (66) involves movement in LF:

(66)   Non pretendo che   tu   arresti nessuno.
          NEG I-require that you arrest   nobody

The quantifier *nessuno* may combine with the negation-marker *non*, so that the sentence is not interpreted as containing two independent negations. The analysis of this is to assume that *nessuno* moves in LF to the

---

[30] The reference here is to Rizzi's paper "Negation, *Wh*-Movement, and the Null Subject Parameter," Rizzi (1982, Chap. 4).

position of *non*. The sentence should then have the following wide-scope interpretation of *nessuno*, and indeed it does.

(67)   There is no person x such that I require that you arrest x.

This shows that *nessuno* can move from the object position. Given the grammaticality of (65), one would expect a similar wide-scope interpretation for *nessuno* in (68):

(68)   Non pretendo che nessuno ti   arresti.
         NEG I-require that nobody you arrest

However, this lacks the expected interpretation:

(69)   *There is no person x such that I require that x arrest you.

This fact suggests that the subject position is not properly governed. Rizzi hypothesized that in fact Italian was just like English with respect to proper government of the preverbal subject position, but that Italian allowed a second option: the subject may appear postverbally, on his analysis adjoined to the VP (cf., (27) above). The following data support this idea.

(70) a. Non pretendo che nessuno sia arrestato.
         NEG I-require that nobody be arrested
     b. Non pretendo che sia arrestato nessuno.
         NEG I-require that be arrested nobody

The latter example, only, allows the wide-scope interpretation for *nessuno*; thus proper government is satisfied in the postverbal position. Rizzi's analysis is that the subject moves from [NP,S] position to adjoin to the VP, where under the weaker definition of c-command the verb will govern, and being a lexical head properly govern, the adjoined position. Movement will therefore be possible from this position.

This account will also explain the grammaticality of (65); the movement will first be to the postverbal position, from where further movement will satisfy the ECP. The idea is that the 'COMP-trace' facts really stem from a prohibition against moving a subject NP over an immediately adjacent COMP (in fact, this is how the constraint was initially formulated in the TG system), but that Italian allows the subject to get to the postverbal position first, and from there further movement is possible.

More recently, confirming evidence for Rizzi's hypothesis has been found in data from dialects of Italian; the crucial cases are reported in Jaeggli (1984), Safir (1985), in which the reader may find further details and references.

9. Binding and NP-types

We finally come to the *Binding Theory*, which characterizes the interpretive relations between NPs, and covers, among other things, the distribution of pronouns and reflexive pronouns. In addition, it plays an important role in the distribution of empty categories.

As stated above in (23), indexing is free at s-structure; it is the Binding Theory that constrains the output of this operation. The definition of *binding* is as follows:

(71)   Binding
         α binds β iff
         (a) α c-commands β, and
         (b) α and β are coindexed.

I will not give examples of this here, as we will see many below.

9.1. Binding Theory and the Typology of Empty Categories

The statement of the Binding Theory partitions the class of NPs into different types and states binding conditions for each. The partitioning is effected by the two-valued features [anaphoric] and [pronominal]; intuitively, 'anaphors' are things that *must* have an antecedent, and 'pronominals' are those things that may have an antecedent. Personal pronouns are [−a, +p] in this system, while, and perhaps less obviously, reflexive pronouns are [+a, −p]. The other remaining (overt) NPs are [−a, −p], and are known as *R-expressions* ('R' for 'referential'). For reasons we will come to, there is no overt NP of the [+a, +p] type.

The unmarked hypothesis is that, if these features are motivated for overt NPs, they should also apply to categorize types of empty category. As noted above, GB recognizes four types of empty category, which correspond to the four possible feature/value-combinations. I list these in (72):

(72)   Types of Empty Category
         $[-a, -p]$ wh-trace (or 'variable')
         $[+a, -p]$ NP-trace
         $[-a, +p]$ pro ('little' or 'small' pro)
         $[+a, +p]$ PRO ('big' PRO)

The first three empty categories share distributional regularities with their overt counterparts, while PRO has a life of its own and its own special theory for relating PRO to its antecedent, the theory of *Control*. There has been some debate in the GB literature as to whether the lexicon should provide four empty categories specified as above, or whether it should provide just one, whose particular binding features would be recoverable (and uniquely predictable), in any given context. This latter view, which has been losing favor, is the so-called 'Functional Determination' of empty categories, about which I will say nothing more (there is a lot of discussion in LGB and Chomsky (1982)).

A rough generalization about pronouns and reflexive pronouns in English is that reflexives must find an antecedent within the same clause while pronouns cannot have an antecedent within that domain. The two types are in *complementary distribution*; some typical examples are given in (73). Coindexing indicates a coreferential interpretation; for instance, example (73)b below is grammatical so long as *him* is not *John*.

(73) a. John_i painted himself_i.

     b.   *John_i painted him_i.

     c.   *Mary_i recalled that John had painted herself_i.

     d. Mary_i recalled that John had painted her_i.

The entire range of data is much more complicated than these few simple examples show, but they give the general idea. The Binding Theory states the following:

(74)   Binding Theory
         Principle A: An anaphor ($[+a]$) is bound
                          in its Governing Category.

         Principle B: A pronominal ($[+p]$) is free
                          in its Governing Category.

         Principle C: An R-expression ($[-a, -p]$) is free.

Principle A says that anything that is [+a] must be bound within some specified local domain, known as the 'Governing Category'; I will discuss this presently. Principle B says that [+p] categories are free (i.e., not bound) in that same domain. Principle C says that R-expressions can never be bound. An important thing to note is that the Binding Theory only applies to A-binding (binding by a category in an A-position), and thus one can classify *wh*-traces as R-expressions without contradiction, for they are $\overline{\text{A}}$-bound.

Some of the examples here, especially those involving pronouns, may strike the reader as grammatical in certain contexts, or with certain intonations, even though I mark them ungrammatical. Principle B is quite weak in a certain sense, and many linguists believe that the facts of 'disjoint reference' for pronouns (such as example (73)b above) are not facts of syntax, but are pragmatically derived. On the other hand, many of the cases that look like counterexamples can themselves be argued to be instances where pragmatics overrides the grammar, and a proponent of this view would claim that it is correct to rule them ungrammatical *on the interpretation indicated*. This is the GB view, and it is not my place to defend it here (though I happen to subscribe to it). More importantly, it is essential to note that the effect of Principle B is not simply to derive disjoint reference for pronouns, but to classify types of NPs, which in turn generates many different predictions, most of which do not admit alternative pragmatic explanations.

The notion of the 'local domain' for certain binding processes is expressed in the Binding Theory in the *Governing Category*, which is a slight variation on the more traditional idea of a clause-nucleus.

(75)   Governing Category
        The Governing Category for β is the smallest NP or S
        containing β and a governor of β.

(The statement of the definition of Governing Category in LGB is somewhat more complicated than this in its final formulation, but the underlying concept is captured in (75).) I will comment on two aspects of this definition, the mention of NP as well as S, and the mention of a governor.

It has been known for quite a long time that the same kinds of syntactic processes apply within NPs and Ss. The simple facts of binding in (76) are just one instance of this (cf., (73)). The brackets indicate an NP contained within a larger NP.

(76) a.   Max$_i$'s painting of himself$_i$

    b.   *Max$_i$'s painting of him$_i$

    c.   *Mary$_i$'s recollection of [John's painting of herself$_i$]

    d.   Mary$_i$'s recollection of [John's painting of her$_i$]

Hence, NP is one of the relevant categories for defining a domain for binding.

The inclusion of a governor in the domain is necessary for the S'-deletion verbs like *believe* and *seem*. This can be illustrated with the examples in (77):

(77) a.   Max$_i$ believes [$_S$ himself$_i$ to be the candidate].

    b.   *Max$_i$ believes [$_S$ him$_i$ to be the candidate].

    c.   *Max$_i$ believes [$_{S'}$ that [$_S$ himself$_i$ is the candidate]].

    d.   Max$_i$ believes [$_{S'}$ that [$_S$ he$_i$ is the candidate]].

In (a), the reflexive must be bound in its Governing Category, according to Principle A. The governor of *himself* is the verb *believes*, and hence the Governing Category is the entire sentence. Similarly, a pronoun must be free in this domain, and so (b) is bad. When we switch to an S' complement, the pattern reverses as this time the governor of the subject position is the INFL of the lower clause, and so the Governing Category is the lower S. Thus, although the reflexive is bound in (c), it is not bound within its Governing Category (for its antecedent is outside of that domain); and the pronoun in (d), although bound, is free in its Governing Category.

A similar pattern to the reflexives holds for NP-trace, which is also [+a, −p] and therefore subject to Principle A.

(78) a.   Mary$_i$ was impressed e$_i$.

    b.   Mary$_i$ seems [$_S$ e$_i$ to be happy].

    c.   *Mary$_i$ seems [$_{S'}$ that [$_S$ e$_i$ is happy]].

In example (c), the empty category is governed by the lower INFL; hence the Governing Category is the lower S. Example (c) is then in violation of Principle A (and, as INFL is not a proper governor, the example also involves an ECP violation).

We have seen some examples of pronouns, subject to Principle B, in the preceding discussion; recall that pronouns are [−a, +p]. Some other relevant examples are shown in (79):

(79) a.   [Mary$_i$'s father] took her$_i$ to the movies.

  b.   Mary$_i$ bought a present for [her$_i$ father].

In (a), the Governing Category for the pronoun is the whole clause, and while the antecedent *Mary* lies within that domain, *Mary* does not bind the pronoun, for it does not c-command it. Hence the pronoun is free and Principle B is satisfied. In (b), the Governing Category for the pronoun is the NP indicated by the bracketing (though I have not said enough about government within NP for this to be obvious to the reader), and again the structure respects Principle B.

The corresponding empty category, pro, does not appear in English. Exactly what properties determine its distribution are not clear, but the classic example of pro is the 'missing' subject that is allowed in many languages where the verb shows person/number inflection, such as the following Spanish examples:[31]

(80) a.   pro llegué   'I arrived.'

  b.   pro llegaste   'You(sg.) arrived.'

  c.   pro llegó   'He/she arrived.' etc.

In such examples, the missing subject shows all the interpretive properties of a regular pronoun, except that it is phonetically null. While pro is supposed to be absent in English, as English verb-inflection is so minimal, the presence of inflection cannot be the sole factor allowing the correct 'identification' of pro, for many highly inflecting languages fail to exhibit missing subjects, and others, such as Japanese, allow any verbal argument to be dropped even though there is no inflection whatsover. So the parameter that determines whether pro will be present in a given language or not has not really been fully isolated yet—though presumably the presence of informative verbal inflection will ultimately be part of that final determination.

---

[31] Recall that pro is an empty category and hence is not pronounced (or, has no phonetic matrix).

The prononimal pro may also be 'expletive' (semantically empty), just like overt pronouns (e.g., English *it*), as in:

(81) a.   pro$_i$ llegó Juan$_i$ 'Juan arrived.'

   b.   pro llueve   'It rains.'

   c.   pro parece que Juan está enfermo
         'It seems that Juan is sick.'

For (a), the nearest English example is something like *There arrived a man*; in the Spanish example *Juan* is within the VP and so does not bind pro, as it does not c-command it. Hence the pronoun (pro) is free in its Governing Category; pro is also free in (b) and (c) as it has no antecedent, and therefore is not bound.

Let us now look at [−a, −p] categories. R-expressions and *wh*-traces, or variables, share the property that they must be A-free in any domain (Principle C). This is seen in the examples in (82).

(82) a.   *He$_i$ likes Max$_i$.

   b.   *Who$_i$ does he$_i$ like e$_i$?

   c.   *He$_i$ thinks that I like Max$_i$.

   d.   *Who$_i$ does he$_i$ think that I like e$_i$?

Examples (b) and (d) show the parallel data with empty categories for the overt categories in (a) and (c). In each case, the R-expression may not be A-bound within any domain. The empty categories are of course Ā-bound, but this is outside of the realm of the Binding Theory. (The observant reader will have noticed that in (81)a, the pronominal pro A-binds the NP *Juan*, in violation of Principle C. Discussion of this problem can be found in Rizzi (1982) and Safir (1985).) If the c-command is broken, as in *His mother likes Max*, then coreference is correctly allowed; as before, if there is no c-command, there is no binding, and therefore despite the fact that the pronoun and *Max* will be coindexed, the pronoun does not bind *Max*.

Examples (b) and (d) above are known as examples of *Strong Cross-over*. This name comes from the transformational account, where the movement of the *wh*-phrase 'crosses over' a coreferential pronoun as it moves into COMP. The GB analysis of this is that as the pronoun c-commands the *wh*-trace, the latter is A-bound, violating Principle C. Reversing the c-command relations, as in (83), gives a grammatical example:

(83)   Who$_i$ e$_i$ thinks that he$_i$ will win?

Here the empty category is correctly A-free (as it is $\overline{A}$-bound by *who*), and though this empty category A-binds the pronoun, the pronoun is A-free in its Governing Category, which is the lower clause.

Finally we come to PRO, the 'pronominal anaphor.' Due to its feature-specification of [+a, +p], PRO is subject to Principles A and B simultaneously, leading to an apparently paradoxical situation. Yet out of this another conclusion is possible: that PRO has no Governing Category; in lacking a Governing Category, it would effectively be immune from the dictates of the binding principles. In this way, GB derives the following statement:

(84)   PRO is ungoverned.

This is a statement about the distribution of PRO. It can only appear in ungoverned positions, for only in those will it lack a Governing Category, in virtue of lacking a governor. In any governed position, it will be required to be both bound and free in the same domain, which is not logically possible. There is one major position that is ungoverned—the subject position of an infinitival clause, as in examples like:

(85) a.   Mary hopes [$_{S'}$ PRO to win].

   b.   [$_{S'}$ PRO to err] is human.

While the tensed INFL governs (though it does not properly govern), the infinitival INFL *to* does not govern at all, allowing the appearance of PRO. The dominating clause must be S', to prevent potential government from outside. Note that the Binding Theory says nothing about the relation of PRO to its antecedent, but rather simply characterizes its distribution. The relation of PRO to its antecedent falls under the theory of *Control*.

As [+a, +p] categories must be ungoverned, by the Binding Theory, no overt category can have this specification; for an overt NP is subject to the Case Filter, but as Case is assigned under government, there is no possibility of satisfying both the Binding Theory and the Case Filter in this case.

Table 3 gives a summary of the Binding Theory and the types of NP. The Governing Category, where relevant, is indicated by unlabelled square brackets if it is not the matrix S.

9.2. Control

The theory of Control is not a homogenous one, in that it seems to involve information coming from syntax, semantics, and pragmatics. I will there-

Table 3
Summary of Binding Theory

NP -type	Binding Features	Binding Principle	
OVERT			
John	−a,−p	C	1. *He$_i$ likes John$_i$ 2. *He$_i$ thinks that I like John$_i$
him	−a,+p	B	1. *John$_i$ likes him$_i$ 2. John$_i$ thinks that [I like him$_i$] 3. *John$_i$ believes him$_i$ to be sick 4. John$_i$'s mother likes him$_i$ 5. His$_i$ mother likes John$_i$
himself	+a,−p	A	1. John$_i$ likes himself$_i$ 2. *John$_i$ thinks that [I like himself$_i$] 3. John$_i$ believes himself$_i$ to be sick 4. *John$_i$'s mother likes himself$_i$
EMPTY			
wh-trace	−a,−p	C	1. *Who$_i$ does he$_i$ like e$_i$? 2. *Who$_i$ does he$_i$ think that I like e$_i$?
pro	−a,+p	B	1. pro habla inglés 2. pro$_i$ llegó Juan$_i$ ayer
NP-trace	+a,−p	A	1. John$_i$ was seen e$_i$ 2. *John$_i$ thinks that [I was seen e$_i$] 3. John$_i$ seems [$_S$ e$_i$ to be here]
PRO	+a,+p	A/B	1. John$_i$ tried PRO$_i$ to sleep 2. John thinks that it is inadvisable PRO to sleep

fore say little about the theory itself, and limit myself to illustration of cases. The idea of classifying PRO as a pronominal anaphor stems in part from the fact that it can be interpreted either as one type or the other, as in:

(86) a.   John$_i$ decided PRO$_i$ to leave.

b.   Mary said that it is unnecessary PRO to cut the grass in winter.

In (a), PRO is subject to *obligatory* control, in that its antecedent must be the subject of the dominating clause. There is a class of predicates with this property, such as *decide, try*, etc.; PRO behaves like an anaphor when it is the subject of a clausal complement to such predicates. Other instances of PRO have *non-obligatory* control; in (86)b the interpretation can be that it is unnecessary for Mary to cut the grass, or for anyone salient in the discourse, or for the speaker, or for anyone in general. In such examples, PRO behaves like a pronoun. The 'anyone in general' interpretation is known as *arbitrary* control, as in *PRO to vote for Johnson is PRO to vote for war;* interestingly, in cases like this with multiple PROs, they are bound together in some way, for the interpretation of this example is like "in each case, for someone to vote for Johnson is for that same person to vote for war."

As I noted above, the clause dominating PRO must be S′, to provide a barrier to external government. Control predicates like *try* show many superficial syntactic similarities with raising predicates like *seem*, but are also in many ways distinct. GB assigns the structures shown in (87):

(87) a.   Mary$_i$ seems [$_S$ e$_i$ to look happy]

b.   Mary$_i$ tried [$_{S′}$ [$_S$ PRO$_i$ to look happy]]

The control verbs also differ from the raising verbs in having a thematic subject; for example *try* assigns the Agent θ-role to its subject. From this, it follows that the subject of a control verb cannot be expletive (for expletives cannot bear θ-roles), as shown in (88); a similar pattern distinguishes *believe* and *persuade*.

(88) a.   It seems that Max is here.

b.   *It tries that Max is here.

c.   There seems to be a fly in the soup.

d.   *There tried to be a fly in the soup.

e.   Max believes it to be obvious that he will win.

f.   *Max persuaded it to be obvious that he will win.

Note that while traces appear in the tails of chains, PRO does not. So, for example, while (Mary, e) is a chain in (87)a, (87)b contains two chains, each with one member. This is necessary, due to the θ-Criterion, for both *Mary* and PRO are assigned θ-roles in (87)b. One diagnostic for PRO is that it must appear in structures where positing a trace would violate the θ-Criterion.

Where To Look Next

A more thorough introduction to GB (on historical lines) can be found in van Riemsdijk and Williams (1986). Possibly the most accessible of Chomsky's recent works is Chomsky (1982), which is a companion to the much fuller and denser presentation in Chomsky (1981). More recent developments in the theory are given in Chomsky (1986a), which also contains a certain amount of philosophical discussion. Chomsky (1986b) explores a radical alternative to the notion of Subjacency.

The work of Kayne and Rizzi has been very important in the development of GB; their papers are collected in Kayne (1984) and Rizzi (1982). Stowell (1981) contains the most detailed discussion of the program to eliminate phrase structure rules from the grammar. The extent to which movement in syntax is paralleled by movement in LF is discussed in Hornstein (1984) and May (1985).

The Japanese data in Section 5.4 comes from Nishigauchi (1984); see also Nishigauchi (to appear) and references there, and Huang (1982) for Chinese. The Chinese word order data alluded to at the end of Section 6 is discussed in Williams (1984) and in more detail in Huang (1982), Koopman (1984) and Travis (1984); Williams (1984) also presents a critical evaluation of Lexical-Functional Grammar from a GB perspective. On Control, see Manzini (1983). On pro, see Rizzi (1986).

Chapter 3

Generalized Phrase Structure Grammar

The theory of Generalized Phrase Structure Grammar (GPSG) developed out of work by Gerald Gazdar at the end of the 1970s, and while practically every detail of the theory has changed in the intervening period, the initial motivation of his original work is preserved. In the present chapter I will provide an overview of the version of GPSG laid out in Gazdar et al. (1985), hereafter 'GKPS.'

Generalized Phrase Structure Grammar is in a sense a very homogeneous theory, in that it posits only one level of syntactic representation, surface structure, and, in its pure conception, only one kind of syntactic object, the phrase structure rule. What GPSG does is augment a phrase structure grammar in certain ways that still leave you with a phrase structure grammar, but one that can handle constructions previously thought to be describable only with the aid of transformations; most well-known is the analysis of '*wh*-movement' type constructions available within GPSG, which caught the attention of many linguists and led to a considerable amount of novel research within the GPSG framework.

Work in Generalized Phrase Structure Grammar has generally taken the idea of formalization quite seriously; consequently, GKPS is full of technical detail to a level almost unprecedented in contemporary grammatical theory. As such, the mathematical properties of GPSG grammars have been and are the focus of much attention, and their relation to a theory of parsing has also been the subject of much recent research. I shall say little about either of these things, except to note that the appearance of a grammatical formalism with relatively well-understood and mild generative power that could handle large chunks of natural languages has brought back to life what was a somewhat dormant area of enquiry: the study of the mathematical properties of human languages. GKPS only allows the system described context-free generative capacity, and as such (admittedly) cannot deal with certain known aspects of human language.

I would take us too far afield to consider the concept of context-freeness and its computational relevance; I simply note that context-free systems are limited in their descriptive power in a way that most linguists have believed is too restricting to deal with natural language syntax. What is interesting, though, is the fact that all of the constructions that have been shown to require greater power than context-freeness are somewhat unusual, and apparently not run-of-the-mill grammatical phenomena. Recently, there have been developments within the GPSG framework[1] that attempt to change it in certain ways to allow coverage of these previously problematic cases, though I shall not discuss them here.

While the emphasis in the development of transformational grammar into Government-Binding Theory was on constraining the transformational component, GPSG takes this emphasis to its conclusion and simply eliminates the transformational component. The claim is thereby advanced that one level of syntactic representation—namely, surface structure—will suffice; but it is important to note that sufficiency does not carry much weight as an argument in linguistics. The difference between the theories described here is not that one can do it one way or another, but that it is an advantage to do it one way: GPSG claims not only that it is possible to have just one level of syntactic representation, but also that in so doing it can solve several long-standing problems whose description required independent stipulations under the transformational grammar account. In its outlook on the architecture of the grammar, GPSG has inherited a tradition from formal language theory and, within the realm of generative grammar, from Montague Grammar. Every syntactic structure is directly paired with a semantic (model-theoretic) interpretation, and while in Montague Grammar syntax very much plays second fiddle, GPSG has explored the potential in the relation between syntax and semantics, in that the one may constrain and interact with the other, and recognizes several 'semantically-driven' syntactic processes.

As currently formulated, there are no phrase structure rules in a GPSG grammar, where we understand phrase structure rules as standing in a direct correspondence to pieces of tree. Rather, the grammar provides various constraints on what informational properties pieces of tree must encode, but does not go through the intermediary representation of phrase

---

[1] In particular, Pollard (1984) and subsequent work.

structure rules. GPSG does have rules, which only represent *immediate dominance*, and are called ID-rules;[2] these are related directly to trees by a *rule-to-tree* definition, which has a series of well-formedness conditions governing it. The overall picture of the grammar is shown in Figure 2, and I will devote most of this chapter to an explication of the different notions contained in it. In Figure 2, I use the term *tree* to refer to a surface structure paired with a semantic interpretation.

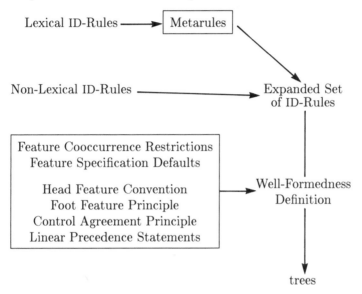

Figure 2.   Generalized Phrase Structure Grammar

Another formal point worth noting is that the grammatical information encoded by rules in GPSG is taken to be constraints on *node-admissibility*, rather than the traditional *rewrite* interpretation given to ordinary phrase structure rules. The difference can be shown with a simple example.

(1)   S   →   NP VP
         NP →   John / _ sleeps
         VP →   sleeps / John _

---

[2] See Section 2.

These are context-sensitive rules; interpreted as rewrite rules, they generate nothing, for once we have rewritten S as NP and VP, we can do no more. We can only rewrite NP in the context of *sleeps* and similarly for VP, but neither context is available. However, interpreted as admissibility conditions, the string *John sleeps* is admitted as an S, for under this interpretation we randomly generate trees and then 'check' them, and this string 'checks out.'

I will say little about Universal Grammar, that is, the general properties of the human language faculty, in this chapter; one reason is that GKPS is devoted to an analysis of English. Whatever universal features of language GPSG will ultimately propose (such as the various properties of the rule-to-tree definition), they will be couched in a rather different fashion than the way Government-Binding Theory states them. The GPSG view is that universals should follow from the very architecture of the theory; as an example, whereas Government-Binding Theory might say that it is a universal property of language that subcategorization is satisfied under government (i.e., in some local domain), GPSG would say that the very nature of the system (using something like phrase structure rules) forces this property, as such rules can only express local relations. Hence constraints, from a GPSG view, derive from the sheer impossibility of stating certain logically prior possibilities, given the primitives of the theory.

1. Features and Syntactic Categories

GPSG relies on being able to pass information around trees, and this information is encoded by means of syntactic features; GPSG is in fact a theory of how syntactic information "flows" within a structure. For example, there might be a feature specification on a given node that indicates that it has a TENSE feature with the value PAST, and an identical specification on the mother of this node. This is a situation where the information is taken to flow or pass from one to the other (the direction of this flow would be a matter for research). Intuitively, a feature (or more precisely, a feature-value pair) is a piece of linguistically significant information, and a feature often has linguistic realization; the feature of TENSE is realized in English as an *-s* on (third person) verb forms when its value is PRES (present), as in *She walks*, and is realized as *-ed* when the value is PAST, as in *She walked*. All syntactic theories use features—to differing degrees—but it is only recently that they have been put to any principled use, rather than simply used for diacritic effect in particular cases. In this section I will focus on various aspects of the GPSG approach to features—the X'-Theory of GKPS, the notion of 'syntactic category' that is adopted, and general properties of the set of features posited.

1.1. X'-Theory

The part of X'-Theory that defines a phrase as a projection of the features of a head is a central part of GPSG, for the information of what is the head determines much of the distribution of syntactic features. GPSG adopts a two-level X'-theory, and defines the major categories N, V, A and P in terms of the primitive features [N] and [V] (see Chap. 2, Table 2). At this point *p. 31* similarity with the Government-Binding Theory version of X'-theory stops; for GPSG proposes that the 'basic' X'-scheme is not to descend level by one, as in Government-Binding Theory, but rather to remain at the same level. This is dealt with by a default mechanism: unless otherwise indicated, the bar-level of a mother and the head daughter will be identical. We will see examples of this below. The motivation for this is essentially economy; GPSG proposes many more rules that do not obey the 'descend-one' idea than rules that do obey it.

A difference that is more immediately demonstrable is the fact that in GPSG S is a projection of V; this is not novel to GPSG but in fact dates back to the earliest work on X'-Theory. There are no abstract categories like INFL in a GPSG grammar as there is no level at which to represent them. Now it is well-attested that information that *ultimately* shows up on the verb must be present on the dominating S-node; for example, the verb *think* subcategorizes for a complement that is tensed:

(2)   a.   Lee thinks (that) Sandy is muscular.

   b.   *Lee thinks (for) Sandy to be muscular.

Information about the presence of tense must therefore pass between the inflection on the verb and the S-node. In Government-Binding Theory this is accomplished by assuming that the information flows up from INFL to its projection S in the syntax, before INFL is combined with the verb in PF. For theories which only allow fully inflected words to be inserted into trees, such an option is not available, and the information must flow directly from V to S. As it is relatively uncontroversial that information of this kind only passes up and down X'-projections, it follows that V must be the head of S in GPSG (given the assumption that words are fully inflected at the point of lexical insertion).

Now, from other considerations it is also desirable to have both VP and S' be maximal projections (i.e., X''s); it is quite common to find rules that affect NP, VP, AP, PP and S'. In order to allow such generalizations to be captured, GPSG assigns the categories VP, S and S' all to the same X' level, namely the maximal projection of V. S is distinguished from VP by a SUBJ feature (for 'subject'), and S' from S by a COMP (for 'complementizer') feature. Independent evidence for this categorization comes from coordination facts; for example, a widely-accepted constraint on coordination is that the coordinating categories must be of the same bar-level. Consider now the example in (3):

(3)   We expect $[_{VP}$ to be there by six] and $[_{S'}$ that we will be too late].

As no other category seems to coordinate with S' under *expect* (e.g., * *We expected a riot and that it would destroy the stadium*), the analysis that we could give for (3) is that *expect* subcategorizes for a complement that is a V^2. (It is usual to express bar-level in GPSG numerically.)

The X'-equivalences for these categories are shown in (4):

(4)   a. $V^2[-SUBJ][COMP\ NIL]$ = VP

    b. $V^2[+SUBJ][COMP\ NIL]$ = S

    c. $V^2[+SUBJ][COMP\ \alpha]$ = S'
       where $\alpha \in \{that,\ for,\ whether,\ if\}$.

1.2. Categories

A syntactic category in GPSG is taken to be a set of feature-value pairs. For example, the label NP (N^2) is taken to be an abbreviation for the set

$$\{<N,+>, <V,->, <BAR, 2>\}$$

where BAR is a feature just like anything else. (Some people find it mysterious that BAR should be a feature, but it is just another piece of information on a node.) The category N would have the same specification, except the value for BAR would be zero. (It is a little unfortunate that the features [N] and [V] are identical with the category names N (noun) and V (verb); I again refer the reader to Chap. 2, Table 2 for clarification.)

However, not every set of feature-value pairs is a possible syntactic category. Categories are taken to be partial functions from features to values. For example, the category NP applied to the feature V gives '−' as a value. Defining categories this way makes axiomatic the elementary observation that no syntactic category has different specifications for the same feature. For example, there are no NPs that bear both nominative and accusative case simultaneously; and

$$\{<N, +>, <V, ->, <BAR, 2>, <CASE, NOM>, <CASE, ACC>\}$$

is not a well-formed category for it is not a function; no function can deliver two values for the same argument.

Major categories are usually taken to be nouns, verbs, adjectives, and prepositions, and GPSG does not depart from this. The rest are known as *minor* categories: things like determiners, complementizers, particles, etc. Major categories participate in the X′-scheme while minor ones do not, and so minor categories can be defined in the following way:

(5)   A category C is a minor category iff C(BAR) is undefined.

That is, a minor category is one that (necessarily) lacks a value for BAR.

1.3. Features

Features in GPSG have two main properties—what kinds of values they take, and what distributional regularities they share with other features. Some features are *atom-valued*, and these are what for most readers will be the familiar case. As the name suggests, the values of such features are atomic, i.e., not susceptible to further analysis. Some sample features and value-sets are shown in (6).

(6)   PLU $+, -$

        BAR   0, 1, 2

        CASE   NOM, ACC, GEN, ...

        PFORM   *by, to, for,* ...

The traditional notion of singular and plural is reconstructed here in the binary-valued feature PLU (it is PLU rather than SING simply as a convention).[3] We have seen the BAR and CASE features above. The PFORM feature is a way of ensuring the right form for prepositions, and is in a sense a syntactic analog to θ-roles. Consider a verb like *give*; it subcategorizes for a PP that is headed by the preposition *to*:

(7)   I gave a book to/*for/*with/*towards Lee.

One way to get this is to assign a thematic role of Goal along with the subcategorization, and make sure that the Goal role is realized by the preposition *to*. Alternatively, one can subcategorize for a PP[PFORM *to*].

Other features in GPSG are *category-valued*; their values are not atomic, but are in fact categories. As an illustration, agreement (say, between a subject and a verb) is dealt with by means of a category-valued feature AGR, and encodes the information "I agree with a category of such-and-such a form," such as a 3rd-person, masculine, plural NP:

(8)   AGR   NP[3 M PL]

I will use [AGR NP[3 M PL]] as an abbreviation for the full specification, which is:

$$\{<AGR, \{<N, +>, <V, ->, <BAR, 2>, <NUM, 3>,$$

$$<GEND, MASC>, <PLU, +>\}>\}$$

in its full form. (I will use [SG] for $<PLU, ->$.)

Finally, any category can in principle label a node in a tree; for example,

$$\{<BAR, 2>\}$$

can label a node in English, and would correspond to the more familiar notation XP (i.e., maximal projection of any major category).

2. ID/LP Format

In the early conceptions of GPSG, the grammar consisted of a set of phrase structure rules, such as:

(9)   VP $\rightarrow$ V NP PP

---

[3] See Sag et al. (1985, 152ff) for more discussion of the feature SING.

Such rules encode two kinds of relation, those of *immediate dominance* and those of *linear precedence*; this particular rule says that VP immediately dominates V and NP and PP, and that the V precedes the NP which precedes the PP. In recent work, these two components are factored out, and phrase structure rules are not used at all. Dominance and precedence requirements are directly stated on nodes in the tree.

2.1. ID/LP

If we look at a set of phrase structure rules, such as those for English VPs given in (10), we notice a certain pattern in ordering of daughter constituents.

(10) a.   VP → V NP   *kiss the bride*

b.   VP → V NP PP   *send the message to Kim*

c.   VP → V NP S′   *tell the class that break is over*

d.   VP → V NP VP   *expect results to be forthcoming*

In all cases, the NP immediately follows the verb, which is always initial in its phrase. Clearly any grammar that just lists these rules is missing something important about English. One could just as easily describe a grammar in which NP preceded the verb if there was also a VP complement, while NP was VP-final if the complement was S′. However, such languages probably do not occur.

Other instances where phrase structure rules seem to be inappropriate are cases where there are few, if any, ordering restrictions. Many languages have rather free constituent order (e.g., the major constituents of S can come in any order in Latin) and for a simple subject-verb-object sentence one finds oneself with six phrase structure rules. The idea of ID/LP format is that these problems are solved by factoring out information of *immediate dominance* (ID) and *linear precedence* (LP). The Latin example would now reduce to:

(11)   S   → V, NP, NP

where the commas indicate that the categories are unordered with respect to each other. Similarly, the English rules above would now be expressed in the format:

(12) a.   VP → V, NP   *kiss the bride*

    b.   VP → V, NP, PP   *send the message to Kim*

    c.   VP → V, NP, S′   *tell the class that break is over*

    d.   VP → V, NP, VP   *expect results to be forthcoming*

    e.   V ≺ NP ≺ XP

This is not the actual GKPS formulation, which I have simplified a little to illustrate the point. The '≺' indicates the precedence relation in the LP-statement (12)e. I will elaborate in a later section on the actual ID-rules and LP-statements proposed for English.

2.2. Heads and Subcategorization

As I have hinted at above, many features are transmitted up and down X'-projections; for example, if a VP is marked as PAST, then the verb heading that VP will be too. The strategy for determining a head that was implicit in generative grammar until recently[4] was the following: look at a rule (like one in (12), or a corresponding tree fragment). Determine which daughter matches the mother in the features [N] and [V]—this is the head. Now copy over all features like person, number, gender, tense, etc., such that the features on the head and mother match.

A head is not defined in this way in GPSG. Essentially, GPSG accords no special role to the features [N] and [V], and copies them over as well. The head is indicated in a rule by the notation 'H,' as in (13).

(13)   VP → H

The idea is that this notation will express the same information (given the feature-passing conventions which I will present below) as the rule VP → V. The class of features that get copied over are called **HEAD** features, and I will say more about them in the section below on the Head Feature Convention. Given that BAR is classified as a **HEAD** feature, the H in (13) would actually be instantiated as a VP, and so we must override the operation of the feature-passing mechanisms with respect to BAR by explicitly mentioning its value. However, as we will see below, the zero bar-level is predictable from other information; that other information relates to subcategorization, which is our next topic.

---

[4] That is, until the appearance of Gazdar and Pullum (1981).

In Chapter 2, I noted that Government-Binding Theory proposed to eliminate the redundancy between phrase structure rules and subcategorization frames by dispensing with the former; in GPSG, the opposite tack has been taken, and verbs do not have a subcategorization frame as such. Rather, they have an indicator that points to the structures in which they occur. So a transitive verb will be marked in such a way as to ensure that it will only be inserted into subtrees that have an NP as sister to the verb. This is again implemented with a feature, SUBCAT, which takes integers as its values. So along with the rules given in (14) there will be the lexical entries in (15).

(14) a.   VP →   H[1]

   b.   VP →   H[2], NP

(15) a. $<weep, [[-N], [+V], [BAR\ 0], [SUBCAT\ 1]], \{wept\},$ **weep′**$>$

   b. $<devour, [[-N], [+V], [BAR\ 0], [SUBCAT\ 2]], \{\},$ **devour′**$>$

These entries also provide information about irregular morphology and a meaning (indicated by the boldface and prime[5]). The SUBCAT feature will ensure that the transitive verb *devour* will only appear in subtrees admitted by rule (14)b; given the view of syntactic categories taken here, failure to respect this feature-specification would be on a par with inserting a noun into a verb position, for example. It is of course possible for a verb to have multiple subcategorizations; each would correspond to a separate, but related, lexical entry.

One consequence of doing subcategorization this way is that it follows that a head can only subcategorize for its sisters; this gives the same results as the stipulation in Government-Binding Theory that subcategorization is satisfied under government, given the definition of c-command that makes reference to the first branching node (the 'stronger' definition). Note that this too entails that subjects are not subcategorized for in English. In this area GPSG may claim that it has accounted for subcategorization without having to stipulate that it must take place in a configuration of government. However, even the strong definition of government does not entirely coin-

---

[5] Note that this prime-notation does not mean the same as the X′-Theory prime-notation. I discuss meanings a little, in Section 4.

cide with the ID-rule system, for government may also go down through an S to a grand-daughter, and so the nature of the comparison is not clear. (This is a point on which Government-Binding Theory and GPSG differ—GPSG must view the sequence after 'object-raising' *believe* as NP VP;[6] for example, this NP corresponds to the subject of the related passive construction, and only sisters of the verb can have this property in GPSG. In Government-Binding Theory the complement must be an S, for no θ-role is assigned to the NP, so it cannot be a (subcategorized) sister of the verb.) Both theories differ from Lexical-Functional Grammar in not subcategorizing for subjects,[7] and this is due in each case to the idea that subcategorization must be satisfied in some local structural domain.

Note that complementizers too bear the SUBCAT feature; we might have the following rule and lexical item:[8]

(16)   a.   S[COMP α] $\rightarrow$ {[SUBCAT α]}, H[COMP NIL]

   b.   <*that*, [SUBCAT *that*]>

The rule says that S with a certain value for COMP can dominate a category with a SUBCAT feature with the same value and an S (the head) without the specification of a complementizer (i.e., [COMP NIL]). Values for COMP are *for*, *that*, *if*, *whether* and NIL.

The notion of 'minor' category is now taken to pick out those categories lacking BAR but having SUBCAT, and the presence of SUBCAT is one way of getting at a wider notion of 'head' than that encoded by the H notation. For example, there are often cases where one wants to treat COMP as the head of S' for some syntactic purpose, such as passing features onto it, while retaining V as the 'ultimate' head. In such cases, the class of functional heads can be accessed by picking out those things with SUBCAT, while the strictly categorial heads will be those things that have both SUBCAT and BAR.

---

[6] As in *believe Kim to be singing*.

[7] Though this is perhaps not so clear in the case of GPSG, as the presence of the AGR feature (see Sec. 5.5 below) to handle subject-verb agreement has the effect of allowing subcategorization for subjects.

[8] Note that the range of values of SUBCAT is now integers plus various names like *that*, *for*, and so on.

3. Rules

Under the general heading of rules, I will discuss in more detail the particular ID-rules that are proposed for English, and then move to a discussion of *metarules*, which are useful ways of stating generalizations across large sets of rules. Metarules are operations on ID-rules that give back new ID-rules, and in this way expand the set of ID-rules. I shall refer to the ID-rules that are listed in the grammar as 'basic' ID-rules and those that are created by metarule as 'derived' rules.

3.1. Lexical and Non-Lexical ID-rules

The class of basic ID-rules partitions into two theoretical domains as far as other operations in the grammar are concerned. In this subsection I will just say what this distinction is, though we will not see until Section 5 why it is useful. Let us look at the rules in (17); the reader will recall that S and VP are abbreviations, as given in (4) above. Similarly, NP and PP are abbreviations, though I hope that these are familiar to the reader by this point.

(17) a.   S   → X^2, H[−SUBJ]
   b.   NP →   Det, H^1
   c. N^1 →   H[30]
   d. N^1 →   H[35], PP[*of*]
   e.   PP →   H[38], NP
   f.   VP →   H[5], NP, NP

The first two rules say that an S-node can consist of any [BAR 2] phrase and a VP (to allow for non-NP 'subjects,' as in *To fight for one's country is noble*), and that an NP can consist of a Determiner and an N^1. The remaining rules differ from these two in that they introduce a *lexical head*, which can be seen from the H[n] notation (a lexical head has both SUBCAT and BAR features). These rules, then, provide the arguments subcategorized for by heads, and are known as *lexical* ID-rules. The non-lexical ID-rules (a) and (b) do not necessarily reflect subcategorization properties of anything, and it is not obvious what generalizations, if any, govern their form.

The rules in (17) will admit the tree in (18) (with some suitable LP-statements).

(18)

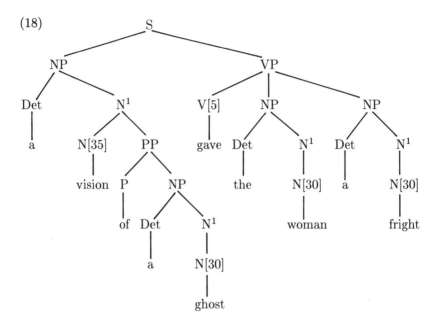

Modifying phrases may be accommodated quite simply, and it is in rules like (19) that we see the full effect of the H notation.

(19)   VP → X^2[+ADV], H

This rule allows an adverbial modifier adjoined to the VP; as the H is fully unspecified, all of the **HEAD** features of the mother will get copied over.[9] The adverbial phrase itself may be any maximal projection—for instance *yesterday* is an NP and *good*, as in *He did it good*, is an AP.

3.2. Metarules

Metarules perform some of the duties in phrase structure grammar that transformations perform in transformational grammar; in a sense, both extend a basic phrase structure grammar in certain ways. Other than this, there are few similarities.

---

[9] I use 'copy' here to give the intuition of the "information flow"; strictly, the GPSG view is that the **HEAD** features on the mother and head daughter are freely instantiated, but are constrained to match.

Let us look at the motivation for metarules. Consider the passive examples in (20); the important parts of these (the bracketed sections) would be admitted by such rules as are shown on the right:

(20) a. Kim was [kissed].   VP → H[PAS]

b. Sandy was [found in the mine].   VP → H[PAS], PP

c. Lee has been [told that it is over]. VP → H[PAS], S[FIN]

The feature PAS indicates the presence of passive morphology on the verb. Clearly it would be a mistake to simply list these rules, for they bear a regular relation to the set of rules that admit 'active' VPs, as we can see in (21) (following GKPS, I mark the [PAS] feature on the mother):

(21) a. VP[PAS] → H[2]   VP → H[2], NP

b. VP[PAS] → H[6], PP   VP → H[6], NP, PP

c. VP[PAS] → H[8], S[FIN]   VP → H[8], NP, S[FIN]

The idea of a metarule is to derive the rules on the left from those on the right. The passive metarule as given in GKPS has the following formulation:

(22)   Passive Metarule

$$VP \rightarrow W, NP$$

$$\Downarrow$$

$$VP[PAS] \rightarrow W, (PP[by])$$

In this metarule, W is a variable over any categories in an ID-rule. The passive feature appears on the VP, but again this is a **HEAD** feature and so the verbal head of the construction will be constrained to be a passive form. The rule says to take any VP-rule that has an NP-daughter, and from that form a new rule with the passive feature indicated on the mother and with the NP missing. Optionally, the new VP-rule may admit a PP daughter; this allows for the agent in a passive to be expressed or not, as in *Dana was arrested/Dana was arrested by the police*.

Note there is no mention of anything becoming a subject in the metarule. This is not necessary for the syntax: the rule effectively intransitivizes verb phrases, and this means that the only NP-position available in a sentence containing such an intransitive verb phrase (as with any intransitive) will be that of the subject. However, the corresponding semantics will change with the Passive Metarule, and will indicate that the NP in the *by*-PP (if there is one) will be interpreted similarly to the syntactic subject in the related active form; the syntactic subject of the passive will likewise have an interpretation corresponding to the interpretation of the object of the active form.

Let us now look at the relation between metarules and transformations. Transformations map trees into new trees, while metarules map rules into new rules. Assuming that the initial trees in a transformational grammar are produced by phrase structure rules, and ignoring empty categories, we can represent the situation in the following way.

(23)

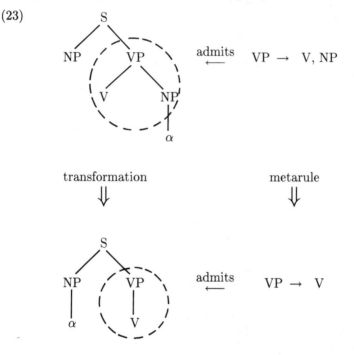

Intuitively, we can either map trees to trees as on the left-hand side of the diagram, or rules to rules as on the right. The former, transformational, way builds sentential structures by phrase structure rules and then transforms them into new structures; the latter uses metarules to expand the set of rules and therefore expand the set of trees admitted. However, the domain over which transformations are defined is much greater than the domain of metarules; potentially the domain of a transformation is an entire tree, while metarules can only apply to rules which admit 'local subtrees,' i.e., subtrees consisting of a mother and some immediately dominated daughter(s). It is impossible, for instance, to define a metarule that mimics the transformational account of 'subject-to-subject raising' (see Chap. 2, Sec. 7) in English, for the metarule cannot mention this much structure.

Another metarule that affects VP-rules is the so-called 'Subject-Aux Inversion' metarule, that allows the grammar to handle the inversion that we find in many English constructions, such as questions (e.g., *Has Robin left?*). The metarule has the following formulation:

(24)   'Subject-Aux Inversion' (SAI) Metarule

$$V^2[-\text{SUBJ}] \rightarrow W$$

$$\Downarrow$$

$$V^2[+\text{INV}, +\text{SUBJ}] \rightarrow W, \text{NP}$$

This rule takes any VP-rule and makes it into an S-rule (note that this gives 'flat' S structures, potentially without a VP), adding in the subject NP and the feature INV that indicates the inversion. This is necessary as matrix questions must be inverted, while embedded questions never are (in most dialects at least):

(25) a.   What has Leslie found?

b.   *What Leslie has found?

c.   *Gerry asked what has Leslie found.

d.   Gerry asked what Leslie has found.

The feature INV is also necessary to correctly account for the distribution of the auxiliary verb form *aren't*, which must appear in an inverted sentence if the subject is first person singular (*I aren't leaving*), and *better*, as in *You better leave now*, which can never be inverted. Finally, we can note in connection with (24) that it is perhaps correct to formulate it so as not to apply to S-rules, for the subject of S can be any [BAR 2] category,[10] but not all such categories show up in inverted sentences:

(26) a.   In these hills have been found gold and silver coins.

    b.   *Have in these hills been found silver and gold coins?

    c.   That Kim ate fish bothered Lou.

    d.   *Did that Kim ate fish bother Lou?

These would suggest that it may not be the case that the distribution of subjects is identical in inverted and non-inverted sentences.

Another independent restriction will prevent any metarule applying to an S-rule. This is the 'Lexical Head Constraint,' which states the following condition on metarule application.

(27)   **Lexical Head Constraint**
       Metarules map from lexical ID-rules to lexical ID-rules.

Although I cannot demonstrate the motivation for this constraint in this section, the effect of it is to limit the domain of metarule application to the domain of lexical subcategorization. Thus metarules cannot create rules that arbitrarily change structure without this being sanctioned by some lexical head.

Finally, in connection with the SAI Metarule, it is worth noting that although the metarule applies to any VP-rule, only those which introduce an auxiliary verb will ever be used in the definition of well-formed trees. This is due to a Feature Cooccurrence Restriction (see (37)a below) which only allows INV to be instantiated on nodes that dominate an auxiliary verb. So, for example, while all of the VP-rules listed in (21) above will be input to the metarule, none of the output rules will lead to well-formed trees. Only those VP-rules that introduce auxiliary verbs as the lexical head will be compatible with both the metarule and the Feature Cooccurrence Restriction. (See Sec. 5.1 for more discussion.)

The next metarule for us to consider is the Extraposition Metarule, which covers cases of extraposition such as those illustrated in (28):

---

[10]   There is some debate (among linguists of all persuasions) as to whether the PP *in these hills* is a subject in (26)a/b. I shall assume that it is, though one might take its failure to allow inversion ((26)b) to indicate that in fact it is not a subject. The main point of these examples is to illustrate that it is not necessary (within GPSG) to relate inverted sentences to non-inverted direct counterparts.

(28) a.   That Dana was arrested upset her mother.

    b.   It upset her mother that Dana was arrested.

    c.   That Lee smokes is obvious.

    d.   It is obvious that Lee smokes.

    e.   That Pat found the treasure seems unfair to Kim.

    f.   It seems unfair to Kim that Pat found the treasure.

The name 'extraposition' comes from the transformational analysis which proposed that a transformation 'extraposed' the clause out of subject position and inserted an *it* subject. The metarule for this has the following specification.

(29)   Extraposition Metarule

$$X^2[\text{AGR S}] \rightarrow W$$

$$\Downarrow$$

$$X^2[\text{AGR NP}[it]] \rightarrow W, \text{S}$$

The presence of a sentential subject is encoded in the agreement feature of the verb, so the metarule only applies to rules that introduce as mother a maximal projection that agrees with (i.e., has) a sentential subject. The metarule says that as an alternative, these predicates may take an *it* subject, with a sentential complement. The metarule thus expresses the dependency between the presence of 'dummy' *it* and the presence of an extraposed clause—this dummy only appears with clausal complements (and correspondingly, the other dummy NP in English, *there*, appears with NP arguments, as in *There is a man sick*, and *There is obvious that Lou is shaking*).

Some verbs, like *seem*, can only appear in the extraposed structure when they have a tensed complement; thus we do not have *That Kim can fly seems*. However, this cannot be a general property of such verbs, as they can appear in non-extraposed structures when combined with other predicates; we could not say, for example, that *seem* always requires extraposition of an S[FIN] subject. This is seen in (28)e/f; it is the adjective *unfair* that licenses the sentential subject, and hence we see that adjective phrases must allow extraposition (which is clear from (28)a/b), a property that may then be 'inherited' by VPs. This is why the metarule mentions X^2 phrases, not VPs. When *seem* takes an infinitival complement it inherits the subcategorization properties of that complement; when it is 'bare,' it is introduced by the rule (30), and hence always has an *it* subject.

(30)   VP[AGR *it*] → H[21], S[FIN]

Finally, we come to the Complement Omission Metarule, which allows the complements of [+N] categories (adjectives and nouns) to be omitted; verbs and prepositions obligatorily take their subcategorized arguments, while with nouns and adjectives, arguments are always optional[11] (even for nouns and adjectives derived from verbs). As complements (i.e., subcategorized arguments) appear under the X'-level, and modifiers do not, this is mentioned in the metarule to prevent gratuitous dropping of modifiers. Some relevant data is given in (32).

(31)   Complement Omission Metarule

[+N, BAR 1] → H, *W*

⇓

[+N, BAR 1] → H

(32) a.   *The enemy destroyed.
     b.   The enemy destroyed the castle.
     c.   the enemy's destruction
     d.   the enemy's destruction of the castle

(33) a.   *Kim respects.
     b.   Kim respects his parents.
     c.   Kim is respectful.
     d.   Kim is respectful to his parents.

---

[11] Exceptions to this, brought to my attention by Tom Wasow, are *fond* and *fondness*.

There are two other metarules given in GKPS, which we will see later in Section 6. This now completes our survey of the basic components of the grammar, with the exception of a brief consideration of the semantics, from which we move to a consideration of the relation between ID-rules and trees.

4. Sketch of Semantics

This will be a good point to give a sketch of the semantics assumed in GPSG, for certain aspects of the semantics are necessary for an understanding of what will follow. What I will present here is a rather crude version of the material in GKPS (Chap. 9).

The semantics adopted in GKPS belongs to a family of closely-related theories of semantics that are usually referred to under the name 'Extended Montague Grammar.' Sentences are assigned a denotation (a meaning) in a model, which corresponds to the way some state of affairs might be. We want our semantics to tell us that in a model where Kim runs that the sentence *Kim runs* is true; of course there may be another model in which Kim does not run, and in that case we would want the sentence to come out false. Rather than dealing directly with model-theoretical objects, which as we will see are things like entities and sets, it is usual to employ an intermediate language of representation, known as *Intensional Logic* (IL).

Following Frege, the denotation of a sentence is taken to be a truth-value, true or false, which are represented by members of the set $\{0, 1\}$; 0 is 'false' and 1 is 'true.' We will take *Kim runs* as our example. What will be the meaning of the noun *Kim*? We can take it to be an *entity*, some kind of thing, and we can represent the denotation of *Kim* by k.

Now what does the VP *runs* mean? We will ignore the tense, and take the denotation of *run* to be the set of things that run. So now we have assigned kinds of meaning to each of the components of our simple sentence. The next step is to decide how those meanings relate to each other. The principle of *compositionality* tells us that the meaning of something is built up out of the meanings of its parts, and practically any linguist will accept this in some form or other. In particular, what we want to say is that the sentence is true iff k is a member of the set of things that run, and false otherwise; this ties everything together. The case where *Kim runs* is true is shown in Figure 3; in that model, *Lee runs* is false.

In general each syntactic category has a unique type of denotation. So for example, the VP *kiss the cook* will denote the set of things that kiss

Universe of Individuals

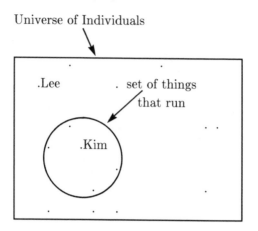

Figure 3

the cook, and the VP *decide that it is time for dessert* will be the set of things that decide that it is time for dessert. However, we do not associate VP-meanings with sets directly. Rather, we associate a VP meaning with the *characteristic function* of a set. The characteristic function of a set tells you, for any given thing, if that thing is in the set or not (true or false). The result of applying the characteristic function of the set of states in the U.S. to 'Oregon' is 1 (true), and 0 if the argument is 'Yorkshire.' Returning to our original example, we have deliberately set up our semantics so that we can view VP-meanings as functions, functions from NP-meanings (entities) to S-meanings (truth-values). The meaning of *runs* is a characteristic function, which when applied to the meaning of the NP *Kim*, will yield a truth-value.

The kind of thing a category denotes is called its *type*. The type of S, represented in GKPS by TYP(S), is symbolized by t; and for NPs that denote entities (not all noun phrases do), TYP(NP) is e. All other types are built up out of these two primitives, truth-values and entities. A VP-meaning is of type $<e, t>$, a function from entities to truth-values. The type of a transitive verb meaning, as a further illustration, will be $<e, <e, t>>$ (a function from entities to a function-from-entities-to-truth-values), while a verb like *tell* will be of type $<t, <e, <e, t>>>$—it takes a sentence and then two NPs as arguments.

In general, we can predict the semantic operation that will combine the meanings of daughter categories in a rule. For example, one typically finds rules of the following sort in the Montague Grammar literature. The prime-notation here is used to represent the meaning of the constituent, and is not related to its usage in X′-Theory.

(34)   S   →   NP, VP; S′ = VP′(NP′)

This says that syntactically an S consists of an NP and an VP, and that you get the S-meaning by treating the VP-meaning as a function on the NP-meaning.[12] Yet given the semantic types we have assigned, there's not much else you can do with a function from entities to truth-values and an entity, to get out a truth-value. In general, the syntax gives enough clues as to what the modes of semantic combination should be that you don't need to specify them; the operation that interprets the syntax in such a way as to build an appropriate denotation for a mother in a rule is known as *functional realization* (this general approach to semantic interpretation has often been described as "shake'n'bake semantics").

In the discussion of agreement to come below, we will need the semantic notion of *predicative category*, which, for the cases we will discuss, will be a category with a VP-type meaning (VPs 'predicate' some property of their subjects). A predicative category is something whose denotation is of type <TYP(NP), TYP(S)>, that is, something which may be predicated truly or falsely of an entity. For example, besides VPs, adjective phrases and predicate nominals (*proud of his children* in *Kim is proud of his children* and *doctor* in *Lee became a doctor*) are also predicative categories; intuitively, like VPs, they denote sets of entities.

I should also mention the role of grammatical relations like 'subject' and 'object' in GPSG. As in Government-Binding Theory, these are not taken to be primitive notions, but are defined in terms of other primitives of the theory. In GPSG, following Dowty (1982), they are defined in terms of the 'semantic structure,' that is, in the function-argument structure of the semantics. For example, a transitive verb like *find* is a two-place function— it needs two arguments to be complete. The subject is defined as the last argument, i.e., the argument to which the application of the function yields a truth-value. Similarly, the object is the next-to-last argument, and so on for indirect object, etc.

---

[12] There are other logical possibilities; for example, in Montague's best-known work "The Proper Treatment of Quantification in Ordinary English," which appears in Montague (1974), it is the NP-meaning that is the function on the VP-meaning.

I have only sketched here those parts of the semantics that are directly relevant to what I want to say below. Many other phenomena are treated in the semantics; for example, the coverage of the Binding Theory in Government-Binding Theory (at least for overt elements) with respect to the binding properties of pronouns and reflexives will have a semantic account in GPSG, although at present one has not really been developed.[13] These topics have been given analyses within the framework of (Extended) Montague Grammar, and such analyses are certainly compatible with a GPSG syntax. I would guide the reader to GKPS, Chapters 9 and 10, for further discussion and references.

5. Projecting From Rules To Trees

The major part of the burden of syntactic description is borne by the relation between ID-rules and trees. The idea is to characterize a function that 'projects' from rules to trees, as shown in (35). I use the notation $C^\dagger$ to indicate the node in a tree corresponding to a category C in an ID-rule.

(35)   rule   tree

The intuition is that the rule 'licenses' the local sub-tree, and that the subtree must include at least the information encoded in the rule, but also may *extend* the rule in various ways. The *projection function* ϕ determines in what ways this 'fleshing out' of information is permissible. For example, from any given VP-rule which does not mention finiteness (the values FIN and INF of the feature VFORM in this system), we would expect to be allowed to have a VP-node in a tree that is specified either as finite or non-finite, and ϕ should sanction this. However, we will want to make sure that the same feature specification that gets put onto the VP also

---

[13] See Pollard and Sag (1983) for an account of reflexives and reciprocals within the closely related 'Head Grammar' framework.

gets put onto the dominating S- and dominated V-nodes in the tree, and ϕ must therefore constrain things accordingly. Clearly we cannot allow a finite ([VFORM FIN]) VP to dominate a non-finite ([VFORM INF]) verb in a tree. We can think of ϕ as composed of various principles that govern what happens with features—in the present example, it would be the Head Feature Convention that governs the distribution of VFORM in the tree.

In this section, we will discuss the various aspects of the grammar which determine that some ϕ is a permissible function for defining a particular local sub-tree with respect to a particular rule. These aspects are: *Feature Cooccurrence Restrictions*, which constrain the class of possible categories in a language (for example, if a category bears a tense feature, then it will be some projection of V); *Feature Specification Defaults*, which specify the 'unmarked' value for a feature (Ss are not inverted unless this is specified via the operation of the SAI metarule; thus INV defaults to $-$); the *Head Feature Convention*, the *Foot Feature Principle*, and the *Control Agreement Principle*, which all determine how features distribute around the tree; and finally the set of *LP-statements*, which determine the order of categories in the tree. (These last four are considered to be principles of Universal Grammar that may be subject to finite variation across languages.) Some particular ϕ will be an *admissible projection*[14] of some rule (or of some category C in a rule) just in case:

- all Feature Cooccurrence Restrictions (FCRs) are true of ϕ(C)

- ϕ(C) is compatible with all Feature Specification Defaults (FSDs)

- ϕ meets the Head Feature Convention, the Foot Feature Principle, and the Control Agreement Principle

- ϕ respects all LP-statements

These switch from being about ϕ(C) to being about ϕ as FCRs and FSDs are defined with respect to categories, but the other principles are defined with respect to local subtrees (and hence refer to the function which relates rules to subtrees). I will work through each of these different component parts of the projection in turn.

---

[14] I am glossing over here the distinction in GKPS between a *candidate* projection and an *admissible* one; a candidate projection satisfies the conditions listed with the exception of the defaults. An admissible projection is a candidate projection that is also compatible with all defaults. See GKPS, 99ff for discussion.

5.1. Feature Cooccurrence Restrictions

Feature Cooccurrence Restrictions (FCRs) express certain dependencies between features, and, as categories are sets of feature-value pairs, express certain restrictions on what is a possible category. Some, such as those shown in (36), are presumably universal while others may be language-specific. The identifying number of each FCR is taken from GKPS.

(36) a. FCR 2:   [VFORM] $\supset$ [−N, +V]

b. FCR 3:   [NFORM] $\supset$ [+N, −V]

c. FCR 4:   [PFORM] $\supset$ [−N, −V]

d. FCR 7:   [BAR 0] $\equiv$ [N]&[V]&[SUBCAT]

e. FCR 8:   [BAR 1] $\supset$ ~[SUBCAT]

f. FCR 9:   [BAR 2] $\supset$ ~[SUBCAT]

The first one says that any category with a VFORM feature specification must be a verb; the '$\supset$' means 'logically implies,' so the FCR says that if a category bears the VFORM feature, then it must also be −N and +V. FCRs 3 and 4 express a similar requirement for nouns and prepositions. The fourth FCR in this list says that any major category with a SUBCAT feature specification is a lexical head ([BAR 0]); '$\equiv$' means 'if and only if,' so the FCR says that a category is ([BAR 0]) if and only if it is defined for N *and* V *and* SUBCAT. The last two FCRs say that projections of lexical heads cannot subcategorize, in that they can not ('~') be specified for SUBCAT. Due to FCR 7, we do not need to mention [BAR 0] in lexical ID-rules, for the head bears the SUBCAT feature.

Similarly, the SAI metarule does not mention 'auxiliary,' due to the English-particular FCR shown in (37)a; other possibly non-universal FCRs follow. (Of course, the distinction between universal and language-particular FCRs has no significance when it comes to the matter of the acceptability of a particular tree.)

(37) a. FCR 1:   [+INV] $\supset$ [+AUX, FIN]

b. FCR 10: [+INV, BAR 2] $\supset$ [+SUBJ]

c. FCR 11: [+SUBJ] $\supset$ [−N, +V, BAR 2]

d. FCR 15: [COMP] $\equiv$ [+SUBJ]

e. FCR 17: [COMP *that*] $\supset$ ([FIN] $\lor$ [BSE])

f. FCR 18: [COMP *for*] $\supset$ [INF]

FCR 1 says that if something is inverted, then it is an auxiliary and it is tensed; this expresses the fact that in English, the only things that invert are (tensed, or finite) auxiliary verbs (the non-finite auxiliary verb *to* does not invert).[15] However, in many languages, any verb may invert, so this is definitely specific to English. FCR 10 ensures that only Ss and not VPs bear the INV feature—that is, there is no such thing as an 'inverted VP' in English.

FCR 11 says that only maximal projections of verbs can be [+SUBJ], i.e., that [+SUBJ] is only defined for the category S. FCR 15 says that only Ss have complementizers, and 17 and 18 ensure that the complementizer *that* only appears in a tensed or subjunctive clause ('∨' means 'or'), and *for* in a non-finite clause. The value BSE of the VFORM feature (on a lexical head) indicates a verb in its 'base,' uninflected form; for example, this form appears in tensed clauses where the tense is carried by an auxiliary, or in subjunctive clauses, as seen in (38).

(38) a.   Kim might *be* there.

    b.   We require that Kim *be* there.

For the sake of completeness, I list here (without comment) the other FCRs that are in GKPS that I will not have cause to refer to later on.

(39) a.   FCR 5:   [PAST] ⊃ [FIN, −SUBJ]

    b.   FCR 12:   [AGR] ⊃ [−N, +V]

    c.   FCR 13:   [FIN, AGR NP] ⊃ [AGR NP[NOM]]

    d.   FCR 14:   ([+PRD] & [VFORM]) ⊃ ([PAS] ∨ [PRP])

So, in projecting from rule to tree, all FCRs must be respected, i.e., they must be true of the node in the tree (or equivalently, they must be true of ϕ applied to the category in the rule).

5.2. Feature Specification Defaults

Feature Specification Defaults (FSDs) are something that all theories use in some way or other, and although the idea is simple, it turns out to be

---

[15] This FCR ensures that the only output rules from the SAI Metarule ((24) above) which will license well-formed trees will be those with a lexical head which is an auxiliary verb. As such verbs appear sister to VP in the basic ID-rules (see Gazdar, Pullum, and Sag (1982)), the metarule-output rules will contain a VP constituent too.

very tricky to state their operation in any formal way. I will just present here the ideas behind the theory of defaults developed in GKPS.

The FSDs in (40) look like candidates for universal FSDs:

(40) a.   FSD   2:   ∼[CONJ]

  b.   FSD   3:   ∼[NULL]

  c.   FSD   4:   ∼[NOM]

  d.   FSD   7:   [BAR 0] ⊃ ∼[PAS]

The first three say that it is marked, i.e., not the usual case, to have a category that is a conjunct, or that is null (phonetically empty), or that bears nominative case. In the special cases where these features do appear, their appearance must be specifically sanctioned by a rule. We can illustrate this with respect to FSD 7, which says that the default for a lexical head is not to be passive; we only want passive verbs to show up when sanctioned by rules created by the Passive Metarule, in which case PAS is explictly mentioned on the rule. If this were not so, we would allow passive verbs to spontaneously appear, and admit things like *Kim was attacked Lee*. In contrast, the PAST feature has no default, and we find past and non-past verbs in any context (roughly speaking).

Let us look at some of the other defaults.

(41) a.   FSD   1:   [−INV]

  b.   FSD   5:   [PFORM] ⊃ [BAR 0]

  c.   FSD   11:   [+V, BAR 0] ⊃ [AGR NP[NFORM NORM]]

These defaults say that things are not inverted unless specifically forced to be so, that the default for the PFORM feature is for it to appear on lexical heads (prepositions, by FCR 4), and that verbs normally agree with 'normal' NPs: the feature NFORM takes three values, NORM, *it*, and *there*, and the last two must be sanctioned by specific rules. The default is then to NORM, as seen in (42)a below. Along with this, I again complete the list of FSDs given in GKPS, again without further comment.

(42) a.   FSD   8:   [NFORM] ⊃ [NFORM NORM]

  b.   FSD   6:   [+ADV] ⊃ [BAR 0]

  c.   FSD   9:   [INF, +SUBJ] ⊃ [COMP *for*]

  d.   FSD   10:   [+N, −V, BAR 2] ≡ [ACC]

5.3. Head Feature Convention

As I have hinted several times in the preceding sections of this chapter, many of the features proposed in GPSG are **HEAD** features, which means that their distribution in a tree is governed in a certain way that crucially involves the notion of a head, indicated by the H symbol in ID-rules.

Under its simplest formulation, the *Head Feature Convention* (HFC), will say that in any local subtree, the **HEAD** features of the mother are identical to the **HEAD** features of the head daughter. This is expressed in the following way.

(43)   Head Feature Convention
$$\phi(C_0) \mid \textbf{HEAD} = \phi(C_h) \mid \textbf{HEAD}$$

Here C_0 and C_h are the mother and head daughter of a rule, respectively; hence ϕ applied to either of these is the corresponding node in the tree. The vertical line '|' represents function restriction—the domain of the function is restricted in the way indicated by what follows the vertical line. Thus, what (43) says is that the features of the mother restricted to **HEAD** features (i.e., just the **HEAD** features on the mother) are identical to the features of the head daughter restricted to **HEAD** features, as desired. The final formulation of the HFC is somewhat more complicated than this, but we will use this version for present purposes.

As an illustration, we will be allowed, by the HFC, to project the subtree in (45) from the rule in (44).

(44)   VP → H[1], NP

(45)

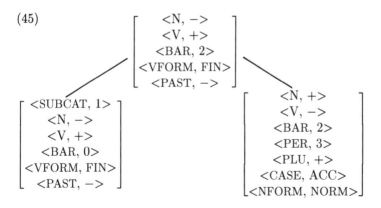

What goes on with the NP node here is irrelevant for current concerns. On the verbal projection, we have added the features VFORM and PAST to the mother; the other features come from the rule. The HFC tells us that *all* of these features (and their values) must be copied over, and most of them are. Note that the value of BAR differs. It has to be 2 on the mother for this is specified in the rule, but it has to be 0 on the daughter due to FCR 7, which says that major categories with SUBCAT are [BAR 0]. One of the subtleties in a final formulation of the HFC is that it must have this 'defaulty' character—features are only forced to match when it is possible for them to match given other constraints that might apply. Similarly, SUBCAT cannot appear on [BAR 1] or [BAR 2] categories, by FCRs 8 and 9, so this feature is present only on the daughter.

The following example shows a subtree that violates the HFC by having different values for PAST indicated on the mother and on the head daughter.

(46)

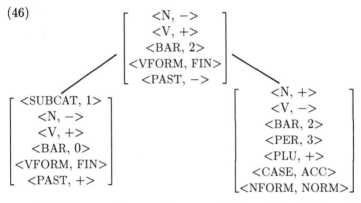

Confusion sometimes arises over the H notation in the rule; why does 'H' not appear in the tree? The answer here is that H is not part of the content of the rule, but rather an instruction about the interpretation of the rule. The daughter H[1] in rule (44) says that there is a [SUBCAT 1] category which *is to be interpreted as* the head of the rule. The H is a metagrammatical symbol; its interpretation can be thought of in the same way as the interpretation of the row of dots in $\{1, 2, \ldots, n\}$: we do not interpret this as the set consisting of four elements, the integers 1 and 2, a row of dots, and some arbitrary number n. Like H, '...' will have a different interpretation depending on context: $\{a, b, \ldots, z\}$ is not interpreted as the set with members a, b, z, and some arbitrary number (23?) of sequential integers.

The HFC, then, largely determines the structure of each X'-projection in a tree. Any arguments and modifiers will have their category specified in the ID-rule that introduces them; of course, their internal structure will again be determined in part by the HFC. The complete list of **HEAD** features presented in GKPS is given in (47).

(47)   Head Features
         {AGR, ADV, AUX, BAR, INV, LOC, N, PAST, PER, PFORM, PLU, PRD, SLASH, SUBCAT, SUBJ, V, VFORM}

We have seen illustrations of most of these; PRD is used to indicate a predicative use of a category—for example, the second complement of *consider* must be a predicative category, and such categories have certain syntactic properties (we will see this in the section below on coordination):

(48) a.   I consider Dr. Jekyll a competent surgeon.

      b.   *I consider Dr. Jekyll Mr. Hyde.

I will postpone discussion of SLASH for the section on unbounded dependencies.

One class of features, then, that distribute around a tree is the class of **HEAD** features; we will see in the next subsection the class of **FOOT** features, which have different properties of distribution. Finally, there are some features which are neither of these types, and they just sit quietly on a node. I list these features in (49) (from GKPS).

(49)   'Non-Propagating' Features
         {CASE, COMP, CONJ, GER, NEG, NFORM, NULL, POSS, RE-MOR, WHMOR}

The feature GER indicates whether something is gerundive or not (we have a gerundive phrase *having been crying* in *Having been crying, Lee looked awful*); the feature POSS indicates the possessive (often called the genitive case in other theories); REMOR indicates whether a pronoun is a reflexive (e.g., *themselves*) or a reciprocal (*each other*), roughly speaking (my use of 'pronoun' is misleading here, but I will not attempt to clarify it more). We will encounter the feature WHMOR (for '*wh*-morphology') in the following subsection.

5.4. Foot Feature Principle

Some features are distributed around a tree without necessarily obeying the Head Feature Convention. For example, it is uncontroversial that the bracketed phrase in (50) somehow 'inherits' a feature of *wh*-ness from the contained relative pronoun *whom*, and that it is this feature that is a criterial part of the syntactic description of the construction. The GPSG analysis of the feature percolation is shown diagrammatically in the tree below, with [+R] indicating the 'relative' feature introduced by the pronoun.

(50)   Kim, [the rumors about whom are totally false], will make a statement later this morning.

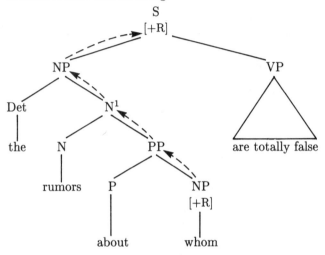

Clearly, in passing up from an NP-node to a PP-node, the feature is not showing the behavior of a **HEAD** feature. Roughly, the idea of the *Foot Feature Principle* is that **FOOT** features will be passed up from *any* daughter in a tree (not just the head), with the upper and lower limits of this propagation determined by prior specification, either in a rule or in a lexical item. For example, we might have the rule in (51) for the nonrestrictive relative clause[16] in (50); I will discuss its role in admitting this example immediately below.

---

[16] A plausible but controversial analysis of relative clauses in English is that restrictive relatives (e.g., in *the man who I met*) are sister to N′, while nonrestrictives (*the man, who I met*) are sister to NP. Note that H in (51) will be instantiated as NP, by the Head Feature Convention. I offer this rule only as an illustration.

(51)   NP →   H, S[+R]

The Foot Feature Principle (FFP) has the following formulation:

(52)   **Foot Feature Principle**

$$\phi(C_0) \mid \mathbf{FOOT} \sim C_0 \;=\; \bigsqcup_{1 \leq i \leq n} \phi(C_i) \mid \mathbf{FOOT} \sim C_i$$

Recall that $\phi(C_n)$ is the node in the tree corresponding to the member C_n in a rule. This time we are restricting the domain of the principle to **FOOT** features, and the new notation '$\sim C_0$' refers to those features *not* on C_0, which is the mother in the ID-rule. Hence, the first part of the principle can be read as "the features on the mother node restricted to **FOOT** features that were not mentioned on the mother in the rule." What the principle is about then, is those **FOOT** features that have been *instantiated* onto the mother node but not *inherited* onto the mother node from the mother category in the rule. The rest of the principle says that these features instantiated on the mother must be identical to the *unification* (the big square cup—see below) of the **FOOT** features instantiated onto all of the daughters. Note again that we are dealing with instantiation on the daughters and not inheritance (due to the '$\sim C_i$'). The basic idea here is that any **FOOT** feature instantiated on a daughter must be matched by one on the mother, and hence the feature appears to "percolate upwards." The notion of unification roughly corresponds to the idea of set-union,[17] and we can think of it as such; so we have that the (set of) **FOOT** features added onto the mother must be identical to the union of the **FOOT** features added onto the daughters.

In the example and tree (50), none of the nodes that bear the [+R] feature are admitted by rules that mention the feature, with the exception of the S-node. If the feature were to "pass up" through this node, we would have the following subtree:

(53)

---

[17] For unification, see also Chapter 4, Section 2.3.

Yet this is exactly the kind of case that the FFP blocks, for the feature has been instantiated on the mother, but not instantiated on any daughters, and so the one is not identical to the other. The daughter bears the feature of course, but in virtue of inheritance. Due to the parallel instantiation on mothers and daughters forced by the FFP, we get the appearance that the feature has actually passed up from the lexical item *whom* to this S-node.

Let us look at some more examples. From the rule in (54), we are licensed by the FFP to admit the subtrees in (55), but not those in (56).

(54)   VP → H[3], NP, PP

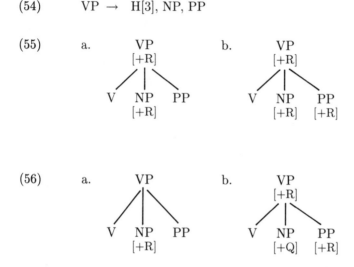

In (55)b, although two tokens of the feature have been instantiated on the daughters, the union of these is just the set {[+R]}; hence this is instantiated on the mother. In (56)a no feature has been instantiated on the mother, while one has on one daughter; and in (56)b two different **FOOT** feature specifications have been added to the daughters, but only one of these to the mother. The notation [+Q] , as I will explain presently, indicates the feature that we find in interrogative pronouns, many of which have relative pronoun counterparts.

The **FOOT** feature WH is ultimately the primitive in the grammar that unifies relative and interrogative pronouns. It is a category-valued feature, as can be seen in the sample parts of lexical entries shown in

(57). The feature WHMOR indicates whether the pronoun's morphology is appropriate to a question, a relative clause, or both.

(57) a.   <*what*, NP[WH NP[WHMOR Q]], ... >

    b.   <*which*, NP[WH NP[WHMOR Q]], ... >

    c.   <*which*, NP[WH NP[WHMOR R]], ... >

    d.   <*which*, Det[WH NP[WHMOR Q]], ... >

    e.   <*which*, Det[WH NP[WHMOR R]], ... >

The pronoun *what* is only an interrogative pronoun (we do not have **the table what you made* in standard dialects); otherwise, most pronouns of this type can be either relative or interrogative. The entry for *what* says that it is an NP with a WH **FOOT** feature whose value is the category NP with the feature specification appropriate to an interrogative pronoun. The word *which*, on the other hand, can be either an NP or a determiner, and either relative or interrogative:

(58) a.   Which do you prefer?

    b.   the tasks which I leave to the housekeeper

    c.   Which tasks do you leave to the housekeeper?

    d.   Here is my list, to which list Kim has added many more ideas.

The relative use of the determiner *which* is limited to the rather formal sounding non-restrictive relative clauses as in (58)d.

Although I have used the metaphor of a **FOOT** feature "passing up" the tree in this section, for this is useful to understand the basic concept, it is not how the system actually works. I will end this present section with another example to illustrate the system directly.

If we take the question *With what did you catch him?*, we again have a similar propagation. To illustrate the operation of the feature instantiation mechanism, I have split the tree for this into subtrees; each subtree will be admitted by one ID-rule. The dotted line is supposed to indicate how the subtrees link together and is not part of the formal representation of the structure. In this example the lower subtree will have a mother PP with the [+Q] **FOOT** feature; this same category will also be a daughter in the subtree rooted in S. For now we can ignore the structure of *did you catch him*, which in GPSG terms is an S/PP (S-missing-a-PP); such structures are the topic of the section on unbounded dependencies.

(59)

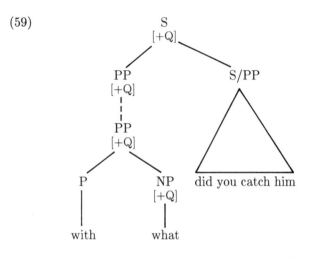

The tree here will be admitted by instantiation of [+Q] on the following rules; I have simplified the structure of PP somewhat in (60)b.

(60) a.   S   → X^2, H/X^2
     b.   PP → H^0, NP

By suitable instantiation, we will admit the subtrees indicated in (59), which will link up, giving the appearance or propagation; something in the grammar will contain the information that S[+Q] is a possible root category (the category of questions). At the "bottom" of the path of [+Q], we will have the category NP[+Q], which may dominate a lexical item like *what*, which, as the reader will recall, is listed as an NP.

I will leave the FFP here, as we will see its operation again (in connection with SLASH) below; GKPS list three **FOOT** features, WH, SLASH (='/'), and RE. The last deals with reflexive and reciprocal pronouns, though I cannot discuss this here (see Pollard and Sag (1983)).

5.5. Control Agreement Principle

The *Control Agreement Principle* (CAP) is part of a theory of agreement that has been the focus of much attention in GPSG. While the 'core' case of agreement is perhaps subject-verb agreement, there are of course many other cases: in some languages, verbs agree with objects, adjectives agree with nouns, and so on. Yet there are also clear constraints—in no language does the subject agree with the object, for example. It is the task of a theory of agreement to predict the existence of just the possibilities that are attested.

The CAP is a 'semantically-based' principle, in that the underlying intuition (due to Ed Keenan—see Keenan (1974)) is that functor categories agree with argument categories. Typically such a functor category is a predicative category, such as a VP, and these categories agree with their *controllers*, such as the subject NP. We thus say that the NP *controls* the VP in virtue of the VP being a predicative category, and the CAP in its crudest form says that controllees agree with their controllers (and not vice versa). This is not to deny a certain symmetry in the agreement relation, but the point is that verbs agree with NPs by showing features that are essentially properties of NPs, such as person, number and gender; we do not find the opposite, say, an NP agreeing with a verb with respect to a 'verbal' feature, such as tense.

The agreement is formally encoded in the AGR feature, which is category-valued, and essentially carries within it a 'copy' of the controller. For example, from the rule in (61) we might admit the tree shown:

(61)   S   →   X², H[−SUBJ]

This might be part of the tree ultimately admitting *Joanna feeds herself*, where the treatment of reflexives will interact with the AGR on the VP to ensure that the reflexive will be a [3 F SG] form. Also, as AGR is a **HEAD** feature, agreement will also show up on the head of the VP, and indeed the verb shows its [3 SG] form (verbs in English do not show agreement for gender).

The statement of the CAP is rather complex, and I will not present any of the formal details here; its effect is to ensure that the projection function ϕ for the rule in (61) only meets the CAP just in case the agreement features of the value of the AGR feature on the VP are identical to the agreement features on the NP. As the theory of agreement predicts what agrees with what, it is not necessary to stipulate this agreement, which distinguishes this version of GPSG from its early predecessors and also, for example, from Government-Binding Theory, where the rule coindexing INFL and the subject NP is simply a statement added to the grammar.

In other cases the controller of a predicative category is not directly its subject, though it is a sister; the definition of controller is formulated so as to ensure that the object NP *Susi* is the controller of the embedded VP in (62).

(62)

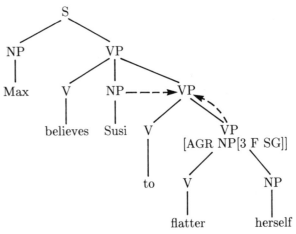

Things are slightly more complex still, as I will outline: in (62), the treatment of reflexive pronouns causes the AGR feature on the lowest VP to have the specification NP[3 F SG]. However, this VP is a predicative category, but it has no controller (no sister NP whose interpretation the interpretation of the VP is predicated of). The CAP says that in such a case the AGR feature passes up to the next node, and so on until a controller is found. This is indicated by the arrows in (62).

This shows what the operation of the CAP does; the reader should consult GKPS for further details. I will turn now to the way GPSG handles the difference between 'raising' verbs like *seem* and *believe* and 'control'[18] verbs like *try* and *persuade*.

---

[18] In the Government-Binding Theory sense of the term. In transformational grammar, such verbs are known as 'Equi-NP Deletion' (or simply 'Equi') verbs.

The examples in (63) will be analysed in part in terms of the syntactic structures shown in (64).

(63) a.   Kim seemed to look puzzled.

　　 b.   Kim tried to look puzzled.

　　 c.   Kim believed Dana to love Lee.

　　 d.   Kim persuaded Dana to love Lee.

(64)

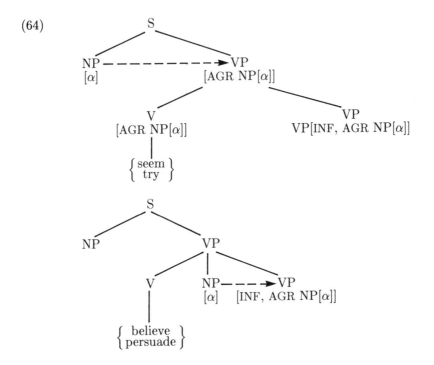

These are the important parts of the structures; with *seem* and *try*, the subject is interpreted as the subject of the lower infinitival VP and controls it (the lower VP has no controller, so the AGR passes up to the higher VP), and with the other verbs it is the object NP that is the controller. Yet there are many differences between the two types of verb; one illustration of this is seen in (65), where the expletive (semantically empty) pronoun *there* cannot appear as an argument of *try* or *persuade*.

(65) a.   There seemed to be a pig in the garden.

     b.   *There tried to be a pig in the garden.

     c.   Kim believed there to be a pig in the garden.

     d.   *Kim persuaded there to be a pig in the garden.

This is handled in the subcategorization for these verbs, that is, in the ID-rules that produce the nodes that immediately dominate them in syntactic structures:

(66) a.   VP →   H[15], VP[INF, +NORM]   *try*

     b.   VP →   H[16], VP[INF]   *seem*

The specification [+NORM] is short for AGR NP[NFORM NORM]. The rules in (66) have the property of allowing any kind of NP to be the subject of *seem*,[19] while ensuring, through agreement, that the subject of *try* is [NFORM NORM], i.e., not *it* or *there*. Directly parallel rules are given for *persuade* and *believe*.

The reader may recall that the feature NFORM defaults to NORM, and so the question arises as to how expletive NPs can ever be licensed at all. This brings us back to very complex problem of how exactly the defaults should work, something far beyond the scope of this chapter. However, I will try to explain what the solution to this problem is.

The feature NFORM should default to NORM on the lexical heads admitted by the rules in (66) (by FSD 11—see (41) above); however, it cannot do so when its sister is a VP[INF], for some of these VP[INF]s require a different value, as will be allowed by rule (66)b. For example, the infinitival VP *to be a pig in the garden* might be the complement of *seem*, and it requires a *there* subject. Hence, the default should not apply when the AGR feature on a lexical head (e.g., *seem*) covaries with the AGR feature on the VP[INF]: this latter category lacks a controller, so the AGR feature specification gets passed up to the dominating VP, and by the HFC down to the verb (*seem*). Under such circumstances, the default is stipulated to become inoperative, and this is a property of the set of like structures—so

---

[19] This is a slight simplification of the GKPS rule, which also allows for an optional PP constituent, as in *seem to Lee to be sick*.

any structure with a lexical head verb sister to a VP[INF] complement will have the default inoperative on that lexical head. By the HFC, the inapplicability of the default will also be true of the dominating VP. This will allow *seem* to take *it* and *there* subjects. Of course, nothing will change for *try*, for its [+NORM] specification comes from the rule, which is an absolute specification.

Similarly, when *seem* takes a tensed complement (as introduced by rule (30) above), there is the specification on the lexical head that the agreement is with an *it* subject. Again, FSD 11 will be inoperative, as just outlined; if this were not so, rule (30) would never be able to do any work in the grammar.

5.6. Linear Precedence Statements

Finally we come to the LP-statements, which dictate the order of sisters in a subtree (as the projection function ϕ is applying to rules, the domain of application of any of the principles in this whole section is the individual rule and/or the corresponding local subtree). The following two statements cover much of English.

(67) a.   [SUBCAT] $\prec$ $\sim$[SUBCAT]

  b.   [+N] $\prec$ P^2 $\prec$ V^2

(67)a means that complementizers precede their sister clauses and that any lexical head precedes its arguments; essentially it says that any terminal symbol (i.e., a lexical item) precedes its sisters. This is potentially a very strong claim and if true (more research is necessary to tell) it would seem to pose a problem for other theories of word order, such as the Government-Binding Theory reliance on Case assignment. For example, while the complementizer *for* assigns Case to a subject and can in Government-Binding Theory be made to precede the S containing the subject as a result, the complementizer *that* assigns nothing yet appears in the same position (however, if COMP is the head of S', then these might fall together as English is head-initial). Similarly, (67)a predicts that, in coordinate structures, conjunction words precede their sister conjuncts[20] in English, as in *two men and four women* and not **two men four women*

---

[20] The constituency assigned in coordinate structures is discussed in Section 6.2.

and, which again appears to admit no explanation in Government-Binding Theory terms.

The other LP-statement orders phrasal categories, and not only covers the order of constituents within VP, but also covers cases where PP-modifiers or -arguments in NP and AP follow intermediate projections, as illustrated in (68):

(68)

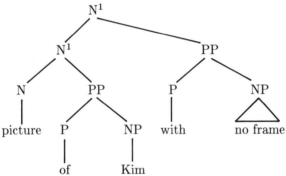

It is clear that LP-statements will be very important in the analysis of cross-linguistic variation, and that LP-statements will indeed vary from language to language.[21] And it is well-known that some languages have a fairly 'fixed' order, while others are rather free. On the other hand, the set of ID-rules is likely to be fairly stable—or more correctly, perhaps, the set of lexical ID-rules, for these express subcategorization properties, and

---

[21] For an analysis of German, see Uszkoreit (1984).

these seem to be quite uniform across languages. The non-lexical ID-rules will vary—many languages, for example, have nothing that corresponds to a complementizer (at least as an independent syntactic unit), and so on. At the phrasal level, some languages seem to lack VP constituent, and one would therefore expect an S-rule that introduces the verb, its subject, and all other arguments as sisters in a 'flat' configuration.

This concludes the review of the components of the rule-to-tree definition. In the final part of this chapter, I will concentrate more on analyses of particular phenomena available within GPSG rather than general properties of the theory.

6. Unbounded Dependencies and Coordination

The phenomenon of 'unbounded dependencies' (I will give examples shortly) was thought for many years to be beyond the scope of a non-transformational grammar; when a phrase structure analysis of such constructions appeared with the earliest versions of GPSG, the theory caught the attention of many linguists, and in particular the interaction of the analysis of unbounded dependencies with the analysis of coordinate structures went beyond the traditional transformational account in its coverage and predictive power. The current formulation of GPSG preserves these earlier insights, while incorporating them in a more general theory of features and principles of Universal Grammar.

6.1. Unbounded Dependencies

Unbounded dependencies appear in many constructions; I just give a few examples here.

(69) a.   Which men does Gerry think are leaving? (question)

  b.   the table on which we left the bottle (relative clause)

  c.   Pictures like this, the Tate Gallery would never want to buy. (topicalization)

All of these constructions have the property that there is what looks like an 'extra' phrase outside of the main clause, while within that main clause a phrase is correspondingly missing. In (69)a, the VP *are leaving* has no subject, in (b) *leave* is missing a locative argument, and in (c) *buy* has no object. The transformational analysis is to generate the phrase in question within the clause, and then move it to a clause-external position, thereby ensuring a one-to-one match between 'extra' phrases and missing phrases. The relation of dependency between these two positions is potentially unbounded, i.e., a subtree of any arbitrary size can intervene.

The apparent problem for a phrase structure analysis is that it seems that we must add to the grammar extra rules like (70)a, and make all (say) NP constituents optional for the S-internal rules, like (70)b. These might be proposed to handle (69)a.

(70) a.   S   →   NP, S

b.   S   →   (NP), VP

That is, sentences can have an extra 'displaced' NP, and any NP position is optional. While a lucky coincidence of choice of the right rules will indeed get (69)a, these rules also predict that *Which man did you meet Lee?* and *are happy* are sentences of English; in the first case we have one NP too many, and in the second one too few. Moreover, there is often agreement between something in the domain of the missing constituent and the displaced phrase (cf., (69)a, *Which men does Gerry think is leaving?*). The solution to this problem is to pass information around the tree, between the displaced position and the missing position, such that a correspondence between the two can be maintained. In particular, GPSG proposes the following rule for dealing with many cases of unbounded dependencies.

(71)   S   → X^2, H/X^2

This rule admits a tree with any [BAR 2] category sister to an S carrying the information that it is missing a [BAR 2] category. (The observant reader will note that nothing in the rule ensures that we have the *same* [BAR 2] category in both cases; the rule is not S → α, S/α, where α is a variable over categories. However, the theory of agreement determines this to be an agreement structure, and the general properties of agreement will ensure a match. The fact that the grammar need not stipulate a match in cases similar to this has consequences for the analysis of coordination.) Now the information of the missing constituent is 'carried down' the tree and is ultimately associated with an appropriate null constituent.

It is again perhaps easier from an expository point of view for me to present the operation of the grammar here as if it were bottom-up. So let us look at what happens at the site of the missing constituent. GPSG uses a feature NULL to encode that a constituent is phonologically null (empty). By FCR 19, this triggers the introduction of the **FOOT** feature SLASH, which is a category-valued feature.

(72)   FCR 19:   [+NULL] ⊃ [SLASH]

The empty string e is listed in the lexicon as belonging to the category $\alpha[+NULL]/\alpha$, and this allows the grammar to license subtrees like (73)a but not (73)b.

(73) a.   NP[NULL, SLASH[NP]]

|
e

b.   *NP[NULL, SLASH[PP]]

|
e

(In fact, as α is a variable over categories here, all the features will have to match, except for [NULL], including person, number, and gender features that I have omitted here.) Only in (73)a can the tree terminate at this point; there is nothing wrong with the dominating category in (73)b, just that it cannot dominate e. So the situation is that the specification of NULL triggers the appearance of SLASH, which, being a **FOOT** feature, will start a 'path' going up the tree. As in the cases we saw in the previous section, the SLASH will stop when it gets to a subtree admitted by a rule that mentions SLASH, such as the rule (71).

The feature NULL defaults to being absent; hence it will only ever appear in a tree when sanctioned by a rule. Such rules will be derived by metarule—in fact, by two. The first for us to consider is Slash Termination Metarule 1 (STM1):

(74)   Slash Termination Metarule 1

$$X \rightarrow W, X^2$$

$$\Downarrow$$

$$X \rightarrow W, X^2[+NULL]$$

This simply says that any [BAR 2] category can be null. We can now put all the pieces together and see how this will work. From the rule in (75)a we get the new rule in (75)b; when we build a subtree, we must instantiate SLASH to respect FCR 19, and I illustrate this in (76), using the ⋆ to indicate the occurrences of SLASH that have been instantiated (and using '/' for SLASH). The example is an embedded question, as in *Lee wonders which woman you saw*; again I show each subtree, to show how the pieces of the tree fit together.

(75) a.   VP →   H[1], NP

  b.   VP →   H[1], NP[+NULL]

(76)

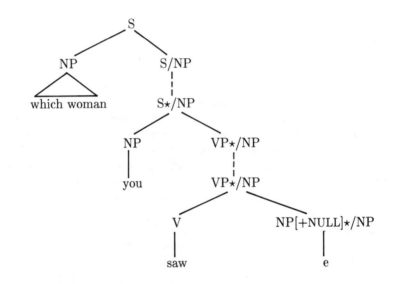

Let us now consider more closely the application of STM1. Essentially, it dictates the distribution of the empty string *e*. (While Government-Binding Theory recognizes four types of empty category, GPSG recognizes only one, which corresponds to *wh*-trace in Government-Binding Theory.) Constraints on the application of this metarule led to the proposal and adoption of the Lexical Head Constraint (LHC), given above in (27), which states that metarules may only apply to lexical ID-rules, those rules that introduce a lexical head as one daughter. Some examples that motivate this are shown below, along with, in each case, the metarule-output rule that would be necessary to sanction the bracketed part of the example.

(77) a.   *Who did Lee say that [_ had arrived]?

   S/NP → NP[+NULL]/NP, VP

   b.   *Kim, the warden gave [_ , who is my brother,] a ticket.

   NP/NP → NP[+NULL]/NP, S[+R]

   c.   *How many did Sandy borrow [_ books]?

   NP/AP → AP[+NULL]/AP, N^1

(78) a.   I wonder who it is [_ that you met]?

   VP/NP → H[44], NP[+NULL]/NP, S[+R]

   b.   Kim, the warden [gave _ a ticket].

   VP/NP → H[5], NP[+NULL]/NP, NP

   c.   How many books did Sandy complain [about _]?

   P^1/NP → H[38], NP[+NULL]/NP

What we notice is that all the good cases have the null category sister to a lexical head, and by imposing the LHC, we can predict the data in (77) and (78). (This is identical in these cases to the part of the ECP in Government-Binding Theory that allows lexical heads to be proper governors, along with the 'strong' definition of government that says you only govern your sisters. The ECP and the LHC were developed independently, and it is striking that they should converge in this way.) No metarule could apply to produce the rules in (77), for the 'source' rules upon which the metarule would operate are non-lexical ID-rules. Hence, the rules given in (77) are not in the grammar of English, and so the examples in (77) are not admissible.

The feature SLASH is categorized not only as a **FOOT** feature, but also as a **HEAD** feature. This has various consequences relating to the distribution of null elements; I will present a simple illustrative example here. It is not generally possible to have a null category inside of an adjunct in English, as seen in the contrast in the examples in (79); the relevant subtrees (in (80)) should both be admissible by the rule (79)c.

(79) a.   Which book did you [buy _ after meeting the author]?

     b.   *Which author did you [buy the book after meeting _]?

     c.   VP → H, PP

(80) a.

$$
\begin{array}{c}
\text{VP/NP} \\
\diagup \quad \diagdown \\
\text{VP/NP} \qquad \text{PP}
\end{array}
$$

     b.

$$
\begin{array}{c}
\text{VP/NP} \\
\diagup \quad \diagdown \\
\text{VP} \qquad \text{PP/NP}
\end{array}
$$

We can predict the difference if we take SLASH to be a **HEAD** feature, for while both subtrees in (80) satisfy the FFP with respect to rule (79)c, only (80)a satisfies the HFC as well. Many other similar cases motivate the dual categorization of SLASH. This requires an additional FCR, to ensure that SLASH does not get down onto a lexical head, for otherwise trees would never terminate.

(81)   FCR 6:   [SUBCAT] ⊃ ~[SLASH]

As the HFC is not an absolute mechanism, it will not override this FCR on lexical heads, but will continue to apply on all projections of lexical heads. The problem that this overcomes is this: if SLASH is a **HEAD** feature, then without FCR 6 we will get nodes labelled V/NP in trees; but these cannot dominate *e*, for no NULL specification is present, and the categories (on either side of the SLASH) do not match. On the other hand, V is a preterminal and cannot dominate any further syntactic structure where we might hope to eliminate the SLASH.[22]

---

[22] In some languages, verbs show special forms when they appear in unbounded dependencies, and this kind of evidence might motivate allowing V/NP as a well-formed category (where the SLASH would 'spell-out' as the special morphology) in such a language. For discussion of relevant cases and issues, see Goldberg (1985) and Zaenen (1983).

The Lexical Head Constraint also has the effect of ruling out NULL subjects, for the subject in English is introduced by a non-lexical ID-rule. This entails that the GPSG analysis of something like *the boy who left* cannot assign the structure shown in (82):

(82)

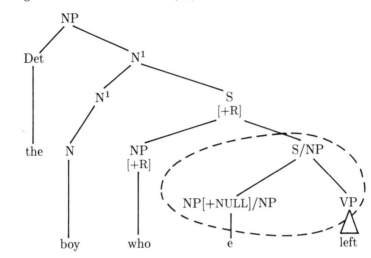

The circled tree in (82) could only be admitted by a rule produced by the application of STM1 to a non-lexical ID-rule (i.e., the rule (17)a above). The analysis must instead be:

(83)

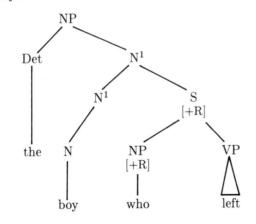

In these cases, there is no displaced phrase, and the relative pronoun appears in the subject position. While this works for simple examples, it does not generalize to cases where the subject really is displaced, as in (69)a above, or in (84):

(84)   the girl who I think has won

Here the verb *think*, which normally takes a sentential complement, appears to have a finite VP as its complement; and this is exactly the structure that GPSG assigns, deriving the required rules via STM2:

(85)   Slash Termination Metarule 2

$$X \rightarrow W, V^2[+\text{SUBJ}, \text{FIN}]$$

$$\Downarrow$$

$$X/NP \rightarrow W, V^2[-\text{SUBJ}]$$

This says that you can take any rule introducing a finite S as one daughter and get back a new rule with a finite VP instead, and with the mother node slashed for NP. Note that this does not introduce NULL, unlike STM1. So from rule (86)a we can get rule (86)b which admits the tree (86)c.

(86) a.   VP →   H[40], S[FIN]

b.   VP/NP →   H[40], VP[FIN]

c.

Principles of agreement interact with SLASH to ensure that the lower VP (which is a predicative category lacking a controller) agrees with the displaced NP (which is *who* in (84), which in turn agrees with *girl*). Invoking STM2 again parallels in part the second Government-Binding Theory definition of what counts for proper government, though the details of the analysis are not so similar, for GPSG sticks to the idea that only lexical heads sanction missing structure.

Although STM2 applies to rule (86)a, it will not apply to the following rule, which introduces a complementizer, for the rule is non-lexical.

(87)   S[COMP *that*] → {[SUBCAT *that*]}, S[COMP NIL]

This means that the grammar will never admit subtrees like:

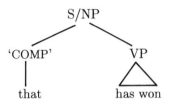

for *that* is not a lexical head ('COMP' here is just an informal way of referring to the {[SUBCAT *that*]} category); in this way, GPSG accounts for the 'COMP-trace' facts shown in (88) (see also Chap. 2, Sec. 8).

(88) a.   Who do you think that Kim saw?

    b.   Who do you think Kim saw?

    c.   *Who do you think that has won?

    d.   Who do you think has won?

Finally, for completeness, I give in (89) the remaining FCRs, though I will not discuss their effects.

(89) a.   FCR 16:   [WH, +SUBJ] ⊃ [COMP NIL]

    b.   FCR 20:   ∼([SLASH]&[WH])

    c.   FCR 21:   [A^1] ⊃ ∼[WH]

    d.   FCR 22:   [VP] ⊃ ∼[WH]

6.2. Coordinate Structures

The traditional wisdom about coordination, which linguists use as a term for both conjunction (with *and* and *but*) and disjunction (with *or*), is that "likes coordinate"; this is generally so—one can coordinate practically any syntactic category with itelf. I will not illustrate the basic facts, but move directly to the more interesting cases whose analysis has influenced the development of GPSG.

The usual analysis for coordinate structures is to posit a rule schema of the form $\alpha \rightarrow \alpha$ *and* α; choosing some value for α (such as NP, A^1, or Det) gives you a particular coordination rule with conjuncts of the same category. Yet such an analysis runs into problems with data like that shown in (90).

(90) a.   Kim is a Republican and proud of it.

b.   Lee is on his way up and looking to take over.

In (a), the coordinated categories are NP and AP, and in (b) we have PP and VP. Clearly this is a problem for the simple analysis, though equally clearly we do not want to give it up completely; for example, all the coordinated phrases in (90) are [BAR 2] categories. In fact, this gives us a clue to the GPSG analysis; the idea is to have what might be considered underspecified categories under certain circumstances. The grammar says that the verb *be* subcategorizes for an X^2 category, and the other principles of the grammar allow this to be compatible with, say, NP and AP. This kind of approach is of course impossible with the coordination schema given above, as the whole point of that is to force categorial identity in all cases.

Consequently, there is a *rule* of coordination, which in its basic form says the following:

(91)   X $\rightarrow$ H, H

This says that the coordination consists of a completely unspecified category as the mother with each daughter being a head; the HFC will force each daughter to match in **HEAD** features with the mother, or almost so (for sometimes the HFC is overriden). Note that this is a rule, and that, other things being equal, could admit a local subtree where each node was just specified as, say, [BAR 1]. In practice, this very rarely happens and much more information must be instantiated to satisfy requirements coming from other parts of the tree.

There are two kinds of coordinate structure in English; one is potentially infinite (*fish, butter, rice, and cake*), and one is binary (*both round and square*). The rules for these are given below; despite what I have said above, they are schemata, for they abstract over the terminal elements (*and* or *or*, etc.). However, with respect to the nature of the syntactic categories that are conjoined, each is a rule.

(92)   Iterating Coordination Schema

$$X \quad \rightarrow \quad H[CONJ \ \alpha_0], \ H[CONJ \ \alpha_1]^+$$

where $\alpha \in \{<and, NIL>, <NIL, and>,$
$<neither, nor>, <or, NIL>, <NIL, or>\}$

(93)   Binary Coordination Schema

$$X \quad \rightarrow \quad H[CONJ \ \alpha_0], \ H[CONJ \ \alpha_1]$$

where $\alpha \in \{<both, and>, <either, or>, <NIL, but>\}$

For simplicity, let us concentrate on the latter.[23] This allows us to build conjuncts like *both the cat* and *and the mat*; there is good evidence that in English the words like *and* form a constituent with the phrase to their right. If the CONJ value is NIL, there is no conjunction word, as in *came but fell asleep*.

The rules which "spell out" the coordinators are shown in (94).

(94) a. $X[CONJ \ NIL] \ \rightarrow \ H$
     b. $X[CONJ \ \alpha] \ \rightarrow \ \{[SUBCAT \ \alpha]\}, \ H$
           where $\alpha \in \{and, both, but, neither, nor, or\}$

Finally, an LP-statement orders the conjuncts according to the value of the CONJ feature.

(95) $[CONJ \ \alpha_0] \prec [CONJ \ \alpha_1]$
            where $\alpha_0 \in \{both, either, neither, NIL\}$
            and $\alpha_1 \in \{and, but, nor, or\}$

---

[23] The '+' notation in (92) indicates a sequence of one or more occurrences of the category.

This now allows subtrees like the following to be admitted:

(96)

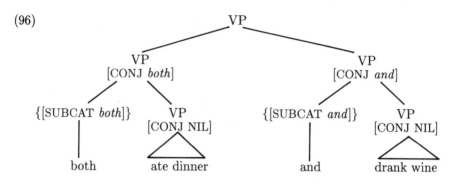

The HFC must also be revised, to allow for the multiple heads that the coordination schemata introduce. Again I present a simplified version of the HFC given in GKPS.

(97)   Head Feature Convention

$$\phi(C_0) \mid \textbf{HEAD} = \bigcap_{C_i \, \in \, W_H} \phi(C_i) \mid \textbf{HEAD}$$

This says that the **HEAD** features on the mother must be the *intersection* (the big upturned cup) of the **HEAD** features on the head daughters, and it reduces to the HFC as given before (in (43)) in the case where there is just one head. Now let us see how this applies to the cases of coordination of non-identical categories given at the beginning of this section. The verb *be* is introduced by the rule (98).

(98)   VP[+AUX] → H[7], X^2[+PRD]

The verb *be* (which behaves like an auxiliary even in its 'main verb' usage), subcategorizes for any predicative [BAR 2] category. Now the intersection of NP and AP is consistent with this—the intersection is in fact {<N, +>, <BAR, 2>}. Hence the following subtree respects the HFC as stated (ignoring the PRD feature).

(99)

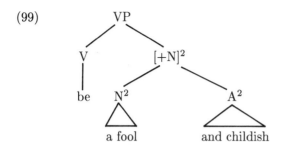

However, in case the mother is more specified, the daughters must be also; we do not get *Kim met a fool and childish* as *meet* subcategorizes for an NP, which would be the mother in the coordinate structure. But the only way for the intersection of each conjunct to be NP is for each conjunct to be at least that highly specified.

Finally we come to the interaction of the analyses of coordination and unbounded dependencies. One general constraint on unbounded dependencies is that, if they go into one conjunct, they must go into all.

(100) a.   the fish that Kim [ate _] [and got sick from _]

     b.   the fish that Kim [ate _] [and hopes not to get sick from _]

     c.   *the fish that Kim [ate _] [and got sick from chicken]

If there is a missing constituent within one conjunct, there must be one missing somewhere in each; examples (a) and (b) indicate that no further 'parallelism' of structure is necessary. (100)c is bad as this condition, known as the *Coordinate Structure Constraint*, is violated.

These facts follow directly from the analysis of SLASH; being a **FOOT** feature, if it appears on one daughter conjunct, then it must be on the mother too, to satisfy the FFP. Once on the mother, it will now be forced to be on every head, i.e., every conjunct, as SLASH is also a **HEAD** feature. As we have just seen, if the mother is specified for some **HEAD** feature, each conjunct must be.

This account also predicts the data in (101), which do show a kind of 'parallelism' effect.

(101) a.   I know a man who Kim likes _ and Lee hired _ .

     b.   I know a man who _ likes Kim and _ adores Lee.

     c.   *I know a man who Lee hired _ and _ likes Kim.

     d.   I know a man who Kim likes _ and Lee hopes _ will be hired.

The generalization in the data is that parallel non-subject 'gaps' are acceptable, or parallel subject gaps (examples (a) and (b)). However, a mix of the two is not possible. The example (101)d shows that the notions of 'subject' and 'non-subject' are relative to the highest clause in the contruction, for in (d) we have paired object and non-highest-clause subject gaps.

These data are predicted by the analysis of subject displacement as involving a VP constituent, while the non-subject cases involve the category S/NP. Under this analysis, (b) has conjoined VPs, while (a) and (d) have conjoined S/NPs. Let us see why (c) is bad; the relevant part of the structure is shown in (102).

(102)

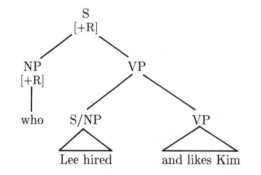

The coordination in (102) violates the FFP as SLASH has been instantiated on the left daughter S but not on the mother; it is impossible to conjoin 'slashed' and 'unslashed' categories for just this reason.

The Coordinate Structure Constraint and the 'parallelism' data are not readily handled within a transformational framework, though it is of course always possible to augment a theory to allow it to cover more data. (In fact, such constraints are somewhat unexpected in a transformational framework, for the idea of movement is to predict a one-to-one correspondence between displaced phrases and missing constituents, but precisely in these cases we have, and must have, a one-to-many correspondence.) Recent analyses of such facts within the Government-Binding Theory framework have indeed introduced additional representations that effectively transmit information through every intervening node between a pre- and post-movement site.

On the other hand, to the extent that there are 'unbounded dependencies' in interpretive phenomena that obey similar constraints to these 'overt' cases, such as with scope of quantifiers and *wh*-phrases, as is claimed by proponents of Government-Binding Theory, there is no way GPSG as presently formulated could account for such correlations. Again, it would be possible to augment the theory by the postulation of **FOOT** features that only have semantic effects to capture such generalizations. However, it has been, and continues to be, a topic of much debate as to just how strong these parallels are.

Where to Look Next

The most complete description of GPSG appears in Gazdar et al. (1985); earlier formulations of the leading ideas can be found in Gazdar (1981), Gazdar (1982), and Gazdar, Pullum, and Sag (1982). The Lexical Head Constraint on metarule application is proposed in Flickinger (1983). Sag et al. (1985) present a much more detailed analysis of coordination than that in Gazdar et al. (1985).

Recently, a related framework known as *Head-driven Phrase Structure Grammar*, or 'HPSG,' has emerged out of the work of Pollard (1984). In this framework, lexical ID-rules as such are eliminated, and subcategorization is stated as a property of lexical heads. This entails that metarules are lexical rules, and arguments for this point of view are given in Pollard (1985). For an overview of this theory, see Sag and Pollard (1986). The analysis of '*wh*-agreement' in Goldberg (1985) is given in terms of this framework. Sag (1986) discusses problems with analysis of linear precedence given in Gazdar et al. (1985), and presents an alternative account in an HPSG formulation.

Chapter 4

Lexical-Functional Grammar

Lexical-Functional Grammar (LFG) was developed initially in the late 1970s by Joan Bresnan and Ron Kaplan; LFG followed *Relational Grammar* in departing from the mainstream of generative grammar by proposing a model of syntax that is not purely structurally-based, or, putting it rather too simply, advocating the view that there is more to syntax than you can express with phrase structure trees.[1] In addition, it differed in being a theory of grammar that was developed with the goal of also serving as the grammatical basis of a computationally precise and psychologically realistic model of human language; many of the theoretical decisions that have been made have been influenced by this aspect of the project (see the introduction to Bresnan (1982)). The most complete description of the formal principles of the theory can be found in Kaplan and Bresnan (1982) (hereafter 'KB').

Lexical-Functional Grammar is the only one of the theories described here that accords the traditional notions of 'subject' and 'object' a distinguished status, in that it alone takes them as primitives (this again is shared with Relational Grammar). The actual theoretical entities are known as *grammatical functions*, and representations which display them are known as *functional structures* (f-structures). The grammatical functions are represented so: SUBJ, OBJ, etc.; and in addition to these the theory recognizes functions that might be less familiar to the reader, like XCOMP, which is an open complement (for example, the participle *laughing* in *She had them laughing in no time*). The name 'function' is chosen not only to indicate the role these objects play in the sentence, such as when we say that *fish* functions as the subject of the predicate *swim* in *Fish swim*,

---

[1] Relational Grammar has been and continues to be a very influential theory of syntax, since its development in the early and mid 1970s; some of the key papers are collected in Perlmutter (1983), and Perlmutter and Rosen (1984).

but is also chosen to indicate the nature of the representation—technically speaking, functional structures are functions, in the mathematical sense, from names to values; so the f-structure for our example will be understood as a function which in this case gives the value *fish* when applied to the name SUBJ. This is analogous (in its mathematical properties) to the Generalized Phrase Structure Grammar idea that categories are functions from features to values, and one can think of SUBJ as the name of a feature (or 'attribute,' as LFG has it).

LFG does not deny that there is a significant aspect of the representation of syntax that is characterized by phrase structure trees, and proposes a level of *constituent structure* (c-structure) that corresponds roughly to the level of PF in Government-Binding Theory and to surface structure in Generalized Phrase Structure Grammar. (Similarly, the level of f-structure corresponds most closely to the level of s-structure in Government-Binding Theory, though the correspondence is weak.) C-structures have things like NPs and Vs in them, and express properties of word order and phrasal structure, which are taken to be subject to great variation across languages. Most of the invariant grammatical constraints, on things like agreement and anaphora, are functionally-based, i.e., stated on f-structure representations.

The *lexical* part of the name of the theory emphasizes a commitment to characterize processes which alter the 'valence' of predicates in the lexicon (and hence render the c-structure component more 'transparent'); for example, the relation between active and passive constructions is determined solely by a lexical process that relates passive forms of verbs to active forms. In a way, lexical rules do the work of Move-α in Government-Binding Theory and metarules in Generalized Phrase Structure Grammar, but there is no formal correspondence nor parallel empirical coverage in these three mechanisms, so I only mention this in the aid of orienting the reader. Finally, it follows from the fact that there is no transformational component that all lexical items are inserted into c-structures in fully inflected form, as in Generalized Phrase Structure Grammar; similarly the argument for a non-transformational grammar is not that one *can* do it, but that it is an advantage to find other mechanisms to do the work once attributed to transformations.

Figure 4 gives a diagrammatic representation of the organization of the grammar.[2]

---

[2] I indicate the mapping to semantics with a dotted line for the reason that, while a semantic component (e.g., a Montague Grammar-style semantics) is

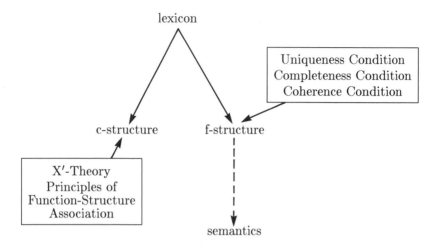

Figure 4.   Lexical-Functional Grammar

While the lexicon and c-structure are the loci of cross-linguistic variation, the level of f-structure is intended to be fairly stable, in the sense that synonymous constructions in different languages might have radically different c-structure representations though very similar f-structures; in general there is no one-to-one correspondence between constituents of a c-structure and constituents of the corresponding f-structure. Indeed, as indicated in Figure 4, while c-structures determine properties of f-structures, there is no direct mapping from c- to f-structures. From a certain point of view, LFG takes the opposite position from Government-Binding Theory as to the nature of the mapping between syntactic levels; while in Government-Binding Theory the idea is that each level differs minimally from the next and is characterized by the same sorts of representations obeying the same sorts of constraints, in LFG the conception is that different levels have different kinds of representations and obey their own constraints. In particular, while the information displayed by an f-structure is *encoded* within the corresponding c-structure, that information is not recoverable solely

understood to be part of the LFG system, the semantics do not interact in any strong way with the syntax (unlike, say, in Generalized Phrase Structure Grammar, where the semantics determine certain aspects of syntactic agreement, for example). I will omit any further discussion of the semantics in this chapter.

from the structural relations in the c-structure, in the sense that there is no isomorphic mapping from c-structures to f-structures. For example, it is typical to find that one language will define the subject 'position' to be a privileged structural position, as in English (the NP immediately dominated by S), while another language will mark its subject with particular grammatical case (often Nominative) and allow the subject to appear in any position (for example, in Japanese, it is a rough generalization that subjects are marked with the case-marker *-ga* and that NPs can appear in any order). In the one instance we have structural encoding of the SUBJ function (i.e., the information of subjecthood comes from the particular structural position), and morphological encoding in the other (it is the *ga*-marked NP that is the subject, no matter where it appears in the structure), yet both contribute exactly the same information to an f-structure.

LFG has so far been cautious in proposing universal constraints on cross-linguistic variation, the emphasis having been on characterizing the diversity that we find among languages; presumably from that research patterns of constraints will emerge that will then be incorporated into the theory in an appropriate way. (This is not to claim that LFG has not proposed universal constraints—many will in fact be discussed in this chapter (see, for example, Bresnan's paper "Control and Complementation," in Bresnan (1982) and Levin (1985)); however, the emphasis on making such proposals has not been as great in LFG as it has been, for example, in Government-Binding Theory.)

1. Constituent Structures

Constituent structures (c-structures) are those objects in LFG that characterize phrasal and sentential syntax in the familiar way; however, as c-structures play a restricted role in the theory we can just look briefly at the properties of the structures they describe and then pay more attention to the information they carry about f-structures.

1.1. Phrase Structure

LFG assumes a fairly standard set of phrase structure rules, such as those given in (1) for English (to be revised shortly).

(1)   a.   S   →   NP VP
      b.   VP →   V NP

Table 4

X′-Equivalences

X	X′	X″
N	N′	NP
V	V′	VP
A	A′	AP
P	P′	PP
	S	S′

Other languages may have rather less structure than English; for example the Australian language Warlpiri appears to form sentences with little internal constituent structure, and suggests a rule like:

(2)   S → X′ Aux X′*

Under this rule (proposed in Simpson (1983)), S consists of some constituent, an Auxiliary, and then any number of further consitituents. The point here is that the sequence is generated directly and is not transformed (by an operation known as 'scrambling') from a more configurational structure which might provide information about what is the subject, what is the object, and so on.

Clearly a rule like (2) is not going to be sufficient for Warlpiri; it would allow a sentence to consist of four NPs and an auxiliary verb, yet we can be sure that no sentence of Warlpiri has this form. All of the properties of the lexical items that will be accessed to 'filter out' this overgeneration (such as subcategorization requirements, etc.) are manifested only in the f-structure, and so while our hypothetical string will indeed be given a c-structure of Warlpiri, well-formedness conditions applying at f-structure will rule it out.

Similarly, in English, *Louise sneezed the banana* will have a well-formed c-structure, but will be unacceptable at the level of f-structure, as *the banana* will have no place in the representation, for *sneeze* is intransitive. Section 2.2 covers functional well-formedness in more detail.

Like the other theories, LFG adopts a version of X′-theory, which I summarize in Table 4. (The reader unfamiliar with the ideas of X′-theory should consult Chap. 2, Sec. 1.) This is rather similar to the Government-Binding Theory formulation of the equivalences, except that S and S′ are not projections of any lexical category in LFG.

The category S has no head in the X′ sense and is said to be *exocentric*, and this permits it to have a variety of 'functional' heads universally, such as VP, or V in some languages, or even N or A. (It is quite common for languages to express such 'predicative' sentences as *Molly is a doctor* by what is literally 'Molly doctor.')

In respect to the status of S, LFG also differs from Generalized Phrase Structure Grammar, in not taking it to be a projection of V. This latter position is more or less essential in Generalized Phrase Structure Grammar, in order that information pass between the verb and S by the Head Feature Convention; but information flow in LFG is not necessarily determined by such considerations (though it may be, as I describe below), and therefore it is free to leave S exocentric.

1.2. Functional Annotations

As I have mentioned, f-structures are not constructed by directly mapping the c-structure representation into some new phrase-structural representation. Rather, c-structures carry information that is displayed in f-structure, and are annotated with *functional schemata*, which intuitively indicate how the functional information contained on a node in the syntax participates in the f-structure. For example, the S-rule in English is annotated in the following way:

$$(3) \qquad S \quad \rightarrow \qquad NP \qquad VP$$
$$(\uparrow \text{SUBJ}) = \downarrow \quad \uparrow = \downarrow$$

The up- and down-arrows ("↑" and "↓") refer to the f-structure that corresponds to the c-structure node built by the rule. The "up" refers to the f-structure of the *mother* node and the "down" refers to the f-structure of the node *itself*. The annotations in (3), which are read "up's SUBJ is down" and "up is down" indicate that (a), all the functional information carried by the NP (i.e., the NP's f-structure) goes into the SUBJ part of the mother's f-structure (i.e., the S's f-structure), and (b), all the functional information carried by the VP (the VP's f-structure) is also direct information about the mother's f-structure. Grossly put, the annotations say of the NP that it is the subject, and of the VP that it is the functional head; in a certain sense, "↑=↓" corresponds to the Head Feature Convention in Generalized Phrase Structure Grammar.

Let us see some other rules for English, and then look at a simple example of the relation between a c-structure and an f-structure.

(4)   VP → V   (NP)   (NP)   PP*   (S′)
                  (↑ OBJ) =↓ (↑ OBJ2) =↓ (↑ (↓ CASE)) =↓ (↑ COMP) =↓

(5) a.   NP → (Det)   N   (PP)
                              (↑ ADJUNCT) =↓

     b.   PP → P   NP
                        (↑ OBJ) =↓

     c.   S′ → COMP   S
                          ↑=↓

The VP-rule says that the VP can contain a verb, then an NP that is the OBJ (direct object), then a second object (OBJ2, as in *give the dog a bone*); these two NPs are optional. Next there can be any number[3] of PPs, whose function is determined by the annotation '(↑ (↓ CASE)) =↓.' The PP will be some kind of oblique phrase, as I will explain later. Finally, there can be an optional S′ constituent, which bears the COMP (complement) function;[4] this will be for things like *that fruit is cheap* as in *We discovered that fruit is cheap*.

Note that there is no functional annotation on the V-node; such an annotation cannot be totally absent, or else the functional information dominated by that node would never get into the f-structure. Rather, there is a general convention that all preterminals are associated with '↑=↓,' so this is not indicated in each rule.

In the NP-rule, then, both the optional Det and the head noun will be associated with '↑=↓,' so here is another case where the distribution of '↑=↓' is not parallel to the distribution of X′-heads. The NP may also contain a PP ADJUNCT; this should probably be Generalized to allow other cases of adjuncts (or modifiers), such as relative clauses and adjectival modifiers, as in *the man asleep at the wheel*.

The PP-rule is quite straightforward, and prepositions govern the function OBJ; note there is no confusion between the OBJ of a verb and the OBJ within a prepositional phrase for in the latter case the OBJ is contained

---

[3] The * notation on the PP node indicates any number of occurrences of that category from zero up. In some LFG work the attribute CASE in the functional annotation is called PCASE.

[4] The reader should not confuse the function COMP and the c-structure category COMP (for 'complementizer'); the latter appears in rule (5)c. I shall have no cause to refer to the category COMP in the remainder of this chapter.

within an oblique function corresponding to the whole PP. The rule for S′ is again straightforward (though see Footnote 4).

Functional information (in fact, most of it) is also carried by lexical items, as we see in the simple example entries given in (6). In the tree in (7), the functional annotations appear above the nodes to indicate which objects the up- and down-arrows 'point to.' The value of each PRED ('predicate') within the quotes indicates the semantic content of the item. The notation (↑ PRED) then can be read as "my mother's f-structure has a PRED value which is ...." The mother node will be the preterminal dominating the lexical item in question, and so in this way functional information passes from lexical items onto (f-structures associated with) constituents of the c-structure.

(6)   a.   *Louise*   N   (↑ PRED) = 'Louise'

   b.   *Tara*   N   (↑ PRED) = 'Tara'

   c.   *paint*   V   (↑ PRED) = 'paint <(↑ SUBJ)(↑ OBJ)>'

(7)

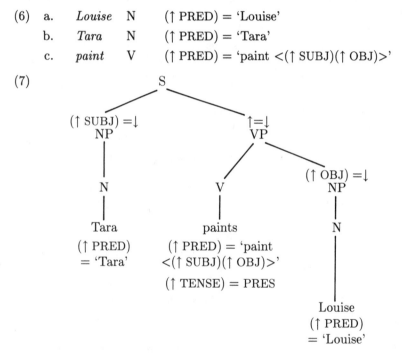

In the entry for the verb, the '<(↑ SUBJ)(↑ OBJ)>' part of the lexical entry indicates that the verb subcategorizes for a SUBJ and an OBJ; this specifies, via the up-arrows, that the mother's f-structure has a SUBJ and an OBJ, though there is no indication as to what the values of those will be (this is what the NPs in a sentence will contribute). The inflection on the verb adds the information that the tense attribute has the value 'present.' The f-structure corresponding to this c-structure is shown in (8).

(8)
$$
\begin{bmatrix}
\text{SUBJ} & [\text{PRED 'Tara'}] \\
\text{OBJ} & [\text{PRED 'Louise'}] \\
\text{TENSE} & \text{PRES} \\
\text{PRED} & \text{'paint} <(\uparrow \text{SUBJ})(\uparrow \text{OBJ})>\text{'}
\end{bmatrix}
$$

Let us work through the way in which this f-structure comes about. The verb carries the information that it has a subject and an object and that the tense is present. In fact, this corresponds to an f-structure, namely:

(9)
$$
\begin{bmatrix}
\text{SUBJ} & [\quad] \\
\text{OBJ} & [\quad] \\
\text{TENSE} & \text{PRES} \\
\text{PRED} & \text{'paint} <(\uparrow \text{SUBJ})(\uparrow \text{OBJ})>\text{'}
\end{bmatrix}
$$

Due to the '$\uparrow = \downarrow$' annotations implicit on the V node and present on VP, this f-structure is also associated with the VP and S nodes.

Within the subject NP, the entry *Tara* carries the information that its mother's f-structure PRED is 'Tara'; hence this is the PRED of the NP. However, the f-structure of the NP is not directly inherited into the f-structure of the S, but rather becomes part of the SUBJ specification within that f-structure. Hence from the subject NP part of the S we get the f-structure shown in (10).

(10)
$$
\begin{bmatrix}
\text{SUBJ} & [\text{PRED 'Tara'}] \\
\\
\end{bmatrix}
$$

This 'merges' (as I will describe below) with the f-structure information coming from the VP; a similar thing happens with the object NP and we end up with (8).

Clearly there is some relation between the flow of information and the projections of X'-theory; for example, any X'-head will in general be associated with '$\uparrow = \downarrow$,' and any maximal projection that appears in a rule will be associated with '($\uparrow$ G) $=\downarrow$,' where G is a variable over grammatical functions. Hence many of the functional annotations in the rules given above are predictable from more general principles of function-structure association. The nature of these relationships has been the focus of much research in LFG, though the theory allows for cases where there is a divergence, say, between the c-structure (X') head of a structure and the functional head (see e.g., Ishikawa (1985) and Simpson (1983)).

This concludes the basic description of the nature of c-structures; we will return to c-structures at the end of the following section, when we consider in more detail the relation between c- and f-structures.

2. Functional Structures

Functional structures (f-structures) encode information about the various functional relations between parts of sentences, information like what is the subject and what is the predicate. In this section, I will discuss the different kinds of information that we find in f-structures (their 'ontology,' so to speak), the well-formedness conditions that apply to f-structures, and then I will provide more detail about the way c-structures give information about f-structures.

2.1. Properties of F-Structure

Formally, f-structures are just sets of attribute-value (or feature-value) pairs; each thing on the left-hand side of an f-structure is an attribute, and on the right is its corresponding value. Thus the whole functional structure is itself a function, from attributes to values. It is as if we represented the squaring function like this:

(11)
$$\begin{bmatrix} 1 & 1 \\ 2 & 4 \\ 3 & 9 \\ \cdots & \cdots \end{bmatrix}$$

Attributes may have three kinds of values:

- the value may be an (atomic) *symbol*, as with SG in the specification [NUM SG]

- the value may be a *semantic form*, which is indicated as the value of PRED and enclosed within '...':
  [PRED 'love<($\uparrow$ SUBJ)($\uparrow$ OBJ)>']

- the value may be an *f-structure*, as in

$$\left[\begin{array}{cc} \text{SUBJ} & \left[\begin{array}{cc} \text{PRED} & \text{'woman'} \\ \text{DEF} & + \end{array} \right] \end{array} \right]$$

Note that in the last example, the values within the inner f-structure are a semantic form and a symbol. Semantic forms provide information necessary for semantic interpretation; for example, presumably 'woman' will be interpreted as denoting the set of women. In addition, semantic forms are *distinct*—no two tokens are the same; we will see the effect of this in Section 2.3.

Certain information that is present in the lexicon or in c-structure does not contribute directly to the construction of an f-structure. While the equations expressed as functional annotations that we have seen so far are *defining* equations, in that they define properties of f-structure, there are also *constraining* equations, which provide well-formedness constraints on f-structures produced by defining equations. We can illustrate this with a simple example. Let us look at the lexical entry for the pronoun *he*.

(12)   *he*   N   ($\uparrow$ PRED) = 'PRO'
                        ($\uparrow$ PERS) = 3
                        ($\uparrow$ NUM) = SG
                        ($\uparrow$ GEN) = MASC
                        ($\uparrow$ CASE) $=_c$ NOM

The first four lines of the lexical entry provide defining equations and describe a simple f-structure. The constraining equation, indicated by the presence of the '$=_c$,' does not provide information directly, but constrains (i.e., checks the appropriateness of) information coming from elsewhere. In the case of (12), unless information that the subject's case is nominative comes from some other part of the c-structure, the f-structure will not be well-formed with respect to this constraining equation; the constraining equation will be violated either if the feature is not specified at all, or if it is specified differently from what the pronoun requires. If we assume that accusative is the unmarked (i.e., general) specification of case in English, then most NP-positions in c-structure will not be specified for case; the constraining equation will correctly prevent *he* from appearing in any of these positions. However, if the case requirement on *he* were a defining equation, then the case attribute would simply be specified in the f-structure to have the value NOM, incorrectly allowing the pronoun to appear. By the constraining equation, *he* will only be allowed (i.e., contribute information about a well-formed f-structure) in just those environments where the case attribute is specified as taking the nominative value.

2.2. Well-Formedness Conditions on F-Structures

There are three main well-formedness conditions imposed on f-structures that 'filter out' most of the overgeneration in c-structure noted above. These are known as the conditions of *Functional Uniqueness* (or *Consistency*), *Completeness*, and *Coherence*. The uniqueness condition ensures that each f-structure is indeed a function, in that each attribute has a unique value (in a given f-structure). Completeness ensures that subcategorization requirements are met, and coherence ensures that every argument is the argument of some predicate; roughly put, completeness ensures that there are not too few arguments for a predicate, and coherence ensures that there are not too many.

I state these conditions in (13)–(15); the last two involve the notion of *governable grammatical function*. For any given language, some function G is a member of the set of governable grammatical functions just in case there is at least one semantic form that subcategorizes for it; that is, G appears within the PRED value of some lexical form. Typically, the governable grammatical functions are SUBJ, OBJ, OBL_{GO}, etc. (OBL_{GO} is the function 'oblique goal,' as in *send flowers to Maria*); things like ADJUNCT are not governable. Hence this is a way of isolating what functions in a given language are associated with arguments.

(13)   Functional Uniqueness
        In a given f-structure, a particular attribute may have at most one value.

(14)   Completeness
An f-structure is *locally complete* if and only if it contains all the governable grammatical functions that its predicate governs. An f-structure is *complete* if and only if it and all its subsidiary f-structures are locally complete.

(15)   Coherence
An f-structure is *locally coherent* if and only if all the governable grammatical functions that it contains are governed by a local predicate. An f-structure is *coherent* if and only if it and all its subsidiary f-structures are locally coherent.

Completeness and coherence are counterparts in a way of the θ-Criterion in Government-Binding Theory. For example, *The girl donated* is incomplete as the verb *donate* governs three functions, SUBJ, OBJ, and OBL$_{GO}$. On the other hand, *The girl donated the school the book* is both incomplete and incoherent; *donate* is missing its OBL$_{GO}$ again, and there is an ungoverned OBJ2 (*the school*), which leads to incoherence. A verb like *give*, which (optionally) governs SUBJ, OBJ, and OBJ2, would then be acceptable if substituted for *donate*.

In contrast to arguments, adjuncts can freely appear (and just as freely fail to do so), and so these are exempt from the conditions outlined here.

2.3. From C-Structures To F-Structures

In this subsection I will provide more of the details of the relation between c- and f-structures. As I have indicated, while f-structures do have certain structural relations of their own, they do not in general stand in any isomorphic structural mapping relation to c-structures. Rather, each piece of c-structure has its own corresponding piece of f-structure, either in virtue of being in a privileged syntactic position (as in the case of English $(\uparrow \text{SUBJ}) = \downarrow$), or in virtue of dominating some lexical content. The main business of the algorithm relating c- and f-structures is to put the different pieces together correctly.

The functional annotations on c-structure, which look like equations, are turned into a set of simultaneous equations by a process known as 'instantiation of metavariables'; the metavariables are the up- and down-arrows. Each piece of the c-structure is assigned a number which is a label for the corresponding piece of f-structure, and then these numbers are substituted for the metavariables.

Let us take as an example *She flew to the moon,* and let us assume that *to the Moon* is an (optional) argument of *fly,* rather than a modifier. After instantiation, the top of the example (16) will be as shown in (17).

(16)

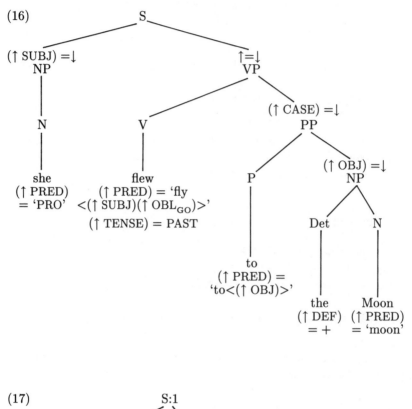

(17)

The f-structure corresponding to S is f_1, with component f-structures f_2 and f_3. The f-structure f_1 is formally the minimal object that is the solution of all these simultaneous equations; the set of such equations is known as an *f-description*. At this point, it is necessary to make clear

ERRATUM

Example (16) on page 148 should be as follows:

the relation between f-descriptions and f-structures (see also KB, 189ff). F-structures are understood as independently existing objects, objects of which f-descriptions may be true. Hence the annotation '↑=↓' indicates that the f-description of the mother node is satisfied by the same object as the f-description of its own node. In all the functional equations, the '=' means 'is identical to' in the sense that both sides of the equation pick out the same object, i.e., some piece of f-structure. While identity in this sense is stated on objects (i.e., models), the implementation of the LFG system manipulates symbolic expressions, using *unification*. The notion of unification was mentioned in connection with the Foot Feature Principle in Chapter 3; it can be thought of as set union for most purposes, and essentially it makes things identical by 'merging' them together.[5] Unification differs from set union in that it fails if some attribute would be specified for conflicting values. Some illustrative examples are given in (18).

(18) a.   [NUM SG] unifies with [PERS 3] to give

$$\begin{bmatrix} \text{NUM} & \text{SG} \\ \text{PERS} & 3 \end{bmatrix}.$$

b.   [NUM SG] unifies with [NUM SG] to give [NUM SG].

c.   [NUM SG] fails to unify with [NUM PL].

The f-structures f_2 and f_3 (from (16) via the instantiation in (17)) are shown below:

(19) f_2
$$\begin{bmatrix} \text{PERS} & 3 \\ \text{NUM} & \text{SG} \\ \text{GEN} & \text{FEM} \\ \text{CASE} & \text{NOM} \\ \text{PRED} & \text{'PRO'} \end{bmatrix}$$

---

[5] The linguistic relevance of unification was first brought out in work by Martin Kay.

(20) f_3

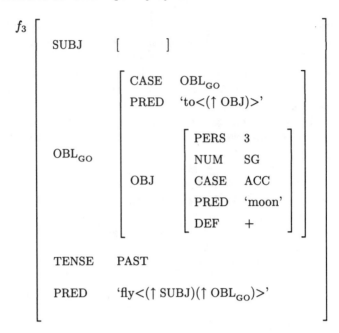

The structure f_3 is inherited directly as f_1, while f_2 is unified as the value of the SUBJ attribute.

Let us now look at the f-structure of the phrase *to the moon*. This involves the PP-rule given in (5) above.

The CASE notation distinguishes different kinds of oblique phrase, and the names indicate thematic roles[6] (so *put* requires an OBJ and an OBL_{LOC} (location), while *give* requires OBJ and OBL_{GO} (goal)). The annotation CASE makes sure that the head of the PP matches the specification on the whole phrase; for example, it ensures that a PP whose f-structure is the value of the OBL_{GO} function will be headed by the preposition in English that regularly marks 'goal,' namely *to*. I will not go into the details of how the CASE equation is actually solved, but simply refer the interested reader to KB, 198ff.

---

[6] In earlier work in LFG, oblique phrases were distiguished by the morphological form of the preposition, such as TO OBJ or BY OBJ; more recently it has become standard to refer to the thematic role associated with the preposition instead.

The information within the value of OBJ in (20) comes from *the moon*, and is unified in as the object of the preposition. The f-structure corresponding to the NP is formed by unifying the f-structures of the determiner and the noun, as specified by the rule (5)a.

Sometimes, a preposition plays a purely grammatical rather than semantic role. In many languages 'grammatical' prepositions are realized as case-markers; for example, German *ihm* as in *Ich habe ihm ein Buch gegeben* 'I have given a book to him.' The difference in the two types of preposition interacts with the system of anaphoric binding, as discussed in Section 4.3. These two functions that prepositions have can be reflected in the lexical entries of prepositions, and in the entries of predicates that subcategorize for such prepositions. For example, *give* will have (as one possibility) the subcategorization shown in (21)a, and the preposition *to* will have the entry shown in (21)b.

(21) a. *give*   V   ($\uparrow$ PRED) = 'give<($\uparrow$ SUBJ)($\uparrow$ OBJ)
                              ($\uparrow$ OBL$_{GO}$ OBJ)>'

     b. *to*   P   (($\uparrow$ PRED) = 'to<($\uparrow$ OBJ)>')
                     ($\uparrow$ CASE) = OBL$_{GO}$

The entry in (21)a shows *give* subcategorizing directly for the object within the OBL$_{GO}$ argument; in this case the preposition has only a grammatical function. The preposition *to* in (21)b is ambiguous, in that it can have an object, or it can allow its c-structure complement to contribute information about the f-structure directly, in which case the preposition becomes a grammatical marker of some kind, with no PRED attribute. It is the former case that we have in example (16).[7] I leave this now and turn to other features of the information that may come from c-structure (or the lexicon, via lexical insertion).

Note that as semantic forms are distinct, it is not possible to unify them. Even something like [PRED 'PRO'] will not unify with [PRED 'PRO']. This general property, that PREDs can never unify, leads to a very simple account of facts such as the following, from Moroccan Arabic, and Spanish.

In Moroccan Arabic, as in many languages, the object argument of a verb may be realized as an NP, or as a clitic on the verb, but not both.

---

[7] Note that in (16) *to* can be replaced by other prepositions expressing similar semantic relations, such as *towards* or *over*. This is not possible with the OBL$_{GO}$ argument of *give*.

(22) a. šra-t   lbent   lxʷebz
         bought-3sgf the-girl the-bread
         'The girl bought the bread.'

   b. šra-t-u   lbent
         bought-3sgf-3sgm the-girl
         'The girl bought it.'

   c. *šra-t-u   lbent   lxʷebz
         bought-3sgf-3sgm the-girl the-bread
         'The girl bought the bread.'

If we assume that the clitic *-u* introduces a [PRED 'PRO'], to indicate the pronominal object in (22)b, then we can explain (22)c by a failure of unification of the two PRED values, 'bread' and 'PRO.' (Hence, the f-structure will be incoherent, for there will be a PRED 'left over.')

In other languages, the appearance of the clitic does not preclude the appearance of an NP object, as in (certain dialects of) Spanish:

(23) a. Juan lo   vio
         Juan him   saw
         'Juan saw him.'

   b. Juan lo   vio   a Pedro
         Juan him   saw   Pedro
         'Juan saw Pedro.'

(We can ignore the *a* in (23)b for our purposes here.) In the Spanish cases, the clitic *can* cooccur with the object NP, which could be handled by making the [PRED 'PRO'] specification optional on the clitic. With this specification optionally absent, (23)a lacks an object PRED, and is incomplete, but (23)b is fine; with this specification present on the clitic, (23)a is good, but in (23)b the failure of unification means that there are two PREDs, violating functional coherence. Hence (23)b is only grammatical if the option is taken of omitting the PRED from the clitic's specification, and conversely for (23)a.[8]

---

[8] On the use of pronominal forms as agreement markers (forms without a PRED), see also Bresnan and Mchombo (1986).

As a final example of how information from different structural sources is represented universally in f-structure, we can consider three different types of language, as illustrated in the c-structures below.

(24) a.

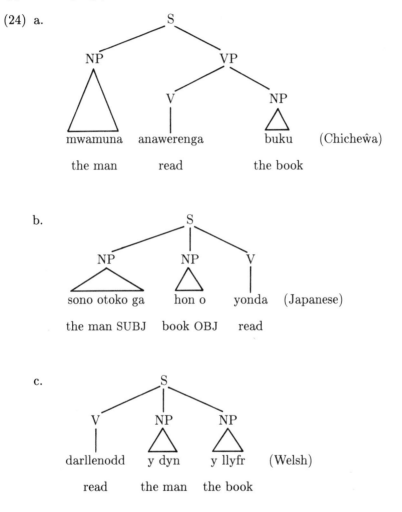

In Chicheŵa, the SUBJ function is encoded structurally; the subject is that NP that is sister to the VP, and Chicheŵa differs from English in that the subject may precede *or* follow the VP—hence *anawerenga buku mwamuna* is acceptable also.

In Japanese, the SUBJ function is encoded morphologically by the *ga* case-marker, and so long as the verb remains final, any order of NPs is in principle possible. In our simple example, *hon o sono otoko ga yonda* is also acceptable.

In Welsh, the SUBJ function is encoded positionally, in that the subject must immediately follow the verb, which must be initial in the clause.

However, all of these types of c-structure encoding lead to the same f-structure, namely that in (25).

(25)

$$
\begin{bmatrix}
\text{SUBJ} & \begin{bmatrix} \text{PRED} & \text{'man'} \\ \text{DEF} & + \end{bmatrix} \\[2em]
\text{OBJ} & \begin{bmatrix} \text{PRED} & \text{'book'} \\ \text{DEF} & + \end{bmatrix} \\[2em]
\text{TENSE} & \text{PAST} \\[1em]
\text{PRED} & \text{'read} <(\uparrow \text{SUBJ})(\uparrow \text{OBJ})>\text{'}
\end{bmatrix}
$$

3. The Lexicon

As I have mentioned, the lexicon is the focus of much attention in LFG, and much of the work done by transformations in transformational grammar is done by lexical rules in LFG; for example, the rule of passive is a lexical rule which essentially adds the passive morpheme to a verb and changes its subcategorization, so that the new form is subcategorizing for a SUBJ and an optional OBL_{AG} (Oblique Agent). Note that subcategorization is for grammatical function in LFG, not grammatical category, as in the other theories that I describe here; this will be one of the topics of this section, along with a consideration of the range of subcategorizable grammatical functions, and a discussion of lexical rules.

3.1. Types of Grammatical Function

The grammatical functions fall into different classes in LFG, and this classification interacts with various other parts of the grammar, such as subcategorization, and control (which we will see later). The major distinctions are shown in (26).

(26)

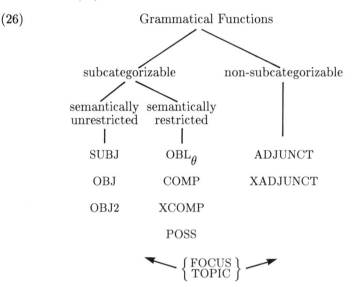

The distinction between the subcategorizable and the non-subcategorizable functions should be quite straightforward; one of the criteria for determining if something is an argument (and hence not an adjunct) is whether it is subcategorized for by some predicate. Recall that COMP is the function assigned to complement clauses; XCOMP is assigned to such complements as infinitival VPs (such as the complement to *try* in *try to kiss Louise*)—see Section 4.1 for more details. The difference between ADJUNCT and XADJUNCT is similarly that the latter has a 'missing' subject, that needs to find an antecedent from elsewhere. The difference is shown in the examples in (27), in which the 'controller' of the XADJUNCT in example (b) is *George*. On the other hand in (a) the ADJUNCT is self-contained.

(27) a.   With George guarding the den, the other boys set off.

b.   Guarding the den, George was scared.

The functions XADJUNCT (open adjunct) and XCOMP (open complement) are known as *open* functions; the rest are *closed*.

The difference between *semantically unrestricted* and *semantically restricted* functions relates to that part of lexical entries that pairs a grammatical predicate with its semantic *predicate-argument* structure. For example, the predicate-argument structure of a verb like *find* will say that *find* denotes a two-place relation between individuals, and that these two individuals will be linked to the thematic roles of Agent and Theme respectively.[9] The unrestricted functions may be linked to any of these argument-types; as an illustration, while subjects are often Agents, they may also be Themes (in a passive construction), or Goals, as in *Max received the prize*, and so on. The unrestricted functions may also realize completely 'non-thematic' arguments, as with the subject of *seem* in *Our goose seems to be cooked*, on the idiomatic interpretation, or with the 'expletive' subjects *it* and *there* as in *It seems that there will be a party*.

The semantically restricted functions are more intimately tied to the semantics, in a sense; for example, the OBL_{GO} function can only be paired with a Goal argument in the predicate-argument structure. The POSS function occurs with the prenominal genitive inside of NP, and is restricted in various ways;[10] for example, we have *the professor's knowledge* but not *chemistry's knowledge* (cf., *knowledge of chemistry*) which suggests that some kind of agency or perhaps sentient feeling is associated with this function (in English, at least). The nature of the semantic restriction on POSS varies with the kind of head noun involved, but the POSS must always be linked to a thematic argument (unlike SUBJ and OBJ). Hence we do not find expletive NPs realizing the POSS function; *it's being obvious that Louise is drunk* and *there's being a party soon* are impossible.

The functions FOCUS and TOPIC are subject to cross-linguistic variation, in that they may be subcategorized for in some languages and not in others; I will not discuss this matter further here.

3.2. Subcategorization

Every form that has a PRED value in its lexical entry is known as a *semantic form*; those that subcategorize for one or more functions are known as

---

[9] For more discussion of these 'thematic roles,' see Chapter 2, Section 3.

[10] These arguments that POSS is a semantically restricted function are due to Rappaport (1983).

lexical forms. For example, if we look at a verb like *seem*, it has the following lexical entry.

(28)   *seem*   V   (↑ PRED) = 'seem<(↑ XCOMP)>(↑ SUBJ)'
                              (↑ SUBJ) = (↑ XCOMP SUBJ)

This entry indicates that *seem* subcategorizes for an XCOMP, which is a (thematic) argument of the predicate (argument-hood is indicated by what is contained within the angle-brackets); thus *seem* also subcategorizes for a non-thematic SUBJ. The equation below the PRED line indicates that the subject of the XCOMP is equal to the subject of *seem*, as I will discuss in detail in the section on Functional Control.

The idea of subcategorizing for functions rather than categories is to allow for a certain category-independence in grammatical processes. For example, it is arguable[11] that in (29), the subject is a PP.

(29)   In this cave dwells a large, ferocious beast.

Given this, then such a PP is expected to undergo subject-to-subject raising (see Chap. 2, Sec. 7) if the rule really makes reference to the *function* of subject, and this appears to be so:

(30)   In this cave seems to dwell a large, ferocious beast.

Thus the LFG analysis is that while the SUBJ function is often realized in English by NP, other maximal projections may be subjects too. This is reflected in the revised S-rule (31).

(31)   S   →   XP   VP
                          (↑ SUBJ) =↓   ↑=↓

Grimshaw (1982) presents other arguments for the functional basis of subcategorization. Other cases of non-NP-subjects were discussed in Chapter 3 (Sec. 3.1); Generalized Phrase Structure Grammar posits an XP position in the syntax too. The facts above are potentially problematic for the Government-Binding Theory account of 'raising' which relies on the Case Filter to force an NP to move to the subject position of *seem* (if it is tensed), for non-NPs should not show the same behavior as they are not subject to the Case Filter.

All lexical forms have a *Predicate-Argument Structure*, each argument of which is linked to a grammatical function. The verb *seem* for example, will have a single argument, that of Proposition, and this will be realized by the XCOMP. The functions outside of the angle-brackets are not linked

---

[11] See e.g., Levin (1985).

to any argument and hence are non-thematic. The *Principle of Function-Argument Biuniqueness* requires that all arguments are paired one-to-one with all (thematic) grammatical functions within any given lexical form.[12] The one allowed exception to this is the case of the null function $\emptyset$, which is the function assigned to the Theme argument of a verb like *drink* in *Lou drinks*. The relevant part of the entry for *drink* is shown in (32).

$$(32) \qquad (\uparrow \text{PRED}) = \text{'drink}< \quad (\uparrow \text{SUBJ}) \quad \emptyset \quad >\text{'}$$
$$\qquad\qquad\qquad\qquad\qquad \text{Agent} \quad\ \text{Theme}$$

This form will be related by a lexical rule to the regular form of *drink*, which pairs the Theme argument with the OBJ function.

Function-argument biuniqueness ensures that each argument is only realized once for each predicate, and hence an example like (33)a will be impossible, for it has two OBL_{AG} arguments. However, we see from example (33)b that this is not a constraint on *by*-phrases *per se*, and indeed so long as the phrases are modifiers, more than one of the same thematic type (Location in (33)c) may appear:

(33) a.   *She was admired by him by the President.

  b.   She was admired by him by the pier/by the hour.

  c.   She was admired by him by the banks of the Ohio by the jetty.

We will return to the topic of the mapping between functions and arguments after the next subsection.

3.3. Some Sample Lexical Entries

To illustrate a few additional points, I present a collection of sample lexical entries that have interesting features.

---

[12] I will not give its definition here; the interested reader may consult Bresnan's paper "The Passive in Lexical Theory," in Bresnan (1982, 163ff), for more details. This principle is rather similar to the θ-Criterion of Government-Binding Theory, in the way it relates semantic arguments and their syntactic realizations.

(34) a. *a*   Det $(\uparrow \text{DEF}) = -$

    b. *girl*   N $(\uparrow \text{PRED}) = \text{'girl'}$
$(\uparrow \text{PERS}) = 3$
$(\uparrow \text{NUM}) = \text{SG}$

    c. *me*   N $(\uparrow \text{PRED}) = \text{'PRO'}$
$(\uparrow \text{PERS}) = 1$
$(\uparrow \text{NUM}) = \text{SG}$
$(\uparrow \text{CASE}) =_c \text{ACC}$

The example of *a* is quite straightforward; it contributes the information that the containing f-structure is not definite.[13] The noun *girl* is unexceptional too—besides its PRED, it contributes the information that it is 3rd person singular (as opposed to *girls*, which is plural). In example (c) we see the use of a constraining equation, to ensure that *me* only shows up in accusative environments (as opposed to nominative *I*). The equation must constrain and not define, to prevent *me* from accidentally appearing in a position that has no case attribute at all, but would have non-accusative case if it were specified (cf., the discussion of *he* in Sec. 2.1).

Consider next the verb *ask*, which has the entry in (35)a.

(35) a. *ask*   V $(\uparrow \text{PRED}) = \text{'ask}<(\uparrow \text{SUBJ})(\uparrow \text{OBJ})(\uparrow \text{COMP})>\text{'}$
$\neg[(\uparrow \text{SUBJ NUM}) = \text{SG} \wedge (\uparrow \text{SUBJ PERS}) = 3]$
$(\uparrow \text{COMP Q}) =_c +$
$(\uparrow \text{TENSE}) = \text{PRES}$

    b. *whether* COMP $(\uparrow \text{Q}) = +$

The inflectional information in this entry is that the verb is present tense, and cannot have a subject which is both 3rd person and singular.[14] The verb subcategorizes for a subject, object, and complement clause that must be interrogative (the Q attribute), in virtue of the constraining equation. Such an attribute is supplied by *wh*-words and -phrases, including *whether*; this ensures that we get *Betsy asked John whether supper was ready* and not **Betsy asked John that supper was ready*. Again, having a defining rather than constraining equation in (35)a would incorrectly de-

---

[13] The attribute I have labelled DEF is called SPEC (for 'specifier') in KB.

[14] The disjunction in (35)a is clearly missing the generalization that the specification of person and number features is the complement (opposite) of the form *asks*; this matter is taken up in Andrews (1984).

fine lots of complement clauses, which were otherwise unspecified, to have [Q +] in their f-structure.

The lexicon will contain various affixes, which also carry functional information. For example, although I have been presenting fully inflected verb forms, in general these will be derived by regular processes of word-formation which combine base forms and affixes. The verbal affix -*s* will have the following entry:

(36)   -*s*   Af   (↑ SUBJ PERS) = SG
                         (↑ SUBJ NUM) = 3
                         (↑ TENSE) = PRES

Such a form, then, regularly contributes the information that the subject of the verb to which it attaches must be 3rd singular, and that the verb carries the information that the clause is present tense.

As another instance of an affix, consider the Spanish 3rd singular present tense affix -*a* (for the appropriate class of verbs). This form may cooccur with (and agree with) an overt subject, or may carry the features of a pronominal subject; so we have *Pedro canta* ('Pedro sings') as well as *canta* ('He/she sings'). Hence the lexical entry for this form might look something like (37).

(37)   -*a*   Af   (↑ SUBJ PERS) = SG
                         (↑ SUBJ NUM) = 3

                         ((↑ SUBJ PRED) = 'PRO')

                         (↑ TENSE) = PRES

This entry says that the affix contributes the information that there is a 3rd singular subject, within an optional pronominal predicate (this is parallel to the case of the Spanish object clitic, discussed in Sec. 2.3).

3.4. Lexical Rules

A lexical rule takes a lexical item as input and gives back a new lexical item; typically a lexical rule is defined over a whole class of items, for example all transitive verbs, or all adjectives with no more than two syllables. Every theory has lexical rules, but uses them to different degrees. For example, in Generalized Phrase Structure Grammar, the lexical part of passive is the operation that converts a base form of the verb into its participial form; the subcategorization of the verb is changed by the Passive Metarule. In Government-Binding Theory, the lexical passive operation again makes the verb participial, takes away the verb's ability to assign Case, and takes away the external (Agent) θ-role. In LFG, the lexical rule of passive directly changes the subcategorization, while performing the conversion to the participial form also.

Ignoring the morphological change, the rule of passive[15] is the following:

(38)   Passive
        (SUBJ) $\longrightarrow$ $\emptyset/(\text{OBL}_{\text{AG}})$

        (OBJ) $\longrightarrow$ (SUBJ)

This takes the argument associated with the object of the active form and makes it the subject, and either assigns the argument paired with the old subject to the null function or to an Oblique Agent phrase (e.g., *eaten by piranhas*). In this latter case, the input and output entries will be as in (39).

(39) a.   ($\uparrow$ PRED) = 'eat< ($\uparrow$ SUBJ) ($\uparrow$ OBJ) >'
                           | |
                        Agent   Theme

     b.   ($\uparrow$ PRED) = 'eat< ($\uparrow$ OBL$_{\text{AG}}$) ($\uparrow$ SUBJ) >'
                           | |
                        Agent   Theme

Evidence for Passive as a lexical rule comes from the interaction of the passive form with other lexical rules. For example, it seems to be the case that in general any verb with a Theme subject in English can function in its participial form as an adjective; this means that there is a rule that makes new adjectives out of verbs. There are some intransitives that do this, as in *fallen leaf* and *lapsed Catholic*; many passives do too, as in *spared prisoners* and *eaten food*. The fact that the subject must be Theme is seen in the contrast between *a much-given present* and **much-given children*, for *give*

---

[15] This is the formulation given in Bresnan's paper "The Passive in Lexical Theory," in Bresnan (1982). Levin (1985) discusses certain redundant aspects (i.e., aspects predictable on general grounds) of this lexical rule, among others.

has two passives, as it has two subcategorizations. The relation between the two active forms of *give* is shown in (40), and active-passive pairs are given in (41).

(40) $(\uparrow \text{PRED}) =$ 'give$<$ $(\uparrow \text{SUBJ})$ $(\uparrow \text{OBJ})$ $(\uparrow \text{OBL}_{GO})$ $>$'

| | | |
Agent   Theme   Goal
| | |
$(\uparrow \text{PRED}) =$ 'give$<$ $(\uparrow \text{SUBJ})$ $(\uparrow \text{OBJ2})$ $(\uparrow \text{OBJ})$ $>$'

(41) a.   Louise gave a present to the children.

   b.   A present was given to the children.

   c.   Louise gave the children a present.

   d.   The children were given a present.

In example (d) the subject is Goal, as the OBJ in the lower entry in (40) is linked to Goal. This shows that the subject of the verbal form must be Theme for it to undergo conversion to an adjective; for while the Goal argument passivizes, as in (d), this verbal form does not undergo conversion (*much-given children*).

The logic of the argument, that Passive must be lexical, should perhaps be made clear. It goes like this: passive forms undergo a rule which only applies to forms with Theme subjects. This shows that the changes induced by passive in subcategorization must be induced in the lexicon, i.e., as a lexical process, in order for such passive forms to be input to the rule. In particular the *give* facts do not admit of a potential counterexplanation— which would be that the adjective conversion rule applies to forms only with a Theme *argument* (this is what Government-Binding Theory passives look like, for the argument that passivizes is the d-structure object, assigned the Theme role)—for (41)d has Theme argument but fails the conversion. Hence, if the generalization is that forms with Theme *subjects* undergo the rule of conversion, and this rule is a lexical rule (which is fairly uncontroversial), then it must be that passive forms have Theme *subjects* as a lexical property. This in turn means that Passive must be a lexical operation.

As a more complex instance of a lexical rule, let us consider the process of causativization in Japanese. The effect of this rule is to add a 'causee' argument to a verb which is morphologically modified by the addition of the *-(s)ase* suffix. This is seen in the examples in (42).

(42) a. Mary ga   aruita.
         Mary SUBJ walk-past
         'Mary walked.'

   b.   John ga   Mary o   aruk-ase-ta.
        John SUBJ Mary OBJ walk-cause-past
        'John made Mary walk.'

(We will not concern ourselves with the particular phonological changes induced in the verb by the past tense suffix and the causative suffix; we will also ignore the rule for causativizing transitive verbs, which is somewhat more complex.) We see from (42) that applying the rule of causative to an intransitive verb makes the argument associated with the SUBJ in (a) appear as the object in (b), and the new 'causee' argument is the SUBJ.

The rule for causativizing an intransitive is given in (43), ignoring the morphological changes induced.

(43)   Causative
         (PRED) $\longrightarrow$ (XCOMP PRED)

         Add: ($\uparrow$ PRED) = 'cause<($\uparrow$ SUBJ)($\uparrow$ OBJ)($\uparrow$ XCOMP)>'

         ($\uparrow$ OBJ) = ($\uparrow$ XCOMP SUBJ)

The effect of causativization is essentially to add one argument, corresponding to the Agent of the causative action. This will be the subject of the new form, and with an intransitive verb the old subject is related to the new object. The lexical rule introduces a new PRED, *cause*, and creates an internal nucleus by making the old PRED the PRED of an XCOMP . The subject of this XCOMP is controlled by the object of the *cause* predicate.[16] The reasons for having this particular analysis are too complex for me to give details here; however the effect is to allow for a simple c-structure as shown in (44) corresponding to a structurally more complex (biclausal) f-structure as shown in (45).

---

[16] This is functional control; see Section 4.1. Roughly, the controlling material is in two places in the f-structure simultaneously.

(44)

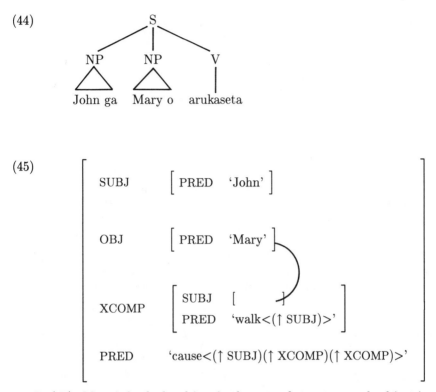

(45)

$$\left[\begin{array}{ll} \text{SUBJ} & \big[\text{ PRED } \quad \text{‘John’} \big] \\ \\ \text{OBJ} & \big[\text{ PRED } \quad \text{‘Mary’} \big] \\ \\ \text{XCOMP} & \left[\begin{array}{ll} \text{SUBJ} & [\qquad] \\ \text{PRED} & \text{‘walk}{<}({\uparrow}\,\text{SUBJ}){>}\text{’} \end{array} \right] \\ \\ \text{PRED} & \text{‘cause}{<}({\uparrow}\,\text{SUBJ})({\uparrow}\,\text{XCOMP})({\uparrow}\,\text{XCOMP}){>}\text{’} \end{array} \right]$$

In (45), *Mary* is both the object in the outer f-structure and subject in the inner one, and there is evidence (from various grammatical processes that pick out subjects and/or objects) that it indeed has the properties of both these functions (the traditional transformational analysis assigns a biclausal structure). On the other hand, there is also evidence with respect to the order of NPs in the causative construction for the simple c-structure (44); the complex f-structure is determined by information from the lexicon, and is not represented directly in the c-structure. As LFG does not directly map between c- and f-structure, it is possible for these two different structures to be assigned to the sentence in question.

4. Control and Binding

The theory of Control (where the Control relation provides the antecedent for a 'missing subject') falls into two parts in LFG, functional control and anaphoric control. Anaphoric control is itself part of a larger theory of anaphoric binding, which includes the binding of overt pronouns and reflexive pronouns. In this section I will discuss each of these topics in some detail.

4.1. Functional Control

Functional Control is the relation that holds between some antecedent and the 'missing subject' in an XCOMP or XADJUNCT. Either of these functions is realized syntactically as any maximal projection of a lexical head in English. Let us concentrate on XCOMP first.

A typical case of XCOMP is the controlled infinitival complement of verbs like *seem* and *try*, as in *Maria seems/tried to work hard*. The control relation between the subject of the verb and the XCOMP's subject is that of functional control in LFG; the relevant parts of the lexical entries are given in (46) and (47).

(46)   *seem*   V   ($\uparrow$ PRED) = 'seem<($\uparrow$ XCOMP)>($\uparrow$ SUBJ)'
                            ($\uparrow$ XCOMP SUBJ) = ($\uparrow$ SUBJ)

(47)   *try*   V   ($\uparrow$ PRED) = 'try<($\uparrow$ XCOMP)($\uparrow$ SUBJ)>'
                            ($\uparrow$ XCOMP SUBJ) = ($\uparrow$ SUBJ)

Note that functional control covers what in Government-Binding Theory is binding of NP-trace in the former case and obligatory control of PRO in the latter case. In Government-Binding Theory the difference in thematic structure determines which empty category will appear; then the difference in empty categories is used to account for the differences in interpretation between *seem* and *try*. (For example, *try* but not *seem* entails the existence of its subject, so that *A unicorn seems to be approaching* can be true even if there are no unicorns. This is reflected in the non-thematic subject of *seem*.) The only difference in LFG in the subcategorization is that the subject of *try* is thematic (linked to Agent). The semantic interpretation assigned to f-structures is sensitive to this difference in subcategorization, and predicts the correct entailments (see Halvorsen (1983)).

The f-structure of *Louise tries to sleep* is shown in (48).

(48)

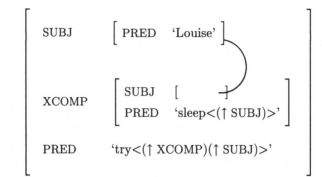

$$
\begin{bmatrix}
\text{SUBJ} & \begin{bmatrix} \text{PRED} & \text{`Louise'} \end{bmatrix} \\
\\
\text{XCOMP} & \begin{bmatrix} \text{SUBJ} & [\quad\quad] \\ \text{PRED} & \text{`sleep<}(\uparrow \text{SUBJ})\text{>'} \end{bmatrix} \\
\\
\text{PRED} & \text{`try<}(\uparrow \text{XCOMP})(\uparrow \text{SUBJ})\text{>'}
\end{bmatrix}
$$

The curved line here indicates the control relation; intuitively, the controlling material belongs in both places at once.

The relation of functional control is determined by the lexical specification of control in the entry for *try*. Due to the fact that functional control is lexically specified, it will have the following properties: it is local, unique, and obligatory. It is local due to a constraint on the syntax of functional equations, known as *Functional Locality*, which only allows at most two attribute-names to appear in any equation;[17] this means that one can specify ($\uparrow$ XCOMP SUBJ) but not ($\uparrow$ XCOMP XCOMP SUBJ) in a Functional Control equation. Secondly, it is unique as attribute-names must be unique, in order to satisfy Functional Uniqueness. Finally, it is obligatory as it is stated in a lexical entry.

Only the unrestricted grammatical functions SUBJ, OBJ, and OBJ2 are allowed to be functional controllers. I will present now some examples which motivate this restriction.

The verbs *persuade* and *promise* both subcategorize for a SUBJ, OBJ, and XCOMP, but differ in the the control of the XCOMP's subject—it is controlled by the OBJ with *persuade* and by the SUBJ with *promise*:

(49) a.   Herb persuaded Louise to follow.
           (($\uparrow$ XCOMP SUBJ) = ($\uparrow$ OBJ))

     b.   Herb promised Louise to follow.
           (($\uparrow$ XCOMP SUBJ) = ($\uparrow$ SUBJ))

---

[17] In a sense, locality (or 'boundedness') comes from the fact that the equation must be written (without variables) into a lexical entry, and therefore can only have at most a finite number of names in it. The particular restriction of this boundedness to two names comes from Functional Locality.

(Hence, in (49)a, Louise is the one who is to do the following, while it is Herb in (49)b.) Now only (49)a has a passive form; this is known as 'Visser's Generalization.'

(50) a. Louise was persuaded to follow.

  b. *Louise was promised to follow.

This is correctly predicted as the control equation for *persuade* after the application of the passive rule is the following,

$$(\uparrow \text{XCOMP SUBJ}) = (\uparrow \text{SUBJ})$$

in which the 'old' OBJ is now the SUBJ. However, with *promise* the 'old' SUBJ becomes either $\emptyset$ or OBL_{AG}, neither of which are possible functional controllers, given the restriction on functional controllers noted above. Hence no control equation can be written for the passivized *promise*.

A related fact (known as 'Bach's Generalization') is that one can 'drop' the object of *promise* but not *persuade*:

(51) a. *Herb persuaded to follow.

  b. Herb promised to follow.

The lexical rule that 'drops' the argument will reassociate an argument linked to the OBJ function with $\emptyset$. With *promise*, this will not affect the control relation, but with *persuade* it will render $\emptyset$ the controller, which again is not permissible.

Linguists consider the verb *promise* to be exceptional, for in general the object will be the controller if an object is present. LFG posits a lexical rule of functional control, which 'fills in' control relations on verbs which are not otherwise marked. As *promise* is exceptional, it will be fully specified independently of this rule, which I give in (52).

(52) Lexical Rule of Functional Control
  Let L be a lexical form and F_L its grammatical function assignment. If XCOMP $\in F_L$, add to the lexical entry of L:
  $(\uparrow \text{XCOMP SUBJ}) = (\uparrow \text{OBJ2})$ if OBJ2 $\in F_L$; otherwise
  $(\uparrow \text{XCOMP SUBJ}) = (\uparrow \text{OBJ})$ if OBJ $\in F_L$; otherwise
  $(\uparrow \text{XCOMP SUBJ}) = (\uparrow \text{SUBJ})$ if SUBJ $\in F_L$.

There are few instances of OBJ2 controllers in English, though there are many, for example, in Japanese.

Returning to the range of possible functional controllers, the facts in (53) are again predicted by the restriction to semantically unrestricted functions.

(53) a.   I presented it to John dead.

b.   *I presented John with it dead.

This time the XCOMP is the AP *dead*, and the controller of its subject is the OBJ in (53)a. However, *present* has a different subcategorization in which the controlling argument would be an oblique (the object of *with*), and this cannot be a functional controller. Consequently control fails in (53)b, and the structure is incomplete in f-structure, for *dead* has no subject. (Independent thematic restrictions prevent the object *John* in (53)b from being a controller.)

In certain cases there appears to be an oblique controller, as in:

(54)   We spoke of her as cowardly.

Yet in this case we can tell that *her* is the object of a complex verb *speak-of*, for it undergoes passive.

(55)   She was spoken of as cowardly.

The availability of passive shows that *her* in (54) is an OBJ, and therefore it is a possible functional controller.

The control of XADJUNCTs is determined by a rule which annotates a control relation to a c-structure (at least in English). For example, a clause-initial adjectival adjunct is obligatorily controlled by the subject of the clause, as seen in the examples in (56).

(56) a.   Sure of winning, Mary entered the competition yesterday.

b.   *Sure of winning, the competition was entered by Mary yesterday.

c.   *Sure of winning, the thought of the competition excited Mary yesterday.

d.   Sure of winning, Mary was excited by the thought of the competition yesterday.

Here it seems to be the grammatical function of SUBJ that is determining the controller; in (56)b/c the controller is determined to be *the competition*, which is semantically anomalous (and hence my * is perhaps a little inappropriate). To account for these examples, we allow AP to appear S-initially, as in (57).

(57)   S   →   (AP)   XP   VP
                    (↑ XADJUNCT) =↓   (↑ SUBJ) =↓   ↑=↓
                    (↑ SUBJ) = (↓ SUBJ)

The annotations here say that the AP is an XADJUNCT and that its subject is (functionally controlled by) the subject of the S.

One important prediction of the LFG system is that there should be instances of identical structural configuration where the functions assigned are different, as it does not accept the view that function can be directly "read off" c-structure. Some examples involving functional control seem to support this view.

The first class of cases to consider involve different subcategorized functions assigned to the same structure.

(58) a.   Susan informed John about the house.

b.   Susan kept John about the house.

In each of these examples, there is no reason to suppose that the constituent structure (in LFG terms) of the verb phrase is anything but V–NP–PP. However, the two verbs have different subcategorizations, as shown in (59).

(59) a.   *inform*   V   (↑ PRED) = 'inform<(↑ SUBJ)(↑ OBJ)
                                         (↑ OBL$_{TH}$)>'

b.   *keep*   V (↑ PRED) = 'keep<(↑ SUBJ)(↑ OBJ)
                                    (↑ XCOMP)>'
            (↑ OBJ) = (↑ XCOMP SUBJ)

That is, while *inform* takes an Oblique Theme argument, *keep* takes an XCOMP (controlled by its OBJ), even though both are realized by the same c-structure configuration.

Given this difference, the following contrasts in anaphora can be predicted.

(60) a.   Susan$_i$ informed John about herself$_i$.

b.   *Susan$_i$ kept John about herself$_i$.

c.   *Susan$_i$ informed John about her$_i$.

d.   Susan$_i$ kept John about her$_i$.

Roughly, what determines the distribution of reflexive and regular pronouns in LFG is whether the pronoun is in the same *nucleus* as its antecedent or not, where a nucleus is defined as a PRED and its subcategorized arguments. In (a) but not (b) the reflexive has an antecedent in the same nucleus (for the XCOMP is a nucleus but OBL$_{TH}$ is not); for regular pronouns, the condition is that the pronoun be free of antecedents in its nucleus, so the pattern of grammaticality reverses. I will discuss pronominal binding in more detail below (Sec. 4.3).

In other cases, we have a contrast between a functionally controlled argument and a functionally controlled adjunct (i.e., the difference between XCOMP and XADJUNCT).

(61) a.   Fred struck me as a fool.

    b.   Louise enjoyed sports as a girl.

    c.   I caught Marcia walking the dog.

    d.   I found the money walking the dog.

In examples (a) and (c) the controlled phrase is an XCOMP argument of the verb; in the other examples it is an XADJUNCT. (Example (c) also has a subject-controlled XADJUNCT interpretation for *walking the dog*.) In the adjunct cases, either of the NPs can be a controller; besides the examples given we can have *I enjoy chess as a hobby* and *I found the money lying under the bathmat*. Hence many examples allow for either an XCOMP or an XADJUNCT analysis, with the same controller; the ambiguity between these can sometimes be teased out, as the range of modification is different. So, for example, in *John will serve the meat raw, raw* is an XCOMP; XCOMPs are semantically constrained in such a way[18] as to rule out **John will serve the fish tasty*. However, the acceptability of *John will serve the fish, tasty and fragrant with herbs* indicates a second analysis, this time with an XADJUNCT, which is not subject to these semantic constraints.

Now while it is possible to prepose the adjuncts in (61), this is not possible with the arguments (keeping the meaning roughly constant—(62)c is good where the preposed phrase is a subject-controlled adjunct):

---

[18] For instance, the contrast here indicates that the XCOMP must express a physical property of the controller.

(62) a.   *As a fool, Fred struck me.

  b.   As a girl, Louise enjoyed sports.

  c.   *Walking the dog, I caught Marcia.

  d.   Walking the dog, I found the money.

On the other hand, it is possible to form a question out of the argument, but not out of the adjunct.

(63) a.   Which dog did you catch Marcia walking?

  b.   *Which dog did you find the money walking?

These facts suggest that the constraints on preposing and questioning (various kinds of 'long-distance dependency,' to be described below) should be sensitive not to constituent structure, which appears to be the same in either case,[19] but to the functions assigned.

4.2. Anaphoric Control

The domain of *Anaphoric Control* is roughly the domain of optional and arbitrary control in Government-Binding Theory (and was the domain of the transformation of "Super-Equi" in transformational grammar). Some typical examples are given in (64).

(64) a.   Maria thinks that watering the lawn before noon is silly.

  b.   John doesn't know that it is necessary to be obedient to the King.

As before, the controlled position is the subject of a gerund or infinitive (though anaphoric control is more restricted than functional control in that the controlled subject can only be the subject of a VP). In the present cases the controlled position may, but need not, be understood as controlled by the subject of the whole clause. In fact, the missing subject behaves like a pronoun, in that it can have a whole range of possible antecedents; (64)a is perhaps most naturally understood 'generically' (i.e. like *that for one to water the lawn ...*). In other cases, the antecedent may be 'split' as in:

(65)   Louise told Tom that eating together would be more economical.

---

[19] Though in such cases Government-Binding Theory would propose different structures, on the view that different functions imply different structures.

Here (under one interpretation) *Louise* and *Tom* jointly control the missing subject of *eating*; for some speakers, this example also allows an antecedent that is 'generic,' or is contextually supplied.

The analysis of this data in English involves an optional rule that assigns the following pair of equations to the lexical entry of a verb.

(66) $\{(\uparrow \text{SUBJ PRED}) = \text{'PRO'},$
         $(\uparrow \text{FIN}) = -\}$

The application of this rule provides a pronominal subject in f-structure (though note that this pronominal has no c-structure realization) which is then subject to whatever constraints hold on anaphoric control; the f-structure of the relevant part of (64)a (the VP *watering the lawn before noon*) is shown below:

(67)

$$
\begin{bmatrix}
\text{SUBJ} & \begin{bmatrix} \text{PRED} & \text{'PRO'} \end{bmatrix} \\
\\
\text{OBJ} & \begin{bmatrix} \text{PRED} & \text{'lawn'} \\ \text{DEF} & + \end{bmatrix} \\
\\
\text{PRED} & \text{'water} < (\uparrow \text{SUBJ})(\uparrow \text{OBJ}) > \text{'} \\
\\
\text{ADJUNCT} & \text{"before noon"}
\end{bmatrix}
$$

One interesting case of the difference between functional and anaphoric control lies in the control patterns of nouns derived from verbs. The LFG analysis of such a 'nominalization' process involves the idea that, while verbs may express their arguments via semantically unrestricted functions, nouns can only subcategorize for semantically restricted functions. This means that with a verb like *order*, the function assignment changes as a consequence of nominalization as shown in (68).

(68) $\text{V} (\uparrow \text{PRED}) = \text{'order} < (\uparrow \text{SUBJ}) \quad (\uparrow \text{OBJ}) \quad (\uparrow \text{XCOMP}) > \text{'}$
                              $|$ $|$ $|$
                         Agent   Goal   Proposition
                              $|$ $|$ $|$
         $\text{N} (\uparrow \text{PRED}) = \text{'order} < (\uparrow \text{POSS}) (\uparrow \text{OBL}_{\text{GO}}) \quad (\uparrow \text{COMP}) > \text{'}$

If all the arguments of the noun are present, we will have the following pair:

(69) a.   Elizabeth ordered the troops to march.

  b.   Elizabeth's order to the troops to march

However, any or all nominal arguments can be missing, so that we can also have things like *the order to march* and *the order*. One interesting difference between the verb and the noun is that the noun can drop its Goal argument, but not the verb.

(70) a.   *Elizabeth ordered to march.

  b.   Elizabeth's order to march.

The reader will recall that verbs of object functional control like *order* cannot drop their objects, for this leaves $\emptyset$ as the functional controller, which is not permissible. However, in the case of the noun, nothing prevents the argument from dropping. This would be predicted if the COMP in the case of the noun were anaphorically controlled.

In fact, this COMP must be so controlled, as there are no candidate functional controllers around; recall that all the arguments of the noun are semantically restricted, but that only semantically unrestricted functions may be functional controllers. Similarly, one can have (71)b but not (71)a.

(71) a.   *We were promised by the King to abdicate.

  b.   the promise by the King to abdicate

The former example is bad as the OBL_{AG} phrase cannot be a functional controller, though it can be an anaphoric controller, in (71)b.

Returning to the example of *order*, we can also "fill in" the controlled subject of the nominal complement, but not of the verb:

(72) a.   *The Queen ordered the general for the troops to leave.

  b.   the Queen's order to the general for the troops to leave

This would again follow if the verb is specified as requiring functional control, but not the noun; in (72)a, there is nothing to be functionally controlled.

4.3. Anaphoric Binding

The topic of *anaphoric binding* covers the binding of overt pronouns and reflexives, in contrast to anaphoric control, which is concerned with the (possibly different) binding of pronouns that have no c-structure representation. There are two properties that are taken to be important in determining the appropriate antecedent for a pronominal,[20] and these are encoded as features, namely:

- [sb]: whether or not the antecedent for the pronominal is a subject
- [ncl]: whether or not the antecedent for the pronominal is in the same nucleus

These are binary-valued features, and the basic English facts in (73) are handled by the assignment of binding specifications in (74).

(73) a. $Mary_i$ defended $herself_i$.

b.   *$Mary_i$ defended her_i.

c.   *$Mary_i$ hopes that Max hires $herself_i$.

d. $Mary_i$ hopes that Max hires her_i.

(74)   Reflexive pronouns in English are [+ncl] and non-reflexive pronouns are [−ncl].

The interpretation of the binding feature specifications are in fact a little more complex than one might initially suspect. In the case of [sb], the idea is that if a pronominal is [+sb] then that means its antecedent must be a grammatical subject (somewhere in the sentence); if a pronominal is [−sb], then its antecedent must not be a grammatical subject. I will discuss [sb], and some additional aspects of its interpretation, in connection with the Norwegian data below.

The interpretation of the feature [ncl] introduces a slight asymmetry; the interpretation is given in (75).

(75)   Pronominals that are [+ncl] must find an antecedent within the minimal nucleus containing the pronominal and a SUBJective function.

Pronominals that are [−ncl] must not find an antecedent within the minimal nucleus.

---

[20] For the remainder of this chapter I will use the term 'pronoun' to refer to non-reflexive pronouns, and 'pronominal' to refer to both pronouns and reflexive pronouns.

A SUBJective function is either SUBJ or POSS (these are notionally the 'subjects' within S and NP respectively). The reader will recall that a *nucleus* is the f-structure domain of a PRED and its subcategorized arguments. For example, the noun *story* subcategorizes for an oblique argument in the examples below, and so creates a nucleus, but that nucleus contains no SUBJective function.

(76) a.   Mary$_i$ liked [the story about herself$_i$].

   b.   Mary$_i$ liked [the story about her$_i$].

In these examples either a reflexive or a pronoun is grammatical; the bracketed domain corresponds to an f-structure nucleus, within which the regular pronoun is free of an antecedent (in (b)), and in (a) the reflexive is able to find an antecedent outside of this nucleus too, as the inner nucleus contains no SUBJective function. If we add such a function, we have:

(77) a.   *Mary$_i$ liked [Louise's story about herself$_i$].

   b.   Mary$_i$ liked [Louise's story about her$_i$].

A similar effect shows up with PPs whose head is a 'semantic' preposition, i.e., a preposition with some semantic content, rather than purely grammatical content as with, say, *to* in *send a book to Max*. The contrast in the examples in (78) stems from this this difference.

(78) a.   Mary$_i$ sent the book to herself$_i$.

   b.   *Mary$_i$ sent the book to her$_i$.

   c.   Mary$_i$ pulled the blanket around herself$_i$.

   d.   Mary$_i$ pulled the blanket around her$_i$.

In these examples an inner nucleus is formed only by the PRED *around*, which subcategorizes for an OBJ argument, and the interpretation assigned to [ncl] again allows for either pronominal form to appear in examples (c/d). Example (b) is bad as the minimal nucleus is the whole clause, but the pronoun is bound within this domain. In the following discussion I will just use the term 'nucleus,' but understand it to be qualified with the SUBJectivity condition.

The interaction of the features [sb] and [ncl] can be illustrated by the following facts of Norwegian, which has four pronominal NPs that we can consider here. The analysis of these in terms of the binding features is given in (79).

(79) a.   *seg selv*   [+sb, +ncl] 'self'

b.   *seg*   [+sb, −ncl] 'self'

c.   *ham selv*   [−sb, +ncl] 'himself'

d.   *ham*   [−ncl]   'him'

In addition to the interpretation of these features given so far, there is another factor that is relevant, and must be brought into the theory. This is known as the *Finite Domain Parameter*, and it specifies the domain in which [sb] is interpreted; if it is positively stated, as it is in Norwegian, it requires that a [+sb] pronominal be bound by a subject *within the minimal tensed (finite) domain* containing the pronominal. Similarly, a [−sb] form must be free of a subject, but only within that minimal domain.

Let us look at some examples involving each of these pronominal forms. With *seg selv*, we have the following distribution.

(80) a.   Ola$_i$ snakket om   seg selv$_i$.

Ola   talked   about self

'Ola talked about himself.'

b.   *Vi fortalte Ola$_i$ om   seg selv$_i$.

We told   Ola   about self

c.   *Ola$_i$ vet   at   vi snakket om   seg selv$_i$.

Ola   knows that we talked   about self

d.   *Ola$_i$ bad   oss snakke om   seg selv$_i$.

Ola   asked us to-talk about self

The form *seg selv* must be bound to a subject within its nucleus; in (80)d, the main verb takes an XCOMP argument, whose subject is controlled by the object *oss*. Hence this is the only possible antecedent for *seg selv*, but as the person and number features of *oss* and *seg selv* conflict, the example is ungrammatical.

Looking now at *seg*, we have a different pattern; *seg* must again take a subject antecedent, but in this case that subject must be outside of the local nucleus of *seg*, and due to the Finite Domain Parameter, that subject must also be within the minimal finite domain. This distinguishes examples (c) and (d) below.

(81) a. *Ola$_i$ snakket om   seg$_i$.
         Ola   talked   about self

   b. *Vi fortalte Ola$_i$ om   seg$_i$.
       We told   Ola   about self

   c. *Ola$_i$ vet   at   vi snakket om   seg$_i$.
       Ola   knows that we talked   about self

   d. Ola$_i$ bad   oss snakke om   seg$_i$.
       Ola   asked   us to-talk about self
       'Ola asked us to talk about him.'

In (c) the pronominal is bound by a subject outside of its minimal finite domain, and so the example is bad. In (d) the embedded clause is non-finite, and this allows *seg* to take the matrix subject as antecedent. The generalization about *seg*, then, is that it must be free in its nucleus and bound to a subject within the minimal tensed clause; hence it will only appear inside of infinitival clauses, and may in principle be arbitrarily far away from its antecedent, so long as only non-finite clauses intervene.

Moving now to *ham selv*, this must be bound by a non-subject within its nucleus:

(82) a. *Ola$_i$ snakket om   ham selv$_i$.
         Ola   talked   about himself

   b. Vi fortalte Ola$_i$ om   ham selv$_i$.
       We told   Ola   about himself
       'We told Ola about himself.'

   c. *Ola$_i$ vet   at   vi snakket om   ham selv$_i$.
       Ola   knows that we talked   about himself

   d. *Ola$_i$ bad   oss snakke om   ham selv$_i$.
       Ola   asked   us to-talk about himself

Finally, *ham* must be free in its nucleus; as it is not specified for [sb], questions of finiteness do not arise, and so both (83)c and (83)d are acceptable.

(83) a.   *Ola$_i$ snakket om   ham$_i$.
          Ola talked   about   him

   b.   *Vi fortalte Ola$_i$ om   ham$_i$.
        We told   Ola about   him

   c.   Ola$_i$ vet   at   vi snakket om   ham$_i$.
        Ola knows   that we talked   about   him
        'Ola knows that we talked about him.'

   d.   Ola$_i$ bad   oss snakke om   ham$_i$.
        Ola asked   us to-talk about him
        'Ola asked us to talk about him.'

An important relation in f-structure that is relevant to anaphoric bind-ing is the relation of *f-command*, which is the corresponding notion in this theory to the notion of c-command in Government-Binding Theory. The idea is that the antecedent of a pronominal must be 'superordinate' in some sense; in LFG, the pronominal must be contained in all the f-structures con-taining the antecedent. As f-structures have a rather different structural configuration from c-structures, the two notions f- and c-command have rather different extensions.

The definition of f-command is given in (84).

(84)   F-Command
          An antecedent *A f-commands* a pronominal *P* iff
          (a) *A* does not contain *P*, and
          (b) every nucleus that contains *A* contains *P*.

Clause (a) need not concern us here, though strictly speaking it is important as we do not want f-command to hold between some piece of structure and another piece that is contained within the first.

The idea of f-command can be simply demonstrated with reflexives; with non-reflexive pronouns, the facts are rather more complicated, and we will therefore avoid them. The contrast in (86) follows from the condition in (85).

(85)   A reflexive pronoun must be f-commanded by its antecedent.

(86) a.   Louise$_i$ dressed herself$_i$.

   b.   *Louise$_i$'s mother dressed herself$_i$.

If we look at the f-structure for (86)b, we can see why the indicated anaphora fails.

(87)

$$
\begin{bmatrix}
\text{SUBJ} & \begin{bmatrix} \text{POSS} & [\text{PRED 'Louise'}] \\ \text{PRED} & \text{'mother}<(\uparrow \text{POSS})>\text{'} \end{bmatrix} \\
\\
\text{OBJ} & \begin{bmatrix} \text{PRED} & \text{'PRO'} \\ \text{REFL} & + \end{bmatrix} \\
\\
\text{PRED} & \text{'dress}<(\uparrow \text{SUBJ})(\uparrow \text{OBJ})>\text{'}
\end{bmatrix}
$$

Here *Louise* fails to f-command the object, for one of the f-structure nuclei containing it does not contain the object (namely the f-structure that is the value of the SUBJ attribute). The f-command condition correctly predicts, of course, that the whole SUBJ 'Louise's mother' is a potential antecedent for the reflexive pronoun.

We will return to the topic of anaphoric binding in the next section. The full system developed in Bresnan et al. (forthcoming) includes a third feature, [log], for the notion of *logophoricity*, which I have not touched on here. The application of this 3-feature system to Japanese is discussed in Kameyama (1984) and in more detail in Kameyama (1985).

5. Long-distance Dependencies and Coordination

In this section I will present two areas of LFG that postdate KB; in the case of coordination, the research (by Bresnan, Kaplan, and Peterson) extends the KB framework, and in the case of long-distance dependencies, the analysis presented here (based on work by Kaplan and Zaenen) is different from that given in KB.

5.1. Long-distance Dependencies

In a *long-distance dependency* (also known as an 'unbounded dependency'), there exists a relation between two positions in syntactic structure, a relation that may stretch over a potentially unbounded portion of tree. A simple illustration is given in (88).

(88)   Which woman did Max say _ has declared herself President?

The phrase *which woman* appears initially, though there is a sense in which it 'belongs' in the position indicated by the ' _ ,' and we have clear syntactic evidence of this from the verb form *has*, which is 3rd singular, and from the reflexive *herself*, which we know independently cannot have an antecedent as 'far away' as the surface position of *which woman*.

The transformational analysis of such constructions is to have a level of structure in which the phrase *which woman* is indeed in the position indicated by the ' _ ,' and then to map via a transformation into a new structure with the surface order of constituents as in (88). In the Government-Binding Theory formulation of this operation, the movement leaves behind an empty category which bears agreement features and is used to ensure the correct form of the verb and the reflexive, etc. As LFG only acknowledges one level of phrase-structure representation (i.e., c-structure), such an analysis is not available.

The idea of the LFG analysis is to use the mechanism of functional control to allow the 'displaced phrase' (i.e., *which woman*) to belong in the f-structure counterparts of *both* places simultaneously. This account differs from the Government-Binding Theory account in that what appears in the place of the ' _ ' at the relevant level of structure is the whole displaced constituent in LFG, in contrast to an empty category bearing only the agreement features of the head of the displaced phrase, in the Government-Binding Theory formulation.

The functions FOCUS and TOPIC are assigned to such displaced phrases, though I will not go into details here about exactly how one decides which of the two is assigned in a particular construction.[21] In a question like (a) below, the italicized phrase is FOCUS; in (b) and (c), a topicalization and a relative clause, it is TOPIC.

(89) a.   *Which picture* do you like _ best?

     b.   *Fresno*, they tell me is nice in winter.

     c.   *the woman* to whom you are responsible

For the purposes of illustration, let us take as an example the topicalization *Maria, Max loves*. If we add to our grammar the rule in (90), and

---

[21] For discussion, see Bresnan and Mchombo (1986, 1987).

allow c-structure nodes to be optional[22] (e.g., the object of *loves*), we will get the f-structure in (91).

(90) $S' \rightarrow$ XP   S
$$\left\{ \begin{array}{l} (\uparrow \text{TOPIC}) = \downarrow \\ (\uparrow \text{FOCUS}) = \downarrow \end{array} \right\} \quad \uparrow = \downarrow$$

(91)

$$
\begin{bmatrix}
\text{TOPIC} & \begin{bmatrix} \text{PRED} & \text{'Maria'} \end{bmatrix} \\
\\
\text{SUBJ} & \begin{bmatrix} \text{PRED} & \text{'Max'} \end{bmatrix} \\
\\
\text{OBJ} & \begin{bmatrix} \quad \end{bmatrix} \\
\\
\text{PRED} & \text{'love}{<}(\uparrow \text{SUBJ})(\uparrow \text{OBJ}){>}'
\end{bmatrix}
$$

As it stands, this f-structure is incomplete as there is no value for OBJ. Clearly what is needed is an extra link that identifies the TOPIC value with the OBJ value. Equally clearly, we must integrate the TOPIC function, or else we would allow the grammar to admit things like *Maria, Max loves Cindy*, which does lead to a complete f-structure given the system as described so far; again, intuitively, what we want in this last case is for the f-structure to be *incoherent*, in that the TOPIC function is not integrated in any way into the rest of the clause. We therefore add two more parts to the account; to rule (90), we add a functional control equation that links (in the example in question) the TOPIC value to the OBJ value, and secondly we extend the *Coherence Condition* to cover TOPIC and FOCUS.[23]

I state this *Extended Coherence Condition* first.

---

[22] The analysis of long-distance dependencies developed by Kaplan and Zaenen does not acknowledge the existence of any kind of empty category; c-structure nodes are optional, rather than being obligatory but being allowed to dominate no lexical material.

[23] This extension was proposed by Fassi Fehri; see Fassi Fehri (to appear).

(92)   Extended Coherence
An f-structure is *locally coherent* if and only if all the governable grammatical functions that it contains are governed by a local predicate. In addition, the functions TOPIC and FOCUS must be linked to predicate-argument structure either by being functionally identified with subcategorized functions or by anaphorically binding subcategorized functions. An f-structure is *coherent* if and only if it and all its subsidiary f-structures are locally coherent.

Here 'functionally identified with' means 'being in the relation of functional control to'; the clause about 'anaphorically binding' need not concern us here: it has to do with those cases where the position indicated by the ' _ ' in the examples above is not a 'missing' constituent in c-structure, but rather some kind of pronominal form.

Let us now consider how to specify the functional control relation. Clearly it would be far too restrictive to specify in the rule (90) something like $(\uparrow \text{TOPIC}) = (\uparrow \text{OBJ})$, for the relation is potentially unbounded; rather, we should say that the TOPIC function is linked to *some* other function, and generalizing maximally, we have the rule in (93).

(93)   S′   →   XP   S
$$\left\{ \begin{array}{l} (\uparrow \text{TOPIC}) = \downarrow \\ (\uparrow \text{FOCUS}) = \downarrow \end{array} \right\} \qquad \uparrow = \downarrow$$
$$(\uparrow \ldots) = \downarrow$$

The notation '...' is taken to range over arbitrary sequences of function names (such as COMP COMP SUBJ, etc.); any restrictions (such as island constraints) on where the ' _ ' may appear will be restrictions on the possible combinations within such sequences, and the uniqueness, completeness, and coherence conditions will ensure that the only good f-structures are those where the function picked out by '...' will have no value coming from anywhere else in the c-structure (i.e., will be a 'missing' constituent in the c-structure). Actually, the '$(\uparrow \ldots) = \downarrow$' annotation builds in the Extended Coherence Condition, in that it requires that FOCUS or TOPIC are identified with some grammatical function; (92) is effectively a hypothesis about this identification. Kaplan and Zaenen (1986) introduce a regular language to describe these paths through the f-structure; for English something like '{COMP ∨ XCOMP}* COMP' is a reasonable first approximation: the path can go through any number (including zero) of COMPs or XCOMPs (or mixtures of both) and ends with any grammatical function *except* COMP.

More formally, the '...' represents the relation of *inclusion* in f-structure. The definition of inclusion is given in (94).

(94)   Inclusion
        f includes g iff there exists an *a* such that $(f\ a) = g$
        or $(f\ a)$ includes *g*.

This says that some f-structure *f* includes another f-structure *g* just in case either *g* is the value of some attribute (function name) *a* in *f*, or *g* is included within the f-structure that is the value of some *a* within *f*. More simply put, it says that *g* is included in *f* just in case *g* is a value somewhere within *f*.

Our example now has the following c- and f-structure representations:

(95)

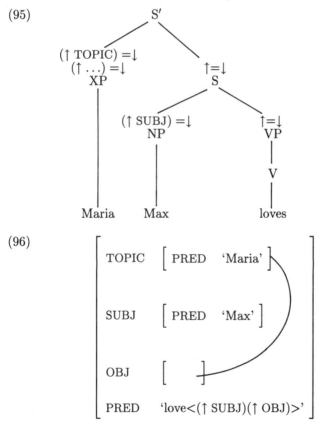

(96)

This particular analysis of long-distance dependencies interacts in an interesting way with the analysis of anaphoric binding, and supports the idea that, in some way, the displaced phrase belongs in two places at the same time.

Many speakers find examples like (97) ambiguous, in that either NP may be the antecedent for the reflexive pronoun.

(97)   Which picture of himself does Max think Larry prefers?

These have been a puzzle for many years in the transformational framework, in that the most natural principles that one would advance for the binding of reflexives fail to predict that *Max* is a possible antecedent. Within the LFG framework, this is indeed a prediction that is made, given the f-command condition on anaphoric binding and the rather 'flat' f-structure configuration that we have just seen (in (96)). The f-structure of the present example has the following form, omitting all but relevant information.

(98)

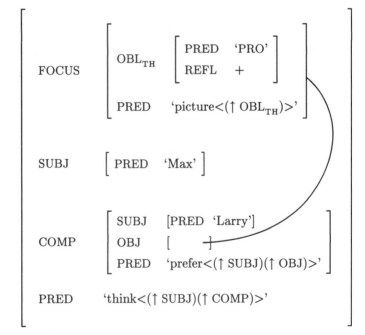

The reader will recall that a reflexive pronoun must be f-commanded by its antecedent, which must also be within the minimal nucleus containing a

SUBJective function. In (98), the reflexive pronoun (the value of the OBL_{TH} attribute) is f-commanded in its position within the FOCUS function by *Max*, and is also f-commanded in its OBJ position by *Larry*; hence either is a potential antecedent. In particular, *Max* may be an antecedent due to the 'flat' f-structure, in which the subcategorized functions of the clause are at the same level as the FOCUS function.

However, if the displaced phrase is an XCOMP, with a controlled subject, then only the controller of that subject will be a potential antecedent. The example (97) contrasts with (99) in this regard.

(99)   How proud of himself does Max think Larry is?

Only *Larry* is a possible antecedent here, as we can see from the f-structure.

(100)

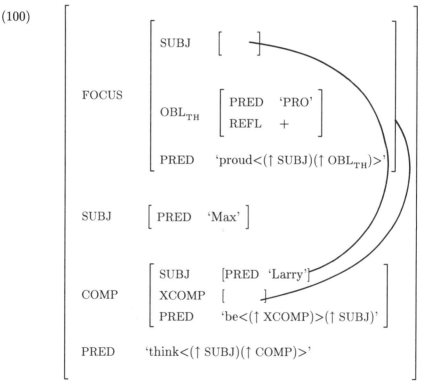

Here the displaced AP is an XCOMP; the verb *be* subcategorizes for an XCOMP and a non-thematic SUBJ which functionally controls the SUBJ of the XCOMP. This means that now the minimal nucleus containing the reflexive also contains a SUBJective function, and so the only possible antecedent for the reflexive pronoun is that SUBJ, whose predicate is 'Larry,' in virtue of the control relation specified by *be*.

5.2. Coordination

As the reader might suspect, the role of functional structure is again important in the LFG account of coordination. While the more common conception in generative grammar is that 'likes coordinate,' where 'like' means identity of syntactic category, in LFG the identity is with functions, in f-structure.

For instance, examples like the following show that identity at the syntactic (categorial) level is not the correct generalization about what can coordinate with what.

(101) a.   We consider him honest and a likely candidate for the next election.

   b.   Maria was asleep and causing a stoppage in the traffic.

The categories of the conjuncts in these examples are AP and NP in the first example, and AP and VP in the second. The Generalized Phrase Structure Grammar solution to this problem is to redefine the way coordination works so that identity is not forced in all cases (see Chap. 3, Sec. 6.2). In LFG, the idea is that there *is* identity in these structures, but identity of function, not of category; in these examples, the function is XCOMP, which may be realized by any maximal projection of a lexical category.

Before getting to the analysis, we must first consider what coordinated f-structures will look like. Rather than single objects, f-structures will now be allowed to be sets; for example, in *Tom and Herb argued*, the value of the SUBJ function will be a set, with two members, which are the f-structures determined by *Tom* and *Herb* respectively. Ultimately, it will be necessary to say what it means for an attribute to have a set as its value, but we can wait for a while before doing this.

The rule of coordination in its simplest form is shown in (102).

(102)   C →   C   Conj   C
                    $\downarrow \in \uparrow$ $\downarrow \in \uparrow$

The *Conj* category is for the conjoining word, *and*, *but*, and so on; I will not say much more about this in the remainder of the discussion. In the rule, 'C' ranges over syntactic categories but is not interpreted as a variable;

the rule might generate a tree with an N dominating a VP and a A′ (though one might want to impose more constraints, such as that the bar-levels of all categories be identical). However, such a tree will be filtered out by the f-structure well-formedness conditions (assuming that these different categories cannot realize the same grammatical functions). Certain cases of categorial mismatch will be allowed, such as in the examples in (101), for the functions are the same.

The annotations '$\downarrow \in \uparrow$' on the categories in the rule indicate that the f-structure of each such category is an element of the f-structure of the mother—that is, that the mother's f-structure is a set.

The interpretation of a set of f-structures is as follows:

(103)   If some f-structure f is a set, then the value of an attribute a in f is v (that is, $(f\ a) = v$) iff for every $g \in f$, $(g\ a)$ includes the information in v.

Using an example to illustrate (103), it says that in a set, the value of the attribute OBJ is [PRED 'Max'] only if the value of OBJ includes the information [PRED 'Max'] in each member of the set.[24]

Let us now look at a simple example, *Louise danced and drank vodka*. The f-structure for (104) is shown in (105).

(104)

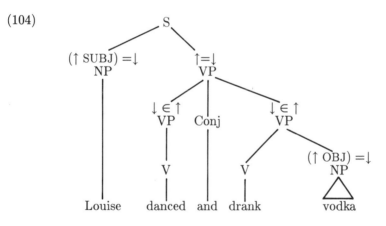

---

[24] The definition in (103) gives much the same results as the statement of the Head Feature Convention for coordinate structures in Generalized Phrase Structure Grammar. In either definition, some attribute (or feature) only has a value if each member of the set has that value, though this is stated

(105)

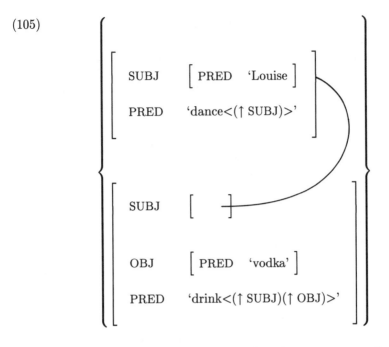

As each verb dictates the basic form of its f-structure, coordinated Vs or VPs lead to the set appearing at the outer level. The subject, *Louise*, is the subject of the coordinated VP, which means that in f-structure it 'distributes' to all the elements of the set representing the conjunction. Given the definition of a value above, it is then the case that the value of SUBJ in (105) is [PRED 'Louise'].

If we consider now the case where we coordinate verbs, we can explain the contrast in (106). In example (a) below, transitive verbs are coordinated and the object *vodka* will distribute to be the value of OBJ for each verb. In example (b), the verb *dance* does not subcategorize for OBJ, but OBJ will distribute to both conjuncts; this makes the nucleus of *dance* incoherent, for it has an OBJ that is not subcategorized by the verb.

---

on f-structures in one case and on surface structures in the other. Moreover, the expression 'includes the information in' allows different information to appear in each conjunct—the value of the attribute being effectively the intersection of the values of that attribute in each conjunct, a conception again similar to that found in Generalized Phrase Structure Grammar.

(106)a.   Louise made and drank vodka.

   b.   *Louise made and danced vodka.

One of the motivating reasons for the change in the treatment of long-distance dependencies from that in KB is the interaction of long-distance dependency constructions with coordination, in particular the phenomenon that was handled in transformational grammar by the *Coordinate Structure Constraint*.[25] The basic facts are shown in (107).

(107)a.   That woman, I interviewed _ and Max hired _ .

   b.   *That woman, I interviewed _ and Max hired a former doctor.

The generalization is that whenever there is a dependency into one conjunct in a coordinate structure, it must be into each conjunct. The treatment this receives is essentially no different from the case considered above of the coordinated transitive and intransitive verbs. For instance, if the FOCUS is functionally identified with some attribute in some member of set of f-structures, then such an identification must take place into each member of the set. This does not happen in (107)b, and so the whole f-structure set has no value for '($\uparrow$ ...) =$\downarrow$' (cf., rule (93)), and the FOCUS is not integrated properly. The f-structure of (107)b is shown in (108)(See p. 190). In this way, the Coordinate Structure Constraint need not be stipulated as an independent condition, for its effect follows as a consequence of the interaction of the analyses of coordination and long-distance dependencies.[26]

LFG currently has not developed an account of the 'COMP-trace' facts of long-distance dependencies (see Chap. 2, Sec. 8, and Chap. 3, Sec. 6.1), nor of the 'parallelism' facts discussed in Chapter 3, Section 6.2. In addition, there is no obvious way to extend its treatment of long-distance dependencies to interpretive phenomena, such as constraints on scope, as discussed in Chapter 2, Sections 5.4 and 8; as noted in Chapter 3, there is some controversy over the convergence in constraints on syntactic and interpretive long-distance phenomena.

---

[25] See also Chapter 3, Section 6.2.

[26] My presentation is somewhat simplified here; see Kaplan and Zaenen (1986) for more details of this interaction.

(108)

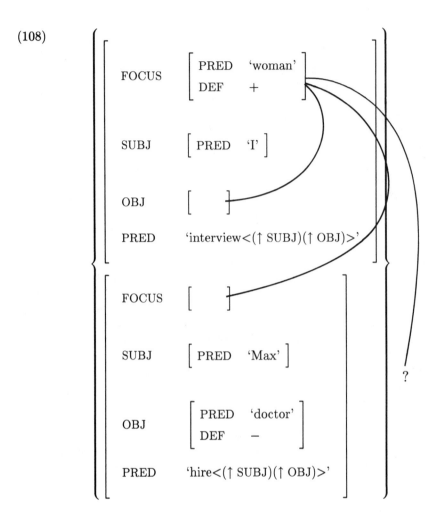

Where to Look Next

The standard source for LFG is the collection of papers in Bresnan (1982), which presents a wide variety of aspects of the theory; see also Levin, Rappaport, and Zaenen (1983), and Iida, Wechsler, and Zec (to appear). The integration of semantic structures into the LFG system is described in Halvorsen (1983).

The Moroccan Arabic data in Section 2.3 is from Wager (1983); the analysis of Japanese causatives in Section 3.4 is drawn from Ishikawa (1985). Levin (1985) presents a study of general principles of function-argument association. On control, see Bresnan, "Control and Complementation" (in Bresnan (1982)), Mohanan (1983) and Simpson and Bresnan (1983); the account of nominalization and its interaction with control (Sec. 4.2) is given in Rappaport (1983).

The basics of the account of anaphoric binding can be found in Kameyama (1984) and in more detail in Kameyama (1985); the Norwegian data is drawn from Bresnan, Halvorsen, and Maling (forthcoming). The discussion in Section 5 is based on the analyses sketched in Saiki (1985); the account of long-distance dependencies is given in more detail in Kaplan and Zaenen (1986). The discussion of the interaction of long-distance dependencies and anaphoric binding is based on material from class lectures given by Joan Bresnan. Fassi Fehri (to appear) presents an account of various aspects of these phenomena based on data from Arabic. On coordination, see Bresnan, Kaplan, and Peterson (1986).

Chapter 5

Postscript

by Thomas Wasow

The preceding chapters have presented an enormous amount of information about the assumptions, mechanisms, and results of three contemporary theories of syntax. To the newcomer, this may seem overwhelming. The purpose of this postscript is to provide a somewhat more global perspective, bringing out some of the important similarities and differences among the theories.[1] Since one important similarity is that they share a common ancestry, I will begin with a few remarks on the recent history of theoretical syntax.

For this purpose, it is useful to note the unique position occupied by Noam Chomsky in the field of theoretical linguistics. Probably no other academic discipline has been so dominated by one individual in recent times. Virtually every innovation that has occurred in this field over the past quarter century has been either an elaboration of or a reaction to some suggestion of Chomsky's. On at least three occasions, Chomsky has revolutionized the way in which syntactic theorizing has been pursued. A brief summary of these changes will be helpful in contrasting the theories covered in this monograph.

---

[1] It should be emphasized that, like much else in syntax, the issue of how much real difference there is among contemporary grammatical theories (and where the differences lie) is quite controversial. By and large, those with the strongest commitment to one theory tend to see greater differences between it and the others than those of us who are less committed. This postscript, then, must be taken as my own personal perspective on the current state of the field. A number of people (including some close colleagues) have taken exception to some of the claims made below.

Three Phases

Chomsky's early work, best exemplified by *Syntactic Structures,* was primarily concerned with establishing the need for generative grammars. At the time, linguists (in America, at least) focussed their attention on methods of data collection and analysis. The goal was to develop precise and objective procedures for classifying corpora of utterances. Chomsky argued that linguists should be concerned primarily with theory construction rather than methodology. He pointed out that languages are infinite and argued that this fact should be of central importance in linguistics. Rather than worrying about the taxonomy of finite corpora, Chomsky proposed that linguists should be writing grammars for infinite languages and testing them against the intuitions of native speakers.

This phase of Chomsky's work was also characterized by a high degree of formal explicitness and an interest in the mathematical properties of grammar formalisms. Chomsky (1959) developed a hierarchy of grammar types (now known as the Chomsky Hierarchy), and proved a number of theorems about what kinds of sets of strings each grammar type could and couldn't generate. These mathematical results, it was claimed, could be used to demonstrate conclusively the inadequacy of certain theories of syntax, on the grounds that natural languages exhibited constructions provably beyond the generative capacity of formalized versions of the theories in question. In the place of the discredited formalisms, Chomsky put forward his theory of transformational grammar. Advocating "the method of rigorously stating a proposed theory and applying it strictly to linguistic material with no attempt to avoid unacceptable conclusions by ad hoc adjustments or loose formulation" (Chomsky, 1957, 5), he presented his analyses in the form of explicit rules for generating a substantial fragment of English.

The emphasis, in short, was largely on what was later to be called "observational adequacy": generating the correct set of strings for a natural language. Meaning was deemed to be outside of the realm of linguistics, and psychological considerations played no role in syntactic theorizing. While some attention was paid to making analyses simple and elegant, top priority was given to developing a theory capable of generating all and only those strings that are well-formed sentences. The major result of this period was the claim that observational adequacy could be achieved with a transformational grammar, but not with a phrase structure grammar.

In the mid-1960's, Chomsky's focus changed dramatically. The so-called 'Standard Theory' of Chomsky (1965) (following earlier work by Fodor, Katz, and Postal) included a semantic component and was explicitly linked to questions of how knowledge of language was represented in the mind. Language was viewed as a system of connections between meanings and sounds, and the job of the linguist was to discover the rules that speakers employ in associating meanings with sounds.

The Standard Theory identified two distinguished levels of representation for sentences: deep and surface structures. Deep structures served as the basis for semantic interpretation, and surface structures as the basis for phonological interpretation. The two levels were related to one another by transformations. Hence, transformations played the central role in connecting meanings with sounds.[2] It was claimed that the same transformational rules needed to distinguish sentences from non-sentences would also serve this connecting function between sounds and meanings. Moreover, it was expected that they would turn out to be "psychologically real," in the sense that they could be shown to play a role in human sentence-processing.[3]

The focus of attention, then, was what Chomsky (1964) called "descriptive adequacy": modeling the ability of speakers to relate meanings and sounds. Interest in the mathematical properties of the theory was subordinated to concern with semantic and psychological questions; consequently, standards of explicitness and rigor were relaxed. The principal result claimed for this period was that descriptive adequacy could be achieved with a transformational grammar of a certain form.[4]

---

[2] This most extreme version of this view was what was called "Generative Semantics," which held that deep structures could be identified with representations of meaning (see Newmeyer (1980, Chaps. 4 and 5) for an overview and references). While Chomsky opposed Generative Semantics, he did at one time endorse the idea that transformations provided the primary link between meaning and sound.

[3] For a survey of literature on this question, see Fodor, Bever, and Garrett (1974).

[4] Some clarification is in order here, for in introducing the distinctions among levels of adequacy for a linguistic theory, Chomsky argued that standard transformational grammar attained (at least on some points) the highest level, namely "explanatory adequacy." Thus, my association of the Standard Theory with concern for descriptive adequacy appears to be in direct conflict with what Chomsky himself asserted at the time. I contend, how-

The widespread acceptance of the Standard Theory lasted only a few years. Beginning with the bitter battle over Generative Semantics in the late sixties, generative grammar became fragmented and factionalized. Until the late seventies, most syntactic research was carried on within some revised and/or extended form of the Standard Theory, though radically different approaches also began to gain visibility.

A common theme in the most important work of this period was the need to constrain the power of transformational grammar. The Standard Theory was so rich in descriptive devices that its ability to provide analyses of particular constructions began to seem rather unremarkable. This intuition was substantiated by Peters and Ritchie (1973), who proved that standard transformational grammars had the power of Turing machines—that is, that they could be used to formalize any procedure that was in principle formalizable. Further, linguists began to take seriously Chomsky's earlier claim that there was a higher level of adequacy than descriptive adequacy to aspire to. A theory would attain "explanatory adequacy" if it provided a means for inferring a grammar on the basis of the facts of the language. In other words, explanatory adequacy is concerned with learnability: it says that syntactic theory should only permit grammars that could be learned on the basis of the primary data available to real language learners. Such a theory could not have the descriptive power of existing versions of generative grammar, which all permitted infinitely many different analyses of any phenomenon.

The third phase of Chomsky's work is dominated by the quest for explanatory adequacy. His books and papers consistently assert that the fundamental question linguistics needs to answer is how language can be learned. The most striking fact about language, he says, is the gap between the small and arbitrary corpora children are exposed to and the unbounded ability people have to produce and understand utterances. This "argument from the poverty of the stimulus" indicates that the innate human language faculty narrowly constrains the class of possible hypotheses available to the child about the structure of the language being learned. Then even a small amount of data about a language may provide the learner with

---

ever, that the overwhelming bulk of the research of the time was concerned with generating the right strings and assigning to them structures which were semantically or psychologically plausible. Little more than lip service was paid to explanatory adequacy, that is, to the goal of establishing a highly constrained theory of universal grammar.

enough information to identify the language uniquely. Thus, this line of reasoning leads to a picture in which as much as possible is factored out of the grammars of particular languages and put into the theory of grammar— or "universal grammar," as it is sometimes called.

It is difficult to pinpoint when this third phase began. As noted in Footnote 3, Chomsky advocated the goal of explanatory adequacy during his second phase. However, the concern with learnability actually did not become a serious motivating force in syntactic analyses until the mid seventies. Government-Binding Theory (GB), introduced by Chomsky (1981), represents the culmination of this tendency. GB research seeks to reduce the grammars of particular languages to settings for a small number of parameters, leaving the remainder to a rich set of universal principles. Because of the focus on universals, the GB literature differs from earlier transformational work in devoting considerable attention to cross-language comparisons. Only in this way can the parameters of language variation be identified and tested.

With the concentration on learnability and universal grammar, many details in the analyses of particular constructions began to receive less attention. Likewise, concern for explicitness and formalization diminished. Indeed, there seems to be quite a general trade-off between theoretical elegance and attention to empirical detail. As Chomsky has sought to attain higher and higher levels of adequacy in his theories, he has concerned himself less and less with analyzing the specifics of particular constructions. Thus, although the discussion of levels of adequacy in the literature claims that attainment of any level presupposes attainment of the lower levels, in actual practice, there has been a cost attached each time the sights have been raised.

The Place of GPSG and LFG

The preceding section described a monotonic course of development in syntactic theorizing over the past thirty years, with formal rigor and attention to grammatical details gradually giving way to an emphasis on universal grammar and larger theoretical questions. Generalized Phrase Structure Grammar (GPSG) and Lexical-Functional Grammar (LFG) can be viewed as attempts to preserve certain attractive features of the earlier phases of generative grammar. More specifically, I will argue that GPSG represents a return to a serious concern for observational adequacy, while LFG's emphasis is on descriptive adequacy. I hasten to add, however, that this is an oversimplification, as both GPSG and LFG do address the question of universals in substantive ways. Nevertheless, I think it is fair to characterize the emphases of the theories in this way, and that it is useful to do so, in trying to fit them into a larger picture.

Like Chomsky's early work, the GPSG literature exhibits a keen interest in the mathematical properties of grammar formalisms. More specifically, Gazdar and others (see especially Pullum and Gazdar (1982)) have revived interest among linguists in questions of "weak generative capacity"—that is, of the sets of strings generable by various types of grammars. In order to investigate such questions, it is necessary that the grammars in question be formulated with considerable precision. Thus, work in GPSG resembles the transformational literature of twenty-five years earlier in its formal rigor. Likewise, GPSG papers typically present explicit grammar fragments, which are evaluated on the basis of the acceptability of the strings they generate.

One striking dissimilarity, however, between GPSG and Chomsky's early theory is the role of semantics. Whereas *Syntactic Structures* excluded the study of meaning from the domain of linguistics, GPSG's semantic analyses are such an integral part of the theory as to be inseparable from the syntactic proposals. More than anything else, this reflects the fact that the intervening decades saw the development of a rigorous formal approach to natural language semantics (Montague Grammar). Unlike the work on meaning by transformationalists in the sixties, no psychological significance has been attached to the semantics of GPSG.

More generally, like the *Syntactic Structures* theory, GPSG has not been tied to any psychological claims, and its proponents have generally been agnostic on the question of the proper relationship between theories of grammar and models of language users.[5] Moreover, though GPSG differs from early transformational grammar in that it makes far stronger claims about universal grammar, its proponents do not invoke the problem of language acquisition as the reason for putting forward such claims. Rather, the motivation appears to stem from general methodological considerations, viz., that universal claims are preferable to existential ones. Thus, even with regard to the quest for linguistic universals, GPSG has been largely free from psychological claims.

LFG, in contrast, has its origin in the concern for the role of grammatical theory in models of processing. Ronald Kaplan, one of the developers of LFG, was trained as a psychologist, and began his career doing ex-

---

[5] There are a few exceptions, e.g., Crain and Fodor (1985).

perimental work on human sentence processing. In an important paper marking the transition from transformational grammar to LFG, Bresnan (1978) argued for the innovations she proposed on the grounds that they were psychologically "realistic." The focus on LFG as a basis for modeling how people process language has been maintained, especially in work by Marilyn Ford. Further, Pinker (1984) has argued that LFG can provide natural explanations for many facts about language acquisition. In short, LFG resembles the work of the Standard Theory period in its emphasis on descriptive adequacy.

LFG and standard transformational grammar are also alike in positing two distinguished levels of grammatical representation, one which is used as the basis for semantic interpretation and one which is used as the basis for phonological interpretation. Of course, the f-structures of LFG do not look like the deep structures of the Standard Theory, but their roles in the two theories are quite similar. Specifically, deep structures and f-structures are the loci of grammatical information and constraints which depend on the predicate-argument relations in sentences. Especially important among these are subcategorization and control relations.

A crucial difference between LFG and transformational grammar is the place of grammatical functions (or "grammatical relations," as they are sometimes called) like 'subject' and 'object' in the two theories. Chomsky (1965) argued that insofar as grammatical functions played a role in linguistic descriptions, they could be defined in terms of configurations in phrase structure trees. For example, he proposed that a subject is an NP directly dominated by S. LFG, in contrast, takes grammatical functions to be primitives of the theory, in terms of which a great many rules and conditions are stated.

In this, LFG is like the theory of Relational Grammar developed by David Perlmutter, Paul Postal, and others over the past dozen years or so. During that period, a large body of literature has been produced, analyzing syntactic phenomena (especially those having to do with the internal structure of clauses) in an impressively wide variety of languagues. Though it is rarely acknowledged, the influence of Relational Grammar on all contemporary work in syntactic theory would be hard to overestimate. Of the theories discussed in this monograph, only LFG adopts the central tenet of Relational Grammar (namely, that grammatical functions are primitive), but proponents of all three have devoted considerable energy to describing phenomena and capturing generalizations first discovered by relational grammarians. Noteworthy examples are Burzio (1981), Dowty (1982), and Bresnan (1982, passim).

I return now to the main theme of this section. The three theories represented in this monograph correspond—at least in what they choose to emphasize—to the three stages of Chomsky's work described in the previous section. The correspondence is not, of course, perfect. However, the styles of doing linguistics, the kind of questions asked, and the criteria for evaluating analyses do match fairly well. It is important to understand that I am not accusing GPSG or LFG of arrested development. As I pointed out above, each stage in Chomsky's work has had its strengths and weaknesses. As the focus changed from observational to descriptive to explanatory adequacy, standards of explicitness, rigor, and attention to empirical detail declined. This is natural, for the larger the questions addressed, the harder it is to give complete answers. Like Chomsky's three stages, the theories under consideration constitute different choices regarding this trade-off.

Some Points of Convergence

In spite of the considerable differences in emphasis, formalism, and substance, there are some respects in which the theories under discussion are surprisingly similar. In this section, I will describe some that have struck me; there may well be others. These points of convergence are of special interest because they indicate areas where linguists may have attained some real new insight transcending the more superficial differences among theories.

Perhaps the most obvious similarity is the reduced role of transformations in the these theories. Their common ancestor, standard transformational grammar, encoded most relationships among the elements of sentences by positing levels of representation at which the related elements were identical or adjacent; it then turned these abstract representations into the actual sentences by means of transformational rules. For example, the Standard Theory posited a transformation of 'Equi-NP Deletion' to remove the subject of a subordinate clause when it was identical with an NP in the main clause; so, the fact that *Pat* is the 'understood' subject of *leave* in *Pat wants to leave* would be encoded by deriving it from *Pat wants Pat to leave* by deletion under identity. None of the theories considered in this monograph adopts this kind of analysis.

More generally, alternative devices for encoding grammatical relationships have supplanted transformations almost everywhere. GPSG and LFG have no transformations, and GB has only one (Move-α). Moreover, most of the real work accomplished by Move-α is a function of the coindexing that is required between the moved element and the pre-movement position. Indeed, Chomsky (1982, 33) goes so far as to say, "It is immaterial ... whether Move-α is regarded as a rule forming s-structure from d-structure, or whether it is regarded as a property of s-structures that are 'base-generated' ... It is in fact far from clear that there is a distinction apart from terminology between these two formulations."

The reduced status of transformations in contemporary linguistic theories can be traced back to the observation that a great many of the transformations in the Standard Theory produced outputs that were structurally identical to base-generated trees. For example, a passive sentence like *The dog was chased by the cat* appears to have the same constituent structure as an active sentence like *The dog was racing by the house*. This fact led Emonds (1976) to develop a theory in which a large class of transformations was required to be 'structure preserving.' This idea is manifested, in a more general form, in the Projection Principle of GB. It also served as an important motivation for eliminating the transformational component altogether in GPSG and LFG. If deep structures and surface structures were isomorphic, it was reasoned, then why relate them by means of rules with the power to alter structure?

There is considerable diversity in the mechanisms proposed in the different theories to do what had formerly been done with transformations. Even here, however, I think that there are significant commonalities. This is most evident in the treatment of unbounded dependencies. In standard transformational grammar, these were handled by means of rules that moved (or deleted) elements across arbitrarily large stretches of a sentence. Contemporary theories, on the other hand, adopt analyses in which the relationship between 'fillers'[6] and 'gaps' is mediated by intervening elements. In GB, this is accomplished by means of 'successive cyclic' movement: *wh*-elements are moved through the COMP nodes of intervening clauses, and the resulting coindexed traces form a chain connecting the surface position of the *wh*-element with its d-structure position. In GPSG, the SLASH feature is passed up the tree along a path of nodes connecting the gap with its filler. In the current LFG analysis, fillers and gaps are connected by means of a sequence of grammatical functions, summarized by the nota-

---

[6] Referred to in the chapters above as 'displaced phrases.'

tion '(↑ ...),' though in this case the path through the f-structure is stated as one expression, not as a series of links.

While the formal mechanisms are different in these three theories, they share the property of effectively reducing unbounded dependencies to sequences of local dependencies, thereby taking the same position on what had been a controversial issue in the transformational literature of the early seventies. The differences among these analyses are slight in comparison with the difference between any of them and any treatment that posits no licensing relation between filler and gap. While clear empirical evidence has been found for the existence of elements sensitive to the presence of unbounded dependencies (see Zaenen (1983)), I know of no direct argument to choose among coindexing, feature passing, and sequences of functions.

Similarly, the three theories agree, roughly speaking, that the gaps in these constructions must, in some sense, be licensed by a lexical element in its clause. In GB, this requirement is embodied in the Empty Category Principle.[7] In GPSG, it follows from the Lexical Head Constraint that the Slash Termination Metarules can only introduce gaps as sisters to lexical heads. Finally, since unbounded dependencies in LFG are handled by means of sequences of grammatical functions, a gap must be identified in terms of the grammatical function it plays with respect to some lexical predicate.[8] In short, not only must fillers and gaps be connected by some chain of intermediate elements, but the gap itself must stand in a special relationship with a lexical head close to it.

These somewhat technical similarities reflect what I believe is a more fundamental insight, namely that unbounded dependencies are permitted only under rather limited circumstances. Standard transformational grammar treated movement or deletion over arbitrary stretches as the norm, specifying certain configurations as 'islands' blocking such operations; contemporary theories, in contrast, treat dependencies between widely separated elements as the exception, requiring special mechanisms to license them.

---

[7] The ECP also permits gaps to be licensed through coindexing, but, as Sells notes, these are in a sense not the "core" cases of the ECP.

[8] An earlier LFG treatment of unbounded dependencies required that for each gap there be a 'lexical signature' (Kaplan and Bresnan (1982, 246ff)). This requirement was even closer to the ECP and the effects of the Lexical Head Constraint than the current LFG treatment.

Another basic idea embodied in these three theories is that clause structure is largely predictable from the semantics of predicates. That is, if you know what a verb (or a predicative adjective or noun) means, you can tell a great deal about what else will occur in a clause it heads. Grammar rules are needed only to state certain language-wide generalizations about how the pieces of sentences are put together and to deal with apparent exceptions to the normal patterns. Most of what was stipulated in the grammars of earlier theories is taken to be a function of lexical semantics.

This idea is clearest in GB. The θ-Criterion says (oversimplifying somewhat) that the meaning of a predicate determines what grammatical arguments it will have. The Projection Principle guarantees that the structure determined by the lexical head's meaning cannot be altered in essential ways. The problem of acquiring a language, then, reduces largely to learning the meanings of words. There is more to it, of course, such as discovering the basic order of constituents, determining what the bounding nodes are, and learning which verbs trigger S'-deletion (such as *seem* and *believe* in English), and so on. In the canonical cases, however, sentence structure is a projection of the semantics of words.

In LFG, the Principle of Function-Argument Biuniqueness ensures that grammatical functions will be paired with thematic roles. The Completeness and Coherence conditions, in turn, see to it that every grammatical function is filled by exactly one constituent in the f-structure. Hence, aside from exceptional predicates permitting non-thematic functions, clause structure is essentially determined by the thematic roles required by the predicate. Again, a certain amount of idiosyncratic information must be stipulated, but far less than in earlier theories.

The version of GPSG presented in Chapter 3 does not really embody this idea of clause structure as a projection of lexical semantics. The closest thing to it is "shake'n'bake semantics": the lexical type of a predicate determines the number and type of arguments that it will combine with; any sentence in which a predicate cooccurred with the wrong number or types of arguments would be uninterpretable. But the alert reader will recall that subcategorization is handled in the syntax, so that a sentence whose verb has the wrong number or category of sister constituents will be ungrammatical, not just semantically anomalous. That is, the lexical meaning of a predicate determines how the semantics of the pieces of a clause should be composed, but it does not determine what those pieces will be.

In recent modifications of GPSG, however, this has been changed. In particular, Pollard's (1984, 1985) work on Head-driven Phrase Structure Grammar involves specifying subcategorization information in lexical entries, rather than in ID-rules. This permits the subcategorization to be linked rather directly to the lexical semantics, while at the same time allowing the ID-rules to be extremely general schemata. Thus, in the most recent incarnations of GPSG, it resembles GB and LFG in deriving canonical clause structure largely from lexical semantics.

Conclusion

It is interesting that contemporary syntactic theories seem to be converging on the idea that sentence structure is generally predictable from word meanings, for this seems to be close to the naive view of a great many non-linguists. The layperson generally equates languages with collections of words, assuming, for example, that learning a new language consists of learning its vocabulary. It might seem unimpressive, then, that linguists are finally coming around to this common-sense view. I contend, quite the contrary, that this is rather remarkable, for the conventional wisdom appears, on closer inspection, to be hopelessly simplistic.

Consider, for example, what happens when one takes a sentence of one language and translates each word into some unrelated language; in general, such word-for-word translations are not only not sentences of the second language, they are not even comprehensible to its speakers. Further, most linguists can produce numerous examples of synonyms or near synonyms that exhibit significant syntactic differences. For example, *likely* takes an infinitival complement (as in *Pat is likely to win*), but *probable* does not (hence, **Pat is probable to win*); and *have,* in the sense of possession, cannot appear in the passive voice, unlike other verbs of possession (hence, *Too many TV stations are owned/*had by fundamentalists*). Thus, the naive view appears at first to be too naive to be taken very seriously; and it was not, as indicated by the emphasis on the study of rule systems in earlier stages of generative grammar.

What has happened to change this is that syntacticians have identified the ways in which languages deviate from the naive view. They have isolated certain kinds of grammatical information that are not predictable from lexical semantics, and have developed theories to permit them to be expressed compactly. The surprising thing (to linguists) has been how little needs to be stipulated beyond lexical meaning. Languages differ (within certain specifiable limits) in constituent and word ordering, in where unbounded dependencies will be permitted, in which constituents can be omitted, in which words have syntactic idiosyncracies, and in a few other ways. They do not, as an earlier generation of linguists maintained, differ without limit. Indeed, the naive view that word meanings determine sentence structure turns out not to be a bad first approximation, though it leaves the most challenging problems in the study of syntax still to be accounted for.

In short, there is evidence here of real progress. Current theories of syntax have focussed on a few key types of phenomena, namely those that aren't fully explainable in terms of what the words in the sentences mean. These are the loci both of cross-language variation and of the most interesting linguistic universals. There is significant disagreement about what the relevant generalizations are and how they should be formulated, but there is even more significant agreement about what the important phenomena are.

Finally, it should be emphasized that all of the theories presented here, as well as the relationships among them, are in the process of fairly rapid change. It is safe to say that most of what appears in this work will be rendered obsolete within a few years. However, if my assessment that genuine progress is taking place is correct, then some familiarity with the current state of these syntactic theories should be useful to the specialist and interested non-specialist alike.

List of Abbreviations

AP	Adjective Phrase
C	variable over syntactic categories
CAP	Control Agreement Principle
COMP	Complementizer node
Det	Determiner node
ECP	Empty Category Principle
FCR	Feature Cooccurrence Restriction
FFP	Foot Feature Principle
FSD	Feature Specification Default
GB	Government-Binding Theory
GKPS	Gazdar, Klein, Pullum, and Sag (1985)
GPSG	Generalized Phrase Structure Grammar
H	head (in an ID-rule)
HFC	Head Feature Convention
ID-rule	Immediate Dominance rule
INFL	Inflection node
KB	Kaplan and Bresnan (1982)
LF	logical form
LFG	Lexical-Functional Grammar
LGB	Chomsky (1981)
LHC	Lexical Head Constraint
LP-statement	Linear Precedence statement
NP	Noun Phrase
PF	phonetic form
PP	Prepositional Phrase
PS-rule	Phrase Structure rule
QR	Quantifier Raising
S	Sentence
SAI	Subject-Auxiliary Inversion
STM	Slash Termination Metarule
TG	Transformational Grammar
UG	Universal Grammar
VP	Verb Phrase
XP	maximal projection of any major category

References

Andrews, Avery. 1984. Lexical Insertion and the Elsewhere Principle in LFG. Ms., Australian National University.

Baltin, Mark. 1982. A Landing Site Theory of Movement Rules, *Linguistic Inquiry* 13:1–38.

Bresnan, Joan. 1978. A Realistic Transformational Grammar. In M. Halle, J. Bresnan, and G. Miller (Eds.), *Linguistic Theory and Psychological Reality*. Cambridge, Mass.: MIT Press, 1–59.

Bresnan, Joan. (Ed.). 1982. *The Mental Representation of Grammatical Relations*. Cambridge, Mass.: MIT Press.

Bresnan, Joan, Per-Kristian Halvorsen, and Joan Maling. Forthcoming. Logophoricity and Bound Anaphors. CSLI, Stanford University.

Bresnan, Joan, Ronald Kaplan, and Peter Peterson. 1986. Coordination and the Flow of Information Through Phrase Structure. Ms., CSLI, Stanford University.

Bresnan, Joan and Sam Mchombo. 1986. Grammatical and Anaphoric Agreement. In A. Farley, P. Farley, and K.-E. McCullough (Eds.), *Papers from the Parasession on Pragmatics and Grammatical Theory at the 22nd Regional Meeting*. Chicago Linguistics Society, Chicago, 278–297.

Bresnan, Joan and Sam Mchombo. 1987. Topic, Pronoun, and Agreement in Chicheŵa. To appear in *Language*.

Burzio, Luigi. 1981. *Intransitive Verbs and Italian Auxiliaries*. Doctoral dissertation, MIT.

Chomsky, Noam. 1957. *Syntactic Structures*. The Hague: Mouton.

Chomsky, Noam. 1959. On Certain Formal Properties of Grammars, *Information and Control* 2:137–167.

Chomsky, Noam. 1964. *Current Issues in Linguistic Theory*. The Hague: Mouton.

Chomsky, Noam. 1965. *Aspects of the Theory of Syntax*. Cambridge, Mass.: MIT Press.

Chomsky, Noam. 1981. *Lectures on Government and Binding.* Dordrecht: Foris.

Chomsky, Noam. 1982. *Some Concepts and Consequences of the Theory of Government and Binding.* Cambridge, Mass.: MIT Press.

Chomsky, Noam. 1986a. *Knowledge of Language: Its Nature, Origins, And Use.* New York: Praeger.

Chomsky, Noam. 1986b. *Barriers.* Cambridge, Mass.: MIT Press.

Crain, Stephen and Janet D. Fodor. 1985. How Can Grammars Help Parsers? In D. Dowty, L. Karttunen, and A. Zwicky (Eds.), *Natural Language Parsing: Psychological, Computational, and Theoretical Perspectives.* New York: Cambridge University Press, 94–128.

Dowty, David. 1982. Grammatical Relations and Montague Grammar. In P. Jacobson and G. K. Pullum (Eds.), *The Nature of Syntactic Representation.* Dordrecht: Reidel, 79–130.

Emonds, Joseph. 1976. *A Transformational Approach to English Syntax.* New York: Academic Press.

Fassi Fehri, Abdelkader. To appear. Agreement in Arabic, Binding, and Coherence. In M. Barlow and C. A. Ferguson (Eds.), *Agreement in Natural Language: Approaches, Theories, Descriptions.* CSLI, Stanford University.

Flickinger, Daniel. 1983. Lexical Heads and Phrasal Gaps. In M. Barlow, D. Flickinger, and M. Wescoat (Eds.), *Proceedings of WCCFL 2.* Stanford Linguistics Association, 89–101.

Fodor, Jerry A., Thomas Bever, and Merrill Garrett. 1974. *The Psychology of Language.* New York: McGraw-Hill.

Gazdar, Gerald. 1981. Unbounded Dependencies and Coordinate Structure, *Linguistic Inquiry* 12:155–184.

Gazdar, Gerald. 1982. Phrase Structure Grammar. In P. Jacobson and G. K. Pullum (Eds.), *The Nature of Syntactic Representation.* Dordrecht: Reidel, 131–186.

Gazdar, Gerald, Ewan Klein, Geoffrey K. Pullum, and Ivan Sag. 1985. *Generalized Phrase Structure Grammar.* Cambridge, Mass.: Harvard University Press.

Gazdar, Gerald and Geoffrey K. Pullum. 1981. Subcategorization, Constituent Order, and the Notion *Head*. In M. Moortgat, H. van der Hulst, and T. Hoekstra (Eds.), *The Scope of Lexical Rules*. Dordrecht: Foris, 107–123.

Gazdar, Gerald, Geoffrey K. Pullum, and Ivan Sag: 1982. Auxiliaries and Related Phenomena in a Restrictive Theory of Grammar, *Language* 58:591–638.

Goldberg, Jeffrey. 1985. Lexical Operations and Unbounded Dependencies. In W. Eilfort, P. Kroeber, and K. Peterson (Eds.), *Papers from the 21st Regional Meeting*. Chicago Linguistics Society, 122–132.

Grimshaw, Jane. 1982. Subcategorization and Grammatical Relations. In A. Zaenen (Ed.), *Subjects and Other Subjects: Proceedings of the Harvard Conference on the Representation of Grammatical Relations*. Bloomington: Indiana University Linguistics Club, 35–55.

Gruber, Jeffrey. 1965. *Studies in Lexical Relations*. Doctoral dissertation, MIT.

Halvorsen, Per-Kristian. 1983. Semantics for Lexical-Functional Grammar, *Linguistic Inquiry* 14:567–615.

Hornstein, Norbert. 1984. *Logic as Grammar*. Cambridge, Mass.: MIT Press.

Huang, C.-T. James. 1982. *Logical Relations in Chinese and the Theory of Grammar*. Doctoral dissertation, MIT.

Iida, Masayo, Stephen Wechsler, and Draga Zec. (Eds.). To appear. *Studies in Grammatical Theory and Discourse Structure, Volume I: Interactions of Morphology, Syntax, and Discourse*. CSLI: Stanford University.

Ishikawa, Akira. 1985. *Complex Predicates and Lexical Operations in Japanese*. Doctoral dissertation, Stanford University.

Jackendoff, Ray. 1972. *Semantic Interpretation in Generative Grammar*. Cambridge, Mass.: MIT Press.

Jaeggli, Osvaldo. 1984. Subject Extraction and the Null Subject Parameter. In C. Jones and P. Sells (Eds.), *Proceedings of NELS* 14. Graduate Linguistic Student Association, University of Massachusetts at Amherst, 132–153.

Kameyama, Megumi. 1984. Subjective/Logophoric Bound Anaphor *Zibun*. In J. Drogo, V. Mishra, and D. Testen (Eds.), *Papers from the 20th Regional Meeting*. Chicago Linguistics Society, Chicago, 228–238.

Kameyama, Megumi. 1985. *Zero Anaphora: The Case of Japanese*. Doctoral dissertation, Stanford University.

Kaplan, Ronald and Joan Bresnan. 1982. Lexical-Functional Grammar: A Formal System for Grammatical Representation. In Bresnan (Ed.), 173–281.

Kaplan, Ronald and Annie Zaenen. 1986. Long-Distance Dependencies and Constituent Structure. Ms., Xerox-PARC.

Kayne, Richie. 1984. *Connectedness and Binary Branching*. Dordrecht: Foris.

Keenan, Edward L. 1974. The Functional Principle: Generalizing the Notion of *Subject Of*. In M. La Galy, R. Fox, and A. Bruck (Eds.), *Papers from the 10th Regional Meeting*. Chicago Linguistics Society, Chicago, 298–309.

Koopman, Hilda. 1984. *The Syntax of Verbs: from Verb Movement Rules in the Kru Languages to Universal Grammar*. Dordrecht: Foris.

Lasnik, Howard and Mamoru Saito. 1984. On the Nature of Proper Government, *Linguistic Inquiry* 15:235–289.

Levin, Lori. 1985. *Operations on Lexical Forms: Unaccusative Rules in Germanic Languages*. Doctoral dissertation, MIT.

Levin, Lori, Malka Rappaport, and Annie Zaenen. (Eds.). 1983. *Papers in Lexical-Functional Grammar*. Bloomington: Indiana University Linguistics Club.

Manzini, Maria Rita. 1983. On Control and Control Theory, *Linguistic Inquiry* 14:421–446.

May, Robert. 1985. *Logical Form: Its Structure and Derivation*. Cambridge, Mass.: MIT Press.

Mohanan, K. P. 1983. Functional and Anaphoric Control, *Linguistic Inquiry* 14:641–674.

Montague, Richard. 1974. *Formal Philosophy: Selected Papers of Richard Montague*, R. Thomason (Ed.). New Haven: Yale University Press.

Newmeyer, Frederick. 1980. *Linguistic Theory in America: The First Quarter-Century of Transformational Generative Grammar*. New York: Academic Press.

Newmeyer, Frederick. 1983. *Grammatical Theory: Its Limits and Its Possibilities*. Chicago: University of Chicago Press.

Nishigauchi, Taisuke. 1984. Japanese LF: Subjacency vs. ECP. To appear in *Seoul Papers On Formal Grammar Theory*.

Nishigauchi, Taisuke. To appear. *Quantification in Syntax*. Doctoral dissertation, University of Massachusetts at Amherst.

Perlmutter, David. (Ed.). 1983. *Studies in Relational Grammar 1*. Chicago: University of Chicago Press.

Perlmutter, David and Carol Rosen. (Eds.). 1984. *Studies in Relational Grammar 2*. Chicago: University of Chicago Press.

Pesetsky, David. 1982. *Paths and Categories*. Doctoral dissertation, MIT.

Peters, Stanley and Robert Ritchie. 1973. On the Generative Power of Transformational Grammars, *Information and Control* 18:483–501.

Pinker, Steven. 1984. *Language Learnability and Language Development*. Cambridge, Mass.: Harvard University Press.

Pollard, Carl. 1984. *Generalized Phrase Structure Grammars, Head Grammars, and Natural Language*. Doctoral dissertation, Stanford University. To appear, Cambridge: Cambridge University Press.

Pollard, Carl. 1985. Phrase Structure Grammar Without Metarules. In J. Goldberg, S. Mackaye, and M. Wescoat (Eds.), *Proceedings of WCCFL 4*. Stanford Linguistics Association, 246–261.

Pollard, Carl and Ivan Sag. 1983. Reflexives and Reciprocals in English: An Alternative to the Binding Theory. In M. Barlow, D. Flickinger, and M. Wescoat (Eds.), *Proceedings of WCCFL 2*. Stanford Linguistics Association, 189–203.

Pullum, Geoffrey K. and Gerald Gazdar. 1982. Natural Languages and Context-free Languages, *Linguistics and Philosophy* 4:471–504.

Rappaport, Malka. 1983. On the Nature of Derived Nominals. In Levin et al., 113–142.

Reinhart, Tanya. 1983. *Anaphora and Semantic Interpretation*. London: Croom Helm.

van Riemsdijk, Henk and Edwin Williams. 1986. *Introduction to the Theory of Grammar*. Cambridge, Mass.: MIT Press.

Rizzi, Luigi. 1982. *Issues in Italian Syntax*. Dordrecht: Foris.

Rizzi, Luigi. 1986. Null Objects in Italian and the Theory of *pro*, *Linguistic Inquiry* 17:501–557.

Safir, Kenneth. 1985. *Syntactic Chains*. New York: Cambridge University Press.

Sag, Ivan. 1986. Grammatical Hierarchy and Linear Precedence. CSLI Report No. 60, Stanford University. Also to appear in G. Huck and A. Ojeda (Eds.), *Discontinuous Constituency (Syntax and Semantics Vol. 20)*. New York: Academic Press.

Sag, Ivan, Gerald Gazdar, Thomas Wasow, and Steven Weisler. 1985. Co-ordination and How to Distinguish Categories, *Natural Language and Linguistic Theory* 3:117–171.

Sag, Ivan and Carl Pollard. 1986. Head-Driven Phrase Structure Grammar: An Informal Synopsis. To appear as a CSLI Report, Stanford University.

Saiki, Mariko. 1985. On the Coordination of Gapped Constituents in Japanese. In W. Eilfort, P. Kroeber, and K. Peterson (Eds.), *Papers from the 21st Regional Meeting*. Chicago Linguistics Society, Chicago, 371–387.

Simpson, Jane. 1983. *Aspects of Warlpiri Morphology and Syntax*. Doctoral dissertation, MIT.

Simpson, Jane and Joan Bresnan. 1983. Control and Obviation in Warlpiri, *Natural Language and Linguistic Theory* 1:49–64.

Sproat, Richard. 1985. Welsh Syntax and VSO Structure, *Natural Language and Linguistic Theory* 3:173–216.

Stowell, Timothy. 1981. *Origins of Phrase Structure*. Doctoral dissertation, MIT.

Travis, Lisa. 1984. *Parameters and Effects of Word Order Variation*. Doctoral dissertation, MIT.

Uszkoreit, Hans. 1984. *Word Order and Constituent Structure in German.* Doctoral dissertation, University of Texas at Austin.

Wager, Jan. 1983. *Complementation in Moroccan Arabic.* Doctoral dissertation, MIT.

Williams, Edwin. 1981. Argument Structure and Morphology, *Linguistic Review* 1:81–114.

Williams, Edwin. 1984. Grammatical Relations, *Linguistic Inquiry* 15:639–673.

Zaenen, Annie. 1983. On Syntactic Binding, *Linguistic Inquiry* 14:469–504.

Index of Names

Index of Subjects

CSLI Publications

Reports

The following titles have been published in the CSLI Reports series. These reports may be obtained from CSLI Publications, Ventura Hall, Stanford University, Stanford, CA 94305.

The Situation in Logic–I. Jon Barwise. CSLI–84–2. ($2.00)

Coordination and How to Distinguish Categories. Ivan Sag, Gerald Gazdar, Thomas Wasow, and Steven Weisler. CSLI–84–3. ($3.50)

Belief and Incompleteness. Kurt Konolige. CSLI–84–4. ($4.50)

Equality, Types, Modules and Generics for Logic Programming. Joseph Goguen and José Meseguer. CSLI–84–5. ($2.50)

Lessons from Bolzano. Johan van Benthem. CSLI–84–6. ($1.50)

Self-propagating Search: A Unified Theory of Memory. Pentti Kanerva. CSLI–84–7. ($9.00)

Reflection and Semantics in LISP. Brian Cantwell Smith. CSLI–84–8. ($2.50)

The Implementation of Procedurally Reflective Languages. Jim des Rivières and Brian Cantwell Smith. CSLI–84–9. ($3.00)

Parameterized Programming. Joseph Goguen. CSLI–84–10. ($3.50)

Morphological Constraints on Scandinavian Tone Accent. Meg Withgott and Per-Kristian Halvorsen. CSLI–84–11. ($2.50)

Partiality and Nonmonotonicity in Classical Logic. Johan van Benthem. CSLI–84–12. ($2.00)

Shifting Situations and Shaken Attitudes. Jon Barwise and John Perry. CSLI–84–13. ($4.50)

Aspectual Classes in Situation Semantics. Robin Cooper. CSLI–85–14-C. ($4.00)

Completeness of Many-Sorted Equational Logic. Joseph Goguen and José Meseguer. CSLI–84–15. ($2.50)

Moving the Semantic Fulcrum. Terry Winograd. CSLI–84–17. ($1.50)

On the Mathematical Properties of Linguistic Theories. C. Raymond Perrault. CSLI–84–18. ($3.00)

A Simple and Efficient Implementation of Higher-order Functions in LISP. Michael P. Georgeff and Stephen F.Bodnar. CSLI–84–19. ($4.50)

On the Axiomatization of "if-then-else". Irène Guessarian and José Meseguer. CSLI–85–20. ($3.00)

The Situation in Logic–II: Conditionals and Conditional Information. Jon Barwise. CSLI–84–21. ($3.00)

Principles of OBJ2. Kokichi Futatsugi, Joseph A. Goguen, Jean-Pierre Jouannaud, and José Meseguer. CSLI–85–22. ($2.00)

Querying Logical Databases. Moshe Vardi. CSLI–85–23. ($1.50)

Computationally Relevant Properties of Natural Languages and Their Grammar. Gerald Gazdar and Geoff Pullum. CSLI–85–24. ($3.50)

An Internal Semantics for Modal Logic: Preliminary Report. Ronald Fagin and Moshe Vardi. CSLI–85–25. ($2.00)

The Situation in Logic–III: Situations, Sets and the Axiom of Foundation. Jon Barwise. CSLI–85–26. ($2.50)

Semantic Automata. Johan van Benthem. CSLI–85–27. ($2.50)

Restrictive and Non-Restrictive Modification. Peter Sells. CSLI–85–28. ($3.00)

228

A Language/Action Perspective on the Design of Cooperative Work Terry Winograd CSLI–87–98. ($3.00)

Implicature and Definite Reference Jerry R. Hobbs CSLI–87–99. ($1.50)

Thinking Machines: Can There be? Are we? Terry Winograd CSLI–87–100. (Forthcoming)

Situation Semantics and Semantic Interpretation in Constraint-Based Grammars Per-Kristian Halvorsen CSLI–87–101. (Forthcoming)

Category Structures Gerald Gazdar, Geoffrey K. Pullum, Robert Carpenter, Ewan Klein, Thomas E. Hukari, Robert D. Levine CSLI–87–102. (Forthcoming)

Cognitive Theories of Emotion Ronald Alan Nash CSLI–87–103. (Forthcoming)

Toward an Architecture for Resource-Bounded Agents Martha E. Pollack, David J. Israel, and Michael E. Bratman CSLI–87–104. (Forthcoming)

Lecture Notes

The titles in this series are distributed by the University of Chicago Press and may be purchased in academic or university bookstores or ordered directly from the distributor at 5801 Ellis Avenue, Chicago, Illinois 60637.

A Manual of Intensional Logic. Johan van Benthem. Lecture Notes No. 1. (Paper $8.95)

Emotion and Focus. Helen Fay Nissenbaum. Lecture Notes No. 2. (Paper $8.95)

Lectures on Contemporary Syntactic Theories. Peter Sells with a Postscript by Thomas Wasow. Lecture Notes No. 3. (Paper $11.95   Cloth $23.95)

An Introduction to Unification-Based Approaches to Grammar. Stuart M. Shieber. Lecture Notes No. 4. (Paper $8.95   Cloth $17.95)

The Semantics of Destructive LISP. Ian A. Mason. Lecture Notes No. 5. (Paper $14.95   Cloth $29.95)

An Essay on Facts. Kenneth Russell Olson. Lecture Notes No. 6. (Paper $11.95   Cloth $23.95)

Logics of Time and Computation. Robert Goldblatt. Lecture Notes No. 7. (Paper $11.95   Cloth $23.95)

Word Order and Constituent Structure in German. Hans Uszkoreit. Lecture Notes No. 8. (Paper $12.95   Cloth $27.50)

Color and Color Perception: A Study in Anthropocentric Realism. David Russel Hilbert. Lecture Notes No. 9. (Forthcoming)

Prolog and Natural-Language Analysis. Fernando C.N. Pereira and Stuart M. Shieber. Lecture Notes No. 10. (Paper $13.95   Cloth $28.95)

Working Papers in Grammatical Theory and Discourse: Interactions of Morphology, Syntax, and Discourse. M. Iida, S. Wechsler, and D. Zec (eds.), with an Introduction by Joan Bresnan. Lecture Notes No. 11. (Paper $14.95   Cloth $35.00)

Information-Based Syntax and Semantics: Volume 1 Fundamentals. Carl Pollard and Ivan Sag. Lecture Notes No. 12. (Forthcoming)

Natural Language Processing in the 1980s: A Bibliography Gerald Gazdar, Roger Evans, Alex Franz, and Karen Osborn. Lecture Notes No. 13. (Forthcoming)

Non-Well-Founded Sets. Peter Aczel. Lecture Notes No. 14. (Forthcoming)

Probability and Induction. Richard Jeffrey. Lecture Notes No. 15. (Forthcoming)

This book was typeset with TeX on Turing, CSLI's principal computer, by the author and Emma Pease in Computer Modern Roman type, designed by Donald Knuth with his digital-font designing program, METAFONT. The cover design is by Nancy Etchemendy, the book design by Dikran Karagueuzian. TeX, which was also created by Knuth, is a trademark of the American Mathematical Society.